I0763314

Famous Works

By

Virginia Woolf

Cover Photograph: archer10 (Dennis)

ISBN:

Contents

Mrs. Dalloway

Mrs. Dalloway said she would buy the flowers herself.

For Lucy had her work cut out for her. The doors would be taken off their hinges; Rumpelmayer's men were coming. And then, thought Clarissa Dalloway, what a morning--fresh as if issued to children on a beach.

What a lark! What a plunge! For so it had always seemed to her, when, with a little squeak of the hinges, which she could hear now, she had burst open the French windows and plunged at Bourton into the open air. How fresh, how calm, stiller than this of course, the air was in the early morning; like the flap of a wave; the kiss of a wave; chill and sharp and yet (for a girl of eighteen as she then was) solemn, feeling as she did, standing there at the open window, that something awful was about to happen; looking at the flowers, at the trees with the smoke winding off them and the rooks rising, falling; standing and looking until Peter Walsh said, "Musing among the vegetables?"--was that it?--"I prefer men to cauliflowers"--was that it? He must have said it at breakfast one morning when she had gone out on to the terrace--Peter Walsh. He would be back from India one of these days, June or July, she forgot which, for his letters were awfully dull; it was his sayings one remembered; his eyes, his pocket-knife, his smile, his grumpiness and, when millions of things had utterly vanished--how strange it was!--a few sayings like this about cabbages.

She stiffened a little on the kerb, waiting for Durtnall's van to pass. A charming woman, Scrope Purvis thought her (knowing her as one does know people who live next door to one in Westminster); a touch of the bird about her, of the jay, blue-green, light, vivacious, though she was over fifty, and grown very white since her illness. There she perched, never seeing him, waiting to cross, very upright.

For having lived in Westminster--how many years now? over twenty,-- one feels even in the midst of the traffic, or waking at night, Clarissa was positive, a particular hush, or solemnity; an indescribable pause; a suspense (but that might be her heart, affected, they said, by influenza) before Big Ben strikes. There! Out it boomed. First a warning, musical; then the hour, irrevocable. The leaden circles dissolved in the air. Such fools we are, she thought, crossing Victoria Street. For Heaven only knows why one loves it so, how one sees it so, making it up, building it round one, tumbling it, creating it every moment afresh; but the veriest frumps, the most dejected of miseries sitting on doorsteps (drink their downfall) do the same; can't be dealt with, she felt positive, by Acts of Parliament for that very reason: they love life. In people's eyes, in the swing, tramp, and trudge; in the bellow and the uproar; the carriages, motor cars, omnibuses, vans, sandwich men shuffling and swinging; brass bands; barrel organs; in the triumph and the jingle and the strange high singing of some aeroplane overhead was what she loved; life; London; this moment of June.

For it was the middle of June. The War was over, except for some one like Mrs. Foxcroft at the Embassy last night eating her heart out because that nice boy was killed and now the old Manor House must go to a cousin; or Lady Bexborough who opened a bazaar, they said, with the telegram in her hand, John, her favourite, killed; but it was over; thank Heaven--over. It was June. The King and Queen were at the Palace. And everywhere, though it was still so early, there was a beating, a stirring of galloping ponies, tapping of cricket bats; Lords, Ascot, Ranelagh and all the rest of it; wrapped in the soft mesh of the grey-blue morning air, which, as the day wore on, would unwind them, and set down on their lawns and pitches the bouncing ponies, whose forefeet just struck the ground and up they sprung, the whirling young men, and laughing girls in their transparent muslins who, even now, after dancing all night, were taking their absurd woolly dogs for a run; and even now, at this hour, discreet old dowagers were shooting out in their motor cars on errands of mystery; and the shopkeepers were fidgeting in their windows with their paste and diamonds, their lovely old sea- green brooches in eighteenth-century settings to tempt Americans (but one must economise, not buy things rashly for Elizabeth), and she, too, loving it as she did with an absurd and faithful passion, being part of it, since her people were courtiers once in the time of the Georges, she, too, was going that very night to kindle and illuminate; to give her party. But how strange, on entering the Park, the silence; the mist; the hum; the slow-swimming happy ducks; the pouched birds waddling; and who should be coming along with his back against the Government buildings, most appropriately, carrying a despatch box stamped with the Royal Arms, who but Hugh Whitbread; her old friend Hugh--the admirable Hugh!

"Good-morning to you, Clarissa!" said Hugh, rather extravagantly, for they had known each other as children. "Where are you off to?"

"I love walking in London," said Mrs. Dalloway. "Really it's better than walking in the country."

They had just come up--unfortunately--to see doctors. Other people came to see pictures; go to the opera; take their daughters out; the Whitbreads came "to see doctors." Times without number Clarissa had visited Evelyn Whitbread in a nursing home. Was Evelyn ill again? Evelyn was a good deal out of sorts, said Hugh, intimating by a kind of pout or swell of his very well-covered, manly, extremely handsome, perfectly upholstered body (he was almost too well dressed always, but presumably had to be, with his little job at Court) that his wife had some internal ailment, nothing serious, which, as an old friend, Clarissa Dalloway would quite understand without requiring him to specify. Ah yes, she did of course; what a nuisance; and felt very sisterly and oddly conscious at the same time of her hat. Not the right hat for the early morning, was that it? For Hugh always made her feel, as he bustled on, raising his hat rather extravagantly and assuring her that she might be a girl of eighteen, and of course he was coming to her party to-night, Evelyn absolutely insisted, only a little late he might be after the party at the Palace to which he had to take one of Jim's boys,--she always felt a little skimpy beside Hugh; schoolgirlish; but attached to him, partly from having known him always, but she did think him a good sort in his own way, though Richard was nearly driven mad by him, and as for Peter Walsh, he had never to this day forgiven her for liking him.

She could remember scene after scene at Bourton--Peter furious; Hugh not, of course, his match in any way, but still not a positive imbecile as Peter made out; not a mere barber's block. When his old mother wanted him to give up shooting or to take her to Bath he did it, without a word; he was really unselfish, and as for saying, as Peter did, that he had no heart, no brain, nothing but the manners and breeding of an English gentleman, that was only her dear Peter at his worst; and he could be intolerable; he could be impossible; but adorable to walk with on a morning like this.

(June had drawn out every leaf on the trees. The mothers of Pimlico gave suck to their young. Messages were passing from the Fleet to the Admiralty. Arlington Street and Piccadilly seemed to chafe the very air in the Park and lift its leaves hotly, brilliantly, on waves of that divine vitality which Clarissa loved. To dance, to ride, she had adored all that.)

For they might be parted for hundreds of years, she and Peter; she never wrote a letter and his were dry sticks; but suddenly it would come over her, If he were with me now what would he say?--some days, some sights bringing him back to her calmly, without the old bitterness; which perhaps was the reward of having cared for people; they came back in the middle of St. James's Park on a fine morning--indeed they did. But Peter--however beautiful the day might be, and the trees and the grass, and the little girl in pink-- Peter never saw a thing of all that. He would put on his spectacles, if she told him to; he would look. It was the state of the world that interested him; Wagner, Pope's poetry, people's characters eternally, and the defects of her own soul. How he scolded her! How they argued! She would marry a Prime Minister and stand at the top of a staircase; the perfect hostess he called her (she had cried over it in her bedroom), she had the makings of the perfect hostess, he said.

So she would still find herself arguing in St. James's Park, still making out that she had been right--and she had too--not to marry him. For in marriage a little licence, a little independence there must be between people living together day in day out in the same house; which Richard gave her, and she him. (Where was he this morning for instance? Some committee, she never asked what.) But with Peter everything had to be shared; everything gone into. And it was intolerable, and when it came to that scene in the little garden by the fountain, she had to break with him or they would have been destroyed, both of them ruined, she was convinced; though she had borne about with her for years like an arrow sticking in her heart the grief, the anguish; and then the horror of the moment when some one told her at a concert that he had married a woman met on the boat going to India! Never should she forget all that! Cold, heartless, a prude, he called her.

Never could she understand how he cared. But those Indian women did presumably-- silly, pretty, flimsy nincompoops. And she wasted her pity. For he was quite happy, he assured her--perfectly happy, though he had never done a thing that they talked of; his whole life had been a failure. It made her angry still.

She had reached the Park gates. She stood for a moment, looking at the omnibuses in Piccadilly.

She would not say of any one in the world now that they were this or were that. She felt very young; at the same time unspeakably aged. She sliced like a knife through everything; at the same time was outside, looking on. She had a perpetual sense, as she watched the taxi cabs, of being out, out, far out to sea and alone; she always had the feeling that it was very, very dangerous to live even one day. Not that she thought herself clever, or much out of the ordinary. How she had got through life on the few twigs of knowledge Fräulein Daniels gave them she could not think. She knew nothing; no language, no history; she scarcely read a book now, except memoirs in bed; and yet to her it was absolutely absorbing; all this; the cabs passing; and she would not say of Peter, she would not say of herself, I am this, I am that.

Her only gift was knowing people almost by instinct, she thought, walking on. If you put her in a room with some one, up went her back like a cat's; or she purred. Devonshire House, Bath House, the house with the china cockatoo, she had seen them all lit up once; and remembered Sylvia, Fred, Sally Seton--such hosts of people; and dancing all night; and the waggons plodding past to market; and driving home across the Park. She remembered once throwing a shilling into the Serpentine. But every one remembered; what she loved was this, here, now, in front of her; the fat lady in the cab. Did it matter then, she asked herself, walking towards Bond Street, did it matter that she must inevitably cease completely; all this must go on without her; did she resent it; or did it not become consoling to believe that death ended absolutely? but that somehow in the streets of London, on the ebb and flow of things, here, there, she survived, Peter survived, lived in each other, she being part, she was positive, of the trees at home; of the house there, ugly, rambling all to bits and pieces as it was; part of people she had never met; being laid out like a mist between the people she knew best, who lifted her on their branches as she had seen the trees lift the mist, but it spread ever so far, her life, herself. But what was she dreaming as she looked into Hatchards' shop window? What was she trying to recover? What image of white dawn in the country, as she read in the book spread open:

Fear no more the heat o' the sun Nor the furious winter's rages.

This late age of the world's experience had bred in them all, all men and women, a well of tears. Tears and sorrows; courage and endurance; a perfectly upright and stoical bearing. Think, for example, of the woman she admired most, Lady Bexborough, opening the bazaar.

There were Jorrocks' Jaunts and Jollities; there were Soapy Sponge and Mrs. Asquith's Memoirs and Big Game Shooting in Nigeria, all spread open. Ever so many books there were; but none that seemed exactly right to take to Evelyn

Whitbread in her nursing home. Nothing that would serve to amuse her and make that indescribably dried-up little woman look, as Clarissa came in, just for a moment cordial; before they settled down for the usual interminable talk of women's ailments. How much she wanted it--that people should look pleased as she came in, Clarissa thought and turned and walked back towards Bond Street, annoyed, because it was silly to have other reasons for doing things. Much rather would she have been one of those people like Richard who did things for themselves, whereas, she thought, waiting to cross, half the time she did things not simply, not for themselves; but to make people think this or that; perfect idiocy she knew (and now the policeman held up his hand) for no one was ever for a second taken in. Oh if she could have had her life over again! she thought, stepping on to the pavement, could have looked even differently!

She would have been, in the first place, dark like Lady Bexborough, with a skin of crumpled leather and beautiful eyes. She would have been, like Lady Bexborough, slow and stately; rather large; interested in politics like a man; with a country house; very dignified, very sincere. Instead of which she had a narrow pea- stick figure; a ridiculous little face, beaked like a bird's. That she held herself well was true; and had nice hands and feet; and dressed well, considering that she spent little. But often now this body she wore (she stopped to look at a Dutch picture), this body, with all its capacities, seemed nothing--nothing at all. She had the oddest sense of being herself invisible; unseen; unknown; there being no more marrying, no more having of children now, but only this astonishing and rather solemn progress with the rest of them, up Bond Street, this being Mrs. Dalloway; not even Clarissa any more; this being Mrs. Richard Dalloway.

Bond Street fascinated her; Bond Street early in the morning in the season; its flags flying; its shops; no splash; no glitter; one roll of tweed in the shop where her father had bought his suits for fifty years; a few pearls; salmon on an iceblock.

"That is all," she said, looking at the fishmonger's. "That is all," she repeated, pausing for a moment at the window of a glove shop where, before the War, you could buy almost perfect gloves. And her old Uncle William used to say a lady is known by her shoes and her gloves. He had turned on his bed one morning in the middle of the War. He had said, "I have had enough." Gloves and shoes; she had a passion for gloves; but her own daughter, her Elizabeth, cared not a straw for either of them.

Not a straw, she thought, going on up Bond Street to a shop where they kept flowers for her when she gave a party. Elizabeth really cared for her dog most of all. The whole house this morning smelt of tar. Still, better poor Grizzle than Miss Kilman; better distemper and tar and all the rest of it than sitting mewed in a stuffy bedroom with a prayer book! Better anything, she was inclined to say. But it might be only a phase, as Richard said, such as all girls go through. It might be falling in love. But why with Miss Kilman? who had been badly treated of course; one must make allowances for that, and Richard said she was very able, had a really historical mind. Anyhow they were inseparable, and Elizabeth, her own daughter, went to Communion; and how she dressed, how she treated people who came to lunch she did not care a bit, it being her experience that the religious ecstasy made people callous (so did causes); dulled their feelings, for Miss Kilman would do anything for the Russians, starved herself for the Austrians, but in private inflicted positive torture, so insensitive was she, dressed in a green mackintosh coat. Year in year out she wore that coat; she perspired; she was never in the room five minutes without making you feel her superiority, your inferiority; how poor she was; how rich you were; how she lived in a slum without a cushion or a bed or a rug or whatever it might be, all her soul rusted with that grievance sticking in it, her dismissal from school during the War--poor embittered unfortunate creature! For it was not her one hated but the idea of her, which undoubtedly had gathered in to itself a great deal that was not Miss Kilman; had become one of those spectres with which one battles in the night; one of those spectres who stand astride us and suck up half our life-blood, dominators and tyrants; for no doubt with another throw of the dice, had the black been uppermost and not the white, she would have loved Miss Kilman! But not in this world. No.

It rasped her, though, to have stirring about in her this brutal monster! to hear twigs cracking and feel hooves planted down in the depths of that leaf-encumbered forest, the soul; never to be content quite, or quite secure, for at any moment the brute would be stirring, this hatred, which, especially since her illness, had power to make her feel scraped, hurt in her spine; gave her physical pain, and made all pleasure in beauty, in friendship, in being well, in being loved and making her home delightful rock, quiver, and bend as if indeed there were a monster grubbing at the roots, as if the whole panoply of content were nothing but self love! this hatred!

Nonsense, nonsense! she cried to herself, pushing through the swing doors of Mulberry's the florists.

She advanced, light, tall, very upright, to be greeted at once by button-faced Miss Pym, whose hands were always bright red, as if they had been stood in cold water with the flowers.

There were flowers: delphiniums, sweet peas, bunches of lilac; and carnations, masses of carnations. There were roses; there were irises. Ah yes--so she breathed in the earthy garden sweet smell as she stood talking to Miss Pym who owed her help, and thought her kind, for kind she had been years ago; very kind, but she looked older, this year, turning her head from side to side among the irises and roses and nodding tufts of lilac with her eyes half closed, snuffing in, after the street uproar, the delicious scent, the exquisite coolness. And then, opening her eyes, how fresh like frilled linen clean from a laundry laid in wicker trays the roses looked; and dark and prim the red carnations, holding their heads up; and all the sweet peas spreading in their bowls, tinged violet, snow white, pale--as if it were the evening and girls in muslin frocks came out to pick sweet peas and roses after the superb summer's day, with its almost blue-black sky, its delphiniums, its carnations, its arum lilies was over; and it was the moment between six and seven when every flower--roses, carnations, irises, lilac-- glows; white, violet, red, deep orange; every flower seems to burn by itself, softly, purely in the misty beds; and how she loved the grey-white moths spinning in and out, over the cherry pie, over the evening primroses!

And as she began to go with Miss Pym from jar to jar, choosing, nonsense, nonsense, she said to herself, more and more gently, as if this beauty, this scent, this colour, and Miss Pym liking her, trusting her, were a wave which she let flow over her and surmount that hatred, that monster, surmount it all; and it lifted her up and up when--oh! a pistol shot in the street outside!

"Dear, those motor cars," said Miss Pym, going to the window to look, and coming back and smiling apologetically with her hands full of sweet peas, as if those motor cars, those tyres of motor cars, were all HER fault.

The violent explosion which made Mrs. Dalloway jump and Miss Pym go to the window and apologise came from a motor car which had drawn to the side of the pavement precisely opposite Mulberry's shop window. Passers-by who, of course, stopped and stared, had just time to see a face of the very greatest importance against the dove-grey upholstery, before a male hand drew the blind and there was nothing to be seen except a square of dove grey.

Yet rumours were at once in circulation from the middle of Bond Street to Oxford Street on one side, to Atkinson's scent shop on the other, passing invisibly, inaudibly, like a cloud, swift, veil- like upon hills, falling indeed with something of a cloud's sudden sobriety and stillness upon faces which a second before had been utterly disorderly. But now mystery had brushed them with her wing; they had heard the voice of authority; the spirit of religion was abroad with her eyes bandaged tight and her lips gaping wide. But nobody knew whose face had been seen. Was it the Prince of Wales's, the Queen's, the Prime Minister's? Whose face was it? Nobody knew.

Edgar J. Watkiss, with his roll of lead piping round his arm, said audibly, humorously of course: "The Proime Minister's kyar."

Septimus Warren Smith, who found himself unable to pass, heard him.

Septimus Warren Smith, aged about thirty, pale-faced, beak-nosed, wearing brown shoes and a shabby overcoat, with hazel eyes which had that look of apprehension in them which makes complete strangers apprehensive too. The world has raised its whip; where will it descend?

Everything had come to a standstill. The throb of the motor engines sounded like a pulse irregularly drumming through an entire body. The sun became extraordinarily hot because the motor car had stopped outside Mulberry's shop window; old ladies on the tops of omnibuses spread their black parasols; here a green, here a red parasol opened with a little pop. Mrs. Dalloway, coming to the window with her arms full of sweet peas, looked out with her little pink face pursed in enquiry. Every one looked at the motor car. Septimus looked. Boys on bicycles sprang off. Traffic accumulated. And there the motor car stood, with drawn blinds, and upon them a curious pattern like a tree, Septimus thought, and this gradual drawing together of everything to one centre before his eyes, as if some horror had come almost to the surface and was about to burst into flames, terrified him. The world wavered and quivered and threatened to burst into flames. It is I who am blocking the way, he thought. Was he not being looked at and pointed at; was he not weighted there, rooted to the pavement, for a purpose? But for what purpose?

"Let us go on, Septimus," said his wife, a little woman, with large eyes in a sallow pointed face; an Italian girl.

But Lucrezia herself could not help looking at the motor car and the tree pattern on the blinds. Was it the Queen in there--the Queen going shopping?

The chauffeur, who had been opening something, turning something, shutting something, got on to the box.

"Come on," said Lucrezia.

But her husband, for they had been married four, five years now, jumped, started, and said, "All right!" angrily, as if she had interrupted him.

People must notice; people must see. People, she thought, looking at the crowd staring at the motor car; the English people, with their children and their horses and their clothes, which she admired in a way; but they were "people" now, because Septimus had said, "I will kill myself"; an awful thing to say. Suppose they had heard him? She looked at the crowd. Help, help! she wanted to cry out to butchers' boys and women. Help! Only last autumn she and Septimus had stood on the Embankment wrapped in the same cloak and, Septimus reading a paper instead of talking, she had snatched it from him and laughed in the old man's face who saw them! But failure one conceals. She must take him away into some park.

"Now we will cross," she said.

She had a right to his arm, though it was without feeling. He would give her, who was so simple, so impulsive, only twenty-four, without friends in England, who had left Italy for his sake, a piece of bone.

The motor car with its blinds drawn and an air of inscrutable reserve proceeded towards Piccadilly, still gazed at, still ruffling the faces on both sides of the street with the same dark breath of veneration whether for Queen, Prince, or Prime Minister nobody knew. The face itself had been seen only once by three people for a few seconds. Even the sex was now in dispute. But there could be no doubt that greatness was seated within; greatness was passing, hidden, down Bond Street, removed only by a hand's- breadth from ordinary people who might now, for the first and last time, be within speaking distance of the majesty of England, of the enduring symbol of the state which will be known to curious antiquaries, sifting the ruins of time, when London is a grass- grown path and all those hurrying along the pavement this Wednesday morning are but bones with a few wedding rings mixed up in their dust and the gold stoppings of innumerable decayed teeth. The face in the motor car will then be known.

It is probably the Queen, thought Mrs. Dalloway, coming out of Mulberry's with her flowers; the Queen. And for a second she wore a look of extreme dignity standing by the flower shop in the sunlight while the car passed at a foot's pace, with its blinds drawn. The Queen going to some hospital; the Queen opening some bazaar, thought Clarissa.

The crush was terrific for the time of day. Lords, Ascot, Hurlingham, what was it? she wondered, for the street was blocked. The British middle classes sitting sideways on the tops of omnibuses with parcels and umbrellas, yes, even furs on a day like this, were, she thought, more ridiculous, more unlike anything there has ever been than one could conceive; and the Queen herself held up; the Queen herself unable to pass. Clarissa was suspended on one side of Brook Street; Sir John Buckhurst, the old Judge on the other, with the car between them (Sir John had laid down the law for years and liked a well-dressed woman) when the chauffeur, leaning ever so slightly, said or showed something to the policeman, who saluted and raised his arm and jerked his head and moved the omnibus to the side and the car passed through. Slowly and very silently it took its way.

Clarissa guessed; Clarissa knew of course; she had seen something white, magical, circular, in the footman's hand, a disc inscribed with a name,--the Queen's, the Prince of Wales's, the Prime Minister's?--which, by force of its own lustre, burnt its way through (Clarissa saw the car diminishing, disappearing), to blaze among candelabras, glittering stars, breasts stiff with oak leaves, Hugh Whitbread and all his colleagues, the gentlemen of England, that night in Buckingham Palace. And Clarissa, too, gave a party. She stiffened a little; so she would stand at the top of her stairs.

The car had gone, but it had left a slight ripple which flowed through glove shops and hat shops and tailors' shops on both sides of Bond Street. For thirty seconds all heads were inclined the same way--to the window. Choosing a pair of gloves--should they be to the elbow or above it, lemon or pale grey?--ladies stopped; when the sentence was finished something had happened. Something so trifling in single instances that no mathematical instrument, though capable of transmitting shocks in China, could register the vibration; yet in its fulness rather formidable and in its common appeal emotional; for in all the hat shops and tailors' shops strangers looked at each other and thought of the dead; of the flag; of Empire. In a public house in a back street a Colonial insulted the House of Windsor which led to words, broken beer glasses, and a general shindy, which echoed strangely across the way in the ears of girls buying white underlinen threaded with pure white ribbon for their weddings. For the surface agitation of the passing car as it sunk grazed something very profound.

Gliding across Piccadilly, the car turned down St. James's Street. Tall men, men of robust physique, well-dressed men with their tail- coats and their white slips and their hair raked back who, for reasons difficult to discriminate, were standing in the bow window of Brooks's with their hands behind the tails of their coats, looking out, perceived instinctively that greatness was passing, and the pale light of the immortal presence fell upon them as it had fallen upon Clarissa Dalloway. At once they stood even straighter, and removed their hands, and seemed ready to attend their Sovereign, if need be, to the cannon's mouth, as their ancestors had done before them. The white busts and the little tables in the background covered with copies of the Tatler and syphons of soda water seemed to approve; seemed to indicate the flowing corn and the manor houses of England; and to return the frail hum of the motor wheels as the walls of a whispering gallery return a single voice expanded and made sonorous by the might of a whole cathedral. Shawled Moll Pratt with her flowers on the pavement wished the dear boy well (it was the Prince of Wales for certain) and would have tossed the price of a pot of beer--a bunch of roses--into St. James's Street out of sheer light-heartedness and contempt of poverty had she not seen the constable's eye upon her, discouraging an old Irishwoman's loyalty. The sentries at St. James's saluted; Queen Alexandra's policeman approved.

A small crowd meanwhile had gathered at the gates of Buckingham Palace. Listlessly, yet confidently, poor people all of them, they waited; looked at the Palace itself with the flag flying; at Victoria, billowing on her mound, admired her shelves of running water, her geraniums; singled out from the motor cars in the Mall first this one, then that; bestowed emotion, vainly, upon commoners out for a drive; recalled their tribute to keep it unspent while this car passed and that; and all the time let rumour accumulate in their veins and thrill the nerves in their thighs at the thought of Royalty looking at them; the Queen bowing; the Prince saluting; at the thought of the heavenly life divinely bestowed upon Kings; of the equerries and deep curtsies; of the Queen's old doll's house; of Princess Mary married to an Englishman, and the Prince--ah! the Prince! who took wonderfully, they said, after old King Edward, but was ever so much slimmer. The Prince lived at St. James's; but he might come along in the morning to visit his mother.

So Sarah Bletchley said with her baby in her arms, tipping her foot up and down as though she were by her own fender in Pimlico, but keeping her eyes on the Mall, while Emily Coates ranged over the Palace windows and thought of the housemaids, the innumerable housemaids, the bedrooms, the innumerable bedrooms. Joined by an elderly gentleman with an Aberdeen terrier, by men without occupation, the crowd increased. Little Mr. Bowley, who had rooms in the Albany and was sealed with wax over the deeper sources of life but could be unsealed suddenly, inappropriately, sentimentally, by this sort of thing--poor women waiting to see the Queen go past-- poor women, nice little children, orphans, widows, the War--tut- tut--actually had tears in his eyes. A breeze flaunting ever so warmly down the Mall through the thin trees, past the bronze heroes, lifted some flag flying in the British breast of Mr. Bowley and he raised his hat as the car turned into the Mall and held it high as the car approached; and let the poor mothers of Pimlico press close to him, and stood very upright. The car came on.

Suddenly Mrs. Coates looked up into the sky. The sound of an aeroplane bored ominously into the ears of the crowd. There it was coming over the trees, letting out white smoke from behind, which curled and twisted, actually writing something! making letters in the sky! Every one looked up.

Dropping dead down the aeroplane soared straight up, curved in a loop, raced, sank, rose, and whatever it did, wherever it went, out fluttered behind it a thick ruffled bar of white smoke which curled and wreathed upon the sky in letters. But what letters? A C was it? an E, then an L? Only for a moment did they lie still; then they moved and melted and were rubbed out up in the sky, and the aeroplane shot further away and again, in a fresh space of sky, began writing a K, an E, a Y perhaps?

"Glaxo," said Mrs. Coates in a strained, awe-stricken voice, gazing straight up, and her baby, lying stiff and white in her arms, gazed straight up.

"Kreemo," murmured Mrs. Bletchley, like a sleep-walker. With his hat held out perfectly still in his hand, Mr. Bowley gazed straight up. All down the Mall people were standing and looking up into the sky. As they looked the whole world became perfectly silent, and a flight of gulls crossed the sky, first one gull leading, then another, and in this extraordinary silence and peace, in this pallor, in this purity, bells struck eleven times, the sound fading up there among the gulls.

The aeroplane turned and raced and swooped exactly where it liked, swiftly, freely, like a skater--

"That's an E," said Mrs. Bletchley--or a dancer--

"It's toffee," murmured Mr. Bowley--(and the car went in at the gates and nobody looked at it), and shutting off the smoke, away and away it rushed, and the smoke faded and assembled itself round the broad white shapes of the clouds.

It had gone; it was behind the clouds. There was no sound. The clouds to which the letters E, G, or L had attached themselves moved freely, as if destined to cross from West to East on a mission of the greatest importance which would never be revealed, and yet certainly so it was--a mission of the greatest importance. Then suddenly, as a train comes out of a tunnel, the aeroplane rushed out of the clouds again, the sound boring into the ears of all people in the Mall, in the Green Park, in Piccadilly, in Regent Street, in Regent's Park, and the bar of smoke curved behind and it dropped down, and it soared up and wrote one letter after another-- but what word was it writing?

Lucrezia Warren Smith, sitting by her husband's side on a seat in Regent's Park in the Broad Walk, looked up.

"Look, look, Septimus!" she cried. For Dr. Holmes had told her to make her husband (who had nothing whatever seriously the matter with him but was a little out of sorts) take an interest in things outside himself.

So, thought Septimus, looking up, they are signalling to me. Not indeed in actual words; that is, he could not read the language yet; but it was plain enough, this beauty, this exquisite beauty, and tears filled his eyes as he looked at the smoke words languishing and melting in the sky and bestowing upon him in their inexhaustible charity and laughing goodness one shape after another of unimaginable beauty and signalling their intention to provide him, for nothing, for ever, for looking merely, with beauty, more beauty! Tears ran down his cheeks.

It was toffee; they were advertising toffee, a nursemaid told Rezia. Together they began to spell t . . . o . . . f . . .

"K . . . R . . ." said the nursemaid, and Septimus heard her say "Kay Arr" close to his ear, deeply, softly, like a mellow organ, but with a roughness in her voice like a grasshopper's, which rasped his spine deliciously and sent running up into his brain waves of sound which, concussing, broke. A marvellous discovery indeed--that the human voice in certain atmospheric conditions (for one must be scientific, above all scientific) can quicken trees into life! Happily Rezia put her hand with a tremendous weight on his knee so that he was weighted down, transfixed, or the excitement of the elm trees rising and falling, rising and falling with all their leaves alight and the colour thinning and thickening from blue to the green of a hollow wave, like plumes on horses' heads, feathers on ladies', so proudly they rose and fell, so superbly, would have sent him mad. But he would not go mad. He would shut his eyes; he would see no more.

But they beckoned; leaves were alive; trees were alive. And the leaves being connected by millions of fibres with his own body, there on the seat, fanned it up and down; when the branch stretched he, too, made that statement. The sparrows fluttering, rising, and falling in jagged fountains were part of the pattern; the white and blue, barred with black branches. Sounds made harmonies with premeditation; the spaces between them were as significant as the sounds. A child cried. Rightly far away a horn sounded. All taken together meant the birth of a new religion--

"Septimus!" said Rezia. He started violently. People must notice.

"I am going to walk to the fountain and back," she said.

For she could stand it no longer. Dr. Holmes might say there was nothing the matter. Far rather would she that he were dead! She could not sit beside him when he stared so and did not see her and made everything terrible; sky and tree, children playing, dragging carts, blowing whistles, falling down; all were terrible. And he would not kill himself; and she could tell no one. "Septimus has been working too hard"--that was all she could say to her own mother. To love makes one solitary, she thought. She could tell nobody, not even Septimus now, and looking back, she saw him sitting in his shabby overcoat alone, on the seat, hunched up, staring. And it was cowardly for a man to say he would kill himself, but Septimus had fought; he was brave; he was not Septimus now. She put on her lace collar. She put on her new hat and he never noticed; and he was happy without her. Nothing could make her happy without him! Nothing! He was selfish. So men are. For he was not ill. Dr. Holmes said there was nothing the matter with him. She spread her hand before her. Look! Her wedding ring slipped--she had grown so thin. It was she who suffered--but she had nobody to tell.

Far was Italy and the white houses and the room where her sisters sat making hats, and the streets crowded every evening with people walking, laughing out loud, not half alive like people here, huddled up in Bath chairs, looking at a few ugly flowers stuck in pots!

"For you should see the Milan gardens," she said aloud. But to whom?

There was nobody. Her words faded. So a rocket fades. Its sparks, having grazed their way into the night, surrender to it, dark descends, pours over the outlines of houses and towers; bleak hillsides soften and fall in. But though they are gone, the night is full of them; robbed of colour, blank of windows, they exist more ponderously, give out what the frank daylight fails to transmit--the trouble and suspense of things conglomerated there in the darkness; huddled together in the darkness; reft of the relief which dawn brings when, washing the walls white and grey, spotting each window-pane, lifting the mist from the fields, showing the red-brown cows peacefully grazing, all is once more decked out to the eye; exists again. I am alone; I am alone! she cried, by the fountain in Regent's Park (staring at the Indian and his cross), as perhaps at midnight, when all boundaries are lost, the country reverts to its ancient shape, as the Romans saw it, lying cloudy, when they landed, and the hills had no names and rivers wound they knew not where--such was her darkness; when suddenly, as if a shelf were shot forth and she stood on it, she said how she was his wife, married years ago in Milan, his wife, and would never, never tell that he was mad! Turning, the shelf fell; down, down she dropped. For he was gone, she thought--gone, as he threatened, to kill himself--to throw himself under a cart! But no; there he was; still sitting alone on the seat, in his shabby overcoat, his legs crossed, staring, talking aloud.

Men must not cut down trees. There is a God. (He noted such revelations on the backs of envelopes.) Change the world. No one kills from hatred. Make it known (he wrote it down). He waited. He listened. A sparrow perched on the railing opposite chirped Septimus, Septimus, four or five times over and went on, drawing its notes out, to sing freshly and piercingly in Greek words how there is no crime and, joined by another sparrow, they sang in voices prolonged and piercing in Greek words, from trees in the meadow of life beyond a river where the dead walk, how there is no death.

There was his hand; there the dead. White things were assembling behind the railings opposite. But he dared not look. Evans was behind the railings!

"What are you saying?" said Rezia suddenly, sitting down by him.

Interrupted again! She was always interrupting.

Away from people--they must get away from people, he said (jumping up), right away over there, where there were chairs beneath a tree and the long slope of the park dipped like a length of green stuff with a ceiling cloth of blue and pink smoke high above, and there was a rampart of far irregular houses hazed in smoke, the traffic hummed in a circle, and on the right, dun-coloured animals stretched long necks over the Zoo palings, barking, howling. There they sat down under a tree.

"Look," she implored him, pointing at a little troop of boys carrying cricket stumps, and one shuffled, spun round on his heel and shuffled, as if he were acting a clown at the music hall.

"Look," she implored him, for Dr. Holmes had told her to make him notice real things, go to a music hall, play cricket--that was the very game, Dr. Holmes said, a nice out-of-door game, the very game for her husband.

"Look," she repeated.

Look the unseen bade him, the voice which now communicated with him who was the greatest of mankind, Septimus, lately taken from life to death, the Lord who had come to renew society, who lay like a coverlet, a snow blanket smitten only by the sun, for ever unwasted, suffering for ever, the scapegoat, the eternal sufferer, but he did not want it, he moaned, putting from him with a wave of his hand that eternal suffering, that eternal loneliness.

"Look," she repeated, for he must not talk aloud to himself out of doors.

"Oh look," she implored him. But what was there to look at? A few sheep. That was all.

The way to Regent's Park Tube station--could they tell her the way to Regent's Park Tube station--Maisie Johnson wanted to know. She was only up from Edinburgh two days ago.

"Not this way--over there!" Rezia exclaimed, waving her aside, lest she should see Septimus.

Both seemed queer, Maisie Johnson thought. Everything seemed very queer. In London for the first time, come to take up a post at her uncle's in Leadenhall Street, and now walking through Regent's Park in the morning, this couple on the chairs gave her quite a turn; the young woman seeming foreign, the man looking queer; so that should she be very old she would still remember and make it jangle again among her memories how she had walked through Regent's Park on a fine summer's morning fifty years ago. For she was only nineteen and had got her way at last, to come to London; and now how queer it was, this couple she had asked the way of, and the girl started and jerked her hand, and the man--he seemed awfully odd; quarrelling, perhaps; parting for ever, perhaps; something was up, she knew; and now all these people (for she returned to the Broad Walk), the stone basins, the prim flowers, the old men and women, invalids most of them in Bath chairs--all seemed, after Edinburgh, so queer. And Maisie Johnson, as she joined that gently trudging, vaguely gazing, breeze-kissed company--squirrels perching and preening, sparrow fountains fluttering for crumbs, dogs busy with the railings, busy with each other, while the soft warm air washed over them and lent to the fixed unsurprised gaze with which they received life something whimsical and mollified--Maisie Johnson positively felt she must cry Oh! (for that young man on the seat had given her quite a turn. Something was up, she knew.)

Horror! horror! she wanted to cry. (She had left her people; they had warned her what would happen.)

Why hadn't she stayed at home? she cried, twisting the knob of the iron railing.

That girl, thought Mrs. Dempster (who saved crusts for the squirrels and often ate her lunch in Regent's Park), don't know a thing yet; and really it seemed to her better to be a little stout, a little slack, a little moderate in one's expectations. Percy drank. Well, better to have a son, thought Mrs. Dempster. She had had a hard time of it, and couldn't help smiling at a girl like that. You'll get married, for you're pretty enough, thought Mrs. Dempster. Get married, she thought, and then you'll know. Oh, the cooks, and so on. Every man has his ways. But whether I'd have chosen quite like that if I could have known, thought Mrs. Dempster, and could not help wishing to whisper a word to Maisie Johnson; to feel on the creased pouch of her worn old face the kiss of pity. For it's been a hard life, thought Mrs. Dempster. What hadn't she given to it? Roses; figure; her feet too. (She drew the knobbed lumps beneath her skirt.)

Roses, she thought sardonically. All trash, m'dear. For really, what with eating, drinking, and mating, the bad days and good, life had been no mere matter of roses, and what was more, let me tell you, Carrie Dempster had no wish to change her lot with any woman's in Kentish Town! But, she implored, pity. Pity, for the loss of roses. Pity she asked of Maisie Johnson, standing by the hyacinth beds.

Ah, but that aeroplane! Hadn't Mrs. Dempster always longed to see foreign parts? She had a nephew, a missionary. It soared and shot. She always went on the sea at Margate, not out o' sight of land, but she had no patience with women who were afraid of water. It swept and fell. Her stomach was in her mouth. Up again. There's a fine young feller aboard of it, Mrs. Dempster wagered, and away and away it went, fast and fading, away and away the aeroplane shot; soaring over Greenwich and all the masts; over the little island of grey churches, St. Paul's and the rest till, on either side of London, fields spread out and dark brown woods where adventurous thrushes hopping boldly, glancing quickly, snatched the snail and tapped him on a stone, once, twice, thrice.

Away and away the aeroplane shot, till it was nothing but a bright spark; an aspiration; a concentration; a symbol (so it seemed to Mr. Bentley, vigorously rolling his strip of turf at Greenwich) of man's soul; of his determination, thought Mr. Bentley, sweeping round the cedar tree, to get outside his body, beyond his house, by means of thought, Einstein, speculation, mathematics, the Mendelian theory--away the aeroplane shot.

Then, while a seedy-looking nondescript man carrying a leather bag stood on the steps of St. Paul's Cathedral, and hesitated, for within was what balm, how great a welcome, how many tombs with banners waving over them, tokens of victories not over armies, but over, he thought, that plaguy spirit of truth seeking which leaves me at present without a situation, and more than that, the cathedral offers company, he thought, invites you to membership of a society; great men belong to it; martyrs have died for it; why not enter in, he thought, put this leather bag stuffed with pamphlets before an altar, a cross, the symbol of something which has soared beyond seeking and questing and knocking of words together and has become all spirit, disembodied, ghostly--why not enter in? he thought and while he hesitated out flew the aeroplane over Ludgate Circus.

It was strange; it was still. Not a sound was to be heard above the traffic. Unguided it seemed; sped of its own free will. And now, curving up and up, straight up, like something mounting in ecstasy, in pure delight, out from behind poured white smoke looping, writing a T, an O, an F.

"What are they looking at?" said Clarissa Dalloway to the maid who opened her door.

The hall of the house was cool as a vault. Mrs. Dalloway raised her hand to her eyes, and, as the maid shut the door to, and she heard the swish of Lucy's skirts, she felt like a nun who has left the world and feels fold round her the familiar veils and the response to old devotions. The cook whistled in the kitchen. She heard the click of the typewriter. It was her life, and, bending her head over the hall table, she bowed beneath the influence, felt blessed and purified, saying to herself, as she took the pad with the telephone message on it, how moments like this are buds on the tree of life, flowers of darkness they are, she thought (as if some lovely rose had blossomed for her eyes only); not for a moment did she believe in God; but all the more, she thought, taking up the pad, must one repay in daily life to servants, yes, to dogs and canaries, above all to Richard her husband, who was the foundation of it--of the gay sounds, of the green lights, of the cook even whistling, for Mrs. Walker was Irish and whistled all day long--one must pay back from this secret deposit of exquisite moments, she thought, lifting the pad, while Lucy stood by her, trying to explain how

"Mr. Dalloway, ma'am"--

Clarissa read on the telephone pad, "Lady Bruton wishes to know if Mr. Dalloway will lunch with her to-day."

"Mr. Dalloway, ma'am, told me to tell you he would be lunching out."

"Dear!" said Clarissa, and Lucy shared as she meant her to her disappointment (but not the pang); felt the concord between them; took the hint; thought how the gentry love; gilded her own future with calm; and, taking Mrs. Dalloway's parasol, handled it like a sacred weapon which a Goddess, having acquitted herself honourably in the field of battle, sheds, and placed it in the umbrella stand.

"Fear no more," said Clarissa. Fear no more the heat o' the sun; for the shock of Lady Bruton asking Richard to lunch without her made the moment in which she had stood shiver, as a plant on the river-bed feels the shock of a passing oar and shivers: so she rocked: so she shivered.

Millicent Bruton, whose lunch parties were said to be extraordinarily amusing, had not asked her. No vulgar jealousy could separate her from Richard. But she feared time itself, and read on Lady Bruton's face, as if it had been a dial cut in impassive stone, the dwindling of life; how year by year her share was sliced; how little the margin that remained was capable any longer of stretching, of absorbing, as in the youthful years, the colours, salts, tones of existence, so that she filled the room she entered, and felt often as she stood hesitating one moment on the threshold of her drawing- room, an exquisite suspense, such as might stay a diver before plunging while the sea darkens and brightens beneath him, and the waves which threaten to break, but only gently split their surface, roll and conceal and encrust as they just turn over the weeds with pearl.

She put the pad on the hall table. She began to go slowly upstairs, with her hand on the bannisters, as if she had left a party, where now this friend now that had flashed back her face, her voice; had shut the door and gone out and stood alone, a single figure against the appalling night, or rather, to be accurate, against the stare of this matter-of-fact June morning; soft with the glow of rose petals for some, she knew, and felt it, as she paused by the open staircase window which let in blinds flapping, dogs barking, let in, she thought, feeling herself suddenly shrivelled, aged, breastless, the grinding, blowing, flowering of the day, out of doors, out of the window, out of her body and brain which now failed, since Lady Bruton, whose lunch parties were said to be extraordinarily amusing, had not asked her.

Like a nun withdrawing, or a child exploring a tower, she went upstairs, paused at the window, came to the bathroom. There was the green linoleum and a tap dripping. There was an emptiness about the heart of life; an attic room. Women must put off their rich apparel. At midday they must disrobe. She pierced the pincushion and laid her feathered yellow hat on the bed. The sheets were clean, tight stretched in a broad white band from side to side. Narrower and narrower would her bed be. The candle was half burnt down and she had read deep in Baron Marbot's Memoirs. She had read late at night of the retreat from Moscow. For the House sat so long that Richard insisted, after her illness, that she must sleep undisturbed. And really she preferred to read of the retreat from Moscow. He knew it. So the room was an attic; the bed narrow; and lying there reading, for she slept badly, she could not dispel a virginity preserved through childbirth which clung to her like a sheet. Lovely in girlhood, suddenly there came a moment--for example on the river beneath the woods at Clieveden-- when, through some contraction of this cold spirit, she had failed him. And then at Constantinople, and again and again. She could see what she lacked. It was not beauty; it was not mind. It was something central which permeated; something warm which broke up surfaces and rippled the cold contact of man and woman, or of women together. For THAT she could dimly perceive. She resented it, had a scruple picked up Heaven knows where, or, as she felt, sent by Nature (who is invariably wise); yet she could not resist sometimes yielding to the charm of a woman, not a girl, of a woman confessing, as to her they often did, some scrape, some folly. And whether it was pity, or their beauty, or that she was older, or some accident--like a faint scent, or a violin next door (so strange is the power of sounds at certain moments), she did undoubtedly then feel what men felt. Only for a moment; but it was enough. It was a sudden revelation, a tinge like a blush which one tried to check and then, as it spread, one yielded to its expansion, and rushed to the farthest verge and there quivered and felt the world come closer, swollen with some astonishing significance, some pressure of rapture, which split its thin skin and gushed and poured with an extraordinary alleviation over the cracks and sores! Then, for that moment, she had seen an illumination; a match burning in a crocus; an inner meaning almost expressed. But the close withdrew; the hard softened. It was over--the moment. Against such moments (with women too) there contrasted (as she laid her hat down) the bed and Baron Marbot and the candle half-burnt. Lying awake, the floor creaked; the lit house was suddenly darkened, and if she raised her head she could just hear the click of the handle released as gently as possible by Richard, who slipped upstairs in his socks and then, as often as not, dropped his hot-water bottle and swore! How she laughed!

But this question of love (she thought, putting her coat away), this falling in love with women. Take Sally Seton; her relation in the old days with Sally Seton. Had not that, after all, been love?

She sat on the floor--that was her first impression of Sally--she sat on the floor with her arms round her knees, smoking a cigarette. Where could it have been? The Mannings? The Kinloch- Jones's? At some party (where, she could not be certain), for she had a distinct recollection of saying to the man she was with, "Who is THAT?" And he had told her, and said that Sally's parents did not get on (how that shocked her--that one's parents should quarrel!). But all that evening she could not take her eyes off Sally. It was an extraordinary beauty of the kind she most admired, dark, large-eyed, with that quality which, since she hadn't got it herself, she always envied--a sort of abandonment, as if she could say anything, do anything; a quality much commoner in foreigners than in Englishwomen. Sally always said she had French blood in her veins, an ancestor had been with Marie Antoinette, had his head cut off, left a ruby ring. Perhaps that summer she came to stay at Bourton, walking in quite unexpectedly without a penny in her pocket, one night after dinner, and upsetting poor Aunt Helena to such an extent that she never forgave her. There had been some quarrel at home. She literally hadn't a penny that night when she came to them--had pawned a brooch to come down. She had rushed off in a passion. They sat up till all hours of the night talking. Sally it was who made her feel, for the first time, how sheltered the life at Bourton was. She knew nothing about sex-- nothing about social problems. She had once seen an old man who had dropped dead in a field--she had seen cows just after their calves were born. But Aunt Helena never liked discussion of anything (when Sally gave her William Morris, it had to be wrapped in brown paper). There they sat, hour after hour, talking in her bedroom at the top of the house, talking about life, how they were to reform the world. They meant to found a society to abolish private property, and actually had a letter written, though not sent out. The ideas were Sally's, of course--but very soon she was just as excited--read Plato in bed before breakfast; read Morris; read Shelley by the hour.

Sally's power was amazing, her gift, her personality. There was her way with flowers, for instance. At Bourton they always had stiff little vases all the way down the table. Sally went out, picked hollyhocks, dahlias--all sorts of flowers that had never been seen together--cut their heads off, and made them swim on the top of water in bowls. The effect was extraordinary--coming in to dinner in the sunset. (Of course Aunt Helena thought it wicked to treat flowers like that.) Then she forgot her sponge, and ran along the passage naked. That grim old housemaid, Ellen Atkins, went about grumbling--"Suppose any of the gentlemen had seen?" Indeed she did shock people. She was untidy, Papa said.

The strange thing, on looking back, was the purity, the integrity, of her feeling for Sally. It was not like one's feeling for a man. It was completely disinterested, and besides, it had a quality which could only exist between women, between women just grown up. It was protective, on her side; sprang from a sense of being in league together, a presentiment of something that was bound to part them (they spoke of marriage always as a catastrophe), which led to this chivalry, this protective feeling which was much more on her side than Sally's. For in those days she was completely reckless; did the most idiotic things out of bravado; bicycled round the parapet on the terrace; smoked cigars. Absurd, she was--very absurd. But the charm was overpowering, to her at least, so that she could remember standing in her bedroom at the top of the house holding the hot-water can in her hands and saying aloud, "She is beneath this roof. . . . She is beneath this roof!"

No, the words meant absolutely nothing to her now. She could not even get an echo of her old emotion. But she could remember going cold with excitement, and doing her hair in a kind of ecstasy (now the old feeling began to come back to her, as she took out her hairpins, laid them on the dressing-table, began to do her hair), with the rooks flaunting up and down in the pink evening light, and dressing, and going downstairs, and feeling as she crossed the hall "if it were now to die 'twere now to be most happy." That was her feeling--Othello's feeling, and she felt it, she was convinced, as strongly as Shakespeare meant Othello to feel it, all because she was coming down to dinner in a white frock to meet Sally Seton!

She was wearing pink gauze--was that possible? She SEEMED, anyhow, all light, glowing, like some bird or air ball that has flown in, attached itself for a moment to a bramble. But nothing is so strange when one is in love (and what was this except being in love?) as the complete indifference of other people. Aunt Helena just wandered off after dinner; Papa read the paper. Peter Walsh might have been there, and old Miss Cummings; Joseph Breitkopf certainly was, for he came every summer, poor old man, for weeks and weeks, and pretended to read German with her, but really played the piano and sang Brahms without any voice.

All this was only a background for Sally. She stood by the fireplace talking, in that beautiful voice which made everything she said sound like a caress, to Papa, who had begun to be attracted rather against his will (he never got over lending her one of his books and finding it soaked on the terrace), when suddenly she said, "What a shame to sit indoors!" and they all went out on to the terrace and walked up and down. Peter Walsh and Joseph Breitkopf went on about Wagner. She and Sally fell a little behind. Then came the most exquisite moment of her whole life passing a stone urn with flowers in it. Sally stopped; picked a flower; kissed her on the lips. The whole world might have turned upside down! The others disappeared; there she was alone with Sally. And she felt that she had been given a present, wrapped up, and told just to keep it, not to look at it--a diamond, something infinitely precious, wrapped up, which, as they walked (up and down, up and down), she uncovered, or the radiance burnt through, the revelation, the religious feeling!--when old Joseph and Peter faced them:

"Star-gazing?" said Peter.

It was like running one's face against a granite wall in the darkness! It was shocking; it was horrible!

Not for herself. She felt only how Sally was being mauled already, maltreated; she felt his hostility; his jealousy; his determination to break into their companionship. All this she saw as one sees a landscape in a flash of lightning--and Sally (never had she admired her so much!) gallantly taking her way unvanquished. She laughed. She made old Joseph tell her the names of the stars, which he liked doing very seriously. She stood there: she listened. She heard the names of the stars.

"Oh this horror!" she said to herself, as if she had known all along that something would interrupt, would embitter her moment of happiness.

Yet, after all, how much she owed to him later. Always when she thought of him she thought of their quarrels for some reason-- because she wanted his good opinion so much, perhaps. She owed him words: "sentimental," "civilised"; they started up every day of her life as if he guarded her. A book was sentimental; an attitude to life sentimental. "Sentimental," perhaps she was to be thinking of the past. What would he think, she wondered, when he came back?

That she had grown older? Would he say that, or would she see him thinking when he came back, that she had grown older? It was true. Since her illness she had turned almost white.

Laying her brooch on the table, she had a sudden spasm, as if, while she mused, the icy claws had had the chance to fix in her. She was not old yet. She had just broken into her fifty-second year. Months and months of it were still untouched. June, July, August! Each still remained almost whole, and, as if to catch the falling drop, Clarissa (crossing to the dressing-table) plunged into the very heart of the moment, transfixed it, there--the moment of this June morning on which was the pressure of all the other mornings, seeing the glass, the dressing-table, and all the bottles afresh, collecting the whole of her at one point (as she looked into the glass), seeing the delicate pink face of the woman who was that very night to give a party; of Clarissa Dalloway; of herself.

How many million times she had seen her face, and always with the same imperceptible contraction! She pursed her lips when she looked in the glass. It was to give her face point. That was her self--pointed; dartlike; definite. That was her self when some effort, some call on her to be her self, drew the parts together, she alone knew how different, how incompatible and composed so for the world only into one centre, one diamond, one woman who sat in her drawing-room and made a meeting-point, a radiancy no doubt in some dull lives, a refuge for the lonely to come to, perhaps; she had helped young people, who were grateful to her; had tried to be the same always, never showing a sign of all the other sides of her--faults, jealousies, vanities, suspicions, like this of Lady Bruton not asking her to lunch; which, she thought (combing her hair finally), is utterly base! Now, where was her dress?

Her evening dresses hung in the cupboard. Clarissa, plunging her hand into the softness, gently detached the green dress and carried it to the window. She had torn it. Some one had trod on the skirt. She had felt it give at the Embassy party at the top among the folds. By artificial light the green shone, but lost its colour now in the sun. She would mend it. Her maids had too much to do. She would wear it to-night. She would take her silks, her scissors, her--what was it?--her thimble, of course, down into the drawing-room, for she must also write, and see that things generally were more or less in order.

Strange, she thought, pausing on the landing, and assembling that diamond shape, that single person, strange how a mistress knows the very moment, the very temper of her house! Faint sounds rose in spirals up the well of the stairs; the swish of a mop; tapping; knocking; a loudness when the front door opened; a voice repeating a message in the basement; the chink of silver on a tray; clean silver for the party. All was for the party.

(And Lucy, coming into the drawing-room with her tray held out, put the giant candlesticks on the mantelpiece, the silver casket in the middle, turned the crystal dolphin towards the clock. They would come; they would stand; they would talk in the mincing tones which she could imitate, ladies and gentlemen. Of all, her mistress was loveliest--mistress of silver, of linen, of china, for the sun, the silver, doors off their hinges, Rumpelmayer's men, gave her a sense, as she laid the paper-knife on the inlaid table, of something achieved. Behold! Behold! she said, speaking to her old friends in the baker's shop, where she had first seen service at Caterham, prying into the glass. She was Lady Angela, attending Princess Mary, when in came Mrs. Dalloway.)

"Oh Lucy," she said, "the silver does look nice!"

"And how," she said, turning the crystal dolphin to stand straight, "how did you enjoy the play last night?" "Oh, they had to go before the end!" she said. "They had to be back at ten!" she said. "So they don't know what happened," she said. "That does seem hard luck," she said (for her servants stayed later, if they asked her). "That does seem rather a shame," she said, taking the old bald- looking cushion in the middle of the sofa and putting it in Lucy's arms, and giving her a little push, and crying:

"Take it away! Give it to Mrs. Walker with my compliments! Take it away!" she cried.

And Lucy stopped at the drawing-room door, holding the cushion, and said, very shyly, turning a little pink, Couldn't she help to mend that dress?

But, said Mrs. Dalloway, she had enough on her hands already, quite enough of her own to do without that.

"But, thank you, Lucy, oh, thank you," said Mrs. Dalloway, and thank you, thank you, she went on saying (sitting down on the sofa with her dress over her knees, her scissors, her silks), thank you, thank you, she went on saying in gratitude to her servants generally for helping her to be like this, to be what she wanted, gentle, generous-hearted. Her servants liked her. And then this dress of hers--where was the tear? and now her needle to be threaded. This was a favourite dress, one of Sally Parker's, the last almost she ever made, alas, for Sally had now retired, living at Ealing, and if ever I have a moment, thought Clarissa (but never would she have a moment any more), I shall go and see her at Ealing. For she was a character, thought Clarissa, a real artist. She thought of little out-of-the-way things; yet her dresses were never queer. You could wear them at Hatfield; at Buckingham Palace. She had worn them at Hatfield; at Buckingham Palace.

Quiet descended on her, calm, content, as her needle, drawing the silk smoothly to its gentle pause, collected the green folds together and attached them, very lightly, to the belt. So on a summer's day waves collect, overbalance, and fall; collect and fall; and the whole world seems to be saying "that is all" more and more ponderously, until even the heart in the body which lies in the sun on the beach says too, That is all. Fear no more, says the heart. Fear no more, says the heart, committing its burden to some sea, which sighs collectively for all sorrows, and renews, begins, collects, lets fall. And the body alone listens to the passing bee; the wave breaking; the dog barking, far away barking and barking.

"Heavens, the front-door bell!" exclaimed Clarissa, staying her needle. Roused, she listened.

"Mrs. Dalloway will see me," said the elderly man in the hall. "Oh yes, she will see ME," he repeated, putting Lucy aside very benevolently, and running upstairs ever so quickly. "Yes, yes, yes," he muttered as he ran upstairs. "She will see me. After five years in India, Clarissa will see me."

"Who can--what can," asked Mrs. Dalloway (thinking it was outrageous to be interrupted at eleven o'clock on the morning of the day she was giving a party), hearing a step on the stairs. She heard a hand upon the door. She made to hide her dress, like a virgin protecting chastity, respecting privacy. Now the brass knob slipped. Now the door opened, and in came--for a single second she could not remember what he was called! so surprised she was to see him, so glad, so shy, so utterly taken aback to have Peter Walsh come to her unexpectedly in the morning! (She had not read his letter.)

"And how are you?" said Peter Walsh, positively trembling; taking both her hands; kissing both her hands. She's grown older, he thought, sitting down. I shan't tell her anything about it, he thought, for she's grown older. She's looking at me, he thought, a sudden embarrassment coming over him, though he had kissed her hands. Putting his hand into his pocket, he took out a large pocket-knife and half opened the blade.

Exactly the same, thought Clarissa; the same queer look; the same check suit; a little out of the straight his face is, a little thinner, dryer, perhaps, but he looks awfully well, and just the same.

"How heavenly it is to see you again!" she exclaimed. He had his knife out. That's so like him, she thought.

He had only reached town last night, he said; would have to go down into the country at once; and how was everything, how was everybody--Richard? Elizabeth?

"And what's all this?" he said, tilting his pen-knife towards her green dress.

He's very well dressed, thought Clarissa; yet he always criticises ME.

Here she is mending her dress; mending her dress as usual, he thought; here she's been sitting all the time I've been in India; mending her dress; playing about; going to parties; running to the House and back and all that, he thought, growing more and more irritated, more and more agitated, for there's nothing in the world so bad for some women as marriage, he thought; and politics; and having a Conservative husband, like the admirable Richard. So it is, so it is, he thought, shutting his knife with a snap.

"Richard's very well. Richard's at a Committee," said Clarissa.

And she opened her scissors, and said, did he mind her just finishing what she was doing to her dress, for they had a party that night?

"Which I shan't ask you to," she said. "My dear Peter!" she said.

But it was delicious to hear her say that--my dear Peter! Indeed, it was all so delicious--the silver, the chairs; all so delicious!

Why wouldn't she ask him to her party? he asked.

Now of course, thought Clarissa, he's enchanting! perfectly enchanting! Now I remember how impossible it was ever to make up my mind--and why did I make up my mind--not to marry him? she wondered, that awful summer?

"But it's so extraordinary that you should have come this morning!" she cried, putting her hands, one on top of another, down on her dress.

"Do you remember," she said, "how the blinds used to flap at Bourton?"

"They did," he said; and he remembered breakfasting alone, very awkwardly, with her father; who had died; and he had not written to Clarissa. But he had never got on well with old Parry, that querulous, weak-kneed old man, Clarissa's father, Justin Parry.

"I often wish I'd got on better with your father," he said.

"But he never liked any one who--our friends," said Clarissa; and could have bitten her tongue for thus reminding Peter that he had wanted to marry her.

Of course I did, thought Peter; it almost broke my heart too, he thought; and was overcome with his own grief, which rose like a moon looked at from a terrace, ghastly beautiful with light from the sunken day. I was more unhappy than I've ever been since, he thought. And as if in truth he were sitting there on the terrace he edged a little towards Clarissa; put his hand out; raised it; let it fall. There above them it hung, that moon. She too seemed to be sitting with him on the terrace, in the moonlight.

"Herbert has it now," she said. "I never go there now," she said.

Then, just as happens on a terrace in the moonlight, when one person begins to feel ashamed that he is already bored, and yet as the other sits silent, very quiet, sadly looking at the moon, does not like to speak, moves his foot, clears his throat, notices some iron scroll on a table leg, stirs a leaf, but says nothing--so Peter Walsh did now. For why go back like this to the past? he thought. Why make him think of it again? Why make him suffer, when she had tortured him so infernally? Why?

"Do you remember the lake?" she said, in an abrupt voice, under the pressure of an emotion which caught her heart, made the muscles of her throat stiff, and contracted her lips in a spasm as she said "lake." For she was a child, throwing bread to the ducks, between her parents, and at the same time a grown woman coming to her parents who stood by the lake, holding her life in her arms which, as she neared them, grew larger and larger in her arms, until it became a whole life, a complete life, which she put down by them and said, "This is what I have made of it! This!" And what had she made of it? What, indeed? sitting there sewing this morning with Peter.

She looked at Peter Walsh; her look, passing through all that time and that emotion, reached him doubtfully; settled on him tearfully; and rose and fluttered away, as a bird touches a branch and rises and flutters away. Quite simply she wiped her eyes.

"Yes," said Peter. "Yes, yes, yes," he said, as if she drew up to the surface something which positively hurt him as it rose. Stop! Stop! he wanted to cry. For he was not old; his life was not over; not by any means. He was only just past fifty. Shall I tell her, he thought, or not? He would like to make a clean breast of it all. But she is too cold, he thought; sewing, with her scissors; Daisy would look ordinary beside Clarissa. And she would think me a failure, which I am in their sense, he thought; in the Dalloways' sense. Oh yes, he had no doubt about that; he was a failure, compared with all this--the inlaid table, the mounted paper-knife, the dolphin and the candlesticks, the chair-covers and the old valuable English tinted prints--he was a failure! I detest the smugness of the whole affair, he thought; Richard's doing, not Clarissa's; save that she married him. (Here Lucy came into the room, carrying silver, more silver, but charming, slender, graceful she looked, he thought, as she stooped to put it down.) And this has been going on all the time! he thought; week after week; Clarissa's life; while I--he thought; and at once everything seemed to radiate from him; journeys; rides; quarrels; adventures; bridge parties; love affairs; work; work, work! and he took out his knife quite openly--his old horn-handled knife which Clarissa could swear he had had these thirty years--and clenched his fist upon it.

What an extraordinary habit that was, Clarissa thought; always playing with a knife. Always making one feel, too, frivolous; empty-minded; a mere silly chatterbox, as he used. But I too, she thought, and, taking up her needle, summoned, like a Queen whose guards have fallen asleep and left her unprotected (she had been quite taken aback by this visit--it had upset her) so that any one can stroll in and have a look at her where she lies with the brambles curving over her, summoned to her help the things she did; the things she liked; her husband; Elizabeth; her self, in short, which Peter hardly knew now, all to come about her and beat off the enemy.

"Well, and what's happened to you?" she said. So before a battle begins, the horses paw the ground; toss their heads; the light shines on their flanks; their necks curve. So Peter Walsh and Clarissa, sitting side by side on the blue sofa, challenged each other. His powers chafed and tossed in him. He assembled from different quarters all sorts of things; praise; his career at Oxford; his marriage, which she knew nothing whatever about; how he had loved; and altogether done his job.

"Millions of things!" he exclaimed, and, urged by the assembly of powers which were now charging this way and that and giving him the feeling at once frightening and extremely exhilarating of being rushed through the air on the shoulders of people he could no longer see, he raised his hands to his forehead.

Clarissa sat very upright; drew in her breath.

"I am in love," he said, not to her however, but to some one raised up in the dark so that you could not touch her but must lay your garland down on the grass in the dark.

"In love," he repeated, now speaking rather dryly to Clarissa Dalloway; "in love with a girl in India." He had deposited his garland. Clarissa could make what she would of it.

"In love!" she said. That he at his age should be sucked under in his little bow-tie by that monster! And there's no flesh on his neck; his hands are red; and he's six months older than I am! her eye flashed back to her; but in her heart she felt, all the same, he is in love. He has that, she felt; he is in love.

But the indomitable egotism which for ever rides down the hosts opposed to it, the river which says on, on, on; even though, it admits, there may be no goal for us whatever, still on, on; this indomitable egotism charged her cheeks with colour; made her look very young; very pink; very bright-eyed as she sat with her dress upon her knee, and her needle held to the end of green silk, trembling a little. He was in love! Not with her. With some younger woman, of course.

"And who is she?" she asked.

Now this statue must be brought from its height and set down between them.

"A married woman, unfortunately," he said; "the wife of a Major in the Indian Army."

And with a curious ironical sweetness he smiled as he placed her in this ridiculous way before Clarissa.

(All the same, he is in love, thought Clarissa.)

"She has," he continued, very reasonably, "two small children; a boy and a girl; and I have come over to see my lawyers about the divorce."

There they are! he thought. Do what you like with them, Clarissa! There they are! And second by second it seemed to him that the wife of the Major in the Indian Army (his Daisy) and her two small children became more and more lovely as Clarissa looked at them; as if he had set light to a grey pellet on a plate and there had risen up a lovely tree in the brisk sea-salted air of their intimacy (for in some ways no one understood him, felt with him, as Clarissa did)--their exquisite intimacy.

She flattered him; she fooled him, thought Clarissa; shaping the woman, the wife of the Major in the Indian Army, with three strokes of a knife. What a waste! What a folly! All his life long Peter had been fooled like that; first getting sent down from Oxford; next marrying the girl on the boat going out to India; now the wife of a Major in the Indian Army--thank Heaven she had refused to marry him! Still, he was in love; her old friend, her dear Peter, he was in love.

"But what are you going to do?" she asked him. Oh the lawyers and solicitors, Messrs. Hooper and Grateley of Lincoln's Inn, they were going to do it, he said. And he actually pared his nails with his pocket-knife.

For Heaven's sake, leave your knife alone! she cried to herself in irrepressible irritation; it was his silly unconventionality, his weakness; his lack of the ghost of a notion what any one else was feeling that annoyed her, had always annoyed her; and now at his age, how silly!

I know all that, Peter thought; I know what I'm up against, he thought, running his finger along the blade of his knife, Clarissa and Dalloway and all the rest of them; but I'll show Clarissa--and then to his utter surprise, suddenly thrown by those uncontrollable forces thrown through the air, he burst into tears; wept; wept without the least shame, sitting on the sofa, the tears running down his cheeks.

And Clarissa had leant forward, taken his hand, drawn him to her, kissed him,--actually had felt his face on hers before she could down the brandishing of silver flashing--plumes like pampas grass in a tropic gale in her breast, which, subsiding, left her holding his hand, patting his knee and, feeling as she sat back extraordinarily at her ease with him and light-hearted, all in a clap it came over her, If I had married him, this gaiety would have been mine all day!

It was all over for her. The sheet was stretched and the bed narrow. She had gone up into the tower alone and left them blackberrying in the sun. The door had shut, and there among the dust of fallen plaster and the litter of birds' nests how distant the view had looked, and the sounds came thin and chill (once on Leith Hill, she remembered), and Richard, Richard! she cried, as a sleeper in the night starts and stretches a hand in the dark for help. Lunching with Lady Bruton, it came back to her. He has left me; I am alone for ever, she thought, folding her hands upon her knee.

Peter Walsh had got up and crossed to the window and stood with his back to her, flicking a bandanna handkerchief from side to side. Masterly and dry and desolate he looked, his thin shoulder-blades lifting his coat slightly; blowing his nose violently. Take me with you, Clarissa thought impulsively, as if he were starting directly upon some great voyage; and then, next moment, it was as if the five acts of a play that had been very exciting and moving were now over and she had lived a lifetime in them and had run away, had lived with Peter, and it was now over.

Now it was time to move, and, as a woman gathers her things together, her cloak, her gloves, her opera-glasses, and gets up to go out of the theatre into the street, she rose from the sofa and went to Peter.

And it was awfully strange, he thought, how she still had the power, as she came tinkling, rustling, still had the power as she came across the room, to make the moon, which he detested, rise at Bourton on the terrace in the summer sky.

"Tell me," he said, seizing her by the shoulders. "Are you happy, Clarissa? Does Richard--"

The door opened.

"Here is my Elizabeth," said Clarissa, emotionally, histrionically, perhaps.

"How d'y do?" said Elizabeth coming forward.

The sound of Big Ben striking the half-hour struck out between them with extraordinary vigour, as if a young man, strong, indifferent, inconsiderate, were swinging dumb-bells this way and that.

"Hullo, Elizabeth!" cried Peter, stuffing his handkerchief into his pocket, going quickly to her, saying "Good-bye, Clarissa" without looking at her, leaving the room quickly, and running downstairs and opening the hall door.

"Peter! Peter!" cried Clarissa, following him out on to the landing. "My party to-night! Remember my party to-night!" she cried, having to raise her voice against the roar of the open air, and, overwhelmed by the traffic and the sound of all the clocks striking, her voice crying "Remember my party to-night!" sounded frail and thin and very far away as Peter Walsh shut the door.

Remember my party, remember my party, said Peter Walsh as he stepped down the street, speaking to himself rhythmically, in time with the flow of the sound, the direct downright sound of Big Ben striking the half-hour. (The leaden circles dissolved in the air.) Oh these parties, he thought; Clarissa's parties. Why does she give these parties, he thought. Not that he blamed her or this effigy of a man in a tail-coat with a carnation in his buttonhole coming towards him. Only one person in the world could be as he was, in love. And there he was, this fortunate man, himself, reflected in the plate-glass window of a motor-car manufacturer in Victoria Street. All India lay behind him; plains, mountains; epidemics of cholera; a district twice as big as Ireland; decisions he had come to alone--he, Peter Walsh; who was now really for the first time in his life, in love. Clarissa had grown hard, he thought; and a trifle sentimental into the bargain, he suspected, looking at the great motor-cars capable of doing--how many miles on how many gallons? For he had a turn for mechanics; had invented a plough in his district, had ordered wheel-barrows from England, but the coolies wouldn't use them, all of which Clarissa knew nothing whatever about.

The way she said "Here is my Elizabeth!"--that annoyed him. Why not "Here's Elizabeth" simply? It was insincere. And Elizabeth didn't like it either. (Still the last tremors of the great booming voice shook the air round him; the half-hour; still early; only half-past eleven still.) For he understood young people; he liked them. There was always something cold in Clarissa, he thought. She had always, even as a girl, a sort of timidity, which in middle age becomes conventionality, and then it's all up, it's all up, he thought, looking rather drearily into the glassy depths, and wondering whether by calling at that hour he had annoyed her; overcome with shame suddenly at having been a fool; wept; been emotional; told her everything, as usual, as usual.

As a cloud crosses the sun, silence falls on London; and falls on the mind. Effort ceases. Time flaps on the mast. There we stop; there we stand. Rigid, the skeleton of habit alone upholds the human frame. Where there is nothing, Peter Walsh said to himself; feeling hollowed out, utterly empty within. Clarissa refused me, he thought. He stood there thinking, Clarissa refused me.

Ah, said St. Margaret's, like a hostess who comes into her drawing- room on the very stroke of the hour and finds her guests there already. I am not late. No, it is precisely half-past eleven, she says. Yet, though she is perfectly right, her voice, being the voice of the hostess, is reluctant to inflict its individuality. Some grief for the past holds it back; some concern for the present. It is half-past eleven, she says, and the sound of St. Margaret's glides into the recesses of the heart and buries itself in ring after ring of sound, like something alive which wants to confide itself, to disperse itself, to be, with a tremor of delight, at rest--like Clarissa herself, thought Peter Walsh, coming down the stairs on the stroke of the hour in white. It is Clarissa herself, he thought, with a deep emotion, and an extraordinarily clear, yet puzzling, recollection of her, as if this bell had come into the room years ago, where they sat at some moment of great intimacy, and had gone from one to the other and had left, like a bee with honey, laden with the moment. But what room? What moment? And why had he been so profoundly happy when the clock was striking? Then, as the sound of St. Margaret's languished, he thought, She has been ill, and the sound expressed languor and suffering. It was her heart, he remembered; and the sudden loudness of the final stroke tolled for death that surprised in the midst of life, Clarissa falling where she stood, in her drawing-room. No! No! he cried. She is not dead! I am not old, he cried, and marched up Whitehall, as if there rolled down to him, vigorous, unending, his future.

He was not old, or set, or dried in the least. As for caring what they said of him--the Dalloways, the Whitbreads, and their set, he cared not a straw--not a straw (though it was true he would have, some time or other, to see whether Richard couldn't help him to some job). Striding, staring, he glared at the statue of the Duke of Cambridge. He had been sent down from Oxford--true. He had been a Socialist, in some sense a failure--true. Still the future of civilisation lies, he thought, in the hands of young men like that; of young men such as he was, thirty years ago; with their love of abstract principles; getting books sent out to them all the way from London to a peak in the Himalayas; reading science; reading philosophy. The future lies in the hands of young men like that, he thought.

A patter like the patter of leaves in a wood came from behind, and with it a rustling, regular thudding sound, which as it overtook him drummed his thoughts, strict in step, up Whitehall, without his doing. Boys in uniform, carrying guns, marched with their eyes ahead of them, marched, their arms stiff, and on their faces an expression like the letters of a legend written round the base of a statue praising duty, gratitude, fidelity, love of England.

It is, thought Peter Walsh, beginning to keep step with them, a very fine training. But they did not look robust. They were weedy for the most part, boys of sixteen, who might, to-morrow, stand behind bowls of rice, cakes of soap on counters. Now they wore on them unmixed with sensual pleasure or daily preoccupations the solemnity of the wreath which they had fetched from Finsbury Pavement to the empty tomb. They had taken their vow. The traffic respected it; vans were stopped.

I can't keep up with them, Peter Walsh thought, as they marched up Whitehall, and sure enough, on they marched, past him, past every one, in their steady way, as if one will worked legs and arms uniformly, and life, with its varieties, its irreticences, had been laid under a pavement of monuments and wreaths and drugged into a stiff yet staring corpse by discipline. One had to respect it; one might laugh; but one had to respect it, he thought. There they go, thought Peter Walsh, pausing at the edge of the pavement; and all the exalted statues, Nelson, Gordon, Havelock, the black, the spectacular images of great soldiers stood looking ahead of them, as if they too had made the same renunciation (Peter Walsh felt he too had made it, the great renunciation), trampled under the same temptations, and achieved at length a marble stare. But the stare Peter Walsh did not want for himself in the least; though he could respect it in others. He could respect it in boys. They don't know the troubles of the flesh yet, he thought, as the marching boys disappeared in the direction of the Strand--all that I've been through, he thought, crossing the road, and standing under Gordon's statue, Gordon whom as a boy he had worshipped; Gordon standing lonely with one leg raised and his arms crossed,--poor Gordon, he thought.

And just because nobody yet knew he was in London, except Clarissa, and the earth, after the voyage, still seemed an island to him, the strangeness of standing alone, alive, unknown, at half-past eleven in Trafalgar Square overcame him. What is it? Where am I? And why, after all, does one do it? he thought, the divorce seeming all moonshine. And down his mind went flat as a marsh, and three great emotions bowled over him; understanding; a vast philanthropy; and finally, as if the result of the others, an irrepressible, exquisite delight; as if inside his brain by another hand strings were pulled, shutters moved, and he, having nothing to do with it, yet stood at the opening of endless avenues, down which if he chose he might wander. He had not felt so young for years.

He had escaped! was utterly free--as happens in the downfall of habit when the mind, like an unguarded flame, bows and bends and seems about to blow from its holding. I haven't felt so young for years! thought Peter, escaping (only of course for an hour or so) from being precisely what he was, and feeling like a child who runs out of doors, and sees, as he runs, his old nurse waving at the wrong window. But she's extraordinarily attractive, he thought, as, walking across Trafalgar Square in the direction of the Haymarket, came a young woman who, as she passed Gordon's statue, seemed, Peter Walsh thought (susceptible as he was), to shed veil after veil, until she became the very woman he had always had in mind; young, but stately; merry, but discreet; black, but enchanting.

Straightening himself and stealthily fingering his pocket-knife he started after her to follow this woman, this excitement, which seemed even with its back turned to shed on him a light which connected them, which singled him out, as if the random uproar of the traffic had whispered through hollowed hands his name, not Peter, but his private name which he called himself in his own thoughts. "You," she said, only "you," saying it with her white gloves and her shoulders. Then the thin long cloak which the wind stirred as she walked past Dent's shop in Cockspur Street blew out with an enveloping kindness, a mournful tenderness, as of arms that would open and take the tired--

But she's not married; she's young; quite young, thought Peter, the red carnation he had seen her wear as she came across Trafalgar Square burning again in his eyes and making her lips red. But she waited at the kerbstone. There was a dignity about her. She was not worldly, like Clarissa; not rich, like Clarissa. Was she, he wondered as she moved, respectable? Witty, with a lizard's flickering tongue, he thought (for one must invent, must allow oneself a little diversion), a cool waiting wit, a darting wit; not noisy.

She moved; she crossed; he followed her. To embarrass her was the last thing he wished. Still if she stopped he would say "Come and have an ice," he would say, and she would answer, perfectly simply, "Oh yes."

But other people got between them in the street, obstructing him, blotting her out. He pursued; she changed. There was colour in her cheeks; mockery in her eyes; he was an adventurer, reckless, he thought, swift, daring, indeed (landed as he was last night from India) a romantic buccaneer, careless of all these damned proprieties, yellow dressing-gowns, pipes, fishing-rods, in the shop windows; and respectability and evening parties and spruce old men wearing white slips beneath their waistcoats. He was a buccaneer. On and on she went, across Piccadilly, and up Regent Street, ahead of him, her cloak, her gloves, her shoulders combining with the fringes and the laces and the feather boas in the windows to make the spirit of finery and whimsy which dwindled out of the shops on to the pavement, as the light of a lamp goes wavering at night over hedges in the darkness.

Laughing and delightful, she had crossed Oxford Street and Great Portland Street and turned down one of the little streets, and now, and now, the great moment was approaching, for now she slackened, opened her bag, and with one look in his direction, but not at him, one look that bade farewell, summed up the whole situation and dismissed it triumphantly, for ever, had fitted her key, opened the door, and gone! Clarissa's voice saying, Remember my party, Remember my party, sang in his ears. The house was one of those flat red houses with hanging flower-baskets of vague impropriety. It was over.

Well, I've had my fun; I've had it, he thought, looking up at the swinging baskets of pale geraniums. And it was smashed to atoms-- his fun, for it was half made up, as he knew very well; invented, this escapade with the girl; made up, as one makes up the better part of life, he thought--making oneself up; making her up; creating an exquisite amusement, and something more. But odd it was, and quite true; all this one could never share--it smashed to atoms.

He turned; went up the street, thinking to find somewhere to sit, till it was time for Lincoln's Inn--for Messrs. Hooper and Grateley. Where should he go? No matter. Up the street, then, towards Regent's Park. His boots on the pavement struck out "no matter"; for it was early, still very early.

It was a splendid morning too. Like the pulse of a perfect heart, life struck straight through the streets. There was no fumbling-- no hesitation. Sweeping and swerving, accurately, punctually, noiselessly, there, precisely at the right instant, the motor-car stopped at the door. The girl, silk-stockinged, feathered, evanescent, but not to him particularly attractive (for he had had his fling), alighted. Admirable butlers, tawny chow dogs, halls laid in black and white lozenges with white blinds blowing, Peter saw through the opened door and approved of. A splendid achievement in its own way, after all, London; the season; civilisation. Coming as he did from a respectable Anglo-Indian family which for at least three generations had administered the affairs of a continent (it's strange, he thought, what a sentiment I have about that, disliking India, and empire, and army as he did), there were moments when civilisation, even of this sort, seemed dear to him as a personal possession; moments of pride in England; in butlers; chow dogs; girls in their security. Ridiculous enough, still there it is, he thought. And the doctors and men of business and capable women all going about their business, punctual, alert, robust, seemed to him wholly admirable, good fellows, to whom one would entrust one's life, companions in the art of living, who would see one through. What with one thing and another, the show was really very tolerable; and he would sit down in the shade and smoke.

There was Regent's Park. Yes. As a child he had walked in Regent's Park--odd, he thought, how the thought of childhood keeps coming back to me--the result of seeing Clarissa, perhaps; for women live much more in the past than we do, he thought. They attach themselves to places; and their fathers--a woman's always proud of her father. Bourton was a nice place, a very nice place, but I could never get on with the old man, he thought. There was quite a scene one night--an argument about something or other, what, he could not remember. Politics presumably.

Yes, he remembered Regent's Park; the long straight walk; the little house where one bought air-balls to the left; an absurd statue with an inscription somewhere or other. He looked for an empty seat. He did not want to be bothered (feeling a little drowsy as he did) by people asking him the time. An elderly grey nurse, with a baby asleep in its perambulator--that was the best he could do for himself; sit down at the far end of the seat by that nurse.

She's a queer-looking girl, he thought, suddenly remembering Elizabeth as she came into the room and stood by her mother. Grown big; quite grown-up, not exactly pretty; handsome rather; and she can't be more than eighteen. Probably she doesn't get on with Clarissa. "There's my Elizabeth"--that sort of thing--why not "Here's Elizabeth" simply?--trying to make out, like most mothers, that things are what they're not. She trusts to her charm too much, he thought. She overdoes it.

The rich benignant cigar smoke eddied coolly down his throat; he puffed it out again in rings which breasted the air bravely for a moment; blue, circular--I shall try and get a word alone with Elizabeth to-night, he thought--then began to wobble into hour- glass shapes and taper away; odd shapes they take, he thought. Suddenly he closed his eyes, raised his hand with an effort, and threw away the heavy end of his cigar. A great brush swept smooth across his mind, sweeping across it moving branches, children's voices, the shuffle of feet, and people passing, and humming traffic, rising and falling traffic. Down, down he sank into the plumes and feathers of sleep, sank, and was muffled over.

The grey nurse resumed her knitting as Peter Walsh, on the hot seat beside her, began snoring. In her grey dress, moving her hands indefatigably yet quietly, she seemed like the champion of the rights of sleepers, like one of those spectral presences which rise in twilight in woods made of sky and branches. The solitary traveller, haunter of lanes, disturber of ferns, and devastator of great hemlock plants, looking up, suddenly sees the giant figure at the end of the ride.

By conviction an atheist perhaps, he is taken by surprise with moments of extraordinary exaltation. Nothing exists outside us except a state of mind, he thinks; a desire for solace, for relief, for something outside these miserable pigmies, these feeble, these ugly, these craven men and women. But if he can conceive of her, then in some sort she exists, he thinks, and advancing down the path with his eyes upon sky and branches he rapidly endows them with womanhood; sees with amazement how grave they become; how majestically, as the breeze stirs them, they dispense with a dark flutter of the leaves charity, comprehension, absolution, and then, flinging themselves suddenly aloft, confound the piety of their aspect with a wild carouse.

Such are the visions which proffer great cornucopias full of fruit to the solitary traveller, or murmur in his ear like sirens lolloping away on the green sea waves, or are dashed in his face like bunches of roses, or rise to the surface like pale faces which fishermen flounder through floods to embrace.

Such are the visions which ceaselessly float up, pace beside, put their faces in front of, the actual thing; often overpowering the solitary traveller and taking away from him the sense of the earth, the wish to return, and giving him for substitute a general peace, as if (so he thinks as he advances down the forest ride) all this fever of living were simplicity itself; and myriads of things merged in one thing; and this figure, made of sky and branches as it is, had risen from the troubled sea (he is elderly, past fifty now) as a shape might be sucked up out of the waves to shower down from her magnificent hands compassion, comprehension, absolution. So, he thinks, may I never go back to the lamplight; to the sitting-room; never finish my book; never knock out my pipe; never ring for Mrs. Turner to clear away; rather let me walk straight on to this great figure, who will, with a toss of her head, mount me on her streamers and let me blow to nothingness with the rest.

Such are the visions. The solitary traveller is soon beyond the wood; and there, coming to the door with shaded eyes, possibly to look for his return, with hands raised, with white apron blowing, is an elderly woman who seems (so powerful is this infirmity) to seek, over a desert, a lost son; to search for a rider destroyed; to be the figure of the mother whose sons have been killed in the battles of the world. So, as the solitary traveller advances down the village street where the women stand knitting and the men dig in the garden, the evening seems ominous; the figures still; as if some august fate, known to them, awaited without fear, were about to sweep them into complete annihilation.

Indoors among ordinary things, the cupboard, the table, the window- sill with its geraniums, suddenly the outline of the landlady, bending to remove the cloth, becomes soft with light, an adorable emblem which only the recollection of cold human contacts forbids us to embrace. She takes the marmalade; she shuts it in the cupboard.

"There is nothing more to-night, sir?"

But to whom does the solitary traveller make reply?

So the elderly nurse knitted over the sleeping baby in Regent's Park. So Peter Walsh snored.

He woke with extreme suddenness, saying to himself, "The death of the soul."

"Lord, Lord!" he said to himself out loud, stretching and opening his eyes. "The death of the soul." The words attached themselves to some scene, to some room, to some past he had been dreaming of. It became clearer; the scene, the room, the past he had been dreaming of.

It was at Bourton that summer, early in the 'nineties, when he was so passionately in love with Clarissa. There were a great many people there, laughing and talking, sitting round a table after tea and the room was bathed in yellow light and full of cigarette smoke. They were talking about a man who had married his housemaid, one of the neighbouring squires, he had forgotten his name. He had married his housemaid, and she had been brought to Bourton to call--an awful visit it had been. She was absurdly over-dressed, "like a cockatoo," Clarissa had said, imitating her, and she never stopped talking. On and on she went, on and on. Clarissa imitated her. Then somebody said--Sally Seton it was--did it make any real difference to one's feelings to know that before they'd married she had had a baby? (In those days, in mixed company, it was a bold thing to say.) He could see Clarissa now, turning bright pink; somehow contracting; and saying, "Oh, I shall never be able to speak to her again!" Whereupon the whole party sitting round the tea-table seemed to wobble. It was very uncomfortable.

He hadn't blamed her for minding the fact, since in those days a girl brought up as she was, knew nothing, but it was her manner that annoyed him; timid; hard; something arrogant; unimaginative; prudish. "The death of the soul." He had said that instinctively, ticketing the moment as he used to do--the death of her soul.

Every one wobbled; every one seemed to bow, as she spoke, and then to stand up different. He could see Sally Seton, like a child who has been in mischief, leaning forward, rather flushed, wanting to talk, but afraid, and Clarissa did frighten people. (She was Clarissa's greatest friend, always about the place, totally unlike her, an attractive creature, handsome, dark, with the reputation in those days of great daring and he used to give her cigars, which she smoked in her bedroom. She had either been engaged to somebody or quarrelled with her family and old Parry disliked them both equally, which was a great bond.) Then Clarissa, still with an air of being offended with them all, got up, made some excuse, and went off, alone. As she opened the door, in came that great shaggy dog which ran after sheep. She flung herself upon him, went into raptures. It was as if she said to Peter--it was all aimed at him, he knew--"I know you thought me absurd about that woman just now; but see how extraordinarily sympathetic I am; see how I love my Rob!"

They had always this queer power of communicating without words. She knew directly he criticised her. Then she would do something quite obvious to defend herself, like this fuss with the dog--but it never took him in, he always saw through Clarissa. Not that he said anything, of course; just sat looking glum. It was the way their quarrels often began.

She shut the door. At once he became extremely depressed. It all seemed useless--going on being in love; going on quarrelling; going on making it up, and he wandered off alone, among outhouses, stables, looking at the horses. (The place was quite a humble one; the Parrys were never very well off; but there were always grooms and stable-boys about--Clarissa loved riding--and an old coachman-- what was his name?--an old nurse, old Moody, old Goody, some such name they called her, whom one was taken to visit in a little room with lots of photographs, lots of bird-cages.)

It was an awful evening! He grew more and more gloomy, not about that only; about everything. And he couldn't see her; couldn't explain to her; couldn't have it out. There were always people about--she'd go on as if nothing had happened. That was the devilish part of her--this coldness, this woodenness, something very profound in her, which he had felt again this morning talking to her; an impenetrability. Yet Heaven knows he loved her. She had some queer power of fiddling on one's nerves, turning one's nerves to fiddle-strings, yes.

He had gone in to dinner rather late, from some idiotic idea of making himself felt, and had sat down by old Miss Parry--Aunt Helena--Mr. Parry's sister, who was supposed to preside. There she sat in her white Cashmere shawl, with her head against the window-- a formidable old lady, but kind to him, for he had found her some rare flower, and she was a great botanist, marching off in thick boots with a black collecting-box slung between her shoulders. He sat down beside her, and couldn't speak. Everything seemed to race past him; he just sat there, eating. And then half-way through dinner he made himself look across at Clarissa for the first time. She was talking to a young man on her right. He had a sudden revelation. "She will marry that man," he said to himself. He didn't even know his name.

For of course it was that afternoon, that very afternoon, that Dalloway had come over; and Clarissa called him "Wickham"; that was the beginning of it all. Somebody had brought him over; and Clarissa got his name wrong. She introduced him to everybody as Wickham. At last he said "My name is Dalloway!"--that was his first view of Richard--a fair young man, rather awkward, sitting on a deck-chair, and blurting out "My name is Dalloway!" Sally got hold of it; always after that she called him "My name is Dalloway!"

He was a prey to revelations at that time. This one--that she would marry Dalloway--was blinding--overwhelming at the moment. There was a sort of--how could he put it?--a sort of ease in her manner to him; something maternal; something gentle. They were talking about politics. All through dinner he tried to hear what they were saying.

Afterwards he could remember standing by old Miss Parry's chair in the drawing-room. Clarissa came up, with her perfect manners, like a real hostess, and wanted to introduce him to some one--spoke as if they had never met before, which enraged him. Yet even then he admired her for it. He admired her courage; her social instinct; he admired her power of carrying things through. "The perfect hostess," he said to her, whereupon she winced all over. But he meant her to feel it. He would have done anything to hurt her after seeing her with Dalloway. So she left him. And he had a feeling that they were all gathered together in a conspiracy against him--laughing and talking--behind his back. There he stood by Miss Parry's chair as though he had been cut out of wood, he talking about wild flowers. Never, never had he suffered so infernally! He must have forgotten even to pretend to listen; at last he woke up; he saw Miss Parry looking rather disturbed, rather indignant, with her prominent eyes fixed. He almost cried out that he couldn't attend because he was in Hell! People began going out of the room. He heard them talking about fetching cloaks; about its being cold on the water, and so on. They were going boating on the lake by moonlight--one of Sally's mad ideas. He could hear her describing the moon. And they all went out. He was left quite alone.

"Don't you want to go with them?" said Aunt Helena--old Miss Parry!--she had guessed. And he turned round and there was Clarissa again. She had come back to fetch him. He was overcome by her generosity--her goodness.

"Come along," she said. "They're waiting." He had never felt so happy in the whole of his life! Without a word they made it up. They walked down to the lake. He had twenty minutes of perfect happiness. Her voice, her laugh, her dress (something floating, white, crimson), her spirit, her adventurousness; she made them all disembark and explore the island; she startled a hen; she laughed; she sang. And all the time, he knew perfectly well, Dalloway was falling in love with her; she was falling in love with Dalloway; but it didn't seem to matter. Nothing mattered. They sat on the ground and talked--he and Clarissa. They went in and out of each other's minds without any effort. And then in a second it was over. He said to himself as they were getting into the boat, "She will marry that man," dully, without any resentment; but it was an obvious thing. Dalloway would marry Clarissa.

Dalloway rowed them in. He said nothing. But somehow as they watched him start, jumping on to his bicycle to ride twenty miles through the woods, wobbling off down the drive, waving his hand and disappearing, he obviously did feel, instinctively, tremendously, strongly, all that; the night; the romance; Clarissa. He deserved to have her.

For himself, he was absurd. His demands upon Clarissa (he could see it now) were absurd. He asked impossible things. He made terrible scenes. She would have accepted him still, perhaps, if he had been less absurd. Sally thought so. She wrote him all that summer long letters; how they had talked of him; how she had praised him, how Clarissa burst into tears! It was an extraordinary summer--all letters, scenes, telegrams--arriving at Bourton early in the morning, hanging about till the servants were up; appalling tête-à-têtes with old Mr. Parry at breakfast; Aunt Helena formidable but kind; Sally sweeping him off for talks in the vegetable garden; Clarissa in bed with headaches.

The final scene, the terrible scene which he believed had mattered more than anything in the whole of his life (it might be an exaggeration--but still so it did seem now) happened at three o'clock in the afternoon of a very hot day. It was a trifle that led up to it--Sally at lunch saying something about Dalloway, and calling him "My name is Dalloway"; whereupon Clarissa suddenly stiffened, coloured, in a way she had, and rapped out sharply, "We've had enough of that feeble joke." That was all; but for him it was precisely as if she had said, "I'm only amusing myself with you; I've an understanding with Richard Dalloway." So he took it. He had not slept for nights. "It's got to be finished one way or the other," he said to himself. He sent a note to her by Sally asking her to meet him by the fountain at three. "Something very important has happened," he scribbled at the end of it.

The fountain was in the middle of a little shrubbery, far from the house, with shrubs and trees all round it. There she came, even before the time, and they stood with the fountain between them, the spout (it was broken) dribbling water incessantly. How sights fix themselves upon the mind! For example, the vivid green moss.

She did not move. "Tell me the truth, tell me the truth," he kept on saying. He felt as if his forehead would burst. She seemed contracted, petrified. She did not move. "Tell me the truth," he repeated, when suddenly that old man Breitkopf popped his head in carrying the Times; stared at them; gaped; and went away. They neither of them moved. "Tell me the truth," he repeated. He felt that he was grinding against something physically hard; she was unyielding. She was like iron, like flint, rigid up the backbone. And when she said, "It's no use. It's no use. This is the end"-- after he had spoken for hours, it seemed, with the tears running down his cheeks--it was as if she had hit him in the face. She turned, she left him, went away.

"Clarissa!" he cried. "Clarissa!" But she never came back. It was over. He went away that night. He never saw her again.

It was awful, he cried, awful, awful!

Still, the sun was hot. Still, one got over things. Still, life had a way of adding day to day. Still, he thought, yawning and beginning to take notice--Regent's Park had changed very little since he was a boy, except for the squirrels--still, presumably there were compensations--when little Elise Mitchell, who had been picking up pebbles to add to the pebble collection which she and her brother were making on the nursery mantelpiece, plumped her handful down on the nurse's knee and scudded off again full tilt into a lady's legs. Peter Walsh laughed out.

But Lucrezia Warren Smith was saying to herself, It's wicked; why should I suffer? she was asking, as she walked down the broad path. No; I can't stand it any longer, she was saying, having left Septimus, who wasn't Septimus any longer, to say hard, cruel, wicked things, to talk to himself, to talk to a dead man, on the seat over there; when the child ran full tilt into her, fell flat, and burst out crying.

That was comforting rather. She stood her upright, dusted her frock, kissed her.

But for herself she had done nothing wrong; she had loved Septimus; she had been happy; she had had a beautiful home, and there her sisters lived still, making hats. Why should SHE suffer?

The child ran straight back to its nurse, and Rezia saw her scolded, comforted, taken up by the nurse who put down her knitting, and the kind-looking man gave her his watch to blow open to comfort her--but why should SHE be exposed? Why not left in Milan? Why tortured? Why?

Slightly waved by tears the broad path, the nurse, the man in grey, the perambulator, rose and fell before her eyes. To be rocked by this malignant torturer was her lot. But why? She was like a bird sheltering under the thin hollow of a leaf, who blinks at the sun when the leaf moves; starts at the crack of a dry twig. She was exposed; she was surrounded by the enormous trees, vast clouds of an indifferent world, exposed; tortured; and why should she suffer? Why?

She frowned; she stamped her foot. She must go back again to Septimus since it was almost time for them to be going to Sir William Bradshaw. She must go back and tell him, go back to him sitting there on the green chair under the tree, talking to himself, or to that dead man Evans, whom she had only seen once for a moment in the shop. He had seemed a nice quiet man; a great friend of Septimus's, and he had been killed in the War. But such things happen to every one. Every one has friends who were killed in the War. Every one gives up something when they marry. She had given up her home. She had come to live here, in this awful city. But Septimus let himself think about horrible things, as she could too, if she tried. He had grown stranger and stranger. He said people were talking behind the bedroom walls. Mrs. Filmer thought it odd. He saw things too--he had seen an old woman's head in the middle of a fern. Yet he could be happy when he chose. They went to Hampton Court on top of a bus, and they were perfectly happy. All the little red and yellow flowers were out on the grass, like floating lamps he said, and talked and chattered and laughed, making up stories. Suddenly he said, "Now we will kill ourselves," when they were standing by the river, and he looked at it with a look which she had seen in his eyes when a train went by, or an omnibus--a look as if something fascinated him; and she felt he was going from her and she caught him by the arm. But going home he was perfectly quiet--perfectly reasonable. He would argue with her about killing themselves; and explain how wicked people were; how he could see them making up lies as they passed in the street. He knew all their thoughts, he said; he knew everything. He knew the meaning of the world, he said.

Then when they got back he could hardly walk. He lay on the sofa and made her hold his hand to prevent him from falling down, down, he cried, into the flames! and saw faces laughing at him, calling him horrible disgusting names, from the walls, and hands pointing round the screen. Yet they were quite alone. But he began to talk aloud, answering people, arguing, laughing, crying, getting very excited and making her write things down. Perfect nonsense it was; about death; about Miss Isabel Pole. She could stand it no longer. She would go back.

She was close to him now, could see him staring at the sky, muttering, clasping his hands. Yet Dr. Holmes said there was nothing the matter with him. What then had happened--why had he gone, then, why, when she sat by him, did he start, frown at her, move away, and point at her hand, take her hand, look at it terrified?

Was it that she had taken off her wedding ring? "My hand has grown so thin," she said. "I have put it in my purse," she told him.

He dropped her hand. Their marriage was over, he thought, with agony, with relief. The rope was cut; he mounted; he was free, as it was decreed that he, Septimus, the lord of men, should be free; alone (since his wife had thrown away her wedding ring; since she had left him), he, Septimus, was alone, called forth in advance of the mass of men to hear the truth, to learn the meaning, which now at last, after all the toils of civilisation--Greeks, Romans, Shakespeare, Darwin, and now himself--was to be given whole to. . . . "To whom?" he asked aloud. "To the Prime Minister," the voices which rustled above his head replied. The supreme secret must be told to the Cabinet; first that trees are alive; next there is no crime; next love, universal love, he muttered, gasping, trembling, painfully drawing out these profound truths which needed, so deep were they, so difficult, an immense effort to speak out, but the world was entirely changed by them for ever.

No crime; love; he repeated, fumbling for his card and pencil, when a Skye terrier snuffed his trousers and he started in an agony of fear. It was turning into a man! He could not watch it happen! It was horrible, terrible to see a dog become a man! At once the dog trotted away.

Heaven was divinely merciful, infinitely benignant. It spared him, pardoned his weakness. But what was the scientific explanation (for one must be scientific above all things)? Why could he see through bodies, see into the future, when dogs will become men? It was the heat wave presumably, operating upon a brain made sensitive by eons of evolution. Scientifically speaking, the flesh was melted off the world. His body was macerated until only the nerve fibres were left. It was spread like a veil upon a rock.

He lay back in his chair, exhausted but upheld. He lay resting, waiting, before he again interpreted, with effort, with agony, to mankind. He lay very high, on the back of the world. The earth thrilled beneath him. Red flowers grew through his flesh; their stiff leaves rustled by his head. Music began clanging against the rocks up here. It is a motor horn down in the street, he muttered; but up here it cannoned from rock to rock, divided, met in shocks of sound which rose in smooth columns (that music should be visible was a discovery) and became an anthem, an anthem twined round now by a shepherd boy's piping (That's an old man playing a penny whistle by the public-house, he muttered) which, as the boy stood still came bubbling from his pipe, and then, as he climbed higher, made its exquisite plaint while the traffic passed beneath. This boy's elegy is played among the traffic, thought Septimus. Now he withdraws up into the snows, and roses hang about him--the thick red roses which grow on my bedroom wall, he reminded himself. The music stopped. He has his penny, he reasoned it out, and has gone on to the next public-house.

But he himself remained high on his rock, like a drowned sailor on a rock. I leant over the edge of the boat and fell down, he thought. I went under the sea. I have been dead, and yet am now alive, but let me rest still; he begged (he was talking to himself again--it was awful, awful!); and as, before waking, the voices of birds and the sound of wheels chime and chatter in a queer harmony, grow louder and louder and the sleeper feels himself drawing to the shores of life, so he felt himself drawing towards life, the sun growing hotter, cries sounding louder, something tremendous about to happen.

He had only to open his eyes; but a weight was on them; a fear. He strained; he pushed; he looked; he saw Regent's Park before him. Long streamers of sunlight fawned at his feet. The trees waved, brandished. We welcome, the world seemed to say; we accept; we create. Beauty, the world seemed to say. And as if to prove it (scientifically) wherever he looked at the houses, at the railings, at the antelopes stretching over the palings, beauty sprang instantly. To watch a leaf quivering in the rush of air was an exquisite joy. Up in the sky swallows swooping, swerving, flinging themselves in and out, round and round, yet always with perfect control as if elastics held them; and the flies rising and falling; and the sun spotting now this leaf, now that, in mockery, dazzling it with soft gold in pure good temper; and now and again some chime (it might be a motor horn) tinkling divinely on the grass stalks-- all of this, calm and reasonable as it was, made out of ordinary things as it was, was the truth now; beauty, that was the truth now. Beauty was everywhere.

"It is time," said Rezia.

The word "time" split its husk; poured its riches over him; and from his lips fell like shells, like shavings from a plane, without his making them, hard, white, imperishable words, and flew to attach themselves to their places in an ode to Time; an immortal ode to Time. He sang. Evans answered from behind the tree. The dead were in Thessaly, Evans sang, among the orchids. There they waited till the War was over, and now the dead, now Evans himself--

"For God's sake don't come!" Septimus cried out. For he could not look upon the dead.

But the branches parted. A man in grey was actually walking towards them. It was Evans! But no mud was on him; no wounds; he was not changed. I must tell the whole world, Septimus cried, raising his hand (as the dead man in the grey suit came nearer), raising his hand like some colossal figure who has lamented the fate of man for ages in the desert alone with his hands pressed to his forehead, furrows of despair on his cheeks, and now sees light on the desert's edge which broadens and strikes the iron-black figure (and Septimus half rose from his chair), and with legions of men prostrate behind him he, the giant mourner, receives for one moment on his face the whole--

"But I am so unhappy, Septimus," said Rezia trying to make him sit down.

The millions lamented; for ages they had sorrowed. He would turn round, he would tell them in a few moments, only a few moments more, of this relief, of this joy, of this astonishing revelation--

"The time, Septimus," Rezia repeated. "What is the time?"

He was talking, he was starting, this man must notice him. He was looking at them.

"I will tell you the time," said Septimus, very slowly, very drowsily, smiling mysteriously. As he sat smiling at the dead man in the grey suit the quarter struck--the quarter to twelve.

And that is being young, Peter Walsh thought as he passed them. To be having an awful scene--the poor girl looked absolutely desperate--in the middle of the morning. But what was it about, he wondered, what had the young man in the overcoat been saying to her to make her look like that; what awful fix had they got themselves into, both to look so desperate as that on a fine summer morning? The amusing thing about coming back to England, after five years, was the way it made, anyhow the first days, things stand out as if one had never seen them before; lovers squabbling under a tree; the domestic family life of the parks. Never had he seen London look so enchanting--the softness of the distances; the richness; the greenness; the civilisation, after India, he thought, strolling across the grass.

This susceptibility to impressions had been his undoing no doubt. Still at his age he had, like a boy or a girl even, these alternations of mood; good days, bad days, for no reason whatever, happiness from a pretty face, downright misery at the sight of a frump. After India of course one fell in love with every woman one met. There was a freshness about them; even the poorest dressed better than five years ago surely; and to his eye the fashions had never been so becoming; the long black cloaks; the slimness; the elegance; and then the delicious and apparently universal habit of paint. Every woman, even the most respectable, had roses blooming under glass; lips cut with a knife; curls of Indian ink; there was design, art, everywhere; a change of some sort had undoubtedly taken place. What did the young people think about? Peter Walsh asked himself.

Those five years--1918 to 1923--had been, he suspected, somehow very important. People looked different. Newspapers seemed different. Now for instance there was a man writing quite openly in one of the respectable weeklies about water-closets. That you couldn't have done ten years ago--written quite openly about water- closets in a respectable weekly. And then this taking out a stick of rouge, or a powder-puff and making up in public. On board ship coming home there were lots of young men and girls--Betty and Bertie he remembered in particular--carrying on quite openly; the old mother sitting and watching them with her knitting, cool as a cucumber. The girl would stand still and powder her nose in front of every one. And they weren't engaged; just having a good time; no feelings hurt on either side. As hard as nails she was--Betty What'shername--; but a thorough good sort. She would make a very good wife at thirty--she would marry when it suited her to marry; marry some rich man and live in a large house near Manchester.

Who was it now who had done that? Peter Walsh asked himself, turning into the Broad Walk,--married a rich man and lived in a large house near Manchester? Somebody who had written him a long, gushing letter quite lately about "blue hydrangeas." It was seeing blue hydrangeas that made her think of him and the old days--Sally Seton, of course! It was Sally Seton--the last person in the world one would have expected to marry a rich man and live in a large house near Manchester, the wild, the daring, the romantic Sally!

But of all that ancient lot, Clarissa's friends--Whitbreads, Kinderleys, Cunninghams, Kinloch-Jones's--Sally was probably the best. She tried to get hold of things by the right end anyhow. She saw through Hugh Whitbread anyhow--the admirable Hugh--when Clarissa and the rest were at his feet.

"The Whitbreads?" he could hear her saying. "Who are the Whitbreads? Coal merchants. Respectable tradespeople."

Hugh she detested for some reason. He thought of nothing but his own appearance, she said. He ought to have been a Duke. He would be certain to marry one of the Royal Princesses. And of course Hugh had the most extraordinary, the most natural, the most sublime respect for the British aristocracy of any human being he had ever come across. Even Clarissa had to own that. Oh, but he was such a dear, so unselfish, gave up shooting to please his old mother-- remembered his aunts' birthdays, and so on.

Sally, to do her justice, saw through all that. One of the things he remembered best was an argument one Sunday morning at Bourton about women's rights (that antediluvian topic), when Sally suddenly lost her temper, flared up, and told Hugh that he represented all that was most detestable in British middle-class life. She told him that she considered him responsible for the state of "those poor girls in Piccadilly"--Hugh, the perfect gentleman, poor Hugh!-- never did a man look more horrified! She did it on purpose she said afterwards (for they used to get together in the vegetable garden and compare notes). "He's read nothing, thought nothing, felt nothing," he could hear her saying in that very emphatic voice which carried so much farther than she knew. The stable boys had more life in them than Hugh, she said. He was a perfect specimen of the public school type, she said. No country but England could have produced him. She was really spiteful, for some reason; had some grudge against him. Something had happened--he forgot what-- in the smoking-room. He had insulted her--kissed her? Incredible! Nobody believed a word against Hugh of course. Who could? Kissing Sally in the smoking-room! If it had been some Honourable Edith or Lady Violet, perhaps; but not that ragamuffin Sally without a penny to her name, and a father or a mother gambling at Monte Carlo. For of all the people he had ever met Hugh was the greatest snob--the most obsequious--no, he didn't cringe exactly. He was too much of a prig for that. A first-rate valet was the obvious comparison-- somebody who walked behind carrying suit cases; could be trusted to send telegrams--indispensable to hostesses. And he'd found his job--married his Honourable Evelyn; got some little post at Court, looked after the King's cellars, polished the Imperial shoe- buckles, went about in knee-breeches and lace ruffles. How re-remorseless life is! A little job at Court!

He had married this lady, the Honourable Evelyn, and they lived hereabouts, so he thought (looking at the pompous houses overlooking the Park), for he had lunched there once in a house which had, like all Hugh's possessions, something that no other house could possibly have--linen cupboards it might have been. You had to go and look at them--you had to spend a great deal of time always admiring whatever it was--linen cupboards, pillow-cases, old oak furniture, pictures, which Hugh had picked up for an old song. But Mrs. Hugh sometimes gave the show away. She was one of those obscure mouse-like little women who admire big men. She was almost negligible. Then suddenly she would say something quite unexpected--something sharp. She had the relics of the grand manner perhaps. The steam coal was a little too strong for her--it made the atmosphere thick. And so there they lived, with their linen cupboards and their old masters and their pillow-cases fringed with real lace at the rate of five or ten thousand a year presumably, while he, who was two years older than Hugh, cadged for a job.

At fifty-three he had to come and ask them to put him into some secretary's office, to find him some usher's job teaching little boys Latin, at the beck and call of some mandarin in an office, something that brought in five hundred a year; for if he married Daisy, even with his pension, they could never do on less. Whitbread could do it presumably; or Dalloway. He didn't mind what he asked Dalloway. He was a thorough good sort; a bit limited; a bit thick in the head; yes; but a thorough good sort. Whatever he took up he did in the same matter-of-fact sensible way; without a touch of imagination, without a spark of brilliancy, but with the inexplicable niceness of his type. He ought to have been a country gentleman--he was wasted on politics. He was at his best out of doors, with horses and dogs--how good he was, for instance, when that great shaggy dog of Clarissa's got caught in a trap and had its paw half torn off, and Clarissa turned faint and Dalloway did the whole thing; bandaged, made splints; told Clarissa not to be a fool. That was what she liked him for perhaps--that was what she needed. "Now, my dear, don't be a fool. Hold this--fetch that," all the time talking to the dog as if it were a human being.

But how could she swallow all that stuff about poetry? How could she let him hold forth about Shakespeare? Seriously and solemnly Richard Dalloway got on his hind legs and said that no decent man ought to read Shakespeare's sonnets because it was like listening at keyholes (besides the relationship was not one that he approved). No decent man ought to let his wife visit a deceased wife's sister. Incredible! The only thing to do was to pelt him with sugared almonds--it was at dinner. But Clarissa sucked it all in; thought it so honest of him; so independent of him; Heaven knows if she didn't think him the most original mind she'd ever met!

That was one of the bonds between Sally and himself. There was a garden where they used to walk, a walled-in place, with rose-bushes and giant cauliflowers--he could remember Sally tearing off a rose, stopping to exclaim at the beauty of the cabbage leaves in the moonlight (it was extraordinary how vividly it all came back to him, things he hadn't thought of for years,) while she implored him, half laughing of course, to carry off Clarissa, to save her from the Hughs and the Dalloways and all the other "perfect gentlemen" who would "stifle her soul" (she wrote reams of poetry in those days), make a mere hostess of her, encourage her worldliness. But one must do Clarissa justice. She wasn't going to marry Hugh anyhow. She had a perfectly clear notion of what she wanted. Her emotions were all on the surface. Beneath, she was very shrewd--a far better judge of character than Sally, for instance, and with it all, purely feminine; with that extraordinary gift, that woman's gift, of making a world of her own wherever she happened to be. She came into a room; she stood, as he had often seen her, in a doorway with lots of people round her. But it was Clarissa one remembered. Not that she was striking; not beautiful at all; there was nothing picturesque about her; she never said anything specially clever; there she was, however; there she was.

No, no, no! He was not in love with her any more! He only felt, after seeing her that morning, among her scissors and silks, making ready for the party, unable to get away from the thought of her; she kept coming back and back like a sleeper jolting against him in a railway carriage; which was not being in love, of course; it was thinking of her, criticising her, starting again, after thirty years, trying to explain her. The obvious thing to say of her was that she was worldly; cared too much for rank and society and getting on in the world--which was true in a sense; she had admitted it to him. (You could always get her to own up if you took the trouble; she was honest.) What she would say was that she hated frumps, fogies, failures, like himself presumably; thought people had no right to slouch about with their hands in their pockets; must do something, be something; and these great swells, these Duchesses, these hoary old Countesses one met in her drawing- room, unspeakably remote as he felt them to be from anything that mattered a straw, stood for something real to her. Lady Bexborough, she said once, held herself upright (so did Clarissa herself; she never lounged in any sense of the word; she was straight as a dart, a little rigid in fact). She said they had a kind of courage which the older she grew the more she respected. In all this there was a great deal of Dalloway, of course; a great deal of the public-spirited, British Empire, tariff-reform, governing-class spirit, which had grown on her, as it tends to do. With twice his wits, she had to see things through his eyes--one of the tragedies of married life. With a mind of her own, she must always be quoting Richard--as if one couldn't know to a tittle what Richard thought by reading the Morning Post of a morning! These parties for example were all for him, or for her idea of him (to do Richard justice he would have been happier farming in Norfolk). She made her drawing-room a sort of meeting-place; she had a genius for it. Over and over again he had seen her take some raw youth, twist him, turn him, wake him up; set him going. Infinite numbers of dull people conglomerated round her of course.

But odd unexpected people turned up; an artist sometimes; sometimes a writer; queer fish in that atmosphere. And behind it all was that network of visiting, leaving cards, being kind to people; running about with bunches of flowers, little presents; So-and-so was going to France--must have an air-cushion; a real drain on her strength; all that interminable traffic that women of her sort keep up; but she did it genuinely, from a natural instinct.

Oddly enough, she was one of the most thoroughgoing sceptics he had ever met, and possibly (this was a theory he used to make up to account for her, so transparent in some ways, so inscrutable in others), possibly she said to herself, As we are a doomed race, chained to a sinking ship (her favourite reading as a girl was Huxley and Tyndall, and they were fond of these nautical metaphors), as the whole thing is a bad joke, let us, at any rate, do our part; mitigate the sufferings of our fellow-prisoners (Huxley again); decorate the dungeon with flowers and air-cushions; be as decent as we possibly can. Those ruffians, the Gods, shan't have it all their own way,--her notion being that the Gods, who never lost a chance of hurting, thwarting and spoiling human lives were seriously put out if, all the same, you behaved like a lady. That phase came directly after Sylvia's death--that horrible affair. To see your own sister killed by a falling tree (all Justin Parry's fault--all his carelessness) before your very eyes, a girl too on the verge of life, the most gifted of them, Clarissa always said, was enough to turn one bitter. Later she wasn't so positive perhaps; she thought there were no Gods; no one was to blame; and so she evolved this atheist's religion of doing good for the sake of goodness.

And of course she enjoyed life immensely. It was her nature to enjoy (though goodness only knows, she had her reserves; it was a mere sketch, he often felt, that even he, after all these years, could make of Clarissa). Anyhow there was no bitterness in her; none of that sense of moral virtue which is so repulsive in good women. She enjoyed practically everything. If you walked with her in Hyde Park now it was a bed of tulips, now a child in a perambulator, now some absurd little drama she made up on the spur of the moment. (Very likely, she would have talked to those lovers, if she had thought them unhappy.) She had a sense of comedy that was really exquisite, but she needed people, always people, to bring it out, with the inevitable result that she frittered her time away, lunching, dining, giving these incessant parties of hers, talking nonsense, sayings things she didn't mean, blunting the edge of her mind, losing her discrimination. There she would sit at the head of the table taking infinite pains with some old buffer who might be useful to Dalloway--they knew the most appalling bores in Europe--or in came Elizabeth and everything must give way to HER. She was at a High School, at the inarticulate stage last time he was over, a round-eyed, pale-faced girl, with nothing of her mother in her, a silent stolid creature, who took it all as a matter of course, let her mother make a fuss of her, and then said "May I go now?" like a child of four; going off, Clarissa explained, with that mixture of amusement and pride which Dalloway himself seemed to rouse in her, to play hockey. And now Elizabeth was "out," presumably; thought him an old fogy, laughed at her mother's friends. Ah well, so be it. The compensation of growing old, Peter Walsh thought, coming out of Regent's Park, and holding his hat in hand, was simply this; that the passions remain as strong as ever, but one has gained--at last!--the power which adds the supreme flavour to existence,--the power of taking hold of experience, of turning it round, slowly, in the light.

A terrible confession it was (he put his hat on again), but now, at the age of fifty-three one scarcely needed people any more. Life itself, every moment of it, every drop of it, here, this instant, now, in the sun, in Regent's Park, was enough. Too much indeed. A whole lifetime was too short to bring out, now that one had acquired the power, the full flavour; to extract every ounce of pleasure, every shade of meaning; which both were so much more solid than they used to be, so much less personal. It was impossible that he should ever suffer again as Clarissa had made him suffer. For hours at a time (pray God that one might say these things without being overheard!), for hours and days he never thought of Daisy.

Could it be that he was in love with her then, remembering the misery, the torture, the extraordinary passion of those days? It was a different thing altogether--a much pleasanter thing--the truth being, of course, that now SHE was in love with HIM. And that perhaps was the reason why, when the ship actually sailed, he felt an extraordinary relief, wanted nothing so much as to be alone; was annoyed to find all her little attentions--cigars, notes, a rug for the voyage--in his cabin. Every one if they were honest would say the same; one doesn't want people after fifty; one doesn't want to go on telling women they are pretty; that's what most men of fifty would say, Peter Walsh thought, if they were honest.

But then these astonishing accesses of emotion--bursting into tears this morning, what was all that about? What could Clarissa have thought of him? thought him a fool presumably, not for the first time. It was jealousy that was at the bottom of it--jealousy which survives every other passion of mankind, Peter Walsh thought, holding his pocket-knife at arm's length. She had been meeting Major Orde, Daisy said in her last letter; said it on purpose he knew; said it to make him jealous; he could see her wrinkling her forehead as she wrote, wondering what she could say to hurt him; and yet it made no difference; he was furious! All this pother of coming to England and seeing lawyers wasn't to marry her, but to prevent her from marrying anybody else. That was what tortured him, that was what came over him when he saw Clarissa so calm, so cold, so intent on her dress or whatever it was; realising what she might have spared him, what she had reduced him to--a whimpering, snivelling old ass. But women, he thought, shutting his pocket- knife, don't know what passion is. They don't know the meaning of it to men. Clarissa was as cold as an icicle. There she would sit on the sofa by his side, let him take her hand, give him one kiss-- Here he was at the crossing.

A sound interrupted him; a frail quivering sound, a voice bubbling up without direction, vigour, beginning or end, running weakly and shrilly and with an absence of all human meaning into

ee um fah um so foo swee too eem oo--

the voice of no age or sex, the voice of an ancient spring spouting from the earth; which issued, just opposite Regent's Park Tube station from a tall quivering shape, like a funnel, like a rusty pump, like a wind-beaten tree for ever barren of leaves which lets the wind run up and down its branches singing

ee um fah um so foo swee too eem oo

and rocks and creaks and moans in the eternal breeze.

Through all ages--when the pavement was grass, when it was swamp, through the age of tusk and mammoth, through the age of silent sunrise, the battered woman--for she wore a skirt--with her right hand exposed, her left clutching at her side, stood singing of love--love which has lasted a million years, she sang, love which prevails, and millions of years ago, her lover, who had been dead these centuries, had walked, she crooned, with her in May; but in the course of ages, long as summer days, and flaming, she remembered, with nothing but red asters, he had gone; death's enormous sickle had swept those tremendous hills, and when at last she laid her hoary and immensely aged head on the earth, now become a mere cinder of ice, she implored the Gods to lay by her side a bunch of purple-heather, there on her high burial place which the last rays of the last sun caressed; for then the pageant of the universe would be over.

As the ancient song bubbled up opposite Regent's Park Tube station still the earth seemed green and flowery; still, though it issued from so rude a mouth, a mere hole in the earth, muddy too, matted with root fibres and tangled grasses, still the old bubbling burbling song, soaking through the knotted roots of infinite ages, and skeletons and treasure, streamed away in rivulets over the pavement and all along the Marylebone Road, and down towards Euston, fertilising, leaving a damp stain.

Still remembering how once in some primeval May she had walked with her lover, this rusty pump, this battered old woman with one hand exposed for coppers the other clutching her side, would still be there in ten million years, remembering how once she had walked in May, where the sea flows now, with whom it did not matter--he was a man, oh yes, a man who had loved her. But the passage of ages had blurred the clarity of that ancient May day; the bright petalled flowers were hoar and silver frosted; and she no longer saw, when she implored him (as she did now quite clearly) "look in my eyes with thy sweet eyes intently," she no longer saw brown eyes, black whiskers or sunburnt face but only a looming shape, a shadow shape, to which, with the bird-like freshness of the very aged she still twittered "give me your hand and let me press it gently" (Peter Walsh couldn't help giving the poor creature a coin as he stepped into his taxi), "and if some one should see, what matter they?" she demanded; and her fist clutched at her side, and she smiled, pocketing her shilling, and all peering inquisitive eyes seemed blotted out, and the passing generations--the pavement was crowded with bustling middle-class people--vanished, like leaves, to be trodden under, to be soaked and steeped and made mould of by that eternal spring--

ee um fah um so foo swee too eem oo

"Poor old woman," said Rezia Warren Smith, waiting to cross.

Oh poor old wretch!

Suppose it was a wet night? Suppose one's father, or somebody who had known one in better days had happened to pass, and saw one standing there in the gutter? And where did she sleep at night?

Cheerfully, almost gaily, the invincible thread of sound wound up into the air like the smoke from a cottage chimney, winding up clean beech trees and issuing in a tuft of blue smoke among the topmost leaves. "And if some one should see, what matter they?"

Since she was so unhappy, for weeks and weeks now, Rezia had given meanings to things that happened, almost felt sometimes that she must stop people in the street, if they looked good, kind people, just to say to them "I am unhappy"; and this old woman singing in the street "if some one should see, what matter they?" made her suddenly quite sure that everything was going to be right. They were going to Sir William Bradshaw; she thought his name sounded nice; he would cure Septimus at once. And then there was a brewer's cart, and the grey horses had upright bristles of straw in their tails; there were newspaper placards. It was a silly, silly dream, being unhappy.

So they crossed, Mr. and Mrs. Septimus Warren Smith, and was there, after all, anything to draw attention to them, anything to make a passer-by suspect here is a young man who carries in him the greatest message in the world, and is, moreover, the happiest man in the world, and the most miserable? Perhaps they walked more slowly than other people, and there was something hesitating, trailing, in the man's walk, but what more natural for a clerk, who has not been in the West End on a weekday at this hour for years, than to keep looking at the sky, looking at this, that and the other, as if Portland Place were a room he had come into when the family are away, the chandeliers being hung in holland bags, and the caretaker, as she lets in long shafts of dusty light upon deserted, queer-looking armchairs, lifting one corner of the long blinds, explains to the visitors what a wonderful place it is; how wonderful, but at the same time, he thinks, as he looks at chairs and tables, how strange.

To look at, he might have been a clerk, but of the better sort; for he wore brown boots; his hands were educated; so, too, his profile-- his angular, big-nosed, intelligent, sensitive profile; but not his lips altogether, for they were loose; and his eyes (as eyes tend to be), eyes merely; hazel, large; so that he was, on the whole, a border case, neither one thing nor the other, might end with a house at Purley and a motor car, or continue renting apartments in back streets all his life; one of those half- educated, self-educated men whose education is all learnt from books borrowed from public libraries, read in the evening after the day's work, on the advice of well-known authors consulted by letter.

As for the other experiences, the solitary ones, which people go through alone, in their bedrooms, in their offices, walking the fields and the streets of London, he had them; had left home, a mere boy, because of his mother; she lied; because he came down to tea for the fiftieth time with his hands unwashed; because he could see no future for a poet in Stroud; and so, making a confidant of his little sister, had gone to London leaving an absurd note behind him, such as great men have written, and the world has read later when the story of their struggles has become famous.

London has swallowed up many millions of young men called Smith; thought nothing of fantastic Christian names like Septimus with which their parents have thought to distinguish them. Lodging off the Euston Road, there were experiences, again experiences, such as change a face in two years from a pink innocent oval to a face lean, contracted, hostile. But of all this what could the most observant of friends have said except what a gardener says when he opens the conservatory door in the morning and finds a new blossom on his plant:--It has flowered; flowered from vanity, ambition, idealism, passion, loneliness, courage, laziness, the usual seeds, which all muddled up (in a room off the Euston Road), made him shy, and stammering, made him anxious to improve himself, made him fall in love with Miss Isabel Pole, lecturing in the Waterloo Road upon Shakespeare.

Was he not like Keats? she asked; and reflected how she might give him a taste of Antony and Cleopatra and the rest; lent him books; wrote him scraps of letters; and lit in him such a fire as burns only once in a lifetime, without heat, flickering a red gold flame infinitely ethereal and insubstantial over Miss Pole; Antony and Cleopatra; and the Waterloo Road. He thought her beautiful, believed her impeccably wise; dreamed of her, wrote poems to her, which, ignoring the subject, she corrected in red ink; he saw her, one summer evening, walking in a green dress in a square. "It has flowered," the gardener might have said, had he opened the door; had he come in, that is to say, any night about this time, and found him writing; found him tearing up his writing; found him finishing a masterpiece at three o'clock in the morning and running out to pace the streets, and visiting churches, and fasting one day, drinking another, devouring Shakespeare, Darwin, The History of Civilisation, and Bernard Shaw.

Something was up, Mr. Brewer knew; Mr. Brewer, managing clerk at Sibleys and Arrowsmiths, auctioneers, valuers, land and estate agents; something was up, he thought, and, being paternal with his young men, and thinking very highly of Smith's abilities, and prophesying that he would, in ten or fifteen years, succeed to the leather arm-chair in the inner room under the skylight with the deed-boxes round him, "if he keeps his health," said Mr. Brewer, and that was the danger--he looked weakly; advised football, invited him to supper and was seeing his way to consider recommending a rise of salary, when something happened which threw out many of Mr. Brewer's calculations, took away his ablest young fellows, and eventually, so prying and insidious were the fingers of the European War, smashed a plaster cast of Ceres, ploughed a hole in the geranium beds, and utterly ruined the cook's nerves at Mr. Brewer's establishment at Muswell Hill.

Septimus was one of the first to volunteer. He went to France to save an England which consisted almost entirely of Shakespeare's plays and Miss Isabel Pole in a green dress walking in a square. There in the trenches the change which Mr. Brewer desired when he advised football was produced instantly; he developed manliness; he was promoted; he drew the attention, indeed the affection of his officer, Evans by name. It was a case of two dogs playing on a hearth-rug; one worrying a paper screw, snarling, snapping, giving a pinch, now and then, at the old dog's ear; the other lying somnolent, blinking at the fire, raising a paw, turning and growling good-temperedly. They had to be together, share with each other, fight with each other, quarrel with each other. But when Evans (Rezia who had only seen him once called him "a quiet man," a sturdy red-haired man, undemonstrative in the company of women), when Evans was killed, just before the Armistice, in Italy, Septimus, far from showing any emotion or recognising that here was the end of a friendship, congratulated himself upon feeling very little and very reasonably. The War had taught him. It was sublime. He had gone through the whole show, friendship, European War, death, had won promotion, was still under thirty and was bound to survive. He was right there. The last shells missed him. He watched them explode with indifference. When peace came he was in Milan, billeted in the house of an innkeeper with a courtyard, flowers in tubs, little tables in the open, daughters making hats, and to Lucrezia, the younger daughter, he became engaged one evening when the panic was on him--that he could not feel.

For now that it was all over, truce signed, and the dead buried, he had, especially in the evening, these sudden thunder-claps of fear. He could not feel. As he opened the door of the room where the Italian girls sat making hats, he could see them; could hear them; they were rubbing wires among coloured beads in saucers; they were turning buckram shapes this way and that; the table was all strewn with feathers, spangles, silks, ribbons; scissors were rapping on the table; but something failed him; he could not feel. Still, scissors rapping, girls laughing, hats being made protected him; he was assured of safety; he had a refuge. But he could not sit there all night. There were moments of waking in the early morning. The bed was falling; he was falling. Oh for the scissors and the lamplight and the buckram shapes! He asked Lucrezia to marry him, the younger of the two, the gay, the frivolous, with those little artist's fingers that she would hold up and say "It is all in them." Silk, feathers, what not were alive to them.

"It is the hat that matters most," she would say, when they walked out together. Every hat that passed, she would examine; and the cloak and the dress and the way the woman held herself. Ill- dressing, over-dressing she stigmatised, not savagely, rather with impatient movements of the hands, like those of a painter who puts from him some obvious well-meant glaring imposture; and then, generously, but always critically, she would welcome a shopgirl who had turned her little bit of stuff gallantly, or praise, wholly, with enthusiastic and professional understanding, a French lady descending from her carriage, in chinchilla, robes, pearls.

"Beautiful!" she would murmur, nudging Septimus, that he might see. But beauty was behind a pane of glass. Even taste (Rezia liked ices, chocolates, sweet things) had no relish to him. He put down his cup on the little marble table. He looked at people outside; happy they seemed, collecting in the middle of the street, shouting, laughing, squabbling over nothing. But he could not taste, he could not feel. In the tea-shop among the tables and the chattering waiters the appalling fear came over him--he could not feel. He could reason; he could read, Dante for example, quite easily ("Septimus, do put down your book," said Rezia, gently shutting the Inferno), he could add up his bill; his brain was perfect; it must be the fault of the world then--that he could not feel.

"The English are so silent," Rezia said. She liked it, she said. She respected these Englishmen, and wanted to see London, and the English horses, and the tailor-made suits, and could remember hearing how wonderful the shops were, from an Aunt who had married and lived in Soho.

It might be possible, Septimus thought, looking at England from the train window, as they left Newhaven; it might be possible that the world itself is without meaning.

At the office they advanced him to a post of considerable responsibility. They were proud of him; he had won crosses. "You have done your duty; it is up to us--" began Mr. Brewer; and could not finish, so pleasurable was his emotion. They took admirable lodgings off the Tottenham Court Road.

Here he opened Shakespeare once more. That boy's business of the intoxication of language--Antony and Cleopatra--had shrivelled utterly. How Shakespeare loathed humanity--the putting on of clothes, the getting of children, the sordidity of the mouth and the belly! This was now revealed to Septimus; the message hidden in the beauty of words. The secret signal which one generation passes, under disguise, to the next is loathing, hatred, despair. Dante the same. Aeschylus (translated) the same. There Rezia sat at the table trimming hats. She trimmed hats for Mrs. Filmer's friends; she trimmed hats by the hour. She looked pale, mysterious, like a lily, drowned, under water, he thought.

"The English are so serious," she would say, putting her arms round Septimus, her cheek against his.

Love between man and woman was repulsive to Shakespeare. The business of copulation was filth to him before the end. But, Rezia said, she must have children. They had been married five years.

They went to the Tower together; to the Victoria and Albert Museum; stood in the crowd to see the King open Parliament. And there were the shops--hat shops, dress shops, shops with leather bags in the window, where she would stand staring. But she must have a boy.

She must have a son like Septimus, she said. But nobody could be like Septimus; so gentle; so serious; so clever. Could she not read Shakespeare too? Was Shakespeare a difficult author? she asked.

One cannot bring children into a world like this. One cannot perpetuate suffering, or increase the breed of these lustful animals, who have no lasting emotions, but only whims and vanities, eddying them now this way, now that.

He watched her snip, shape, as one watches a bird hop, flit in the grass, without daring to move a finger. For the truth is (let her ignore it) that human beings have neither kindness, nor faith, nor charity beyond what serves to increase the pleasure of the moment. They hunt in packs. Their packs scour the desert and vanish screaming into the wilderness. They desert the fallen. They are plastered over with grimaces. There was Brewer at the office, with his waxed moustache, coral tie-pin, white slip, and pleasurable emotions--all coldness and clamminess within,--his geraniums ruined in the War--his cook's nerves destroyed; or Amelia What'shername, handing round cups of tea punctually at five--a leering, sneering obscene little harpy; and the Toms and Berties in their starched shirt fronts oozing thick drops of vice. They never saw him drawing pictures of them naked at their antics in his notebook. In the street, vans roared past him; brutality blared out on placards; men were trapped in mines; women burnt alive; and once a maimed file of lunatics being exercised or displayed for the diversion of the populace (who laughed aloud), ambled and nodded and grinned past him, in the Tottenham Court Road, each half apologetically, yet triumphantly, inflicting his hopeless woe. And would HE go mad?

At tea Rezia told him that Mrs. Filmer's daughter was expecting a baby. SHE could not grow old and have no children! She was very lonely, she was very unhappy! She cried for the first time since they were married. Far away he heard her sobbing; he heard it accurately, he noticed it distinctly; he compared it to a piston thumping. But he felt nothing.

His wife was crying, and he felt nothing; only each time she sobbed in this profound, this silent, this hopeless way, he descended another step into the pit.

At last, with a melodramatic gesture which he assumed mechanically and with complete consciousness of its insincerity, he dropped his head on his hands. Now he had surrendered; now other people must help him. People must be sent for. He gave in.

Nothing could rouse him. Rezia put him to bed. She sent for a doctor--Mrs. Filmer's Dr. Holmes. Dr. Holmes examined him. There was nothing whatever the matter, said Dr. Holmes. Oh, what a relief! What a kind man, what a good man! thought Rezia. When he felt like that he went to the Music Hall, said Dr. Holmes. He took a day off with his wife and played golf. Why not try two tabloids of bromide dissolved in a glass of water at bedtime? These old Bloomsbury houses, said Dr. Holmes, tapping the wall, are often full of very fine panelling, which the landlords have the folly to paper over. Only the other day, visiting a patient, Sir Somebody Something in Bedford Square--

So there was no excuse; nothing whatever the matter, except the sin for which human nature had condemned him to death; that he did not feel. He had not cared when Evans was killed; that was worst; but all the other crimes raised their heads and shook their fingers and jeered and sneered over the rail of the bed in the early hours of the morning at the prostrate body which lay realising its degradation; how he had married his wife without loving her; had lied to her; seduced her; outraged Miss Isabel Pole, and was so pocked and marked with vice that women shuddered when they saw him in the street. The verdict of human nature on such a wretch was death.

Dr. Holmes came again. Large, fresh coloured, handsome, flicking his boots, looking in the glass, he brushed it all aside-- headaches, sleeplessness, fears, dreams--nerve symptoms and nothing more, he said. If Dr. Holmes found himself even half a pound below eleven stone six, he asked his wife for another plate of porridge at breakfast. (Rezia would learn to cook porridge.) But, he continued, health is largely a matter in our own control. Throw yourself into outside interests; take up some hobby. He opened Shakespeare--Antony and Cleopatra; pushed Shakespeare aside. Some hobby, said Dr. Holmes, for did he not owe his own excellent health (and he worked as hard as any man in London) to the fact that he could always switch off from his patients on to old furniture? And what a very pretty comb, if he might say so, Mrs. Warren Smith was wearing!

When the damned fool came again, Septimus refused to see him. Did he indeed? said Dr. Holmes, smiling agreeably. Really he had to give that charming little lady, Mrs. Smith, a friendly push before he could get past her into her husband's bedroom.

"So you're in a funk," he said agreeably, sitting down by his patient's side. He had actually talked of killing himself to his wife, quite a girl, a foreigner, wasn't she? Didn't that give her a very odd idea of English husbands? Didn't one owe perhaps a duty to one's wife? Wouldn't it be better to do something instead of lying in bed? For he had had forty years' experience behind him; and Septimus could take Dr. Holmes's word for it--there was nothing whatever the matter with him. And next time Dr. Holmes came he hoped to find Smith out of bed and not making that charming little lady his wife anxious about him.

Human nature, in short, was on him--the repulsive brute, with the blood-red nostrils. Holmes was on him. Dr. Holmes came quite regularly every day. Once you stumble, Septimus wrote on the back of a postcard, human nature is on you. Holmes is on you. Their only chance was to escape, without letting Holmes know; to Italy-- anywhere, anywhere, away from Dr. Holmes.

But Rezia could not understand him. Dr. Holmes was such a kind man. He was so interested in Septimus. He only wanted to help them, he said. He had four little children and he had asked her to tea, she told Septimus.

So he was deserted. The whole world was clamouring: Kill yourself, kill yourself, for our sakes. But why should he kill himself for their sakes? Food was pleasant; the sun hot; and this killing oneself, how does one set about it, with a table knife, uglily, with floods of blood,--by sucking a gaspipe? He was too weak; he could scarcely raise his hand. Besides, now that he was quite alone, condemned, deserted, as those who are about to die are alone, there was a luxury in it, an isolation full of sublimity; a freedom which the attached can never know. Holmes had won of course; the brute with the red nostrils had won. But even Holmes himself could not touch this last relic straying on the edge of the world, this outcast, who gazed back at the inhabited regions, who lay, like a drowned sailor, on the shore of the world.

It was at that moment (Rezia gone shopping) that the great revelation took place. A voice spoke from behind the screen. Evans was speaking. The dead were with him.

"Evans, Evans!" he cried.

Mr. Smith was talking aloud to himself, Agnes the servant girl cried to Mrs. Filmer in the kitchen. "Evans, Evans," he had said as she brought in the tray. She jumped, she did. She scuttled downstairs.

And Rezia came in, with her flowers, and walked across the room, and put the roses in a vase, upon which the sun struck directly, and it went laughing, leaping round the room.

She had had to buy the roses, Rezia said, from a poor man in the street. But they were almost dead already, she said, arranging the roses.

So there was a man outside; Evans presumably; and the roses, which Rezia said were half dead, had been picked by him in the fields of Greece. "Communication is health; communication is happiness, communication--" he muttered.

"What are you saying, Septimus?" Rezia asked, wild with terror, for he was talking to himself.

She sent Agnes running for Dr. Holmes. Her husband, she said, was mad. He scarcely knew her.

"You brute! You brute!" cried Septimus, seeing human nature, that is Dr. Holmes, enter the room.

"Now what's all this about?" said Dr. Holmes in the most amiable way in the world. "Talking nonsense to frighten your wife?" But he would give him something to make him sleep. And if they were rich people, said Dr. Holmes, looking ironically round the room, by all means let them go to Harley Street; if they had no confidence in him, said Dr. Holmes, looking not quite so kind.

It was precisely twelve o'clock; twelve by Big Ben; whose stroke was wafted over the northern part of London; blent with that of other clocks, mixed in a thin ethereal way with the clouds and wisps of smoke, and died up there among the seagulls--twelve o'clock struck as Clarissa Dalloway laid her green dress on her bed, and the Warren Smiths walked down Harley Street. Twelve was the hour of their appointment. Probably, Rezia thought, that was Sir William Bradshaw's house with the grey motor car in front of it. The leaden circles dissolved in the air.

Indeed it was--Sir William Bradshaw's motor car; low, powerful, grey with plain initials' interlocked on the panel, as if the pomps of heraldry were incongruous, this man being the ghostly helper, the priest of science; and, as the motor car was grey, so to match its sober suavity, grey furs, silver grey rugs were heaped in it, to keep her ladyship warm while she waited. For often Sir William would travel sixty miles or more down into the country to visit the rich, the afflicted, who could afford the very large fee which Sir William very properly charged for his advice. Her ladyship waited with the rugs about her knees an hour or more, leaning back, thinking sometimes of the patient, sometimes, excusably, of the wall of gold, mounting minute by minute while she waited; the wall of gold that was mounting between them and all shifts and anxieties (she had borne them bravely; they had had their struggles) until she felt wedged on a calm ocean, where only spice winds blow; respected, admired, envied, with scarcely anything left to wish for, though she regretted her stoutness; large dinner-parties every

Thursday night to the profession; an occasional bazaar to be opened; Royalty greeted; too little time, alas, with her husband, whose work grew and grew; a boy doing well at Eton; she would have liked a daughter too; interests she had, however, in plenty; child welfare; the after-care of the epileptic, and photography, so that if there was a church building, or a church decaying, she bribed the sexton, got the key and took photographs, which were scarcely to be distinguished from the work of professionals, while she waited.

Sir William himself was no longer young. He had worked very hard; he had won his position by sheer ability (being the son of a shopkeeper); loved his profession; made a fine figurehead at ceremonies and spoke well--all of which had by the time he was knighted given him a heavy look, a weary look (the stream of patients being so incessant, the responsibilities and privileges of his profession so onerous), which weariness, together with his grey hairs, increased the extraordinary distinction of his presence and gave him the reputation (of the utmost importance in dealing with nerve cases) not merely of lightning skill, and almost infallible accuracy in diagnosis but of sympathy; tact; understanding of the human soul. He could see the first moment they came into the room (the Warren Smiths they were called); he was certain directly he saw the man; it was a case of extreme gravity. It was a case of complete breakdown--complete physical and nervous breakdown, with every symptom in an advanced stage, he ascertained in two or three minutes (writing answers to questions, murmured discreetly, on a pink card).

How long had Dr. Holmes been attending him?

Six weeks.

Prescribed a little bromide? Said there was nothing the matter? Ah yes (those general practitioners! thought Sir William. It took half his time to undo their blunders. Some were irreparable).

"You served with great distinction in the War?"

The patient repeated the word "war" interrogatively.

He was attaching meanings to words of a symbolical kind. A serious symptom, to be noted on the card.

"The War?" the patient asked. The European War--that little shindy of schoolboys with gunpowder? Had he served with distinction? He really forgot. In the War itself he had failed.

"Yes, he served with the greatest distinction," Rezia assured the doctor; "he was promoted."

"And they have the very highest opinion of you at your office?" Sir William murmured, glancing at Mr. Brewer's very generously worded letter. "So that you have nothing to worry you, no financial anxiety, nothing?"

He had committed an appalling crime and been condemned to death by human nature.

"I have--I have," he began, "committed a crime--"

"He has done nothing wrong whatever," Rezia assured the doctor. If Mr. Smith would wait, said Sir William, he would speak to Mrs. Smith in the next room. Her husband was very seriously ill, Sir William said. Did he threaten to kill himself?

Oh, he did, she cried. But he did not mean it, she said. Of course not. It was merely a question of rest, said Sir William; of rest, rest, rest; a long rest in bed. There was a delightful home down in the country where her husband would be perfectly looked after. Away from her? she asked. Unfortunately, yes; the people we care for most are not good for us when we are ill. But he was not mad, was he? Sir William said he never spoke of "madness"; he called it not having a sense of proportion. But her husband did not like doctors. He would refuse to go there. Shortly and kindly Sir William explained to her the state of the case. He had threatened to kill himself. There was no alternative. It was a question of law. He would lie in bed in a beautiful house in the country. The nurses were admirable. Sir William would visit him once a week. If Mrs. Warren Smith was quite sure she had no more questions to ask--he never hurried his patients--they would return to her husband. She had nothing more to ask--not of Sir William.

So they returned to the most exalted of mankind; the criminal who faced his judges; the victim exposed on the heights; the fugitive; the drowned sailor; the poet of the immortal ode; the Lord who had gone from life to death; to Septimus Warren Smith, who sat in the arm-chair under the skylight staring at a photograph of Lady Bradshaw in Court dress, muttering messages about beauty.

"We have had our little talk," said Sir William.

"He says you are very, very ill," Rezia cried.

"We have been arranging that you should go into a home," said Sir William.

"One of Holmes's homes?" sneered Septimus.

The fellow made a distasteful impression. For there was in Sir William, whose father had been a tradesman, a natural respect for breeding and clothing, which shabbiness nettled; again, more profoundly, there was in Sir William, who had never had time for reading, a grudge, deeply buried, against cultivated people who came into his room and intimated that doctors, whose profession is a constant strain upon all the highest faculties, are not educated men.

"One of MY homes, Mr. Warren Smith," he said, "where we will teach you to rest."

And there was just one thing more.

He was quite certain that when Mr. Warren Smith was well he was the last man in the world to frighten his wife. But he had talked of killing himself.

"We all have our moments of depression," said Sir William.

Once you fall, Septimus repeated to himself, human nature is on you. Holmes and Bradshaw are on you. They scour the desert. They fly screaming into the wilderness. The rack and the thumbscrew are applied. Human nature is remorseless.

"Impulses came upon him sometimes?" Sir William asked, with his pencil on a pink card.

That was his own affair, said Septimus.

"Nobody lives for himself alone," said Sir William, glancing at the photograph of his wife in Court dress.

"And you have a brilliant career before you," said Sir William. There was Mr. Brewer's letter on the table. "An exceptionally brilliant career."

But if he confessed? If he communicated? Would they let him off then, his torturers?

"I--I--" he stammered.

But what was his crime? He could not remember it.

"Yes?" Sir William encouraged him. (But it was growing late.)

Love, trees, there is no crime--what was his message?

He could not remember it.

"I--I--" Septimus stammered.

"Try to think as little about yourself as possible," said Sir William kindly. Really, he was not fit to be about.

Was there anything else they wished to ask him? Sir William would make all arrangements (he murmured to Rezia) and he would let her know between five and six that evening he murmured.

"Trust everything to me," he said, and dismissed them.

Never, never had Rezia felt such agony in her life! She had asked for help and been deserted! He had failed them! Sir William Bradshaw was not a nice man.

The upkeep of that motor car alone must cost him quite a lot, said Septimus, when they got out into the street.

She clung to his arm. They had been deserted.

But what more did she want?

To his patients he gave three-quarters of an hour; and if in this exacting science which has to do with what, after all, we know nothing about--the nervous system, the human brain--a doctor loses his sense of proportion, as a doctor he fails. Health we must have; and health is proportion; so that when a man comes into your room and says he is Christ (a common delusion), and has a message, as they mostly have, and threatens, as they often do, to kill himself, you invoke proportion; order rest in bed; rest in solitude; silence and rest; rest without friends, without books, without messages; six months' rest; until a man who went in weighing seven stone six comes out weighing twelve.

Proportion, divine proportion, Sir William's goddess, was acquired by Sir William walking hospitals, catching salmon, begetting one son in Harley Street by Lady Bradshaw, who caught salmon herself and took photographs scarcely to be distinguished from the work of professionals. Worshipping proportion, Sir William not only prospered himself but made England prosper, secluded her lunatics, forbade childbirth, penalised despair, made it impossible for the unfit to propagate their views until they, too, shared his sense of proportion--his, if they were men, Lady Bradshaw's if they were women (she embroidered, knitted, spent four nights out of seven at home with her son), so that not only did his colleagues respect him, his subordinates fear him, but the friends and relations of his patients felt for him the keenest gratitude for insisting that these prophetic Christs and Christesses, who prophesied the end of the world, or the advent of God, should drink milk in bed, as Sir William ordered; Sir William with his thirty years' experience of these kinds of cases, and his infallible instinct, this is madness, this sense; in fact, his sense of proportion.

But Proportion has a sister, less smiling, more formidable, a Goddess even now engaged--in the heat and sands of India, the mud and swamp of Africa, the purlieus of London, wherever in short the climate or the devil tempts men to fall from the true belief which is her own--is even now engaged in dashing down shrines, smashing idols, and setting up in their place her own stern countenance. Conversion is her name and she feasts on the wills of the weakly, loving to impress, to impose, adoring her own features stamped on the face of the populace. At Hyde Park Corner on a tub she stands preaching; shrouds herself in white and walks penitentially disguised as brotherly love through factories and parliaments; offers help, but desires power; smites out of her way roughly the dissentient, or dissatisfied; bestows her blessing on those who, looking upward, catch submissively from her eyes the light of their own. This lady too (Rezia Warren Smith divined it) had her dwelling in Sir William's heart, though concealed, as she mostly is, under some plausible disguise; some venerable name; love, duty, self sacrifice. How he would work--how toil to raise funds, propagate reforms, initiate institutions! But conversion, fastidious Goddess, loves blood better than brick, and feasts most subtly on the human will. For example, Lady Bradshaw. Fifteen years ago she had gone under. It was nothing you could put your finger on; there had been no scene, no snap; only the slow sinking, water-logged, of her will into his. Sweet was her smile, swift her submission; dinner in Harley Street, numbering eight or nine courses, feeding ten or fifteen guests of the professional classes, was smooth and urbane. Only as the evening wore on a very slight dulness, or uneasiness perhaps, a nervous twitch, fumble, stumble and confusion indicated, what it was really painful to believe-- that the poor lady lied. Once, long ago, she had caught salmon freely: now, quick to minister to the craving which lit her husband's eye so oilily for dominion, for power, she cramped, squeezed, pared, pruned, drew back, peeped through; so that without knowing precisely what made the evening disagreeable, and caused this pressure on the top of the head (which might well be imputed to the professional conversation, or the fatigue of a great doctor whose life, Lady Bradshaw said, "is not his own but his patients'") disagreeable it was: so that guests, when the clock struck ten, breathed in the air of Harley Street even with rapture; which relief, however, was denied to his patients.

There in the grey room, with the pictures on the wall, and the valuable furniture, under the ground glass skylight, they learnt the extent of their transgressions; huddled up in arm-chairs, they watched him go through, for their benefit, a curious exercise with the arms, which he shot out, brought sharply back to his hip, to prove (if the patient was obstinate) that Sir William was master of his own actions, which the patient was not. There some weakly broke down; sobbed, submitted; others, inspired by Heaven knows what intemperate madness, called

Sir William to his face a damnable humbug; questioned, even more impiously, life itself. Why live? they demanded. Sir William replied that life was good. Certainly Lady Bradshaw in ostrich feathers hung over the mantelpiece, and as for his income it was quite twelve thousand a year. But to us, they protested, life has given no such bounty. He acquiesced. They lacked a sense of proportion. And perhaps, after all, there is no God? He shrugged his shoulders. In short, this living or not living is an affair of our own? But there they were mistaken. Sir William had a friend in Surrey where they taught, what Sir William frankly admitted was a difficult art--a sense of proportion. There were, moreover, family affection; honour; courage; and a brilliant career. All of these had in Sir William a resolute champion. If they failed him, he had to support police and the good of society, which, he remarked very quietly, would take care, down in Surrey, that these unsocial impulses, bred more than anything by the lack of good blood, were held in control. And then stole out from her hiding-place and mounted her throne that Goddess whose lust is to override opposition, to stamp indelibly in the sanctuaries of others the image of herself. Naked, defenceless, the exhausted, the friendless received the impress of Sir William's will. He swooped; he devoured. He shut people up. It was this combination of decision and humanity that endeared Sir William so greatly to the relations of his victims.

But Rezia Warren Smith cried, walking down Harley Street, that she did not like that man.

Shredding and slicing, dividing and subdividing, the clocks of Harley Street nibbled at the June day, counselled submission, upheld authority, and pointed out in chorus the supreme advantages of a sense of proportion, until the mound of time was so far diminished that a commercial clock, suspended above a shop in Oxford Street, announced, genially and fraternally, as if it were a pleasure to Messrs. Rigby and Lowndes to give the information gratis, that it was half-past one.

Looking up, it appeared that each letter of their names stood for one of the hours; subconsciously one was grateful to Rigby and Lowndes for giving one time ratified by Greenwich; and this gratitude (so Hugh Whitbread ruminated, dallying there in front of the shop window), naturally took the form later of buying off Rigby and Lowndes socks or shoes. So he ruminated. It was his habit. He did not go deeply. He brushed surfaces; the dead languages, the living, life in Constantinople, Paris, Rome; riding, shooting, tennis, it had been once. The malicious asserted that he now kept guard at Buckingham Palace, dressed in silk stockings and knee- breeches, over what nobody knew. But he did it extremely efficiently. He had been afloat on the cream of English society for fifty-five years. He had known Prime Ministers. His affections were understood to be deep. And if it were true that he had not taken part in any of the great movements of the time or held important office, one or two humble reforms stood to his credit; an improvement in public shelters was one; the protection of owls in Norfolk another; servant girls had reason to be grateful to him; and his name at the end of letters to the Times, asking for funds, appealing to the public to protect, to preserve, to clear up litter, to abate smoke, and stamp out immorality in parks, commanded respect.

A magnificent figure he cut too, pausing for a moment (as the sound of the half hour died away) to look critically, magisterially, at socks and shoes; impeccable, substantial, as if he beheld the world from a certain eminence, and dressed to match; but realised the obligations which size, wealth, health, entail, and observed punctiliously even when not absolutely necessary, little courtesies, old-fashioned ceremonies which gave a quality to his manner, something to imitate, something to remember him by, for he would never lunch, for example, with Lady Bruton, whom he had known these twenty years, without bringing her in his outstretched hand a bunch of carnations and asking Miss Brush, Lady Bruton's secretary, after her brother in South Africa, which, for some reason, Miss Brush, deficient though she was in every attribute of female charm, so much resented that she said "Thank you, he's doing very well in South Africa," when, for half a dozen years, he had been doing badly in Portsmouth.

Lady Bruton herself preferred Richard Dalloway, who arrived at the next moment. Indeed they met on the doorstep.

Lady Bruton preferred Richard Dalloway of course. He was made of much finer material. But she wouldn't let them run down her poor dear Hugh. She could never forget his kindness--he had been really remarkably kind--she forgot precisely upon what occasion. But he had been--remarkably kind. Anyhow, the difference between one man and another does not amount to much. She had never seen the sense of cutting people up, as Clarissa Dalloway did--cutting them up and sticking them together again; not at any rate when one was sixty- two. She took Hugh's carnations with her angular grim smile. There was nobody else coming, she said. She had got them there on false pretences, to help her out of a difficulty--

"But let us eat first," she said.

And so there began a soundless and exquisite passing to and fro through swing doors of aproned white-capped maids, handmaidens not of necessity, but adepts in a mystery or grand deception practised by hostesses in Mayfair from one-thirty to two, when, with a wave of the hand, the traffic ceases, and there rises instead this profound illusion in the first place about the food--how it is not paid for; and then that the table spreads itself voluntarily with glass and silver, little mats, saucers of red fruit; films of brown cream mask turbot; in casseroles severed chickens swim; coloured, undomestic, the fire burns; and with the wine and the coffee (not paid for) rise jocund visions before musing eyes; gently speculative eyes; eyes to whom life appears musical, mysterious; eyes now kindled to observe genially the beauty of the red carnations which Lady Bruton (whose movements were always angular) had laid beside her plate, so that Hugh Whitbread, feeling at peace with the entire universe and at the same time completely sure of his standing, said, resting his fork,

"Wouldn't they look charming against your lace?"

Miss Brush resented this familiarity intensely. She thought him an underbred fellow. She made Lady Bruton laugh.

Lady Bruton raised the carnations, holding them rather stiffly with much the same attitude with which the General held the scroll in the picture behind her; she remained fixed, tranced. Which was she now, the General's great-grand-daughter? great-great-grand- daughter? Richard Dalloway asked himself. Sir Roderick, Sir Miles, Sir Talbot--that was it. It was remarkable how in that family the likeness persisted in the women. She should have been a general of dragoons herself. And Richard would have served under her, cheerfully; he had the greatest respect for her; he cherished these romantic views about well-set-up old women of pedigree, and would have liked, in his good-humoured way, to bring some young hot-heads of his acquaintance to lunch with her; as if a type like hers could be bred of amiable tea-drinking enthusiasts! He knew her country. He knew her people. There was a vine, still bearing, which either Lovelace or Herrick--she never read a word poetry of herself, but so the story ran--had sat under. Better wait to put before them the question that bothered her (about making an appeal to the public; if so, in what terms and so on), better wait until they have had their coffee, Lady Bruton thought; and so laid the carnations down beside her plate.

"How's Clarissa?" she asked abruptly.

Clarissa always said that Lady Bruton did not like her. Indeed, Lady Bruton had the reputation of being more interested in politics than people; of talking like a man; of having had a finger in some notorious intrigue of the eighties, which was now beginning to be mentioned in memoirs. Certainly there was an alcove in her drawing-room, and a table in that alcove, and a photograph upon that table of General Sir Talbot Moore, now deceased, who had written there (one evening in the eighties) in Lady Bruton's presence, with her cognisance, perhaps advice, a telegram ordering the British troops to advance upon an historical occasion. (She kept the pen and told the story.) Thus, when she said in her offhand way "How's Clarissa?" husbands had difficulty in persuading their wives and indeed, however devoted, were secretly doubtful themselves, of her interest in women who often got in their husbands' way, prevented them from accepting posts abroad, and had to be taken to the seaside in the middle of the session to recover from influenza. Nevertheless her inquiry, "How's Clarissa?" was known by women infallibly, to be a signal from a well-wisher, from an almost silent companion, whose utterances (half a dozen perhaps in the course of a lifetime) signified recognition of some feminine comradeship which went beneath masculine lunch parties and united Lady Bruton and Mrs. Dalloway, who seldom met, and appeared when they did meet indifferent and even hostile, in a singular bond.

"I met Clarissa in the Park this morning," said Hugh Whitbread, diving into the casserole, anxious to pay himself this little tribute, for he had only to come to London and he met everybody at once; but greedy, one of the greediest men she had ever known, Milly Brush thought, who observed men with unflinching rectitude, and was capable of everlasting devotion, to her own sex in particular, being knobbed, scraped, angular, and entirely without feminine charm.

"D'you know who's in town?" said Lady Bruton suddenly bethinking her. "Our old friend, Peter Walsh."

They all smiled. Peter Walsh! And Mr. Dalloway was genuinely glad, Milly Brush thought; and Mr. Whitbread thought only of his chicken.

Peter Walsh! All three, Lady Bruton, Hugh Whitbread, and Richard Dalloway, remembered the same thing--how passionately Peter had been in love; been rejected; gone to India; come a cropper; made a mess of things; and Richard Dalloway had a very great liking for the dear old fellow too. Milly Brush saw that; saw a depth in the brown of his eyes; saw him hesitate; consider; which interested her, as Mr. Dalloway always interested her, for what was he thinking, she wondered, about Peter Walsh?

That Peter Walsh had been in love with Clarissa; that he would go back directly after lunch and find Clarissa; that he would tell her, in so many words, that he loved her. Yes, he would say that.

Milly Brush once might almost have fallen in love with these silences; and Mr. Dalloway was always so dependable; such a gentleman too. Now, being forty, Lady Bruton had only to nod, or turn her head a little abruptly, and Milly Brush took the signal, however deeply she might be sunk in these reflections of a detached spirit, of an uncorrupted soul whom life could not bamboozle, because life had not offered her a trinket of the slightest value; not a curl, smile, lip, cheek, nose; nothing whatever; Lady Bruton had only to nod, and Perkins was instructed to quicken the coffee.

"Yes; Peter Walsh has come back," said Lady Bruton. It was vaguely flattering to them all. He had come back, battered, unsuccessful, to their secure shores. But to help him, they reflected, was impossible; there was some flaw in his character. Hugh Whitbread said one might of course mention his name to So-and-so. He wrinkled lugubriously, consequentially, at the thought of the letters he would write to the heads of Government offices about "my old friend, Peter Walsh," and so on. But it wouldn't lead to anything--not to anything permanent, because of his character.

"In trouble with some woman," said Lady Bruton. They had all guessed that THAT was at the bottom of it.

"However," said Lady Bruton, anxious to leave the subject, "we shall hear the whole story from Peter himself."

(The coffee was very slow in coming.)

"The address?" murmured Hugh Whitbread; and there was at once a ripple in the grey tide of service which washed round Lady Bruton day in, day out, collecting, intercepting, enveloping her in a fine tissue which broke concussions, mitigated interruptions, and spread round the house in Brook Street a fine net where things lodged and were picked out accurately, instantly, by grey-haired Perkins, who had been with Lady Bruton these thirty years and now wrote down the address; handed it to Mr. Whitbread, who took out his pocket-book, raised his eyebrows, and slipping it in among documents of the highest importance, said that he would get Evelyn to ask him to lunch.

(They were waiting to bring the coffee until Mr. Whitbread had finished.)

Hugh was very slow, Lady Bruton thought. He was getting fat, she noticed. Richard always kept himself in the pink of condition. She was getting impatient; the whole of her being was setting positively, undeniably, domineeringly brushing aside all this unnecessary trifling (Peter Walsh and his affairs) upon that subject which engaged her attention, and not merely her attention, but that fibre which was the ramrod of her soul, that essential part of her without which Millicent Bruton would not have been Millicent Bruton; that project for emigrating young people of both sexes born of respectable parents and setting them up with a fair prospect of doing well in Canada. She exaggerated. She had perhaps lost her sense of proportion. Emigration was not to others the obvious remedy, the sublime conception. It was not to them (not to Hugh, or Richard, or even to devoted Miss Brush) the liberator of the pent egotism, which a strong martial woman, well nourished, well descended, of direct impulses, downright feelings, and little introspective power (broad and simple--why could not every one be broad and simple? she asked) feels rise within her, once youth is past, and must eject upon some object--it may be Emigration, it may be Emancipation; but whatever it be, this object round which the essence of her soul is daily secreted, becomes inevitably prismatic, lustrous, half looking-glass, half precious stone; now carefully hidden in case people should sneer at it; now proudly displayed. Emigration had become, in short, largely Lady Bruton.

But she had to write. And one letter to the Times, she used to say to Miss Brush, cost her more than to organise an expedition to South Africa (which she had done in the war). After a morning's battle beginning, tearing up, beginning again, she used to feel the futility of her own womanhood as she felt it on no other occasion, and would turn gratefully to the thought of Hugh Whitbread who possessed--no one could doubt it--the art of writing letters to the Times.

A being so differently constituted from herself, with such a command of language; able to put things as editors like them put; had passions which one could not call simply greed. Lady Bruton often suspended judgement upon men in deference to the mysterious accord in which they, but no woman, stood to the laws of the universe; knew how to put things; knew what was said; so that if Richard advised her, and Hugh wrote for her, she was sure of being somehow right. So she let Hugh eat his soufflé; asked after poor Evelyn; waited until they were smoking, and then said,

"Milly, would you fetch the papers?"

And Miss Brush went out, came back; laid papers on the table; and Hugh produced his fountain pen; his silver fountain pen, which had done twenty years' service, he said, unscrewing the cap. It was still in perfect order; he had shown it to the makers; there was no reason, they said, why it should ever wear out; which was somehow to Hugh's credit, and to the credit of the sentiments which his pen expressed (so Richard Dalloway felt) as Hugh began carefully writing capital letters with rings round them in the margin, and thus marvellously reduced Lady Bruton's tangles to sense, to grammar such as the editor of the Times, Lady Bruton felt, watching the marvellous transformation, must respect. Hugh was slow. Hugh was pertinacious. Richard said one must take risks. Hugh proposed modifications in deference to people's feelings, which, he said rather tartly when Rich-Richard laughed, "had to be considered," and read out "how, therefore, we are of opinion that the times are ripe . . . the superfluous youth of our ever-increasing population . . . what we owe to the dead . . ." which Richard thought all stuffing and bunkum, but no harm in it, of course, and Hugh went on drafting sentiments in alphabetical order of the highest nobility, brushing the cigar ash from his waistcoat, and summing up now and then the progress they had made until, finally, he read out the draft of a letter which Lady Bruton felt certain was a masterpiece. Could her own meaning sound like that?

Hugh could not guarantee that the editor would put it in; but he would be meeting somebody at luncheon.

Whereupon Lady Bruton, who seldom did a graceful thing, stuffed all Hugh's carnations into the front of her dress, and flinging her hands out called him "My Prime Minister!" What she would have done without them both she did not know. They rose. And Richard Dalloway strolled off as usual to have a look at the General's portrait, because he meant, whenever he had a moment of leisure, to write a history of Lady Bruton's family.

And Millicent Bruton was very proud of her family. But they could wait, they could wait, she said, looking at the picture; meaning that her family, of military men, administrators, admirals, had been men of action, who had done their duty; and Richard's first duty was to his country, but it was a fine face, she said; and all the papers were ready for Richard down at Aldmixton whenever the time came; the Labour Government she meant. "Ah, the news from India!" she cried.

And then, as they stood in the hall taking yellow gloves from the bowl on the malachite table and Hugh was offering Miss Brush with quite unnecessary courtesy some discarded ticket or other compliment, which she loathed from the depths of her heart and blushed brick red, Richard turned to Lady Bruton, with his hat in his hand, and said,

"We shall see you at our party to-night?" whereupon Lady Bruton resumed the magnificence which letter-writing had shattered. She might come; or she might not come. Clarissa had wonderful energy. Parties terrified Lady Bruton. But then, she was getting old. So she intimated, standing at her doorway; handsome; very erect; while her chow stretched behind her, and Miss Brush disappeared into the background with her hands full of papers.

And Lady Bruton went ponderously, majestically, up to her room, lay, one arm extended, on the sofa. She sighed, she snored, not that she was asleep, only drowsy and heavy, drowsy and heavy, like a field of clover in the sunshine this hot June day, with the bees going round and about and the yellow butterflies. Always she went back to those fields down in Devonshire, where she had jumped the brooks on Patty, her pony, with Mortimer and Tom, her brothers. And there were the dogs; there were the rats; there were her father and mother on the lawn under the trees, with the tea-things out, and the beds of dahlias, the hollyhocks, the pampas grass; and they, little wretches, always up to some mischief! stealing back through the shrubbery, so as not to be seen, all bedraggled from some roguery. What old nurse used to say about her frocks!

Ah dear, she remembered--it was Wednesday in Brook Street. Those kind good fellows, Richard Dalloway, Hugh Whitbread, had gone this hot day through the streets whose growl came up to her lying on the sofa. Power was hers, position, income. She had lived in the forefront of her time. She had had good friends; known the ablest men of her day. Murmuring London flowed up to her, and her hand, lying on the sofa back, curled upon some imaginary baton such as her grandfathers might have held, holding which she seemed, drowsy and heavy, to be commanding battalions marching to Canada, and those good fellows walking across London, that territory of theirs, that little bit of carpet, Mayfair.

And they went further and further from her, being attached to her by a thin thread (since they had lunched with her) which would stretch and stretch, get thinner and thinner as they walked across London; as if one's friends were attached to one's body, after lunching with them, by a thin thread, which (as she dozed there) became hazy with the sound of bells, striking the hour or ringing to service, as a single spider's thread is blotted with rain-drops, and, burdened, sags down. So she slept.

And Richard Dalloway and Hugh Whitbread hesitated at the corner of Conduit Street at the very moment that Millicent Bruton, lying on the sofa, let the thread snap; snored. Contrary winds buffeted at the street corner. They looked in at a shop window; they did not wish to buy or to talk but to part, only with contrary winds buffeting the street corner, with some sort of lapse in the tides of the body, two forces meeting in a swirl, morning and afternoon, they paused. Some newspaper placard went up in the air, gallantly, like a kite at first, then paused, swooped, fluttered; and a lady's veil hung. Yellow awnings trembled. The speed of the morning traffic slackened, and single carts rattled carelessly down half-empty streets. In Norfolk, of which Richard Dalloway was half thinking, a soft warm wind blew back the petals; confused the waters; ruffled the flowering grasses. Haymakers, who had pitched beneath hedges to sleep away the morning toil, parted curtains of green blades; moved trembling globes of cow parsley to see the sky; the blue, the steadfast, the blazing summer sky.

Aware that he was looking at a silver two-handled Jacobean mug, and that Hugh Whitbread admired condescendingly with airs of connoisseurship a Spanish necklace which he thought of asking the price of in case Evelyn might like it--still Richard was torpid; could not think or move. Life had thrown up this wreckage; shop windows full of coloured paste, and one stood stark with the lethargy of the old, stiff with the rigidity of the old, looking in. Evelyn Whitbread might like to buy this Spanish necklace--so she might. Yawn he must. Hugh was going into the shop.

"Right you are!" said Richard, following.

Goodness knows he didn't want to go buying necklaces with Hugh. But there are tides in the body. Morning meets afternoon. Borne like a frail shallop on deep, deep floods, Lady Bruton's great- grandfather and his memoir and his campaigns in North America were whelmed and sunk. And Millicent Bruton too. She went under. Richard didn't care a straw what became of Emigration; about that letter, whether the editor put it in or not. The necklace hung stretched between Hugh's admirable fingers. Let him give it to a girl, if he must buy jewels--any girl, any girl in the street. For the worthlessness of this life did strike Richard pretty forcibly-- buying necklaces for Evelyn. If he'd had a boy he'd have said, Work, work. But he had his Elizabeth; he adored his Elizabeth.

"I should like to see Mr. Dubonnet," said Hugh in his curt worldly way. It appeared that this Dubonnet had the measurements of Mrs. Whitbread's neck, or, more strangely still, knew her views upon Spanish jewellery and the extent of her possessions in that line (which Hugh could not remember). All of which seemed to Richard Dalloway awfully odd. For he never gave Clarissa presents, except a bracelet two or three years ago, which had not been a success. She never wore it. It pained him to remember that she never wore it. And as a single spider's thread after wavering here and there attaches itself to the point of a leaf, so Richard's mind, recovering from its lethargy, set now on his wife, Clarissa, whom Peter Walsh had loved so passionately; and Richard had had a sudden vision of her there at luncheon; of himself and Clarissa; of their life together; and he drew the tray of old jewels towards him, and taking up first this brooch then that ring, "How much is that?" he asked, but doubted his own taste. He wanted to open the drawing- room door and come in holding out something; a present for Clarissa. Only what? But Hugh was on his legs again. He was unspeakably pompous. Really, after dealing here for thirty-five years he was not going to be put off by a mere boy who did not know his business. For Dubonnet, it seemed, was out, and Hugh would not buy anything until Mr. Dubonnet chose to be in; at which the youth flushed and bowed his correct little bow. It was all perfectly correct. And yet Richard couldn't have said that to save his life! Why these people stood that damned insolence he could not conceive. Hugh was becoming an intolerable ass. Richard Dalloway could not stand more than an hour of his society. And, flicking his bowler hat by way of farewell, Richard turned at the corner of Conduit Street eager, yes, very eager, to travel that spider's thread of attachment between himself and Clarissa; he would go straight to her, in Westminster.

But he wanted to come in holding something. Flowers? Yes, flowers, since he did not trust his taste in gold; any number of flowers, roses, orchids, to celebrate what was, reckoning things as you will, an event; this feeling about her when they spoke of Peter Walsh at luncheon; and they never spoke of it; not for years had they spoken of it; which, he thought, grasping his red and white roses together (a vast bunch in tissue paper), is the greatest mistake in the world. The time comes when it can't be said; one's too shy to say it, he thought, pocketing his sixpence or two of change, setting off with his great bunch held against his body to Westminster to say straight out in so many words (whatever she might think of him), holding out his flowers, "I love you." Why not? Really it was a miracle thinking of the war, and thousands of poor chaps, with all their lives before them, shovelled together, already half forgotten; it was a miracle. Here he was walking across London to say to Clarissa in so many words that he loved her. Which one never does say, he thought. Partly one's lazy; partly one's shy. And Clarissa--it was difficult to think of her; except in starts, as at luncheon, when he saw her quite distinctly; their whole life. He stopped at the crossing; and repeated--being simple by nature, and undebauched, because he had tramped, and shot; being pertinacious and dogged, having championed the down- trodden and followed his instincts in the House of Commons; being preserved in his simplicity yet at the same time grown rather speechless, rather stiff--he repeated that it was a miracle that he should have married Clarissa; a miracle--his life had been a miracle, he thought; hesitating to cross. But it did make his blood boil to see little creatures of five or six crossing Piccadilly alone. The police ought to have stopped the traffic at once. He had no illusions about the London police. Indeed, he was collecting evidence of their malpractices; and those costermongers, not allowed to stand their barrows in the streets; and prostitutes, good Lord, the fault wasn't in them, nor in young men either, but in our detestable social system and so forth; all of which he considered, could be seen considering, grey, dogged, dapper, clean, as he walked across the Park to tell his wife that he loved her.

For he would say it in so many words, when he came into the room. Because it is a thousand pities never to say what one feels, he thought, crossing the Green Park and observing with pleasure how in the shade of the trees whole families, poor families, were sprawling; children kicking up their legs; sucking milk; paper bags thrown about, which could easily be picked up (if people objected) by one of those fat gentlemen in livery; for he was of opinion that every park, and every square, during the summer months should be open to children (the grass of the park flushed and faded, lighting up the poor mothers of Westminster and their crawling babies, as if a yellow lamp were moved beneath). But what could be done for female vagrants like that poor creature, stretched on her elbow (as if she had flung herself on the earth, rid of all ties, to observe curiously, to speculate boldly, to consider the whys and the wherefores, impudent, loose-lipped, humorous), he did not know. Bearing his flowers like a weapon, Richard Dalloway approached her; intent he passed her; still there was time for a spark between them--she laughed at the sight of him, he smiled good-humouredly, considering the problem of the female vagrant; not that they would ever speak. But he would tell Clarissa that he loved her, in so many words. He had, once upon a time, been jealous of Peter Walsh; jealous of him and Clarissa. But she had often said to him that she had been right not to marry Peter Walsh; which, knowing Clarissa, was obviously true; she wanted support. Not that she was weak; but she wanted support.

As for Buckingham Palace (like an old prima donna facing the audience all in white) you can't deny it a certain dignity, he considered, nor despise what does, after all, stand to millions of people (a little crowd was waiting at the gate to see the King drive out) for a symbol, absurd though it is; a child with a box of bricks could have done better, he thought; looking at the memorial to Queen Victoria (whom he could remember in her horn spectacles driving through Kensington), its white mound, its billowing motherliness; but he liked being ruled by the descendant of Horsa; he liked continuity; and the sense of handing on the traditions of the past. It was a great age in which to have lived. Indeed, his own life was a miracle; let him make no mistake about it; here he was, in the prime of life, walking to his house in Westminster to tell Clarissa that he loved her. Happiness is this he thought.

It is this, he said, as he entered Dean's Yard. Big Ben was beginning to strike, first the warning, musical; then the hour, irrevocable. Lunch parties waste the entire afternoon, he thought, approaching his door.

The sound of Big Ben flooded Clarissa's drawing-room, where she sat, ever so annoyed, at her writing-table; worried; annoyed. It was perfectly true that she had not asked Ellie Henderson to her party; but she had done it on purpose. Now Mrs. Marsham wrote "she had told Ellie Henderson she would ask Clarissa--Ellie so much wanted to come."

But why should she invite all the dull women in London to her parties? Why should Mrs. Marsham interfere? And there was Elizabeth closeted all this time with Doris Kilman. Anything more nauseating she could not conceive. Prayer at this hour with that woman. And the sound of the bell flooded the room with its melancholy wave; which receded, and gathered itself together to fall once more, when she heard, distractingly, something fumbling, something scratching at the door. Who at this hour? Three, good Heavens! Three already! For with overpowering directness and dignity the clock struck three; and she heard nothing else; but the door handle slipped round and in came Richard! What a surprise! In came Richard, holding out flowers. She had failed him, once at Constantinople; and Lady Bruton, whose lunch parties were said to be extraordinarily amusing, had not asked her. He was holding out flowers--roses, red and white roses. (But he could not bring himself to say he loved her; not in so many words.)

But how lovely, she said, taking his flowers. She understood; she understood without his speaking; his Clarissa. She put them in vases on the mantelpiece. How lovely they looked! she said. And was it amusing, she asked? Had Lady Bruton asked after her? Peter Walsh was back. Mrs. Marsham had written. Must she ask Ellie Henderson? That woman Kilman was upstairs.

"But let us sit down for five minutes," said Richard.

It all looked so empty. All the chairs were against the wall. What had they been doing? Oh, it was for the party; no, he had not forgotten, the party. Peter Walsh was back. Oh yes; she had had him. And he was going to get a divorce; and he was in love with some woman out there. And he hadn't changed in the slightest. There she was, mending her dress. . . .

"Thinking of Bourton," she said.

"Hugh was at lunch," said Richard. She had met him too! Well, he was getting absolutely intolerable. Buying Evelyn necklaces; fatter than ever; an intolerable ass.

"And it came over me 'I might have married you,'" she said, thinking of Peter sitting there in his little bow-tie; with that knife, opening it, shutting it. "Just as he always was, you know."

They were talking about him at lunch, said Richard. (But he could not tell her he loved her. He held her hand. Happiness is this, he thought.) They had been writing a letter to the Times for Millicent Bruton. That was about all Hugh was fit for.

"And our dear Miss Kilman?" he asked. Clarissa thought the roses absolutely lovely; first bunched together; now of their own accord starting apart.

"Kilman arrives just as we've done lunch," she said. "Elizabeth turns pink. They shut themselves up. I suppose they're praying."

Lord! He didn't like it; but these things pass over if you let them.

"In a mackintosh with an umbrella," said Clarissa.

He had not said "I love you"; but he held her hand. Happiness is this, is this, he thought.

"But why should I ask all the dull women in London to my parties?" said Clarissa. And if Mrs. Marsham gave a party, did SHE invite her guests?

"Poor Ellie Henderson," said Richard--it was a very odd thing how much Clarissa minded about her parties, he thought.

But Richard had no notion of the look of a room. However--what was he going to say?

If she worried about these parties he would not let her give them. Did she wish she had married Peter? But he must go.

He must be off, he said, getting up. But he stood for a moment as if he were about to say something; and she wondered what? Why? There were the roses.

"Some Committee?" she asked, as he opened the door.

"Armenians," he said; or perhaps it was "Albanians."

And there is a dignity in people; a solitude; even between husband and wife a gulf; and that one must respect, thought Clarissa, watching him open the door; for one would not part with it oneself, or take it, against his will, from one's husband, without losing one's independence, one's self-respect--something, after all, priceless.

He returned with a pillow and a quilt.

"An hour's complete rest after luncheon," he said. And he went.

How like him! He would go on saying "An hour's complete rest after luncheon" to the end of time, because a doctor had ordered it once. It was like him to take what doctors said literally; part of his adorable, divine simplicity, which no one had to the same extent; which made him go and do the thing while she and Peter frittered their time away bickering. He was already halfway to the House of Commons, to his Armenians, his Albanians, having settled her on the sofa, looking at his roses. And people would say, "Clarissa Dalloway is spoilt." She cared much more for her roses than for the Armenians. Hunted out of existence, maimed, frozen, the victims of cruelty and injustice (she had heard Richard say so over and over again)--no, she could feel nothing for the Albanians, or was it the

Armenians? but she loved her roses (didn't that help the Armenians?)--the only flowers she could bear to see cut. But Richard was already at the House of Commons; at his Committee, having settled all her difficulties. But no; alas, that was not true. He did not see the reasons against asking Ellie Henderson. She would do it, of course, as he wished it. Since he had brought the pillows, she would lie down. . . . But--but--why did she suddenly feel, for no reason that she could discover, desperately unhappy? As a person who has dropped some grain of pearl or diamond into the grass and parts the tall blades very carefully, this way and that, and searches here and there vainly, and at last spies it there at the roots, so she went through one thing and another; no, it was not Sally Seton saying that Richard would never be in the Cabinet because he had a second-class brain (it came back to her); no, she did not mind that; nor was it to do with Elizabeth either and Doris Kilman; those were facts. It was a feeling, some unpleasant feeling, earlier in the day perhaps; something that Peter had said, combined with some depression of her own, in her bedroom, taking off her hat; and what Richard had said had added to it, but what had he said? There were his roses. Her parties! That was it! Her parties! Both of them criticised her very unfairly, laughed at her very unjustly, for her parties. That was it! That was it!

Well, how was she going to defend herself? Now that she knew what it was, she felt perfectly happy. They thought, or Peter at any rate thought, that she enjoyed imposing herself; liked to have famous people about her; great names; was simply a snob in short. Well, Peter might think so. Richard merely thought it foolish of her to like excitement when she knew it was bad for her heart. It was childish, he thought. And both were quite wrong. What she liked was simply life.

"That's what I do it for," she said, speaking aloud, to life.

Since she was lying on the sofa, cloistered, exempt, the presence of this thing which she felt to be so obvious became physically existent; with robes of sound from the street, sunny, with hot breath, whispering, blowing out the blinds. But suppose Peter said to her, "Yes, yes, but your parties--what's the sense of your parties?" all she could say was (and nobody could be expected to understand): They're an offering; which sounded horribly vague. But who was Peter to make out that life was all plain sailing?-- Peter always in love, always in love with the wrong woman? What's your love? she might say to him. And she knew his answer; how it is the most important thing in the world and no woman possibly understood it. Very well. But could any man understand what she meant either? about life? She could not imagine Peter or Richard taking the trouble to give a party for no reason whatever.

But to go deeper, beneath what people said (and these judgements, how superficial, how fragmentary they are!) in her own mind now, what did it mean to her, this thing she called life? Oh, it was very queer. Here was So-and-so in South Kensington; some one up in Bayswater; and somebody else, say, in Mayfair. And she felt quite continuously a sense of their existence; and she felt what a waste;

and she felt what a pity; and she felt if only they could be brought together; so she did it. And it was an offering; to combine, to create; but to whom?

An offering for the sake of offering, perhaps. Anyhow, it was her gift. Nothing else had she of the slightest importance; could not think, write, even play the piano. She muddled Armenians and Turks; loved success; hated discomfort; must be liked; talked oceans of nonsense: and to this day, ask her what the Equator was, and she did not know. All the same, that one day should follow another; Wednesday, Thursday, Friday, Saturday; that one should wake up in the morning; see the sky; walk in the park; meet Hugh Whitbread; then suddenly in came Peter; then these roses; it was enough. After that, how unbelievable death was!--that it must end; and no one in the whole world would know how she had loved it all; how, every instant . . .

The door opened. Elizabeth knew that her mother was resting. She came in very quietly. She stood perfectly still. Was it that some Mongol had been wrecked on the coast of Norfolk (as Mrs. Hilbery said), had mixed with the Dalloway ladies, perhaps, a hundred years ago? For the Dalloways, in general, were fair-haired; blue-eyed; Elizabeth, on the contrary, was dark; had Chinese eyes in a pale face; an Oriental mystery; was gentle, considerate, still. As a child, she had had a perfect sense of humour; but now at seventeen, why, Clarissa could not in the least understand, she had become very serious; like a hyacinth, sheathed in glossy green, with buds just tinted, a hyacinth which has had no sun.

She stood quite still and looked at her mother; but the door was ajar, and outside the door was Miss Kilman, as Clarissa knew; Miss Kilman in her mackintosh, listening to whatever they said.

Yes, Miss Kilman stood on the landing, and wore a mackintosh; but had her reasons. First, it was cheap; second, she was over forty; and did not, after all, dress to please. She was poor, moreover; degradingly poor. Otherwise she would not be taking jobs from people like the Dalloways; from rich people, who liked to be kind. Mr. Dalloway, to do him justice, had been kind. But Mrs. Dalloway had not. She had been merely condescending. She came from the most worthless of all classes--the rich, with a smattering of culture. They had expensive things everywhere; pictures, carpets, lots of servants. She considered that she had a perfect right to anything that the Dalloways did for her.

She had been cheated. Yes, the word was no exaggeration, for surely a girl has a right to some kind of happiness? And she had never been happy, what with being so clumsy and so poor. And then, just as she might have had a chance at Miss Dolby's school, the war came; and she had never been able to tell lies. Miss Dolby thought she would be happier with people who shared her views about the Germans. She had had to go. It was true that the family was of German origin; spelt the name Kiehlman in the eighteenth century; but her brother had been killed. They turned her out because she would not pretend that the Germans were all villains--when she had German friends, when the only happy days of her life had been spent in Germany! And after all, she could read history. She had had to take whatever she could get. Mr. Dalloway had come across her working for the

Friends. He had allowed her (and that was really generous of him) to teach his daughter history. Also she did a little Extension lecturing and so on. Then Our Lord had come to her (and here she always bowed her head). She had seen the light two years and three months ago. Now she did not envy women like Clarissa Dalloway; she pitied them.

She pitied and despised them from the bottom of her heart, as she stood on the soft carpet, looking at the old engraving of a little girl with a muff. With all this luxury going on, what hope was there for a better state of things? Instead of lying on a sofa-- "My mother is resting," Elizabeth had said--she should have been in a factory; behind a counter; Mrs. Dalloway and all the other fine ladies!

Bitter and burning, Miss Kilman had turned into a church two years three months ago. She had heard the Rev. Edward Whittaker preach; the boys sing; had seen the solemn lights descend, and whether it was the music, or the voices (she herself when alone in the evening found comfort in a violin; but the sound was excruciating; she had no ear), the hot and turbulent feelings which boiled and surged in her had been assuaged as she sat there, and she had wept copiously, and gone to call on Mr. Whittaker at his private house in Kensington. It was the hand of God, he said. The Lord had shown her the way. So now, whenever the hot and painful feelings boiled within her, this hatred of Mrs. Dalloway, this grudge against the world, she thought of God. She thought of Mr. Whittaker. Rage was succeeded by calm. A sweet savour filled her veins, her lips parted, and, standing formidable upon the landing in her mackintosh, she looked with steady and sinister serenity at Mrs. Dalloway, who came out with her daughter.

Elizabeth said she had forgotten her gloves. That was because Miss Kilman and her mother hated each other. She could not bear to see them together. She ran upstairs to find her gloves.

But Miss Kilman did not hate Mrs. Dalloway. Turning her large gooseberry-coloured eyes upon Clarissa, observing her small pink face, her delicate body, her air of freshness and fashion, Miss Kilman felt, Fool! Simpleton! You who have known neither sorrow nor pleasure; who have trifled your life away! And there rose in her an overmastering desire to overcome her; to unmask her. If she could have felled her it would have eased her. But it was not the body; it was the soul and its mockery that she wished to subdue; make feel her mastery. If only she could make her weep; could ruin her; humiliate her; bring her to her knees crying, You are right! But this was God's will, not Miss Kilman's. It was to be a religious victory. So she glared; so she glowered.

Clarissa was really shocked. This a Christian--this woman! This woman had taken her daughter from her! She in touch with invisible presences! Heavy, ugly, commonplace, without kindness or grace, she know the meaning of life!

"You are taking Elizabeth to the Stores?" Mrs. Dalloway said.

Miss Kilman said she was. They stood there. Miss Kilman was not going to make herself agreeable. She had always earned her living. Her knowledge of modern history was thorough in the extreme. She did out of her meagre income set aside so much for causes she believed in; whereas this woman did nothing, believed nothing; brought up her daughter--but here was Elizabeth, rather out of breath, the beautiful girl.

So they were going to the Stores. Odd it was, as Miss Kilman stood there (and stand she did, with the power and taciturnity of some prehistoric monster armoured for primeval warfare), how, second by second, the idea of her diminished, how hatred (which was for ideas, not people) crumbled, how she lost her malignity, her size, became second by second merely Miss Kilman, in a mackintosh, whom Heaven knows Clarissa would have liked to help.

At this dwindling of the monster, Clarissa laughed. Saying good- bye, she laughed.

Off they went together, Miss Kilman and Elizabeth, downstairs.

With a sudden impulse, with a violent anguish, for this woman was taking her daughter from her, Clarissa leant over the bannisters and cried out, "Remember the party! Remember our party tonight!"

But Elizabeth had already opened the front door; there was a van passing; she did not answer.

Love and religion! thought Clarissa, going back into the drawing- room, tingling all over. How detestable, how detestable they are! For now that the body of Miss Kilman was not before her, it overwhelmed her--the idea. The cruelest things in the world, she thought, seeing them clumsy, hot, domineering, hypocritical, eavesdropping, jealous, infinitely cruel and unscrupulous, dressed in a mackintosh coat, on the landing; love and religion. Had she ever tried to convert any one herself? Did she not wish everybody merely to be themselves? And she watched out of the window the old lady opposite climbing upstairs. Let her climb upstairs if she wanted to; let her stop; then let her, as Clarissa had often seen her, gain her bedroom, part her curtains, and disappear again into the background. Somehow one respected that--that old woman looking out of the window, quite unconscious that she was being watched. There was something solemn in it--but love and religion would destroy that, whatever it was, the privacy of the soul. The odious Kilman would destroy it. Yet it was a sight that made her want to cry.

Love destroyed too. Everything that was fine, everything that was true went. Take Peter Walsh now. There was a man, charming, clever, with ideas about everything. If you wanted to know about Pope, say, or Addison, or just to talk nonsense, what people were like, what things meant, Peter knew better than any one. It was Peter who had helped her; Peter who had lent her books. But look at the women he loved--vulgar, trivial, commonplace. Think of Peter in love--he came to see her after all these years, and what did he talk about? Himself. Horrible passion! she thought. Degrading passion! she thought, thinking of Kilman and her Elizabeth walking to the Army and Navy Stores.

Big Ben struck the half-hour.

How extraordinary it was, strange, yes, touching, to see the old lady (they had been neighbours ever so many years) move away from the window, as if she were attached to that sound, that string. Gigantic as it was, it had something to do with her. Down, down, into the midst of ordinary things the finger fell making the moment solemn. She was forced, so Clarissa imagined, by that sound, to move, to go--but where? Clarissa tried to follow her as she turned and disappeared, and could still just see her white cap moving at the back of the bedroom. She was still there moving about at the other end of the room. Why creeds and prayers and mackintoshes? when, thought Clarissa, that's the miracle, that's the mystery; that old lady, she meant, whom she could see going from chest of drawers to dressing-table. She could still see her. And the supreme mystery which Kilman might say she had solved, or Peter might say he had solved, but Clarissa didn't believe either of them had the ghost of an idea of solving, was simply this: here was one room; there another. Did religion solve that, or love?

Love--but here the other clock, the clock which always struck two minutes after Big Ben, came shuffling in with its lap full of odds and ends, which it dumped down as if Big Ben were all very well with his majesty laying down the law, so solemn, so just, but she must remember all sorts of little things besides--Mrs. Marsham, Ellie Henderson, glasses for ices--all sorts of little things came flooding and lapping and dancing in on the wake of that solemn stroke which lay flat like a bar of gold on the sea. Mrs. Marsham, Ellie Henderson, glasses for ices. She must telephone now at once.

Volubly, troublously, the late clock sounded, coming in on the wake of Big Ben, with its lap full of trifles. Beaten up, broken up by the assault of carriages, the brutality of vans, the eager advance of myriads of angular men, of flaunting women, the domes and spires of offices and hospitals, the last relics of this lap full of odds and ends seemed to break, like the spray of an exhausted wave, upon the body of Miss Kilman standing still in the street for a moment to mutter "It is the flesh."

It was the flesh that she must control. Clarissa Dalloway had insulted her. That she expected. But she had not triumphed; she had not mastered the flesh. Ugly, clumsy, Clarissa Dalloway had laughed at her for being that; and had revived the fleshly desires, for she minded looking as she did beside Clarissa. Nor could she talk as she did. But why wish to resemble her? Why? She despised Mrs. Dalloway from the bottom of her heart. She was not serious. She was not good. Her life was a tissue of vanity and deceit. Yet Doris Kilman had been overcome. She had, as a matter of fact, very nearly burst into tears when Clarissa Dalloway laughed at her. "It is the flesh, it is the flesh," she muttered (it being her habit to talk aloud) trying to subdue this turbulent and painful feeling as she walked down Victoria Street. She prayed to God. She could not help being ugly; she could not afford to buy pretty clothes. Clarissa Dalloway had laughed--but she would concentrate her mind upon something else until she had reached the pillar-box. At any rate she had got Elizabeth. But she would think of something else; she would think of Russia; until she reached the pillar-box.

How nice it must be, she said, in the country, struggling, as Mr. Whittaker had told her, with that violent grudge against the world which had scorned her, sneered at her, cast her off, beginning with this indignity--the infliction of her unlovable body which people could not bear to see. Do her hair as she might, her forehead remained like an egg, bald, white. No clothes suited her. She might buy anything. And for a woman, of course, that meant never meeting the opposite sex. Never would she come first with any one. Sometimes lately it had seemed to her that, except for Elizabeth, her food was all that she lived for; her comforts; her dinner, her tea; her hot-water bottle at night. But one must fight; vanquish; have faith in God. Mr. Whittaker had said she was there for a purpose. But no one knew the agony! He said, pointing to the crucifix, that God knew. But why should she have to suffer when other women, like Clarissa Dalloway, escaped? Knowledge comes through suffering, said Mr. Whittaker.

She had passed the pillar-box, and Elizabeth had turned into the cool brown tobacco department of the Army and Navy Stores while she was still muttering to herself what Mr. Whittaker had said about knowledge coming through suffering and the flesh. "The flesh," she muttered.

What department did she want? Elizabeth interrupted her.

"Petticoats," she said abruptly, and stalked straight on to the lift.

Up they went. Elizabeth guided her this way and that; guided her in her abstraction as if she had been a great child, an unwieldy battleship. There were the petticoats, brown, decorous, striped, frivolous, solid, flimsy; and she chose, in her abstraction, portentously, and the girl serving thought her mad.

Elizabeth rather wondered, as they did up the parcel, what Miss Kilman was thinking. They must have their tea, said Miss Kilman, rousing, collecting herself. They had their tea.

Elizabeth rather wondered whether Miss Kilman could be hungry. It was her way of eating, eating with intensity, then looking, again and again, at a plate of sugared cakes on the table next them; then, when a lady and a child sat down and the child took the cake, could Miss Kilman really mind it? Yes, Miss Kilman did mind it. She had wanted that cake--the pink one. The pleasure of eating was almost the only pure pleasure left her, and then to be baffled even in that!

When people are happy, they have a reserve, she had told Elizabeth, upon which to draw, whereas she was like a wheel without a tyre (she was fond of such metaphors), jolted by every pebble, so she would say staying on after the lesson standing by the fire-place with her bag of books, her "satchel," she called it, on a Tuesday morning, after the lesson was over. And she talked too about the war. After all, there were people who did not think the English invariably right. There were books. There were meetings. There were other points of view. Would Elizabeth like to come with her to listen to So-and-so (a most extraordinary looking old man)? Then Miss Kilman took her to some church in Kensington and they had tea with a clergyman. She had lent her books. Law, medicine, politics, all professions are open to women of your generation, said Miss Kilman. But for herself, her career was absolutely ruined and was it her fault? Good gracious, said Elizabeth, no.

And her mother would come calling to say that a hamper had come from Bourton and would Miss Kilman like some flowers? To Miss Kilman she was always very, very nice, but Miss Kilman squashed the flowers all in a bunch, and hadn't any small talk, and what interested Miss Kilman bored her mother, and Miss Kilman and she were terrible together; and Miss Kilman swelled and looked very plain. But then Miss Kilman was frightfully clever. Elizabeth had never thought about the poor. They lived with everything they wanted,--her mother had breakfast in bed every day; Lucy carried it up; and she liked old women because they were Duchesses, and being descended from some Lord. But Miss Kilman said (one of those Tuesday mornings when the lesson was over), "My grandfather kept an oil and colour shop in Kensington." Miss Kilman made one feel so small.

Miss Kilman took another cup of tea. Elizabeth, with her oriental bearing, her inscrutable mystery, sat perfectly upright; no, she did not want anything more. She looked for her gloves--her white gloves. They were under the table. Ah, but she must not go! Miss Kilman could not let her go! this youth, that was so beautiful, this girl, whom she genuinely loved! Her large hand opened and shut on the table.

But perhaps it was a little flat somehow, Elizabeth felt. And really she would like to go.

But said Miss Kilman, "I've not quite finished yet."

Of course, then, Elizabeth would wait. But it was rather stuffy in here.

"Are you going to the party to-night?" Miss Kilman said. Elizabeth supposed she was going; her mother wanted her to go. She must not let parties absorb her, Miss Kilman said, fingering the last two inches of a chocolate éclair.

She did not much like parties, Elizabeth said. Miss Kilman opened her mouth, slightly projected her chin, and swallowed down the last inches of the chocolate éclair, then wiped her fingers, and washed the tea round in her cup.

She was about to split asunder, she felt. The agony was so terrific. If she could grasp her, if she could clasp her, if she could make her hers absolutely and forever and then die; that was all she wanted. But to sit here, unable to think of anything to say; to see Elizabeth turning against her; to be felt repulsive even by her--it was too much; she could not stand it. The thick fingers curled inwards.

"I never go to parties," said Miss Kilman, just to keep Elizabeth from going. "People don't ask me to parties"--and she knew as she said it that it was this egotism that was her undoing; Mr. Whittaker had warned her; but she could not help it. She had suffered so horribly. "Why should they ask me?" she said. "I'm plain, I'm unhappy." She knew it was idiotic. But it was all those people passing--people with parcels who despised her, who made her say it. However, she was Doris Kilman. She had her degree. She was a woman who had made her way in the world. Her knowledge of modern history was more than respectable.

"I don't pity myself," she said. "I pity"--she meant to say "your mother" but no, she could not, not to Elizabeth. "I pity other people," she said, "more."

Like some dumb creature who has been brought up to a gate for an unknown purpose, and stands there longing to gallop away, Elizabeth Dalloway sat silent. Was Miss Kilman going to say anything more?

"Don't quite forget me," said Doris Kilman; her voice quivered. Right away to the end of the field the dumb creature galloped in terror.

The great hand opened and shut.

Elizabeth turned her head. The waitress came. One had to pay at the desk, Elizabeth said, and went off, drawing out, so Miss Kilman felt, the very entrails in her body, stretching them as she crossed the room, and then, with a final twist, bowing her head very politely, she went.

She had gone. Miss Kilman sat at the marble table among the éclairs, stricken once, twice, thrice by shocks of suffering. She had gone. Mrs. Dalloway had triumphed. Elizabeth had gone. Beauty had gone, youth had gone.

So she sat. She got up, blundered off among the little tables, rocking slightly from side to side, and somebody came after her with her petticoat, and she lost her way, and was hemmed in by trunks specially prepared for taking to India; next got among the accouchement sets, and baby linen; through all the commodities of the world, perishable and permanent, hams, drugs, flowers, stationery, variously smelling, now sweet, now sour she lurched; saw herself thus lurching with her hat askew, very red in the face, full length in a looking-glass; and at last came out into the street.

The tower of Westminster Cathedral rose in front of her, the habitation of God. In the midst of the traffic, there was the habitation of God. Doggedly she set off with her parcel to that other sanctuary, the Abbey, where, raising her hands in a tent before her face, she sat beside those driven into shelter too; the variously assorted worshippers, now divested of social rank, almost of sex, as they raised their hands before their faces; but once they removed them, instantly reverent, middle class, English men and women, some of them desirous of seeing the wax works.

But Miss Kilman held her tent before her face. Now she was deserted; now rejoined. New worshippers came in from the street to replace the strollers, and still, as people gazed round and shuffled past the tomb of the Unknown Warrior, still she barred her eyes with her fingers and tried in this double darkness, for the light in the Abbey was bodiless, to aspire above the vanities, the desires, the commodities, to rid herself both of hatred and of love. Her hands twitched. She seemed to struggle. Yet to others God was accessible and the path to Him smooth. Mr. Fletcher, retired, of the Treasury, Mrs. Gorham, widow of the famous K.C., approached Him simply, and having done their praying, leant back, enjoyed the music (the organ pealed sweetly), and saw Miss Kilman at the end of the row, praying, praying, and, being still on the threshold of their underworld, thought of her sympathetically as a soul haunting the same territory; a soul cut out of immaterial substance; not a woman, a soul.

But Mr. Fletcher had to go. He had to pass her, and being himself neat as a new pin, could not help being a little distressed by the poor lady's disorder; her hair down; her parcel on the floor. She did not at once let him pass. But, as he stood gazing about him, at the white marbles, grey window panes, and accumulated treasures (for he was extremely proud of the Abbey), her largeness, robustness, and power as she sat there shifting her knees from time to time (it was so rough the approach to her God--so tough her desires) impressed him, as they had impressed Mrs. Dalloway (she could not get the thought of her out of her mind that afternoon), the Rev. Edward Whittaker, and Elizabeth too.

And Elizabeth waited in Victoria Street for an omnibus. It was so nice to be out of doors. She thought perhaps she need not go home just yet. It was so nice to be out in the air. So she would get on to an omnibus. And already, even as she stood there, in her very well cut clothes, it was beginning. . . . People were beginning to compare her to poplar trees, early dawn, hyacinths, fawns, running water, and garden lilies; and it made her life a burden to her, for she so much preferred being left alone to do what she liked in the country, but they would compare her to lilies, and she had to go to parties, and London was so dreary compared with being alone in the country with her father and the dogs.

Buses swooped, settled, were off--garish caravans, glistening with red and yellow varnish. But which should she get on to? She had no preferences. Of course, she would not push her way. She inclined to be passive. It was expression she needed, but her eyes were fine, Chinese, oriental, and, as her mother said, with such nice shoulders and holding herself so straight, she was always charming to look at; and lately, in the evening especially, when she was interested, for she never seemed excited, she looked almost beautiful, very stately, very serene. What could she be thinking? Every man fell in love with her, and she was really awfully bored. For it was beginning. Her mother could see that--the compliments were beginning. That she did not care more about it--for instance for her clothes--sometimes worried Clarissa, but perhaps it was as well with all those puppies and guinea pigs about having distemper, and it gave her a charm. And now there was this odd friendship with Miss Kilman. Well, thought Clarissa about three o'clock in the morning, reading Baron Marbot for she could not sleep, it proves she has a heart.

Suddenly Elizabeth stepped forward and most competently boarded the omnibus, in front of everybody. She took a seat on top. The impetuous creature--a pirate--started forward, sprang away; she had to hold the rail to steady herself, for a pirate it was, reckless, unscrupulous, bearing down ruthlessly, circumventing dangerously, boldly snatching a passenger, or ignoring a passenger, squeezing eel-like and arrogant in between, and then rushing insolently all sails spread up Whitehall. And did Elizabeth give one thought to poor Miss Kilman who loved her without jealousy, to whom she had been a fawn in the open, a moon in a glade? She was delighted to be free. The fresh air was so delicious. It had been so stuffy in the Army and Navy Stores. And now it was like riding, to be rushing up Whitehall; and to each movement of the omnibus the beautiful body in the fawn-coloured coat responded freely like a rider, like the figure-head of a ship, for the breeze slightly disarrayed her; the heat gave her cheeks the pallor of white painted wood; and her fine eyes, having no eyes to meet, gazed ahead, blank, bright, with the staring incredible innocence of sculpture.

It was always talking about her own sufferings that made Miss Kilman so difficult. And was she right? If it was being on committees and giving up hours and hours every day (she hardly ever saw him in London) that helped the poor, her father did that, goodness knows,--if that was what Miss Kilman meant about being a Christian; but it was so difficult to say. Oh, she would like to go a little further. Another penny was it to the Strand? Here was another penny then. She would go up the Strand.

She liked people who were ill. And every profession is open to the women of your generation, said Miss Kilman. So she might be a doctor. She might be a farmer. Animals are often ill. She might own a thousand acres and have people under her. She would go and see them in their cottages. This was Somerset House. One might be a very good farmer--and that, strangely enough though Miss Kilman had her share in it, was almost entirely due to Somerset House. It looked so splendid, so serious, that great grey building. And she liked the feeling of people working. She liked those churches, like shapes of grey paper, breasting the stream of the Strand. It was quite different here from Westminster, she thought, getting off at Chancery Lane. It was so serious; it was so busy. In short, she would like to have a profession. She would become a doctor, a farmer, possibly go into Parliament, if she found it necessary, all because of the Strand.

The feet of those people busy about their activities, hands putting stone to stone, minds eternally occupied not with trivial chatterings (comparing women to poplars--which was rather exciting, of course, but very silly), but with thoughts of ships, of business, of law, of administration, and with it all so stately (she was in the Temple), gay (there was the river), pious (there was the Church), made her quite determined, whatever her mother might say, to become either a farmer or a doctor. But she was, of course, rather lazy.

And it was much better to say nothing about it. It seemed so silly. It was the sort of thing that did sometimes happen, when one was alone--buildings without architects' names, crowds of people coming back from the city having more power than single clergymen in Kensington, than any of the books Miss Kilman had lent her, to stimulate what lay slumbrous, clumsy, and shy on the mind's sandy floor to break surface, as a child suddenly stretches its arms; it was just that, perhaps, a sigh, a stretch of the arms, an impulse, a revelation, which has its effects for ever, and then down again it went to the sandy floor. She must go home. She must dress for dinner. But what was the time?--where was a clock?

She looked up Fleet Street. She walked just a little way towards St. Paul's, shyly, like some one penetrating on tiptoe, exploring a strange house by night with a candle, on edge lest the owner should suddenly fling wide his bedroom door and ask her business, nor did she dare wander off into queer alleys, tempting bye-streets, any more than in a strange house open doors which might be bedroom doors, or sitting-room doors, or lead straight to the larder. For no Dalloways came down the Strand daily; she was a pioneer, a stray, venturing, trusting.

In many ways, her mother felt, she was extremely immature, like a child still, attached to dolls, to old slippers; a perfect baby; and that was charming. But then, of course, there was in the Dalloway family the tradition of public service. Abbesses, principals, head mistresses, dignitaries, in the republic of women--without being brilliant, any of them, they were that. She penetrated a little further in the direction of St. Paul's. She liked the geniality, sisterhood, motherhood, brotherhood of this uproar. It seemed to her good. The noise was tremendous; and suddenly there were trumpets (the unemployed) blaring, rattling about in the uproar; military music; as if people were marching; yet had they been dying--had some woman breathed her last and whoever was watching, opening the window of the room where she had just brought off that act of supreme dignity, looked down on Fleet Street, that uproar, that military music would have come triumphing up to him, consolatory, indifferent.

It was not conscious. There was no recognition in it of one fortune, or fate, and for that very reason even to those dazed with watching for the last shivers of consciousness on the faces of the dying, consoling. Forgetfulness in people might wound, their ingratitude corrode, but this voice, pouring endlessly, year in year out, would take whatever it might be; this vow; this van; this life; this procession, would wrap them all about and carry them on, as in the rough stream of a glacier the ice holds a splinter of bone, a blue petal, some oak trees, and rolls them on.

But it was later than she thought. Her mother would not like her to be wandering off alone like this. She turned back down the Strand.

A puff of wind (in spite of the heat, there was quite a wind) blew a thin black veil over the sun and over the Strand. The faces faded; the omnibuses suddenly lost their glow. For although the clouds were of mountainous white so that one could fancy hacking hard chips off with a hatchet, with broad golden slopes, lawns of celestial pleasure gardens, on their flanks, and had all the appearance of settled habitations assembled for the conference of gods above the world, there was a perpetual movement among them. Signs were interchanged, when, as if to fulfil some scheme arranged already, now a summit dwindled, now a whole block of pyramidal size which had kept its station inalterably advanced into the midst or gravely led the procession to fresh anchorage. Fixed though they seemed at their posts, at rest in perfect unanimity, nothing could be fresher, freer, more sensitive superficially than the snow-white or gold-kindled surface; to change, to go, to dismantle the solemn assemblage was immediately possible; and in spite of the grave fixity, the accumulated robustness and solidity, now they struck light to the earth, now darkness.

Calmly and competently, Elizabeth Dalloway mounted the Westminster omnibus.

Going and coming, beckoning, signalling, so the light and shadow which now made the wall grey, now the bananas bright yellow, now made the Strand grey, now made the omnibuses bright yellow, seemed to Septimus Warren Smith lying on the sofa in the sitting-room; watching the watery gold glow and fade with the astonishing sensibility of some live creature on the roses, on the wall-paper. Outside the trees dragged their leaves like nets through the depths of the air; the sound of water was in the room and through the waves came the voices of birds singing. Every power poured its treasures on his head, and his hand lay there on the back of the sofa, as he had seen his hand lie when he was bathing, floating, on the top of the waves, while far away on shore he heard dogs barking and barking far away. Fear no more, says the heart in the body; fear no more.

He was not afraid. At every moment Nature signified by some laughing hint like that gold spot which went round the wall--there, there, there--her determination to show, by brandishing her plumes, shaking her tresses, flinging her mantle this way and that, beautifully, always beautifully, and standing close up to breathe through her hollowed hands Shakespeare's words, her meaning.

Rezia, sitting at the table twisting a hat in her hands, watched him; saw him smiling. He was happy then. But she could not bear to see him smiling. It was not marriage; it was not being one's husband to look strange like that, always to be starting, laughing, sitting hour after hour silent, or clutching her and telling her to write. The table drawer was full of those writings; about war; about Shakespeare; about great discoveries; how there is no death. Lately he had become excited suddenly for no reason (and both Dr. Holmes and Sir William Bradshaw said excitement was the worst thing for him), and waved his hands and cried out that he knew the truth! He knew everything! That man, his friend who was killed, Evans, had come, he said. He was singing behind the screen. She wrote it down just as he spoke it. Some things were very beautiful; others sheer nonsense. And he was always stopping in the middle, changing his mind; wanting to add something; hearing something new; listening with his hand up.

But she heard nothing.

And once they found the girl who did the room reading one of these papers in fits of laughter. It was a dreadful pity. For that made Septimus cry out about human cruelty--how they tear each other to pieces. The fallen, he said, they tear to pieces. "Holmes is on us," he would say, and he would invent stories about Holmes; Holmes eating porridge; Holmes reading Shakespeare--making himself roar with laughter or rage, for Dr. Holmes seemed to stand for something horrible to him. "Human nature," he called him. Then there were the visions. He was drowned, he used to say, and lying on a cliff with the gulls screaming over him. He would look over the edge of the sofa down into the sea. Or he was hearing music. Really it was only a barrel organ or some man crying in the street. But "Lovely!" he used to cry, and the tears would run down his cheeks, which was to her the most dreadful thing of all, to see a man like Septimus, who had fought, who was brave, crying. And he would lie listening until suddenly he would cry that he was falling down, down into the flames! Actually she would look for flames, it was so vivid. But there was nothing. They were alone in the room. It was a dream, she would tell him and so quiet him at last, but sometimes she was frightened too. She sighed as she sat sewing.

Her sigh was tender and enchanting, like the wind outside a wood in the evening. Now she put down her scissors; now she turned to take something from the table. A little stir, a little crinkling, a little tapping built up something on the table there, where she sat sewing. Through his eyelashes he could see her blurred outline; her little black body; her face and hands; her turning movements at the table, as she took up a reel, or looked (she was apt to lose things) for her silk. She was making a hat for Mrs. Filmer's married daughter, whose name was--he had forgotten her name.

"What is the name of Mrs. Filmer's married daughter?" he asked.

"Mrs. Peters," said Rezia. She was afraid it was too small, she said, holding it before her. Mrs. Peters was a big woman; but she did not like her. It was only because Mrs. Filmer had been so good to them. "She gave me grapes this morning," she said--that Rezia wanted to do something to show that they were grateful. She had come into the room the other evening and found Mrs. Peters, who thought they were out, playing the gramophone.

"Was it true?" he asked. She was playing the gramophone? Yes; she had told him about it at the time; she had found Mrs. Peters playing the gramophone.

He began, very cautiously, to open his eyes, to see whether a gramophone was really there. But real things--real things were too exciting. He must be cautious. He would not go mad. First he looked at the fashion papers on the lower shelf, then, gradually at the gramophone with the green trumpet. Nothing could be more exact. And so, gathering courage, he looked at the sideboard; the plate of bananas; the engraving of Queen Victoria and the Prince Consort; at the mantelpiece, with the jar of roses. None of these things moved. All were still; all were real.

"She is a woman with a spiteful tongue," said Rezia.

"What does Mr. Peters do?" Septimus asked.

"Ah," said Rezia, trying to remember. She thought Mrs. Filmer had said that he travelled for some company. "Just now he is in Hull," she said.

"Just now!" She said that with her Italian accent. She said that herself. He shaded his eyes so that he might see only a little of her face at a time, first the chin, then the nose, then the forehead, in case it were deformed, or had some terrible mark on it. But no, there she was, perfectly natural, sewing, with the pursed lips that women have, the set, the melancholy expression, when sewing. But there was nothing terrible about it, he assured himself, looking a second time, a third time at her face, her hands, for what was frightening or disgusting in her as she sat there in broad daylight, sewing? Mrs. Peters had a spiteful tongue. Mr. Peters was in Hull. Why then rage and prophesy? Why fly scourged and outcast? Why be made to tremble and sob by the clouds? Why seek truths and deliver messages when Rezia sat sticking pins into the front of her dress, and Mr. Peters was in Hull? Miracles, revelations, agonies, loneliness, falling through the sea, down, down into the flames, all were burnt out, for he had a sense, as he watched Rezia trimming the straw hat for Mrs. Peters, of a coverlet of flowers.

"It's too small for Mrs. Peters," said Septimus.

For the first time for days he was speaking as he used to do! Of course it was--absurdly small, she said. But Mrs. Peters had chosen it.

He took it out of her hands. He said it was an organ grinder's monkey's hat.

How it rejoiced her that! Not for weeks had they laughed like this together, poking fun privately like married people. What she meant was that if Mrs. Filmer had come in, or Mrs. Peters or anybody they would not have understood what she and Septimus were laughing at.

"There," she said, pinning a rose to one side of the hat. Never had she felt so happy! Never in her life!

But that was still more ridiculous, Septimus said. Now the poor woman looked like a pig at a fair. (Nobody ever made her laugh as Septimus did.)

What had she got in her work-box? She had ribbons and beads, tassels, artificial flowers. She tumbled them out on the table. He began putting odd colours together--for though he had no fingers, could not even do up a parcel, he had a wonderful eye, and often he was right, sometimes absurd, of course, but sometimes wonderfully right.

"She shall have a beautiful hat!" he murmured, taking up this and that, Rezia kneeling by his side, looking over his shoulder. Now it was finished--that is to say the design; she must stitch it together. But she must be very, very careful, he said, to keep it just as he had made it.

So she sewed. When she sewed, he thought, she made a sound like a kettle on the hob; bubbling, murmuring, always busy, her strong little pointed fingers pinching and poking; her needle flashing straight. The sun might go in and out, on the tassels, on the wall-paper, but he would wait, he thought, stretching out his feet, looking at his ringed sock at the end of the sofa; he would wait in this warm place, this pocket of still air, which one comes on at the edge of a wood sometimes in the evening, when, because of a fall in the ground, or some arrangement of the trees (one must be scientific above all, scientific), warmth lingers, and the air buffets the cheek like the wing of a bird.

"There it is," said Rezia, twirling Mrs. Peters' hat on the tips of her fingers. "That'll do for the moment. Later . . ." her sentence bubbled away drip, drip, drip, like a contented tap left running.

It was wonderful. Never had he done anything which made him feel so proud. It was so real, it was so substantial, Mrs. Peters' hat.

"Just look at it," he said.

Yes, it would always make her happy to see that hat. He had become himself then, he had laughed then. They had been alone together. Always she would like that hat.

He told her to try it on.

"But I must look so queer!" she cried, running over to the glass and looking first this side then that. Then she snatched it off again, for there was a tap at the door. Could it be Sir William Bradshaw? Had he sent already?

No! it was only the small girl with the evening paper.

What always happened, then happened--what happened every night of their lives. The small girl sucked her thumb at the door; Rezia went down on her knees; Rezia cooed and kissed; Rezia got a bag of sweets out of the table drawer. For so it always happened. First one thing, then another. So she built it up, first one thing and then another. Dancing, skipping, round and round the room they went. He took the paper. Surrey was all out, he read. There was a heat wave.

Rezia repeated: Surrey was all out. There was a heat wave, making it part of the game she was playing with Mrs. Filmer's grandchild, both of them laughing, chattering at the same time, at their game. He was very tired. He was very happy. He would sleep. He shut his eyes. But directly he saw nothing the sounds of the game became fainter and stranger and sounded like the cries of people seeking and not finding, and passing further and further away. They had lost him!

He started up in terror. What did he see? The plate of bananas on the sideboard. Nobody was there (Rezia had taken the child to its mother. It was bedtime). That was it: to be alone forever. That was the doom pronounced in Milan when he came into the room and saw them cutting out buckram shapes with their scissors; to be alone forever.

He was alone with the sideboard and the bananas. He was alone, exposed on this bleak eminence, stretched out--but not on a hill- top; not on a crag; on Mrs. Filmer's sitting-room sofa. As for the visions, the faces, the voices of the dead, where were they? There was a screen in front of him, with black bulrushes and blue swallows. Where he had once seen mountains, where he had seen faces, where he had seen beauty, there was a screen.

"Evans!" he cried. There was no answer. A mouse had squeaked, or a curtain rustled. Those were the voices of the dead. The screen, the coalscuttle, the sideboard remained to him. Let him then face the screen, the coal-scuttle and the sideboard . . . but Rezia burst into the room chattering.

Some letter had come. Everybody's plans were changed. Mrs. Filmer would not be able to go to Brighton after all. There was no time to let Mrs. Williams know, and really Rezia thought it very, very annoying, when she caught sight of the hat and thought . . . perhaps . . . she . . . might just make a little. . . . Her voice died out in contented melody.

"Ah, damn!" she cried (it was a joke of theirs, her swearing), the needle had broken. Hat, child, Brighton, needle. She built it up; first one thing, then another, she built it up, sewing.

She wanted him to say whether by moving the rose she had improved the hat. She sat on the end of the sofa.

They were perfectly happy now, she said, suddenly, putting the hat down. For she could say anything to him now. She could say whatever came into her head. That was almost the first thing she had felt about him, that night in the café when he had come in with his English friends. He had come in, rather shyly, looking round him, and his hat had fallen when he hung it up. That she could remember. She knew he was English, though not one of the large Englishmen her sister admired, for he was always thin; but he had a beautiful fresh colour; and with his big nose, his bright eyes, his way of sitting a little hunched made her think, she had often told him, of a young hawk, that first evening she saw him, when they were playing dominoes, and he had come in--of a young hawk; but with her he was always very gentle. She had never seen him wild or drunk, only suffering sometimes through this terrible war, but even so, when she came in, he would put it all away. Anything, anything in the whole world, any little bother with her work, anything that struck her to say she would tell him, and he understood at once. Her own family even were not the same. Being older than she was and being so clever--how serious he was, wanting her to read Shakespeare before she could even read a child's story in English!-- being so much more experienced, he could help her. And she too could help him.

But this hat now. And then (it was getting late) Sir William Bradshaw.

She held her hands to her head, waiting for him to say did he like the hat or not, and as she sat there, waiting, looking down, he could feel her mind, like a bird, falling from branch to branch, and always alighting, quite rightly; he could follow her mind, as she sat there in one of those loose lax poses that came to her naturally and, if he should say anything, at once she smiled, like a bird alighting with all its claws firm upon the bough.

But he remembered Bradshaw said, "The people we are most fond of are not good for us when we are ill." Bradshaw said, he must be taught to rest. Bradshaw said they must be separated.

"Must," "must," why "must"? What power had Bradshaw over him? "What right has Bradshaw to say 'must' to me?" he demanded.

"It is because you talked of killing yourself," said Rezia. (Mercifully, she could now say anything to Septimus.)

So he was in their power! Holmes and Bradshaw were on him! The brute with the red nostrils was snuffing into every secret place! "Must" it could say! Where were his papers? the things he had written?

She brought him his papers, the things he had written, things she had written for him. She tumbled them out on to the sofa. They looked at them together. Diagrams, designs, little men and women brandishing sticks for arms, with wings--were they?--on their backs; circles traced round shillings and sixpences--the suns and stars; zigzagging precipices with mountaineers ascending roped together, exactly like knives and forks; sea pieces with little faces laughing out of what might perhaps be waves: the map of the world. Burn them! he cried. Now for his writings; how the dead sing behind rhododendron bushes; odes to Time; conversations with Shakespeare; Evans, Evans, Evans--his messages from the dead; do not cut down trees; tell the Prime Minister. Universal love: the meaning of the world. Burn them! he cried.

But Rezia laid her hands on them. Some were very beautiful, she thought. She would tie them up (for she had no envelope) with a piece of silk.

Even if they took him, she said, she would go with him. They could not separate them against their wills, she said.

Shuffling the edges straight, she did up the papers, and tied the parcel almost without looking, sitting beside him, he thought, as if all her petals were about her. She was a flowering tree; and through her branches looked out the face of a lawgiver, who had reached a sanctuary where she feared no one; not Holmes; not Bradshaw; a miracle, a triumph, the last and greatest. Staggering he saw her mount the appalling staircase, laden with Holmes and Bradshaw, men who never weighed less than eleven stone six, who sent their wives to Court, men who made ten thousand a year and talked of proportion; who different in their verdicts (for Holmes said one thing, Bradshaw another), yet judges they were; who mixed the vision and the sideboard; saw nothing clear, yet ruled, yet inflicted. "Must" they said. Over them she triumphed.

"There!" she said. The papers were tied up. No one should get at them. She would put them away.

And, she said, nothing should separate them. She sat down beside him and called him by the name of that hawk or crow which being malicious and a great destroyer of crops was precisely like him. No one could separate them, she said.

Then she got up to go into the bedroom to pack their things, but hearing voices downstairs and thinking that Dr. Holmes had perhaps called, ran down to prevent him coming up.

Septimus could hear her talking to Holmes on the staircase.

"My dear lady, I have come as a friend," Holmes was saying.

"No. I will not allow you to see my husband," she said.

He could see her, like a little hen, with her wings spread barring his passage. But Holmes persevered.

"My dear lady, allow me . . ." Holmes said, putting her aside (Holmes was a powerfully built man).

Holmes was coming upstairs. Holmes would burst open the door. Holmes would say "In a funk, eh?" Holmes would get him. But no; not Holmes; not Bradshaw. Getting up rather unsteadily, hopping indeed from foot to foot, he considered Mrs. Filmer's nice clean bread knife with "Bread" carved on the handle. Ah, but one mustn't spoil that. The gas fire? But it was too late now. Holmes was coming. Razors he might have got, but Rezia, who always did that sort of thing, had packed them. There remained only the window, the large Bloomsbury-lodging house window, the tiresome, the troublesome, and rather melodramatic business of opening the window and throwing himself out. It was their idea of tragedy, not his or Rezia's (for she was with him). Holmes and Bradshaw like that sort of thing. (He sat on the sill.) But he would wait till the very last moment. He did not want to die. Life was good. The sun hot. Only human beings--what did THEY want? Coming down the staircase opposite an old man stopped and stared at him. Holmes was at the door. "I'll give it you!" he cried, and flung himself vigorously, violently down on to Mrs. Filmer's area railings.

"The coward!" cried Dr. Holmes, bursting the door open. Rezia ran to the window, she saw; she understood. Dr. Holmes and Mrs. Filmer collided with each other. Mrs. Filmer flapped her apron and made her hide her eyes in the bedroom. There was a great deal of running up and down stairs. Dr. Holmes came in--white as a sheet, shaking all over, with a glass in his hand. She must be brave and drink something, he said (What was it? Something sweet), for her husband was horribly mangled, would not recover consciousness, she must not see him, must be spared as much as possible, would have the inquest to go through, poor young woman. Who could have foretold it? A sudden impulse, no one was in the least to blame (he told Mrs. Filmer). And why the devil he did it, Dr. Holmes could not conceive.

It seemed to her as she drank the sweet stuff that she was opening long windows, stepping out into some garden. But where? The clock was striking--one, two, three: how sensible the sound was; compared with all this thumping and whispering; like Septimus himself. She was falling asleep. But the clock went on striking, four, five, six and Mrs. Filmer waving her apron (they wouldn't bring the body in here, would they?) seemed part of that garden; or a flag. She had once seen a flag slowly rippling out from a mast when she stayed with her aunt at Venice. Men killed in battle were thus saluted, and Septimus had been through the War. Of her memories, most were happy.

She put on her hat, and ran through cornfields--where could it have been?--on to some hill, somewhere near the sea, for there were ships, gulls, butterflies; they sat on a cliff. In London too, there they sat, and, half dreaming, came to her through the bedroom door, rain falling, whisperings, stirrings among dry corn, the caress of the sea, as it seemed to her, hollowing them in its arched shell and murmuring to her laid on shore, strewn she felt, like flying flowers over some tomb.

"He is dead," she said, smiling at the poor old woman who guarded her with her honest light-blue eyes fixed on the door. (They wouldn't bring him in here, would they?) But Mrs. Filmer pooh- poohed. Oh no, oh no! They were carrying him away now. Ought she not to be told? Married people ought to be together, Mrs. Filmer thought. But they must do as the doctor said.

"Let her sleep," said Dr. Holmes, feeling her pulse. She saw the large outline of his body standing dark against the window. So that was Dr. Holmes.

One of the triumphs of civilisation, Peter Walsh thought. It is one of the triumphs of civilisation, as the light high bell of the ambulance sounded. Swiftly, cleanly the ambulance sped to the hospital, having picked up instantly, humanely, some poor devil; some one hit on the head, struck down by disease, knocked over perhaps a minute or so ago at one of these crossings, as might happen to oneself. That was civilisation. It struck him coming back from the East--the efficiency, the organisation, the communal spirit of London. Every cart or carriage of its own accord drew aside to let the ambulance pass. Perhaps it was morbid; or was it not touching rather, the respect which they showed this ambulance with its victim inside--busy men hurrying home yet instantly bethinking them as it passed of some wife; or presumably how easily it might have been them there, stretched on a shelf with a doctor and a nurse. . . . Ah, but thinking became morbid, sentimental, directly one began conjuring up doctors, dead bodies; a little glow of pleasure, a sort of lust too over the visual impression warned one not to go on with that sort of thing any more--fatal to art, fatal to friendship. True. And yet, thought Peter Walsh, as the ambulance turned the corner though the light high bell could be heard down the next street and still farther as it crossed the Tottenham Court Road, chiming constantly, it is the privilege of loneliness; in privacy one may do as one chooses. One might weep if no one saw. It had been his undoing--this susceptibility--in Anglo-Indian society; not weeping at the right time, or laughing either. I have that in me, he thought standing by the pillar-box, which could now dissolve in tears. Why, Heaven knows. Beauty of some sort probably, and the weight of the day, which beginning with that visit to Clarissa had exhausted him with its heat, its intensity, and the drip, drip, of one impression after another down into that cellar where they stood, deep, dark, and no one would ever know. Partly for that reason, its secrecy, complete and inviolable, he had found life like an unknown garden, full of turns and corners, surprising, yes; really it took one's breath away, these moments; there coming to him by the pillar-box opposite the British Museum one of them, a moment, in which things came together; this ambulance; and life and death. It was as if he were sucked up to some very high roof by that rush of emotion and the rest of him, like a white shell-sprinkled beach, left bare. It had been his undoing in Anglo-Indian society--this susceptibility.

Clarissa once, going on top of an omnibus with him somewhere, Clarissa superficially at least, so easily moved, now in despair, now in the best of spirits, all aquiver in those days and such good company, spotting queer little scenes, names, people from the top of a bus, for they used to explore London and bring back bags full of treasures from the Caledonian market--Clarissa had a theory in those days--they had heaps of theories, always theories, as young people have. It was to explain the feeling they had of dissatisfaction; not knowing people; not being known. For how could they know each other? You met every day; then not for six months, or years. It was unsatisfactory, they agreed, how little one knew people. But she said, sitting on the bus going up Shaftesbury Avenue, she felt herself everywhere; not "here, here, here"; and she tapped the back of the seat; but everywhere. She waved her hand, going up Shaftesbury Avenue. She was all that. So that to know her, or any one, one must seek out the people who completed them; even the places. Odd affinities she had with people she had never spoken to, some woman in the street, some man behind a counter--even trees, or barns. It ended in a transcendental theory which, with her horror of death, allowed her to believe, or say that she believed (for all her scepticism), that since our apparitions, the part of us which appears, are so momentary compared with the other, the unseen part of us, which spreads wide, the unseen might survive, be recovered somehow attached to this person or that, or even haunting certain places after death . . . perhaps-- perhaps.

Looking back over that long friendship of almost thirty years her theory worked to this extent. Brief, broken, often painful as their actual meetings had been what with his absences and interruptions (this morning, for instance, in came Elizabeth, like a long-legged colt, handsome, dumb, just as he was beginning to talk to Clarissa) the effect of them on his life was immeasurable. There was a mystery about it. You were given a sharp, acute, uncomfortable grain--the actual meeting; horribly painful as often as not; yet in absence, in the most unlikely places, it would flower out, open, shed its scent, let you touch, taste, look about you, get the whole feel of it and understanding, after years of lying lost. Thus she had come to him; on board ship; in the Himalayas; suggested by the oddest things (so Sally Seton, generous, enthusiastic goose! thought of HIM when she saw blue hydrangeas). She had influenced him more than any person he had ever known. And always in this way coming before him without his wishing it, cool, lady-like, critical; or ravishing, romantic, recalling some field or English harvest. He saw her most often in the country, not in London. One scene after another at Bourton. . . .

He had reached his hotel. He crossed the hall, with its mounds of reddish chairs and sofas, its spike-leaved, withered-looking plants. He got his key off the hook. The young lady handed him some letters. He went upstairs--he saw her most often at Bourton, in the late summer, when he stayed there for a week, or fortnight even, as people did in those days. First on top of some hill there she would stand, hands clapped to her hair, her cloak blowing out, pointing, crying to them--she saw the Severn beneath. Or in a wood, making the kettle boil--very ineffective with her fingers; the smoke curtseying, blowing in their faces; her little pink face showing through; begging water from an old woman in a cottage, who came to the door to watch them go. They walked always; the others drove. She was bored driving, disliked all animals, except that dog. They tramped miles along roads. She would break off to get her bearings, pilot him back across country; and all the time they argued, discussed poetry, discussed people, discussed politics (she was a Radical then); never noticing a thing except when she stopped, cried out at a view or a tree, and made him look with her; and so on again, through stubble fields, she walking ahead, with a flower for her aunt, never tired of walking for all her delicacy; to drop down on Bourton in the dusk. Then, after dinner, old Breitkopf would open the piano and sing without any voice, and they would lie sunk in arm-chairs, trying not to laugh, but always breaking down and laughing, laughing--laughing at nothing. Breitkopf was supposed not to see. And then in the morning, flirting up and down like a wagtail in front of the house. . . .

Oh it was a letter from her! This blue envelope; that was her hand. And he would have to read it. Here was another of those meetings, bound to be painful! To read her letter needed the devil of an effort. "How heavenly it was to see him. She must tell him that." That was all.

But it upset him. It annoyed him. He wished she hadn't written it. Coming on top of his thoughts, it was like a nudge in the ribs. Why couldn't she let him be? After all, she had married Dalloway, and lived with him in perfect happiness all these years.

These hotels are not consoling places. Far from it. Any number of people had hung up their hats on those pegs. Even the flies, if you thought of it, had settled on other people's noses. As for the cleanliness which hit him in the face, it wasn't cleanliness, so much as bareness, frigidity; a thing that had to be. Some arid matron made her rounds at dawn sniffing, peering, causing blue- nosed maids to scour, for all the world as if the next visitor were a joint of meat to be served on a perfectly clean platter. For sleep, one bed; for sitting in, one armchair; for cleaning one's teeth and shaving one's chin, one tumbler, one looking-glass. Books, letters, dressing-gown, slipped about on the impersonality of the horsehair like incongruous impertinences. And it was Clarissa's letter that made him see all this. "Heavenly to see you. She must say so!" He folded the paper; pushed it away; nothing would induce him to read it again!

To get that letter to him by six o'clock she must have sat down and written it directly he left her; stamped it; sent somebody to the post. It was, as people say, very like her. She was upset by his visit. She had felt a great deal; had for a moment, when she kissed his hand, regretted, envied him even, remembered possibly (for he saw her look it) something he had said--how they would change the world if she married him perhaps; whereas, it was this; it was middle age; it was mediocrity; then forced herself with her indomitable vitality to put all that aside, there being in her a thread of life which for toughness, endurance, power to overcome obstacles, and carry her triumphantly through he had never known the like of. Yes; but there would come a reaction directly he left the room. She would be frightfully sorry for him; she would think what in the world she could do to give him pleasure (short always of the one thing) and he could see her with the tears running down her cheeks going to her writing-table and dashing off that one line which he was to find greeting him. . . . "Heavenly to see you!" And she meant it.

Peter Walsh had now unlaced his boots.

But it would not have been a success, their marriage. The other thing, after all, came so much more naturally.

It was odd; it was true; lots of people felt it. Peter Walsh, who had done just respectably, filled the usual posts adequately, was liked, but thought a little cranky, gave himself airs--it was odd that HE should have had, especially now that his hair was grey, a contented look; a look of having reserves. It was this that made him attractive to women who liked the sense that he was not altogether manly. There was something unusual about him, or something behind him. It might be that he was bookish--never came to see you without taking up the book on the table (he was now reading, with his bootlaces trailing on the floor); or that he was a gentleman, which showed itself in the way he knocked the ashes out of his pipe, and in his manners of course to women. For it was very charming and quite ridiculous how easily some girl without a grain of sense could twist him round her finger. But at her own risk. That is to say, though he might be ever so easy, and indeed with his gaiety and good-breeding fascinating to be with, it was only up to a point. She said something--no, no; he saw through that. He wouldn't stand that--no, no. Then he could shout and rock and hold his sides together over some joke with men. He was the best judge of cooking in India. He was a man. But not the sort of man one had to respect--which was a mercy; not like Major Simmons, for instance; not in the least like that, Daisy thought, when, in spite of her two small children, she used to compare them.

He pulled off his boots. He emptied his pockets. Out came with his pocket-knife a snapshot of Daisy on the verandah; Daisy all in white, with a fox-terrier on her knee; very charming, very dark; the best he had ever seen of her. It did come, after all so naturally; so much more naturally than Clarissa. No fuss. No bother. No finicking and fidgeting. All plain sailing. And the dark, adorably pretty girl on the verandah exclaimed (he could hear her). Of course, of course she would give him everything! she cried (she had no sense of discretion) everything he wanted! she cried, running to meet him, whoever might be looking. And she was only twenty-four. And she had two children. Well, well!

Well indeed he had got himself into a mess at his age. And it came over him when he woke in the night pretty forcibly. Suppose they did marry? For him it would be all very well, but what about her? Mrs. Burgess, a good sort and no chatterbox, in whom he had confided, thought this absence of his in England, ostensibly to see lawyers might serve to make Daisy reconsider, think what it meant. It was a question of her position, Mrs. Burgess said; the social barrier; giving up her children. She'd be a widow with a past one of these days, draggling about in the suburbs, or more likely, indiscriminate (you know, she said, what such women get like, with too much paint). But Peter Walsh pooh-poohed all that. He didn't mean to die yet. Anyhow she must settle for herself; judge for herself, he thought, padding about the room in his socks, smoothing out his dress-shirt, for he might go to Clarissa's party, or he might go to one of the Halls, or he might settle in and read an absorbing book written by a man he used to know at Oxford. And if he did retire, that's what he'd do--write books. He would go to Oxford and poke about in the Bodleian. Vainly the dark, adorably pretty girl ran to the end of the terrace; vainly waved her hand; vainly cried she didn't care a straw what people said. There he was, the man she thought the world of, the perfect gentleman, the fascinating, the distinguished (and his age made not the least difference to her), padding about a room in an hotel in Bloomsbury, shaving, washing, continuing, as he took up cans, put down razors, to poke about in the Bodleian, and get at the truth about one or two little matters that interested him. And he would have a chat with whoever it might be, and so come to disregard more and more precise hours for lunch, and miss engagements, and when Daisy asked him, as she would, for a kiss, a scene, fail to come up to the scratch (though he was genuinely devoted to her)--in short it might be happier, as Mrs. Burgess said, that she should forget him, or merely remember him as he was in August 1922, like a figure standing at the cross roads at dusk, which grows more and more remote as the dog-cart spins away, carrying her securely fastened to the back seat, though her arms are outstretched, and as she sees the figure dwindle and disappear still she cries out how she would do anything in the world, anything, anything, anything. . . .

He never knew what people thought. It became more and more difficult for him to concentrate. He became absorbed; he became busied with his own concerns; now surly, now gay; dependent on women, absent-minded, moody, less and less able (so he thought as he shaved) to understand why Clarissa couldn't simply find them a lodging and be nice to Daisy; introduce her. And then he could just--just do what? just haunt and hover (he was at the moment actually engaged in sorting out various keys, papers), swoop and taste, be alone, in short, sufficient to himself; and yet nobody of course was more dependent upon others (he buttoned his waistcoat); it had been his undoing. He could not keep out of smoking-rooms, liked colonels, liked golf, liked bridge, and above all women's society, and the fineness of their companionship, and their faithfulness and audacity and greatness in loving which though it had its drawbacks seemed to him (and the dark, adorably pretty face was on top of the envelopes) so wholly admirable, so splendid a flower to grow on the crest of human life, and yet he could not come up to the scratch, being always apt to see round things (Clarissa had sapped something in him permanently), and to tire very easily of mute devotion and to want variety in love, though it would make him furious if Daisy loved anybody else, furious! for he was jealous, uncontrollably jealous by temperament. He suffered tortures! But where was his knife; his watch; his seals, his note- case, and Clarissa's letter which he would not read again but liked to think of, and Daisy's photograph? And now for dinner.

They were eating.

Sitting at little tables round vases, dressed or not dressed, with their shawls and bags laid beside them, with their air of false composure, for they were not used to so many courses at dinner, and confidence, for they were able to pay for it, and strain, for they had been running about London all day shopping, sightseeing; and their natural curiosity, for they looked round and up as the nice- looking gentleman in horn-rimmed spectacles came in, and their good nature, for they would have been glad to do any little service, such as lend a time-table or impart useful information, and their desire, pulsing in them, tugging at them subterraneously, somehow to establish connections if it were only a birthplace (Liverpool, for example) in common or friends of the same name; with their furtive glances, odd silences, and sudden withdrawals into family jocularity and isolation; there they sat eating dinner when Mr. Walsh came in and took his seat at a little table by the curtain.

It was not that he said anything, for being solitary he could only address himself to the waiter; it was his way of looking at the menu, of pointing his forefinger to a particular wine, of hitching himself up to the table, of addressing himself seriously, not gluttonously to dinner, that won him their respect; which, having to remain unexpressed for the greater part of the meal, flared up at the table where the Morrises sat when Mr. Walsh was heard to say at the end of the meal, "Bartlett pears." Why he should have spoken so moderately yet firmly, with the air of a disciplinarian well within his rights which are founded upon justice, neither young Charles Morris, nor old Charles, neither Miss Elaine nor Mrs. Morris knew. But when he said, "Bartlett pears," sitting alone at his table, they felt that he counted on their support in some lawful demand; was champion of a cause which immediately became their own, so that their eyes met his eyes sympathetically, and when they all reached the smoking-room simultaneously, a little talk between them became inevitable.

It was not very profound--only to the effect that London was crowded; had changed in thirty years; that Mr. Morris preferred Liverpool; that Mrs. Morris had been to the Westminster flower- show, and that they had all seen the Prince of Wales. Yet, thought Peter Walsh, no family in the world can compare with the

Morrises; none whatever; and their relations to each other are perfect, and they don't care a hang for the upper classes, and they like what they like, and Elaine is training for the family business, and the boy has won a scholarship at Leeds, and the old lady (who is about his own age) has three more children at home; and they have two motor cars, but Mr. Morris still mends the boots on Sunday: it is superb, it is absolutely superb, thought Peter Walsh, swaying a little backwards and forwards with his liqueur glass in his hand among the hairy red chairs and ash-trays, feeling very well pleased with himself, for the Morrises liked him. Yes, they liked a man who said, "Bartlett pears." They liked him, he felt.

He would go to Clarissa's party. (The Morrises moved off; but they would meet again.) He would go to Clarissa's party, because he wanted to ask Richard what they were doing in India--the conservative duffers. And what's being acted? And music. . . . Oh yes, and mere gossip.

For this is the truth about our soul, he thought, our self, who fish-like inhabits deep seas and plies among obscurities threading her way between the boles of giant weeds, over sun-flickered spaces and on and on into gloom, cold, deep, inscrutable; suddenly she shoots to the surface and sports on the wind-wrinkled waves; that is, has a positive need to brush, scrape, kindle herself, gossiping. What did the Government mean--Richard Dalloway would know--to do about India?

Since it was a very hot night and the paper boys went by with placards proclaiming in huge red letters that there was a heat- wave, wicker chairs were placed on the hotel steps and there, sipping, smoking, detached gentlemen sat. Peter Walsh sat there. One might fancy that day, the London day, was just beginning. Like a woman who had slipped off her print dress and white apron to array herself in blue and pearls, the day changed, put off stuff, took gauze, changed to evening, and with the same sigh of exhilaration that a woman breathes, tumbling petticoats on the floor, it too shed dust, heat, colour; the traffic thinned; motor cars, tinkling, darting, succeeded the lumber of vans; and here and there among the thick foliage of the squares an intense light hung. I resign, the evening seemed to say, as it paled and faded above the battlements and prominences, moulded, pointed, of hotel, flat, and block of shops, I fade, she was beginning, I disappear, but London would have none of it, and rushed her bayonets into the sky, pinioned her, constrained her to partnership in her revelry.

For the great revolution of Mr. Willett's summer time had taken place since Peter Walsh's last visit to England. The prolonged evening was new to him. It was inspiriting, rather. For as the young people went by with their despatch-boxes, awfully glad to be free, proud too, dumbly, of stepping this famous pavement, joy of a kind, cheap, tinselly, if you like, but all the same rapture, flushed their faces. They dressed well too; pink stockings; pretty shoes. They would now have two hours at the pictures. It sharpened, it refined them, the yellow-blue evening light; and on the leaves in the square shone lurid, livid--they looked as if dipped in sea water--the foliage of a submerged city. He was astonished by the beauty; it was encouraging too, for where the returned Anglo-Indian sat by rights (he knew crowds of them) in the Oriental Club biliously summing up the ruin of the world, here was he, as young as ever; envying young people their summer time and the rest of it, and more than suspecting from the words of a girl, from a housemaid's laughter--intangible things you couldn't lay your hands on--that shift in the whole pyramidal accumulation which in his youth had seemed immovable. On top of them it had pressed; weighed them down, the women especially, like those flowers Clarissa's Aunt Helena used to press between sheets of grey blotting-paper with Littré's dictionary on top, sitting under the lamp after dinner. She was dead now. He had heard of her, from Clarissa, losing the sight of one eye. It seemed so fitting--one of nature's masterpieces--that old Miss Parry should turn to glass. She would die like some bird in a frost gripping her perch. She belonged to a different age, but being so entire, so complete, would always stand up on the horizon, stone-white, eminent, like a lighthouse marking some past stage on this adventurous, long, long voyage, this interminable (he felt for a copper to buy a paper and read about Surrey and Yorkshire--he had held out that copper millions of times. Surrey was all out once more)--this interminable life. But cricket was no mere game. Cricket was important. He could never help reading about cricket. He read the scores in the stop press first, then how it was a hot day; then about a murder case. Having done things millions of times enriched them, though it might be said to take the surface off. The past enriched, and experience, and having cared for one or two people, and so having acquired the power which the young lack, of cutting short, doing what one likes, not caring a rap what people say and coming and going without any very great expectations (he left his paper on the table and moved off), which however (and he looked for his hat and coat) was not altogether true of him, not to-night, for here he was starting to go to a party, at his age, with the belief upon him that he was about to have an experience. But what?

Beauty anyhow. Not the crude beauty of the eye. It was not beauty pure and simple--Bedford Place leading into Russell Square. It was straightness and emptiness of course; the symmetry of a corridor; but it was also windows lit up, a piano, a gramophone sounding; a sense of pleasure-making hidden, but now and again emerging when, through the uncurtained window, the window left open, one saw parties sitting over tables, young people slowly circling, conversations between men and women, maids idly looking out (a strange comment theirs, when work was done), stockings drying on top ledges, a parrot, a few plants. Absorbing, mysterious, of infinite richness, this life. And in the large square where the cabs shot and swerved so quick, there were loitering couples, dallying, embracing, shrunk up under the shower of a tree; that was moving; so silent, so absorbed, that one passed, discreetly, timidly, as if in the presence of some sacred ceremony to interrupt which would have been impious. That was interesting. And so on into the flare and glare.

His light overcoat blew open, he stepped with indescribable idiosyncrasy, lent a little forward, tripped, with his hands behind his back and his eyes still a little hawklike; he tripped through London, towards Westminster, observing.

Was everybody dining out, then? Doors were being opened here by a footman to let issue a high-stepping old dame, in buckled shoes, with three purple ostrich feathers in her hair. Doors were being opened for ladies wrapped like mummies in shawls with bright flowers on them, ladies with bare heads. And in respectable quarters with stucco pillars through small front gardens lightly swathed with combs in their hair (having run up to see the children), women came; men waited for them, with their coats blowing open, and the motor started. Everybody was going out. What with these doors being opened, and the descent and the start, it seemed as if the whole of London were embarking in little boats moored to the bank, tossing on the waters, as if the whole place were floating off in carnival. And Whitehall was skated over, silver beaten as it was, skated over by spiders, and there was a sense of midges round the arc lamps; it was so hot that people stood about talking. And here in Westminster was a retired Judge, presumably, sitting four square at his house door dressed all in white. An Anglo-Indian presumably.

And here a shindy of brawling women, drunken women; here only a policeman and looming houses, high houses, domed houses, churches, parliaments, and the hoot of a steamer on the river, a hollow misty cry. But it was her street, this, Clarissa's; cabs were rushing round the corner, like water round the piers of a bridge, drawn together, it seemed to him because they bore people going to her party, Clarissa's party.

The cold stream of visual impressions failed him now as if the eye were a cup that overflowed and let the rest run down its china walls unrecorded. The brain must wake now. The body must contract now, entering the house, the lighted house, where the door stood open, where the motor cars were standing, and bright women descending: the soul must brave itself to endure. He opened the big blade of his pocket-knife.

Lucy came running full tilt downstairs, having just nipped in to the drawing-room to smooth a cover, to straighten a chair, to pause a moment and feel whoever came in must think how clean, how bright, how beautifully cared for, when they saw the beautiful silver, the brass fire-irons, the new chair-covers, and the curtains of yellow chintz: she appraised each; heard a roar of voices; people already coming up from dinner; she must fly!

The Prime Minister was coming, Agnes said: so she had heard them say in the dining-room, she said, coming in with a tray of glasses. Did it matter, did it matter in the least, one Prime Minister more or less? It made no difference at this hour of the night to Mrs. Walker among the plates, saucepans, cullenders, frying-pans, chicken in aspic, ice-cream freezers, pared crusts of bread, lemons, soup tureens, and pudding basins which, however hard they washed up in the scullery seemed to be all on top of her, on the kitchen table, on chairs, while the fire blared and roared, the electric lights glared, and still supper had to be laid. All she felt was, one Prime Minister more or less made not a scrap of difference to Mrs. Walker.

The ladies were going upstairs already, said Lucy; the ladies were going up, one by one, Mrs. Dalloway walking last and almost always sending back some message to the kitchen, "My love to Mrs. Walker," that was it one night. Next morning they would go over the dishes-- the soup, the salmon; the salmon, Mrs. Walker knew, as usual underdone, for she always got nervous about the pudding and left it to Jenny; so it happened, the salmon was always underdone. But some lady with fair hair and silver ornaments had said, Lucy said, about the entrée, was it really made at home? But it was the salmon that bothered Mrs. Walker, as she spun the plates round and round, and pulled in dampers and pulled out dampers; and there came a burst of laughter from the dining-room; a voice speaking; then another burst of laughter--the gentlemen enjoying themselves when the ladies had gone. The tokay, said Lucy running in. Mr. Dalloway had sent for the tokay, from the Emperor's cellars, the Imperial Tokay.

It was borne through the kitchen. Over her shoulder Lucy reported how Miss Elizabeth looked quite lovely; she couldn't take her eyes off her; in her pink dress, wearing the necklace Mr. Dalloway had given her. Jenny must remember the dog, Miss Elizabeth's fox- terrier, which, since it bit, had to be shut up and might, Elizabeth thought, want something. Jenny must remember the dog. But Jenny was not going upstairs with all those people about. There was a motor at the door already! There was a ring at the bell--and the gentlemen still in the dining-room, drinking tokay!

There, they were going upstairs; that was the first to come, and now they would come faster and faster, so that Mrs. Parkinson (hired for parties) would leave the hall door ajar, and the hall would be full of gentlemen waiting (they stood waiting, sleeking down their hair) while the ladies took their cloaks off in the room along the passage; where Mrs. Barnet helped them, old Ellen Barnet, who had been with the family for forty years, and came every summer to help the ladies, and remembered mothers when they were girls, and though very unassuming did shake hands; said "milady" very respectfully, yet had a humorous way with her, looking at the young ladies, and ever so tactfully helping Lady Lovejoy, who had some trouble with her underbodice. And they could not help feeling, Lady Lovejoy and Miss Alice, that some little privilege in the matter of brush and comb, was awarded them having known Mrs. Barnet--"thirty years, milady," Mrs. Barnet supplied her. Young ladies did not use to rouge, said Lady Lovejoy, when they stayed at Bourton in the old days. And Miss Alice didn't need rouge, said Mrs. Barnet, looking at her fondly. There Mrs. Barnet would sit, in the cloak-room, patting down the furs, smoothing out the Spanish shawls, tidying the dressing-table, and knowing perfectly well, in spite of the furs and the embroideries, which were nice ladies, which were not. The dear old body, said Lady Lovejoy, mounting the stairs, Clarissa's old nurse.

And then Lady Lovejoy stiffened. "Lady and Miss Lovejoy," she said to Mr. Wilkins (hired for parties). He had an admirable manner, as he bent and straightened himself, bent and straightened himself and announced with perfect impartiality "Lady and Miss Lovejoy . . . Sir John and Lady Needham . . . Miss Weld . . . Mr. Walsh." His manner was admirable; his family life must be irreproachable, except that it seemed impossible that a being with greenish lips and shaven cheeks could ever have blundered into the nuisance of children.

"How delightful to see you!" said Clarissa. She said it to every one. How delightful to see you! She was at her worst--effusive, insincere. It was a great mistake to have come. He should have stayed at home and read his book, thought Peter Walsh; should have gone to a music hall; he should have stayed at home, for he knew no one.

Oh dear, it was going to be a failure; a complete failure, Clarissa felt it in her bones as dear old Lord Lexham stood there apologising for his wife who had caught cold at the Buckingham Palace garden party. She could see Peter out of the tail of her eye, criticising her, there, in that corner. Why, after all, did she do these things? Why seek pinnacles and stand drenched in fire? Might it consume her anyhow! Burn her to cinders! Better anything, better brandish one's torch and hurl it to earth than taper and dwindle away like some Ellie Henderson! It was extraordinary how Peter put her into these states just by coming and standing in a corner. He made her see herself; exaggerate. It was idiotic. But why did he come, then, merely to criticise? Why always take, never give? Why not risk one's one little point of view? There he was wandering off, and she must speak to him. But she would not get the chance. Life was that--humiliation, renunciation. What Lord Lexham was saying was that his wife would not wear her furs at the garden party because "my dear, you ladies are all alike"--Lady Lexham being seventy-five at least! It was delicious, how they petted each other, that old couple. She did like old Lord Lexham. She did think it mattered, her party, and it made her feel quite sick to know that it was all going wrong, all falling flat. Anything, any explosion, any horror was better than people wandering aimlessly, standing in a bunch at a corner like Ellie Henderson, not even caring to hold themselves upright.

Gently the yellow curtain with all the birds of Paradise blew out and it seemed as if there were a flight of wings into the room, right out, then sucked back. (For the windows were open.) Was it draughty, Ellie Henderson wondered? She was subject to chills. But it did not matter that she should come down sneezing tomorrow; it was the girls with their naked shoulders she thought of, being trained to think of others by an old father, an invalid, late vicar of Bourton, but he was dead now; and her chills never went to her chest, never. It was the girls she thought of, the young girls with their bare shoulders, she herself having always been a wisp of a creature, with her thin hair and meagre profile; though now, past fifty, there was beginning to shine through some mild beam, something purified into distinction by years of self-abnegation but obscured again, perpetually, by her distressing gentility, her panic fear, which arose from three hundred pounds' income, and her weaponless state (she could not earn a penny) and it made her timid, and more and more disqualified year by year to meet well- dressed people who did this sort of thing every night of the season, merely telling their maids "I'll wear so and so," whereas Ellie Henderson ran out nervously and bought cheap pink flowers, half a dozen, and then threw a shawl over her old black dress. For her invitation to Clarissa's party had come at the last moment. She was not quite happy about it. She had a sort of feeling that Clarissa had not meant to ask her this year.

Why should she? There was no reason really, except that they had always known each other. Indeed, they were cousins. But naturally they had rather drifted apart, Clarissa being so sought after. It was an event to her, going to a party. It was quite a treat just to see the lovely clothes. Wasn't that Elizabeth, grown up, with her hair done in the fashionable way, in the pink dress? Yet she could not be more than seventeen. She was very, very handsome. But girls when they first came out didn't seem to wear white as they used. (She must remember everything to tell Edith.) Girls wore straight frocks, perfectly tight, with skirts well above the ankles. It was not becoming, she thought.

So, with her weak eyesight, Ellie Henderson craned rather forward, and it wasn't so much she who minded not having any one to talk to (she hardly knew anybody there), for she felt that they were all such interesting people to watch; politicians presumably; Richard Dalloway's friends; but it was Richard himself who felt that he could not let the poor creature go on standing there all the evening by herself.

"Well, Ellie, and how's the world treating YOU?" he said in his genial way, and Ellie Henderson, getting nervous and flushing and feeling that it was extraordinarily nice of him to come and talk to her, said that many people really felt the heat more than the cold.

"Yes, they do," said Richard Dalloway. "Yes."

But what more did one say?

"Hullo, Richard," said somebody, taking him by the elbow, and, good Lord, there was old Peter, old Peter Walsh. He was delighted to see him--ever so pleased to see him! He hadn't changed a bit. And off they went together walking right across the room, giving each other little pats, as if they hadn't met for a long time, Ellie Henderson thought, watching them go, certain she knew that man's face. A tall man, middle aged, rather fine eyes, dark, wearing spectacles, with a look of John Burrows. Edith would be sure to know.

The curtain with its flight of birds of Paradise blew out again. And Clarissa saw--she saw Ralph Lyon beat it back, and go on talking. So it wasn't a failure after all! it was going to be all right now--her party. It had begun. It had started. But it was still touch and go. She must stand there for the present. People seemed to come in a rush.

Colonel and Mrs. Garrod . . . Mr. Hugh Whitbread . . . Mr. Bowley . . . Mrs. Hilbery . . . Lady Mary Maddox . . . Mr. Quin . . . intoned Wilkin. She had six or seven words with each, and they went on, they went into the rooms; into something now, not nothing, since Ralph Lyon had beat back the curtain.

And yet for her own part, it was too much of an effort. She was not enjoying it. It was too much like being--just anybody, standing there; anybody could do it; yet this anybody she did a little admire, couldn't help feeling that she had, anyhow, made this happen, that it marked a stage, this post that she felt herself to have become, for oddly enough she had quite forgotten what she looked like, but felt herself a stake driven in at the top of her stairs. Every time she gave a party she had this feeling of being something not herself, and that every one was unreal in one way; much more real in another. It was, she thought, partly their clothes, partly being taken out of their ordinary ways, partly the background, it was possible to say things you couldn't say anyhow else, things that needed an effort; possible to go much deeper. But not for her; not yet anyhow.

"How delightful to see you!" she said. Dear old Sir Harry! He would know every one.

And what was so odd about it was the sense one had as they came up the stairs one after another, Mrs. Mount and Celia, Herbert Ainsty, Mrs. Dakers--oh and Lady Bruton!

"How awfully good of you to come!" she said, and she meant it--it was odd how standing there one felt them going on, going on, some quite old, some . . .

WHAT name? Lady Rosseter? But who on earth was Lady Rosseter?

"Clarissa!" That voice! It was Sally Seton! Sally Seton! after all these years! She loomed through a mist. For she hadn't looked like THAT, Sally Seton, when Clarissa grasped the hot water can, to think of her under this roof, under this roof! Not like that!

All on top of each other, embarrassed, laughing, words tumbled out-- passing through London; heard from Clara Haydon; what a chance of seeing you! So I thrust myself in--without an invitation. . . .

One might put down the hot water can quite composedly. The lustre had gone out of her. Yet it was extraordinary to see her again, older, happier, less lovely. They kissed each other, first this cheek then that, by the drawing-room door, and Clarissa turned, with Sally's hand in hers, and saw her rooms full, heard the roar of voices, saw the candlesticks, the blowing curtains, and the roses which Richard had given her.

"I have five enormous boys," said Sally.

She had the simplest egotism, the most open desire to be thought first always, and Clarissa loved her for being still like that. "I can't believe it!" she cried, kindling all over with pleasure at the thought of the past.

But alas, Wilkins; Wilkins wanted her; Wilkins was emitting in a voice of commanding authority as if the whole company must be admonished and the hostess reclaimed from frivolity, one name:

"The Prime Minister," said Peter Walsh.

The Prime Minister? Was it really? Ellie Henderson marvelled. What a thing to tell Edith!

One couldn't laugh at him. He looked so ordinary. You might have stood him behind a counter and bought biscuits--poor chap, all rigged up in gold lace. And to be fair, as he went his rounds, first with Clarissa then with Richard escorting him, he did it very well. He tried to look somebody. It was amusing to watch. Nobody looked at him. They just went on talking, yet it was perfectly plain that they all knew, felt to the marrow of their bones, this majesty passing; this symbol of what they all stood for, English society. Old Lady Bruton, and she looked very fine too, very stalwart in her lace, swam up, and they withdrew into a little room which at once became spied upon, guarded, and a sort of stir and rustle rippled through every one, openly: the Prime Minister!

Lord, lord, the snobbery of the English! thought Peter Walsh, standing in the corner. How they loved dressing up in gold lace and doing homage! There! That must be, by Jove it was, Hugh Whitbread, snuffing round the precincts of the great, grown rather fatter, rather whiter, the admirable Hugh!

He looked always as if he were on duty, thought Peter, a privileged, but secretive being, hoarding secrets which he would die to defend, though it was only some little piece of tittle- tattle dropped by a court footman, which would be in all the papers tomorrow. Such were his rattles, his baubles, in playing with which he had grown white, come to the verge of old age, enjoying the respect and affection of all who had the privilege of knowing this type of the English public school man. Inevitably one made up things like that about Hugh; that was his style; the style of those admirable letters which Peter had read thousands of miles across the sea in the Times, and had thanked God he was out of that pernicious hubble-bubble if it were only to hear baboons chatter and coolies beat their wives. An olive-skinned youth from one of the Universities stood obsequiously by. Him he would patronise, initiate, teach how to get on. For he liked nothing better than doing kindnesses, making the hearts of old ladies palpitate with the joy of being thought of in their age, their affliction, thinking themselves quite forgotten, yet here was dear Hugh driving up and spending an hour talking of the past, remembering trifles, praising the home-made cake, though Hugh might eat cake with a Duchess any day of his life, and, to look at him, probably did spend a good deal of time in that agreeable occupation. The All- judging, the All-merciful, might excuse. Peter Walsh had no mercy. Villains there must be, and God knows the rascals who get hanged for battering the brains of a girl out in a train do less harm on the whole than Hugh Whitbread and his kindness. Look at him now, on tiptoe, dancing forward, bowing and scraping, as the Prime Minister and Lady Bruton emerged, intimating for all the world to see that he was privileged to say something, something private, to Lady Bruton as she passed. She stopped. She wagged her fine old head. She was thanking him presumably for some piece of servility. She had her toadies, minor officials in Government offices who ran about putting through little jobs on her behalf, in return for which she gave them luncheon. But she derived from the eighteenth century. She was all right.

And now Clarissa escorted her Prime Minister down the room, prancing, sparkling, with the stateliness of her grey hair. She wore ear-rings, and a silver-green mermaid's dress. Lolloping on the waves and braiding her tresses she seemed, having that gift still; to be; to exist; to sum it all up in the moment as she passed; turned, caught her scarf in some other woman's dress, unhitched it, laughed, all with the most perfect ease and air of a creature floating in its element. But age had brushed her; even as a mermaid might behold in her glass the setting sun on some very clear evening over the waves. There was a breath of tenderness; her severity, her prudery, her woodenness were all warmed through now, and she had about her as she said good-bye to the thick gold- laced man who was doing his best, and good luck to him, to look important, an inexpressible dignity; an exquisite cordiality; as if she wished the whole world well, and must now, being on the very verge and rim of things, take her leave. So she made him think. (But he was not in love.)

Indeed, Clarissa felt, the Prime Minister had been good to come. And, walking down the room with him, with Sally there and Peter there and Richard very pleased, with all those people rather inclined, perhaps, to envy, she had felt that intoxication of the moment, that dilatation of the nerves of the heart itself till it seemed to quiver, steeped, upright;--yes, but after all it was what other people felt, that; for, though she loved it and felt it tingle and sting, still these semblances, these triumphs (dear old Peter, for example, thinking her so brilliant), had a hollowness; at arm's length they were, not in the heart; and it might be that she was growing old but they satisfied her no longer as they used; and suddenly, as she saw the Prime Minister go down the stairs, the gilt rim of the Sir Joshua picture of the little girl with a muff brought back Kilman with a rush; Kilman her enemy. That was satisfying; that was real. Ah, how she hated her--hot, hypocritical, corrupt; with all that power; Elizabeth's seducer; the woman who had crept in to steal and defile (Richard would say, What nonsense!). She hated her: she loved her. It was enemies one wanted, not friends--not Mrs. Durrant and Clara, Sir William and Lady Bradshaw, Miss Truelock and Eleanor Gibson (whom she saw coming upstairs). They must find her if they wanted her. She was for the party!

There was her old friend Sir Harry.

"Dear Sir Harry!" she said, going up to the fine old fellow who had produced more bad pictures than any other two Academicians in the whole of St. John's Wood (they were always of cattle, standing in sunset pools absorbing moisture, or signifying, for he had a certain range of gesture, by the raising of one foreleg and the toss of the antlers, "the Approach of the Stranger"--all his activities, dining out, racing, were founded on cattle standing absorbing moisture in sunset pools).

"What are you laughing at?" she asked him. For Willie Titcomb and Sir Harry and Herbert Ainsty were all laughing. But no. Sir Harry could not tell Clarissa Dalloway (much though he liked her; of her type he thought her perfect, and threatened to paint her) his stories of the music hall stage. He chaffed her about her party. He missed his brandy. These circles, he said, were above him. But he liked her; respected her, in spite of her damnable, difficult upper-class refinement, which made it impossible to ask Clarissa Dalloway to sit on his knee. And up came that wandering will-o'- the-wisp, that vagulous phosphorescence, old Mrs. Hilbery, stretching her hands to the blaze of his laughter (about the Duke and the Lady), which, as she heard it across the room, seemed to reassure her on a point which sometimes bothered her if she woke early in the morning and did not like to call her maid for a cup of tea; how it is certain we must die.

"They won't tell us their stories," said Clarissa.

"Dear Clarissa!" exclaimed Mrs. Hilbery. She looked to-night, she said, so like her mother as she first saw her walking in a garden in a grey hat.

And really Clarissa's eyes filled with tears. Her mother, walking in a garden! But alas, she must go.

For there was Professor Brierly, who lectured on Milton, talking to little Jim Hutton (who was unable even for a party like this to compass both tie and waist-coat or make his hair lie flat), and even at this distance they were quarrelling, she could see. For Professor Brierly was a very queer fish. With all those degrees, honours, lectureships between him and the scribblers he suspected instantly an atmosphere not favourable to his queer compound; his prodigious learning and timidity; his wintry charm without cordiality; his innocence blent with snobbery; he quivered if made conscious by a lady's unkempt hair, a youth's boots, of an underworld, very creditable doubtless, of rebels, of ardent young people; of would-be geniuses, and intimated with a little toss of the head, with a sniff--Humph!--the value of moderation; of some slight training in the classics in order to appreciate Milton. Professor Brierly (Clarissa could see) wasn't hitting it off with little Jim Hutton (who wore red socks, his black being at the laundry) about Milton. She interrupted.

She said she loved Bach. So did Hutton. That was the bond between them, and Hutton (a very bad poet) always felt that Mrs. Dalloway was far the best of the great ladies who took an interest in art. It was odd how strict she was. About music she was purely impersonal. She was rather a prig. But how charming to look at! She made her house so nice if it weren't for her Professors. Clarissa had half a mind to snatch him off and set him down at the piano in the back room. For he played divinely.

"But the noise!" she said. "The noise!"

"The sign of a successful party." Nodding urbanely, the Professor stepped delicately off.

"He knows everything in the whole world about Milton," said Clarissa.

"Does he indeed?" said Hutton, who would imitate the Professor throughout Hampstead; the Professor on Milton; the Professor on moderation; the Professor stepping delicately off.

But she must speak to that couple, said Clarissa, Lord Gayton and Nancy Blow.

Not that THEY added perceptibly to the noise of the party. They were not talking (perceptibly) as they stood side by side by the yellow curtains. They would soon be off elsewhere, together; and never had very much to say in any circumstances. They looked; that was all. That was enough. They looked so clean, so sound, she with an apricot bloom of powder and paint, but he scrubbed, rinsed, with the eyes of a bird, so that no ball could pass him or stroke surprise him. He struck, he leapt, accurately, on the spot. Ponies' mouths quivered at the end of his reins. He had his honours, ancestral monuments, banners hanging in the church at home. He had his duties; his tenants; a mother and sisters; had been all day at Lords, and that was what they were talking about-- cricket, cousins, the movies--when Mrs. Dalloway came up. Lord Gayton liked her most awfully. So did Miss Blow. She had such charming manners.

"It is angelic--it is delicious of you to have come!" she said. She loved Lords; she loved youth, and Nancy, dressed at enormous expense by the greatest artists in Paris, stood there looking as if her body had merely put forth, of its own accord, a green frill.

"I had meant to have dancing," said Clarissa.

For the young people could not talk. And why should they? Shout, embrace, swing, be up at dawn; carry sugar to ponies; kiss and caress the snouts of adorable chows; and then all tingling and streaming, plunge and swim. But the enormous resources of the English language, the power it bestows, after all, of communicating feelings (at their age, she and Peter would have been arguing all the evening), was not for them. They would solidify young. They would be good beyond measure to the people on the estate, but alone, perhaps, rather dull.

"What a pity!" she said. "I had hoped to have dancing."

It was so extraordinarily nice of them to have come! But talk of dancing! The rooms were packed.

There was old Aunt Helena in her shawl. Alas, she must leave them-- Lord Gayton and Nancy Blow. There was old Miss Parry, her aunt.

For Miss Helena Parry was not dead: Miss Parry was alive. She was past eighty. She ascended staircases slowly with a stick. She was placed in a chair (Richard had seen to it). People who had known Burma in the 'seventies were always led up to her. Where had Peter got to? They used to be such friends. For at the mention of India, or even Ceylon, her eyes (only one was glass) slowly deepened, became blue, beheld, not human beings--she had no tender memories, no proud illusions about Viceroys, Generals, Mutinies--it was orchids she saw, and mountain passes and herself carried on the backs of coolies in the 'sixties over solitary peaks; or descending to uproot orchids (startling blossoms, never beheld before) which she painted in water-colour; an indomitable Englishwoman, fretful if disturbed by the War, say, which dropped a bomb at her very door, from her deep meditation over orchids and her own figure journeying in the 'sixties in India--but here was Peter.

"Come and talk to Aunt Helena about Burma," said Clarissa.

And yet he had not had a word with her all the evening!

"We will talk later," said Clarissa, leading him up to Aunt Helena, in her white shawl, with her stick.

"Peter Walsh," said Clarissa.

That meant nothing.

Clarissa had asked her. It was tiring; it was noisy; but Clarissa had asked her. So she had come. It was a pity that they lived in London--Richard and Clarissa. If only for Clarissa's health it would have been better to live in the country. But Clarissa had always been fond of society.

"He has been in Burma," said Clarissa.

Ah. She could not resist recalling what Charles Darwin had said about her little book on the orchids of Burma.

(Clarissa must speak to Lady Bruton.)

No doubt it was forgotten now, her book on the orchids of Burma, but it went into three editions before 1870, she told Peter. She remembered him now. He had been at Bourton (and he had left her, Peter Walsh remembered, without a word in the drawing-room that night when Clarissa had asked him to come boating).

"Richard so much enjoyed his lunch party," said Clarissa to Lady Bruton.

"Richard was the greatest possible help," Lady Bruton replied. "He helped me to write a letter. And how are you?"

"Oh, perfectly well!" said Clarissa. (Lady Bruton detested illness in the wives of politicians.)

"And there's Peter Walsh!" said Lady Bruton (for she could never think of anything to say to Clarissa; though she liked her. She had lots of fine qualities; but they had nothing in common--she and Clarissa. It might have been better if Richard had married a woman with less charm, who would have helped him more in his work. He had lost his chance of the Cabinet). "There's Peter Walsh!" she said, shaking hands with that agreeable sinner, that very able fellow who should have made a name for himself but hadn't (always in difficulties with women), and, of course, old Miss Parry. Wonderful old lady!

Lady Bruton stood by Miss Parry's chair, a spectral grenadier, draped in black, inviting Peter Walsh to lunch; cordial; but without small talk, remembering nothing whatever about the flora or fauna of India. She had been there, of course; had stayed with three Viceroys; thought some of the Indian civilians uncommonly fine fellows; but what a tragedy it was--the state of India! The Prime Minister had just been telling her (old Miss Parry huddled up in her shawl, did not care what the Prime Minister had just been telling her), and Lady Bruton would like to have Peter Walsh's opinion, he being fresh from the centre, and she would get Sir Sampson to meet him, for really it prevented her from sleeping at night, the folly of it, the wickedness she might say, being a soldier's daughter. She was an old woman now, not good for much. But her house, her servants, her good friend Milly Brush--did he remember her?--were all there only asking to be used if--if they could be of help, in short. For she never spoke of England, but this isle of men, this dear, dear land, was in her blood (without reading Shakespeare), and if ever a woman could have worn the helmet and shot the arrow, could have led troops to attack, ruled with indomitable justice barbarian hordes and lain under a shield noseless in a church, or made a green grass mound on some primeval hillside, that woman was Millicent Bruton. Debarred by her sex and some truancy, too, of the logical faculty (she found it impossible to write a letter to the Times), she had the thought of Empire always at hand, and had acquired from her association with that armoured goddess her ramrod bearing, her robustness of demeanour, so that one could not figure her even in death parted from the earth or roaming territories over which, in some spiritual shape, the Union Jack had ceased to fly. To be not English even among the dead--no, no! Impossible!

But was it Lady Bruton (whom she used to know)? Was it Peter Walsh grown grey? Lady Rosseter asked herself (who had been Sally Seton). It was old Miss Parry certainly--the old aunt who used to be so cross when she stayed at Bourton. Never should she forget running along the passage naked, and being sent for by Miss Parry! And Clarissa! oh Clarissa! Sally caught her by the arm.

Clarissa stopped beside them.

"But I can't stay," she said. "I shall come later. Wait," she said, looking at Peter and Sally. They must wait, she meant, until all these people had gone.

"I shall come back," she said, looking at her old friends, Sally and Peter, who were shaking hands, and Sally, remembering the past no doubt, was laughing.

But her voice was wrung of its old ravishing richness; her eyes not aglow as they used to be, when she smoked cigars, when she ran down the passage to fetch her sponge bag, without a stitch of clothing on her, and Ellen Atkins asked, What if the gentlemen had met her? But everybody forgave her. She stole a chicken from the larder because she was hungry in the night; she smoked cigars in her bedroom; she left a priceless book in the punt. But everybody adored her (except perhaps Papa). It was her warmth; her vitality-- she would paint, she would write. Old women in the village never to this day forgot to ask after "your friend in the red cloak who seemed so bright." She accused Hugh Whitbread, of all people (and there he was, her old friend Hugh, talking to the Portuguese Ambassador), of kissing her in the smoking-room to punish her for saying that women should have votes. Vulgar men did, she said. And Clarissa remembered having to persuade her not to denounce him at family prayers--which she was capable of doing with her daring, her recklessness, her melodramatic love of being the centre of everything and creating scenes, and it was bound, Clarissa used to think, to end in some awful tragedy; her death; her martyrdom; instead of which she had married, quite unexpectedly, a bald man with a large buttonhole who owned, it was said, cotton mills at Manchester. And she had five boys!

She and Peter had settled down together. They were talking: it seemed so familiar--that they should be talking. They would discuss the past. With the two of them (more even than with Richard) she shared her past; the garden; the trees; old Joseph Breitkopf singing Brahms without any voice; the drawing-room wallpaper; the smell of the mats. A part of this Sally must always be; Peter must always be. But she must leave them. There were the Bradshaws, whom she disliked. She must go up to Lady Bradshaw (in grey and silver, balancing like a sea-lion at the edge of its tank, barking for invitations, Duchesses, the typical successful man's wife), she must go up to Lady Bradshaw and say . . .

But Lady Bradshaw anticipated her.

"We are shockingly late, dear Mrs. Dalloway, we hardly dared to come in," she said.

And Sir William, who looked very distinguished, with his grey hair and blue eyes, said yes; they had not been able to resist the temptation. He was talking to

Richard about that Bill probably, which they wanted to get through the Commons. Why did the sight of him, talking to Richard, curl her up? He looked what he was, a great doctor. A man absolutely at the head of his profession, very powerful, rather worn. For think what cases came before him-- people in the uttermost depths of misery; people on the verge of insanity; husbands and wives. He had to decide questions of appalling difficulty. Yet--what she felt was, one wouldn't like Sir William to see one unhappy. No; not that man.

"How is your son at Eton?" she asked Lady Bradshaw.

He had just missed his eleven, said Lady Bradshaw, because of the mumps. His father minded even more than he did, she thought "being," she said, "nothing but a great boy himself."

Clarissa looked at Sir William, talking to Richard. He did not look like a boy--not in the least like a boy. She had once gone with some one to ask his advice. He had been perfectly right; extremely sensible. But Heavens--what a relief to get out to the street again! There was some poor wretch sobbing, she remembered, in the waiting-room. But she did not know what it was--about Sir William; what exactly she disliked. Only Richard agreed with her, "didn't like his taste, didn't like his smell." But he was extraordinarily able. They were talking about this Bill. Some case, Sir William was mentioning, lowering his voice. It had its bearing upon what he was saying about the deferred effects of shell shock. There must be some provision in the Bill.

Sinking her voice, drawing Mrs. Dalloway into the shelter of a common femininity, a common pride in the illustrious qualities of husbands and their sad tendency to overwork, Lady Bradshaw (poor goose--one didn't dislike her) murmured how, "just as we were starting, my husband was called up on the telephone, a very sad case. A young man (that is what Sir William is telling Mr. Dalloway) had killed himself. He had been in the army." Oh! thought Clarissa, in the middle of my party, here's death, she thought.

She went on, into the little room where the Prime Minister had gone with Lady Bruton. Perhaps there was somebody there. But there was nobody. The chairs still kept the impress of the Prime Minister and Lady Bruton, she turned deferentially, he sitting four-square, authoritatively. They had been talking about India. There was nobody. The party's splendour fell to the floor, so strange it was to come in alone in her finery.

What business had the Bradshaws to talk of death at her party? A young man had killed himself. And they talked of it at her party-- the Bradshaws, talked of death. He had killed himself--but how? Always her body went through it first, when she was told, suddenly, of an accident; her dress flamed, her body burnt. He had thrown himself from a window. Up had flashed the ground; through him, blundering, bruising, went the rusty spikes. There he lay with a thud, thud, thud in his brain, and then a suffocation of blackness. So she saw it. But why had he done it? And the Bradshaws talked of it at her party!

She had once thrown a shilling into the Serpentine, never anything more. But he had flung it away. They went on living (she would have to go back; the rooms were still crowded; people kept on coming). They (all day she had been thinking of Bourton, of Peter, of Sally), they would grow old. A thing there was that mattered; a thing, wreathed about with chatter, defaced, obscured in her own life, let drop every day in corruption, lies, chatter. This he had preserved. Death was defiance. Death was an attempt to communicate; people feeling the impossibility of reaching the centre which, mystically, evaded them; closeness drew apart; rapture faded, one was alone. There was an embrace in death.

But this young man who had killed himself--had he plunged holding his treasure? "If it were now to die, 'twere now to be most happy," she had said to herself once, coming down in white.

Or there were the poets and thinkers. Suppose he had had that passion, and had gone to Sir William Bradshaw, a great doctor yet to her obscurely evil, without sex or lust, extremely polite to women, but capable of some indescribable outrage--forcing your soul, that was it--if this young man had gone to him, and Sir William had impressed him, like that, with his power, might he not then have said (indeed she felt it now), Life is made intolerable; they make life intolerable, men like that?

Then (she had felt it only this morning) there was the terror; the overwhelming incapacity, one's parents giving it into one's hands, this life, to be lived to the end, to be walked with serenely; there was in the depths of her heart an awful fear. Even now, quite often if Richard had not been there reading the Times, so that she could crouch like a bird and gradually revive, send roaring up that immeasurable delight, rubbing stick to stick, one thing with another, she must have perished. But that young man had killed himself.

Somehow it was her disaster--her disgrace. It was her punishment to see sink and disappear here a man, there a woman, in this profound darkness, and she forced to stand here in her evening dress. She had schemed; she had pilfered. She was never wholly admirable. She had wanted success. Lady Bexborough and the rest of it. And once she had walked on the terrace at Bourton.

It was due to Richard; she had never been so happy. Nothing could be slow enough; nothing last too long. No pleasure could equal, she thought, straightening the chairs, pushing in one book on the shelf, this having done with the triumphs of youth, lost herself in the process of living, to find it, with a shock of delight, as the sun rose, as the day sank. Many a time had she gone, at Bourton when they were all talking, to look at the sky; or seen it between people's shoulders at dinner; seen it in London when she could not sleep. She walked to the window.

It held, foolish as the idea was, something of her own in it, this country sky, this sky above Westminster. She parted the curtains; she looked. Oh, but how surprising!--in the room opposite the old lady stared straight at her! She was going to bed. And the sky. It will be a solemn sky, she had thought, it will be a dusky sky, turning away its cheek in beauty. But there it was--ashen pale, raced over quickly by tapering vast clouds. It was new to her. The wind must have risen. She was going to bed, in the room opposite. It was fascinating to watch her, moving about, that old lady, crossing the room, coming to the window. Could she see her? It was fascinating, with people still laughing and shouting in the drawing-room, to watch that old woman, quite quietly, going to bed. She pulled the blind now. The clock began striking. The young man had killed himself; but she did not pity him; with the clock striking the hour, one, two, three, she did not pity him, with all this going on. There! the old lady had put out her light! the whole house was dark now with this going on, she repeated, and the words came to her, Fear no more the heat of the sun. She must go back to them. But what an extraordinary night! She felt somehow very like him--the young man who had killed himself. She felt glad that he had done it; thrown it away. The clock was striking. The leaden circles dissolved in the air. He made her feel the beauty; made her feel the fun. But she must go back. She must assemble. She must find Sally and Peter. And she came in from the little room.

"But where is Clarissa?" said Peter. He was sitting on the sofa with Sally. (After all these years he really could not call her "Lady Rosseter.") "Where's the woman gone to?" he asked. "Where's Clarissa?"

Sally supposed, and so did Peter for the matter of that, that there were people of importance, politicians, whom neither of them knew unless by sight in the picture papers, whom Clarissa had to be nice to, had to talk to. She was with them. Yet there was Richard Dalloway not in the Cabinet. He hadn't been a success, Sally supposed? For herself, she scarcely ever read the papers. She sometimes saw his name mentioned. But then--well, she lived a very solitary life, in the wilds, Clarissa would say, among great merchants, great manufacturers, men, after all, who did things. She had done things too!

"I have five sons!" she told him.

Lord, Lord, what a change had come over her! the softness of motherhood; its egotism too. Last time they met, Peter remembered, had been among the cauliflowers in the moonlight, the leaves "like rough bronze" she had said, with her literary turn; and she had picked a rose. She had marched him up and down that awful night, after the scene by the fountain; he was to catch the midnight train. Heavens, he had wept!

That was his old trick, opening a pocket-knife, thought Sally, always opening and shutting a knife when he got excited. They had been very, very intimate, she and Peter Walsh, when he was in love with Clarissa, and there was that dreadful, ridiculous scene over Richard Dalloway at lunch. She had called Richard "Wickham." Why not call Richard "Wickham"? Clarissa had flared up! and indeed they had never seen each other since, she and Clarissa, not more than half a dozen times perhaps in the last ten years. And Peter Walsh had gone off to India, and she had heard vaguely that he had made an unhappy marriage, and she didn't know whether he had any children, and she couldn't ask him, for he had changed. He was rather shrivelled-looking, but kinder, she felt, and she had a real affection for him, for he was connected with her youth, and she still had a little Emily Brontë he had given her, and he was to write, surely? In those days he was to write.

"Have you written?" she asked him, spreading her hand, her firm and shapely hand, on her knee in a way he recalled.

"Not a word!" said Peter Walsh, and she laughed.

She was still attractive, still a personage, Sally Seton. But who was this Rosseter? He wore two camellias on his wedding day--that was all Peter knew of him. "They have myriads of servants, miles of conservatories," Clarissa wrote; something like that. Sally owned it with a shout of laughter.

"Yes, I have ten thousand a year"--whether before the tax was paid or after, she couldn't remember, for her husband, "whom you must meet," she said, "whom you would like," she said, did all that for her.

And Sally used to be in rags and tatters. She had pawned her grandmother's ring which Marie Antoinette had given her great- grandfather to come to Bourton.

Oh yes, Sally remembered; she had it still, a ruby ring which Marie Antoinette had given her great-grandfather. She never had a penny to her name in those days, and going to Bourton always meant some frightful pinch. But going to Bourton had meant so much to her-- had kept her sane, she believed, so unhappy had she been at home. But that was all a thing of the past--all over now, she said. And Mr. Parry was dead; and Miss Parry was still alive. Never had he had such a shock in his life! said Peter. He had been quite certain she was dead. And the marriage had been, Sally supposed, a success? And that very handsome, very self-possessed young woman was Elizabeth, over there, by the curtains, in red.

(She was like a poplar, she was like a river, she was like a hyacinth, Willie Titcomb was thinking. Oh how much nicer to be in the country and do what she liked! She could hear her poor dog howling, Elizabeth was certain.) She was not a bit like Clarissa, Peter Walsh said.

"Oh, Clarissa!" said Sally.

What Sally felt was simply this. She had owed Clarissa an enormous amount. They had been friends, not acquaintances, friends, and she still saw Clarissa all in white going about the house with her hands full of flowers--to this day tobacco plants made her think of Bourton. But--did Peter understand?--she lacked something. Lacked what was it? She had charm; she had extraordinary charm. But to be frank (and she felt that Peter was an old friend, a real friend-- did absence matter? did distance matter? She had often wanted to write to him, but torn it up, yet felt he understood, for people understand without things being said, as one realises growing old, and old she was, had been that afternoon to see her sons at Eton, where they had the mumps), to be quite frank then, how could Clarissa have done it?--married Richard Dalloway? a sportsman, a man who cared only for dogs. Literally, when he came into the room he smelt of the stables. And then all this? She waved her hand.

Hugh Whitbread it was, strolling past in his white waistcoat, dim, fat, blind, past everything he looked, except self-esteem and comfort.

"He's not going to recognise US," said Sally, and really she hadn't the courage--so that was Hugh! the admirable Hugh!

"And what does he do?" she asked Peter.

He blacked the King's boots or counted bottles at Windsor, Peter told her. Peter kept his sharp tongue still! But Sally must be frank, Peter said. That kiss now, Hugh's.

On the lips, she assured him, in the smoking-room one evening. She went straight to Clarissa in a rage. Hugh didn't do such things! Clarissa said, the admirable Hugh! Hugh's socks were without exception the most beautiful she had ever seen--and now his evening dress. Perfect! And had he children?

"Everybody in the room has six sons at Eton," Peter told her, except himself. He, thank God, had none. No sons, no daughters, no wife. Well, he didn't seem to mind, said Sally. He looked younger, she thought, than any of them.

But it had been a silly thing to do, in many ways, Peter said, to marry like that; "a perfect goose she was," he said, but, he said, "we had a splendid time of it," but how could that be? Sally wondered; what did he mean? and how odd it was to know him and yet not know a single thing that had happened to him. And did he say it out of pride? Very likely, for after all it must be galling for him (though he was an oddity, a sort of sprite, not at all an ordinary man), it must be lonely at his age to have no home, nowhere to go to. But he must stay with them for weeks and weeks. Of course he would; he would love to stay with them, and that was how it came out. All these years the Dalloways had never been once. Time after time they had asked them. Clarissa (for it was Clarissa of course) would not come. For, said Sally, Clarissa was at heart a snob--one had to admit it, a snob. And it was that that was between them, she was convinced. Clarissa thought she had married beneath her, her husband being--she was proud of it--a miner's son. Every penny they had he had earned. As a little boy (her voice trembled) he had carried great sacks.

(And so she would go on, Peter felt, hour after hour; the miner's son; people thought she had married beneath her; her five sons; and what was the other thing--plants, hydrangeas, syringas, very, very rare hibiscus lilies that never grow north of the Suez Canal, but she, with one gardener in a suburb near Manchester, had beds of them, positively beds! Now all that Clarissa had escaped, unmaternal as she was.)

A snob was she? Yes, in many ways. Where was she, all this time? It was getting late.

"Yet," said Sally, "when I heard Clarissa was giving a party, I felt I couldn't NOT come--must see her again (and I'm staying in Victoria Street, practically next door). So I just came without an invitation. But," she whispered, "tell me, do. Who is this?"

It was Mrs. Hilbery, looking for the door. For how late it was getting! And, she murmured, as the night grew later, as people went, one found old friends; quiet nooks and corners; and the loveliest views. Did they know, she asked, that they were surrounded by an enchanted garden? Lights and trees and wonderful gleaming lakes and the sky. Just a few fairy lamps, Clarissa Dalloway had said, in the back garden! But she was a magician! It was a park. . . . And she didn't know their names, but friends she knew they were, friends without names, songs without words, always the best. But there were so many doors, such unexpected places, she could not find her way.

"Old Mrs. Hilbery," said Peter; but who was that? that lady standing by the curtain all the evening, without speaking? He knew her face; connected her with Bourton. Surely she used to cut up underclothes at the large table in the window? Davidson, was that her name?

"Oh, that is Ellie Henderson," said Sally. Clarissa was really very hard on her. She was a cousin, very poor. Clarissa WAS hard on people.

She was rather, said Peter. Yet, said Sally, in her emotional way, with a rush of that enthusiasm which Peter used to love her for, yet dreaded a little now, so effusive she might become--how generous to her friends Clarissa was! and what a rare quality one found it, and how sometimes at night or on Christmas Day, when she counted up her blessings, she put that friendship first. They were young; that was it. Clarissa was pure-hearted; that was it. Peter would think her sentimental. So she was. For she had come to feel that it was the only thing worth saying--what one felt. Cleverness was silly. One must say simply what one felt.

"But I do not know," said Peter Walsh, "what I feel."

Poor Peter, thought Sally. Why did not Clarissa come and talk to them? That was what he was longing for. She knew it. All the time he was thinking only of Clarissa, and was fidgeting with his knife.

He had not found life simple, Peter said. His relations with Clarissa had not been simple. It had spoilt his life, he said. (They had been so intimate--he and Sally Seton, it was absurd not to say it.) One could not be in love twice, he said. And what could she say? Still, it is better to have loved (but he would think her sentimental--he used to be so sharp). He must come and stay with them in Manchester. That is all very true, he said. All very true. He would love to come and stay with them, directly he had done what he had to do in London.

And Clarissa had cared for him more than she had ever cared for Richard. Sally was positive of that.

"No, no, no!" said Peter (Sally should not have said that--she went too far). That good fellow--there he was at the end of the room, holding forth, the same as ever, dear old Richard. Who was he talking to? Sally asked, that very distinguished-looking man? Living in the wilds as she did, she had an insatiable curiosity to know who people were. But Peter did not know. He did not like his looks, he said, probably a Cabinet Minister. Of them all, Richard seemed to him the best, he said--the most disinterested.

"But what has he done?" Sally asked. Public work, she supposed. And were they happy together? Sally asked (she herself was extremely happy); for, she admitted, she knew nothing about them, only jumped to conclusions, as one does, for what can one know even of the people one lives with every day? she asked. Are we not all prisoners? She had read a wonderful play about a man who scratched on the wall of his cell, and she had felt that was true of life-- one scratched on the wall. Despairing of human relationships (people were so difficult), she often went into her garden and got from her flowers a peace which men and women never gave her. But no; he did not like cabbages; he preferred human beings, Peter said. Indeed, the young are beautiful, Sally said, watching Elizabeth cross the room. How unlike Clarissa at her age! Could he make anything of her? She would not open her lips. Not much, not yet, Peter admitted. She was like a lily, Sally said, a lily by the side of a pool. But Peter did not agree that we know nothing. We know everything, he said; at least he did.

But these two, Sally whispered, these two coming now (and really she must go, if Clarissa did not come soon), this distinguished- looking man and his rather common-looking wife who had been talking to Richard--what could one know about people like that?

"That they're damnable humbugs," said Peter, looking at them casually. He made Sally laugh.

But Sir William Bradshaw stopped at the door to look at a picture. He looked in the corner for the engraver's name. His wife looked too. Sir William Bradshaw was so interested in art.

When one was young, said Peter, one was too much excited to know people. Now that one was old, fifty-two to be precise (Sally was fifty-five, in body, she said, but her heart was like a girl's of twenty); now that one was mature then, said Peter, one could watch, one could understand, and one did not lose the power of feeling, he said. No, that is true, said Sally. She felt more deeply, more passionately, every year. It increased, he said, alas, perhaps, but one should be glad of it--it went on increasing in his experience. There was some one in India. He would like to tell Sally about her. He would like Sally to know her. She was married, he said. She had two small children. They must all come to Manchester, said Sally--he must promise before they left.

There's Elizabeth, he said, she feels not half what we feel, not yet. But, said Sally, watching Elizabeth go to her father, one can see they are devoted to each other. She could feel it by the way Elizabeth went to her father.

For her father had been looking at her, as he stood talking to the Bradshaws, and he had thought to himself, Who is that lovely girl? And suddenly he realised that it was his Elizabeth, and he had not recognised her, she looked so lovely in her pink frock! Elizabeth had felt him looking at her as she talked to Willie Titcomb. So she went to him and they stood together, now that the party was almost over, looking at the people going, and the rooms getting emptier and emptier, with things scattered on the floor. Even Ellie Henderson was going, nearly last of all, though no one had spoken to her, but she had wanted to see everything, to tell Edith. And Richard and Elizabeth were rather glad it was over, but Richard was proud of his daughter. And he had not meant to tell her, but he could not help telling her. He had looked at her, he said, and he had wondered, Who is that lovely girl? and it was his daughter! That did make her happy. But her poor dog was howling.

"Richard has improved. You are right," said Sally. "I shall go and talk to him. I shall say goodnight. What does the brain matter," said Lady Rosseter, getting up, "compared with the heart?"

"I will come," said Peter, but he sat on for a moment. What is this terror? what is this ecstasy? he thought to himself. What is it that fills me with extraordinary excitement?

It is Clarissa, he said.

For there she was.

THE END

To the Lighthouse

THE WINDOW

1

"Yes, of course, if it's fine tomorrow," said Mrs. Ramsay. "But you'll have to be up with the lark," she added.

To her son these words conveyed an extraordinary joy, as if it were settled, the expedition were bound to take place, and the wonder to which he had looked forward, for years and years it seemed, was, after a night's darkness and a day's sail, within touch. Since he belonged, even at the age of six, to that great clan which cannot keep this feeling separate from that, but must let future prospects, with their joys and sorrows, cloud what is actually at hand, since to such people even in earliest childhood any turn in the wheel of sensation has the power to crystallise and transfix the moment upon which its gloom or radiance rests, James Ramsay, sitting on the floor cutting out pictures from the illustrated catalogue of the Army and Navy stores, endowed the picture of a refrigerator, as his mother spoke, with heavenly bliss. It was fringed with joy. The wheelbarrow, the lawnmower, the sound of poplar trees, leaves whitening before rain, rooks cawing, brooms knocking, dresses rustling--all these were so coloured and distinguished in his mind that he had already his private code, his secret language, though he appeared the image of stark and uncompromising severity, with his high forehead and his fierce blue eyes, impeccably candid and pure, frowning slightly at the sight of human frailty, so that his mother, watching him guide his scissors neatly round the refrigerator, imagined him all red and ermine on the Bench or directing a stern and momentous enterprise in some crisis of public affairs.

"But," said his father, stopping in front of the drawing-room window, "it won't be fine."

Had there been an axe handy, a poker, or any weapon that would have gashed a hole in his father's breast and killed him, there and then, James would have seized it. Such were the extremes of emotion that Mr. Ramsay excited in his children's breasts by his mere presence; standing, as now, lean as a knife, narrow as the blade of one, grinning sarcastically, not only with the pleasure of disillusioning his son and casting ridicule upon his wife, who was ten thousand times better in every way than he was (James thought), but also with some secret conceit at his own accuracy of judgement. What he said was true. It was always true. He was incapable of untruth; never tampered with a fact; never altered a disagreeable word to suit the pleasure or convenience of any mortal being, least of all of his own children, who, sprung from his loins, should be aware from childhood that life is difficult; facts uncompromising; and the passage to that fabled land where our brightest hopes are extinguished, our frail barks founder in darkness (here Mr. Ramsay would straighten his back and narrow his little blue eyes upon the horizon), one that needs, above all, courage, truth, and the power to endure.

"But it may be fine--I expect it will be fine," said Mrs. Ramsay, making some little twist of the reddish brown stocking she was knitting, impatiently. If she finished it tonight, if they did go to the Lighthouse after all, it was to be given to the Lighthouse keeper for his little boy, who was threatened with a tuberculous hip; together with a pile of old magazines, and some tobacco, indeed, whatever she could find lying about, not really wanted, but only littering the room, to give those poor fellows, who must be bored to death sitting all day with nothing to do but polish the lamp and trim the wick and rake about on their scrap of garden, something to amuse them. For how would you like to be shut up for a whole month at a time, and possibly more in stormy weather, upon a rock the size of a tennis lawn? she would ask; and to have no letters or newspapers, and to see nobody; if you were married, not to see your wife, not to know how your children were,--if they were ill, if they had fallen down and broken their legs or arms; to see the same dreary waves breaking week after week, and then a dreadful storm coming, and the windows covered with spray, and birds dashed against the lamp, and the whole place rocking, and not be able to put your nose out of doors for fear of being swept into the sea? How would you like that? she asked, addressing herself particularly to her daughters. So she added, rather differently, one must take them whatever comforts one can.

"It's due west," said the atheist Tansley, holding his bony fingers spread so that the wind blew through them, for he was sharing Mr. Ramsay's evening walk up and down, up and down the terrace. That is to say, the wind blew from the worst possible direction for landing at the Lighthouse. Yes, he did say disagreeable things, Mrs. Ramsay admitted; it was odious of him to rub this in, and make James still more disappointed; but at the same time, she would not let them laugh at him. "The atheist," they called him; "the little atheist." Rose mocked him; Prue mocked him; Andrew, Jasper, Roger mocked him; even old Badger without a tooth in his head had bit him, for being (as Nancy put it) the hundred and tenth young man to chase them all the way up to the Hebrides when it was ever so much nicer to be alone.

"Nonsense," said Mrs. Ramsay, with great severity. Apart from the habit of exaggeration which they had from her, and from the implication (which was true) that she asked too many people to stay, and had to lodge some in the town, she could not bear incivility to her guests, to young men in particular, who were poor as churchmice, "exceptionally able," her husband said, his great admirers, and come there for a holiday. Indeed, she had the whole of the other sex under her protection; for reasons she could not explain, for their chivalry and valour, for the fact that they negotiated treaties, ruled India, controlled finance; finally for an attitude towards herself which no woman could fail to feel or to find agreeable, something trustful, childlike, reverential; which an old woman could take from a young man without loss of dignity, and woe betide the girl--pray Heaven it was none of her daughters!--who did not feel the worth of it, and all that it implied, to the marrow of her bones!

She turned with severity upon Nancy. He had not chased them, she said. He had been asked.

They must find a way out of it all. There might be some simpler way, some less laborious way, she sighed. When she looked in the glass and saw her hair grey, her cheek sunk, at fifty, she thought, possibly she might have managed things better--her husband; money; his books. But for her own part she would never for a single second regret her decision, evade difficulties, or slur over duties. She was now formidable to behold, and it was only in silence, looking up from their plates, after she had spoken so severely about Charles Tansley, that her daughters, Prue, Nancy, Rose--could sport with infidel ideas which they had brewed for themselves of a life different from hers; in Paris, perhaps; a wilder life; not always taking care of some man or other; for there was in all their minds a mute questioning of deference and chivalry, of the Bank of England and the Indian Empire, of ringed fingers and lace, though to them all there was something in this of the essence of beauty, which called out the manliness in their girlish hearts, and made them, as they sat at table beneath their mother's eyes, honour her strange severity, her extreme courtesy, like a queen's raising from the mud to wash a beggar's dirty foot, when she admonished them so very severely about that wretched atheist who had chased them--or, speaking accurately, been invited to stay with them--in the Isle of Skye.

"There'll be no landing at the Lighthouse tomorrow," said Charles Tansley, clapping his hands together as he stood at the window with her husband. Surely, he had said enough. She wished they would both leave her and James alone and go on talking. She looked at him. He was such a miserable specimen, the children said, all humps and hollows. He couldn't play cricket; he poked; he shuffled. He was a sarcastic brute, Andrew said. They knew what he liked best--to be for ever walking up and down, up and down, with Mr. Ramsay, and saying who had won this, who had won that, who was a "first rate man" at Latin verses, who was "brilliant but I think fundamentally unsound," who was undoubtedly the "ablest fellow in Balliol," who had buried his light temporarily at Bristol or Bedford, but was bound to be heard of later when his Prolegomena, of which Mr. Tansley had the first pages in proof with him if Mr. Ramsay would like to see them, to some branch of mathematics or philosophy saw the light of day. That was what they talked about.

She could not help laughing herself sometimes. She said, the other day, something about "waves mountains high." Yes, said Charles Tansley, it was a little rough. "Aren't you drenched to the skin?" she had said. "Damp, not wet through," said Mr. Tansley, pinching his sleeve, feeling his socks.

But it was not that they minded, the children said. It was not his face; it was not his manners. It was him--his point of view. When they talked about something interesting, people, music, history, anything, even said it was a fine evening so why not sit out of doors, then what they complained of about Charles Tansley was that until he had turned the whole thing round and made it somehow reflect himself and disparage them--he was not satisfied. And he would go to picture galleries they said, and he would ask one, did one like his tie? God knows, said Rose, one did not.

Disappearing as stealthily as stags from the dinner-table directly the meal was over, the eight sons and daughters of Mr. and Mrs. Ramsay sought their bedrooms, their fastness in a house where there was no other privacy to debate anything, everything; Tansley's tie; the passing of the Reform Bill; sea birds and butterflies; people; while the sun poured into those attics, which a plank alone separated from each other so that every footstep could be plainly heard and the Swiss girl sobbing for her father who was dying of cancer in a valley of the Grisons, and lit up bats, flannels, straw hats, ink-pots, paint-pots, beetles, and the skulls of small birds, while it drew from the long frilled strips of seaweed pinned to the wall a smell of salt and weeds, which was in the towels too, gritty with sand from bathing.

Strife, divisions, difference of opinion, prejudices twisted into the very fibre of being, oh, that they should begin so early, Mrs. Ramsay deplored. They were so critical, her children. They talked such nonsense. She went from the dining-room, holding James by the hand, since he would not go with the others. It seemed to her such nonsense--inventing differences, when people, heaven knows, were different enough without that. The real differences, she thought, standing by the drawing-room window, are enough, quite enough. She had in mind at the moment, rich and poor, high and low; the great in birth receiving from her, half grudging, some respect, for had she not in her veins the blood of that very noble, if slightly mythical, Italian house, whose daughters, scattered about English drawing-rooms in the nineteenth century, had lisped so charmingly, had stormed so wildly, and all her wit and her bearing and her temper came from them, and not from the sluggish English, or the cold Scotch; but more profoundly, she ruminated the other problem, of rich and poor, and the things she saw with her own eyes, weekly, daily, here or in London, when she visited this widow, or that struggling wife in person with a bag on her arm, and a note-book and pencil with which she wrote down in columns carefully ruled for the purpose wages and spendings, employment and unemployment, in the hope that thus she would cease to be a private woman whose charity was half a sop to her own indignation, half a relief to her own curiosity, and become what with her untrained mind she greatly admired, an investigator, elucidating the social problem.

Insoluble questions they were, it seemed to her, standing there, holding James by the hand. He had followed her into the drawing-room, that young man they laughed at; he was standing by the table, fidgeting with something, awkwardly, feeling himself out of things, as she knew without looking round. They had all gone--the children; Minta Doyle and Paul Rayley; Augustus Carmichael; her husband--they had all gone. So she turned with a sigh and said, "Would it bore you to come with me, Mr. Tansley?"

She had a dull errand in the town; she had a letter or two to write; she would be ten minutes perhaps; she would put on her hat. And, with her basket and her parasol, there she was again, ten minutes later, giving out a sense of being ready, of being equipped for a jaunt, which, however, she must interrupt for a moment, as they passed the tennis lawn, to ask Mr. Carmichael, who was basking with his yellow cat's eyes ajar, so that like a cat's they seemed to reflect the branches moving or the clouds passing, but to give no inkling of any inner thoughts or emotion whatsoever, if he wanted anything.

For they were making the great expedition, she said, laughing. They were going to the town. "Stamps, writing-paper, tobacco?" she suggested, stopping by his side. But no, he wanted nothing. His hands clasped themselves over his capacious paunch, his eyes blinked, as if he would have liked to reply kindly to these blandishments (she was seductive but a little nervous) but could not, sunk as he was in a grey-green somnolence which embraced them all, without need of words, in a vast and benevolent lethargy of well-wishing; all the house; all the world; all the people in it, for he had slipped into his glass at lunch a few drops of something, which accounted, the children thought, for the vivid streak of canary-yellow in moustache and beard that were otherwise milk white. No, nothing, he murmured.

He should have been a great philosopher, said Mrs. Ramsay, as they went down the road to the fishing village, but he had made an unfortunate marriage. Holding her black parasol very erect, and moving with an indescribable air of expectation, as if she were going to meet some one round the corner, she told the story; an affair at Oxford with some girl; an early marriage; poverty; going to India; translating a little poetry "very beautifully, I believe," being willing to teach the boys Persian or Hindustanee, but what really was the use of that?--and then lying, as they saw him, on the lawn.

It flattered him; snubbed as he had been, it soothed him that Mrs. Ramsay should tell him this. Charles Tansley revived. Insinuating, too, as she did the greatness of man's intellect, even in its decay, the subjection of all wives--not that she blamed the girl, and the marriage had been happy enough, she believed--to their husband's labours, she made him feel better pleased with himself than he had done yet, and he would have liked, had they taken a cab, for example, to have paid the fare. As for her little bag, might he not carry that? No, no, she said, she always carried THAT herself. She did too. Yes, he felt that in her. He felt many things, something in particular that excited him and disturbed him for reasons which he could not give. He would like her to see him, gowned and hooded, walking in a procession. A fellowship, a professorship, he felt capable of anything and saw himself--but what was she looking at? At a man pasting a bill. The vast flapping sheet flattened itself out, and each shove of the brush revealed fresh legs, hoops, horses, glistening reds and blues, beautifully smooth, until half the wall was covered with the advertisement of a circus; a hundred horsemen, twenty performing seals, lions, tigers ... Craning forwards, for she was short-sighted, she read it out ... "will visit this town," she read. It was terribly dangerous work for a one-armed man, she exclaimed, to stand on top of a ladder like that--his left arm had been cut off in a reaping machine two years ago.

"Let us all go!" she cried, moving on, as if all those riders and horses had filled her with childlike exultation and made her forget her pity.

"Let's go," he said, repeating her words, clicking them out, however, with a self-consciousness that made her wince. "Let us all go to the circus." No. He could not say it right. He could not feel it right. But why not? she wondered. What was wrong with him then? She liked him warmly, at the moment. Had they not been taken, she asked, to circuses when they were children? Never, he answered, as if she asked the very thing he wanted; had been longing all these days to say, how they did not go to circuses. It was a large family, nine brothers and sisters, and his father was a working man. "My father is a chemist, Mrs. Ramsay. He keeps a shop." He himself had paid his own way since he was thirteen. Often he went without a greatcoat in winter. He could never "return hospitality" (those were his parched stiff words) at college. He had to make things last twice the time other people did; he smoked the cheapest tobacco; shag; the same the old men did in the quays. He worked hard--seven hours a day; his subject was now the influence of something upon somebody--they were walking on and Mrs. Ramsay did not quite catch the meaning, only the words, here and there ... dissertation ... fellowship ... readership ... lectureship. She could not follow the ugly academic jargon, that rattled itself off so glibly, but said to herself that she saw now why going to the circus had knocked him off his perch, poor little man, and why he came out, instantly, with all that about his father and mother and brothers and sisters, and she would see to it that they didn't laugh at him any more; she would tell Prue about it. What he would have liked, she supposed, would have been to say how he had gone not to the circus but to Ibsen with the Ramsays. He was an awful prig--oh yes, an insufferable bore. For, though they had reached the town now and were in the main street, with carts grinding past on the cobbles, still he went on talking, about settlements, and teaching, and working men, and helping our own class, and lectures, till she gathered that he had got back entire self-confidence, had recovered from the circus, and was about (and now again she liked him warmly) to tell her--but here, the houses falling away on both sides, they came out on the quay, and the whole bay spread before them and Mrs. Ramsay could not help exclaiming, "Oh, how beautiful!" For the great plateful of blue water was before her; the hoary Lighthouse, distant, austere, in the midst; and on the right, as far as the eye could see, fading and falling, in soft low pleats, the green sand dunes with the wild flowing grasses on them, which always seemed to be running away into some moon country, uninhabited of men.

That was the view, she said, stopping, growing greyer-eyed, that her husband loved.

She paused a moment. But now, she said, artists had come here. There indeed, only a few paces off, stood one of them, in Panama hat and yellow boots, seriously, softly, absorbedly, for all that he was watched by ten little boys, with an air of profound contentment on his round red face gazing, and then, when he had gazed, dipping; imbuing the tip of his brush in some soft mound of green or pink. Since Mr. Paunceforte had been there, three years before, all the pictures were like that, she said, green and grey, with lemon-coloured sailing-boats, and pink women on the beach.

But her grandmother's friends, she said, glancing discreetly as they passed, took the greatest pains; first they mixed their own colours, and then they ground them, and then they put damp cloths to keep them moist.

So Mr. Tansley supposed she meant him to see that that man's picture was skimpy, was that what one said? The colours weren't solid? Was that what one said? Under the influence of that extraordinary emotion which had been growing all the walk, had begun in the garden when he had wanted to take her bag, had increased in the town when he had wanted to tell her everything about himself, he was coming to see himself, and everything he had ever known gone crooked a little. It was awfully strange.

There he stood in the parlour of the poky little house where she had taken him, waiting for her, while she went upstairs a moment to see a woman. He heard her quick step above; heard her voice cheerful, then low; looked at the mats, tea-caddies, glass shades; waited quite impatiently; looked forward eagerly to the walk home; determined to carry her bag; then heard her come out; shut a door; say they must keep the windows open and the doors shut, ask at the house for anything they wanted (she must be talking to a child) when, suddenly, in she came, stood for a moment silent (as if she had been pretending up there, and for a moment let herself be now), stood quite motionless for a moment against a picture of Queen Victoria wearing the blue ribbon of the Garter; when all at once he realised that it was this: it was this:--she was the most beautiful person he had ever seen.

With stars in her eyes and veils in her hair, with cyclamen and wild violets--what nonsense was he thinking? She was fifty at least; she had eight children. Stepping through fields of flowers and taking to her breast buds that had broken and lambs that had fallen; with the stars in her eyes and the wind in her hair--He had hold of her bag.

"Good-bye, Elsie," she said, and they walked up the street, she holding her parasol erect and walking as if she expected to meet some one round the corner, while for the first time in his life Charles Tansley felt an extraordinary pride; a man digging in a drain stopped digging and looked at her, let his arm fall down and looked at her; for the first time in his life Charles Tansley felt an extraordinary pride; felt the wind and the cyclamen and the violets for he was walking with a beautiful woman. He had hold of her bag.

2

"No going to the Lighthouse, James," he said, as trying in deference to Mrs. Ramsay to soften his voice into some semblance of geniality at least.

Odious little man, thought Mrs. Ramsay, why go on saying that?

3

"Perhaps you will wake up and find the sun shining and the birds singing," she said compassionately, smoothing the little boy's hair, for her husband, with his caustic saying that it would not be fine, had dashed his spirits she could see. This going to the Lighthouse was a passion of his, she saw, and then, as if her husband had not said enough, with his caustic saying that it would not be fine tomorrow, this odious little man went and rubbed it in all over again.

"Perhaps it will be fine tomorrow," she said, smoothing his hair.

All she could do now was to admire the refrigerator, and turn the pages of the Stores list in the hope that she might come upon something like a rake, or a mowing-machine, which, with its prongs and its handles, would need the greatest skill and care in cutting out. All these young men parodied her husband, she reflected; he said it would rain; they said it would be a positive tornado.

But here, as she turned the page, suddenly her search for the picture of a rake or a mowing-machine was interrupted. The gruff murmur, irregularly broken by the taking out of pipes and the putting in of pipes which had kept on assuring her, though she could not hear what was said (as she sat in the window which opened on the terrace), that the men were happily talking; this sound, which had lasted now half an hour and had taken its place soothingly in the scale of sounds pressing on top of her, such as the tap of balls upon bats, the sharp, sudden bark now and then, "How's that? How's that?" of the children playing cricket, had ceased; so that the monotonous fall of the waves on the beach, which for the most part beat a measured and soothing tattoo to her thoughts and seemed consolingly to repeat over and over again as she sat with the children the words of some old cradle song, murmured by nature, "I am guarding you--I am your support," but at other times suddenly and unexpectedly, especially when her mind raised itself slightly from the task actually in hand, had no such kindly meaning, but like a ghostly roll of drums remorselessly beat the measure of life, made one think of the destruction of the island and its engulfment in the sea, and warned her whose day had slipped past in one quick doing after another that it was all ephemeral as a rainbow--this sound which had been obscured and concealed under the other sounds suddenly thundered hollow in her ears and made her look up with an impulse of terror.

They had ceased to talk; that was the explanation. Falling in one second from the tension which had gripped her to the other extreme which, as if to recoup her for her unnecessary expense of emotion, was cool, amused, and even faintly malicious, she concluded that poor Charles Tansley had been shed. That was of little account to her. If her husband required sacrifices (and indeed he did) she cheerfully offered up to him Charles Tansley, who had snubbed her little boy.

One moment more, with her head raised, she listened, as if she waited for some habitual sound, some regular mechanical sound; and then, hearing something rhythmical, half said, half chanted, beginning in the garden, as her husband beat up and down the terrace, something between a croak and a song, she was soothed once more, assured again that all was well, and looking down at the book on her knee found the picture of a pocket knife with six blades which could only be cut out if James was very careful.

Suddenly a loud cry, as of a sleep-walker, half roused, something about

Stormed at with shot and shell

sung out with the utmost intensity in her ear, made her turn apprehensively to see if anyone had heard him. Only Lily Briscoe, she was glad to find; and that did not matter. But the sight of the girl standing on the edge of the lawn painting reminded her; she was supposed to be keeping her head as much in the same position as possible for Lily's picture. Lily's picture! Mrs. Ramsay smiled. With her little Chinese eyes and her puckered-up face, she would never marry; one could not take her painting very seriously; she was an independent little creature, and Mrs. Ramsay liked her for it; so, remembering her promise, she bent her head.

4

Indeed, he almost knocked her easel over, coming down upon her with his hands waving shouting out, "Boldly we rode and well," but, mercifully, he turned sharp, and rode off, to die gloriously she supposed upon the heights of Balaclava. Never was anybody at once so ridiculous and so alarming. But so long as he kept like that, waving, shouting, she was safe; he would not stand still and look at her picture. And that was what Lily Briscoe could not have endured. Even while she looked at the mass, at the line, at the colour, at Mrs. Ramsay sitting in the window with James, she kept a feeler on her surroundings lest some one should creep up, and suddenly she should find her picture looked at. But now, with all her senses quickened as they were, looking, straining, till the colour of the wall and the jacmanna beyond burnt into her eyes, she was aware of someone coming out of the house, coming towards her; but somehow divined, from the footfall, William Bankes, so that though her brush quivered, she did not, as she would have done had it been Mr. Tansley, Paul Rayley, Minta Doyle, or practically anybody else, turn her canvas upon the grass, but let it stand. William Bankes stood beside her.

They had rooms in the village, and so, walking in, walking out, parting late on door-mats, had said little things about the soup, about the children, about one thing and another which made them allies; so that when he stood beside her now in his judicial way (he was old enough to be her father too, a botanist, a widower, smelling of soap, very scrupulous and clean) she just stood there. He just stood there. Her shoes were excellent, he observed. They allowed the toes their natural expansion. Lodging in the same house with her, he had noticed too, how orderly she was, up before breakfast and off to paint, he believed, alone: poor, presumably, and without the complexion or the allurement of Miss Doyle certainly, but with a good sense which made her in his eyes superior to that young lady. Now, for instance, when Ramsay bore down on them, shouting, gesticulating, Miss Briscoe, he felt certain, understood.

Some one had blundered.

Mr. Ramsay glared at them. He glared at them without seeming to see them. That did make them both vaguely uncomfortable. Together they had seen a thing they had not been meant to see. They had encroached upon a privacy. So, Lily thought, it was probably an excuse of his for moving, for getting out of earshot, that made Mr. Bankes almost immediately say something about its being chilly and suggested taking a stroll. She would come, yes. But it was with difficulty that she took her eyes off her picture.

The jacmanna was bright violet; the wall staring white. She would not have considered it honest to tamper with the bright violet and the staring white, since she saw them like that, fashionable though it was, since Mr. Paunceforte's visit, to see everything pale, elegant, semitransparent. Then beneath the colour there was the shape. She could see it all so clearly, so commandingly, when she looked: it was when she took her brush in hand that the whole thing changed. It was in that moment's flight between the picture and her canvas that the demons set on her who often brought her to the verge of tears and made this passage from conception to work as dreadful as any down a dark passage for a child. Such she often felt herself--struggling against terrific odds to maintain her courage; to say: "But this is what I see; this is what I see," and so to clasp some miserable remnant of her vision to her breast, which a thousand forces did their best to pluck from her. And it was then too, in that chill and windy way, as she began to paint, that there forced themselves upon her other things, her own inadequacy, her insignificance, keeping house for her father off the Brompton Road, and had much ado to control her impulse to fling herself (thank Heaven she had always resisted so far) at Mrs. Ramsay's knee and say to her--but what could one say to her? "I'm in love with you?" No, that was not true. "I'm in love with this all," waving her hand at the hedge, at the house, at the children. It was absurd, it was impossible. So now she laid her brushes neatly in the box, side by side, and said to William Bankes:

"It suddenly gets cold. The sun seems to give less heat," she said, looking about her, for it was bright enough, the grass still a soft deep green, the house starred in its greenery with purple passion flowers, and rooks dropping cool cries from the high blue. But something moved, flashed, turned a silver wing in the air. It was September after all, the middle of September, and past six in the evening. So off they strolled down the garden in the usual direction, past the tennis lawn, past the pampas grass, to that break in the thick hedge, guarded by red hot pokers like brasiers of clear burning coal, between which the blue waters of the bay looked bluer than ever.

They came there regularly every evening drawn by some need. It was as if the water floated off and set sailing thoughts which had grown stagnant on dry land, and gave to their bodies even some sort of physical relief. First, the pulse of colour flooded the bay with blue, and the heart expanded with it and the body swam, only the next instant to be checked and chilled by the prickly blackness on the ruffled waves. Then, up behind the great black rock, almost every evening spurted irregularly, so that one had to watch for it and it was a delight when it came, a fountain of white water; and then, while one waited for that, one watched, on the pale semicircular beach, wave after wave shedding again and again smoothly, a film of mother of pearl.

They both smiled, standing there. They both felt a common hilarity, excited by the moving waves; and then by the swift cutting race of a sailing boat, which, having sliced a curve in the bay, stopped; shivered; let its sails drop down; and then, with a natural instinct to complete the picture, after this swift movement, both of them looked at the dunes far away, and instead of merriment felt come over them some sadness--because the thing was completed partly, and partly because distant views seem to outlast by a million years (Lily thought) the gazer and to be communing already with a sky which beholds an earth entirely at rest.

Looking at the far sand hills, William Bankes thought of Ramsay: thought of a road in Westmorland, thought of Ramsay striding along a road by himself hung round with that solitude which seemed to be his natural air. But this was suddenly interrupted, William Bankes remembered (and this must refer to some actual incident), by a hen, straddling her wings out in protection of a covey of little chicks, upon which Ramsay, stopping, pointed his stick and said "Pretty--pretty," an odd illumination in to his heart, Bankes had thought it, which showed his simplicity, his sympathy with humble things; but it seemed to him as if their friendship had ceased, there, on that stretch of road. After that, Ramsay had married. After that, what with one thing and another, the pulp had gone out of their friendship. Whose fault it was he could not say, only, after a time, repetition had taken the place of newness. It was to repeat that they met. But in this dumb colloquy with the sand dunes he maintained that his affection for Ramsay had in no way diminished; but there, like the body of a young man laid up in peat for a century, with the red fresh on his lips, was his friendship, in its acuteness and reality, laid up across the bay among the sandhills.

He was anxious for the sake of this friendship and perhaps too in order to clear himself in his own mind from the imputation of having dried and shrunk--for Ramsay lived in a welter of children, whereas Bankes was childless and a widower--he was anxious that Lily Briscoe should not disparage Ramsay (a great man in his own way) yet should understand how things stood between them. Begun long years ago, their friendship had petered out on a Westmorland road, where the hen spread her wings before her chicks; after which Ramsay had married, and their paths lying different ways, there had been, certainly for no one's fault, some tendency, when they met, to repeat.

Yes. That was it. He finished. He turned from the view. And, turning to walk back the other way, up the drive, Mr. Bankes was alive to things which would not have struck him had not those sandhills revealed to him the body of his friendship lying with the red on its lips laid up in peat--for instance, Cam, the little girl, Ramsay's youngest daughter. She was picking Sweet Alice on the bank. She was wild and fierce. She would not "give a flower to the gentleman" as the nursemaid told her. No! no! no! she would not! She clenched her fist. She stamped. And Mr. Bankes felt aged and saddened and somehow put into the wrong by her about his friendship. He must have dried and shrunk.

The Ramsays were not rich, and it was a wonder how they managed to contrive it all. Eight children! To feed eight children on philosophy! Here was another of them, Jasper this time, strolling past, to have a shot at a bird, he said, nonchalantly, swinging Lily's hand like a pump-handle as he passed, which caused Mr. Bankes to say, bitterly, how SHE was a favourite. There was education now to be considered (true, Mrs. Ramsay had something of her own perhaps) let alone the daily wear and tear of shoes and stockings which those "great fellows," all well grown, angular, ruthless youngsters, must require. As for being sure which was which, or in what order they came, that was beyond him. He called them privately after the Kings and Queens of England; Cam the Wicked, James the Ruthless, Andrew the Just, Prue the Fair--for Prue would have beauty, he thought, how could she help it?--and Andrew brains. While he walked up the drive and Lily Briscoe said yes and no and capped his comments (for she was in love with them all, in love with this world) he weighed Ramsay's case, commiserated him, envied him, as if he had seen him divest himself of all those glories of isolation and austerity which crowned him in youth to cumber himself definitely with fluttering wings and clucking domesticities. They gave him something--William Bankes acknowledged that; it would have been pleasant if Cam had stuck a flower in his coat or clambered over his shoulder, as over her father's, to look at a picture of Vesuvius in eruption; but they had also, his old friends could not but feel, destroyed something. What would a stranger think now? What did this Lily Briscoe think? Could one help noticing that habits grew on him? eccentricities, weaknesses perhaps? It was astonishing that a man of his intellect could stoop so low as he did--but that was too harsh a phrase--could depend so much as he did upon people's praise.

"Oh, but," said Lily, "think of his work!"

Whenever she "thought of his work" she always saw clearly before her a large kitchen table. It was Andrew's doing. She asked him what his father's books were about. "Subject and object and the nature of reality," Andrew had said. And when she said Heavens, she had no notion what that meant. "Think of a kitchen table then," he told her, "when you're not there."

So now she always saw, when she thought of Mr. Ramsay's work, a scrubbed kitchen table. It lodged now in the fork of a pear tree, for they had reached the orchard. And with a painful effort of concentration, she focused her mind, not upon the silver-bossed bark of the tree, or upon its fish-shaped leaves, but upon a phantom kitchen table, one of those scrubbed board tables, grained and knotted, whose virtue seems to have been laid bare by years of muscular integrity, which stuck there, its four legs in air. Naturally, if one's days were passed in this seeing of angular essences, this reducing of lovely evenings, with all their flamingo clouds and blue and silver to a white deal four-legged table (and it was a mark of the finest minds to do so), naturally one could not be judged like an ordinary person.

Mr. Bankes liked her for bidding him "think of his work." He had thought of it, often and often. Times without number, he had said, "Ramsay is one of those men who do their best work before they are forty." He had made a definite contribution to philosophy in one little book when he was only five and twenty; what came after was more or less amplification, repetition. But the number of men who make a definite contribution to anything whatsoever is very small, he said, pausing by the pear tree, well brushed, scrupulously exact, exquisitely judicial. Suddenly, as if the movement of his hand had released it, the load of her accumulated impressions of him tilted up, and down poured in a ponderous avalanche all she felt about him. That was one sensation. Then up rose in a fume the essence of his being. That was another. She felt herself transfixed by the intensity of her perception; it was his severity; his goodness. I respect you (she addressed silently him in person) in every atom; you are not vain; you are entirely impersonal; you are finer than Mr. Ramsay; you are the finest human being that I know; you have neither wife nor child (without any sexual feeling, she longed to cherish that loneliness), you live for science (involuntarily, sections of potatoes rose before her eyes); praise would be an insult to you; generous, pure-hearted, heroic man! But simultaneously, she remembered how he had brought a valet all the way up here; objected to dogs on chairs; would prose for hours (until Mr. Ramsay slammed out of the room) about salt in vegetables and the iniquity of English cooks.

How then did it work out, all this? How did one judge people, think of them? How did one add up this and that and conclude that it was liking one felt or disliking? And to those words, what meaning attached, after all? Standing now, apparently transfixed, by the pear tree, impressions poured in upon her of those two men, and to follow her thought was like following a voice which speaks too quickly to be taken down by one's pencil, and the voice was her own voice saying without prompting undeniable, everlasting, contradictory things, so that even the fissures and humps on the bark of the pear tree were irrevocably fixed there for eternity. You have greatness, she continued, but Mr. Ramsay has none of it. He is petty, selfish, vain, egotistical; he is spoilt; he is a tyrant; he wears Mrs. Ramsay to death; but he has what you (she addressed Mr. Bankes) have not; a fiery unworldliness; he knows nothing about trifles; he loves dogs and his children. He has eight. Mr. Bankes has none. Did he not come down in two coats the other night and let Mrs. Ramsay trim his hair into a pudding basin? All of this danced up and down, like a company of gnats, each separate but all marvellously controlled in an invisible elastic net--danced up and down in Lily's mind, in and about the branches of the pear tree, where still hung in effigy the scrubbed kitchen table, symbol of her profound respect for Mr. Ramsay's mind, until her thought which had spun quicker and quicker exploded of its own intensity; she felt released; a shot went off close at hand, and there came, flying from its fragments, frightened, effusive, tumultuous, a flock of starlings.

"Jasper!" said Mr. Bankes. They turned the way the starlings flew, over the terrace. Following the scatter of swift-flying birds in the sky they stepped through the gap in the high hedge straight into Mr. Ramsay, who boomed tragically at them, "Some one had blundered!"

His eyes, glazed with emotion, defiant with tragic intensity, met theirs for a second, and trembled on the verge of recognition; but then, raising his hand, half-way to his face as if to avert, to brush off, in an agony of peevish shame, their normal gaze, as if he begged them to withhold for a moment what he knew to be inevitable, as if he impressed upon them his own child-like resentment of interruption, yet even in the moment of discovery was not to be routed utterly, but was determined to hold fast to something of this delicious emotion, this impure rhapsody of which he was ashamed, but in which he revelled--he turned abruptly, slammed his private door on them; and, Lily Briscoe and Mr. Bankes, looking uneasily up into the sky, observed that the flock of starlings which Jasper had routed with his gun had settled on the tops of the elm trees.

5

"And even if it isn't fine tomorrow," said Mrs. Ramsay, raising her eyes to glance at William Bankes and Lily Briscoe as they passed, "it will be another day. And now," she said, thinking that Lily's charm was her Chinese eyes, aslant in her white, puckered little face, but it would take a clever man to see it, "and now stand up, and let me measure your leg," for they might go to the Lighthouse after all, and she must see if the stocking did not need to be an inch or two longer in the leg.

Smiling, for it was an admirable idea, that had flashed upon her this very second--William and Lily should marry--she took the heather-mixture stocking, with its criss-cross of steel needles at the mouth of it, and measured it against James's leg.

"My dear, stand still," she said, for in his jealousy, not liking to serve as measuring block for the Lighthouse keeper's little boy, James fidgeted purposely; and if he did that, how could she see, was it too long, was it too short? she asked.

She looked up--what demon possessed him, her youngest, her cherished?--and saw the room, saw the chairs, thought them fearfully shabby. Their entrails, as Andrew said the other day, were all over the floor; but then what was the point, she asked, of buying good chairs to let them spoil up here all through the winter when the house, with only one old woman to see to it, positively dripped with wet? Never mind, the rent was precisely twopence half-penny; the children loved it; it did her husband good to be three thousand, or if she must be accurate, three hundred miles from his libraries and his lectures and his disciples; and there was room for visitors. Mats, camp beds, crazy ghosts of chairs and tables whose London life of service was done--they did well enough here; and a photograph or two, and books. Books, she thought, grew of themselves. She never had time to read them. Alas! even the books that had been given her and inscribed by the hand of the poet himself: "For her whose wishes must be obeyed" ... "The happier Helen of our days" ... disgraceful to say, she had never read them. And Croom on the Mind and Bates on the Savage Customs of Polynesia ("My dear, stand still," she said)--neither of those could one send to the Lighthouse. At a certain moment, she supposed, the house would become so shabby that something must be done. If they could be taught to wipe their feet and not bring the beach in with them--that would be something. Crabs, she had to allow, if Andrew really wished to dissect them, or if Jasper believed that one could make soup from seaweed, one could not prevent it; or Rose's objects--shells, reeds, stones; for they were gifted, her children, but all in quite different ways. And the result of it was, she sighed, taking in the whole room from floor to ceiling, as she held the stocking against James's leg, that things got shabbier and got shabbier summer after summer. The mat was fading; the wall-paper was flapping. You couldn't tell any more that those were roses on it. Still, if every door in a house is left perpetually open, and no lockmaker in the whole of Scotland can mend a bolt, things must spoil. What was the use of flinging a green Cashemere shawl over the edge of a picture frame? In two weeks it would be the colour of pea soup. But it was the doors that annoyed her; every door was left open. She listened. The drawing-room door was open; the hall door was open; it sounded as if the bedroom doors were open; and certainly the window on the landing was open, for that she had opened herself. That windows should be open, and doors shut--simple as it was, could none of them remember it? She would go into the maids' bedrooms at night and find them sealed like ovens, except for Marie's, the Swiss girl, who would rather go without a bath than without fresh air, but then at home, she had said, "the mountains are so beautiful." She had said that last night looking out of the window with tears in her eyes. "The mountains are so beautiful." Her father was dying there, Mrs. Ramsay knew. He was leaving them fatherless. Scolding and demonstrating (how to make a bed, how to open a window, with hands that shut and spread like a Frenchwoman's) all had folded itself quietly about her, when the girl spoke, as, after a flight through the sunshine the wings of a bird fold themselves quietly and the blue of its plumage changes from bright steel to soft purple. She had stood there silent for there was nothing to be said. He had cancer of the throat. At the recollection--how she had stood there, how the girl had said, "At home the mountains are so beautiful," and there was no hope, no hope whatever, she had a spasm of irritation, and speaking sharply, said to James:

"Stand still. Don't be tiresome," so that he knew instantly that her severity was real, and straightened his leg and she measured it.

The stocking was too short by half an inch at least, making allowance for the fact that Sorley's little boy would be less well grown than James.

"It's too short," she said, "ever so much too short."

Never did anybody look so sad. Bitter and black, half-way down, in the darkness, in the shaft which ran from the sunlight to the depths, perhaps a tear formed; a tear fell; the waters swayed this way and that, received it, and were at rest. Never did anybody look so sad.

But was it nothing but looks, people said? What was there behind it--her beauty and splendour? Had he blown his brains out, they asked, had he died the week before they were married--some other, earlier lover, of whom rumours reached one? Or was there nothing? nothing but an incomparable beauty which she lived behind, and could do nothing to disturb? For easily though she might have said at some moment of intimacy when stories of great passion, of love foiled, of ambition thwarted came her way how she too had known or felt or been through it herself, she never spoke. She was silent always. She knew then--she knew without having learnt. Her simplicity fathomed what clever people falsified. Her singleness of mind made her drop plumb like a stone, alight exact as a bird, gave her, naturally, this swoop and fall of the spirit upon truth which delighted, eased, sustained--falsely perhaps.

("Nature has but little clay," said Mr. Bankes once, much moved by her voice on the telephone, though she was only telling him a fact about a train, "like that of which she moulded you." He saw her at the end of the line, Greek, blue-eyed, straight-nosed. How incongruous it seemed to be telephoning to a woman like that. The Graces assembling seemed to have joined hands in meadows of asphodel to compose that face. Yes, he would catch the 10:30 at Euston.

"But she's no more aware of her beauty than a child," said Mr. Bankes, replacing the receiver and crossing the room to see what progress the workmen were making with an hotel which they were building at the back of his house. And he thought of Mrs. Ramsay as he looked at that stir among the unfinished walls. For always, he thought, there was something incongruous to be worked into the harmony of her face. She clapped a deer-stalker's hat on her head; she ran across the lawn in galoshes to snatch a child from mischief. So that if it was her beauty merely that one thought of, one must remember the quivering thing, the living thing (they were carrying bricks up a little plank as he watched them), and work it into the picture; or if one thought of her simply as a woman, one must endow her with some freak of idiosyncrasy--she did not like admiration--or suppose some latent desire to doff her royalty of form as if her beauty bored her and all that men say of beauty, and she wanted only to be like other people, insignificant. He did not know. He did not know. He must go to his work.)

Knitting her reddish-brown hairy stocking, with her head outlined absurdly by the gilt frame, the green shawl which she had tossed over the edge of the frame, and the authenticated masterpiece by Michael Angelo, Mrs. Ramsay smoothed out what had been harsh in her manner a moment before, raised his head, and kissed her little boy on the forehead. "Let us find another picture to cut out," she said.

6

But what had happened?

Some one had blundered.

Starting from her musing she gave meaning to words which she had held meaningless in her mind for a long stretch of time. "Some one had blundered"-- Fixing her short-sighted eyes upon her husband, who was now bearing down upon her, she gazed steadily until his closeness revealed to her (the jingle mated itself in her head) that something had happened, some one had blundered. But she could not for the life of her think what.

He shivered; he quivered. All his vanity, all his satisfaction in his own splendour, riding fell as a thunderbolt, fierce as a hawk at the head of his men through the valley of death, had been shattered, destroyed. Stormed at by shot and shell, boldly we rode and well, flashed through the valley of death, volleyed and thundered--straight into Lily Briscoe and William Bankes. He quivered; he shivered.

Not for the world would she have spoken to him, realising, from the familiar signs, his eyes averted, and some curious gathering together of his person, as if he wrapped himself about and needed privacy into which to regain his equilibrium, that he was outraged and anguished. She stroked James's head; she transferred to him what she felt for her husband, and, as she watched him chalk yellow the white dress shirt of a gentleman in the Army and Navy Stores catalogue, thought what a delight it would be to her should he turn out a great artist; and why should he not? He had a splendid forehead. Then, looking up, as her husband passed her once more, she was relieved to find that the ruin was veiled; domesticity triumphed; custom crooned its soothing rhythm, so that when stopping deliberately, as his turn came round again, at the window he bent quizzically and whimsically to tickle James's bare calf with a sprig of something, she twitted him for having dispatched "that poor young man," Charles Tansley. Tansley had had to go in and write his dissertation, he said.

"James will have to write HIS dissertation one of these days," he added ironically, flicking his sprig.

Hating his father, James brushed away the tickling spray with which in a manner peculiar to him, compound of severity and humour, he teased his youngest son's bare leg.

She was trying to get these tiresome stockings finished to send to Sorley's little boy tomorrow, said Mrs. Ramsay.

There wasn't the slightest possible chance that they could go to the Lighthouse tomorrow, Mr. Ramsay snapped out irascibly.

How did he know? she asked. The wind often changed.

The extraordinary irrationality of her remark, the folly of women's minds enraged him. He had ridden through the valley of death, been shattered and shivered; and now, she flew in the face of facts, made his children hope what was utterly out of the question, in effect, told lies. He stamped his foot on the stone step. "Damn you," he said. But what had she said? Simply that it might be fine tomorrow. So it might.

Not with the barometer falling and the wind due west.

To pursue truth with such astonishing lack of consideration for other people's feelings, to rend the thin veils of civilization so wantonly, so brutally, was to her so horrible an outrage of human decency that, without replying, dazed and blinded, she bent her head as if to let the pelt of jagged hail, the drench of dirty water, bespatter her unrebuked. There was nothing to be said.

He stood by her in silence. Very humbly, at length, he said that he would step over and ask the Coastguards if she liked.

There was nobody whom she reverenced as she reverenced him.

She was quite ready to take his word for it, she said. Only then they need not cut sandwiches--that was all. They came to her, naturally, since she was a woman, all day long with this and that; one wanting this, another that; the children were growing up; she often felt she was nothing but a sponge sopped full of human emotions. Then he said, Damn you. He said, It must rain. He said, It won't rain; and instantly a Heaven of security opened before her. There was nobody she reverenced more. She was not good enough to tie his shoe strings, she felt.

Already ashamed of that petulance, of that gesticulation of the hands when charging at the head of his troops, Mr. Ramsay rather sheepishly prodded his son's bare legs once more, and then, as if he had her leave for it, with a movement which oddly reminded his wife of the great sea lion at the Zoo tumbling backwards after swallowing his fish and walloping off so that the water in the tank washes from side to side, he dived into the evening air which, already thinner, was taking the substance from leaves and hedges but, as if in return, restoring to roses and pinks a lustre which they had not had by day.

"Some one had blundered," he said again, striding off, up and down the terrace.

But how extraordinarily his note had changed! It was like the cuckoo; "in June he gets out of tune"; as if he were trying over, tentatively seeking, some phrase for a new mood, and having only this at hand, used it, cracked though it was. But it sounded ridiculous--"Some one had blundered"--said like that, almost as a question, without any conviction, melodiously. Mrs. Ramsay could not help smiling, and soon, sure enough, walking up and down, he hummed it, dropped it, fell silent.

He was safe, he was restored to his privacy. He stopped to light his pipe, looked once at his wife and son in the window, and as one raises one's eyes from a page in an express train and sees a farm, a tree, a cluster of cottages as an illustration, a confirmation of something on the printed page to which one returns, fortified, and satisfied, so without his distinguishing either his son or his wife, the sight of them fortified him and satisfied him and consecrated his effort to arrive at a perfectly clear understanding of the problem which now engaged the energies of his splendid mind.

It was a splendid mind. For if thought is like the keyboard of a piano, divided into so many notes, or like the alphabet is ranged in twenty-six letters all in order, then his splendid mind had no sort of difficulty in running over those letters one by one, firmly and accurately, until it had reached, say, the letter Q. He reached Q. Very few people in the whole of England ever reach Q. Here, stopping for one moment by the stone urn which held the geraniums, he saw, but now far, far away, like children picking up shells, divinely innocent and occupied with little trifles at their feet and somehow entirely defenceless against a doom which he perceived, his wife and son, together, in the window. They needed his protection; he gave it them. But after Q? What comes next? After Q there are a number of letters the last of which is scarcely visible to mortal eyes, but glimmers red in the distance. Z is only reached once by one man in a generation. Still, if he could reach R it would be something. Here at least was Q. He dug his heels in at Q. Q he was sure of. Q he could demonstrate. If Q then is Q--R--. Here he knocked his pipe out, with two or three resonant taps on the handle of the urn, and proceeded. "Then R ..." He braced himself. He clenched himself.

Qualities that would have saved a ship's company exposed on a broiling sea with six biscuits and a flask of water--endurance and justice, foresight, devotion, skill, came to his help. R is then--what is R?

A shutter, like the leathern eyelid of a lizard, flickered over the intensity of his gaze and obscured the letter R. In that flash of darkness he heard people saying--he was a failure--that R was beyond him. He would never reach R. On to R, once more. R--

Qualities that in a desolate expedition across the icy solitudes of the Polar region would have made him the leader, the guide, the counsellor, whose temper, neither sanguine nor despondent, surveys with equanimity what is to be and faces it, came to his help again. R--

The lizard's eye flickered once more. The veins on his forehead bulged. The geranium in the urn became startlingly visible and, displayed among its leaves, he could see, without wishing it, that old, that obvious distinction between the two classes of men; on the one hand the steady goers of superhuman strength who, plodding and persevering, repeat the whole alphabet in order, twenty-six letters in all, from start to finish; on the other the gifted, the inspired who, miraculously, lump all the letters together in one flash--the way of genius. He had not genius; he laid no claim to that: but he had, or might have had, the power to repeat every letter of the alphabet from A to Z accurately in order. Meanwhile, he stuck at Q. On, then, on to R.

Feelings that would not have disgraced a leader who, now that the snow has begun to fall and the mountain top is covered in mist, knows that he must lay himself down and die before morning comes, stole upon him, paling the colour of his eyes, giving him, even in the two minutes of his turn on the terrace, the bleached look of withered old age. Yet he would not die lying down; he would find some crag of rock, and there, his eyes fixed on the storm, trying to the end to pierce the darkness, he would die standing. He would never reach R.

He stood stock-still, by the urn, with the geranium flowing over it. How many men in a thousand million, he asked himself, reach Z after all? Surely the leader of a forlorn hope may ask himself that, and answer, without treachery to the expedition behind him, "One perhaps." One in a generation. Is he to be blamed then if he is not that one? provided he has toiled honestly, given to the best of his power, and till he has no more left to give? And his fame lasts how long? It is permissible even for a dying hero to think before he dies how men will speak of him hereafter. His fame lasts perhaps two thousand years. And what are two thousand years? (asked Mr. Ramsay ironically, staring at the hedge). What, indeed, if you look from a mountain top down the long wastes of the ages? The very stone one kicks with one's boot will outlast Shakespeare. His own little light would shine, not very brightly, for a year or two, and would then be merged in some bigger light, and that in a bigger still. (He looked into the hedge, into the intricacy of the twigs.) Who then could blame the leader of that forlorn party which after all has climbed high enough to see the waste of the years and the perishing of the stars, if before death stiffens his limbs beyond the power of movement he does a little consciously raise his numbed fingers to his brow, and square his shoulders, so that when the search party comes they will find him dead at his post, the fine figure of a soldier? Mr. Ramsay squared his shoulders and stood very upright by the urn.

Who shall blame him, if, so standing for a moment he dwells upon fame, upon search parties, upon cairns raised by grateful followers over his bones? Finally, who shall blame the leader of the doomed expedition, if, having adventured to the uttermost, and used his strength wholly to the last ounce and fallen asleep not much caring if he wakes or not, he now perceives by some pricking in his toes that he lives, and does not on the whole object to live, but requires sympathy, and whisky, and some one to tell the story of his suffering to at once? Who shall blame him? Who will not secretly rejoice when the hero puts his armour off, and halts by the window and gazes at his wife and son, who, very distant at first, gradually come closer and closer, till lips and book and head are clearly before him, though still lovely and unfamiliar from the intensity of his isolation and the waste of ages and the perishing of the stars, and finally putting his pipe in his pocket and bending his magnificent head before her--who will blame him if he does homage to the beauty of the world?

7

But his son hated him. He hated him for coming up to them, for stopping and looking down on them; he hated him for interrupting them; he hated him for the exaltation and sublimity of his gestures; for the magnificence of his head; for his exactingness and egotism (for there he stood, commanding them to attend to him) but most of all he hated the twang and twitter of his father's emotion which, vibrating round them, disturbed the perfect simplicity and good sense of his relations with his mother. By looking fixedly at the page, he hoped to make him move on; by pointing his finger at a word, he hoped to recall his mother's attention, which, he knew angrily, wavered instantly his father stopped. But, no. Nothing would make Mr. Ramsay move on. There he stood, demanding sympathy.

Mrs. Ramsay, who had been sitting loosely, folding her son in her arm, braced herself, and, half turning, seemed to raise herself with an effort, and at once to pour erect into the air a rain of energy, a column of spray, looking at the same time animated and alive as if all her energies were being fused into force, burning and illuminating (quietly though she sat, taking up her stocking again), and into this delicious fecundity, this fountain and spray of life, the fatal sterility of the male plunged itself, like a beak of brass, barren and bare. He wanted sympathy. He was a failure, he said. Mrs. Ramsay flashed her needles. Mr. Ramsay repeated, never taking his eyes from her face, that he was a failure. She blew the words back at him. "Charles Tansley..." she said. But he must have more than that. It was sympathy he wanted, to be assured of his genius, first of all, and then to be taken within the circle of life, warmed and soothed, to have his senses restored to him, his barrenness made fertile, and all the rooms of the house made full of life--the drawing-room; behind the drawing-room the kitchen; above the kitchen the bedrooms; and beyond them the nurseries; they must be furnished, they must be filled with life.

Charles Tansley thought him the greatest metaphysician of the time, she said. But he must have more than that. He must have sympathy. He must be assured that he too lived in the heart of life; was needed; not only here, but all over the world. Flashing her needles, confident, upright, she created drawing-room and kitchen, set them all aglow; bade him take his ease there, go in and out, enjoy himself. She laughed, she knitted. Standing between her knees, very stiff, James felt all her strength flaring up to be drunk and quenched by the beak of brass, the arid scimitar of the male, which smote mercilessly, again and again, demanding sympathy.

He was a failure, he repeated. Well, look then, feel then. Flashing her needles, glancing round about her, out of the window, into the room, at James himself, she assured him, beyond a shadow of a doubt, by her laugh, her poise, her competence (as a nurse carrying a light across a dark room assures a fractious child), that it was real; the house was full; the garden blowing. If he put implicit faith in her, nothing should hurt him; however deep he buried himself or climbed high, not for a second should he find himself without her. So boasting of her capacity to surround and protect, there was scarcely a shell of herself left for her to know herself by; all was so lavished and spent; and James, as he stood stiff between her knees, felt her rise in a rosy-flowered fruit tree laid with leaves and dancing boughs into which the beak of brass, the arid scimitar of his father, the egotistical man, plunged and smote, demanding sympathy.

Filled with her words, like a child who drops off satisfied, he said, at last, looking at her with humble gratitude, restored, renewed, that he would take a turn; he would watch the children playing cricket. He went.

Immediately, Mrs. Ramsey seemed to fold herself together, one petal closed in another, and the whole fabric fell in exhaustion upon itself, so that she had only strength enough to move her finger, in exquisite abandonment to exhaustion, across the page of Grimm's fairy story, while there throbbed through her, like a pulse in a spring which has expanded to its full width and now gently ceases to beat, the rapture of successful creation.

Every throb of this pulse seemed, as he walked away, to enclose her and her husband, and to give to each that solace which two different notes, one high, one low, struck together, seem to give each other as they combine. Yet as the resonance died, and she turned to the Fairy Tale again, Mrs. Ramsey felt not only exhausted in body (afterwards, not at the time, she always felt this) but also there tinged her physical fatigue some faintly disagreeable sensation with another origin. Not that, as she read aloud the story of the Fisherman's Wife, she knew precisely what it came from; nor did she let herself put into words her dissatisfaction when she realized, at the turn of the page when she stopped and heard dully, ominously, a wave fall, how it came from this: she did not like, even for a second, to feel finer than her husband; and further, could not bear not being entirely sure, when she spoke to him, of the truth of what she said. Universities and people wanting him, lectures and books and their being of the highest importance--all that she did not doubt for a moment; but it was their relation, and his coming to her like that, openly, so that any one could see, that discomposed her; for then people said he depended on her, when they must know that of the two he was infinitely the more important, and what she gave the world, in comparison with what he gave, negligible. But then again, it was the other thing too--not being able to tell him the truth, being afraid, for instance, about the greenhouse roof and the expense it would be, fifty pounds perhaps to mend it; and then about his books, to be afraid that he might guess, what she a little suspected, that his last book was not quite his best book (she gathered that from William Bankes); and then to hide small daily things, and the children seeing it, and the burden it laid on them--all this diminished the entire joy, the pure joy, of the two notes sounding together, and let the sound die on her ear now with a dismal flatness.

A shadow was on the page; she looked up. It was Augustus Carmichael shuffling past, precisely now, at the very moment when it was painful to be reminded of the inadequacy of human relationships, that the most perfect was flawed, and could not bear the examination which, loving her husband, with her instinct for truth, she turned upon it; when it was painful to feel herself convicted of unworthiness, and impeded in her proper function by these lies, these exaggerations,--it was at this moment when she was fretted thus ignobly in the wake of her exaltation, that Mr. Carmichael shuffled past, in his yellow slippers, and some demon in her made it necessary for her to call out, as he passed,

"Going indoors Mr. Carmichael?"

8

He said nothing. He took opium. The children said he had stained his beard yellow with it. Perhaps. What was obvious to her was that the poor man was unhappy, came to them every year as an escape; and yet every year she felt the same thing; he did not trust her. She said, "I am going to the town. Shall I get you stamps, paper, tobacco?" and she felt him wince. He did not trust her. It was his wife's doing. She remembered that iniquity of his wife's towards him, which had made her turn to steel and adamant there, in the horrible little room in St John's Wood, when with her own eyes she had seen that odious woman turn him out of the house. He was unkempt; he dropped things on his coat; he had the tiresomeness of an old man with nothing in the world to do; and she turned him out of the room. She said, in her odious way, "Now, Mrs. Ramsay and I want to have a little talk together," and Mrs. Ramsay could see, as if before her eyes, the innumerable miseries of his life. Had he money enough to buy tobacco? Did he have to ask her for it? half a crown? eighteenpence? Oh, she could not bear to think of the little indignities she made him suffer. And always now (why, she could not guess, except that it came probably from that woman somehow) he shrank from her. He never told her anything. But what more could she have done? There was a sunny room given up to him. The children were good to him. Never did she show a sign of not wanting him. She went out of her way indeed to be friendly. Do you want stamps, do you want tobacco? Here's a book you might like and so on. And after all--after all (here insensibly she drew herself together, physically, the sense of her own beauty becoming, as it did so seldom, present to her) after all, she had not generally any difficulty in making people like her; for instance, George Manning; Mr. Wallace; famous as they were, they would come to her of an evening, quietly, and talk alone over her fire. She bore about with her, she could not help knowing it, the torch of her beauty; she carried it erect into any room that she entered; and after all, veil it as she might, and shrink from the monotony of bearing that it imposed on her, her beauty was apparent. She had been admired. She had been loved. She had entered rooms where mourners sat. Tears had flown in her presence. Men, and women too, letting go to the multiplicity of things, had allowed themselves with her the relief of simplicity. It injured her that he should shrink. It hurt her. And yet not cleanly, not rightly. That was what she minded, coming as it did on top of her discontent with her husband; the sense she had now when Mr. Carmichael shuffled past, just nodding to her question, with a book beneath his arm, in his yellow slippers, that she was suspected; and that all this desire of hers to give, to help, was vanity. For her own self-satisfaction was it that she wished so instinctively to help, to give, that people might say of her, "O Mrs. Ramsay! dear Mrs. Ramsay ... Mrs. Ramsay, of course!" and need her and send for her and admire her? Was it not secretly this that she wanted, and therefore when Mr. Carmichael shrank away from her, as he did at this moment, making off to some corner where he did acrostics endlessly, she did not feel merely snubbed back in her instinct, but made aware of the pettiness of some part of her, and of human relations, how flawed they are, how despicable, how self-seeking, at their best. Shabby and worn out, and not presumably (her cheeks were hollow, her hair was white) any longer a sight that filled the eyes with joy, she had better devote her mind to the story of the Fisherman and his Wife and so pacify that bundle of sensitiveness (none of her children was as sensitive as he was), her son James.

"The man's heart grew heavy," she read aloud, "and he would not go. He said to himself, 'It is not right,' and yet he went. And when he came to the sea the water was quite purple and dark blue, and grey and thick, and no longer so green and yellow, but it was still quiet. And he stood there and said--"

Mrs. Ramsay could have wished that her husband had not chosen that moment to stop. Why had he not gone as he said to watch the children playing cricket? But he did not speak; he looked; he nodded; he approved; he went on. He slipped, seeing before him that hedge which had over and over again rounded some pause, signified some conclusion, seeing his wife and child, seeing again the urns with the trailing of red geraniums which had so often decorated processes of thought, and bore, written up among their leaves, as if they were scraps of paper on which one scribbles notes in the rush of reading--he slipped, seeing all this, smoothly into speculation suggested by an article in THE TIMES about the number of Americans who visit Shakespeare's house every year. If Shakespeare had never existed, he asked, would the world have differed much from what it is today? Does the progress of civilization depend upon great men? Is the lot of the average human being better now than in the time of the Pharaohs? Is the lot of the average human being, however, he asked himself, the criterion by which we judge the measure of civilization? Possibly not. Possibly the greatest good requires the existence of a slave class. The liftman in the Tube is an eternal necessity. The thought was distasteful to him. He tossed his head. To avoid it, he would find some way of snubbing the predominance of the arts. He would argue that the world exists for the average human being; that the arts are merely a decoration imposed on the top of human life; they do not express it. Nor is Shakespeare necessary to it. Not knowing precisely why it was that he wanted to disparage Shakespeare and come to the rescue of the man who stands eternally in the door of the lift, he picked a leaf sharply from the hedge. All this would have to be dished up for the young men at Cardiff next month, he thought; here, on his terrace, he was merely foraging and picnicking (he threw away the leaf that he had picked so peevishly) like a man who reaches from his horse to pick a bunch of roses, or stuffs his pockets with nuts as he ambles at his ease through the lanes and fields of a country known to him from boyhood. It was all familiar; this turning, that stile, that cut across the fields. Hours he would spend thus, with his pipe, of an evening, thinking up and down and in and out of the old familiar lanes and commons, which were all stuck about with the history of that campaign there, the life of this statesman here, with poems and with anecdotes, with figures too, this thinker, that soldier; all very brisk and clear; but at length the lane, the field, the common, the fruitful nut-tree and the flowering hedge led him on to that further turn of the road where he dismounted always, tied his horse to a tree, and proceeded on foot alone. He reached the edge of the lawn and looked out on the bay beneath.

It was his fate, his peculiarity, whether he wished it or not, to come out thus on a spit of land which the sea is slowly eating away, and there to stand, like a desolate sea-bird, alone. It was his power, his gift, suddenly to shed all superfluities, to shrink and diminish so that he looked barer and felt sparer, even physically, yet lost none of his intensity of mind, and so to stand on his little ledge facing the dark of human ignorance, how we know nothing and the sea eats away the ground we stand on--that was his fate, his gift. But having thrown away, when he dismounted, all gestures and fripperies, all trophies of nuts and roses, and shrunk so that not only fame but even his own name was forgotten by him, kept even in that desolation a vigilance which spared no phantom and luxuriated in no vision, and it was in this guise that he inspired in William Bankes (intermittently) and in Charles Tansley (obsequiously)and in his wife now, when she looked up and saw him standing at the edge of the lawn, profoundly, reverence, and pity, and gratitude too, as a stake driven into the bed of a channel upon which the gulls perch and the waves beat inspires in merry boat-loads a feeling of gratitude for the duty it is taking upon itself of marking the channel out there in the floods alone.

"But the father of eight children has no choice." Muttering half aloud, so he broke off, turned, sighed, raised his eyes, sought the figure of his wife reading stories to his little boy, filled his pipe. He turned from the sight of human ignorance and human fate and the sea eating the ground we stand on, which, had he been able to contemplate it fixedly might have led to something; and found consolation in trifles so slight compared with the august theme just now before him that he was disposed to slur that comfort over, to deprecate it, as if to be caught happy in a world of misery was for an honest man the most despicable of crimes. It was true; he was for the most part happy; he had his wife; he had his children; he had promised in six weeks' time to talk "some nonsense" to the young men of Cardiff about Locke, Hume, Berkeley, and the causes of the French Revolution. But this and his pleasure in it, his glory in the phrases he made, in the ardour of youth, in his wife's beauty, in the tributes that reached him from Swansea, Cardiff, Exeter, Southampton, Kidderminster, Oxford, Cambridge--all had to be deprecated and concealed under the phrase "talking nonsense," because, in effect, he had not done the thing he might have done. It was a disguise; it was the refuge of a man afraid to own his own feelings, who could not say, This is what I like--this is what I am; and rather pitiable and distasteful to William Bankes and Lily Briscoe, who wondered why such concealments should be necessary; why he needed always praise; why so brave a man in thought should be so timid in life; how strangely he was venerable and laughable at one and the same time.

Teaching and preaching is beyond human power, Lily suspected. (She was putting away her things.) If you are exalted you must somehow come a cropper. Mrs. Ramsay gave him what he asked too easily. Then the change must be so upsetting, Lily said. He comes in from his books and finds us all playing games and talking nonsense. Imagine what a change from the things he thinks about, she said.

He was bearing down upon them. Now he stopped dead and stood looking in silence at the sea. Now he had turned away again.

9

Yes, Mr. Bankes said, watching him go. It was a thousand pities. (Lily had said something about his frightening her--he changed from one mood to another so suddenly.) Yes, said Mr. Bankes, it was a thousand pities that Ramsay could not behave a little more like other people. (For he liked Lily Briscoe; he could discuss Ramsay with her quite openly.) It was for that reason, he said, that the young don't read Carlyle. A crusty old grumbler who lost his temper if the porridge was cold, why should he preach to us? was what Mr. Bankes understood that young people said nowadays. It was a thousand pities if you thought, as he did, that Carlyle was one of the great teachers of mankind. Lily was ashamed to say that she had not read Carlyle since she was at school. But in her opinion one liked Mr. Ramsay all the better for thinking that if his little finger ached the whole world must come to an end. It was not THAT she minded. For who could be deceived by him? He asked you quite openly to flatter him, to admire him, his little dodges deceived nobody. What she disliked was his narrowness, his blindness, she said, looking after him.

"A bit of a hypocrite?" Mr. Bankes suggested, looking too at Mr. Ramsay's back, for was he not thinking of his friendship, and of Cam refusing to give him a flower, and of all those boys and girls, and his own house, full of comfort, but, since his wife's death, quiet rather? Of course, he had his work... All the same, he rather wished Lily to agree that Ramsay was, as he said, "a bit of a hypocrite."

Lily Briscoe went on putting away her brushes, looking up, looking down. Looking up, there he was--Mr. Ramsay--advancing towards them, swinging, careless, oblivious, remote. A bit of a hypocrite? she repeated. Oh, no--the most sincere of men, the truest (here he was), the best; but, looking down, she thought, he is absorbed in himself, he is tyrannical, he is unjust; and kept looking down, purposely, for only so could she keep steady, staying with the Ramsays. Directly one looked up and saw them, what she called "being in love" flooded them. They became part of that unreal but penetrating and exciting universe which is the world seen through the eyes of love. The sky stuck to them; the birds sang through them. And, what was even more exciting, she felt, too, as she saw Mr. Ramsay bearing down and retreating, and Mrs. Ramsay sitting with James in the window and the cloud moving and the tree bending, how life, from being made up of little separate incidents which one lived one by one, became curled and whole like a wave which bore one up and threw one down with it, there, with a dash on the beach.

Mr. Bankes expected her to answer. And she was about to say something criticizing Mrs. Ramsay, how she was alarming, too, in her way, high-handed, or words to that effect, when Mr. Bankes made it entirely unnecessary for her to speak by his rapture. For such it was considering his age, turned sixty, and his cleanliness and his impersonality, and the white scientific coat which seemed to clothe him. For him to gaze as Lily saw him gazing at Mrs. Ramsay was a rapture, equivalent, Lily felt, to the loves of dozens of young men (and perhaps Mrs. Ramsay had never excited the loves of dozens of young men). It was love, she thought, pretending to move her canvas, distilled and filtered; love that never attempted to clutch its object; but, like the love which mathematicians bear their symbols, or poets their phrases, was meant to be spread over the world and become part of the human gain. So it was indeed. The world by all means should have shared it, could Mr. Bankes have said why that woman pleased him so; why the sight of her reading a fairy tale to her boy had upon him precisely the same effect as the solution of a scientific problem, so that he rested in contemplation of it, and felt, as he felt when he had proved something absolute about the digestive system of plants, that barbarity was tamed, the reign of chaos subdued.

Such a rapture--for by what other name could one call it?--made Lily Briscoe forget entirely what she had been about to say. It was nothing of importance; something about Mrs. Ramsay. It paled beside this "rapture," this silent stare, for which she felt intense gratitude; for nothing so solaced her, eased her of the perplexity of life, and miraculously raised its burdens, as this sublime power, this heavenly gift, and one would no more disturb it, while it lasted, than break up the shaft of sunlight, lying level across the floor.

That people should love like this, that Mr. Bankes should feel this for Mrs. Ramsey (she glanced at him musing) was helpful, was exalting. She wiped one brush after another upon a piece of old rag, menially, on purpose. She took shelter from the reverence which covered all women; she felt herself praised. Let him gaze; she would steal a look at her picture.

She could have wept. It was bad, it was bad, it was infinitely bad! She could have done it differently of course; the colour could have been thinned and faded; the shapes etherealised; that was how Paunceforte would have seen it. But then she did not see it like that. She saw the colour burning on a framework of steel; the light of a butterfly's wing lying upon the arches of a cathedral. Of all that only a few random marks scrawled upon the canvas remained. And it would never be seen; never be hung even, and there was Mr. Tansley whispering in her ear, "Women can't paint, women can't write ..."

She now remembered what she had been going to say about Mrs. Ramsay. She did not know how she would have put it; but it would have been something critical. She had been annoyed the other night by some highhandedness. Looking along the level of Mr. Bankes's glance at her, she thought that no woman could worship another woman in the way he worshipped; they could only seek shelter under the shade which Mr. Bankes extended over them both. Looking along his beam she added to it her different ray, thinking that she was unquestionably the loveliest of people (bowed over her book); the best perhaps; but also, different too from the perfect shape which one saw there. But why different, and how different? she asked herself, scraping her palette of all those mounds of blue and green which seemed to her like clods with no life in them now, yet she vowed, she would inspire them, force them to move, flow, do her bidding tomorrow. How did she differ? What was the spirit in her, the essential thing, by which, had you found a crumpled glove in the corner of a sofa, you would have known it, from its twisted finger, hers indisputably? She was like a bird for speed, an arrow for directness. She was willful; she was commanding (of course, Lily reminded herself, I am thinking of her relations with women, and I am much younger, an insignificant person, living off the Brompton Road). She opened bedroom windows. She shut doors. (So she tried to start the tune of Mrs. Ramsay in her head.) Arriving late at night, with a light tap on one's bedroom door, wrapped in an old fur coat (for the setting of her beauty was always that--hasty, but apt), she would enact again whatever it might be--Charles Tansley losing his umbrella; Mr. Carmichael snuffling and sniffing; Mr. Bankes saying, "The vegetable salts are lost." All this she would adroitly shape; even maliciously twist; and, moving over to the window, in pretence that she must go,--it was dawn, she could see the sun rising,--half turn back, more intimately, but still always laughing, insist that she must, Minta must, they all must marry, since in the whole world whatever laurels might be tossed to her (but Mrs. Ramsay cared not a fig for her painting), or triumphs won by her (probably Mrs. Ramsay had had her share of those), and here she saddened, darkened, and came back to her chair, there could be no disputing this: an unmarried woman (she lightly took her hand for a moment), an unmarried woman has missed the best of life. The house seemed full of children sleeping and Mrs. Ramsay listening; shaded lights and regular breathing.

Oh, but, Lily would say, there was her father; her home; even, had she dared to say it, her painting. But all this seemed so little, so virginal, against the other. Yet, as the night wore on, and white lights parted the curtains, and even now and then some bird chirped in the garden, gathering a desperate courage she would urge her own exemption from the universal law; plead for it; she liked to be alone; she liked to be herself; she was not made for that; and so have to meet a serious stare from eyes of unparalleled depth, and confront Mrs. Ramsay's simple certainty (and she was childlike now) that her dear Lily, her little Brisk, was a fool. Then, she remembered, she had laid her head on Mrs. Ramsay's lap and laughed and laughed and laughed, laughed almost hysterically at the thought of Mrs. Ramsay presiding with immutable calm over destinies which she completely failed to understand. There she sat, simple, serious. She had recovered her sense of her now--this was the glove's twisted finger. But into what sanctuary had one penetrated? Lily Briscoe had looked up at last, and there was Mrs. Ramsay, unwitting entirely what had caused her laughter, still presiding, but now with every trace of wilfulness abolished, and in its stead, something clear as the space which the clouds at last uncover--the little space of sky which sleeps beside the moon.

Was it wisdom? Was it knowledge? Was it, once more, the deceptiveness of beauty, so that all one's perceptions, half way to truth, were tangled in a golden mesh? or did she lock up within her some secret which certainly Lily Briscoe believed people must have for the world to go on at all? Every one could not be as helter skelter, hand to mouth as she was. But if they knew, could they tell one what they knew? Sitting on the floor with her arms round Mrs. Ramsay's knees, close as she could get, smiling to think that Mrs. Ramsay would never know the reason of that pressure, she imagined how in the chambers of the mind and heart of the woman who was, physically, touching her, were stood, like the treasures in the tombs of kings, tablets bearing sacred inscriptions, which if one could spell them out, would teach one everything, but they would never be offered openly, never made public. What art was there, known to love or cunning, by which one pressed through into those secret chambers? What device for becoming, like waters poured into one jar, inextricably the same, one with the object one adored? Could the body achieve, or the mind, subtly mingling in the intricate passages of the brain? or the heart? Could loving, as people called it, make her and Mrs. Ramsay one? for it was not knowledge but unity that she desired, not inscriptions on tablets, nothing that could be written in any language known to men, but intimacy itself, which is knowledge, she had thought, leaning her head on Mrs. Ramsay's knee.

Nothing happened. Nothing! Nothing! as she leant her head against Mrs. Ramsay's knee. And yet, she knew knowledge and wisdom were stored up in Mrs. Ramsay's heart. How, then, she had asked herself, did one know one thing or another thing about people, sealed as they were? Only like a bee, drawn by some sweetness or sharpness in the air intangible to touch or taste, one haunted the dome-shaped hive, ranged the wastes of the air over the countries of the world alone, and then haunted the hives with their murmurs and their stirrings; the hives, which were people. Mrs. Ramsay rose. Lily rose. Mrs. Ramsay went. For days there hung about her, as after a dream some subtle change is felt in the person one has dreamt of, more vividly than anything she said, the sound of murmuring and, as she sat in the wicker arm-chair in the drawing-room window she wore, to Lily's eyes, an august shape; the shape of a dome.

This ray passed level with Mr. Bankes's ray straight to Mrs. Ramsay sitting reading there with James at her knee. But now while she still looked, Mr. Bankes had done. He had put on his spectacles. He had stepped back. He had raised his hand. He had slightly narrowed his clear blue eyes, when Lily, rousing herself, saw what he was at, and winced like a dog who sees a hand raised to strike it. She would have snatched her picture off the easel, but she said to herself, One must. She braced herself to stand the awful trial of some one looking at her picture. One must, she said, one must. And if it must be seen, Mr. Bankes was less alarming than another. But that any other eyes should see the residue of her thirty-three years, the deposit of each day's living mixed with something more secret than she had ever spoken or shown in the course of all those days was an agony. At the same time it was immensely exciting.

Nothing could be cooler and quieter. Taking out a pen-knife, Mr. Bankes tapped the canvas with the bone handle. What did she wish to indicate by the triangular purple shape, "just there"? he asked.

It was Mrs. Ramsay reading to James, she said. She knew his objection-- that no one could tell it for a human shape. But she had made no attempt at likeness, she said. For what reason had she introduced them then? he asked. Why indeed?--except that if there, in that corner, it was bright, here, in this, she felt the need of darkness. Simple, obvious, commonplace, as it was, Mr. Bankes was interested. Mother and child then--objects of universal veneration, and in this case the mother was famous for her beauty--might be reduced, he pondered, to a purple shadow without irreverence.

But the picture was not of them, she said. Or, not in his sense. There were other senses too in which one might reverence them. By a shadow here and a light there, for instance. Her tribute took that form if, as she vaguely supposed, a picture must be a tribute. A mother and child might be reduced to a shadow without irreverence. A light here required a shadow there. He considered. He was interested. He took it scientifically in complete good faith. The truth was that all his prejudices were on the other side, he explained. The largest picture in his drawing-room, which painters had praised, and valued at a higher price than he had given for it, was of the cherry trees in blossom on the banks of the Kennet. He had spent his honeymoon on the banks of the Kennet, he said. Lily must come and see that picture, he said. But now--he turned, with his glasses raised to the scientific examination of her canvas. The question being one of the relations of masses, of lights and shadows, which, to be honest, he had never considered before, he would like to have it explained--what then did she wish to make of it? And he indicated the scene before them. She looked. She could not show him what she wished to make of it, could not see it even herself, without a brush in her hand. She took up once more her old painting position with the dim eyes and the absent-minded manner, subduing all her impressions as a woman to something much more general; becoming once more under the power of that vision which she had seen clearly once and must now grope for among hedges and houses and mothers and children--her picture. It was a question, she remembered, how to connect this mass on the right hand with that on the left. She might do it by bringing the line of the branch across so; or break the vacancy in the foreground by an object (James perhaps) so. But the danger was that by doing that the unity of the whole might be broken. She stopped; she did not want to bore him; she took the canvas lightly off the easel.

But it had been seen; it had been taken from her. This man had shared with her something profoundly intimate. And, thanking Mr. Ramsay for it and Mrs. Ramsay for it and the hour and the place, crediting the world with a power which she had not suspected--that one could walk away down that long gallery not alone any more but arm in arm with somebody--the strangest feeling in the world, and the most exhilarating--she nicked the catch of her paint-box to, more firmly than was necessary, and the nick seemed to surround in a circle forever the paint-box, the lawn, Mr. Bankes, and that wild villain, Cam, dashing past.

10

For Cam grazed the easel by an inch; she would not stop for Mr. Bankes and Lily Briscoe; though Mr. Bankes, who would have liked a daughter of his own, held out his hand; she would not stop for her father, whom she grazed also by an inch; nor for her mother, who called "Cam! I want you a moment!" as she dashed past. She was off like a bird, bullet, or arrow, impelled by what desire, shot by whom, at what directed, who could say? What, what? Mrs. Ramsay pondered, watching her. It might be a vision--of a shell, of a wheelbarrow, of a fairy kingdom on the far side of the hedge; or it might be the glory of speed; no one knew. But when Mrs. Ramsay called "Cam!" a second time, the projectile dropped in mid career, and Cam came lagging back, pulling a leaf by the way, to her mother.

What was she dreaming about, Mrs. Ramsay wondered, seeing her engrossed, as she stood there, with some thought of her own, so that she had to repeat the message twice--ask Mildred if Andrew, Miss Doyle, and Mr. Rayley have come back?--The words seemed to be dropped into a well, where, if the waters were clear, they were also so extraordinarily distorting that, even as they descended, one saw them twisting about to make Heaven knows what pattern on the floor of the child's mind. What message would Cam give the cook? Mrs. Ramsay wondered. And indeed it was only by waiting patiently, and hearing that there was an old woman in the kitchen with very red cheeks, drinking soup out of a basin, that Mrs. Ramsay at last prompted that parrot-like instinct which had picked up Mildred's words quite accurately and could now produce them, if one waited, in a colourless singsong. Shifting from foot to foot, Cam repeated the words, "No, they haven't, and I've told Ellen to clear away tea."

Minta Doyle and Paul Rayley had not come back then. That could only mean, Mrs. Ramsay thought, one thing. She must accept him, or she must refuse him. This going off after luncheon for a walk, even though Andrew was with them--what could it mean? except that she had decided, rightly, Mrs. Ramsay thought (and she was very, very fond of Minta), to accept that good fellow, who might not be brilliant, but then, thought Mrs. Ramsay, realising that James was tugging at her, to make her go on reading aloud the Fisherman and his Wife, she did in her own heart infinitely prefer boobies to clever men who wrote dissertations; Charles Tansley, for instance. Anyhow it must have happened, one way or the other, by now.

But she read, "Next morning the wife awoke first, and it was just daybreak, and from her bed she saw the beautiful country lying before her. Her husband was still stretching himself..."

But how could Minta say now that she would not have him? Not if she agreed to spend whole afternoons trapesing about the country alone--for Andrew would be off after his crabs--but possibly Nancy was with them. She tried to recall the sight of them standing at the hall door after lunch. There they stood, looking at the sky, wondering about the weather, and she had said, thinking partly to cover their shyness, partly to encourage them to be off (for her sympathies were with Paul),

"There isn't a cloud anywhere within miles," at which she could feel little Charles Tansley, who had followed them out, snigger. But she did it on purpose. Whether Nancy was there or not, she could not be certain, looking from one to the other in her mind's eye.

She read on: "Ah, wife," said the man, "why should we be King? I do not want to be King." "Well," said the wife, "if you won't be King, I will; go to the Flounder, for I will be King."

"Come in or go out, Cam," she said, knowing that Cam was attracted only by the word "Flounder" and that in a moment she would fidget and fight with James as usual. Cam shot off. Mrs. Ramsay went on reading, relieved, for she and James shared the same tastes and were comfortable together.

"And when he came to the sea, it was quite dark grey, and the water heaved up from below, and smelt putrid. Then he went and stood by it and said,

'Flounder, flounder, in the sea, Come, I pray thee, here to me; For my wife, good Ilsabil, Wills not as I'd have her will.'

'Well, what does she want then?' said the Flounder." And where were they now? Mrs. Ramsay wondered, reading and thinking, quite easily, both at the same time; for the story of the Fisherman and his Wife was like the bass gently accompanying a tune, which now and then ran up unexpectedly into the melody. And when should she be told? If nothing happened, she would have to speak seriously to Minta. For she could not go trapesing about all over the country, even if Nancy were with them (she tried again, unsuccessfully, to visualize their backs going down the path, and to count them). She was responsible to Minta's parents--the Owl and the Poker. Her nicknames for them shot into her mind as she read. The Owl and the Poker--yes, they would be annoyed if they heard--and they were certain to hear--that Minta, staying with the Ramsays, had been seen etcetera, etcetera, etcetera. "He wore a wig in the House of Commons and she ably assisted him at the head of the stairs," she repeated, fishing them up out of her mind by a phrase which, coming back from some party, she had made to amuse her husband. Dear, dear, Mrs. Ramsay said to herself, how did they produce this incongruous daughter? this tomboy Minta, with a hole in her stocking? How did she exist in that portentous atmosphere where the maid was always removing in a dust-pan the sand that the parrot had scattered, and conversation was almost entirely reduced to the exploits--interesting perhaps, but limited after all--of that bird? Naturally, one had asked her to lunch, tea, dinner, finally to stay with them up at Finlay, which had resulted in some friction with the Owl, her mother, and more calling, and more conversation, and more sand, and really at the end of it, she had told enough lies about parrots to last her a lifetime (so she had said to her husband that night, coming back from the party). However, Minta came...Yes, she came, Mrs. Ramsay thought, suspecting some thorn in the tangle of this thought; and disengaging it found it to be this: a woman had once accused her of "robbing her of her daughter's affections"; something Mrs. Doyle had said made her remember that charge again. Wishing to dominate, wishing to interfere, making people do what she wished--that was the charge against her, and she thought it most unjust.

How could she help being "like that" to look at? No one could accuse her of taking pains to impress. She was often ashamed of her own shabbiness. Nor was she domineering, nor was she tyrannical. It was more true about hospitals and drains and the dairy. About things like that she did feel passionately, and would, if she had the chance, have liked to take people by the scruff of their necks and make them see. No hospital on the whole island. It was a disgrace. Milk delivered at your door in London positively brown with dirt. It should be made illegal. A model dairy and a hospital up here--those two things she would have liked to do, herself. But how? With all these children? When they were older, then perhaps she would have time; when they were all at school.

Oh, but she never wanted James to grow a day older! or Cam either. These two she would have liked to keep for ever just as they were, demons of wickedness, angels of delight, never to see them grow up into long-legged monsters. Nothing made up up for the loss. When she read just now to James, "and there were numbers of soldiers with kettledrums and trumpets," and his eyes darkened, she thought, why should they grow up and lose all that? He was the most gifted, the most sensitive of her children. But all, she thought, were full of promise. Prue, a perfect angel with the others, and sometimes now, at night especially, she took one's breath away with her beauty. Andrew--even her husband admitted that his gift for mathematics was extraordinary. And Nancy and Roger, they were both wild creatures now, scampering about over the country all day long. As for Rose, her mouth was too big, but she had a wonderful gift with her hands. If they had charades, Rose made the dresses; made everything; liked best arranging tables, flowers, anything. She did not like it that Jasper should shoot birds; but it was only a stage; they all went through stages. Why, she asked, pressing her chin on James's head, should they grow up so fast? Why should they go to school? She would have liked always to have had a baby. She was happiest carrying one in her arms. Then people might say she was tyrannical, domineering, masterful, if they chose; she did not mind. And, touching his hair with her lips, she thought, he will never be so happy again, but stopped herself, remembering how it angered her husband that she should say that. Still, it was true. They were happier now than they would ever be again. A tenpenny tea set made Cam happy for days. She heard them stamping and crowing on the floor above her head the moment they awoke. They came bustling along the passage. Then the door sprang open and in they came, fresh as roses, staring, wide awake, as if this coming into the dining-room after breakfast, which they did every day of their lives, was a positive event to them, and so on, with one thing after another, all day long, until she went up to say good-night to them, and found them netted in their cots like birds among cherries and raspberries, still making up stories about some little bit of rubbish--something they had heard, something they had picked up in the garden. They all had their little treasures... And so she went down and said to her husband, Why must they grow up and lose it all? Never will they be so happy again. And he was angry. Why take such a gloomy view of life? he said. It is not sensible. For it was odd; and she believed it to be true; that with all his gloom and desperation he was happier, more hopeful on the whole, than she was. Less exposed to human worries--perhaps that was it. He had always his work to fall back on. Not that she herself was "pessimistic," as he accused her of being. Only she thought life--and a little strip of time presented itself to her eyes--her fifty years. There it was before her--life. Life, she thought--but she did not finish her thought. She took a look at life, for she had a clear sense of it there, something real, something private, which she shared neither with her children nor with her husband. A sort of transaction went on between them, in which she was on one side, and life was on another, and she was always trying to get the better of it, as it was of her; and sometimes they parleyed (when she sat alone); there were, she remembered, great reconciliation scenes; but for the most part, oddly enough, she must admit that she felt this thing that she called life terrible, hostile, and quick to pounce on you if you gave it a chance. There were eternal problems: suffering; death; the poor. There was always a woman dying of cancer even here. And yet she had said to all these children, You shall go through it all. To eight people she had said relentlessly that (and the bill for the greenhouse would be fifty pounds). For that reason, knowing what was before them--love and ambition and being wretched alone in dreary places--she had often the feeling, Why must they grow up and lose it all? And then she said to herself, brandishing her sword at life, Nonsense. They will be perfectly happy. And here she was, she reflected, feeling life rather sinister again, making Minta marry Paul Rayley; because whatever she might feel about her own transaction, she had had experiences which need not happen to every one (she did not name them to herself); she was driven on, too quickly she knew, almost as if it were an escape for her too, to say that people must marry; people must have children.

Was she wrong in this, she asked herself, reviewing her conduct for the past week or two, and wondering if she had indeed put any pressure upon Minta, who was only twenty-four, to make up her mind. She was uneasy. Had she not laughed about it? Was she not forgetting again how strongly she influenced people? Marriage needed--oh, all sorts of qualities (the bill for the greenhouse would be fifty pounds); one--she need not name it--that was essential; the thing she had with her husband. Had they that?

"Then he put on his trousers and ran away like a madman," she read. "But outside a great storm was raging and blowing so hard that he could scarcely keep his feet; houses and trees toppled over, the mountains trembled, rocks rolled into the sea, the sky was pitch black, and it thundered and lightened, and the sea came in with black waves as high as church towers and mountains, and all with white foam at the top."

She turned the page; there were only a few lines more, so that she would finish the story, though it was past bed-time. It was getting late. The light in the garden told her that; and the whitening of the flowers and something grey in the leaves conspired together, to rouse in her a feeling of anxiety. What it was about she could not think at first. Then she remembered; Paul and Minta and Andrew had not come back. She summoned before her again the little group on the terrace in front of the hall door, standing looking up into the sky. Andrew had his net and basket. That meant he was going to catch crabs and things. That meant he would climb out on to a rock; he would be cut off. Or coming back single file on one of those little paths above the cliff one of them might slip. He would roll and then crash. It was growing quite dark.

But she did not let her voice change in the least as she finished the story, and added, shutting the book, and speaking the last words as if she had made them up herself, looking into James's eyes: "And there they are living still at this very time."

"And that's the end," she said, and she saw in his eyes, as the interest of the story died away in them, something else take its place; something wondering, pale, like the reflection of a light, which at once made him gaze and marvel. Turning, she looked across the bay, and there, sure enough, coming regularly across the waves first two quick strokes and then one long steady stroke, was the light of the Lighthouse. It had been lit.

In a moment he would ask her, "Are we going to the Lighthouse?" And she would have to say, "No: not tomorrow; your father says not." Happily, Mildred came in to fetch them, and the bustle distracted them. But he kept looking back over his shoulder as Mildred carried him out, and she was certain that he was thinking, we are not going to the Lighthouse tomorrow; and she thought, he will remember that all his life.

11

No, she thought, putting together some of the pictures he had cut out-- a refrigerator, a mowing machine, a gentleman in evening dress-- children never forget. For this reason, it was so important what one said, and what one did, and it was a relief when they went to bed. For now she need not think about anybody. She could be herself, by herself. And that was what now she often felt the need of--to think; well, not even to think. To be silent; to be alone. All the being and the doing, expansive, glittering, vocal, evaporated; and one shrunk, with a sense of solemnity, to being oneself, a wedge-shaped core of darkness, something invisible to others. Although she continued to knit, and sat upright, it was thus that she felt herself; and this self having shed its attachments was free for the strangest adventures. When life sank down for a moment, the range of experience seemed limitless. And to everybody there was always this sense of unlimited resources, she supposed; one after another, she, Lily, Augustus Carmichael, must feel, our apparitions, the things you know us by, are simply childish. Beneath it is all dark, it is all spreading, it is unfathomably deep; but now and again we rise to the surface and that is what you see us by. Her horizon seemed to her limitless. There were all the places she had not seen; the Indian plains; she felt herself pushing aside the thick leather curtain of a church in Rome. This core of darkness could go anywhere, for no one saw it. They could not stop it, she thought, exulting. There was freedom, there was peace, there was, most welcome of all, a summoning together, a resting on a platform of stability. Not as oneself did one find rest ever, in her experience (she accomplished here something dexterous with her needles) but as a wedge of darkness. Losing personality, one lost the fret, the hurry, the stir; and there rose to her lips always some exclamation of triumph over life when things came together in this peace, this rest, this eternity; and pausing there she looked out to meet that stroke of the Lighthouse, the long steady stroke, the last of the three, which was her stroke, for watching them in this mood always at this hour one could not help attaching oneself to one thing especially of the things one saw; and this thing, the long steady stroke, was her stroke. Often she found herself sitting and looking, sitting and looking, with her work in her hands until she became the thing she looked at--that light, for example. And it would lift up on it some little phrase or other which had been lying in her mind like that--"Children don't forget, children don't forget"--which she would repeat and begin adding to it, It will end, it will end, she said. It will come, it will come, when suddenly she added, We are in the hands of the Lord.

But instantly she was annoyed with herself for saying that. Who had said it? Not she; she had been trapped into saying something she did not mean. She looked up over her knitting and met the third stroke and it seemed to her like her own eyes meeting her own eyes, searching as she alone could search into her mind and her heart, purifying out of existence that lie, any lie. She praised herself in praising the light, without vanity, for she was stern, she was searching, she was beautiful like that light. It was odd, she thought, how if one was alone, one leant to inanimate things; trees, streams, flowers; felt they expressed one; felt they became one; felt they knew one, in a sense were one; felt an irrational tenderness thus (she looked at that long steady light) as for oneself. There rose, and she looked and looked with her needles suspended, there curled up off the floor of the mind, rose from the lake of one's being, a mist, a bride to meet her lover.

What brought her to say that: "We are in the hands of the Lord?" she wondered. The insincerity slipping in among the truths roused her, annoyed her. She returned to her knitting again. How could any Lord have made this world? she asked. With her mind she had always seized the fact that there is no reason, order, justice: but suffering, death, the poor. There was no treachery too base for the world to commit; she knew that. No happiness lasted; she knew that. She knitted with firm composure, slightly pursing her lips and, without being aware of it, so stiffened and composed the lines of her face in a habit of sternness that when her husband passed, though he was chuckling at the thought that Hume, the philosopher, grown enormously fat, had stuck in a bog, he could not help noting, as he passed, the sternness at the heart of her beauty. It saddened him, and her remoteness pained him, and he felt, as he passed, that he could not protect her, and, when he reached the hedge, he was sad. He could do nothing to help her. He must stand by and watch her. Indeed, the infernal truth was, he made things worse for her. He was irritable--he was touchy. He had lost his temper over the Lighthouse. He looked into the hedge, into its intricacy, its darkness.

Always, Mrs. Ramsay felt, one helped oneself out of solitude reluctantly by laying hold of some little odd or end, some sound, some sight. She listened, but it was all very still; cricket was over; the children were in their baths; there was only the sound of the sea. She stopped knitting; she held the long reddish-brown stocking dangling in her hands a moment. She saw the light again. With some irony in her interrogation, for when one woke at all, one's relations changed, she looked at the steady light, the pitiless, the remorseless, which was so much her, yet so little her, which had her at its beck and call (she woke in the night and saw it bent across their bed, stroking the floor), but for all that she thought, watching it with fascination, hypnotised, as if it were stroking with its silver fingers some sealed vessel in her brain whose bursting would flood her with delight, she had known happiness, exquisite happiness, intense happiness, and it silvered the rough waves a little more brightly, as daylight faded, and the blue went out of the sea and it rolled in waves of pure lemon which curved and swelled and broke upon the beach and the ecstasy burst in her eyes and waves of pure delight raced over the floor of her mind and she felt, It is enough! It is enough!

He turned and saw her. Ah! She was lovely, lovelier now than ever he thought. But he could not speak to her. He could not interrupt her. He wanted urgently to speak to her now that James was gone and she was alone at last. But he resolved, no; he would not interrupt her. She was aloof from him now in her beauty, in her sadness. He would let her be, and he passed her without a word, though it hurt him that she should look so distant, and he could not reach her, he could do nothing to help her. And again he would have passed her without a word had she not, at that very moment, given him of her own free will what she knew he would never ask, and called to him and taken the green shawl off the picture frame, and gone to him. For he wished, she knew, to protect her.

12

She folded the green shawl about her shoulders. She took his arm. His beauty was so great, she said, beginning to speak of Kennedy the gardener, at once he was so awfully handsome, that she couldn't dismiss him. There was a ladder against the greenhouse, and little lumps of putty stuck about, for they were beginning to mend the greenhouse. Yes, but as she strolled along with her husband, she felt that that particular source of worry had been placed. She had it on the tip of her tongue to say, as they strolled, "It'll cost fifty pounds," but instead, for her heart failed her about money, she talked about Jasper shooting birds, and he said, at once, soothing her instantly, that it was natural in a boy, and he trusted he would find better ways of amusing himself before long. Her husband was so sensible, so just. And so she said, "Yes; all children go through stages," and began considering the dahlias in the big bed, and wondering what about next year's flowers, and had he heard the children's nickname for Charles Tansley, she asked. The atheist, they called him, the little atheist. "He's not a polished specimen," said Mr. Ramsay. "Far from it," said Mrs. Ramsay.

She supposed it was all right leaving him to his own devices, Mrs. Ramsay said, wondering whether it was any use sending down bulbs; did they plant them? "Oh, he has his dissertation to write," said Mr. Ramsay. She knew all about THAT, said Mrs. Ramsay. He talked of nothing else. It was about the influence of somebody upon something. "Well, it's all he has to count on," said Mr. Ramsay. "Pray Heaven he won't fall in love with Prue," said Mrs. Ramsay. He'd disinherit her if she married him, said Mr. Ramsay. He did not look at the flowers, which his wife was considering, but at a spot about a foot or so above them. There was no harm in him, he added, and was just about to say that anyhow he was the only young man in England who admired his--when he choked it back. He would not bother her again about his books. These flowers seemed creditable, Mr. Ramsay said, lowering his gaze and noticing something red, something brown. Yes, but then these she had put in with her own hands, said Mrs. Ramsay. The question was, what happened if she sent bulbs down; did Kennedy plant them? It was his incurable laziness; she added, moving on. If she stood over him all day long with a spade in her hand, he did sometimes do a stroke of work. So they strolled along, towards the red-hot pokers. "You're teaching your daughters to exaggerate," said Mr. Ramsay, reproving her. Her Aunt Camilla was far worse than she was, Mrs. Ramsay remarked. "Nobody ever held up your Aunt Camilla as a model of virtue that I'm aware of," said Mr. Ramsay. "She was the most beautiful woman I ever saw," said Mrs. Ramsay. "Somebody else was that," said Mr. Ramsay. Prue was going to be far more beautiful than she was, said Mrs. Ramsay. He saw no trace of it, said Mr. Ramsay. "Well, then, look tonight," said Mrs. Ramsay. They paused. He wished Andrew could be induced to work harder. He would lose every chance of a scholarship if he didn't. "Oh, scholarships!" she said. Mr. Ramsay thought her foolish for saying that, about a serious thing, like a scholarship. He should be very proud of Andrew if he got a scholarship, he said. She would be just as proud of him if he didn't, she answered. They disagreed always about this, but it did not matter. She liked him to believe in scholarships, and he liked her to be proud of Andrew whatever he did. Suddenly she remembered those little paths on the edge of the cliffs.

Wasn't it late? she asked. They hadn't come home yet. He flicked his watch carelessly open. But it was only just past seven. He held his watch open for a moment, deciding that he would tell her what he had felt on the terrace. To begin with, it was not reasonable to be so nervous. Andrew could look after himself. Then, he wanted to tell her that when he was walking on the terrace just now--here he became uncomfortable, as if he were breaking into that solitude, that aloofness, that remoteness of hers. But she pressed him. What had he wanted to tell her, she asked, thinking it was about going to the Lighthouse; that he was sorry he had said "Damn you." But no. He did not like to see her look so sad, he said. Only wool gathering, she protested, flushing a little. They both felt uncomfortable, as if they did not know whether to go on or go back. She had been reading fairy tales to James, she said. No, they could not share that; they could not say that.

They had reached the gap between the two clumps of red-hot pokers, and there was the Lighthouse again, but she would not let herself look at it. Had she known that he was looking at her, she thought, she would not have let herself sit there, thinking. She disliked anything that reminded her that she had been seen sitting thinking. So she looked over her shoulder, at the town. The lights were rippling and running as if they were drops of silver water held firm in a wind. And all the poverty, all the suffering had turned to that, Mrs. Ramsay thought. The lights of the town and of the harbour and of the boats seemed like a phantom net floating there to mark something which had sunk. Well, if he could not share her thoughts, Mr. Ramsay said to himself, he would be off, then, on his own. He wanted to go on thinking, telling himself the story how Hume was stuck in a bog; he wanted to laugh. But first it was nonsense to be anxious about Andrew. When he was Andrew's age he used to walk about the country all day long, with nothing but a biscuit in his pocket and nobody bothered about him, or thought that he had fallen over a cliff. He said aloud he thought he would be off for a day's walk if the weather held. He had had about enough of Bankes and of Carmichael. He would like a little solitude. Yes, she said. It annoyed him that she did not protest. She knew that he would never do it. He was too old now to walk all day long with a biscuit in his pocket. She worried about the boys, but not about him. Years ago, before he had married, he thought, looking across the bay, as they stood between the clumps of red-hot pokers, he had walked all day. He had made a meal off bread and cheese in a public house. He had worked ten hours at a stretch; an old woman just popped her head in now and again and saw to the fire. That was the country he liked best, over there; those sandhills dwindling away into darkness. One could walk all day without meeting a soul. There was not a house scarcely, not a single village for miles on end. One could worry things out alone. There were little sandy beaches where no one had been since the beginning of time. The seals sat up and looked at you. It sometimes seemed to him that in a little house out there, alone--he broke off, sighing. He had no right. The father of eight children--he reminded himself. And he would have been a beast and a cur to wish a single thing altered. Andrew would be a better man than he had been. Prue would be a beauty, her mother said. They would stem the flood a bit. That was a good bit of work on the whole--his eight children. They showed he did not damn the poor little universe entirely, for on an evening like this, he thought, looking at the land dwindling away, the little island seemed pathetically small, half swallowed up in the sea.

"Poor little place," he murmured with a sigh.

She heard him. He said the most melancholy things, but she noticed that directly he had said them he always seemed more cheerful than usual. All this phrase-making was a game, she thought, for if she had said half what he said, she would have blown her brains out by now.

It annoyed her, this phrase-making, and she said to him, in a matter- of-fact way, that it was a perfectly lovely evening. And what was he groaning about, she asked, half laughing, half complaining, for she guessed what he was thinking--he would have written better books if he had not married.

He was not complaining, he said. She knew that he did not complain. She knew that he had nothing whatever to complain of. And he seized her hand and raised it to his lips and kissed it with an intensity that brought the tears to her eyes, and quickly he dropped it.

They turned away from the view and began to walk up the path where the silver-green spear-like plants grew, arm in arm. His arm was almost like a young man's arm, Mrs. Ramsay thought, thin and hard, and she thought with delight how strong he still was, though he was over sixty, and how untamed and optimistic, and how strange it was that being convinced, as he was, of all sorts of horrors, seemed not to depress him, but to cheer him. Was it not odd, she reflected? Indeed he seemed to her sometimes made differently from other people, born blind, deaf, and dumb, to the ordinary things, but to the extraordinary things, with an eye like an eagle's. His understanding often astonished her. But did he notice the flowers? No. Did he notice the view? No. Did he even notice his own daughter's beauty, or whether there was pudding on his plate or roast beef? He would sit at table with them like a person in a dream. And his habit of talking aloud, or saying poetry aloud, was growing on him, she was afraid; for sometimes it was awkward--

Best and brightest come away!

poor Miss Giddings, when he shouted that at her, almost jumped out of her skin. But then, Mrs. Ramsay, though instantly taking his side against all the silly Giddingses in the world, then, she thought, intimating by a little pressure on his arm that he walked up hill too fast for her, and she must stop for a moment to see whether those were fresh molehills on the bank, then, she thought, stooping down to look, a great mind like his must be different in every way from ours. All the great men she had ever known, she thought, deciding that a rabbit must have got in, were like that, and it was good for young men (though the atmosphere of lecture-rooms was stuffy and depressing to her beyond endurance almost) simply to hear him, simply to look at him. But without shooting rabbits, how was one to keep them down? she wondered. It might be a rabbit; it might be a mole. Some creature anyhow was ruining her Evening Primroses. And looking up, she saw above the thin trees the first pulse of the full-throbbing star, and wanted to make her husband look at it; for the sight gave her such keen pleasure. But she stopped herself. He never looked at things. If he did, all he would say would be, Poor little world, with one of his sighs.

At that moment, he said, "Very fine," to please her, and pretended to admire the flowers. But she knew quite well that he did not admire them, or even realise that they were there. It was only to please her. Ah, but was that not Lily Briscoe strolling along with William Bankes? She focussed her short-sighted eyes upon the backs of a retreating couple. Yes, indeed it was. Did that not mean that they would marry? Yes, it must! What an admirable idea! They must marry!

13

He had been to Amsterdam, Mr. Bankes was saying as he strolled across the lawn with Lily Briscoe. He had seen the Rembrandts. He had been to Madrid. Unfortunately, it was Good Friday and the Prado was shut. He had been to Rome. Had Miss Briscoe never been to Rome? Oh, she should--It would be a wonderful experience for her--the Sistine Chapel; Michael Angelo; and Padua, with its Giottos. His wife had been in bad health for many years, so that their sight-seeing had been on a modest scale.

She had been to Brussels; she had been to Paris but only for a flying visit to see an aunt who was ill. She had been to Dresden; there were masses of pictures she had not seen; however, Lily Briscoe reflected, perhaps it was better not to see pictures: they only made one hopelessly discontented with one's own work. Mr. Bankes thought one could carry that point of view too far. We can't all be Titians and we can't all be Darwins, he said; at the same time he doubted whether you could have your Darwin and your Titian if it weren't for humble people like ourselves. Lily would have liked to pay him a compliment; you're not humble, Mr. Bankes, she would have liked to have said. But he did not want compliments (most men do, she thought), and she was a little ashamed of her impulse and said nothing while he remarked that perhaps what he was saying did not apply to pictures. Anyhow, said Lily, tossing off her little insincerity, she would always go on painting, because it interested her. Yes, said Mr. Bankes, he was sure she would, and, as they reached the end of the lawn he was asking her whether she had difficulty in finding subjects in London when they turned and saw the Ramsays. So that is marriage, Lily thought, a man and a woman looking at a girl throwing a ball. That is what Mrs. Ramsay tried to tell me the other night, she thought. For she was wearing a green shawl, and they were standing close together watching Prue and Jasper throwing catches. And suddenly the meaning which, for no reason at all, as perhaps they are stepping out of the Tube or ringing a doorbell, descends on people, making them symbolical, making them representative, came upon them, and made them in the dusk standing, looking, the symbols of marriage, husband and wife. Then, after an instant, the symbolical outline which transcended the real figures sank down again, and they became, as they met them, Mr. and Mrs. Ramsay watching the children throwing catches. But still for a moment, though Mrs. Ramsay greeted them with her usual smile (oh, she's thinking we're going to get married, Lily thought) and said, "I have triumphed tonight," meaning that for once Mr. Bankes had agreed to dine with them and not run off to his own lodging where his man cooked vegetables properly; still, for one moment, there was a sense of things having been blown apart, of space, of irresponsibility as the ball soared high, and they followed it and lost it and saw the one star and the draped branches. In the failing light they all looked sharp-edged and ethereal and divided by great distances. Then, darting backwards over the vast space (for it seemed as if solidity had vanished altogether), Prue ran full tilt into them and caught the ball brilliantly high up in her left hand, and her mother said, "Haven't they come back yet?" whereupon the spell was broken. Mr. Ramsay felt free now to laugh out loud at the thought that Hume had stuck in a bog and an old woman rescued him on condition he said the Lord's Prayer, and chuckling to himself he strolled off to his study. Mrs. Ramsay, bringing Prue back into throwing catches again, from which she had escaped, asked,

"Did Nancy go with them?"

14

(Certainly, Nancy had gone with them, since Minta Doyle had asked it with her dumb look, holding out her hand, as Nancy made off, after lunch, to her attic, to escape the horror of family life. She supposed she must go then. She did not want to go. She did not want to be drawn into it all. For as they walked along the road to the cliff Minta kept on taking her hand. Then she would let it go. Then she would take it again. What was it she wanted? Nancy asked herself. There was something, of course, that people wanted; for when Minta took her hand and held it, Nancy, reluctantly, saw the whole world spread out beneath her, as if it were Constantinople seen through a mist, and then, however heavy-eyed one might be, one must needs ask, "Is that Santa Sofia?" "Is that the Golden Horn?" So Nancy asked, when Minta took her hand. "What is it that she wants? Is it that?" And what was that? Here and there emerged from the mist (as Nancy looked down upon life spread beneath her) a pinnacle, a dome; prominent things, without names. But when Minta dropped her hand, as she did when they ran down the hillside, all that, the dome, the pinnacle, whatever it was that had protruded through the mist, sank down into it and disappeared. Minta, Andrew observed, was rather a good walker. She wore more sensible clothes that most women. She wore very short skirts and black knickerbockers. She would jump straight into a stream and flounder across. He liked her rashness, but he saw that it would not do--she would kill herself in some idiotic way one of these days. She seemed to be afraid of nothing--except bulls. At the mere sight of a bull in a field she would throw up her arms and fly screaming, which was the very thing to enrage a bull of course. But she did not mind owning up to it in the least; one must admit that. She knew she was an awful coward about bulls, she said. She thought she must have been tossed in her perambulator when she was a baby. She didn't seem to mind what she said or did. Suddenly now she pitched down on the edge of the cliff and began to sing some song about

Damn your eyes, damn your eyes.

They all had to join in and sing the chorus, and shout out together:

Damn your eyes, damn your eyes,

but it would be fatal to let the tide come in and cover up all the good hunting-grounds before they got on to the beach.

"Fatal," Paul agreed, springing up, and as they went slithering down, he kept quoting the guide-book about "these islands being justly celebrated for their park-like prospects and the extent and variety of their marine curiosities." But it would not do altogether, this shouting and damning your eyes, Andrew felt, picking his way down the cliff, this clapping him on the back, and calling him "old fellow" and all that; it would not altogether do. It was the worst of taking women on walks. Once on the beach they separated, he going out on to the Pope's Nose, taking his shoes off, and rolling his socks in them and letting that couple look after themselves; Nancy waded out to her own rocks and searched her own pools and let that couple look after themselves. She crouched low down and touched the smooth rubber-like sea anemones, who were stuck like lumps of jelly to the side of the rock. Brooding, she changed the pool into the sea, and made the minnows into sharks and whales, and cast vast clouds over this tiny world by holding her hand against the sun, and so brought darkness and desolation, like God himself, to millions of ignorant and innocent creatures, and then took her hand away suddenly and let the sun stream down. Out on the pale criss-crossed sand, high-stepping, fringed, gauntleted, stalked some fantastic leviathan (she was still enlarging the pool), and slipped into the vast fissures of the mountain side. And then, letting her eyes slide imperceptibly above the pool and rest on that wavering line of sea and sky, on the tree trunks which the smoke of steamers made waver on the horizon, she became with all that power sweeping savagely in and inevitably withdrawing, hypnotised, and the two senses of that vastness and this tininess (the pool had diminished again) flowering within it made her feel that she was bound hand and foot and unable to move by the intensity of feelings which reduced her own body, her own life, and the lives of all the people in the world, for ever, to nothingness. So listening to the waves, crouching over the pool, she brooded.

And Andrew shouted that the sea was coming in, so she leapt splashing through the shallow waves on to the shore and ran up the beach and was carried by her own impetuosity and her desire for rapid movement right behind a rock and there--oh, heavens! in each other's arms, were Paul and Minta kissing probably. She was outraged, indignant. She and Andrew put on their shoes and stockings in dead silence without saying a thing about it. Indeed they were rather sharp with each other. She might have called him when she saw the crayfish or whatever it was, Andrew grumbled. However, they both felt, it's not our fault. They had not wanted this horrid nuisance to happen. All the same it irritated Andrew that Nancy should be a woman, and Nancy that Andrew should be a man, and they tied their shoes very neatly and drew the bows rather tight.

It was not until they had climbed right up on to the top of the cliff again that Minta cried out that she had lost her grandmother's brooch-- her grandmother's brooch, the sole ornament she possessed--a weeping willow, it was (they must remember it) set in pearls. They must have seen it, she said, with the tears running down her cheeks, the brooch which her grandmother had fastened her cap with till the last day of her life. Now she had lost it. She would rather have lost anything than that! She would go back and look for it. They all went back. They poked and peered and looked. They kept their heads very low, and said things shortly and gruffly. Paul Rayley searched like a madman all about the rock where they had been sitting. All this pother about a brooch really didn't do at all, Andrew thought, as Paul told him to make a "thorough search between this point and that." The tide was coming in fast. The sea would cover the place where they had sat in a minute. There was not a ghost of a chance of their finding it now. "We shall be cut off!" Minta shrieked, suddenly terrified. As if there were any danger of that! It was the same as the bulls all over again--she had no control over her emotions, Andrew thought. Women hadn't. The wretched Paul had to pacify her. The men (Andrew and Paul at once became manly, and different from usual) took counsel briefly and decided that they would plant Rayley's stick where they had sat and come back at low tide again. There was nothing more that could be done now. If the brooch was there, it would still be there in the morning, they assured her, but Minta still sobbed, all the way up to the top of the cliff. It was her grandmother's brooch; she would rather have lost anything but that, and yet Nancy felt, it might be true that she minded losing her brooch, but she wasn't crying only for that. She was crying for something else. We might all sit down and cry, she felt. But she did not know what for.

They drew ahead together, Paul and Minta, and he comforted her, and said how famous he was for finding things. Once when he was a little boy he had found a gold watch. He would get up at daybreak and he was positive he would find it. It seemed to him that it would be almost dark, and he would be alone on the beach, and somehow it would be rather dangerous. He began telling her, however, that he would certainly find it, and she said that she would not hear of his getting up at dawn: it was lost: she knew that: she had had a presentiment when she put it on that afternoon. And secretly he resolved that he would not tell her, but he would slip out of the house at dawn when they were all asleep and if he could not find it he would go to Edinburgh and buy her another, just like it but more beautiful. He would prove what he could do. And as they came out on the hill and saw the lights of the town beneath them, the lights coming out suddenly one by one seemed like things that were going to happen to him--his marriage, his children, his house; and again he thought, as they came out on to the high road, which was shaded with high bushes, how they would retreat into solitude together, and walk on and on, he always leading her, and she pressing close to his side (as she did now). As they turned by the cross roads he thought what an appalling experience he had been through, and he must tell some one--Mrs. Ramsay of course, for it took his breath away to think what he had been and done. It had been far and away the worst moment of his life when he asked Minta to marry him. He would go straight to Mrs. Ramsay, because he felt somehow that she was the person who had made him do it. She had made him think he could do anything. Nobody else took him seriously. But she made him believe that he could do whatever he wanted. He had felt her eyes on him all day today, following him about (though she never said a word) as if she were saying, "Yes, you can do it. I believe in you. I expect it of you." She had made him feel all that, and directly they got back (he looked for the lights of the house above the bay) he would go to her and say, "I've done it, Mrs. Ramsay; thanks to you." And so turning into the lane that led to the house he could see lights moving about in the upper windows.

They must be awfully late then. People were getting ready for dinner. The house was all lit up, and the lights after the darkness made his eyes feel full, and he said to himself, childishly, as he walked up the drive, Lights, lights, lights, and repeated in a dazed way, Lights, lights, lights, as they came into the house staring about him with his face quite stiff. But, good heavens, he said to himself, putting his hand to his tie, I must not make a fool of myself.)

15

"Yes," said Prue, in her considering way, answering her mother's question, "I think Nancy did go with them."

16

Well then, Nancy had gone with them, Mrs. Ramsay supposed, wondering, as she put down a brush, took up a comb, and said "Come in" to a tap at the door (Jasper and Rose came in), whether the fact that Nancy was with them made it less likely or more likely that anything would happen; it made it less likely, somehow, Mrs. Ramsay felt, very irrationally, except that after all holocaust on such a scale was not probable. They could not all be drowned. And again she felt alone in the presence of her old antagonist, life.

Jasper and Rose said that Mildred wanted to know whether she should wait dinner.

"Not for the Queen of England," said Mrs. Ramsay emphatically.

"Not for the Empress of Mexico," she added, laughing at Jasper; for he shared his mother's vice: he, too, exaggerated.

And if Rose liked, she said, while Jasper took the message, she might choose which jewels she was to wear. When there are fifteen people sitting down to dinner, one cannot keep things waiting for ever. She was now beginning to feel annoyed with them for being so late; it was inconsiderate of them, and it annoyed her on top of her anxiety about them, that they should choose this very night to be out late, when, in fact, she wished the dinner to be particularly nice, since William Bankes had at last consented to dine with them; and they were having Mildred's masterpiece--BOEUF EN DAUBE. Everything depended upon things being served up to the precise moment they were ready. The beef, the bayleaf, and the wine--all must be done to a turn. To keep it waiting was out of the question. Yet of course tonight, of all nights, out they went, and they came in late, and things had to be sent out, things had to be kept hot; the BOEUF EN DAUBE would be entirely spoilt.

Jasper offered her an opal necklace; Rose a gold necklace. Which looked best against her black dress? Which did indeed, said Mrs. Ramsay absent-mindedly, looking at her neck and shoulders (but avoiding her face) in the glass. And then, while the children rummaged among her things, she looked out of the window at a sight which always amused her--the rooks trying to decide which tree to settle on.

Every time, they seemed to change their minds and rose up into the air again, because, she thought, the old rook, the father rook, old Joseph was her name for him, was a bird of a very trying and difficult disposition. He was a disreputable old bird, with half his wing feathers missing. He was like some seedy old gentleman in a top hat she had seen playing the horn in front of a public house.

"Look!" she said, laughing. They were actually fighting. Joseph and Mary were fighting. Anyhow they all went up again, and the air was shoved aside by their black wings and cut into exquisite scimitar shapes. The movements of the wings beating out, out, out--she could never describe it accurately enough to please herself--was one of the loveliest of all to her. Look at that, she said to Rose, hoping that Rose would see it more clearly than she could. For one's children so often gave one's own perceptions a little thrust forwards.

But which was it to be? They had all the trays of her jewel-case open. The gold necklace, which was Italian, or the opal necklace, which Uncle James had brought her from India; or should she wear her amethysts?

"Choose, dearests, choose," she said, hoping that they would make haste.

But she let them take their time to choose: she let Rose, particularly, take up this and then that, and hold her jewels against the black dress, for this little ceremony of choosing jewels, which was gone through every night, was what Rose liked best, she knew. She had some hidden reason of her own for attaching great importance to this choosing what her mother was to wear. What was the reason, Mrs. Ramsay wondered, standing still to let her clasp the necklace she had chosen, divining, through her own past, some deep, some buried, some quite speechless feeling that one had for one's mother at Rose's age. Like all feelings felt for oneself, Mrs. Ramsay thought, it made one sad. It was so inadequate, what one could give in return; and what Rose felt was quite out of proportion to anything she actually was. And Rose would grow up; and Rose would suffer, she supposed, with these deep feelings, and she said she was ready now, and they would go down, and Jasper, because he was the gentleman, should give her his arm, and Rose, as she was the lady, should carry her handkerchief (she gave her the handkerchief), and what else? oh, yes, it might be cold: a shawl. Choose me a shawl, she said, for that would please Rose, who was bound to suffer so. "There," she said, stopping by the window on the landing, "there they are again." Joseph had settled on another tree- top. "Don't you think they mind," she said to Jasper, "having their wings broken?" Why did he want to shoot poor old Joseph and Mary? He shuffled a little on the stairs, and felt rebuked, but not seriously, for she did not understand the fun of shooting birds; and they did not feel; and being his mother she lived away in another division of the world, but he rather liked her stories about Mary and Joseph. She made him laugh. But how did she know that those were Mary and Joseph? Did she think the same birds came to the same trees every night? he asked. But here, suddenly, like all grown-up people, she ceased to pay him the least attention. She was listening to a clatter in the hall.

"They've come back!" she exclaimed, and at once she felt much more annoyed with them than relieved. Then she wondered, had it happened? She would go down and they would tell her--but no. They could not tell her anything, with all these people about. So she must go down and begin dinner and wait. And, like some queen who, finding her people gathered in the hall, looks down upon them, and descends among them, and acknowledges their tributes silently, and accepts their devotion and their prostration before her (Paul did not move a muscle but looked straight before him as she passed) she went down, and crossed the hall and bowed her head very slightly, as if she accepted what they could not say: their tribute to her beauty.

But she stopped. There was a smell of burning. Could they have let the BOEUF EN DAUBE overboil? she wondered, pray heaven not! when the great clangour of the gong announced solemnly, authoritatively, that all those scattered about, in attics, in bedrooms, on little perches of their own, reading, writing, putting the last smooth to their hair, or fastening dresses, must leave all that, and the little odds and ends on their washing-tables and dressing tables, and the novels on the bed- tables, and the diaries which were so private, and assemble in the dining-room for dinner.

17

But what have I done with my life? thought Mrs. Ramsay, taking her place at the head of the table, and looking at all the plates making white circles on it. "William, sit by me," she said. "Lily," she said, wearily, "over there." They had that--Paul Rayley and Minta Doyle--she, only this--an infinitely long table and plates and knives. At the far end was her husband, sitting down, all in a heap, frowning. What at? She did not know. She did not mind. She could not understand how she had ever felt any emotion or affection for him. She had a sense of being past everything, through everything, out of everything, as she helped the soup, as if there was an eddy--there-- and one could be in it, or one could be out of it, and she was out of it. It's all come to an end, she thought, while they came in one after another, Charles Tansley--"Sit there, please," she said--Augustus Carmichael--and sat down. And meanwhile she waited, passively, for some one to answer her, for something to happen. But this is not a thing, she thought, ladling out soup, that one says.

Raising her eyebrows at the discrepancy--that was what she was thinking, this was what she was doing--ladling out soup--she felt, more and more strongly, outside that eddy; or as if a shade had fallen, and, robbed of colour, she saw things truly. The room (she looked round it) was very shabby. There was no beauty anywhere. She forebore to look at Mr. Tansley. Nothing seemed to have merged. They all sat separate. And the whole of the effort of merging and flowing and creating rested on her. Again she felt, as a fact without hostility, the sterility of men, for if she did not do it nobody would do it, and so, giving herself a little shake that one gives a watch that has stopped, the old familiar pulse began beating, as the watch begins ticking--one, two, three, one, two, three. And so on and so on, she repeated, listening to it, sheltering and fostering the still feeble pulse as one might guard a weak flame with a news-paper. And so then, she concluded, addressing herself by bending silently in his direction to William Bankes--poor man! who had no wife, and no children and dined alone in lodgings except for tonight; and in pity for him, life being now strong enough to bear her on again, she began all this business, as a sailor not without weariness sees the wind fill his sail and yet hardly wants to be off again and thinks how, had the ship sunk, he would have whirled round and round and found rest on the floor of the sea.

"Did you find your letters? I told them to put them in the hall for you," she said to William Bankes.

Lily Briscoe watched her drifting into that strange no-man's land where to follow people is impossible and yet their going inflicts such a chill on those who watch them that they always try at least to follow them with their eyes as one follows a fading ship until the sails have sunk beneath the horizon.

How old she looks, how worn she looks, Lily thought, and how remote. Then when she turned to William Bankes, smiling, it was as if the ship had turned and the sun had struck its sails again, and Lily thought with some amusement because she was relieved, Why does she pity him? For that was the impression she gave, when she told him that his letters were in the hall. Poor William Bankes, she seemed to be saying, as if her own weariness had been partly pitying people, and the life in her, her resolve to live again, had been stirred by pity. And it was not true, Lily thought; it was one of those misjudgments of hers that seemed to be instinctive and to arise from some need of her own rather than of other people's. He is not in the least pitiable. He has his work, Lily said to herself. She remembered, all of a sudden as if she had found a treasure, that she had her work. In a flash she saw her picture, and thought, Yes, I shall put the tree further in the middle; then I shall avoid that awkward space. That's what I shall do. That's what has been puzzling me. She took up the salt cellar and put it down again on a flower pattern in the table-cloth, so as to remind herself to move the tree.

"It's odd that one scarcely gets anything worth having by post, yet one always wants one's letters," said Mr. Bankes.

What damned rot they talk, thought Charles Tansley, laying down his spoon precisely in the middle of his plate, which he had swept clean, as if, Lily thought (he sat opposite to her with his back to the window precisely in the middle of view), he were determined to make sure of his meals. Everything about him had that meagre fixity, that bare unloveliness. But nevertheless, the fact remained, it was impossible to dislike any one if one looked at them. She liked his eyes; they were blue, deep set, frightening.

"Do you write many letters, Mr. Tansley?" asked Mrs. Ramsay, pitying him too, Lily supposed; for that was true of Mrs. Ramsay--she pitied men always as if they lacked something--women never, as if they had something. He wrote to his mother; otherwise he did not suppose he wrote one letter a month, said Mr. Tansley, shortly.

For he was not going to talk the sort of rot these condescended to by these silly women. He had been reading in his room, and now he came down and it all seemed to him silly, superficial, flimsy. Why did they dress? He had come down in his ordinary clothes. He had not got any dress clothes. "One never gets anything worth having by post"--that was the sort of thing they were always saying. They made men say that sort of thing. Yes, it was pretty well true, he thought. They never got anything worth having from one year's end to another. They did nothing but talk, talk, talk, eat, eat, eat. It was the women's fault. Women made civilisation impossible with all their "charm," all their silliness.

"No going to the Lighthouse tomorrow, Mrs. Ramsay," he said, asserting himself. He liked her; he admired her; he still thought of the man in the drain-pipe looking up at her; but he felt it necessary to assert himself.

He was really, Lily Briscoe thought, in spite of his eyes, but then look at his nose, look at his hands, the most uncharming human being she had ever met. Then why did she mind what he said? Women can't write, women can't paint--what did that matter coming from him, since clearly it was not true to him but for some reason helpful to him, and that was why he said it? Why did her whole being bow, like corn under a wind, and erect itself again from this abasement only with a great and rather painful effort? She must make it once more. There's the sprig on the table-cloth; there's my painting; I must move the tree to the middle; that matters--nothing else. Could she not hold fast to that, she asked herself, and not lose her temper, and not argue; and if she wanted revenge take it by laughing at him?

"Oh, Mr. Tansley," she said, "do take me to the Lighthouse with you. I should so love it."

She was telling lies he could see. She was saying what she did not mean to annoy him, for some reason. She was laughing at him. He was in his old flannel trousers. He had no others. He felt very rough and isolated and lonely. He knew that she was trying to tease him for some reason; she didn't want to go to the Lighthouse with him; she despised him: so did Prue Ramsay; so did they all. But he was not going to be made a fool of by women, so he turned deliberately in his chair and looked out of the window and said, all in a jerk, very rudely, it would be too rough for her tomorrow. She would be sick.

It annoyed him that she should have made him speak like that, with Mrs. Ramsay listening. If only he could be alone in his room working, he thought, among his books. That was where he felt at his ease. And he had never run a penny into debt; he had never cost his father a penny since he was fifteen; he had helped them at home out of his savings; he was educating his sister. Still, he wished he had known how to answer Miss Briscoe properly; he wished it had not come out all in a jerk like that. "You'd be sick." He wished he could think of something to say to Mrs. Ramsay, something which would show her that he was not just a dry prig. That was what they all thought him. He turned to her. But Mrs. Ramsay was talking about people he had never heard of to William Bankes.

"Yes, take it away," she said briefly, interrupting what she was saying to William Bankes to speak to the maid. "It must have been fifteen-- no, twenty years ago--that I last saw her," she was saying, turning back to him again as if she could not lose a moment of their talk, for she was absorbed by what they were saying. So he had actually heard from her this evening! And was Carrie still living at Marlow, and was everything still the same? Oh, she could remember it as if it were yesterday--on the river, feeling it as if it were yesterday--going on the river, feeling very cold. But if the Mannings made a plan they stuck to it. Never should she forget Herbert killing a wasp with a teaspoon on the bank! And it was still going on, Mrs. Ramsay mused, gliding like a ghost among the chairs and tables of that drawing-room on the banks of the Thames where she had been so very, very cold twenty years ago; but now she went among them like a ghost; and it fascinated her, as if, while she had changed, that particular day, now become very still and beautiful, had remained there, all these years. Had Carrie written to him herself? she asked.

"Yes. She says they're building a new billiard room," he said. No! No! That was out of the question! Building a new billiard room! It seemed to her impossible.

Mr. Bankes could not see that there was anything very odd about it. They were very well off now. Should he give her love to Carrie?

"Oh," said Mrs. Ramsay with a little start, "No," she added, reflecting that she did not know this Carrie who built a new billiard room. But how strange, she repeated, to Mr. Bankes's amusement, that they should be going on there still. For it was extraordinary to think that they had been capable of going on living all these years when she had not thought of them more than once all that time. How eventful her own life had been, during those same years. Yet perhaps Carrie Manning had not thought about her, either. The thought was strange and distasteful.

"People soon drift apart," said Mr. Bankes, feeling, however, some satisfaction when he thought that after all he knew both the Mannings and the Ramsays. He had not drifted apart he thought, laying down his spoon and wiping his clean-shaven lips punctiliously. But perhaps he was rather unusual, he thought, in this; he never let himself get into a groove. He had friends in all circles... Mrs. Ramsay had to break off here to tell the maid something about keeping food hot. That was why he preferred dining alone. All those interruptions annoyed him. Well, thought William Bankes, preserving a demeanour of exquisite courtesy and merely spreading the fingers of his left hand on the table-cloth as a mechanic examines a tool beautifully polished and ready for use in an interval of leisure, such are the sacrifices one's friends ask of one. It would have hurt her if he had refused to come. But it was not worth it for him. Looking at his hand he thought that if he had been alone dinner would have been almost over now; he would have been free to work. Yes, he thought, it is a terrible waste of time. The children were dropping in still. "I wish one of you would run up to Roger's room," Mrs. Ramsay was saying. How trifling it all is, how boring it all is, he thought, compared with the other thing-- work. Here he sat drumming his fingers on the table-cloth when he might have been--he took a flashing bird's-eye view of his work. What a waste of time it all was to be sure! Yet, he thought, she is one of my oldest friends. I am by way of being devoted to her. Yet now, at this moment her presence meant absolutely nothing to him: her beauty meant nothing to him; her sitting with her little boy at the window-- nothing, nothing. He wished only to be alone and to take up that book. He felt uncomfortable; he felt treacherous, that he could sit by her side and feel nothing for her. The truth was that he did not enjoy family life. It was in this sort of state that one asked oneself, What does one live for? Why, one asked oneself, does one take all these pains for the human race to go on? Is it so very desirable? Are we attractive as a species? Not so very, he thought, looking at those rather untidy boys. His favourite, Cam, was in bed, he supposed. Foolish questions, vain questions, questions one never asked if one was occupied. Is human life this? Is human life that? One never had time to think about it. But here he was asking himself that sort of question, because Mrs. Ramsay was giving orders to servants, and also because it had struck him, thinking how surprised Mrs. Ramsay was that Carrie Manning should still exist, that friendships, even the best of them, are frail things. One drifts apart. He reproached himself again. He was sitting beside Mrs. Ramsay and he had nothing in the world to say to her.

"I'm so sorry," said Mrs. Ramsy, turning to him at last. He felt rigid and barren, like a pair of boots that have been soaked and gone dry so that you can hardly force your feet into them. Yet he must force his feet into them. He must make himself talk. Unless he were very careful, she would find out this treachery of his; that he did not care a straw for her, and that would not be at all pleasant, he thought. So he bent his head courteously in her direction.

"How you must detest dining in this bear garden," she said, making use, as she did when she was distracted, of her social manner. So, when there is a strife of tongues, at some meeting, the chairman, to obtain unity, suggests that every one shall speak in French. Perhaps it is bad French; French may not contain the words that express the speaker's thoughts; nevertheless speaking French imposes some order, some uniformity. Replying to her in the same language, Mr. Bankes said, "No, not at all," and Mr. Tansley, who had no knowledge of this language, even spoke thus in words of one syllable, at once suspected its insincerity. They did talk nonsense, he thought, the Ramsays; and he pounced on this fresh instance with joy, making a note which, one of these days, he would read aloud, to one or two friends. There, in a society where one could say what one liked he would sarcastically describe "staying with the Ramsays" and what nonsense they talked. It was worth while doing it once, he would say; but not again. The women bored one so, he would say. Of course Ramsay had dished himself by marrying a beautiful woman and having eight children. It would shape itself something like that, but now, at this moment, sitting stuck there with an empty seat beside him, nothing had shaped itself at all. It was all in scraps and fragments. He felt extremely, even physically, uncomfortable. He wanted somebody to give him a chance of asserting himself. He wanted it so urgently that he fidgeted in his chair, looked at this person, then at that person, tried to break into their talk, opened his mouth and shut it again. They were talking about the fishing industry. Why did no one ask him his opinion? What did they know about the fishing industry?

Lily Briscoe knew all that. Sitting opposite him, could she not see, as in an X-ray photograph, the ribs and thigh bones of the young man's desire to impress himself, lying dark in the mist of his flesh--that thin mist which convention had laid over his burning desire to break into the conversation? But, she thought, screwing up her Chinese eyes, and remembering how he sneered at women, "can't paint, can't write," why should I help him to relieve himself?

There is a code of behaviour, she knew, whose seventh article (it may be) says that on occasions of this sort it behoves the woman, whatever her own occupation might be, to go to the help of the young man opposite so that he may expose and relieve the thigh bones, the ribs, of his vanity, of his urgent desire to assert himself; as indeed it is their duty, she reflected, in her old maidenly fairness, to help us, suppose the Tube were to burst into flames. Then, she thought, I should certainly expect Mr. Tansley to get me out. But how would it be, she thought, if neither of us did either of these things? So she sat there smiling.

"You're not planning to go to the Lighthouse, are you, Lily," said Mrs. Ramsay. "Remember poor Mr. Langley; he had been round the world dozens of times, but he told me he never suffered as he did when my husband took him there. Are you a good sailor, Mr. Tansley?" she asked.

Mr. Tansley raised a hammer: swung it high in air; but realising, as it descended, that he could not smite that butterfly with such an instrument as this, said only that he had never been sick in his life. But in that one sentence lay compact, like gunpowder, that his grandfather was a fisherman; his father a chemist; that he had worked his way up entirely himself; that he was proud of it; that he was Charles Tansley--a fact that nobody there seemed to realise; but one of these days every single person would know it. He scowled ahead of him. He could almost pity these mild cultivated people, who would be blown sky high, like bales of wool and barrels of apples, one of these days by the gunpowder that was in him.

"Will you take me, Mr. Tansley?" said Lily, quickly, kindly, for, of course, if Mrs. Ramsay said to her, as in effect she did, "I am drowning, my dear, in seas of fire. Unless you apply some balm to the anguish of this hour and say something nice to that young man there, life will run upon the rocks--indeed I hear the grating and the growling at this minute. My nerves are taut as fiddle strings. Another touch and they will snap"--when Mrs. Ramsay said all this, as the glance in her eyes said it, of course for the hundred and fiftieth time Lily Briscoe had to renounce the experiment--what happens if one is not nice to that young man there--and be nice.

Judging the turn in her mood correctly--that she was friendly to him now--he was relieved of his egotism, and told her how he had been thrown out of a boat when he was a baby; how his father used to fish him out with a boat-hook; that was how he had learnt to swim. One of his uncles kept the light on some rock or other off the Scottish coast, he said. He had been there with him in a storm. This was said loudly in a pause. They had to listen to him when he said that he had been with his uncle in a lighthouse in a storm. Ah, thought Lily Briscoe, as the conversation took this auspicious turn, and she felt Mrs. Ramsay's gratitude (for

Mrs. Ramsay was free now to talk for a moment herself), ah, she thought, but what haven't I paid to get it for you? She had not been sincere.

She had done the usual trick--been nice. She would never know him. He would never know her. Human relations were all like that, she thought, and the worst (if it had not been for Mr. Bankes) were between men and women. Inevitably these were extremely insincere she thought. Then her eye caught the salt cellar, which she had placed there to remind her, and she remembered that next morning she would move the tree further towards the middle, and her spirits rose so high at the thought of painting tomorrow that she laughed out loud at what Mr. Tansley was saying. Let him talk all night if he liked it.

"But how long do they leave men on a Lighthouse?" she asked. He told her. He was amazingly well informed. And as he was grateful, and as he liked her, and as he was beginning to enjoy himself, so now, Mrs. Ramsay thought, she could return to that dream land, that unreal but fascinating place, the Mannings' drawing-room at Marlow twenty years ago; where one moved about without haste or anxiety, for there was no future to worry about. She knew what had happened to them, what to her. It was like reading a good book again, for she knew the end of that story, since it had happened twenty years ago, and life, which shot down even from this dining-room table in cascades, heaven knows where, was sealed up there, and lay, like a lake, placidly between its banks. He said they had built a billiard room--was it possible? Would William go on talking about the Mannings? She wanted him to. But, no--for some reason he was no longer in the mood. She tried. He did not respond. She could not force him. She was disappointed.

"The children are disgraceful," she said, sighing. He said something about punctuality being one of the minor virtues which we do not acquire until later in life.

"If at all," said Mrs. Ramsay merely to fill up space, thinking what an old maid William was becoming. Conscious of his treachery, conscious of her wish to talk about something more intimate, yet out of mood for it at present, he felt come over him the disagreeableness of life, sitting there, waiting. Perhaps the others were saying something interesting? What were they saying?

That the fishing season was bad; that the men were emigrating. They were talking about wages and unemployment. The young man was abusing the government. William Bankes, thinking what a relief it was to catch on to something of this sort when private life was disagreeable, heard him say something about "one of the most scandalous acts of the present government." Lily was listening; Mrs. Ramsay was listening; they were all listening. But already bored, Lily felt that something was lacking; Mr. Bankes felt that something was lacking. Pulling her shawl round her Mrs. Ramsay felt that something was lacking. All of them bending themselves to listen thought, "Pray heaven that the inside of my mind may not be exposed," for each thought, "The others are feeling this. They are outraged and indignant with the government about the fishermen. Whereas, I feel nothing at all." But perhaps, thought Mr. Bankes, as he looked at Mr. Tansley, here is the man. One was always waiting for the man. There was always a chance.

At any moment the leader might arise; the man of genius, in politics as in anything else. Probably he will be extremely disagreeable to us old fogies, thought Mr. Bankes, doing his best to make allowances, for he knew by some curious physical sensation, as of nerves erect in his spine, that he was jealous, for himself partly, partly more probably for his work, for his point of view, for his science; and therefore he was not entirely open- minded or altogether fair, for Mr. Tansley seemed to be saying, You have wasted your lives. You are all of you wrong. Poor old fogies, you're hopelessly behind the times. He seemed to be rather cocksure, this young man; and his manners were bad. But Mr. Bankes bade himself observe, he had courage; he had ability; he was extremely well up in the facts. Probably, Mr. Bankes thought, as Tansley abused the government, there is a good deal in what he says.

"Tell me now..." he said. So they argued about politics, and Lily looked at the leaf on the table-cloth; and Mrs. Ramsay, leaving the argument entirely in the hands of the two men, wondered why she was so bored by this talk, and wished, looking at her husband at the other end of the table, that he would say something. One word, she said to herself. For if he said a thing, it would make all the difference. He went to the heart of things. He cared about fishermen and their wages. He could not sleep for thinking of them. It was altogether different when he spoke; one did not feel then, pray heaven you don't see how little I care, because one did care. Then, realising that it was because she admired him so much that she was waiting for him to speak, she felt as if somebody had been praising her husband to her and their marriage, and she glowed all over without realising that it was she herself who had praised him. She looked at him thinking to find this in his face; he would be looking magnificent... But not in the least! He was screwing his face up, he was scowling and frowning, and flushing with anger. What on earth was it about? she wondered. What could be the matter? Only that poor old Augustus had asked for another plate of soup--that was all. It was unthinkable, it was detestable (so he signalled to her across the table) that Augustus should be beginning his soup over again. He loathed people eating when he had finished. She saw his anger fly like a pack of hounds into his eyes, his brow, and she knew that in a moment something violent would explode, and then--thank goodness! she saw him clutch himself and clap a brake on the wheel, and the whole of his body seemed to emit sparks but not words. He sat there scowling. He had said nothing, he would have her observe. Let her give him the credit for that! But why after all should poor Augustus not ask for another plate of soup? He had merely touched Ellen's arm and said:

"Ellen, please, another plate of soup," and then Mr. Ramsay scowled like that.

And why not? Mrs. Ramsay demanded. Surely they could let Augustus have his soup if he wanted it. He hated people wallowing in food, Mr. Ramsay frowned at her. He hated everything dragging on for hours like this. But he had controlled himself, Mr. Ramsay would have her observe, disgusting though the sight was. But why show it so plainly, Mrs. Ramsay demanded (they looked at each other down the long table sending these questions and answers across, each knowing exactly what the other felt). Everybody could see, Mrs. Ramsay thought. There was Rose gazing at her father, there was Roger gazing at his father; both would be off in spasms of laughter in another second, she knew, and so she said promptly (indeed it was time):

"Light the candles," and they jumped up instantly and went and fumbled at the sideboard.

Why could he never conceal his feelings? Mrs. Ramsay wondered, and she wondered if Augustus Carmichael had noticed. Perhaps he had; perhaps he had not. She could not help respecting the composure with which he sat there, drinking his soup. If he wanted soup, he asked for soup. Whether people laughed at him or were angry with him he was the same. He did not like her, she knew that; but partly for that very reason she respected him, and looking at him, drinking soup, very large and calm in the failing light, and monumental, and contemplative, she wondered what he did feel then, and why he was always content and dignified; and she thought how devoted he was to Andrew, and would call him into his room, and Andrew said, "show him things." And there he would lie all day long on the lawn brooding presumably over his poetry, till he reminded one of a cat watching birds, and then he clapped his paws together when he had found the word, and her husband said, "Poor old Augustus--he's a true poet," which was high praise from her husband.

Now eight candles were stood down the table, and after the first stoop the flames stood upright and drew with them into visibility the long table entire, and in the middle a yellow and purple dish of fruit. What had she done with it, Mrs. Ramsay wondered, for Rose's arrangement of the grapes and pears, of the horny pink-lined shell, of the bananas, made her think of a trophy fetched from the bottom of the sea, of Neptune's banquet, of the bunch that hangs with vine leaves over the shoulder of Bacchus (in some picture), among the leopard skins and the torches lolloping red and gold... Thus brought up suddenly into the light it seemed possessed of great size and depth, was like a world in which one could take one's staff and climb hills, she thought, and go down into valleys, and to her pleasure (for it brought them into sympathy momentarily) she saw that Augustus too feasted his eyes on the same plate of fruit, plunged in, broke off a bloom there, a tassel here, and returned, after feasting, to his hive. That was his way of looking, different from hers. But looking together united them.

Now all the candles were lit up, and the faces on both sides of the table were brought nearer by the candle light, and composed, as they had not been in the twilight, into a party round a table, for the night was now shut off by panes of glass, which, far from giving any accurate view of the outside world, rippled it so strangely that here, inside the room, seemed to be order and dry land; there, outside, a reflection in which things waved and vanished, waterily.

Some change at once went through them all, as if this had really happened, and they were all conscious of making a party together in a hollow, on an island; had their common cause against that fluidity out there. Mrs. Ramsay, who had been uneasy, waiting for Paul and Minta to come in, and unable, she felt, to settle to things, now felt her uneasiness changed to expectation. For now they must come, and Lily Briscoe, trying to analyse the cause of the sudden exhilaration, compared it with that moment on the tennis lawn, when solidity suddenly vanished, and such vast spaces lay between them; and now the same effect was got by the many candles in the sparely furnished room, and the uncurtained windows, and the bright mask-like look of faces seen by candlelight. Some weight was taken off them; anything might happen, she felt. They must come now, Mrs. Ramsay thought, looking at the door, and at that instant, Minta Doyle, Paul Rayley, and a maid carrying a great dish in her hands came in together. They were awfully late; they were horribly late, Minta said, as they found their way to different ends of the table.

"I lost my brooch--my grandmother's brooch," said Minta with a sound of lamentation in her voice, and a suffusion in her large brown eyes, looking down, looking up, as she sat by Mr. Ramsay, which roused his chivalry so that he bantered her.

How could she be such a goose, he asked, as to scramble about the rocks in jewels?

She was by way of being terrified of him--he was so fearfully clever, and the first night when she had sat by him, and he talked about George Eliot, she had been really frightened, for she had left the third volume of MIDDLEMARCH in the train and she never knew what happened in the end; but afterwards she got on perfectly, and made herself out even more ignorant than she was, because he liked telling her she was a fool. And so tonight, directly he laughed at her, she was not frightened. Besides, she knew, directly she came into the room that the miracle had happened; she wore her golden haze. Sometimes she had it; sometimes not. She never knew why it came or why it went, or if she had it until she came into the room and then she knew instantly by the way some man looked at her. Yes, tonight she had it, tremendously; she knew that by the way Mr. Ramsay told her not to be a fool. She sat beside him, smiling.

It must have happened then, thought Mrs. Ramsay; they are engaged. And for a moment she felt what she had never expected to feel again-- jealousy. For he, her husband, felt it too--Minta's glow; he liked these girls, these golden-reddish girls, with something flying, something a little wild and harum-scarum about them, who didn't "scrape their hair off," weren't, as he said about poor Lily Briscoe, "skimpy". There was some quality which she herself had not, some lustre, some richness, which attracted him, amused him, led him to make favourites of girls like Minta. They might cut his hair from him, plait him watch-chains, or interrupt him at his work, hailing him (she heard them), "Come along, Mr. Ramsay; it's our turn to beat them now," and out he came to play tennis.

But indeed she was not jealous, only, now and then, when she made herself look in her glass, a little resentful that she had grown old, perhaps, by her own fault. (The bill for the greenhouse and all the rest of it.) She was grateful to them for laughing at him. ("How many pipes have you smoked today, Mr. Ramsay?" and so on), till he seemed a young man; a man very attractive to women, not burdened, not weighed down with the greatness of his labours and the sorrows of the world and his fame or his failure, but again as she had first known him, gaunt but gallant; helping her out of a boat, she remembered; with delightful ways, like that (she looked at him, and he looked astonishingly young, teasing Minta). For herself--"Put it down there," she said, helping the Swiss girl to place gently before her the huge brown pot in which was the BOEUF EN DAUBE--for her own part, she liked her boobies. Paul must sit by her. She had kept a place for him. Really, she sometimes thought she liked the boobies best. They did not bother one with their dissertations. How much they missed, after all, these very clever men! How dried up they did become, to be sure. There was something, she thought as he sat down, very charming about Paul. His manners were delightful to her, and his sharp cut nose and his bright blue eyes. He was so considerate. Would he tell her--now that they were all talking again--what had happened?

"We went back to look for Minta's brooch," he said, sitting down by her. "We"--that was enough. She knew from the effort, the rise in his voice to surmount a difficult word that it was the first time he had said "we." "We did this, we did that." They'll say that all their lives, she thought, and an exquisite scent of olives and oil and juice rose from the great brown dish as Marthe, with a little flourish, took the cover off. The cook had spent three days over that dish. And she must take great care, Mrs. Ramsay thought, diving into the soft mass, to choose a specially tender piece for William Bankes. And she peered into the dish, with its shiny walls and its confusion of savoury brown and yellow meats and its bay leaves and its wine, and thought, This will celebrate the occasion--a curious sense rising in her, at once freakish and tender, of celebrating a festival, as if two emotions were called up in her, one profound--for what could be more serious than the love of man for woman, what more commanding, more impressive, bearing in its bosom the seeds of death; at the same time these lovers, these people entering into illusion glittering eyed, must be danced round with mockery, decorated with garlands.

"It is a triumph," said Mr. Bankes, laying his knife down for a moment. He had eaten attentively. It was rich; it was tender. It was perfectly cooked. How did she manage these things in the depths of the country? he asked her. She was a wonderful woman. All his love, all his reverence, had returned; and she knew it.

"It is a French recipe of my grandmother's," said Mrs. Ramsay, speaking with a ring of great pleasure in her voice. Of course it was French. What passes for cookery in England is an abomination (they agreed). It is putting cabbages in water. It is roasting meat till it is like leather. It is cutting off the delicious skins of vegetables. "In which," said Mr. Bankes, "all the virtue of the vegetable is contained." And the waste, said Mrs. Ramsay. A whole French family could live on what an English cook throws away. Spurred on by her sense that William's affection had come back to her, and that everything was all right again, and that her suspense was over, and that now she was free both to triumph and to mock, she laughed, she gesticulated, till Lily thought, How childlike, how absurd she was, sitting up there with all her beauty opened again in her, talking about the skins of vegetables. There was something frightening about her. She was irresistible. Always she got her own way in the end, Lily thought. Now she had brought this off--Paul and Minta, one might suppose, were engaged. Mr. Bankes was dining here. She put a spell on them all, by wishing, so simply, so directly, and Lily contrasted that abundance with her own poverty of spirit, and supposed that it was partly that belief (for her face was all lit up--without looking young, she looked radiant) in this strange, this terrifying thing, which made Paul Rayley, sitting at her side, all of a tremor, yet abstract, absorbed, silent. Mrs. Ramsay, Lily felt, as she talked about the skins of vegetables, exalted that, worshipped that; held her hands over it to warm them, to protect it, and yet, having brought it all about, somehow laughed, led her victims, Lily felt, to the altar. It came over her too now--the emotion, the vibration, of love. How inconspicuous she felt herself by Paul's side! He, glowing, burning; she, aloof, satirical; he, bound for adventure; she, moored to the shore; he, launched, incautious; she solitary, left out--and, ready to implore a share, if it were a disaster, in his disaster, she said shyly:

"When did Minta lose her brooch?"

He smiled the most exquisite smile, veiled by memory, tinged by dreams. He shook his head. "On the beach," he said.

"I'm going to find it," he said, "I'm getting up early." This being kept secret from Minta, he lowered his voice, and turned his eyes to where she sat, laughing, beside Mr. Ramsay.

Lily wanted to protest violently and outrageously her desire to help him, envisaging how in the dawn on the beach she would be the one to pounce on the brooch half-hidden by some stone, and thus herself be included among the sailors and adventurers. But what did he reply to her offer? She actually said with an emotion that she seldom let appear, "Let me come with you," and he laughed. He meant yes or no-- either perhaps. But it was not his meaning--it was the odd chuckle he gave, as if he had said, Throw yourself over the cliff if you like, I don't care. He turned on her cheek the heat of love, its horror, its cruelty, its unscrupulosity. It scorched her, and Lily, looking at Minta, being charming to Mr. Ramsay at the other end of the table, flinched for her exposed to these fangs, and was thankful. For at any rate, she said to herself, catching sight of the salt cellar on the pattern, she need not marry, thank Heaven: she need not undergo that degradation. She was saved from that dilution. She would move the tree rather more to the middle.

Such was the complexity of things. For what happened to her, especially staying with the Ramsays, was to be made to feel violently two opposite things at the same time; that's what you feel, was one; that's what I feel, was the other, and then they fought together in her mind, as now. It is so beautiful, so exciting, this love, that I tremble on the verge of it, and offer, quite out of my own habit, to look for a brooch on a beach; also it is the stupidest, the most barbaric of human passions, and turns a nice young man with a profile like a gem's (Paul's was exquisite) into a bully with a crowbar (he was swaggering, he was insolent) in the Mile End Road. Yet, she said to herself, from the dawn of time odes have been sung to love; wreaths heaped and roses; and if you asked nine people out of ten they would say they wanted nothing but this--love; while the women, judging from her own experience, would all the time be feeling, This is not what we want; there is nothing more tedious, puerile, and inhumane than this; yet it is also beautiful and necessary. Well then, well then? she asked, somehow expecting the others to go on with the argument, as if in an argument like this one threw one's own little bolt which fell short obviously and left the others to carry it on. So she listened again to what they were saying in case they should throw any light upon the question of love.

"Then," said Mr. Bankes, "there is that liquid the English call coffee."

"Oh, coffee!" said Mrs. Ramsay. But it was much rather a question (she was thoroughly roused, Lily could see, and talked very emphatically) of real butter and clean milk. Speaking with warmth and eloquence, she described the iniquity of the English dairy system, and in what state milk was delivered at the door, and was about to prove her charges, for she had gone into the matter, when all round the table, beginning with Andrew in the middle, like a fire leaping from tuft to tuft of furze, her children laughed; her husband laughed; she was laughed at, fire- encircled, and forced to veil her crest, dismount her batteries, and only retaliate by displaying the raillery and ridicule of the table to Mr. Bankes as an example of what one suffered if one attacked the prejudices of the British Public.

Purposely, however, for she had it on her mind that Lily, who had helped her with Mr. Tansley, was out of things, she exempted her from the rest; said "Lily anyhow agrees with me," and so drew her in, a little fluttered, a little startled. (For she was thinking about love.) They were both out of things, Mrs. Ramsay had been thinking, both Lily and Charles Tansley. Both suffered from the glow of the other two. He, it was clear, felt himself utterly in the cold; no woman would look at him with Paul Rayley in the room. Poor fellow! Still, he had his dissertation, the influence of somebody upon something: he could take care of himself. With Lily it was different. She faded, under Minta's glow; became more inconspicuous than ever, in her little grey dress with her little puckered face and her little Chinese eyes. Everything about her was so small. Yet, thought Mrs. Ramsay, comparing her with Minta, as she claimed her help (for Lily should bear her out she talked no more about her dairies than her husband did about his boots--he would talk by the hour about his boots) of the two, Lily at forty will be the better. There was in Lily a thread of something; a flare of something; something of her own which Mrs. Ramsay liked very much indeed, but no man would, she feared. Obviously, not, unless it were a much older man, like William Bankes. But then he cared, well, Mrs. Ramsay sometimes thought that he cared, since his wife's death, perhaps for her. He was not "in love" of course; it was one of those unclassified affections of which there are so many. Oh, but nonsense, she thought; William must marry Lily. They have so many things in common. Lily is so fond of flowers. They are both cold and aloof and rather self-sufficing. She must arrange for them to take a long walk together.

Foolishly, she had set them opposite each other. That could be remedied tomorrow. If it were fine, they should go for a picnic. Everything seemed possible. Everything seemed right. Just now (but this cannot last, she thought, dissociating herself from the moment while they were all talking about boots) just now she had reached security; she hovered like a hawk suspended; like a flag floated in an element of joy which filled every nerve of her body fully and sweetly, not noisily, solemnly rather, for it arose, she thought, looking at them all eating there, from husband and children and friends; all of which rising in this profound stillness (she was helping William Bankes to one very small piece more, and peered into the depths of the earthenware pot) seemed now for no special reason to stay there like a smoke, like a fume rising upwards, holding them safe together. Nothing need be said; nothing could be said. There it was, all round them. It partook, she felt, carefully helping Mr. Bankes to a specially tender piece, of eternity; as she had already felt about something different once before that afternoon; there is a coherence in things, a stability; something, she meant, is immune from change, and shines out (she glanced at the window with its ripple of reflected lights) in the face of the flowing, the fleeting, the spectral, like a ruby; so that again tonight she had the feeling she had had once today, already, of peace, of rest. Of such moments, she thought, the thing is made that endures.

"Yes," she assured William Bankes, "there is plenty for everybody."

"Andrew," she said, "hold your plate lower, or I shall spill it." (The BOEUF EN DAUBE was a perfect triumph.) Here, she felt, putting the spoon down, where one could move or rest; could wait now (they were all helped) listening; could then, like a hawk which lapses suddenly from its high station, flaunt and sink on laughter easily, resting her whole weight upon what at the other end of the table her husband was saying about the square root of one thousand two hundred and fifty-three. That was the number, it seemed, on his watch.

What did it all mean? To this day she had no notion. A square root? What was that? Her sons knew. She leant on them; on cubes and square roots; that was what they were talking about now; on Voltaire and Madame de Stael; on the character of Napoleon; on the French system of land tenure; on Lord Rosebery; on Creevey's Memoirs: she let it uphold her and sustain her, this admirable fabric of the masculine intelligence, which ran up and down, crossed this way and that, like iron girders spanning the swaying fabric, upholding the world, so that she could trust herself to it utterly, even shut her eyes, or flicker them for a moment, as a child staring up from its pillow winks at the myriad layers of the leaves of a tree. Then she woke up. It was still being fabricated. William Bankes was praising the Waverly novels.

He read one of them every six months, he said. And why should that make Charles Tansley angry? He rushed in (all, thought Mrs. Ramsay, because Prue will not be nice to him) and denounced the Waverly novels when he knew nothing about it, nothing about it whatsoever, Mrs. Ramsay thought, observing him rather than listening to what he said. She could see how it was from his manner--he wanted to assert himself, and so it would always be with him till he got his

Professorship or married his wife, and so need not be always saying, "I--I--I." For that was what his criticism of poor Sir Walter, or perhaps it was Jane Austen, amounted to. "I---I---I." He was thinking of himself and the impression he was making, as she could tell by the sound of his voice, and his emphasis and his uneasiness. Success would be good for him. At any rate they were off again. Now she need not listen. It could not last, she knew, but at the moment her eyes were so clear that they seemed to go round the table unveiling each of these people, and their thoughts and their feelings, without effort like a light stealing under water so that its ripples and the reeds in it and the minnows balancing themselves, and the sudden silent trout are all lit up hanging, trembling. So she saw them; she heard them; but whatever they said had also this quality, as if what they said was like the movement of a trout when, at the same time, one can see the ripple and the gravel, something to the right, something to the left; and the whole is held together; for whereas in active life she would be netting and separating one thing from another; she would be saying she liked the Waverly novels or had not read them; she would be urging herself forward; now she said nothing. For the moment, she hung suspended.

"Ah, but how long do you think it'll last?" said somebody. It was as if she had antennae trembling out from her, which, intercepting certain sentences, forced them upon her attention. This was one of them. She scented danger for her husband. A question like that would lead, almost certainly, to something being said which reminded him of his own failure. How long would he be read--he would think at once. William Bankes (who was entirely free from all such vanity) laughed, and said he attached no importance to changes in fashion. Who could tell what was going to last--in literature or indeed in anything else?

"Let us enjoy what we do enjoy," he said. His integrity seemed to Mrs. Ramsay quite admirable. He never seemed for a moment to think, But how does this affect me? But then if you had the other temperament, which must have praise, which must have encouragement, naturally you began (and she knew that Mr. Ramsay was beginning) to be uneasy; to want somebody to say, Oh, but your work will last, Mr. Ramsay, or something like that. He showed his uneasiness quite clearly now by saying, with some irritation, that, anyhow, Scott (or was it Shakespeare ?) would last him his lifetime. He said it irritably. Everybody, she thought, felt a little uncomfortable, without knowing why. Then Minta Doyle, whose instinct was fine, said bluffly, absurdly, that she did not believe that any one really enjoyed reading Shakespeare. Mr. Ramsay said grimly (but his mind was turned away again) that very few people liked it as much as they said they did. But, he added, there is considerable merit in some of the plays nevertheless, and Mrs. Ramsay saw that it would be all right for the moment anyhow; he would laugh at Minta, and she, Mrs. Ramsay saw, realising his extreme anxiety about himself, would, in her own way, see that he was taken care of, and praise him, somehow or other. But she wished it was not necessary: perhaps it was her fault that it was necessary. Anyhow, she was free now to listen to what Paul Rayley was trying to say about books one had read as a boy. They lasted, he said. He had read some of Tolstoi at school. There was one he always remembered, but he had forgotten the name. Russian names were impossible, said Mrs. Ramsay. "Vronsky," said Paul. He remembered that because he always thought it such a good name for a villain. "Vronsky," said Mrs. Ramsay; "Oh, ANNA KARENINA," but that did not take them very far; books were not in their line. No, Charles Tansley would put them both right in a second about books, but it was all so mixed up with, Am I saying the right thing? Am I making a good impression? that, after all, one knew more about him than about Tolstoi, whereas, what Paul said was about the thing, simply, not himself, nothing else. Like all stupid people, he had a kind of modesty too, a consideration for what you were feeling, which, once in a way at least, she found attractive. Now he was thinking, not about himself, or about Tolstoi, but whether she was cold, whether she felt a draught, whether she would like a pear.

No, she said, she did not want a pear. Indeed she had been keeping guard over the dish of fruit (without realising it) jealously, hoping that nobody would touch it. Her eyes had been going in and out among the curves and shadows of the fruit, among the rich purples of the lowland grapes, then over the horny ridge of the shell, putting a yellow against a purple, a curved shape against a round shape, without knowing why she did it, or why, every time she did it, she felt more and more serene; until, oh, what a pity that they should do it--a hand reached out, took a pear, and spoilt the whole thing. In sympathy she looked at Rose. She looked at Rose sitting between Jasper and Prue. How odd that one's child should do that!

How odd to see them sitting there, in a row, her children, Jasper, Rose, Prue, Andrew, almost silent, but with some joke of their own going on, she guessed, from the twitching at their lips. It was something quite apart from everything else, something they were hoarding up to laugh over in their own room. It was not about their father, she hoped. No, she thought not. What was it, she wondered, sadly rather, for it seemed to her that they would laugh when she was not there. There was all that hoarded behind those rather set, still, mask-like faces, for they did not join in easily; they were like watchers, surveyors, a little raised or set apart from the grown-up people. But when she looked at Prue tonight, she saw that this was not now quite true of her. She was just beginning, just moving, just descending. The faintest light was on her face, as if the glow of Minta opposite, some excitement, some anticipation of happiness was reflected in her, as if the sun of the love of men and women rose over the rim of the table-cloth, and without knowing what it was she bent towards it and greeted it. She kept looking at Minta, shyly, yet curiously, so that Mrs. Ramsay looked from one to the other and said, speaking to Prue in her own mind, You will be as happy as she is one of these days. You will be much happier, she added, because you are my daughter, she meant; her own daughter must be happier than other people's daughters. But dinner was over. It was time to go. They were only playing with things on their plates. She would wait until they had done laughing at some story her husband was telling. He was having a joke with Minta about a bet. Then she would get up.

She liked Charles Tansley, she thought, suddenly; she liked his laugh. She liked him for being so angry with Paul and Minta. She liked his awkwardness. There was a lot in that young man after all. And Lily, she thought, putting her napkin beside her plate, she always has some joke of her own. One need never bother about Lily. She waited. She tucked her napkin under the edge of her plate. Well, were they done now? No. That story had led to another story. Her husband was in great spirits tonight, and wishing, she supposed, to make it all right with old Augustus after that scene about the soup, had drawn him in-- they were telling stories about some one they had both known at college. She looked at the window in which the candle flames burnt brighter now that the panes were black, and looking at that outside the voices came to her very strangely, as if they were voices at a service in a cathedral, for she did not listen to the words. The sudden bursts of laughter and then one voice (Minta's) speaking alone, reminded her of men and boys crying out the Latin words of a service in some Roman Catholic cathedral. She waited. Her husband spoke. He was repeating something, and she knew it was poetry from the rhythm and the ring of exultation, and melancholy in his voice:

Come out and climb the garden path, Luriana Lurilee. The China rose is all abloom and buzzing with the yellow bee.

The words (she was looking at the window) sounded as if they were floating like flowers on water out there, cut off from them all, as if no one had said them, but they had come into existence of themselves.

And all the lives we ever lived and all the lives to be Are full of trees and changing leaves.

She did not know what they meant, but, like music, the words seemed to be spoken by her own voice, outside her self, saying quite easily and naturally what had been in her mind the whole evening while she said different things. She knew, without looking round, that every one at the table was listening to the voice saying:

I wonder if it seems to you, Luriana, Lurilee

with the same sort of relief and pleasure that she had, as if this were, at last, the natural thing to say, this were their own voice speaking.

But the voice had stopped. She looked round. She made herself get up. Augustus Carmichael had risen and, holding his table napkin so that it looked like a long white robe he stood chanting:

To see the Kings go riding by Over lawn and daisy lea With their palm leaves and cedar Luriana, Lurilee,

and as she passed him, he turned slightly towards her repeating the last words:

Luriana, Lurilee

and bowed to her as if he did her homage. Without knowing why, she felt that he liked her better than he ever had done before; and with a feeling of relief and gratitude she returned his bow and passed through the door which he held open for her.

It was necessary now to carry everything a step further. With her foot on the threshold she waited a moment longer in a scene which was vanishing even as she looked, and then, as she moved and took Minta's arm and left the room, it changed, it shaped itself differently; it had become, she knew, giving one last look at it over her shoulder, already the past.

18

As usual, Lily thought. There was always something that had to be done at that precise moment, something that Mrs. Ramsay had decided for reasons of her own to do instantly, it might be with every one standing about making jokes, as now, not being able to decide whether they were going into the smoking-room, into the drawing-room, up to the attics. Then one saw Mrs. Ramsay in the midst of this hubbub standing there with Minta's arm in hers, bethink her, "Yes, it is time for that now," and so make off at once with an air of secrecy to do something alone. And directly she went a sort of disintegration set in; they wavered about, went different ways, Mr. Bankes took Charles Tansley by the arm and went off to finish on the terrace the discussion they had begun at dinner about politics, thus giving a turn to the whole poise of the evening, making the weight fall in a different direction, as if, Lily thought, seeing them go, and hearing a word or two about the policy of the Labour Party, they had gone up on to the bridge of the ship and were taking their bearings; the change from poetry to politics struck her like that; so Mr. Bankes and Charles Mrs. Ramsay going upstairs in the lamplight alone. Where, Lily wondered, was she going so quickly?

Not that she did in fact run or hurry; she went indeed rather slowly. She felt rather inclined just for a moment to stand still after all that chatter, and pick out one particular thing; the thing that mattered; to detach it; separate it off; clean it of all the emotions and odds and ends of things, and so hold it before her, and bring it to the tribunal where, ranged about in conclave, sat the judges she had set up to decide these things. Is it good, is it bad, is it right or wrong? Where are we all going to? and so on. So she righted herself after the shock of the event, and quite unconsciously and incongruously, used the branches of the elm trees outside to help her to stabilise her position. Her world was changing: they were still. The event had given her a sense of movement. All must be in order. She must get that right and that right, she thought, insensibly approving of the dignity of the trees' stillness, and now again of the superb upward rise (like the beak of a ship up a wave) of the elm branches as the wind raised them. For it was windy (she stood a moment to look out). It was windy, so that the leaves now and then brushed open a star, and the stars themselves seemed to be shaking and darting light and trying to flash out between the edges of the leaves. Yes, that was done then, accomplished; and as with all things done, became solemn. Now one thought of it, cleared of chatter and emotion, it seemed always to have been, only was shown now and so being shown, struck everything into stability. They would, she thought, going on again, however long they lived, come back to this night; this moon; this wind; this house: and to her too. It flattered her, where she was most susceptible of flattery, to think how, wound about in their hearts, however long they lived she would be woven; and this, and this, and this, she thought, going upstairs, laughing, but affectionately, at the sofa on the landing (her mother's); at the rocking-chair (her father's); at the map of the Hebrides. All that would be revived again in the lives of Paul and Minta; "the Rayleys"--she tried the new name over; and she felt, with her hand on the nursery door, that community of feeling with other people which emotion gives as if the walls of partition had become so thin that practically (the feeling was one of relief and happiness) it was all one stream, and chairs, tables, maps, were hers, were theirs, it did not matter whose, and Paul and Minta would carry it on when she was dead.

She turned the handle, firmly, lest it should squeak, and went in, pursing her lips slightly, as if to remind herself that she must not speak aloud. But directly she came in she saw, with annoyance, that the precaution was not needed. The children were not asleep. It was most annoying. Mildred should be more careful. There was James wide awake and Cam sitting bolt upright, and Mildred out of bed in her bare feet, and it was almost eleven and they were all talking. What was the matter? It was that horrid skull again. She had told Mildred to move it, but Mildred, of course, had forgotten, and now there was Cam wide awake, and James wide awake quarreling when they ought to have been asleep hours ago. What had possessed Edward to send them this horrid skull? She had been so foolish as to let them nail it up there. It was nailed fast, Mildred said, and Cam couldn't go to sleep with it in the room, and James screamed if she touched it.

Then Cam must go to sleep (it had great horns said Cam)--must go to sleep and dream of lovely palaces, said Mrs. Ramsay, sitting down on the bed by her side. She could see the horns, Cam said, all over the room. It was true. Wherever they put the light (and James could not sleep without a light) there was always a shadow somewhere.

"But think, Cam, it's only an old pig," said Mrs. Ramsay, "a nice black pig like the pigs at the farm." But Cam thought it was a horrid thing, branching at her all over the room.

"Well then," said Mrs. Ramsay, "we will cover it up," and they all watched her go to the chest of drawers, and open the little drawers quickly one after another, and not seeing anything that would do, she quickly took her own shawl off and wound it round the skull, round and round and round, and then she came back to Cam and laid her head almost flat on the pillow beside Cam's and said how lovely it looked now; how the fairies would love it; it was like a bird's nest; it was like a beautiful mountain such as she had seen abroad, with valleys and flowers and bells ringing and birds singing and little goats and antelopes and... She could see the words echoing as she spoke them rhythmically in Cam's mind, and Cam was repeating after her how it was like a mountain, a bird's nest, a garden, and there were little antelopes, and her eyes were opening and shutting, and Mrs. Ramsay went on speaking still more monotonously, and more rhythmically and more nonsensically, how she must shut her eyes and go to sleep and dream of mountains and valleys and stars falling and parrots and antelopes and gardens, and everything lovely, she said, raising her head very slowly and speaking more and more mechanically, until she sat upright and saw that Cam was asleep.

Now, she whispered, crossing over to his bed, James must go to sleep too, for see, she said, the boar's skull was still there; they had not touched it; they had done just what he wanted; it was there quite unhurt. He made sure that the skull was still there under the shawl. But he wanted to ask her something more. Would they go to the Lighthouse tomorrow?

No, not tomorrow, she said, but soon, she promised him; the next fine day. He was very good. He lay down. She covered him up. But he would never forget, she knew, and she felt angry with Charles Tansley, with her husband, and with herself, for she had raised his hopes. Then feeling for her shawl and remembering that she had wrapped it round the boar's skull, she got up, and pulled the window down another inch or two, and heard the wind, and got a breath of the perfectly indifferent chill night air and murmured good night to Mildred and left the room and let the tongue of the door slowly lengthen in the lock and went out.

She hoped he would not bang his books on the floor above their heads, she thought, still thinking how annoying Charles Tansley was. For neither of them slept well; they were excitable children, and since he said things like that about the Lighthouse, it seemed to her likely that he would knock a pile of books over, just as they were going to sleep, clumsily sweeping them off the table with his elbow. For she supposed that he had gone upstairs to work. Yet he looked so desolate; yet she would feel relieved when he went; yet she would see that he was better treated tomorrow; yet he was admirable with her husband; yet his manners certainly wanted improving; yet she liked his laugh--thinking this, as she came downstairs, she noticed that she could now see the moon itself through the staircase window--the yellow harvest moon-- and turned, and they saw her, standing above them on the stairs.

"That's my mother," thought Prue. Yes; Minta should look at her; Paul Rayley should look at her. That is the thing itself, she felt, as if there were only one person like that in the world; her mother. And, from having been quite grown up, a moment before, talking with the others, she became a child again, and what they had been doing was a game, and would her mother sanction their game, or condemn it, she wondered. And thinking what a chance it was for Minta and Paul and Lily to see her, and feeling what an extraordinary stroke of fortune it was for her, to have her, and how she would never grow up and never leave home, she said, like a child, "We thought of going down to the beach to watch the waves."

Instantly, for no reason at all, Mrs. Ramsay became like a girl of twenty, full of gaiety. A mood of revelry suddenly took possession of her. Of course they must go; of course they must go, she cried, laughing; and running down the last three or four steps quickly, she began turning from one to the other and laughing and drawing Minta's wrap round her and saying she only wished she could come too, and would they be very late, and had any of them got a watch?

"Yes, Paul has," said Minta. Paul slipped a beautiful gold watch out of a little wash-leather case to show her. And as he held it in the palm of his hand before her, he felt, "She knows all about it. I need not say anything." He was saying to her as he showed her the watch, "I've done it, Mrs. Ramsay. I owe it all to you." And seeing the gold watch lying in his hand, Mrs. Ramsay felt, How extraordinarily lucky Minta is! She is marrying a man who has a gold watch in a wash- leather bag!

"How I wish I could come with you!" she cried. But she was withheld by something so strong that she never even thought of asking herself what it was. Of course it was impossible for her to go with them. But she would have liked to go, had it not been for the other thing, and tickled by the absurdity of her thought (how lucky to marry a man with a wash-leather bag for his watch) she went with a smile on her lips into the other room, where her husband sat reading.

19

Of course, she said to herself, coming into the room, she had to come here to get something she wanted. First she wanted to sit down in a particular chair under a particular lamp. But she wanted something more, though she did not know, could not think what it was that she wanted. She looked at her husband (taking up her stocking and beginning to knit), and saw that he did not want to be interrupted-- that was clear. He was reading something that moved him very much. He was half smiling and then she knew he was controlling his emotion. He was tossing the pages over. He was acting it--perhaps he was thinking himself the person in the book. She wondered what book it was. Oh, it was one of old Sir Walter's she saw, adjusting the shade of her lamp so that the light fell on her knitting. For Charles Tansley had been saying (she looked up as if she expected to hear the crash of books on the floor above), had been saying that people don't read Scott any more. Then her husband thought, "That's what they'll say of me;" so he went and got one of those books. And if he came to the conclusion "That's true" what Charles Tansley said, he would accept it about Scott. (She could see that he was weighing, considering, putting this with that as he read.) But not about himself. He was always uneasy about himself. That troubled her. He would always be worrying about his own books--will they be read, are they good, why aren't they better, what do people think of me? Not liking to think of him so, and wondering if they had guessed at dinner why he suddenly became irritable when they talked about fame and books lasting, wondering if the children were laughing at that, she twitched the stockings out, and all the fine gravings came drawn with steel instruments about her lips and forehead, and she grew still like a tree which has been tossing and quivering and now, when the breeze falls, settles, leaf by leaf, into quiet.

It didn't matter, any of it, she thought. A great man, a great book, fame--who could tell? She knew nothing about it. But it was his way with him, his truthfulness--for instance at dinner she had been thinking quite instinctively, If only he would speak! She had complete trust in him. And dismissing all this, as one passes in diving now a weed, now a straw, now a bubble, she felt again, sinking deeper, as she had felt in the hall when the others were talking, There is something I want--something I have come to get, and she fell deeper and deeper without knowing quite what it was, with her eyes closed. And she waited a little, knitting, wondering, and slowly rose those words they had said at dinner, "the China rose is all abloom and buzzing with the honey bee," began washing from side to side of her mind rhythmically, and as they washed, words, like little shaded lights, one red, one blue, one yellow, lit up in the dark of her mind, and seemed leaving their perches up there to fly across and across, or to cry out and to be echoed; so she turned and felt on the table beside her for a book.

And all the lives we ever lived And all the lives to be, Are full of trees and changing leaves,

she murmured, sticking her needles into the stocking. And she opened the book and began reading here and there at random, and as she did so, she felt that she was climbing backwards, upwards, shoving her way up under petals that curved over her, so that she only knew this is white, or this is red. She did not know at first what the words meant at all.

Steer, hither steer your winged pines, all beaten Mariners

she read and turned the page, swinging herself, zigzagging this way and that, from one line to another as from one branch to another, from one red and white flower to another, until a little sound roused her--her husband slapping his thighs. Their eyes met for a second; but they did not want to speak to each other. They had nothing to say, but something seemed, nevertheless, to go from him to her. It was the life, it was the power of it, it was the tremendous humour, she knew, that made him slap his thighs. Don't interrupt me, he seemed to be saying, don't say anything; just sit there. And he went on reading. His lips twitched. It filled him. It fortified him. He clean forgot all the little rubs and digs of the evening, and how it bored him unutterably to sit still while people ate and drank interminably, and his being so irritable with his wife and so touchy and minding when they passed his books over as if they didn't exist at all. But now, he felt, it didn't matter a damn who reached Z (if thought ran like an alphabet from A to Z). Somebody would reach it--if not he, then another. This man's strength and sanity, his feeling for straight forward simple things, these fishermen, the poor old crazed creature in Mucklebackit's cottage made him feel so vigorous, so relieved of something that he felt roused and triumphant and could not choke back his tears. Raising the book a little to hide his face, he let them fall and shook his head from side to side and forgot himself completely (but not one or two reflections about morality and French novels and English novels and Scott's hands being tied but his view perhaps being as true as the other view), forgot his own bothers and failures completely in poor Steenie's drowning and Mucklebackit's sorrow (that was Scott at his best) and the astonishing delight and feeling of vigour that it gave him.

Well, let them improve upon that, he thought as he finished the chapter. He felt that he had been arguing with somebody, and had got the better of him. They could not improve upon that, whatever they might say; and his own position became more secure. The lovers were fiddlesticks, he thought, collecting it all in his mind again. That's fiddlesticks, that's first-rate, he thought, putting one thing beside another. But he must read it again. He could not remember the whole shape of the thing. He had to keep his judgement in suspense. So he returned to the other thought--if young men did not care for this, naturally they did not care for him either. One ought not to complain, thought Mr. Ramsay, trying to stifle his desire to complain to his wife that young men did not admire him. But he was determined; he would not bother her again. Here he looked at her reading. She looked very peaceful, reading. He liked to think that every one had taken themselves off and that he and she were alone. The whole of life did not consist in going to bed with a woman, he thought, returning to Scott and Balzac, to the English novel and the French novel.

Mrs. Ramsay raised her head and like a person in a light sleep seemed to say that if he wanted her to wake she would, she really would, but otherwise, might she go on sleeping, just a little longer, just a little longer? She was climbing up those branches, this way and that, laying hands on one flower and then another.

Nor praise the deep vermilion in the rose,

she read, and so reading she was ascending, she felt, on to the top, on to the summit. How satisfying! How restful! All the odds and ends of the day stuck to this magnet; her mind felt swept, felt clean. And then there it was, suddenly entire; she held it in her hands, beautiful and reasonable, clear and complete, here--the sonnet.

But she was becoming conscious of her husband looking at her. He was smiling at her, quizzically, as if he were ridiculing her gently for being asleep in broad daylight, but at the same time he was thinking, Go on reading. You don't look sad now, he thought. And he wondered what she was reading, and exaggerated her ignorance, her simplicity, for he liked to think that she was not clever, not book-learned at all. He wondered if she understood what she was reading. Probably not, he thought. She was astonishingly beautiful. Her beauty seemed to him, if that were possible, to increase

Yet seem'd it winter still, and, you away, As with your shadow I with these did play,

she finished.

"Well?" she said, echoing his smile dreamily, looking up from her book.

As with your shadow I with these did play,

she murmured, putting the book on the table.

What had happened, she wondered, as she took up her knitting, since she had seen him alone? She remembered dressing, and seeing the moon; Andrew holding his plate too high at dinner; being depressed by something William had said; the birds in the trees; the sofa on the landing; the children being awake; Charles Tansley waking them with his books falling--oh, no, that she had invented; and Paul having a wash- leather case for his watch. Which should she tell him about?

"They're engaged," she said, beginning to knit, "Paul and Minta."

"So I guessed," he said. There was nothing very much to be said about it. Her mind was still going up and down, up and down with the poetry; he was still feeling very vigorous, very forthright, after reading about Steenie's funeral. So they sat silent. Then she became aware that she wanted him to say something.

Anything, anything, she thought, going on with her knitting. Anything will do.

"How nice it would be to marry a man with a wash-leather bag for his watch," she said, for that was the sort of joke they had together.

He snorted. He felt about this engagement as he always felt about any engagement; the girl is much too good for that young man. Slowly it came into her head, why is it then that one wants people to marry? What was the value, the meaning of things? (Every word they said now would be true.) Do say something, she thought, wishing only to hear his voice. For the shadow, the thing folding them in was beginning, she felt, to close round her again. Say anything, she begged, looking at him, as if for help.

He was silent, swinging the compass on his watch-chain to and fro, and thinking of Scott's novels and Balzac's novels. But through the crepuscular walls of their intimacy, for they were drawing together, involuntarily, coming side by side, quite close, she could feel his mind like a raised hand shadowing her mind; and he was beginning, now that her thoughts took a turn he disliked--towards this "pessimism" as he called it--to fidget, though he said nothing, raising his hand to his forehead, twisting a lock of hair, letting it fall again.

"You won't finish that stocking tonight," he said, pointing to her stocking. That was what she wanted--the asperity in his voice reproving her. If he says it's wrong to be pessimistic probably it is wrong, she thought; the marriage will turn out all right.

"No," she said, flattening the stocking out upon her knee, "I shan't finish it."

And what then? For she felt that he was still looking at her, but that his look had changed. He wanted something--wanted the thing she always found it so difficult to give him; wanted her to tell him that she loved him. And that, no, she could not do. He found talking so much easier than she did. He could say things--she never could. So naturally it was always he that said the things, and then for some reason he would mind this suddenly, and would reproach her. A heartless woman he called her; she never told him that she loved him. But it was not so--it was not so. It was only that she never could say what she felt. Was there no crumb on his coat? Nothing she could do for him? Getting up, she stood at the window with the reddish-brown stocking in her hands, partly to turn away from him, partly because she remembered how beautiful it often is--the sea at night. But she knew that he had turned his head as she turned; he was watching her. She knew that he was thinking, You are more beautiful than ever. And she felt herself very beautiful. Will you not tell me just for once that you love me? He was thinking that, for he was roused, what with Minta and his book, and its being the end of the day and their having quarrelled about going to the Lighthouse. But she could not do it; she could not say it. Then, knowing that he was watching her, instead of saying anything she turned, holding her stocking, and looked at him. And as she looked at him she began to smile, for though she had not said a word, he knew, of course he knew, that she loved him. He could not deny it. And smiling she looked out of the window and said (thinking to herself, Nothing on earth can equal this happiness)--

"Yes, you were right. It's going to be wet tomorrow. You won't be able to go." And she looked at him smiling. For she had triumphed again. She had not said it: yet he knew.

TIME PASSES

1

"Well, we must wait for the future to show," said Mr. Bankes, coming in from the terrace.

"It's almost too dark to see," said Andrew, coming up from the beach.

"One can hardly tell which is the sea and which is the land," said Prue.

"Do we leave that light burning?" said Lily as they took their coats off indoors.

"No," said Prue, "not if every one's in."

"Andrew," she called back, "just put out the light in the hall."

One by one the lamps were all extinguished, except that Mr. Carmichael, who liked to lie awake a little reading Virgil, kept his candle burning rather longer than the rest.

2

So with the lamps all put out, the moon sunk, and a thin rain drumming on the roof a downpouring of immense darkness began. Nothing, it seemed, could survive the flood, the profusion of darkness which, creeping in at keyholes and crevices, stole round window blinds, came into bedrooms, swallowed up here a jug and basin, there a bowl of red and yellow dahlias, there the sharp edges and firm bulk of a chest of drawers. Not only was furniture confounded; there was scarcely anything left of body or mind by which one could say, "This is he" or "This is she." Sometimes a hand was raised as if to clutch something or ward off something, or somebody groaned, or somebody laughed aloud as if sharing a joke with nothingness.

Nothing stirred in the drawing-room or in the dining-room or on the staircase. Only through the rusty hinges and swollen sea-moistened woodwork certain airs, detached from the body of the wind (the house was ramshackle after all) crept round corners and ventured indoors. Almost one might imagine them, as they entered the drawing-room questioning and wondering, toying with the flap of hanging wall-paper, asking, would it hang much longer, when would it fall? Then smoothly brushing the walls, they passed on musingly as if asking the red and yellow roses on the wall-paper whether they would fade, and questioning (gently, for there was time at their disposal) the torn letters in the wastepaper basket, the flowers, the books, all of which were now open to them and asking, Were they allies? Were they enemies? How long would they endure?

So some random light directing them with its pale footfall upon stair and mat, from some uncovered star, or wandering ship, or the Lighthouse even, with its pale footfall upon stair and mat, the little airs mounted the staircase and nosed round bedroom doors. But here surely, they must cease. Whatever else may perish and disappear, what lies here is steadfast. Here one might say to those sliding lights, those fumbling airs that breathe and bend over the bed itself, here you can neither touch nor destroy. Upon which, wearily, ghostlily, as if they had feather-light fingers and the light persistency of feathers, they would look, once, on the shut eyes, and the loosely clasping fingers, and fold their garments wearily and disappear. And so, nosing, rubbing, they went to the window on the staircase, to the servants' bedrooms, to the boxes in the attics; descending, blanched the apples on the dining-room table, fumbled the petals of roses, tried the picture on the easel, brushed the mat and blew a little sand along the floor. At length, desisting, all ceased together, gathered together, all sighed together; all together gave off an aimless gust of lamentation to which some door in the kitchen replied; swung wide; admitted nothing; and slammed to.

[Here Mr. Carmichael, who was reading Virgil, blew out his candle. It was past midnight.]

3

But what after all is one night? A short space, especially when the darkness dims so soon, and so soon a bird sings, a cock crows, or a faint green quickens, like a turning leaf, in the hollow of the wave. Night, however, succeeds to night. The winter holds a pack of them in store and deals them equally, evenly, with indefatigable fingers. They lengthen; they darken. Some of them hold aloft clear planets, plates of brightness. The autumn trees, ravaged as they are, take on the flash of tattered flags kindling in the gloom of cool cathedral caves where gold letters on marble pages describe death in battle and how bones bleach and burn far away in Indian sands. The autumn trees gleam in the yellow moonlight, in the light of harvest moons, the light which mellows the energy of labour, and smooths the stubble, and brings the wave lapping blue to the shore.

It seemed now as if, touched by human penitence and all its toil, divine goodness had parted the curtain and displayed behind it, single, distinct, the hare erect; the wave falling; the boat rocking; which, did we deserve them, should be ours always. But alas, divine goodness, twitching the cord, draws the curtain; it does not please him; he covers his treasures in a drench of hail, and so breaks them, so confuses them that it seems impossible that their calm should ever return or that we should ever compose from their fragments a perfect whole or read in the littered pieces the clear words of truth. For our penitence deserves a glimpse only; our toil respite only.

The nights now are full of wind and destruction; the trees plunge and bend and their leaves fly helter skelter until the lawn is plastered with them and they lie packed in gutters and choke rain pipes and scatter damp paths. Also the sea tosses itself and breaks itself, and should any sleeper fancying that he might find on the beach an answer to his doubts, a sharer of his solitude, throw off his bedclothes and go down by himself to walk on the sand, no image with semblance of serving and divine promptitude comes readily to hand bringing the night to order and making the world reflect the compass of the soul. The hand dwindles in his hand; the voice bellows in his ear. Almost it would appear that it is useless in such confusion to ask the night those questions as to what, and why, and wherefore, which tempt the sleeper from his bed to seek an answer.

[Mr. Ramsay, stumbling along a passage one dark morning, stretched his arms out, but Mrs. Ramsay having died rather suddenly the night before, his arms, though stretched out, remained empty.]]

4

So with the house empty and the doors locked and the mattresses rolled round, those stray airs, advance guards of great armies, blustered in, brushed bare boards, nibbled and fanned, met nothing in bedroom or drawing-room that wholly resisted them but only hangings that flapped, wood that creaked, the bare legs of tables, saucepans and china already furred, tarnished, cracked. What people had shed and left--a pair of shoes, a shooting cap, some faded skirts and coats in wardrobes--those alone kept the human shape and in the emptiness indicated how once they were filled and animated; how once hands were busy with hooks and buttons; how once the looking-glass had held a face; had held a world hollowed out in which a figure turned, a hand flashed, the door opened, in came children rushing and tumbling; and went out again. Now, day after day, light turned, like a flower reflected in water, its sharp image on the wall opposite. Only the shadows of the trees, flourishing in the wind, made obeisance on the wall, and for a moment darkened the pool in which light reflected itself; or birds, flying, made a soft spot flutter slowly across the bedroom floor.

So loveliness reigned and stillness, and together made the shape of loveliness itself, a form from which life had parted; solitary like a pool at evening, far distant, seen from a train window, vanishing so quickly that the pool, pale in the evening, is scarcely robbed of its solitude, though once seen. Loveliness and stillness clasped hands in the bedroom, and among the shrouded jugs and sheeted chairs even the prying of the wind, and the soft nose of the clammy sea airs, rubbing, snuffling, iterating, and reiterating their questions--"Will you fade? Will you perish?"--scarcely disturbed the peace, the indifference, the air of pure integrity, as if the question they asked scarcely needed that they should answer: we remain.

Nothing it seemed could break that image, corrupt that innocence, or disturb the swaying mantle of silence which, week after week, in the empty room, wove into itself the falling cries of birds, ships hooting, the drone and hum of the fields, a dog's bark, a man's shout, and folded them round the house in silence. Once only a board sprang on the landing; once in the middle of the night with a roar, with a rupture, as after centuries of quiescence, a rock rends itself from the mountain and hurtles crashing into the valley, one fold of the shawl loosened and swung to and fro. Then again peace descended; and the shadow wavered; light bent to its own image in adoration on the bedroom wall; and Mrs. McNab, tearing the veil of silence with hands that had stood in the wash-tub, grinding it with boots that had crunched the shingle, came as directed to open all windows, and dust the bedrooms.

5

As she lurched (for she rolled like a ship at sea) and leered (for her eyes fell on nothing directly, but with a sidelong glance that deprecated the scorn and anger of the world--she was witless, she knew it), as she clutched the banisters and hauled herself upstairs and rolled from room to room, she sang. Rubbing the glass of the long looking-glass and leering sideways at her swinging figure a sound issued from her lips--something that had been gay twenty years before on the stage perhaps, had been hummed and danced to, but now, coming from the toothless, bonneted, care-taking woman, was robbed of meaning, was like the voice of witlessness, humour, persistency itself, trodden down but springing up again, so that as she lurched, dusting, wiping, she seemed to say how it was one long sorrow and trouble, how it was getting up and going to bed again, and bringing things out and putting them away again. It was not easy or snug this world she had known for close on seventy years. Bowed down she was with weariness. How long, she asked, creaking and groaning on her knees under the bed, dusting the boards, how long shall it endure? but hobbled to her feet again, pulled herself up, and again with her sidelong leer which slipped and turned aside even from her own face, and her own sorrows, stood and gaped in the glass, aimlessly smiling, and began again the old amble and hobble, taking up mats, putting down china, looking sideways in the glass, as if, after all, she had her consolations, as if indeed there twined about her dirge some incorrigible hope. Visions of joy there must have been at the wash- tub, say with her children (yet two had been base-born and one had deserted her), at the public-house, drinking; turning over scraps in her drawers. Some cleavage of the dark there must have been, some channel in the depths of obscurity through which light enough issued to twist her face grinning in the glass and make her, turning to her job again, mumble out the old music hall song. The mystic, the visionary, walking the beach on a fine night, stirring a puddle, looking at a stone, asking themselves "What am I," "What is this?" had suddenly an answer vouchsafed them: (they could not say what it was) so that they were warm in the frost and had comfort in the desert. But Mrs. McNab continued to drink and gossip as before.

6

The Spring without a leaf to toss, bare and bright like a virgin fierce in her chastity, scornful in her purity, was laid out on fields wide- eyed and watchful and entirely careless of what was done or thought by the beholders. [Prue Ramsay, leaning on her father's arm, was given in marriage. What, people said, could have been more fitting? And, they added, how beautiful she looked!]

As summer neared, as the evenings lengthened, there came to the wakeful, the hopeful, walking the beach, stirring the pool, imaginations of the strangest kind--of flesh turned to atoms which drove before the wind, of stars flashing in their hearts, of cliff, sea, cloud, and sky brought purposely together to assemble outwardly the scattered parts of the vision within. In those mirrors, the minds of men, in those pools of uneasy water, in which clouds for ever turn and shadows form, dreams persisted, and it was impossible to resist the strange intimation which every gull, flower, tree, man and woman, and the white earth itself seemed to declare (but if questioned at once to withdraw) that good triumphs, happiness prevails, order rules; or to resist the extraordinary stimulus to range hither and thither in search of some absolute good, some crystal of intensity, remote from the known pleasures and familiar virtues, something alien to the processes of domestic life, single, hard, bright, like a diamond in the sand, which would render the possessor secure. Moreover, softened and acquiescent, the spring with her bees humming and gnats dancing threw her cloak about her, veiled her eyes, averted her head, and among passing shadows and flights of small rain seemed to have taken upon her a knowledge of the sorrows of mankind.

[Prue Ramsay died that summer in some illness connected with childbirth, which was indeed a tragedy, people said, everything, they said, had promised so well.]

And now in the heat of summer the wind sent its spies about the house again. Flies wove a web in the sunny rooms; weeds that had grown close to the glass in the night tapped methodically at the window pane. When darkness fell, the stroke of the Lighthouse, which had laid itself with such authority upon the carpet in the darkness, tracing its pattern, came now in the softer light of spring mixed with moonlight gliding gently as if it laid its caress and lingered steathily and looked and came lovingly again. But in the very lull of this loving caress, as the long stroke leant upon the bed, the rock was rent asunder; another fold of the shawl loosened; there it hung, and swayed. Through the short summer nights and the long summer days, when the empty rooms seemed to murmur with the echoes of the fields and the hum of flies, the long streamer waved gently, swayed aimlessly; while the sun so striped and barred the rooms and filled them with yellow haze that Mrs. McNab, when she broke in and lurched about, dusting, sweeping, looked like a tropical fish oaring its way through sun-lanced waters.

But slumber and sleep though it might there came later in the summer ominous sounds like the measured blows of hammers dulled on felt, which, with their repeated shocks still further loosened the shawl and cracked the tea-cups. Now and again some glass tinkled in the cupboard as if a giant voice had shrieked so loud in its agony that tumblers stood inside a cupboard vibrated too. Then again silence fell; and then, night after night, and sometimes in plain mid-day when the roses were bright and light turned on the wall its shape clearly there seemed to drop into this silence, this indifference, this integrity, the thud of something falling.

[A shell exploded. Twenty or thirty young men were blown up in France, among them Andrew Ramsay, whose death, mercifully, was instantaneous.]

At that season those who had gone down to pace the beach and ask of the sea and sky what message they reported or what vision they affirmed had to consider among the usual tokens of divine bounty--the sunset on the sea, the pallor of dawn, the moon rising, fishing-boats against the moon, and children making mud pies or pelting each other with handfuls of grass, something out of harmony with this jocundity and this serenity. There was the silent apparition of an ashen-coloured ship for instance, come, gone; there was a purplish stain upon the bland surface of the sea as if something had boiled and bled, invisibly, beneath. This intrusion into a scene calculated to stir the most sublime reflections and lead to the most comfortable conclusions stayed their pacing. It was difficult blandly to overlook them; to abolish their significance in the landscape; to continue, as one walked by the sea, to marvel how beauty outside mirrored beauty within.

Did Nature supplement what man advanced? Did she complete what he began? With equal complacence she saw his misery, his meanness, and his torture. That dream, of sharing, completing, of finding in solitude on the beach an answer, was then but a reflection in a mirror, and the mirror itself was but the surface glassiness which forms in quiescence when the nobler powers sleep beneath? Impatient, despairing yet loth to go (for beauty offers her lures, has her consolations), to pace the beach was impossible; contemplation was unendurable; the mirror was broken.

[Mr. Carmichael brought out a volume of poems that spring, which had an unexpected success. The war, people said, had revived their interest in poetry.]

7

Night after night, summer and winter, the torment of storms, the arrow- like stillness of fine (had there been any one to listen) from the upper rooms of the empty house only gigantic chaos streaked with lightning could have been heard tumbling and tossing, as the winds and waves disported themselves like the amorphous bulks of leviathans whose brows are pierced by no light of reason, and mounted one on top of another, and lunged and plunged in the darkness or the daylight (for night and day, month and year ran shapelessly together) in idiot games, until it seemed as if the universe were battling and tumbling, in brute confusion and wanton lust aimlessly by itself.

In spring the garden urns, casually filled with wind-blown plants, were gay as ever. Violets came and daffodils. But the stillness and the brightness of the day were as strange as the chaos and tumult of night, with the trees standing there, and the flowers standing there, looking before them, looking up, yet beholding nothing, eyeless, and so terrible.

8

Thinking no harm, for the family would not come, never again, some said, and the house would be sold at Michaelmas perhaps, Mrs. McNab stooped and picked a bunch of flowers to take home with her. She laid them on the table while she dusted. She was fond of flowers. It was a pity to let them waste. Suppose the house were sold (she stood arms akimbo in front of the looking-glass) it would want seeing to--it would. There it had stood all these years without a soul in it. The books and things were mouldy, for, what with the war and help being hard to get, the house had not been cleaned as she could have wished. It was beyond one person's strength to get it straight now. She was too old. Her legs pained her. All those books needed to be laid out on the grass in the sun; there was plaster fallen in the hall; the rain-pipe had blocked over the study window and let the water in; the carpet was ruined quite. But people should come themselves; they should have sent somebody down to see. For there were clothes in the cupboards; they had left clothes in all the bedrooms. What was she to do with them? They had the moth in them--Mrs. Ramsay's things. Poor lady! She would never want THEM again. She was dead, they said; years ago, in London. There was the old grey cloak she wore gardening (Mrs. McNab fingered it). She could see her, as she came up the drive with the washing, stooping over her flowers (the garden was a pitiful sight now, all run to riot, and rabbits scuttling at you out of the beds)--she could see her with one of the children by her in that grey cloak. There were boots and shoes; and a brush and comb left on the dressing-table, for all the world as if she expected to come back tomorrow. (She had died very sudden at the end, they said.) And once they had been coming, but had put off coming, what with the war, and travel being so difficult these days; they had never come all these years; just sent her money; but never wrote, never came, and expected to find things as they had left them, ah, dear! Why the dressing-table drawers were full of things (she pulled them open), handkerchiefs, bits of ribbon. Yes, she could see Mrs. Ramsay as she came up the drive with the washing.

"Good-evening, Mrs. McNab," she would say.

She had a pleasant way with her. The girls all liked her. But, dear, many things had changed since then (she shut the drawer); many families had lost their dearest. So she was dead; and Mr. Andrew killed; and Miss Prue dead too, they said, with her first baby; but everyone had lost some one these years. Prices had gone up shamefully, and didn't come down again neither. She could well remember her in her grey cloak.

"Good-evening, Mrs. McNab," she said, and told cook to keep a plate of milk soup for her--quite thought she wanted it, carrying that heavy basket all the way up from town. She could see her now, stooping over her flowers; and faint and flickering, like a yellow beam or the circle at the end of a telescope, a lady in a grey cloak, stooping over her flowers, went wandering over the bedroom wall, up the dressing-table, across the wash-stand, as Mrs. McNab hobbled and ambled, dusting, straightening. And cook's name now? Mildred? Marian?--some name like that. Ah, she had forgotten--she did forget things. Fiery, like all red-haired women. Many a laugh they had had. She was always welcome in the kitchen. She made them laugh, she did. Things were better then than now.

She sighed; there was too much work for one woman. She wagged her head this side and that. This had been the nursery. Why, it was all damp in here; the plaster was falling. Whatever did they want to hang a beast's skull there? gone mouldy too. And rats in all the attics. The rain came in. But they never sent; never came. Some of the locks had gone, so the doors banged. She didn't like to be up here at dusk alone neither. It was too much for one woman, too much, too much. She creaked, she moaned. She banged the door. She turned the key in the lock, and left the house alone, shut up, locked.

9

The house was left; the house was deserted. It was left like a shell on a sandhill to fill with dry salt grains now that life had left it. The long night seemed to have set in; the trifling airs, nibbling, the clammy breaths, fumbling, seemed to have triumphed. The saucepan had rusted and the mat decayed. Toads had nosed their way in. Idly, aimlessly, the swaying shawl swung to and fro. A thistle thrust itself between the tiles in the larder. The swallows nested in the drawing- room; the floor was strewn with straw; the plaster fell in shovelfuls; rafters were laid bare; rats carried off this and that to gnaw behind the wainscots. Tortoise-shell butterflies burst from the chrysalis and pattered their life out on the window-pane. Poppies sowed themselves among the dahlias; the lawn waved with long grass; giant artichokes towered among roses; a fringed carnation flowered among the cabbages; while the gentle tapping of a weed at the window had become, on winters' nights, a drumming from sturdy trees and thorned briars which made the whole room green in summer.

What power could now prevent the fertility, the insensibility of nature? Mrs. McNab's dream of a lady, of a child, of a plate of milk soup? It had wavered over the walls like a spot of sunlight and vanished. She had locked the door; she had gone. It was beyond the strength of one woman, she said. They never sent. They never wrote. There were things up there rotting in the drawers--it was a shame to leave them so, she said. The place was gone to rack and ruin. Only the Lighthouse beam entered the rooms for a moment, sent its sudden stare over bed and wall in the darkness of winter, looked with equanimity at the thistle and the swallow, the rat and the straw. Nothing now withstood them; nothing said no to them. Let the wind blow; let the poppy seed itself and the carnation mate with the cabbage. Let the swallow build in the drawing-room, and the thistle thrust aside the tiles, and the butterfly sun itself on the faded chintz of the arm-chairs. Let the broken glass and the china lie out on the lawn and be tangled over with grass and wild berries.

For now had come that moment, that hesitation when dawn trembles and night pauses, when if a feather alight in the scale it will be weighed down. One feather, and the house, sinking, falling, would have turned and pitched downwards to the depths of darkness. In the ruined room, picnickers would have lit their kettles; lovers sought shelter there, lying on the bare boards; and the shepherd stored his dinner on the bricks, and the tramp slept with his coat round him to ward off the cold. Then the roof would have fallen; briars and hemlocks would have blotted out path, step and window; would have grown, unequally but lustily over the mound, until some trespasser, losing his way, could have told only by a red-hot poker among the nettles, or a scrap of china in the hemlock, that here once some one had lived; there had been a house.

If the feather had fallen, if it had tipped the scale downwards, the whole house would have plunged to the depths to lie upon the sands of oblivion. But there was a force working; something not highly conscious; something that leered, something that lurched; something not inspired to go about its work with dignified ritual or solemn chanting. Mrs. McNab groaned; Mrs. Bast creaked. They were old; they were stiff; their legs ached. They came with their brooms and pails at last; they got to work. All of a sudden, would Mrs. McNab see that the house was ready, one of the young ladies wrote: would she get this done; would she get that done; all in a hurry. They might be coming for the summer; had left everything to the last; expected to find things as they had left them. Slowly and painfully, with broom and pail, mopping, scouring, Mrs. McNab, Mrs. Bast, stayed the corruption and the rot; rescued from the pool of Time that was fast closing over them now a basin, now a cupboard; fetched up from oblivion all the Waverley novels and a tea-set one morning; in the afternoon restored to sun and air a brass fender and a set of steel fire-irons. George, Mrs. Bast's son, caught the rats, and cut the grass. They had the builders. Attended with the creaking of hinges and the screeching of bolts, the slamming and banging of damp-swollen woodwork, some rusty laborious birth seemed to be taking place, as the women, stooping, rising, groaning, singing, slapped and slammed, upstairs now, now down in the cellars. Oh, they said, the work!

They drank their tea in the bedroom sometimes, or in the study; breaking off work at mid-day with the smudge on their faces, and their old hands clasped and cramped with the broom handles. Flopped on chairs, they contemplated now the magnificent conquest over taps and bath; now the more arduous, more partial triumph over long rows of books, black as ravens once, now white-stained, breeding pale mushrooms and secreting furtive spiders. Once more, as she felt the tea warm in her, the telescope fitted itself to Mrs. McNab's eyes, and in a ring of light she saw the old gentleman, lean as a rake, wagging his head, as she came up with the washing, talking to himself, she supposed, on the lawn. He never noticed her.

Some said he was dead; some said she was dead. Which was it? Mrs. Bast didn't know for certain either. The young gentleman was dead. That she was sure. She had read his name in the papers.

There was the cook now, Mildred, Marian, some such name as that--a red-headed woman, quick-tempered like all her sort, but kind, too, if you knew the way with her. Many a laugh they had had together. She saved a plate of soup for Maggie; a bite of ham, sometimes; whatever was over. They lived well in those days. They had everything they wanted (glibly, jovially, with the tea hot in her, she unwound her ball of memories, sitting in the wicker arm-chair by the nursery fender). There was always plenty doing, people in the house, twenty staying sometimes, and washing up till long past midnight.

Mrs. Bast (she had never known them; had lived in Glasgow at that time) wondered, putting her cup down, whatever they hung that beast's skull there for? Shot in foreign parts no doubt.

It might well be, said Mrs. McNab, wantoning on with her memories; they had friends in eastern countries; gentlemen staying there, ladies in evening dress; she had seen them once through the dining-room door all sitting at dinner. Twenty she dared say all in their jewellery, and she asked to stay help wash up, might be till after midnight.

Ah, said Mrs. Bast, they'd find it changed. She leant out of the window. She watched her son George scything the grass. They might well ask, what had been done to it? seeing how old Kennedy was supposed to have charge of it, and then his leg got so bad after he fell from the cart; and perhaps then no one for a year, or the better part of one; and then Davie Macdonald, and seeds might be sent, but who should say if they were ever planted? They'd find it changed.

She watched her son scything. He was a great one for work--one of those quiet ones. Well they must be getting along with the cupboards, she supposed. They hauled themselves up.

At last, after days of labour within, of cutting and digging without, dusters were flicked from the windows, the windows were shut to, keys were turned all over the house; the front door was banged; it was finished.

And now as if the cleaning and the scrubbing and the scything and the mowing had drowned it there rose that half-heard melody, that intermittent music which the ear half catches but lets fall; a bark, a bleat; irregular, intermittent, yet somehow related; the hum of an insect, the tremor of cut grass, disevered yet somehow belonging; the jar of a dorbeetle, the squeak of a wheel, loud, low, but mysteriously related; which the ear strains to bring together and is always on the verge of harmonising, but they are never quite heard, never fully harmonised, and at last, in the evening, one after another the sounds die out, and the harmony falters, and silence falls. With the sunset sharpness was lost, and like mist rising, quiet rose, quiet spread, the wind settled; loosely the world shook itself down to sleep, darkly here without a light to it, save what came green suffused through leaves, or pale on the white flowers in the bed by the window.

[Lily Briscoe had her bag carried up to the house late one evening in September. Mr. Carmichael came by the same train.]

10

Then indeed peace had come. Messages of peace breathed from the sea to the shore. Never to break its sleep any more, to lull it rather more deeply to rest, and whatever the dreamers dreamt holily, dreamt wisely, to confirm--what else was it murmuring--as Lily Briscoe laid her head on the pillow in the clean still room and heard the sea. Through the open window the voice of the beauty of the world came murmuring, too softly to hear exactly what it said--but what mattered if the meaning were plain? entreating the sleepers (the house was full again; Mrs. Beckwith was staying there, also Mr. Carmichael), if they would not actually come down to the beach itself at least to lift the blind and look out. They would see then night flowing down in purple; his head crowned; his sceptre jewelled; and how in his eyes a child might look. And if they still faltered (Lily was tired out with travelling and slept almost at once; but Mr. Carmichael read a book by candlelight), if they still said no, that it was vapour, this splendour of his, and the dew had more power than he, and they preferred sleeping; gently then without complaint, or argument, the voice would sing its song. Gently the waves would break (Lily heard them in her sleep); tenderly the light fell (it seemed to come through her eyelids). And it all looked, Mr. Carmichael thought, shutting his book, falling asleep, much as it used to look.

Indeed the voice might resume, as the curtains of dark wrapped themselves over the house, over Mrs. Beckwith, Mr. Carmichael, and Lily Briscoe so that they lay with several folds of blackness on their eyes, why not accept this, be content with this, acquiesce and resign? The sigh of all the seas breaking in measure round the isles soothed them; the night wrapped them; nothing broke their sleep, until, the birds beginning and the dawn weaving their thin voices in to its whiteness, a cart grinding, a dog somewhere barking, the sun lifted the curtains, broke the veil on their eyes, and Lily Briscoe stirring in her sleep. She clutched at her blankets as a faller clutches at the turf on the edge of a cliff. Her eyes opened wide. Here she was again, she thought, sitting bold upright in bed. Awake.

THE LIGHTHOUSE

1

What does it mean then, what can it all mean? Lily Briscoe asked herself, wondering whether, since she had been left alone, it behoved her to go to the kitchen to fetch another cup of coffee or wait here. What does it mean?--a catchword that was, caught up from some book, fitting her thought loosely, for she could not, this first morning with the Ramsays, contract her feelings, could only make a phrase resound to cover the blankness of her mind until these vapours had shrunk. For really, what did she feel, come back after all these years and Mrs. Ramsay dead? Nothing, nothing--nothing that she could express at all.

She had come late last night when it was all mysterious, dark. Now she was awake, at her old place at the breakfast table, but alone. It was very early too, not yet eight. There was this expedition--they were going to the Lighthouse, Mr. Ramsay, Cam, and James. They should have gone already--they had to catch the tide or something. And Cam was not ready and James was not ready and Nancy had forgotten to order the sandwiches and Mr. Ramsay had lost his temper and banged out of the room.

"What's the use of going now?" he had stormed.

Nancy had vanished. There he was, marching up and down the terrace in a rage. One seemed to hear doors slamming and voices calling all over the house. Now Nancy burst in, and asked, looking round the room, in a queer half dazed, half desperate way, "What does one send to the Lighthouse?" as if she were forcing herself to do what she despaired of ever being able to do.

What does one send to the Lighthouse indeed! At any other time Lily could have suggested reasonably tea, tobacco, newspapers. But this morning everything seemed so extraordinarily queer that a question like Nancy's--What does one send to the Lighthouse?--opened doors in one's mind that went banging and swinging to and fro and made one keep asking, in a stupefied gape, What does one send? What does one do? Why is one sitting here, after all?

Sitting alone (for Nancy went out again) among the clean cups at the long table, she felt cut off from other people, and able only to go on watching, asking, wondering. The house, the place, the morning, all seemed strangers to her. She had no attachment here, she felt, no relations with it, anything might happen, and whatever did happen, a step outside, a voice calling ("It's not in the cupboard; it's on the landing," some one cried), was a question, as if the link that usually bound things together had been cut, and they floated up here, down there, off, anyhow. How aimless it was,, how chaotic, how unreal it was, she thought, looking at her empty coffee cup. Mrs. Ramsay dead; Andrew killed; Prue dead too--repeat it as she might, it roused no feeling in her. And we all get together in a house like this on a morning like this, she said, looking out of the window. It was a beautiful still day.

2

Suddenly Mr. Ramsay raised his head as he passed and looked straight at her, with his distraught wild gaze which was yet so penetrating, as if he saw you, for one second, for the first time, for ever; and she pretended to drink out of her empty coffee cup so as to escape him--to escape his demand on her, to put aside a moment longer that imperious need. And he shook his head at her, and strode on ("Alone" she heard him say, "Perished" she heard him say) and like everything else this strange morning the words became symbols, wrote themselves all over the grey-green walls. If only she could put them together, she felt, write them out in some sentence, then she would have got at the truth of things. Old Mr. Carmichael came padding softly in, fetched his coffee, took his cup and made off to sit in the sun. The extraordinary unreality was frightening; but it was also exciting. Going to the Lighthouse. But what does one send to the Lighthouse? Perished. Alone. The grey-green light on the wall opposite. The empty places. Such were some of the parts, but how bring them together? she asked. As if any interruption would break the frail shape she was building on the table she turned her back to the window lest Mr. Ramsay should see her. She must escape somewhere, be alone somewhere. Suddenly she remembered. When she had sat there last ten years ago there had been a little sprig or leaf pattern on the table-cloth, which she had looked at in a moment of revelation. There had been a problem about a foreground of a picture. Move the tree to the middle, she had said. She had never finished that picture. She would paint that picture now. It had been knocking about in her mind all these years. Where were her paints, she wondered? Her paints, yes. She had left them in the hall last night. She would start at once. She got up quickly, before Mr. Ramsay turned.

She fetched herself a chair. She pitched her easel with her precise old-maidish movements on the edge of the lawn, not too close to Mr. Carmichael, but close enough for his protection. Yes, it must have been precisely here that she had stood ten years ago. There was the wall; the hedge; the tree. The question was of some relation between those masses. She had borne it in her mind all these years. It seemed as if the solution had come to her: she knew now what she wanted to do.

But with Mr. Ramsay bearing down on her, she could do nothing. Every time he approached--he was walking up and down the terrace--ruin approached, chaos approached. She could not paint. She stooped, she turned; she took up this rag; she squeezed that tube. But all she did was to ward him off a moment. He made it impossible for her to do anything. For if she gave him the least chance, if he saw her disengaged a moment, looking his way a moment, he would be on her, saying, as he had said last night, "You find us much changed." Last night he had got up and stopped before her, and said that. Dumb and staring though they had all sat, the six children whom they used to call after the Kings and Queens of England--the Red, the Fair, the Wicked, the Ruthless--she felt how they raged under it. Kind old Mrs. Beckwith said something sensible. But it was a house full of unrelated passions--she had felt that all the evening. And on top of this chaos Mr. Ramsay got up, pressed her hand, and said: "You will find us much changed" and none of them had moved or had spoken; but had sat there as if they were forced to let him say it. Only James (certainly the Sullen) scowled at the lamp; and Cam screwed her handkerchief round her finger. Then he reminded them that they were going to the Lighthouse tomorrow. They must be ready, in the hall, on the stroke of half-past seven. Then, with his hand on the door, he stopped; he turned upon them. Did they not want to go? he demanded. Had they dared say No (he had some reason for wanting it) he would have flung himself tragically backwards into the bitter waters of despair. Such a gift he had for gesture. He looked like a king in exile. Doggedly James said yes. Cam stumbled more wretchedly. Yes, oh, yes, they'd both be ready, they said. And it struck her, this was tragedy--not palls, dust, and the shroud; but children coerced, their spirits subdued. James was sixteen, Cam, seventeen, perhaps. She had looked round for some one who was not there, for Mrs. Ramsay, presumably. But there was only kind Mrs. Beckwith turning over her sketches under the lamp. Then, being tired, her mind still rising and falling with the sea, the taste and smell that places have after long absence possessing her, the candles wavering in her eyes, she had lost herself and gone under. It was a wonderful night, starlit; the waves sounded as they went upstairs; the moon surprised them, enormous, pale, as they passed the staircase window. She had slept at once.

She set her clean canvas firmly upon the easel, as a barrier, frail, but she hoped sufficiently substantial to ward off Mr. Ramsay and his exactingness. She did her best to look, when his back was turned, at her picture; that line there, that mass there. But it was out of the question. Let him be fifty feet away, let him not even speak to you, let him not even see you, he permeated, he prevailed, he imposed himself. He changed everything. She could not see the colour; she could not see the lines; even with his back turned to her, she could only think, But he'll be down on me in a moment, demanding--something she felt she could not give him. She rejected one brush; she chose another. When would those children come? When would they all be off? she fidgeted. That man, she thought, her anger rising in her, never gave; that man took. She, on the other hand, would be forced to give. Mrs. Ramsay had given. Giving, giving, giving, she had died--and had left all this. Really, she was angry with Mrs. Ramsay. With the brush slightly trembling in her fingers she looked at the hedge, the step, the wall. It was all Mrs. Ramsay's doing.

She was dead. Here was Lily, at forty-four, wasting her time, unable to do a thing, standing there, playing at painting, playing at the one thing one did not play at, and it was all Mrs. Ramsay's fault. She was dead. The step where she used to sit was empty. She was dead.

But why repeat this over and over again? Why be always trying to bring up some feeling she had not got? There was a kind of blasphemy in it. It was all dry: all withered: all spent. They ought not to have asked her; she ought not to have come. One can't waste one's time at forty- four, she thought. She hated playing at painting. A brush, the one dependable thing in a world of strife, ruin, chaos--that one should not play with, knowingly even: she detested it. But he made her. You shan't touch your canvas, he seemed to say, bearing down on her, till you've given me what I want of you. Here he was, close upon her again, greedy, distraught. Well, thought Lily in despair, letting her right hand fall at her side, it would be simpler then to have it over. Surely, she could imitate from recollection the glow, the rhapsody, the self-surrender, she had seen on so many women's faces (on Mrs. Ramsay's, for instance) when on some occasion like this they blazed up--she could remember the look on Mrs. Ramsay's face--into a rapture of sympathy, of delight in the reward they had, which, though the reason of it escaped her, evidently conferred on them the most supreme bliss of which human nature was capable. Here he was, stopped by her side. She would give him what she could.

3

She seemed to have shrivelled slightly, he thought. She looked a little skimpy, wispy; but not unattractive. He liked her. There had been some talk of her marrying William Bankes once, but nothing had come of it. His wife had been fond of her. He had been a little out of temper too at breakfast. And then, and then--this was one of those moments when an enormous need urged him, without being conscious what it was, to approach any woman, to force them, he did not care how, his need was so great, to give him what he wanted: sympathy.

Was anybody looking after her? he said. Had she everything she wanted?

"Oh, thanks, everything," said Lily Briscoe nervously. No; she could not do it. She ought to have floated off instantly upon some wave of sympathetic expansion: the pressure on her was tremendous. But she remained stuck. There was an awful pause. They both looked at the sea. Why, thought Mr. Ramsay, should she look at the sea when I am here? She hoped it would be calm enough for them to land at the Lighthouse, she said. The Lighthouse! The Lighthouse! What's that got to do with it? he thought impatiently. Instantly, with the force of some primeval gust (for really he could not restrain himself any longer), there issued from him such a groan that any other woman in the whole world would have done something, said something--all except myself, thought Lily, girding at herself bitterly, who am not a woman, but a peevish, ill-tempered, dried-up old maid, presumably.

[Mr. Ramsay sighed to the full. He waited. Was she not going to say anything? Did she not see what he wanted from her? Then he said he had a particular reason for wanting to go to the Lighthouse. His wife used to send the men things. There was a poor boy with a tuberculous hip, the lightkeeper's son. He sighed profoundly. He sighed significantly. All Lily wished was that this enormous flood of grief, this insatiable hunger for sympathy, this demand that she should surrender herself up to him entirely, and even so he had sorrows enough to keep her supplied for ever, should leave her, should be diverted (she kept looking at the house, hoping for an interruption) before it swept her down in its flow.

"Such expeditions," said Mr. Ramsay, scraping the ground with his toe, "are very painful." Still Lily said nothing. (She is a stock, she is a stone, he said to himself.) "They are very exhausting," he said, looking, with a sickly look that nauseated her (he was acting, she felt, this great man was dramatising himself), at his beautiful hands. It was horrible, it was indecent. Would they never come, she asked, for she could not sustain this enormous weight of sorrow, support these heavy draperies of grief (he had assumed a pose of extreme decreptitude; he even tottered a little as he stood there) a moment longer.

Still she could say nothing; the whole horizon seemed swept bare of objects to talk about; could only feel, amazedly, as Mr. Ramsay stood there, how his gaze seemed to fall dolefully over the sunny grass and discolour it, and cast over the rubicund, drowsy, entirely contented figure of Mr. Carmichael, reading a French novel on a deck-chair, a veil of crape, as if such an existence, flaunting its prosperity in a world of woe, were enough to provoke the most dismal thoughts of all. Look at him, he seemed to be saying, look at me; and indeed, all the time he was feeling, Think of me, think of me. Ah, could that bulk only be wafted alongside of them, Lily wished; had she only pitched her easel a yard or two closer to him; a man, any man, would staunch this effusion, would stop these lamentations. A woman, she had provoked this horror; a woman, she should have known how to deal with it. It was immensely to her discredit, sexually, to stand there dumb. One said--what did one say?--Oh, Mr. Ramsay! Dear Mr. Ramsay! That was what that kind old lady who sketched, Mrs. Beckwith, would have said instantly, and rightly. But, no. They stood there, isolated from the rest of the world. His immense self-pity, his demand for sympathy poured and spread itself in pools at their feet, and all she did, miserable sinner that she was, was to draw her skirts a little closer round her ankles, lest she should get wet. In complete silence she stood there, grasping her paint brush.

Heaven could never be sufficiently praised! She heard sounds in the house. James and Cam must be coming. But Mr. Ramsay, as if he knew that his time ran short, exerted upon her solitary figure the immense pressure of his concentrated woe; his age; his frailty: his desolation; when suddenly, tossing his head impatiently, in his annoyance--for after all, what woman could resist him?--he noticed that his boot-laces were untied. Remarkable boots they were too, Lily thought, looking down at them: sculptured; colossal; like everything that Mr. Ramsay wore, from his frayed tie to his half-buttoned waistcoat, his own indisputably. She could see them walking to his room of their own accord, expressive in his absence of pathos, surliness, ill-temper, charm.

"What beautiful boots!" she exclaimed. She was ashamed of herself. To praise his boots when he asked her to solace his soul; when he had shown her his bleeding hands, his lacerated heart, and asked her to pity them, then to say, cheerfully, "Ah, but what beautiful boots you wear!" deserved, she knew, and she looked up expecting to get it in one of his sudden roars of ill-temper complete annihilation.

Instead, Mr. Ramsay smiled. His pall, his draperies, his infirmities fell from him. Ah, yes, he said, holding his foot up for her to look at, they were first-rate boots. There was only one man in England who could make boots like that. Boots are among the chief curses of mankind, he said. "Bootmakers make it their business," he exclaimed, "to cripple and torture the human foot." They are also the most obstinate and perverse of mankind. It had taken him the best part of his youth to get boots made as they should be made. He would have her observe (he lifted his right foot and then his left) that she had never seen boots made quite that shape before. They were made of the finest leather in the world, also. Most leather was mere brown paper and cardboard. He looked complacently at his foot, still held in the air. They had reached, she felt, a sunny island where peace dwelt, sanity reigned and the sun for ever shone, the blessed island of good boots. Her heart warmed to him. "Now let me see if you can tie a knot," he said. He poohpoohed her feeble system. He showed her his own invention. Once you tied it, it never came undone. Three times he knotted her shoe; three times he unknotted it.

Why, at this completely inappropriate moment, when he was stooping over her shoe, should she be so tormented with sympathy for him that, as she stooped too, the blood rushed to her face, and, thinking of her callousness (she had called him a play-actor) she felt her eyes swell and tingle with tears? Thus occupied he seemed to her a figure of infinite pathos. He tied knots. He bought boots. There was no helping Mr. Ramsay on the journey he was going. But now just as she wished to say something, could have said something, perhaps, here they were--Cam and James. They appeared on the terrace. They came, lagging, side by side, a serious, melancholy couple.

But why was it like THAT that they came? She could not help feeling annoyed with them; they might have come more cheerfully; they might have given him what, now that they were off, she would not have the chance of giving him. For she felt a sudden emptiness; a frustration. Her feeling had come too late; there it was ready; but he no longer needed it. He had become a very distinguished, elderly man, who had no need of her whatsoever. She felt snubbed. He slung a knapsack round his shoulders. He shared out the parcels--there were a number of them, ill tied in brown paper. He sent Cam for a cloak. He had all the appearance of a leader making ready for an expedition. Then, wheeling about, he led the way with his firm military tread, in those wonderful boots, carrying brown paper parcels, down the path, his children following him. They looked, she thought, as if fate had devoted them to some stern enterprise, and they went to it, still young enough to be drawn acquiescent in their father's wake, obediently, but with a pallor in their eyes which made her feel that they suffered something beyond their years in silence. So they passed the edge of the lawn, and it seemed to Lily that she watched a procession go, drawn on by some stress of common feeling which made it, faltering and flagging as it was, a little company bound together and strangely impressive to her. Politely, but very distantly, Mr. Ramsay raised his hand and saluted her as they passed.

But what a face, she thought, immediately finding the sympathy which she had not been asked to give troubling her for expression. What had made it like that? Thinking, night after night, she supposed--about the reality of kitchen tables, she added, remembering the symbol which in her vagueness as to what Mr. Ramsay did think about Andrew had given her. (He had been killed by the splinter of a shell instantly, she bethought her.) The kitchen table was something visionary, austere; something bare, hard, not ornamental. There was no colour to it; it was all edges and angles; it was uncompromisingly plain. But Mr. Ramsay kept always his eyes fixed upon it, never allowed himself to be distracted or deluded, until his face became worn too and ascetic and partook of this unornamented beauty which so deeply impressed her. Then, she recalled (standing where he had left her, holding her brush), worries had fretted it--not so nobly. He must have had his doubts about that table, she supposed; whether the table was a real table; whether it was worth the time he gave to it; whether he was able after all to find it. He had had doubts, she felt, or he would have asked less of people. That was what they talked about late at night sometimes, she suspected; and then next day Mrs. Ramsay looked tired, and Lily flew into a rage with him over some absurd little thing. But now he had nobody to talk to about that table, or his boots, or his knots; and he was like a lion seeking whom he could devour, and his face had that touch of desperation, of exaggeration in it which alarmed her, and made her pull her skirts about her. And then, she recalled, there was that sudden revivification, that sudden flare (when she praised his boots), that sudden recovery of vitality and interest in ordinary human things, which too passed and changed (for he was always changing, and hid nothing) into that other final phase which was new to her and had, she owned, made herself ashamed of her own irritability, when it seemed as if he had shed worries and ambitions, and the hope of sympathy and the desire for praise, had entered some other region, was drawn on, as if by curiosity, in dumb colloquy, whether with himself or another, at the head of that little procession out of one's range. An extraordinary face! The gate banged.

4

So they're gone, she thought, sighing with relief and disappointment. Her sympathy seemed to be cast back on her, like a bramble sprung across her face. She felt curiously divided, as if one part of her were drawn out there--it was a still day, hazy; the Lighthouse looked this morning at an immense distance; the other had fixed itself doggedly, solidly, here on the lawn. She saw her canvas as if it had floated up and placed itself white and uncompromising directly before her. It seemed to rebuke her with its cold stare for all this hurry and agitation; this folly and waste of emotion; it drastically recalled her and spread through her mind first a peace, as her disorderly sensations (he had gone and she had been so sorry for him and she had said nothing) trooped off the field; and then, emptiness. She looked blankly at the canvas, with its uncompromising white stare; from the canvas to the garden. There was something (she stood screwing up her little Chinese eyes in her small puckered face), something she remembered in the relations of those lines cutting across, slicing down, and in the mass of the hedge with its green cave of blues and browns, which had stayed in her mind; which had tied a knot in her mind so that at odds and ends of time, involuntarily, as she walked along the Brompton Road, as she brushed her hair, she found herself painting that picture, passing her eye over it, and untying the knot in imagination. But there was all the difference in the world between this planning airily away from the canvas and actually taking her brush and making the first mark.

She had taken the wrong brush in her agitation at Mr. Ramsay's presence, and her easel, rammed into the earth so nervously, was at the wrong angle. And now that she had put that right, and in so doing had subdued the impertinences and irrelevances that plucked her attention and made her remember how she was such and such a person, had such and such relations to people, she took her hand and raised her brush. For a moment it stayed trembling in a painful but exciting ecstasy in the air. Where to begin?--that was the question at what point to make the first mark? One line placed on the canvas committed her to innumerable risks, to frequent and irrevocable decisions. All that in idea seemed simple became in practice immediately complex; as the waves shape themselves symmetrically from the cliff top, but to the swimmer among them are divided by steep gulfs, and foaming crests. Still the risk must be run; the mark made.

With a curious physical sensation, as if she were urged forward and at the same time must hold herself back, she made her first quick decisive stroke. The brush descended. It flickered brown over the white canvas; it left a running mark. A second time she did it--a third time. And so pausing and so flickering, she attained a dancing rhythmical movement, as if the pauses were one part of the rhythm and the strokes another, and all were related; and so, lightly and swiftly pausing, striking, she scored her canvas with brown running nervous lines which had no sooner settled there than they enclosed (she felt it looming out at her) a space. Down in the hollow of one wave she saw the next wave towering higher and higher above her. For what could be more formidable than that space? Here she was again, she thought, stepping back to look at it, drawn out of gossip, out of living, out of community with people into the presence of this formidable ancient enemy of hers--this other thing, this truth, this reality, which suddenly laid hands on her, emerged stark at the back of appearances and commanded her attention. She was half unwilling, half reluctant. Why always be drawn out and hauled away? Why not left in peace, to talk to Mr. Carmichael on the lawn? It was an exacting form of intercourse anyhow. Other worshipful objects were content with worship; men, women, God, all let one kneel prostrate; but this form, were it only the shape of a white lamp-shade looming on a wicker table, roused one to perpetual combat, challenged one to a fight in which one was bound to be worsted.

Always (it was in her nature, or in her sex, she did not know which) before she exchanged the fluidity of life for the concentration of painting she had a few moments of nakedness when she seemed like an unborn soul, a soul reft of body, hesitating on some windy pinnacle and exposed without protection to all the blasts of doubt. Why then did she do it? She looked at the canvas, lightly scored with running lines. It would be hung in the servants' bedrooms. It would be rolled up and stuffed under a sofa. What was the good of doing it then, and she heard some voice saying she couldn't paint, saying she couldn't create, as if she were caught up in one of those habitual currents in which after a certain time experience forms in the mind, so that one repeats words without being aware any longer who originally spoke them.

Can't paint, can't write, she murmured monotonously, anxiously considering what her plan of attack should be. For the mass loomed before her; it protruded; she felt it pressing on her eyeballs. Then, as if some juice necessary for the lubrication of her faculties were spontaneously squirted, she began precariously dipping among the blues and umbers, moving her brush hither and thither, but it was now heavier and went slower, as if it had fallen in with some rhythm which was dictated to her (she kept looking at the hedge, at the canvas) by what she rhythm was strong enough to bear her along with it on its current. Certainly she was losing consciousness of outer things. And as she lost consciousness of outer things, and her name and her personality and her appearance, and whether Mr. Carmichael was there or not, her mind kept throwing up from its depths, scenes, and names, and sayings, and memories and ideas, like a fountain spurting over that glaring, hideously difficult white space, while she modelled it with greens and blues.

Charles Tansley used to say that, she remembered, women can't paint, can't write. Coming up behind her, he had stood close beside her, a thing she hated, as she painted her on this very spot. "Shag tobacco," he said, "fivepence an ounce," parading his poverty, his principles. (But the war had drawn the sting of her femininity. Poor devils, one thought, poor devils, of both sexes.) He was always carrying a book about under his arm--a purple book. He "worked." He sat, she remembered, working in a blaze of sun. At dinner he would sit right in the middle of the view. But after all, she reflected, there was the scene on the beach. One must remember that. It was a windy morning. They had all gone down to the beach. Mrs. Ramsay sat down and wrote letters by a rock. She wrote and wrote. "Oh," she said, looking up at something floating in the sea, "is it a lobster pot? Is it an upturned boat?" She was so short-sighted that she could not see, and then Charles Tansley became as nice as he could possibly be. He began playing ducks and drakes. They chose little flat black stones and sent them skipping over the waves. Every now and then Mrs. Ramsay looked up over her spectacles and laughed at them. What they said she could not remember, but only she and Charles throwing stones and getting on very well all of a sudden and Mrs. Ramsay watching them. She was highly conscious of that. Mrs. Ramsay, she thought, stepping back and screwing up her eyes. (It must have altered the design a good deal when she was sitting on the step with James. There must have been a shadow.) When she thought of herself and Charles throwing ducks and drakes and of the whole scene on the beach, it seemed to depend somehow upon Mrs. Ramsay sitting under the rock, with a pad on her knee, writing letters. (She wrote innumerable letters, and sometimes the wind took them and she and Charles just saved a page from the sea.) But what a power was in the human soul! she thought. That woman sitting there writing under the rock resolved everything into simplicity; made these angers, irritations fall off like old rags; she brought together this and that and then this, and so made out of that miserable silliness and spite (she and Charles squabbling, sparring, had been silly and spiteful) something--this scene on the beach for example, this moment of friendship and liking--which survived, after all these years complete, so that she dipped into it to re-fashion her memory of him, and there it stayed in the mind affecting one almost like a work of art.

"Like a work of art," she repeated, looking from her canvas to the drawing-room steps and back again. She must rest for a moment. And, resting, looking from one to the other vaguely, the old question which traversed the sky of the soul perpetually, the vast, the general question which was apt to particularise itself at such moments as these, when she released faculties that had been on the strain, stood over her, paused over her, darkened over her. What is the meaning of life? That was all--a simple question; one that tended to close in on one with years. The great revelation had never come. The great revelation perhaps never did come. Instead there were little daily miracles, illuminations, matches struck unexpectedly in the dark; here was one. This, that, and the other; herself and Charles Tansley and the breaking wave; Mrs. Ramsay bringing them together; Mrs. Ramsay saying, "Life stand still here"; Mrs. Ramsay making of the moment something permanent (as in another sphere Lily herself tried to make of the moment something permanent)--this was of the nature of a revelation. In the midst of chaos there was shape; this eternal passing and flowing (she looked at the clouds going and the leaves shaking) was struck into stability. Life stand still here, Mrs. Ramsay said. "Mrs. Ramsay! Mrs. Ramsay!" she repeated. She owed it all to her.

All was silence. Nobody seemed yet to be stirring in the house. She looked at it there sleeping in the early sunlight with its windows green and blue with the reflected leaves. The faint thought she was thinking of Mrs. Ramsay seemed in consonance with this quiet house; this smoke; this fine early morning air. Faint and unreal, it was amazingly pure and exciting. She hoped nobody would open the window or come out of the house, but that she might be left alone to go on thinking, to go on painting. She turned to her canvas. But impelled by some curiosity, driven by the discomfort of the sympathy which she held undischarged, she walked a pace or so to the end of the lawn to see whether, down there on the beach, she could see that little company setting sail. Down there among the little boats which floated, some with their sails furled, some slowly, for it was very calm moving away, there was one rather apart from the others. The sail was even now being hoisted. She decided that there in that very distant and entirely silent little boat Mr. Ramsay was sitting with Cam and James. Now they had got the sail up; now after a little flagging and silence, she watched the boat take its way with deliberation past the other boats out to sea.

5

The sails flapped over their heads. The water chuckled and slapped the sides of the boat, which drowsed motionless in the sun. Now and then the sails rippled with a little breeze in them, but the ripple ran over them and ceased. The boat made no motion at all. Mr. Ramsay sat in the middle of the boat. He would be impatient in a moment, James thought, and Cam thought, looking at her father, who sat in the middle of the boat between them (James steered; Cam sat alone in the bow) with his legs tightly curled. He hated hanging about. Sure enough, after fidgeting a second or two, he said something sharp to Macalister's boy, who got out his oars and began to row. But their father, they knew, would never be content until they were flying along. He would keep looking for a breeze, fidgeting, saying things under his breath, which Macalister and Macalister's boy would overhear, and they would both be made horribly uncomfortable. He had made them come. He had forced them to come. In their anger they hoped that the breeze would never rise, that he might be thwarted in every possible way, since he had forced them to come against their wills.

All the way down to the beach they had lagged behind together, though he bade them "Walk up, walk up," without speaking. Their heads were bent down, their heads were pressed down by some remorseless gale. Speak to him they could not. They must come; they must follow. They must walk behind him carrying brown paper parcels. But they vowed, in silence, as they walked, to stand by each other and carry out the great compact--to resist tyranny to the death. So there they would sit, one at one end of the boat, one at the other, in silence. They would say nothing, only look at him now and then where he sat with his legs twisted, frowning and fidgeting, and pishing and pshawing and muttering things to himself, and waiting impatiently for a breeze. And they hoped it would be calm. They hoped he would be thwarted. They hoped the whole expedition would fail, and they would have to put back, with their parcels, to the beach.

But now, when Macalister's boy had rowed a little way out, the sails slowly swung round, the boat quickened itself, flattened itself, and shot off. Instantly, as if some great strain had been relieved, Mr. Ramsay uncurled his legs, took out his tobacco pouch, handed it with a little grunt to Macalister, and felt, they knew, for all they suffered, perfectly content. Now they would sail on for hours like this, and Mr. Ramsay would ask old Macalister a question--about the great storm last winter probably--and old Macalister would answer it, and they would puff their pipes together, and Macalister would take a tarry rope in his fingers, tying or untying some knot, and the boy would fish, and never say a word to any one. James would be forced to keep his eye all the time on the sail. For if he forgot, then the sail puckered and shivered, and the boat slackened, and Mr. Ramsay would say sharply, "Look out! Look out!" and old Macalister would turn slowly on his seat.

So they heard Mr. Ramsay asking some question about the great storm at Christmas. "She comes driving round the point," old Macalister said, describing the great storm last Christmas, when ten ships had been driven into the bay for shelter, and he had seen "one there, one there, one there" (he pointed slowly round the bay. Mr. Ramsay followed him, turning his head). He had seen four men clinging to the mast. Then she was gone. "And at last we shoved her off," he went on (but in their anger and their silence they only caught a word here and there, sitting at opposite ends of the boat, united by their compact to fight tyranny to the death). At last they had shoved her off, they had launched the lifeboat, and they had got her out past the point--Macalister told the story; and though they only caught a word here and there, they were conscious all the time of their father--how he leant forward, how he brought his voice into tune with Macalister's voice; how, puffing at his pipe, and looking there and there where Macalister pointed, he relished the thought of the storm and the dark night and the fishermen striving there. He liked that men should labour and sweat on the windy beach at night; pitting muscle and brain against the waves and the wind; he liked men to work like that, and women to keep house, and sit beside sleeping children indoors, while men were drowned, out there in a storm. So James could tell, so Cam could tell (they looked at him, they looked at each other), from his toss and his vigilance and the ring in his voice, and the little tinge of Scottish accent which came into his voice, making him seem like a peasant himself, as he questioned Macalister about the eleven ships that had been driven into the bay in a storm. Three had sunk.

He looked proudly where Macalister pointed; and Cam thought, feeling proud of him without knowing quite why, had he been there he would have launched the lifeboat, he would have reached the wreck, Cam thought. He was so brave, he was so adventurous, Cam thought. But she remembered. There was the compact; to resist tyranny to the death. Their grievance weighed them down. They had been forced; they had been bidden. He had borne them down once more with his gloom and his authority, making them do his bidding, on this fine morning, come, because he wished it, carrying these parcels, to the Lighthouse; take part in these rites he went through for his own pleasure in memory of dead people, which they hated, so that they lagged after him, all the pleasure of the day was spoilt.

Yes, the breeze was freshening. The boat was leaning, the water was sliced sharply and fell away in green cascades, in bubbles, in cataracts. Cam looked down into the foam, into the sea with all its treasure in it, and its speed hypnotised her, and the tie between her and James sagged a little. It slackened a little. She began to think, How fast it goes. Where are we going? and the movement hypnotised her, while James, with his eye fixed on the sail and on the horizon, steered grimly. But he began to think as he steered that he might escape; he might be quit of it all. They might land somewhere; and be free then. Both of them, looking at each other for a moment, had a sense of escape and exaltation, what with the speed and the change. But the breeze bred in Mr. Ramsay too the same excitement, and, as old Macalister turned to fling his line overboard, he cried out aloud,

"We perished," and then again, "each alone." And then with his usual spasm of repentance or shyness, pulled himself up, and waved his hand towards the shore.

"See the little house," he said pointing, wishing Cam to look. She raised herself reluctantly and looked. But which was it? She could no longer make out, there on the hillside, which was their house. All looked distant and peaceful and strange. The shore seemed refined, far away, unreal. Already the little distance they had sailed had put them far from it and given it the changed look, the composed look, of something receding in which one has no longer any part. Which was their house? She could not see it.

"But I beneath a rougher sea," Mr. Ramsay murmured. He had found the house and so seeing it, he had also seen himself there; he had seen himself walking on the terrace, alone. He was walking up and down between the urns; and he seemed to himself very old and bowed. Sitting in the boat, he bowed, he crouched himself, acting instantly his part-- the part of a desolate man, widowed, bereft; and so called up before him in hosts people sympathising with him; staged for himself as he sat in the boat, a little drama; which required of him decrepitude and exhaustion and sorrow (he raised his hands and looked at the thinness of them, to confirm his dream) and then there was given him in abundance women's sympathy, and he imagined how they would soothe him and sympathise with him, and so getting in his dream some reflection of the exquisite pleasure women's sympathy was to him, he sighed and said gently and mournfully:

But I beneath a rougher sea Was whelmed in deeper gulfs than he,

so that the mournful words were heard quite clearly by them all. Cam half started on her seat. It shocked her--it outraged her. The movement roused her father; and he shuddered, and broke off, exclaiming: "Look! Look!" so urgently that James also turned his head to look over his shoulder at the island. They all looked. They looked at the island.

But Cam could see nothing. She was thinking how all those paths and the lawn, thick and knotted with the lives they had lived there, were gone: were rubbed out; were past; were unreal, and now this was real; the boat and the sail with its patch; Macalister with his earrings; the noise of the waves--all this was real. Thinking this, she was murmuring to herself, "We perished, each alone," for her father's words broke and broke again in her mind, when her father, seeing her gazing so vaguely, began to tease her. Didn't she know the points of the compass? he asked. Didn't she know the North from the South? Did she really think they lived right out there? And he pointed again, and showed her where their house was, there, by those trees. He wished she would try to be more accurate, he said: "Tell me--which is East, which is West?" he said, half laughing at her, half scolding her, for he could not understand the state of mind of any one, not absolutely imbecile, who did not know the points of the compass. Yet she did not know. And seeing her gazing, with her vague, now rather frightened, eyes fixed where no house was Mr. Ramsay forgot his dream; how he walked up and down between the urns on the terrace; how the arms were stretched out to him. He thought, women are always like that; the vagueness of their minds is hopeless; it was a thing he had never been able to understand; but so it was. It had been so with her--his wife. They could not keep anything clearly fixed in their minds. But he had been wrong to be angry with her; moreover, did he not rather like this vagueness in women? It was part of their extraordinary charm. I will make her smile at me, he thought. She looks frightened. She was so silent. He clutched his fingers, and determined that his voice and his face and all the quick expressive gestures which had been at his command making people pity him and praise him all these years should subdue themselves. He would make her smile at him. He would find some simple easy thing to say to her. But what? For, wrapped up in his work as he was, he forgot the sort of thing one said. There was a puppy. They had a puppy. Who was looking after the puppy today? he asked. Yes, thought James pitilessly, seeing his sister's head against the sail, now she will give way. I shall be left to fight the tyrant alone. The compact would be left to him to carry out. Cam would never resist tyranny to the death, he thought grimly, watching her face, sad, sulky, yielding. And as sometimes happens when a cloud falls on a green hillside and gravity descends and there among all the surrounding hills is gloom and sorrow, and it seems as if the hills themselves must ponder the fate of the clouded, the darkened, either in pity, or maliciously rejoicing in her dismay: so Cam now felt herself overcast, as she sat there among calm, resolute people and wondered how to answer her father about the puppy; how to resist his entreaty--forgive me, care for me; while James the lawgiver, with the tablets of eternal wisdom laid open on his knee (his hand on the tiller had become symbolical to her), said, Resist him. Fight him. He said so rightly; justly. For they must fight tyranny to the death, she thought. Of all human qualities she reverenced justice most. Her brother was most god-like, her father most suppliant. And to which did she yield, she thought, sitting between them, gazing at the shore whose points were all unknown to her, and thinking how the lawn and the terrace and the house were smoothed away now and peace dwelt there.

"Jasper," she said sullenly. He'd look after the puppy.

And what was she going to call him? her father persisted. He had had a dog when he was a little boy, called Frisk. She'll give way, James thought, as he watched a look come upon her face, a look he remembered. They look down he thought, at their knitting or something. Then suddenly they look up. There was a flash of blue, he remembered, and then somebody sitting with him laughed, surrendered, and he was very angry. It must have been his mother, he thought, sitting on a low chair, with his father standing over her. He began to search among the infinite series of impressions which time had laid down, leaf upon leaf, fold upon fold softly, incessantly upon his brain; among scents, sounds; voices, harsh, hollow, sweet; and lights passing, and brooms tapping; and the wash and hush of the sea, how a man had marched up and down and stopped dead, upright, over them. Meanwhile, he noticed, Cam dabbled her fingers in the water, and stared at the shore and said nothing. No, she won't give way, he thought; she's different, he thought. Well, if Cam would not answer him, he would not bother her Mr. Ramsay decided, feeling in his pocket for a book. But she would answer him; she wished, passionately, to move some obstacle that lay upon her tongue and to say, Oh, yes, Frisk. I'll call him Frisk. She wanted even to say, Was that the dog that found its way over the moor alone? But try as she might, she could think of nothing to say like that, fierce and loyal to the compact, yet passing on to her father, unsuspected by James, a private token of the love she felt for him. For she thought, dabbling her hand (and now Macalister's boy had caught a mackerel, and it lay kicking on the floor, with blood on its gills) for she thought, looking at James who kept his eyes dispassionately on the sail, or glanced now and then for a second at the horizon, you're not exposed to it, to this pressure and division of feeling, this extraordinary temptation. Her father was feeling in his pockets; in another second, he would have found his book. For no one attracted her more; his hands were beautiful, and his feet, and his voice, and his words, and his haste, and his temper, and his oddity, and his passion, and his saying straight out before every one, we perish, each alone, and his remoteness. (He had opened his book.) But what remained intolerable, she thought, sitting upright, and watching Macalister's boy tug the hook out of the gills of another fish, was that crass blindness and tyranny of his which had poisoned her childhood and raised bitter storms, so that even now she woke in the night trembling with rage and remembered some command of his; some insolence: "Do this," "Do that," his dominance: his "Submit to me."

So she said nothing, but looked doggedly and sadly at the shore, wrapped in its mantle of peace; as if the people there had fallen asleep, she thought; were free like smoke, were free to come and go like ghosts. They have no suffering there, she thought.

6

Yes, that is their boat, Lily Briscoe decided, standing on the edge of the lawn. It was the boat with greyish-brown sails, which she saw now flatten itself upon the water and shoot off across the bay. There he sits, she thought, and the children are quite silent still. And she could not reach him either. The sympathy she had not given him weighed her down. It made it difficult for her to paint.

She had always found him difficult. She never had been able to praise him to his face, she remembered. And that reduced their relationship to something neutral, without that element of sex in it which made his manner to Minta so gallant, almost gay. He would pick a flower for her, lend her his books. But could he believe that Minta read them? She dragged them about the garden, sticking in leaves to mark the place.

"D'you remember, Mr. Carmichael?" she was inclined to ask, looking at the old man. But he had pulled his hat half over his forehead; he was asleep, or he was dreaming, or he was lying there catching words, she supposed.

"D'you remember?" she felt inclined to ask him as she passed him, thinking again of Mrs. Ramsay on the beach; the cask bobbing up and down; and the pages flying. Why, after all these years had that survived, ringed round, lit up, visible to the last detail, with all before it blank and all after it blank, for miles and miles?

"Is it a boat? Is it a cork?" she would say, Lily repeated, turning back, reluctantly again, to her canvas. Heaven be praised for it, the problem of space remained, she thought, taking up her brush again. It glared at her. The whole mass of the picture was poised upon that weight. Beautiful and bright it should be on the surface, feathery and evanescent, one colour melting into another like the colours on a butterfly's wing; but beneath the fabric must be clamped together with bolts of iron. It was to be a thing you could ruffle with your breath; and a thing you could not dislodge with a team of horses. And she began to lay on a red, a grey, and she began to model her way into the hollow there. At the same time, she seemed to be sitting beside Mrs. Ramsay on the beach.

"Is it a boat? Is it a cask?" Mrs. Ramsay said. And she began hunting round for her spectacles. And she sat, having found them, silent, looking out to sea. And Lily, painting steadily, felt as if a door had opened, and one went in and stood gazing silently about in a high cathedral-like place, very dark, very solemn. Shouts came from a world far away. Steamers vanished in stalks of smoke on the horizon. Charles threw stones and sent them skipping.

Mrs. Ramsay sat silent. She was glad, Lily thought, to rest in silence, uncommunicative; to rest in the extreme obscurity of human relationships. Who knows what we are, what we feel? Who knows even at the moment of intimacy, This is knowledge? Aren't things spoilt then, Mrs. Ramsay may have asked (it seemed to have happened so often, this silence by her side) by saying them? Aren't we more expressive thus? The moment at least seemed extraordinarily fertile. She rammed a little hole in the sand and covered it up, by way of burying in it the perfection of the moment. It was like a drop of silver in which one dipped and illumined the darkness of the past.

Lily stepped back to get her canvas--so--into perspective. It was an odd road to be walking, this of painting. Out and out one went, further, until at last one seemed to be on a narrow plank, perfectly alone, over the sea. And as she dipped into the blue paint, she dipped too into the past there. Now Mrs. Ramsay got up, she remembered. It was time to go back to the house--time for luncheon. And they all walked up from the beach together, she walking behind with William Bankes, and there was Minta in front of them with a hole in her stocking. How that little round hole of pink heel seemed to flaunt itself before them! How William Bankes deplored it, without, so far as she could remember, saying anything about it! It meant to him the annihilation of womanhood, and dirt and disorder, and servants leaving and beds not made at mid-day--all the things he most abhorred. He had a way of shuddering and spreading his fingers out as if to cover an unsightly object which he did now--holding his hand in front of him. And Minta walked on ahead, and presumably Paul met her and she went off with Paul in the garden.

The Rayleys, thought Lily Briscoe, squeezing her tube of green paint. She collected her impressions of the Rayleys. Their lives appeared to her in a series of scenes; one, on the staircase at dawn. Paul had come in and gone to bed early; Minta was late. There was Minta, wreathed, tinted, garish on the stairs about three o'clock in the morning. Paul came out in his pyjamas carrying a poker in case of burglars. Minta was eating a sandwich, standing half-way up by a window, in the cadaverous early morning light, and the carpet had a hole in it. But what did they say? Lily asked herself, as if by looking she could hear them. Minta went on eating her sandwich, annoyingly, while he spoke something violent, abusing her, in a mutter so as not to wake the children, the two little boys. He was withered, drawn; she flamboyant, careless. For things had worked loose after the first year or so; the marriage had turned out rather badly.

And this, Lily thought, taking the green paint on her brush, this making up scenes about them, is what we call "knowing" people, "thinking" of them, "being fond" of them! Not a word of it was true; she had made it up; but it was what she knew them by all the same. She went on tunnelling her way into her picture, into the past.

Another time, Paul said he "played chess in coffee-houses." She had built up a whole structure of imagination on that saying too. She remembered how, as he said it, she thought how he rang up the servant, and she said, "Mrs. Rayley's out, sir," and he decided that he would not come home either. She saw him sitting in the corner of some lugubrious place where the smoke attached itself to the red plush seats, and the waitresses got to know you, and he played chess with a little man who was in the tea trade and lived at Surbiton, but that was all Paul knew about him. And then Minta was out when he came home and then there was that scene on the stairs, when he got the poker in case of burglars (no doubt to frighten her too) and spoke so bitterly, saying she had ruined his life. At any rate when she went down to see them at a cottage near Rickmansworth, things were horribly strained. Paul took her down the garden to look at the Belgian hares which he bred, and Minta followed them, singing, and put her bare arm on his shoulder, lest he should tell her anything.

Minta was bored by hares, Lily thought. But Minta never gave herself away. She never said things like that about playing chess in coffee- houses. She was far too conscious, far too wary. But to go on with their story--they had got through the dangerous stage by now. She had been staying with them last summer some time and the car broke down and Minta had to hand him his tools. He sat on the road mending the car, and it was the way she gave him the tools--business-like, straightforward, friendly--that proved it was all right now. They were "in love" no longer; no, he had taken up with another woman, a serious woman, with her hair in a plait and a case in her hand (Minta had described her gratefully, almost admiringly), who went to meetings and shared Paul's views (they had got more and more pronounced) about the taxation of land values and a capital levy. Far from breaking up the marriage, that alliance had righted it. They were excellent friends, obviously, as he sat on the road and she handed him his tools.

So that was the story of the Rayleys, Lily thought. She imagined herself telling it to Mrs. Ramsay, who would be full of curiosity to know what had become of the Rayleys. She would feel a little triumphant, telling Mrs. Ramsay that the marriage had not been a success.

But the dead, thought Lily, encountering some obstacle in her design which made her pause and ponder, stepping back a foot or so, oh, the dead! she murmured, one pitied them, one brushed them aside, one had even a little contempt for them. They are at our mercy. Mrs. Ramsay has faded and gone, she thought. We can over-ride her wishes, improve away her limited, old-fashioned ideas. She recedes further and further from us. Mockingly she seemed to see her there at the end of the corridor of years saying, of all incongruous things, "Marry, marry!" (sitting very upright early in the morning with the birds beginning to cheep in the garden outside). And one would have to say to her, It has all gone against your wishes. They're happy like that; I'm happy like this. Life has changed completely. At that all her being, even her beauty, became for a moment, dusty and out of date. For a moment Lily, standing there, with the sun hot on her back, summing up the Rayleys, triumphed over Mrs. Ramsay, who would never know how Paul went to coffee-houses and had a mistress; how he sat on the ground and Minta handed him his tools; how she stood here painting, had never married, not even William Bankes.

Mrs. Ramsay had planned it. Perhaps, had she lived, she would have compelled it. Already that summer he was "the kindest of men." He was "the first scientist of his age, my husband says." He was also "poor William--it makes me so unhappy, when I go to see him, to find nothing nice in his house--no one to arrange the flowers." So they were sent for walks together, and she was told, with that faint touch of irony that made Mrs. Ramsay slip through one's fingers, that she had a scientific mind; she liked flowers; she was so exact. What was this mania of hers for marriage? Lily wondered, stepping to and fro from her easel.

(Suddenly, as suddenly as a star slides in the sky, a reddish light seemed to burn in her mind, covering Paul Rayley, issuing from him. It rose like a fire sent up in token of some celebration by savages on a distant beach. She heard the roar and the crackle. The whole sea for miles round ran red and gold. Some winey smell mixed with it and intoxicated her, for she felt again her own headlong desire to throw herself off the cliff and be drowned looking for a pearl brooch on a beach. And the roar and the crackle repelled her with fear and disgust, as if while she saw its splendour and power she saw too how it fed on the treasure of the house, greedily, disgustingly, and she loathed it. But for a sight, for a glory it surpassed everything in her experience, and burnt year after year like a signal fire on a desert island at the edge of the sea, and one had only to say "in love" and instantly, as happened now, up rose Paul's fire again. And it sank and she said to herself, laughing, "The Rayleys"; how Paul went to coffee-houses and played chess.)

She had only escaped by the skin of her teeth though, she thought. She had been looking at the table-cloth, and it had flashed upon her that she would move the tree to the middle, and need never marry anybody, and she had felt an enormous exultation. She had felt, now she could stand up to Mrs. Ramsay--a tribute to the astonishing power that Mrs. Ramsay had over one. Do this, she said, and one did it. Even her shadow at the window with James was full of authority. She remembered how William Bankes had been shocked by her neglect of the significance of mother and son. Did she not admire their beauty? he said. But William, she remembered, had listened to her with his wise child's eyes when she explained how it was not irreverence: how a light there needed a shadow there and so on. She did not intend to disparage a subject which, they agreed, Raphael had treated divinely. She was not cynical. Quite the contrary. Thanks to his scientific mind he understood--a proof of disinterested intelligence which had pleased her and comforted her enormously. One could talk of painting then seriously to a man. Indeed, his friendship had been one of the pleasures of her life. She loved William Bankes.

They went to Hampton Court and he always left her, like the perfect gentleman he was, plenty of time to wash her hands, while he strolled by the river. That was typical of their relationship. Many things were left unsaid. Then they strolled through the courtyards, and admired, summer after summer, the proportions and the flowers, and he would tell her things, about perspective, about architecture, as they walked, and he would stop to look at a tree, or the view over the lake, and admire a child--(it was his great grief--he had no daughter) in the vague aloof way that was natural to a man who spent so much time in laboratories that the world when he came out seemed to dazzle him, so that he walked slowly, lifted his hand to screen his eyes and paused, with his head thrown back, merely to breathe the air. Then he would tell her how his housekeeper was on her holiday; he must buy a new carpet for the staircase. Perhaps she would go with him to buy a new carpet for the staircase. And once something led him to talk about the Ramsays and he had said how when he first saw her she had been wearing a grey hat; she was not more than nineteen or twenty. She was astonishingly beautiful. There he stood looking down the avenue at Hampton Court as if he could see her there among the fountains.

She looked now at the drawing-room step. She saw, through William's eyes, the shape of a woman, peaceful and silent, with downcast eyes. She sat musing, pondering (she was in grey that day, Lily thought). Her eyes were bent. She would never lift them. Yes, thought Lily, looking intently, I must have seen her look like that, but not in grey; nor so still, nor so young, nor so peaceful. The figure came readily enough. She was astonishingly beautiful, as William said. But beauty was not everything. Beauty had this penalty--it came too readily, came too completely. It stilled life--froze it. One forgot the little agitations; the flush, the pallor, some queer distortion, some light or shadow, which made the face unrecognisable for a moment and yet added a quality one saw for ever after. It was simpler to smooth that all out under the cover of beauty. But what was the look she had, Lily wondered, when she clapped her deer-stalkers's hat on her head, or ran across the grass, or scolded Kennedy, the gardener? Who could tell her? Who could help her?

Against her will she had come to the surface, and found herself half out of the picture, looking, little dazedly, as if at unreal things, at Mr. Carmichael. He lay on his chair with his hands clasped above his paunch not reading, or sleeping, but basking like a creature gorged with existence. His book had fallen on to the grass.

She wanted to go straight up to him and say, "Mr. Carmichael!" Then he would look up benevolently as always, from his smoky vague green eyes. But one only woke people if one knew what one wanted to say to them. And she wanted to say not one thing, but everything. Little words that broke up the thought and dismembered it said nothing. "About life, about death; about Mrs. Ramsay"--no, she thought, one could say nothing to nobody. The urgency of the moment always missed its mark. Words fluttered sideways and struck the object inches too low. Then one gave it up; then the idea sunk back again; then one became like most middle-aged people, cautious, furtive, with wrinkles between the eyes and a look of perpetual apprehension. For how could one express in words these emotions of the body? express that emptiness there? (She was looking at the drawing-room steps; they looked extraordinarily empty.) It was one's body feeling, not one's mind. The physical sensations that went with the bare look of the steps had become suddenly extremely unpleasant. To want and not to have, sent all up her body a hardness, a hollowness, a strain. And then to want and not to have--to want and want--how that wrung the heart, and wrung it again and again! Oh, Mrs. Ramsay! she called out silently, to that essence which sat by the boat, that abstract one made of her, that woman in grey, as if to abuse her for having gone, and then having gone, come back again. It had seemed so safe, thinking of her. Ghost, air, nothingness, a thing you could play with easily and safely at any time of day or night, she had been that, and then suddenly she put her hand out and wrung the heart thus. Suddenly, the empty drawing-room steps, the frill of the chair inside, the puppy tumbling on the terrace, the whole wave and whisper of the garden became like curves and arabesques flourishing round a centre of complete emptiness.

"What does it mean? How do you explain it all?" she wanted to say, turning to Mr. Carmichael again. For the whole world seemed to have dissolved in this early morning hour into a pool of thought, a deep basin of reality, and one could almost fancy that had Mr. Carmichael spoken, for instance, a little tear would have rent the surface pool. And then? Something would emerge. A hand would be shoved up, a blade would be flashed. It was nonsense of course.

A curious notion came to her that he did after all hear the things she could not say. He was an inscrutable old man, with the yellow stain on his beard, and his poetry, and his puzzles, sailing serenely through a world which satisfied all his wants, so that she thought he had only to put down his hand where he lay on the lawn to fish up anything he wanted. She looked at her picture. That would have been his answer, presumably--how "you" and "I" and "she" pass and vanish; nothing stays; all changes; but not words, not paint. Yet it would be hung in the attics, she thought; it would be rolled up and flung under a sofa; yet even so, even of a picture like that, it was true. One might say, even of this scrawl, not of that actual picture, perhaps, but of what it attempted, that it "remained for ever," she was going to say, or, for the words spoken sounded even to herself, too boastful, to hint, wordlessly; when, looking at the picture, she was surprised to find that she could not see it. Her eyes were full of a hot liquid (she did not think of tears at first) which, without disturbing the firmness of her lips, made the air thick, rolled down her cheeks. She had perfect control of herself--Oh, yes!--in every other way. Was she crying then for Mrs. Ramsay, without being aware of any unhappiness? She addressed old Mr. Carmichael again. What was it then? What did it mean? Could things thrust their hands up and grip one; could the blade cut; the fist grasp? Was there no safety? No learning by heart of the ways of the world? No guide, no shelter, but all was miracle, and leaping from the pinnacle of a tower into the air? Could it be, even for elderly people, that this was life?--startling, unexpected, unknown? For one moment she felt that if they both got up, here, now on the lawn, and demanded an explanation, why was it so short, why was it so inexplicable, said it with violence, as two fully equipped human beings from whom nothing should be hid might speak, then, beauty would roll itself up; the space would fill; those empty flourishes would form into shape; if they shouted loud enough Mrs. Ramsay would return. "Mrs. Ramsay!" she said aloud, "Mrs. Ramsay!" The tears ran down her face.

7

[Macalister's boy took one of the fish and cut a square out of its side to bait his hook with. The mutilated body (it was alive still) was thrown back into the sea.]

8

"Mrs. Ramsay!" Lily cried, "Mrs. Ramsay!" But nothing happened. The pain increased. That anguish could reduce one to such a pitch of imbecility, she thought! Anyhow the old man had not heard her. He remained benignant, calm--if one chose to think it, sublime. Heaven be praised, no one had heard her cry that ignominious cry, stop pain, stop! She had not obviously taken leave of her senses. No one had seen her step off her strip of board into the waters of annihilation. She remained a skimpy old maid, holding a paint-brush.

And now slowly the pain of the want, and the bitter anger (to be called back, just as she thought she would never feel sorrow for Mrs. Ramsay again. Had she missed her among the coffee cups at breakfast? not in the least) lessened; and of their anguish left, as antidote, a relief that was balm in itself, and also, but more mysteriously, a sense of some one there, of Mrs. Ramsay, relieved for a moment of the weight that the world had put on her, staying lightly by her side and then (for this was Mrs. Ramsay in all her beauty) raising to her forehead a wreath of white flowers with which she went. Lily squeezed her tubes again. She attacked that problem of the hedge. It was strange how clearly she saw her, stepping with her usual quickness across fields among whose folds, purplish and soft, among whose flowers, hyacinth or lilies, she vanished. It was some trick of the painter's eye. For days after she had heard of her death she had seen her thus, putting her wreath to her forehead and going unquestioningly with her companion, a shade across the fields. The sight, the phrase, had its power to console. Wherever she happened to be, painting, here, in the country or in London, the vision would come to her, and her eyes, half closing, sought something to base her vision on. She looked down the railway carriage, the omnibus; took a line from shoulder or cheek; looked at the windows opposite; at Piccadilly, lamp-strung in the evening. All had been part of the fields of death. But always something--it might be a face, a voice, a paper boy crying STANDARD, NEWS--thrust through, snubbed her, waked her, required and got in the end an effort of attention, so that the vision must be perpetually remade. Now again, moved as she was by some instinctive need of distance and blue, she looked at the bay beneath her, making hillocks of the blue bars of the waves, and stony fields of the purpler spaces, again she was roused as usual by something incongruous. There was a brown spot in the middle of the bay. It was a boat. Yes, she realised that after a second. But whose boat? Mr. Ramsay's boat, she replied. Mr. Ramsay; the man who had marched past her, with his hand raised, aloof, at the head of a procession, in his beautiful boots, asking her for sympathy, which she had refused. The boat was now half way across the bay.

So fine was the morning except for a streak of wind here and there that the sea and sky looked all one fabric, as if sails were stuck high up in the sky, or the clouds had dropped down into the sea. A steamer far out at sea had drawn in the air a great scroll of smoke which stayed there curving and circling decoratively, as if the air were a fine gauze which held things and kept them softly in its mesh, only gently swaying them this way and that. And as happens sometimes when the weather is very fine, the cliffs looked as if they were conscious of the ships, and the ships looked as if they were conscious of the cliffs, as if they signalled to each other some message of their own. For sometimes quite close to the shore, the Lighthouse looked this morning in the haze an enormous distance away.

"Where are they now?" Lily thought, looking out to sea. Where was he, that very old man who had gone past her silently, holding a brown paper parcel under his arm? The boat was in the middle of the bay.

9

They don't feel a thing there, Cam thought, looking at the shore, which, rising and falling, became steadily more distant and more peaceful. Her hand cut a trail in the sea, as her mind made the green swirls and streaks into patterns and, numbed and shrouded, wandered in imagination in that underworld of waters where the pearls stuck in clusters to white sprays, where in the green light a change came over one's entire mind and one's body shone half transparent enveloped in a green cloak.

Then the eddy slackened round her hand. The rush of the water ceased; the world became full of little creaking and squeaking sounds. One heard the waves breaking and flapping against the side of the boat as if they were anchored in harbour. Everything became very close to one. For the sail, upon which James had his eyes fixed until it had become to him like a person whom he knew, sagged entirely; there they came to a stop, flapping about waiting for a breeze, in the hot sun, miles from shore, miles from the Lighthouse. Everything in the whole world seemed to stand still. The Lighthouse became immovable, and the line of the distant shore became fixed. The sun grew hotter and everybody seemed to come very close together and to feel each other's presence, which they had almost forgotten. Macalister's fishing line went plumb down into the sea. But Mr. Ramsay went on reading with his legs curled under him.

He was reading a little shiny book with covers mottled like a plover's egg. Now and again, as they hung about in that horrid calm, he turned a page. And James felt that each page was turned with a peculiar gesture aimed at him; now assertively, now commandingly; now with the intention of making people pity him; and all the time, as his father read and turned one after another of those little pages, James kept dreading the moment when he would look up and speak sharply to him about something or other. Why were they lagging about here? he would demand, or something quite unreasonable like that. And if he does, James thought, then I shall take a knife and strike him to the heart.

He had always kept this old symbol of taking a knife and striking his father to the heart. Only now, as he grew older, and sat staring at his father in an impotent rage, it was not him, that old man reading, whom he wanted to kill, but it was the thing that descended on him--without his knowing it perhaps: that fierce sudden black-winged harpy, with its talons and its beak all cold and hard, that struck and struck at you (he could feel the beak on his bare legs, where it had struck when he was a child) and then made off, and there he was again, an old man, very sad, reading his book. That he would kill, that he would strike to the heart. Whatever he did--(and he might do anything, he felt, looking at the Lighthouse and the distant shore) whether he was in a business, in a bank, a barrister, a man at the head of some enterprise, that he would fight, that he would track down and stamp out--tyranny, despotism, he called it--making people do what they did not want to do, cutting off their right to speak. How could any of them say, But I won't, when he said, Come to the Lighthouse. Do this. Fetch me that. The black wings spread, and the hard beak tore. And then next moment, there he sat reading his book; and he might look up--one never knew--quite reasonably. He might talk to the Macalisters. He might be pressing a sovereign into some frozen old woman's hand in the street, James thought, and he might be shouting out at some fisherman's sports; he might be waving his arms in the air with excitement. Or he might sit at the head of the table dead silent from one end of dinner to the other. Yes, thought James, while the boat slapped and dawdled there in the hot sun; there was a waste of snow and rock very lonely and austere; and there he had come to feel, quite often lately, when his father said something or did something which surprised the others, there were two pairs of footprints only; his own and his father's. They alone knew each other. What then was this terror, this hatred? Turning back among the many leaves which the past had folded in him, peering into the heart of that forest where light and shade so chequer each other that all shape is distorted, and one blunders, now with the sun in one's eyes, now with a dark shadow, he sought an image to cool and detach and round off his feeling in a concrete shape. Suppose then that as a child sitting helpless in a perambulator, or on some one's knee, he had seen a waggon crush ignorantly and innocently, some one's foot? Suppose he had seen the foot first, in the grass, smooth, and whole; then the wheel; and the same foot, purple, crushed. But the wheel was innocent. So now, when his father came striding down the passage knocking them up early in the morning to go to the Lighthouse down it came over his foot, over Cam's foot, over anybody's foot. One sat and watched it.

But whose foot was he thinking of, and in what garden did all this happen? For one had settings for these scenes; trees that grew there; flowers; a certain light; a few figures. Everything tended to set itself in a garden where there was none of this gloom. None of this throwing of hands about; people spoke in an ordinary tone of voice. They went in and out all day long. There was an old woman gossiping in the kitchen; and the blinds were sucked in and out by the breeze; all was blowing, all was growing; and over all those plates and bowls and tall brandishing red and yellow flowers a very thin yellow veil would be drawn, like a vine leaf, at night. Things became stiller and darker at night. But the leaf-like veil was so fine, that lights lifted it, voices crinkled it; he could see through it a figure stooping, hear, coming close, going away, some dress rustling, some chain tinkling.

It was in this world that the wheel went over the person's foot. Something, he remembered, stayed flourished up in the air, something arid and sharp descended even there, like a blade, a scimitar, smiting through the leaves and flowers even of that happy world and making it shrivel and fall.

"It will rain," he remembered his father saying. "You won't be able to go to the Lighthouse."

The Lighthouse was then a silvery, misty-looking tower with a yellow eye, that opened suddenly, and softly in the evening. Now--

James looked at the Lighthouse. He could see the white-washed rocks; the tower, stark and straight; he could see that it was barred with black and white; he could see windows in it; he could even see washing spread on the rocks to dry. So that was the Lighthouse, was it?

No, the other was also the Lighthouse. For nothing was simply one thing. The other Lighthouse was true too. It was sometimes hardly to be seen across the bay. In the evening one looked up and saw the eye opening and shutting and the light seemed to reach them in that airy sunny garden where they sat.

But he pulled himself up. Whenever he said "they" or "a person," and then began hearing the rustle of some one coming, the tinkle of some one going, he became extremely sensitive to the presence of whoever might be in the room. It was his father now. The strain was acute. For in one moment if there was no breeze, his father would slap the covers of his book together, and say: "What's happening now? What are we dawdling about here for, eh?" as, once before he had brought his blade down among them on the terrace and she had gone stiff all over, and if there had been an axe handy, a knife, or anything with a sharp point he would have seized it and struck his father through the heart. She had gone stiff all over, and then, her arm slackening, so that he felt she listened to him no longer, she had risen somehow and gone away and left him there, impotent, ridiculous, sitting on the floor grasping a pair of scissors.

Not a breath of wind blew. The water chuckled and gurgled in the bottom of the boat where three or four mackerel beat their tails up and down in a pool of water not deep enough to cover them. At any moment Mr. Ramsay (he scarcely dared look at him) might rouse himself, shut his book, and say something sharp; but for the moment he was reading, so that James stealthily, as if he were stealing downstairs on bare feet, afraid of waking a watchdog by a creaking board, went on thinking what was she like, where did she go that day? He began following her from room to room and at last they came to a room where in a blue light, as if the reflection came from many china dishes, she talked to somebody; he listened to her talking. She talked to a servant, saying simply whatever came into her head. She alone spoke the truth; to her alone could he speak it. That was the source of her everlasting attraction for him, perhaps; she was a person to whom one could say what came into one's head. But all the time he thought of her, he was conscious of his father following his thought, surveying it, making it shiver and falter. At last he ceased to think.

There he sat with his hand on the tiller in the sun, staring at the Lighthouse, powerless to move, powerless to flick off these grains of misery which settled on his mind one after another. A rope seemed to bind him there, and his father had knotted it and he could only escape by taking a knife and plunging it... But at that moment the sail swung slowly round, filled slowly out, the boat seemed to shake herself, and then to move off half conscious in her sleep, and then she woke and shot through the waves. The relief was extraordinary. They all seemed to fall away from each other again and to be at their ease, and the fishing-lines slanted taut across the side of the boat. But his father did not rouse himself. He only raised his right hand mysteriously high in the air, and let it fall upon his knee again as if he were conducting some secret symphony.

10

[The sea without a stain on it, thought Lily Briscoe, still standing and looking out over the bay. The sea stretched like silk across the bay. Distance had an extraordinary power; they had been swallowed up in it, she felt, they were gone for ever, they had become part of the nature of things. It was so calm; it was so quiet. The steamer itself had vanished, but the great scroll of smoke still hung in the air and drooped like a flag mournfully in valediction.]

11

It was like that then, the island, thought Cam, once more drawing her fingers through the waves. She had never seen it from out at sea before. It lay like that on the sea, did it, with a dent in the middle and two sharp crags, and the sea swept in there, and spread away for miles and miles on either side of the island. It was very small; shaped something like a leaf stood on end. So we took a little boat, she thought, beginning to tell herself a story of adventure about escaping from a sinking ship. But with the sea streaming through her fingers, a spray of seaweed vanishing behind them, she did not want to tell herself seriously a story; it was the sense of adventure and escape that she wanted, for she was thinking, as the boat sailed on, how her father's anger about the points of the compass, James's obstinacy about the compact, and her own anguish, all had slipped, all had passed, all had streamed away. What then came next? Where were they going? From her hand, ice cold, held deep in the sea, there spurted up a fountain of joy at the change, at the escape, at the adventure (that she should be alive, that she should be there). And the drops falling from this sudden and unthinking fountain of joy fell here and there on the dark, the slumbrous shapes in her mind; shapes of a world not realised but turning in their darkness, catching here and there, a spark of light; Greece, Rome, Constantinople. Small as it was, and shaped something like a leaf stood on its end with the gold- sprinkled waters flowing in and about it, it had, she supposed, a place in the universe--even that little island? The old gentlemen in the study she thought could have told her. Sometimes she strayed in from the garden purposely to catch them at it. There they were (it might be Mr. Carmichael or Mr. Bankes who was sitting with her father) sitting opposite each other in their low arm-chairs. They were crackling in front of them the pages of THE TIMES, when she came in from the garden, all in a muddle, about something some one had said about Christ, or hearing that a mammoth had been dug up in a London street, or wondering what Napoleon was like. Then they took all this with their clean hands (they wore grey-coloured clothes; they smelt of heather) and they brushed the scraps together, turning the paper, crossing their knees, and said something now and then very brief. Just to please herself she would take a book from the shelf and stand there, watching her father write, so equally, so neatly from one side of the page to another, with a little cough now and then, or something said briefly to the other old gentleman opposite. And she thought, standing there with her book open, one could let whatever one thought expand here like a leaf in water; and if it did well here, among the old gentlemen smoking and THE TIMES crackling then it was right. And watching her father as he wrote in his study, she thought (now sitting in the boat) he was not vain, nor a tyrant and did not wish to make you pity him. Indeed, if he saw she was there, reading a book, he would ask her, as gently as any one could, Was there nothing he could give her?

Lest this should be wrong, she looked at him reading the little book with the shiny cover mottled like a plover's egg. No; it was right. Look at him now, she wanted to say aloud to James. (But James had his eye on the sail.) He is a sarcastic brute, James would say. He brings the talk round to himself and his books, James would say. He is intolerably egotistical. Worst of all, he is a tyrant. But look! she said, looking at him. Look at him now. She looked at him reading the little book with his legs curled; the little book whose yellowish pages she knew, without knowing what was written on them. It was small; it was closely printed; on the fly-leaf, she knew, he had written that he had spent fifteen francs on dinner; the wine had been so much; he had given so much to the waiter; all was added up neatly at the bottom of the page. But what might be written in the book which had rounded its edges off in his pocket, she did not know. What he thought they none of them knew. But he was absorbed in it, so that when he looked up, as he did now for an instant, it was not to see anything; it was to pin down some thought more exactly. That done, his mind flew back again and he plunged into his reading. He read, she thought, as if he were guiding something, or wheedling a large flock of sheep, or pushing his way up and up a single narrow path; and sometimes he went fast and straight, and broke his way through the bramble, and sometimes it seemed a branch struck at him, a bramble blinded him, but he was not going to let himself be beaten by that; on he went, tossing over page after page. And she went on telling herself a story about escaping from a sinking ship, for she was safe, while he sat there; safe, as she felt herself when she crept in from the garden, and took a book down, and the old gentleman, lowering the paper suddenly, said something very brief over the top of it about the character of Napoleon.

She gazed back over the sea, at the island. But the leaf was losing its sharpness. It was very small; it was very distant. The sea was more important now than the shore. Waves were all round them, tossing and sinking, with a log wallowing down one wave; a gull riding on another. About here, she thought, dabbling her fingers in the water, a ship had sunk, and she murmured, dreamily half asleep, how we perished, each alone.

12

So much depends then, thought Lily Briscoe, looking at the sea which had scarcely a stain on it, which was so soft that the sails and the clouds seemed set in its blue, so much depends, she thought, upon distance: whether people are near us or far from us; for her feeling for Mr. Ramsay changed as he sailed further and further across the bay. It seemed to be elongated, stretched out; he seemed to become more and more remote. He and his children seemed to be swallowed up in that blue, that distance; but here, on the lawn, close at hand, Mr. Carmichael suddenly grunted. She laughed. He clawed his book up from the grass. He settled into his chair again puffing and blowing like some sea monster. That was different altogether, because he was so near. And now again all was quiet. They must be out of bed by this time, she supposed, looking at the house, but nothing appeared there. But then, she remembered, they had always made off directly a meal was over, on business of their own. It was all in keeping with this silence, this emptiness, and the unreality of the early morning hour. It was a way things had sometimes, she thought, lingering for a moment and looking at the long glittering windows and the plume of blue smoke: they became illness, before habits had spun themselves across the surface, one felt that same unreality, which was so startling; felt something emerge. Life was most vivid then. One could be at one's ease. Mercifully one need not say, very briskly, crossing the lawn to greet old Mrs. Beckwith, who would be coming out to find a corner to sit in, "Oh, good-morning, Mrs. Beckwith! What a lovely day! Are you going to be so bold as to sit in the sun? Jasper's hidden the chairs. Do let me find you one!" and all the rest of the usual chatter. One need not speak at all. One glided, one shook one's sails (there was a good deal of movement in the bay, boats were starting off) between things, beyond things. Empty it was not, but full to the brim. She seemed to be standing up to the lips in some substance, to move and float and sink in it, yes, for these waters were unfathomably deep. Into them had spilled so many lives. The Ramsays'; the children's; and all sorts of waifs and strays of things besides. A washer-woman with her basket; a rook, a red-hot poker; the purples and grey-greens of flowers: some common feeling which held the whole together.

It was some such feeling of completeness perhaps which, ten years ago, standing almost where she stood now, had made her say that she must be in love with the place. Love had a thousand shapes. There might be lovers whose gift it was to choose out the elements of things and place them together and so, giving them a wholeness not theirs in life, make of some scene, or meeting of people (all now gone and separate), one of those globed compacted things over which thought lingers, and love plays.

Her eyes rested on the brown speck of Mr. Ramsay's sailing boat. They would be at the Lighthouse by lunch time she supposed. But the wind had freshened, and, as the sky changed slightly and the sea changed slightly and the boats altered their positions, the view, which a moment before had seemed miraculously fixed, was now unsatisfactory. The wind had blown the trail of smoke about; there was something displeasing about the placing of the ships.

The disproportion there seemed to upset some harmony in her own mind. She felt an obscure distress. It was confirmed when she turned to her picture. She had been wasting her morning. For whatever reason she could not achieve that razor edge of balance between two opposite forces; Mr. Ramsay and the picture; which was necessary. There was something perhaps wrong with the design? Was it, she wondered, that the line of the wall wanted breaking, was it that the mass of the trees was too heavy? She smiled ironically; for had she not thought, when she began, that she had solved her problem?

What was the problem then? She must try to get hold of something that evaded her. It evaded her when she thought of Mrs. Ramsay; it evaded her now when she thought of her picture. Phrases came. Visions came. Beautiful pictures. Beautiful phrases. But what she wished to get hold of was that very jar on the nerves, the thing itself before it has been made anything. Get that and start afresh; get that and start afresh; she said desperately, pitching herself firmly again before her easel. It was a miserable machine, an inefficient machine, she thought, the human apparatus for painting or for feeling; it always broke down at the critical moment; heroically, one must force it on. She stared, frowning. There was the hedge, sure enough. But one got nothing by soliciting urgently. One got only a glare in the eye from looking at the line of the wall, or from thinking--she wore a grey hat. She was astonishingly beautiful. Let it come, she thought, if it will come. For there are moments when one can neither think nor feel. And if one can neither think nor feel, she thought, where is one?

Here on the grass, on the ground, she thought, sitting down, and examining with her brush a little colony of plantains. For the lawn was very rough. Here sitting on the world, she thought, for she could not shake herself free from the sense that everything this morning was happening for the first time, perhaps for the last time, as a traveller, even though he is half asleep, knows, looking out of the train window, that he must look now, for he will never see that town, or that mule-cart, or that woman at work in the fields, again. The lawn was the world; they were up here together, on this exalted station, she thought, looking at old Mr. Carmichael, who seemed (though they had not said a word all this time) to share her thoughts. And she would never see him again perhaps. He was growing old. Also, she remembered, smiling at the slipper that dangled from his foot, he was growing famous. People said that his poetry was "so beautiful." They went and published things he had written forty years ago. There was a famous man now called Carmichael, she smiled, thinking how many shapes one person might wear, how he was that in the newspapers, but here the same as he had always been. He looked the same--greyer, rather. Yes, he looked the same, but somebody had said, she recalled, that when he had heard of Andrew Ramsay's death (he was killed in a second by a shell; he should have been a great mathematician) Mr. Carmichael had "lost all interest in life." What did it mean--that? she wondered. Had he marched through Trafalgar Square grasping a big stick? Had he turned pages over and over, without reading them, sitting in his room in St. John's Wood alone? She did not know what he had done, when he heard that Andrew was killed, but she felt it in him all the same. They only mumbled at each other on staircases; they looked up at the sky and said it will be fine or it won't be fine. But this was one way of knowing people, she thought: to know the outline, not the detail, to sit in one's garden and look at the slopes of a hill running purple down into the distant heather. She knew him in that way. She knew that he had changed somehow. She had never read a line of his poetry. She thought that she knew how it went though, slowly and sonorously. It was seasoned and mellow. It was about the desert and the camel. It was about the palm tree and the sunset. It was extremely impersonal; it said something about death; it said very little about love. There was an impersonality about him. He wanted very little of other people. Had he not always lurched rather awkwardly past the drawing-room window with some newspaper under his arm, trying to avoid Mrs. Ramsay whom for some reason he did not much like? On that account, of course, she would always try to make him stop. He would bow to her. He would halt unwillingly and bow profoundly. Annoyed that he did not want anything of her, Mrs. Ramsay would ask him (Lily could hear her) wouldn't he like a coat, a rug, a newspaper? No, he wanted nothing. (Here he bowed.) There was some quality in her which he did not much like. It was perhaps her masterfulness, her positiveness, something matter-of-fact in her. She was so direct.

(A noise drew her attention to the drawing-room window--the squeak of a hinge. The light breeze was toying with the window.)

There must have been people who disliked her very much, Lily thought (Yes; she realised that the drawing-room step was empty, but it had no effect on her whatever. She did not want Mrs. Ramsay now.)--People who thought her too sure, too drastic.

Also, her beauty offended people probably. How monotonous, they would say, and the same always! They preferred another type--the dark, the vivacious. Then she was weak with her husband. She let him make those scenes. Then she was reserved. Nobody knew exactly what had happened to her. And (to go back to Mr. Carmichael and his dislike) one could not imagine Mrs. Ramsay standing painting, lying reading, a whole morning on the lawn. It was unthinkable. Without saying a word, the only token of her errand a basket on her arm, she went off to the town, to the poor, to sit in some stuffy little bedroom. Often and often Lily had seen her go silently in the midst of some game, some discussion, with her basket on her arm, very upright. She had noted her return. She had thought, half laughing (she was so methodical with the tea cups), half moved (her beauty took one's breath away), eyes that are closing in pain have looked on you. You have been with them there.

And then Mrs. Ramsay would be annoyed because somebody was late, or the butter not fresh, or the teapot chipped. And all the time she was saying that the butter was not fresh one would be thinking of Greek temples, and how beauty had been with them there in that stuffy little room. She never talked of it--she went, punctually, directly. It was her instinct to go, an instinct like the swallows for the south, the artichokes for the sun, turning her infallibly to the human race, making her nest in its heart. And this, like all instincts, was a little distressing to people who did not share it; to Mr. Carmichael perhaps, to herself certainly. Some notion was in both of them about the ineffectiveness of action, the supremacy of thought. Her going was a reproach to them, gave a different twist to the world, so that they were led to protest, seeing their own prepossessions disappear, and clutch at them vanishing. Charles Tansley did that too: it was part of the reason why one disliked him. He upset the proportions of one's world. And what had happened to him, she wondered, idly stirring the plantains with her brush. He had got his fellowship. He had married; he lived at Golder's Green.

She had gone one day into a Hall and heard him speaking during the war. He was denouncing something: he was condemning somebody. He was preaching brotherly love. And all she felt was how could he love his kind who did not know one picture from another, who had stood behind her smoking shag ("fivepence an ounce, Miss Briscoe") and making it his business to tell her women can't write, women can't paint, not so much that he believed it, as that for some odd reason he wished it? There he was lean and red and raucous, preaching love from a platform (there were ants crawling about among the plantains which she disturbed with her brush--red, energetic, shiny ants, rather like Charles Tansley). She had looked at him ironically from her seat in the half-empty hall, pumping love into that chilly space, and suddenly, there was the old cask or whatever it was bobbing up and down among the waves and Mrs. Ramsay looking for her spectacle case among the pebbles. "Oh, dear! What a nuisance! Lost again. Don't bother, Mr. Tansley. I lose thousands every summer," at which he pressed his chin back against his collar, as if afraid to sanction such exaggeration, but could stand it in her whom he liked, and smiled very charmingly. He must have confided in her on one of those long expeditions when people got separated and walked back alone. He was educating his little sister, Mrs. Ramsay had told her. It was immensely to his credit. Her own idea of him was grotesque, Lily knew well, stirring the plantains with her brush. Half one's notions of other people were, after all, grotesque. They served private purposes of one's own. He did for her instead of a whipping-boy. She found herself flagellating his lean flanks when she was out of temper. If she wanted to be serious about him she had to help herself to Mrs. Ramsay's sayings, to look at him through her eyes.

She raised a little mountain for the ants to climb over. She reduced them to a frenzy of indecision by this interference in their cosmogony. Some ran this way, others that.

One wanted fifty pairs of eyes to see with, she reflected. Fifty pairs of eyes were not enough to get round that one woman with, she thought. Among them, must be one that was stone blind to her beauty. One wanted most some secret sense, fine as air, with which to steal through keyholes and surround her where she sat knitting, talking, sitting silent in the window alone; which took to itself and treasured up like the air which held the smoke of the steamer, her thoughts, her imaginations, her desires. What did the hedge mean to her, what did the garden mean to her, what did it mean to her when a wave broke? (Lily looked up, as she had seen Mrs. Ramsay look up; she too heard a wave falling on the beach.) And then what stirred and trembled in her mind when the children cried, "How's that? How's that?" cricketing? She would stop knitting for a second. She would look intent. Then she would lapse again, and suddenly Mr. Ramsay stopped dead in his pacing in front of her and some curious shock passed through her and seemed to rock her in profound agitation on its breast when stopping there he stood over her and looked down at her. Lily could see him.

He stretched out his hand and raised her from her chair. It seemed somehow as if he had done it before; as if he had once bent in the same way and raised her from a boat which, lying a few inches off some island, had required that the ladies should thus be helped on shore by the gentlemen. An old-fashioned scene that was, which required, very nearly, crinolines and peg-top trousers. Letting herself be helped by him, Mrs. Ramsay had thought (Lily supposed) the time has come now. Yes, she would say it now. Yes, she would marry him. And she stepped slowly, quietly on shore. Probably she said one word only, letting her hand rest still in his. I will marry you, she might have said, with her hand in his; but no more. Time after time the same thrill had passed between them--obviously it had, Lily thought, smoothing a way for her ants. She was not inventing; she was only trying to smooth out something she had been given years ago folded up; something she had seen. For in the rough and tumble of daily life, with all those children about, all those visitors, one had constantly a sense of repetition--of one thing falling where another had fallen, and so setting up an echo which chimed in the air and made it full of vibrations.

But it would be a mistake, she thought, thinking how they walked off together, arm in arm, past the greenhouse, to simplify their relationship. It was no monotony of bliss--she with her impulses and quicknesses; he with his shudders and glooms. Oh, no. The bedroom door would slam violently early in the morning. He would start from the table in a temper. He would whizz his plate through the window. Then all through the house there would be a sense of doors slamming and blinds fluttering, as if a gusty wind were blowing and people scudded about trying in a hasty way to fasten hatches and make things ship- shape. She had met Paul Rayley like that one day on the stairs. They had laughed and laughed, like a couple of children, all because Mr. Ramsay, finding an earwig in his milk at breakfast had sent the whole thing flying through the air on to the terrace outside. 'An earwig, Prue murmured, awestruck, 'in his milk.' Other people might find centipedes. But he had built round him such a fence of sanctity, and occupied the space with such a demeanour of majesty that an earwig in his milk was a monster.

But it tired Mrs. Ramsay, it cowed her a little--the plates whizzing and the doors slamming. And there would fall between them sometimes long rigid silences, when, in a state of mind which annoyed Lily in her, half plaintive, half resentful, she seemed unable to surmount the tempest calmly, or to laugh as they laughed, but in her weariness perhaps concealed something. She brooded and sat silent. After a time he would hang stealthily about the places where she was--roaming under the window where she sat writing letters or talking, for she would take care to be busy when he passed, and evade him, and pretend not to see him. Then he would turn smooth as silk, affable, urbane, and try to win her so. Still she would hold off, and now she would assert for a brief season some of those prides and airs the due of her beauty which she was generally utterly without; would turn her head; would look so, over her shoulder, always with some Minta, Paul, or William Bankes at her side. At length, standing outside the group the very figure of a famished wolfhound (Lily got up off the grass and stood looking at the steps, at the window, where she had seen him), he would say her name, once only, for all the world like a wolf barking in the snow, but still she held back; and he would say it once more, and this time something in the tone would rouse her, and she would go to him, leaving them all of a sudden, and they would walk off together among the pear trees, the cabbages, and the raspberry beds. They would have it out together. But with what attitudes and with what words? Such a dignity was theirs in this relationship that, turning away, she and Paul and Minta would hide their curiosity and their discomfort, and begin picking flowers, throwing balls, chattering, until it was time for dinner, and there they were, he at one end of the table, she at the other, as usual.

"Why don't some of you take up botany?.. With all those legs and arms why doesn't one of you...?" So they would talk as usual, laughing, among the children. All would be as usual, save only for some quiver, as of a blade in the air, which came and went between them as if the usual sight of the children sitting round their soup plates had freshened itself in their eyes after that hour among the pears and the cabbages. Especially, Lily thought, Mrs. Ramsay would glance at Prue. She sat in the middle between brothers and sisters, always occupied, it seemed, seeing that nothing went wrong so that she scarcely spoke herself. How Prue must have blamed herself for that earwig in the milk How white she had gone when Mr. Ramsay threw his plate through the window! How she drooped under those long silences between them! Anyhow, her mother now would seem to be making it up to her; assuring her that everything was well; promising her that one of these days that same happiness would be hers. She had enjoyed it for less than a year, however.

She had let the flowers fall from her basket, Lily thought, screwing up her eyes and standing back as if to look at her picture, which she was not touching, however, with all her faculties in a trance, frozen over superficially but moving underneath with extreme speed.

She let her flowers fall from her basket, scattered and tumbled them on to the grass and, reluctantly and hesitatingly, but without question or complaint--had she not the faculty of obedience to perfection?--went too. Down fields, across valleys, white, flower-strewn--that was how she would have painted it. The hills were austere. It was rocky; it was steep. The waves sounded hoarse on the stones beneath. They went, the three of them together, Mrs. Ramsay walking rather fast in front, as if she expected to meet some one round the corner.

Suddenly the window at which she was looking was whitened by some light stuff behind it. At last then somebody had come into the drawing-room; somebody was sitting in the chair. For Heaven's sake, she prayed, let them sit still there and not come floundering out to talk to her. Mercifully, whoever it was stayed still inside; had settled by some stroke of luck so as to throw an odd-shaped triangular shadow over the step. It altered the composition of the picture a little. It was interesting. It might be useful. Her mood was coming back to her. One must keep on looking without for a second relaxing the intensity of emotion, the determination not to be put off, not to be bamboozled. One must hold the scene--so--in a vice and let nothing come in and spoil it. One wanted, she thought, dipping her brush deliberately, to be on a level with ordinary experience, to feel simply that's a chair, that's a table, and yet at the same time, It's a miracle, it's an ecstasy. The problem might be solved after all. Ah, but what had happened? Some wave of white went over the window pane. The air must have stirred some flounce in the room. Her heart leapt at her and seized her and tortured her.

"Mrs. Ramsay! Mrs. Ramsay!" she cried, feeling the old horror come back--to want and want and not to have. Could she inflict that still? And then, quietly, as if she refrained, that too became part of ordinary experience, was on a level with the chair, with the table. Mrs. Ramsay--it was part of her perfect goodness--sat there quite simply, in the chair, flicked her needles to and fro, knitted her reddish-brown stocking, cast her shadow on the step. There she sat.

And as if she had something she must share, yet could hardly leave her easel, so full her mind was of what she was thinking, of what she was seeing, Lily went past Mr. Carmichael holding her brush to the edge of the lawn. Where was that boat now? And Mr. Ramsay? She wanted him.

13

Mr. Ramsay had almost done reading. One hand hovered over the page as if to be in readiness to turn it the very instant he had finished it. He sat there bareheaded with the wind blowing his hair about, extraordinarily exposed to everything. He looked very old. He looked, James thought, getting his head now against the Lighthouse, now against the waste of waters running away into the open, like some old stone lying on the sand; he looked as if he had become physically what was always at the back of both of their minds--that loneliness which was for both of them the truth about things.

He was reading very quickly, as if he were eager to get to the end. Indeed they were very close to the Lighthouse now. There it loomed up, stark and straight, glaring white and black, and one could see the waves breaking in white splinters like smashed glass upon the rocks. One could see lines and creases in the rocks. One could see the windows clearly; a dab of white on one of them, and a little tuft of green on the rock. A man had come out and looked at them through a glass and gone in again. So it was like that, James thought, the Lighthouse one had seen across the bay all these years; it was a stark tower on a bare rock. It satisfied him. It confirmed some obscure feeling of his about his own character. The old ladies, he thought, thinking of the garden at home, went dragging their chairs about on the lawn. Old Mrs. Beckwith, for example, was always saying how nice it was and how sweet it was and how they ought to be so proud and they ought to be so happy, but as a matter of fact, James thought, looking at the Lighthouse stood there on its rock, it's like that. He looked at his father reading fiercely with his legs curled tight. They shared that knowledge. "We are driving before a gale--we must sink," he began saying to himself, half aloud, exactly as his father said it.

Nobody seemed to have spoken for an age. Cam was tired of looking at the sea. Little bits of black cork had floated past; the fish were dead in the bottom of the boat. Still her father read, and James looked at him and she looked at him, and they vowed that they would fight tyranny to the death, and he went on reading quite unconscious of what they thought. It was thus that he escaped, she thought. Yes, with his great forehead and his great nose, holding his little mottled book firmly in front of him, he escaped. You might try to lay hands on him, but then like a bird, he spread his wings, he floated off to settle out of your reach somewhere far away on some desolate stump. She gazed at the immense expanse of the sea. The island had grown so small that it scarcely looked like a leaf any longer. It looked like the top of a rock which some wave bigger than the rest would cover. Yet in its frailty were all those paths, those terraces, those bedrooms-- all those innumberable things. But as, just before sleep, things simplify themselves so that only one of all the myriad details has power to assert itself, so, she felt, looking drowsily at the island, all those paths and terraces and bedrooms were fading and disappearing, and nothing was left but a pale blue censer swinging rhythmically this way and that across her mind. It was a hanging garden; it was a valley, full of birds, and flowers, and antelopes... She was falling asleep.

"Come now," said Mr. Ramsay, suddenly shutting his book.

Come where? To what extraordinary adventure? She woke with a start. To land somewhere, to climb somewhere? Where was he leading them? For after his immense silence the words startled them. But it was absurd. He was hungry, he said. It was time for lunch. Besides, look, he said. "There's the Lighthouse. We're almost there."

"He's doing very well," said Macalister, praising James. "He's keeping her very steady."

But his father never praised him, James thought grimly.

Mr. Ramsay opened the parcel and shared out the sandwiches among them. Now he was happy, eating bread and cheese with these fishermen. He would have liked to live in a cottage and lounge about in the harbour spitting with the other old men, James thought, watching him slice his cheese into thin yellow sheets with his penknife.

This is right, this is it, Cam kept feeling, as she peeled her hard- boiled egg. Now she felt as she did in the study when the old men were reading THE TIMES. Now I can go on thinking whatever I like, and I shan't fall over a precipice or be drowned, for there he is, keeping his eye on me, she thought.

At the same time they were sailing so fast along by the rocks that it was very exciting--it seemed as if they were doing two things at once; they were eating their lunch here in the sun and they were also making for safety in a great storm after a shipwreck. Would the water last? Would the provisions last? she asked herself, telling herself a story but knowing at the same time what was the truth.

They would soon be out of it, Mr. Ramsay was saying to old Macalister; but their children would see some strange things. Macalister said he was seventy-five last March; Mr. Ramsay was seventy-one. Macalister said he had never seen a doctor; he had never lost a tooth. And that's the way I'd like my children to live-- Cam was sure that her father was thinking that, for he stopped her throwing a sandwich into the sea and told her, as if he were thinking of the fishermen and how they lived, that if she did not want it she should put it back in the parcel. She should not waste it. He said it so wisely, as if he knew so well all the things that happened in the world that she put it back at once, and then he gave her, from his own parcel, a gingerbread nut, as if he were a great Spanish gentleman, she thought, handing a flower to a lady at a window (so courteous his manner was). He was shabby, and simple, eating bread and cheese; and yet he was leading them on a great expedition where, for all she knew, they would be drowned.

"That was where she sunk," said Macalister's boy suddenly.

Three men were drowned where we are now, the old man said. He had seen them clinging to the mast himself. And Mr. Ramsay taking a look at the spot was about, James and Cam were afraid, to burst out:

But I beneath a rougher sea,

and if he did, they could not bear it; they would shriek aloud; they could not endure another explosion of the passion that boiled in him; but to their surprise all he said was "Ah" as if he thought to himself. But why make a fuss about that? Naturally men are drowned in a storm, but it is a perfectly straightforward affair, and the depths of the sea (he sprinkled the crumbs from his sandwich paper over them) are only water after all. Then having lighted his pipe he took out his watch. He looked at it attentively; he made, perhaps, some mathematical calculation. At last he said, triumphantly:

"Well done!" James had steered them like a born sailor.

There! Cam thought, addressing herself silently to James. You've got it at last. For she knew that this was what James had been wanting, and she knew that now he had got it he was so pleased that he would not look at her or at his father or at any one. There he sat with his hand on the tiller sitting bolt upright, looking rather sulky and frowning slightly. He was so pleased that he was not going to let anybody share a grain of his pleasure. His father had praised him. They must think that he was perfectly indifferent. But you've got it now, Cam thought.

They had tacked, and they were sailing swiftly, buoyantly on long rocking waves which handed them on from one to another with an extraordinary lilt and exhilaration beside the reef. On the left a row of rocks showed brown through the water which thinned and became greener and on one, a higher rock, a wave incessantly broke and spurted a little column of drops which fell down in a shower. One could hear the slap of the water and the patter of falling drops and a kind of hushing and hissing sound from the waves rolling and gambolling and slapping the rocks as if they were wild creatures who were perfectly free and tossed and tumbled and sported like this for ever.

Now they could see two men on the Lighthouse, watching them and making ready to meet them.

Mr. Ramsay buttoned his coat, and turned up his trousers. He took the large, badly packed, brown paper parcel which Nancy had got ready and sat with it on his knee. Thus in complete readiness to land he sat looking back at the island. With his long-sighted eyes perhaps he could see the dwindled leaf-like shape standing on end on a plate of gold quite clearly. What could he see? Cam wondered. It was all a blur to her. What was he thinking now? she wondered. What was it he sought, so fixedly, so intently, so silently? They watched him, both of them, sitting bareheaded with his parcel on his knee staring and staring at the frail blue shape which seemed like the vapour of something that had burnt itself away.

What do you want? they both wanted to ask. They both wanted to say, Ask us anything and we will give it you. But he did not ask them anything. He sat and looked at the island and he might be thinking, We perished, each alone, or he might be thinking, I have reached it. I have found it; but he said nothing.

Then he put on his hat.

"Bring those parcels," he said, nodding his head at the things Nancy had done up for them to take to the Lighthouse. "The parcels for the Lighthouse men," he said. He rose and stood in the bow of the boat, very straight and tall, for all the world, James thought, as if he were saying, "There is no God," and Cam thought, as if he were leaping into space, and they both rose to follow him as he sprang, lightly like a young man, holding his parcel, on to the rock.

14

"He must have reached it," said Lily Briscoe aloud, feeling suddenly completely tired out. For the Lighthouse had become almost invisible, had melted away into a blue haze, and the effort of looking at it and the effort of thinking of him landing there, which both seemed to be one and the same effort, had stretched her body and mind to the utmost. Ah, but she was relieved. Whatever she had wanted to give him, when he left her that morning, she had given him at last.

"He has landed," she said aloud. "It is finished." Then, surging up, puffing slightly, old Mr. Carmichael stood beside her, looking like an old pagan god, shaggy, with weeds in his hair and the trident (it was only a French novel) in his hand. He stood by her on the edge of the lawn, swaying a little in his bulk and said, shading his eyes with his hand: "They will have landed," and she felt that she had been right. They had not needed to speak. They had been thinking the same things and he had answered her without her asking him anything. He stood there as if he were spreading his hands over all the weakness and suffering of mankind; she thought he was surveying, tolerantly and compassionately, their final destiny. Now he has crowned the occasion, she thought, when his hand slowly fell, as if she had seen him let fall from his great height a wreath of violets and asphodels which, fluttering slowly, lay at length upon the earth.

Quickly, as if she were recalled by something over there, she turned to her canvas. There it was--her picture. Yes, with all its greens and blues, its lines running up and across, its attempt at something. It would be hung in the attics, she thought; it would be destroyed. But what did that matter? she asked herself, taking up her brush again. She looked at the steps; they were empty; she looked at her canvas; it was blurred. With a sudden intensity, as if she saw it clear for a second, she drew a line there, in the centre. It was done; it was finished. Yes, she thought, laying down her brush in extreme fatigue, I have had my vision.

THE END

Orlando A Biography

TO
V. SACKVILLE-WEST.

PREFACE.

Many friends have helped me in writing this book. Some are dead and so illustrious that I scarcely dare name them, yet no one can read or write without being perpetually in the debt of Defoe, Sir Thomas Browne, Sterne, Sir Walter Scott, Lord Macaulay, Emily Bronte, De Quincey, and Walter Pater,--to name the first that come to mind. Others are alive, and though perhaps as illustrious in their own way, are less formidable for that very reason. I am specially indebted to Mr C.P. Sanger, without whose knowledge of the law of real property this book could never have been written. Mr Sydney-Turner's wide and peculiar erudition has saved me, I hope, some lamentable blunders. I have had the advantage--how great I alone can estimate--of Mr Arthur Waley's knowledge of Chinese. Madame Lopokova (Mrs J.M. Keynes) has been at hand to correct my Russian. To the unrivalled sympathy and imagination of Mr Roger Fry I owe whatever understanding of the art of painting I may possess. I have, I hope, profited in another department by the singularly penetrating, if severe, criticism of my nephew Mr Julian Bell. Miss M.K. Snowdon's indefatigable researches in the archives of Harrogate and Cheltenham were none the less arduous for being vain. Other friends have helped me in ways too various to specify. I must content myself with naming Mr Angus Davidson; Mrs Cartwright; Miss Janet Case; Lord Berners (whose knowledge of Elizabethan music has proved invaluable); Mr Francis Birrell; my brother, Dr Adrian Stephen; Mr F.L. Lucas; Mr and Mrs Desmond Maccarthy; that most inspiriting of critics, my brother-in-law, Mr Clive Bell; Mr G.H. Rylands; Lady Colefax; Miss Nellie Boxall; Mr J.M. Keynes; Mr Hugh Walpole; Miss Violet Dickinson; the Hon. Edward Sackville West; Mr and Mrs St. John Hutchinson; Mr Duncan Grant; Mr and Mrs Stephen Tomlin; Mr and Lady Ottoline Morrell; my mother-in-law, Mrs Sydney Woolf; Mr Osbert Sitwell; Madame Jacques Raverat; Colonel Cory Bell; Miss Valerie Taylor; Mr J.T. Sheppard; Mr and Mrs T.S. Eliot; Miss Ethel Sands; Miss Nan Hudson; my nephew Mr Quentin Bell (an old and valued collaborator in fiction); Mr Raymond Mortimer; Lady Gerald Wellesley; Mr Lytton Strachey; the Viscountess Cecil; Miss Hope Mirrlees; Mr E.M. Forster; the Hon. Harold Nicolson; and my sister, Vanessa Bell--but the list threatens to grow too long and is already far too distinguished. For while it rouses in me memories of the pleasantest kind it will inevitably wake expectations in the reader which the book itself can only disappoint. Therefore I will conclude by thanking the officials of the British Museum and Record Office for their wonted courtesy; my niece Miss Angelica Bell, for a service which none but she could have rendered; and my husband for the patience with which he has invariably helped my researches and for the profound historical knowledge to which these pages owe whatever degree of accuracy they may attain. Finally, I would thank, had I not lost his name and address, a gentleman in America, who has generously and gratuitously corrected the punctuation, the botany, the entomology, the geography, and the chronology of previous works of mine and will, I hope, not spare his services on the present occasion.

CHAPTER 1.

He--for there could be no doubt of his sex, though the fashion of the time did something to disguise it--was in the act of slicing at the head of a Moor which swung from the rafters. It was the colour of an old football, and more or less the shape of one, save for the sunken cheeks and a strand or two of coarse, dry hair, like the hair on a cocoanut. Orlando's father, or perhaps his grandfather, had struck it from the shoulders of a vast Pagan who had started up under the moon in the barbarian fields of Africa; and now it swung, gently, perpetually, in the breeze which never ceased blowing through the attic rooms of the gigantic house of the lord who had slain him.

Orlando's fathers had ridden in fields of asphodel, and stony fields, and fields watered by strange rivers, and they had struck many heads of many colours off many shoulders, and brought them back to hang from the rafters. So too would Orlando, he vowed. But since he was sixteen only, and too young to ride with them in Africa or France, he would steal away from his mother and the peacocks in the garden and go to his attic room and there lunge and plunge and slice the air with his blade. Sometimes he cut the cord so that the skull bumped on the floor and he had to string it up again, fastening it with some chivalry almost out of reach so that his enemy grinned at him through shrunk, black lips triumphantly. The skull swung to and fro, for the house, at the top of which he lived, was so vast that there seemed trapped in it the wind itself, blowing this way, blowing that way, winter and summer. The green arras with the hunters on it moved perpetually. His fathers had been noble since they had been at all. They came out of the northern mists wearing coronets on their heads. Were not the bars of darkness in the room, and the yellow pools which chequered the floor, made by the sun falling through the stained glass of a vast coat of arms in the window? Orlando stood now in the midst of the yellow body of an heraldic leopard. When he put his hand on the window-sill to push the window open, it was instantly coloured red, blue, and yellow like a butterfly's wing. Thus, those who like symbols, and have a turn for the deciphering of them, might observe that though the shapely legs, the handsome body, and the well-set shoulders were all of them decorated with various tints of heraldic light, Orlando's face, as he threw the window open, was lit solely by the sun itself. A more candid, sullen face it would be impossible to find. Happy the mother who bears, happier still the biographer who records the life of such a one! Never need she vex herself, nor he invoke the help of novelist or poet. From deed to deed, from glory to glory, from office to office he must go, his scribe following after, till they reach whatever seat it may be that is the height of their desire. Orlando, to look at, was cut out precisely for some such career. The red of the cheeks was covered with peach down; the down on the lips was only a little thicker than the down on the cheeks. The lips themselves were short and slightly drawn back over teeth of an exquisite and almond whiteness. Nothing disturbed the arrowy nose in its short, tense flight; the hair was dark, the ears small, and fitted closely to the head. But, alas, that these catalogues of youthful beauty cannot end without mentioning forehead and eyes. Alas, that people are seldom born devoid of all three; for directly we glance at Orlando standing by the window, we must admit that he had eyes like drenched violets, so large that the water seemed to have brimmed in them and widened them; and a brow like the swelling of a marble dome pressed between the two blank medallions which were his temples. Directly we glance at eyes and forehead, thus do we rhapsodize. Directly we glance at eyes and forehead, we have to admit a thousand disagreeables which it is the aim of every good biographer to ignore. Sights disturbed him, like that of his mother, a very beautiful lady in green walking out to feed the peacocks with Twitchett, her maid, behind her; sights exalted him--the birds and the trees; and made him in love with death--the evening sky, the homing rooks; and so, mounting up the spiral stairway into his brain--which was a roomy one--all these sights, and the garden sounds too, the hammer beating, the wood chopping, began that riot and confusion of the passions and emotions which every good biographer detests, But to continue--Orlando slowly drew in his head, sat down at the table, and, with the half-conscious air of one doing what they do every day of their lives at this hour, took out a writing book labelled 'Aethelbert: A Tragedy in Five Acts,' and dipped an old stained goose quill in the ink.

Soon he had covered ten pages and more with poetry. He was fluent, evidently, but he was abstract. Vice, Crime, Misery were the personages of his drama; there were Kings and Queens of impossible territories; horrid plots confounded them; noble sentiments suffused them; there was never a word said as he himself would have said it, but all was turned with a fluency and sweetness which, considering his age--he was not yet seventeen--and that the sixteenth century had still some years of its course to run, were remarkable enough. At last, however, he came to a halt. He was describing, as all young poets are for ever describing, nature, and in order to match the shade of green precisely he looked (and here he showed more audacity than most) at the thing itself, which happened to be a laurel bush growing beneath the window. After that, of course, he could write no more. Green in nature is one thing, green in literature another. Nature and letters seem to have a natural antipathy; bring them together and they tear each other to pieces. The shade of green Orlando now saw spoilt his rhyme and split his metre. Moreover, nature has tricks of her own. Once look out of a window at bees among flowers, at a yawning dog, at the sun setting, once think 'how many more suns shall I see set', etc. etc. (the thought is too well known to be worth writing out) and one drops the pen, takes one's cloak, strides out of the room, and catches one's foot on a painted chest as one does so. For Orlando was a trifle clumsy.

He was careful to avoid meeting anyone. There was Stubbs, the gardener, coming along the path. He hid behind a tree till he had passed. He let himself out at a little gate in the garden wall. He skirted all stables, kennels, breweries, carpenters' shops, washhouses, places where they make tallow candles, kill oxen, forge horse-shoes, stitch jerkins--for the house was a town ringing with men at work at their various crafts--and gained the ferny path leading uphill through the park unseen. There is perhaps a kinship among qualities; one draws another along with it; and the biographer should here call attention to the fact that this clumsiness is often mated with a love of solitude. Having stumbled over a chest, Orlando naturally loved solitary places, vast views, and to feel himself for ever and ever and ever alone.

So, after a long silence, 'I am alone', he breathed at last, opening his lips for the first time in this record. He had walked very quickly uphill through ferns and hawthorn bushes, startling deer and wild birds, to a place crowned by a single oak tree. It was very high, so high indeed that nineteen English counties could be seen beneath; and on clear days thirty or perhaps forty, if the weather was very fine. Sometimes one could see the English Channel, wave reiterating upon wave. Rivers could be seen and pleasure boats gliding on them; and galleons setting out to sea; and armadas with puffs of smoke from which came the dull thud of cannon firing; and forts on the coast; and castles among the meadows; and here a watch tower; and there a fortress; and again some vast mansion like that of Orlando's father, massed like a town in the valley circled by walls. To the east there were the spires of London and the smoke of the city; and perhaps on the very sky line, when the wind was in the right quarter, the craggy top and serrated edges of Snowdon herself showed mountainous among the clouds. For a moment Orlando stood counting, gazing, recognizing. That was his father's house; that his uncle's. His aunt owned those three great turrets among the trees there. The heath was theirs and the forest; the pheasant and the deer, the fox, the badger, and the butterfly.

He sighed profoundly, and flung himself--there was a passion in his movements which deserves the word--on the earth at the foot of the oak tree. He loved, beneath all this summer transiency, to feel the earth's spine beneath him; for such he took the hard root of the oak tree to be; or, for image followed image, it was the back of a great horse that he was riding, or the deck of a tumbling ship--it was anything indeed, so long as it was hard, for he felt the need of something which he could attach his floating heart to; the heart that tugged at his side; the heart that seemed filled with spiced and amorous gales every evening about this time when he walked out. To the oak tree he tied it and as he lay there, gradually the flutter in and about him stilled itself; the little leaves hung, the deer stopped; the pale summer clouds stayed; his limbs grew heavy on the ground; and he lay so still that by degrees the deer stepped nearer and the rooks wheeled round him and the swallows dipped and circled and the dragonflies shot past, as if all the fertility and amorous activity of a summer's evening were woven web-like about his body.

After an hour or so--the sun was rapidly sinking, the white clouds had turned red, the hills were violet, the woods purple, the valleys black--a trumpet sounded. Orlando leapt to his feet. The shrill sound came from the valley. It came from a dark spot down there; a spot compact and mapped out; a maze; a town, yet girt about with walls; it came from the heart of his own great house in the valley, which, dark before, even as he looked and the single trumpet duplicated and reduplicated itself with other shriller sounds, lost its darkness and became pierced with lights. Some were small hurrying lights, as if servants dashed along corridors to answer summonses; others were high and lustrous lights, as if they burnt in empty banqueting-halls made ready to receive guests who had not come; and others dipped and waved and sank and rose, as if held in the hands of troops of serving men, bending, kneeling, rising, receiving, guarding, and escorting with all dignity indoors a great Princess alighting from her chariot. Coaches turned and wheeled in the courtyard. Horses tossed their plumes. The Queen had come.

Orlando looked no more. He dashed downhill. He let himself in at a wicket gate. He tore up the winding staircase. He reached his room. He tossed his stockings to one side of the room, his jerkin to the other. He dipped his head. He scoured his hands. He pared his finger nails. With no more than six inches of looking-glass and a pair of old candles to help him, he had thrust on crimson breeches, lace collar, waistcoat of taffeta, and shoes with rosettes on them as big as double dahlias in less than ten minutes by the stable clock. He was ready. He was flushed. He was excited, But he was terribly late.

By short cuts known to him, he made his way now through the vast congeries of rooms and staircases to the banqueting-hall, five acres distant on the other side of the house. But half-way there, in the back quarters where the servants lived, he stopped. The door of Mrs Stewkley's sitting-room stood open--she was gone, doubtless, with all her keys to wait upon her mistress. But there, sitting at the servant's dinner table with a tankard beside him and paper in front of him, sat a rather fat, shabby man, whose ruff was a thought dirty, and whose clothes were of hodden brown. He held a pen in his hand, but he was not writing. He seemed in the act of rolling some thought up and down, to and fro in his mind till it gathered shape or momentum to his liking. His eyes, globed and clouded like some green stone of curious texture, were fixed. He did not see Orlando. For all his hurry, Orlando stopped dead. Was this a poet? Was he writing poetry? 'Tell me', he wanted to say, 'everything in the whole world'--for he had the wildest, most absurd, extravagant ideas about poets and poetry--but how speak to a man who does not see you? who sees ogres, satyrs, perhaps the depths of the sea instead? So Orlando stood gazing while the man turned his pen in his fingers, this way and that way; and gazed and mused; and then, very quickly, wrote half-a-dozen lines and looked up. Whereupon Orlando, overcome with shyness, darted off and reached the banqueting-hall only just in time to sink upon his knees and, hanging his head in confusion, to offer a bowl of rose water to the great Queen herself.

Such was his shyness that he saw no more of her than her ringed hands in water; but it was enough. It was a memorable hand; a thin hand with long fingers always curling as if round orb or sceptre; a nervous, crabbed, sickly hand; a commanding hand too; a hand that had only to raise itself for a head to fall; a hand, he guessed, attached to an old body that smelt like a cupboard in which furs are kept in camphor; which body was yet caparisoned in all sorts of brocades and gems; and held itself very upright though perhaps in pain from sciatica; and never flinched though strung together by a thousand fears; and the Queen's eyes were light yellow. All this he felt as the great rings flashed in the water and then something pressed his hair--which, perhaps, accounts for his seeing nothing more likely to be of use to a historian. And in truth, his mind was such a welter of opposites--of the night and the blazing candles, of the shabby poet and the great Queen, of silent fields and the clatter of serving men--that he could see nothing; or only a hand.

By the same showing, the Queen herself can have seen only a head. But if it is possible from a hand to deduce a body, informed with all the attributes of a great Queen, her crabbedness, courage, frailty, and terror, surely a head can be as fertile, looked down upon from a chair of state by a lady whose eyes were always, if the waxworks at the Abbey are to be trusted, wide open. The long, curled hair, the dark head bent so reverently, so innocently before her, implied a pair of the finest legs that a young nobleman has ever stood upright upon; and violet eyes; and a heart of gold; and loyalty and manly charm--all qualities which the old woman loved the more the more they failed her. For she was growing old and worn and bent before her time. The sound of cannon was always in her ears. She saw always the glistening poison drop and the long stiletto. As she sat at table she listened; she heard the guns in the Channel; she dreaded--was that a curse, was that a whisper? Innocence, simplicity, were all the more dear to her for the dark background she set them against. And it was that same night, so tradition has it, when Orlando was sound asleep, that she made over formally, putting her hand and seal finally to the parchment, the gift of the great monastic house that had been the Archbishop's and then the King's to Orlando's father.

Orlando slept all night in ignorance. He had been kissed by a queen without knowing it. And perhaps, for women's hearts are intricate, it was his ignorance and the start he gave when her lips touched him that kept the memory of her young cousin (for they had blood in common) green in her mind. At any rate, two years of this quiet country life had not passed, and Orlando had written no more perhaps than twenty tragedies and a dozen histories and a score of sonnets when a message came that he was to attend the Queen at Whitehall.

'Here', she said, watching him advance down the long gallery towards her, 'comes my innocent!' (There was a serenity about him always which had the look of innocence when, technically, the word was no longer applicable.)

'Come!' she said. She was sitting bolt upright beside the fire. And she held him a foot's pace from her and looked him up and down. Was she matching her speculations the other night with the truth now visible? Did she find her guesses justified? Eyes, mouth, nose, breast, hips, hands--she ran them over; her lips twitched visibly as she looked; but when she saw his legs she laughed out loud. He was the very image of a noble gentleman. But inwardly? She flashed her yellow hawk's eyes upon him as if she would pierce his soul. The young man withstood her gaze blushing only a damask rose as became him. Strength, grace, romance, folly, poetry, youth--she read him like a page. Instantly she plucked a ring from her finger (the joint was swollen rather) and as she fitted it to his, named him her Treasurer and Steward; next hung about him chains of office; and bidding him bend his knee, tied round it at the slenderest part the jewelled order of the Garter. Nothing after that was denied him. When she drove in state he rode at her carriage door. She sent him to Scotland on a sad embassy to the unhappy Queen. He was about to sail for the Polish wars when she recalled him. For how could she bear to think of that tender flesh torn and that curly head rolled in the dust? She kept him with her. At the height of her triumph when the guns were booming at the Tower and the air was thick enough with gunpowder to make one sneeze and the huzzas of the people rang beneath the windows, she pulled him down among the cushions where her women had laid her (she was so worn and old) and made him bury his face in that astonishing composition--she had not changed her dress for a month--which smelt for all the world, he thought, recalling his boyish memory, like some old cabinet at home where his mother's furs were stored. He rose, half suffocated from the embrace. 'This', she breathed, 'is my victory!'--even as a rocket roared up and dyed her cheeks scarlet.

For the old woman loved him. And the Queen, who knew a man when she saw one, though not, it is said, in the usual way, plotted for him a splendid ambitious career. Lands were given him, houses assigned him. He was to be the son of her old age; the limb of her infirmity; the oak tree on which she leant her degradation. She croaked out these promises and strange domineering tendernesses (they were at Richmond now) sitting bolt upright in her stiff brocades by the fire which, however high they piled it, never kept her warm.

Meanwhile, the long winter months drew on. Every tree in the Park was lined with frost. The river ran sluggishly. One day when the snow was on the ground and the dark panelled rooms were full of shadows and the stags were barking in the Park, she saw in the mirror, which she kept for fear of spies always by her, through the door, which she kept for fear of murderers always open, a boy--could it be Orlando?--kissing a girl--who in the Devil's name was the brazen hussy? Snatching at her golden-hilted sword she struck violently at the mirror. The glass crashed; people came running; she was lifted and set in her chair again; but she was stricken after that and groaned much, as her days wore to an end, of man's treachery.

It was Orlando's fault perhaps; yet, after all, are we to blame Orlando? The age was the Elizabethan; their morals were not ours; nor their poets; nor their climate; nor their vegetables even. Everything was different. The weather itself, the heat and cold of summer and winter, was, we may believe, of another temper altogether. The brilliant amorous day was divided as sheerly from the night as land from water. Sunsets were redder and more intense; dawns were whiter and more auroral. Of our crepuscular half-lights and lingering twilights they knew nothing. The rain fell vehemently, or not at all. The sun blazed or there was darkness. Translating this to the spiritual regions as their wont is, the poets sang beautifully how roses fade and petals fall. The moment is brief they sang; the moment is over; one long night is then to be slept by all. As for using the artifices of the greenhouse or conservatory to prolong or preserve these fresh pinks and roses, that was not their way. The withered intricacies and ambiguities of our more gradual and doubtful age were unknown to them. Violence was all. The flower bloomed and faded. The sun rose and sank. The lover loved and went. And what the poets said in rhyme, the young translated into practice. Girls were roses, and their seasons were short as the flowers'. Plucked they must be before nightfall; for the day was brief and the day was all. Thus, if Orlando followed the leading of the climate, of the poets, of the age itself, and plucked his flower in the window-seat even with the snow on the ground and the Queen vigilant in the corridor we can scarcely bring ourselves to blame him. He was young; he was boyish; he did but as nature bade him do. As for the girl, we know no more than Queen Elizabeth herself did what her name was. It may have been Doris, Chloris, Delia, or Diana, for he made rhymes to them all in turn; equally, she may have been a court lady, or some serving maid. For Orlando's taste was broad; he was no lover of garden flowers only; the wild and the weeds even had always a fascination for him.

Here, indeed, we lay bare rudely, as a biographer may, a curious trait in him, to be accounted for, perhaps, by the fact that a certain grandmother of his had worn a smock and carried milkpails. Some grains of the Kentish or Sussex earth were mixed with the thin, fine fluid which came to him from Normandy. He held that the mixture of brown earth and blue blood was a good one. Certain it is that he had always a liking for low company, especially for that of lettered people whose wits so often keep them under, as if there were the sympathy of blood between them. At this season of his life, when his head brimmed with rhymes and he never went to bed without striking off some conceit, the cheek of an innkeeper's daughter seemed fresher and the wit of a gamekeeper's niece seemed quicker than those of the ladies at Court. Hence, he began going frequently to Wapping Old Stairs and the beer gardens at night, wrapped in a grey cloak to hide the star at his neck and the garter at his knee. There, with a mug before him, among the sanded alleys and bowling greens and all the simple architecture of such places, he listened to sailors' stories of hardship and horror and cruelty on the Spanish main; how some had lost their toes, others their noses--for the spoken story was never so rounded or so finely coloured as the written. Especially he loved to hear them volley forth their songs of 'the Azores, while the parrakeets, which they had brought from those parts, pecked at the rings in their ears, tapped with their hard acquisitive beaks at the rubies on their fingers, and swore as vilely as their masters. The women were scarcely less bold in their speech and less free in their manner than the birds. They perched on his knee, flung their arms round his neck and, guessing that something out of the common lay hid beneath his duffle cloak, were quite as eager to come at the truth of the matter as Orlando himself.

Nor was opportunity lacking. The river was astir early and late with barges, wherries, and craft of all description. Every day sailed to sea some fine ship bound for the Indies; now and again another blackened and ragged with hairy men on board crept painfully to anchor. No one missed a boy or girl if they dallied a little on the water after sunset; or raised an eyebrow if gossip had seen them sleeping soundly among the treasure sacks safe in each other's arms. Such indeed was the adventure that befel Orlando, Sukey, and the Earl of Cumberland. The day was hot; their loves had been active; they had fallen asleep among the rubies. Late that night the Earl, whose fortunes were much bound up in the Spanish ventures, came to check the booty alone with a lantern. He flashed the light on a barrel. He started back with an oath. Twined about the cask two spirits lay sleeping. Superstitious by nature, and his conscience laden with many a crime, the Earl took the couple--they were wrapped in a red cloak, and Sukey's bosom was almost as white as the eternal snows of Orlando's poetry--for a phantom sprung from the graves of drowned sailors to upbraid him. He crossed himself. He vowed repentance. The row of alms houses still standing in the Sheen Road is the visible fruit of that moment's panic. Twelve poor old women of the parish today drink tea and tonight bless his Lordship for a roof above their heads; so that illicit love in a treasure ship--but we omit the moral.

Soon, however, Orlando grew tired, not only of the discomfort of this way of life, and of the crabbed streets of the neighbourhood, but of the primitive manner of the people. For it has to be remembered that crime and poverty had none of the attraction for the Elizabethans that they have for us. They had none of our modern shame of book learning; none of our belief that to be born the son of a butcher is a blessing and to be unable to read a virtue; no fancy that what we call 'life' and 'reality' are somehow connected with ignorance and brutality; nor, indeed, any equivalent for these two words at all. It was not to seek 'life' that Orlando went among them; not in quest of 'reality' that he left them. But when he had heard a score of times how Jakes had lost his nose and Sukey her honour--and they told the stories admirably, it must be admitted--he began to be a little weary of the repetition, for a nose can only be cut off in one way and maidenhood lost in another--or so it seemed to him--whereas the arts and the sciences had a diversity about them which stirred his curiosity profoundly. So, always keeping them in happy memory, he left off frequenting the beer gardens and the skittle alleys, hung his grey cloak in his wardrobe, let his star shine at his neck and his garter twinkle at his knee, and appeared once more at the Court of King James. He was young, he was rich, he was handsome. No one could have been received with greater acclamation than he was.

It is certain indeed that many ladies were ready to show him their favours. The names of three at least were freely coupled with his in marriage--Clorinda, Favilla, Euphrosyne--so he called them in his sonnets.

To take them in order; Clorinda was a sweet-mannered gentle lady enough;--indeed Orlando was greatly taken with her for six months and a half; but she had white eyelashes and could not bear the sight of blood. A hare brought up roasted at her father's table turned her faint. She was much under the influence of the Priests too, and stinted her underlinen in order to give to the poor. She took it on her to reform Orlando of his sins, which sickened him, so that he drew back from the marriage, and did not much regret it when she died soon after of the small-pox.

Favilla, who comes next, was of a different sort altogether. She was the daughter of a poor Somersetshire gentleman; who, by sheer assiduity and the use of her eyes had worked her way up at court, where her address in horsemanship, her fine instep, and her grace in dancing won the admiration of all. Once, however, she was so ill-advised as to whip a spaniel that had torn one of her silk stockings (and it must be said in justice that Favilla had few stockings and those for the most part of drugget) within an inch of its life beneath Orlando's window. Orlando, who was a passionate lover of animals, now noticed that her teeth were crooked, and the two front turned inward, which, he said, is a sure sign of a perverse and cruel disposition in women, and so broke the engagement that very night for ever.

The third, Euphrosyne, was by far the most serious of his flames. She was by birth one of the Irish Desmonds and had therefore a family tree of her own as old and deeply rooted as Orlando's itself. She was fair, florid, and a trifle phlegmatic. She spoke Italian well, had a perfect set of teeth in the upper jaw, though those on the lower were slightly discoloured. She was never without a whippet or spaniel at her knee; fed them with white bread from her own plate; sang sweetly to the virginals; and was never dressed before mid-day owing to the extreme care she took of her person. In short, she would have made a perfect wife for such a nobleman as Orlando, and matters had gone so far that the lawyers on both sides were busy with covenants, jointures, settlements, messuages, tenements, and whatever is needed before one great fortune can mate with another when, with the suddenness and severity that then marked the English climate, came the Great Frost.

The Great Frost was, historians tell us, the most severe that has ever visited these islands. Birds froze in mid-air and fell like stones to the ground. At Norwich a young countrywoman started to cross the road in her usual robust health and was seen by the onlookers to turn visibly to powder and be blown in a puff of dust over the roofs as the icy blast struck her at the street corner. The mortality among sheep and cattle was enormous. Corpses froze and could not be drawn from the sheets. It was no uncommon sight to come upon a whole herd of swine frozen immovable upon the road. The fields were full of shepherds, ploughmen, teams of horses, and little bird-scaring boys all struck stark in the act of the moment, one with his hand to his nose, another with the bottle to his lips, a third with a stone raised to throw at the ravens who sat, as if stuffed, upon the hedge within a yard of him. The severity of the frost was so extraordinary that a kind of petrifaction sometimes ensued; and it was commonly supposed that the great increase of rocks in some parts of Derbyshire was due to no eruption, for there was none, but to the solidification of unfortunate wayfarers who had been turned literally to stone where they stood. The Church could give little help in the matter, and though some landowners had these relics blessed, the most part preferred to use them either as landmarks, scratching-posts for sheep, or, when the form of the stone allowed, drinking troughs for cattle, which purposes they serve, admirably for the most part, to this day.

But while the country people suffered the extremity of want, and the trade of the country was at a standstill, London enjoyed a carnival of the utmost brilliancy. The Court was at Greenwich, and the new King seized the opportunity that his coronation gave him to curry favour with the citizens. He directed that the river, which was frozen to a depth of twenty feet and more for six or seven miles on either side, should be swept, decorated and given all the semblance of a park or pleasure ground, with arbours, mazes, alleys, drinking booths, etc. at his expense. For himself and the courtiers, he reserved a certain space immediately opposite the Palace gates; which, railed off from the public only by a silken rope, became at once the centre of the most brilliant society in England. Great statesmen, in their beards and ruffs, despatched affairs of state under the crimson awning of the Royal Pagoda. Soldiers planned the conquest of the Moor and the downfall of the Turk in striped arbours surmounted by plumes of ostrich feathers. Admirals strode up and down the narrow pathways, glass in hand, sweeping the horizon and telling stories of the north-west passage and the Spanish Armada. Lovers dallied upon divans spread with sables. Frozen roses fell in showers when the Queen and her ladies walked abroad. Coloured balloons hovered motionless in the air. Here and there burnt vast bonfires of cedar and oak wood, lavishly salted, so that the flames were of green, orange, and purple fire. But however fiercely they burnt, the heat was not enough to melt the ice which, though of singular transparency, was yet of the hardness of steel. So clear indeed was it that there could be seen, congealed at a depth of several feet, here a porpoise, there a flounder. Shoals of eels lay motionless in a trance, but whether their state was one of death or merely of suspended animation which the warmth would revive puzzled the philosophers. Near London Bridge, where the river had frozen to a depth of some twenty fathoms, a wrecked wherry boat was plainly visible, lying on the bed of the river where it had sunk last autumn, overladen with apples. The old bumboat woman, who was carrying her fruit to market on the Surrey side, sat there in her plaids and farthingales with her lap full of apples, for all the world as if she were about to serve a customer, though a certain blueness about the lips hinted the truth. 'Twas a sight King James specially liked to look upon, and he would bring a troupe of courtiers to gaze with him. In short, nothing could exceed the brilliancy and gaiety of the scene by day. But it was at night that the carnival was at its merriest. For the frost continued unbroken; the nights were of perfect stillness; the moon and stars blazed with the hard fixity of diamonds, and to the fine music of flute and trumpet the courtiers danced.

Orlando, it is true, was none of those who tread lightly the corantoe and lavolta; he was clumsy and a little absentminded. He much preferred the plain dances of his own country, which he danced as a child to these fantastic foreign measures. He had indeed just brought his feet together about six in the evening of the seventh of January at the finish of some such quadrille or minuet when he beheld, coming from the pavilion of the Muscovite Embassy, a figure, which, whether boy's or woman's, for the loose tunic and trousers of the Russian fashion served to disguise the sex, filled him with the highest curiosity. The person, whatever the name or sex, was about middle height, very slenderly fashioned, and dressed entirely in oyster-coloured velvet, trimmed with some unfamiliar greenish-coloured fur. But these details were obscured by the extraordinary seductiveness which issued from the whole person. Images, metaphors of the most extreme and extravagant twined and twisted in his mind. He called her a melon, a pineapple, an olive tree, an emerald, and a fox in the snow all in the space of three seconds; he did not know whether he had heard her, tasted her, seen her, or all three together. (For though we must pause not a moment in the narrative we may here hastily note that all his images at this time were simple in the extreme to match his senses and were mostly taken from things he had liked the taste of as a boy. But if his senses were simple they were at the same time extremely strong. To pause therefore and seek the reasons of things is out of the question.)...A melon, an emerald, a fox in the snow--so he raved, so he stared. When the boy, for alas, a boy it must be--no woman could skate with such speed and vigour--swept almost on tiptoe past him, Orlando was ready to tear his hair with vexation that the person was of his own sex, and thus all embraces were out of the question. But the skater came closer. Legs, hands, carriage, were a boy's, but no boy ever had a mouth like that; no boy had those breasts; no boy had eyes which looked as if they had been fished from the bottom of the sea. Finally, coming to a stop and sweeping a curtsey with the utmost grace to the King, who was shuffling past on the arm of some Lord-in-waiting, the unknown skater came to a standstill. She was not a handsbreadth off. She was a woman. Orlando stared; trembled; turned hot; turned cold; longed to hurl himself through the summer air; to crush acorns beneath his feet; to toss his arm with the beech trees and the oaks. As it was, he drew his lips up over his small white teeth; opened them perhaps half an inch as if to bite; shut them as if he had bitten. The Lady Euphrosyne hung upon his arm.

The stranger's name, he found, was the Princess Marousha Stanilovska Dagmar Natasha Iliana Romanovitch, and she had come in the train of the Muscovite Ambassador, who was her uncle perhaps, or perhaps her father, to attend the coronation. Very little was known of the Muscovites. In their great beards and furred hats they sat almost silent; drinking some black liquid which they spat out now and then upon the ice. None spoke English, and French with which some at least were familiar was then little spoken at the English Court.

It was through this accident that Orlando and the Princess became acquainted. They were seated opposite each other at the great table spread under a huge awning for the entertainment of the notables. The Princess was placed between two young Lords, one Lord Francis Vere and the other the young Earl of Moray. It was laughable to see the predicament she soon had them in, for though both were fine lads in their way, the babe unborn had as much knowledge of the French tongue as they had. When at the beginning of dinner the Princess turned to the Earl and said, with a grace which ravished his heart, 'Je crois avoir fait la connaissance d'un gentilhomme qui vous etait apparente en Pologne l'ete dernier,' or 'La beaute des dames de la cour d'Angleterre me met dans le ravissement. On ne peut voir une dame plus gracieuse que votre reine, ni une coiffure plus belle que la sienne,' both Lord Francis and the Earl showed the highest embarrassment. The one helped her largely to horse-radish sauce, the other whistled to his dog and made him beg for a marrow bone. At this the Princess could no longer contain her laughter, and Orlando, catching her eyes across the boars' heads and stuffed peacocks, laughed too. He laughed, but the laugh on his lips froze in wonder. Whom had he loved, what had he loved, he asked himself in a tumult of emotion, until now? An old woman, he answered, all skin and bone. Red-cheeked trulls too many to mention. A puling nun. A hard-bitten cruel-mouthed adventuress. A nodding mass of lace and ceremony. Love had meant to him nothing but sawdust and cinders. The joys he had had of it tasted insipid in the extreme. He marvelled how he could have gone through with it without yawning. For as he looked the thickness of his blood melted; the ice turned to wine in his veins; he heard the waters flowing and the birds singing; spring broke over the hard wintry landscape; his manhood woke; he grasped a sword in his hand; he charged a more daring foe than Pole or Moor; he dived in deep water; he saw the flower of danger growing in a crevice; he stretched his hand--in fact he was rattling off one of his most impassioned sonnets when the Princess addressed him, 'Would you have the goodness to pass the salt?'

He blushed deeply.

'With all the pleasure in the world, Madame,' he replied, speaking French with a perfect accent. For, heaven be praised, he spoke the tongue as his own; his mother's maid had taught him. Yet perhaps it would have been better for him had he never learnt that tongue; never answered that voice; never followed the light of those eyes...

The Princess continued. Who were those bumpkins, she asked him, who sat beside her with the manners of stablemen? What was the nauseating mixture they had poured on her plate? Did the dogs eat at the same table with the men in England? Was that figure of fun at the end of the table with her hair rigged up like a Maypole (comme une grande perche mal fagotee) really the Queen? And did the King always slobber like that? And which of those popinjays was George Villiers? Though these questions rather discomposed Orlando at first, they were put with such archness and drollery that he could not help but laugh; and he saw from the blank faces of the company that nobody understood a word, he answered her as freely as she asked him, speaking, as she did, in perfect French.

Thus began an intimacy between the two which soon became the scandal of the Court.

Soon it was observed Orlando paid the Muscovite far more attention than mere civility demanded. He was seldom far from her side, and their conversation, though unintelligible to the rest, was carried on with such animation, provoked such blushes and laughter, that the dullest could guess the subject. Moreover, the change in Orlando himself was extraordinary. Nobody had ever seen him so animated. In one night he had thrown off his boyish clumsiness; he was changed from a sulky stripling, who could not enter a ladies' room without sweeping half the ornaments from the table, to a nobleman, full of grace and manly courtesy. To see him hand the Muscovite (as she was called) to her sledge, or offer her his hand for the dance, or catch the spotted kerchief which she had let drop, or discharge any other of those manifold duties which the supreme lady exacts and the lover hastens to anticipate was a sight to kindle the dull eyes of age, and to make the quick pulse of youth beat faster. Yet over it all hung a cloud. The old men shrugged their shoulders. The young tittered between their fingers. All knew that a Orlando was betrothed to another. The Lady Margaret O'Brien O'Dare O'Reilly Tyrconnel (for that was the proper name of Euphrosyne of the Sonnets) wore Orlando's splendid sapphire on the second finger of her left hand. It was she who had the supreme right to his attentions. Yet she might drop all the handkerchiefs in her wardrobe (of which she had many scores) upon the ice and Orlando never stooped to pick them up. She might wait twenty minutes for him to hand her to her sledge, and in the end have to be content with the services of her Blackamoor. When she skated, which she did rather clumsily, no one was at her elbow to encourage her, and, if she fell, which she did rather heavily, no one raised her to her feet and dusted the snow from her petticoats. Although she was naturally phlegmatic, slow to take offence, and more reluctant than most people to believe that a mere foreigner could oust her from Orlando's affections, still even the Lady Margaret herself was brought at last to suspect that something was brewing against her peace of mind.

Indeed, as the days passed, Orlando took less and less care to hide his feelings. Making some excuse or other, he would leave the company as soon as they had dined, or steal away from the skaters, who were forming sets for a quadrille. Next moment it would be seen that the Muscovite was missing too. But what most outraged the Court, and stung it in its tenderest part, which is its vanity, was that the couple was often seen to slip under the silken rope, which railed off the Royal enclosure from the public part of the river and to disappear among the crowd of common people. For suddenly the Princess would stamp her foot and cry, 'Take me away. I detest your English mob,' by which she meant the English Court itself. She could stand it no longer. It was full of prying old women, she said, who stared in one's face, and of bumptious young men who trod on one's toes. They smelt bad. Their dogs ran between her legs. It was like being in a cage. In Russia they had rivers ten miles broad on which one could gallop six horses abreast all day long without meeting a soul. Besides, she wanted to see the Tower, the Beefeaters, the Heads on Temple Bar, and the jewellers' shops in the city. Thus, it came about that Orlando took her into the city, showed her the Beefeaters and the rebels' heads, and bought her whatever took her fancy in the Royal Exchange. But this was not enough. Each increasingly desired the other's company in privacy all day long where there were none to marvel or to stare. Instead of taking the road to London, therefore, they turned the other way about and were soon beyond the crowd among the frozen reaches of the Thames where, save for sea birds and some old country woman hacking at the ice in a vain attempt to draw a pailful of water or gathering what sticks or dead leaves she could find for firing, not a living soul ever came their way. The poor kept closely to their cottages, and the better sort, who could afford it, crowded for warmth and merriment to the city.

Hence, Orlando and Sasha, as he called her for short, and because it was the name of a white Russian fox he had had as a boy--a creature soft as snow, but with teeth of steel, which bit him so savagely that his father had it killed--hence, they had the river to themselves. Hot with skating and with love they would throw themselves down in some solitary reach, where the yellow osiers fringed the bank, and wrapped in a great fur cloak Orlando would take her in his arms, and know, for the first time, he murmured, the delights of love. Then, when the ecstasy was over and they lay lulled in a swoon on the ice, he would tell her of his other loves, and how, compared with her, they had been of wood, of sackcloth, and of cinders. And laughing at his vehemence, she would turn once more in his arms and give him for love's sake, one more embrace. And then they would marvel that the ice did not melt with their heat, and pity the poor old woman who had no such natural means of thawing it, but must hack at it with a chopper of cold steel. And then, wrapped in their sables, they would talk of everything under the sun; of sights and travels; of Moor and Pagan; of this man's beard and that woman's skin; of a rat that fed from her hand at table; of the arras that moved always in the hall at home; of a face; of a feather. Nothing was too small for such converse, nothing was too great.

Then suddenly, Orlando would fall into one of his moods of melancholy; the sight of the old woman hobbling over the ice might be the cause of it, or nothing; and would fling himself face downwards on the ice and look into the frozen waters and think of death. For the philosopher is right who says that nothing thicker than a knife's blade separates happiness from melancholy; and he goes on to opine that one is twin fellow to the other; and draws from this the conclusion that all extremes of feeling are allied to madness; and so bids us take refuge in the true Church (in his view the Anabaptist), which is the only harbour, port, anchorage, etc., he said, for those tossed on this sea.

'All ends in death,' Orlando would say, sitting upright, his face clouded with gloom. (For that was the way his mind worked now, in violent see-saws from life to death, stopping at nothing in between, so that the biographer must not stop either, but must fly as fast as he can and so keep pace with the unthinking passionate foolish actions and sudden extravagant words in which, it is impossible to deny, Orlando at this time of his life indulged.)

'All ends in death,' Orlando would say, sitting upright on the ice. But Sasha who after all had no English blood in her but was from Russia where the sunsets are longer, the dawns less sudden, and sentences often left unfinished from doubt as to how best to end them--Sasha stared at him, perhaps sneered at him, for he must have seemed a child to her, and said nothing. But at length the ice grew cold beneath them, which she disliked, so pulling him to his feet again, she talked so enchantingly, so wittily, so wisely (but unfortunately always in French, which notoriously loses its flavour in translation) that he forgot the frozen waters or night coming or the old woman or whatever it was, and would try to tell her--plunging and splashing among a thousand images which had gone as stale as the women who inspired them--what she was like. Snow, cream, marble, cherries, alabaster, golden wire? None of these. She was like a fox, or an olive tree; like the waves of the sea when you look down upon them from a height; like an emerald; like the sun on a green hill which is yet clouded--like nothing he had seen or known in England. Ransack the language as he might, words failed him. He wanted another landscape, and another tongue. English was too frank, too candid, too honeyed a speech for Sasha. For in all she said, however open she seemed and voluptuous, there was something hidden; in all she did, however daring, there was something concealed. So the green flame seems hidden in the emerald, or the sun prisoned in a hill. The clearness was only outward; within was a wandering flame. It came; it went; she never shone with the steady beam of an Englishwoman--here, however, remembering the Lady Margaret and her petticoats, Orlando ran wild in his transports and swept her over the ice, faster, faster, vowing that he would chase the flame, dive for the gem, and so on and so on, the words coming on the pants of his breath with the passion of a poet whose poetry is half pressed out of him by pain.

But Sasha was silent. When Orlando had done telling her that she was a fox, an olive tree, or a green hill-top, and had given her the whole history of his family; how their house was one of the most ancient in Britain; how they had come from Rome with the Caesars and had the right to walk down the Corso (which is the chief street in Rome) under a tasselled palanquin, which he said is a privilege reserved only for those of imperial blood (for there was an orgulous credulity about him which was pleasant enough), he would pause and ask her, Where was her own house? What was her father? Had she brothers? Why was she here alone with her uncle? Then, somehow, though she answered readily enough, an awkwardness would come between them. He suspected at first that her rank was not as high as she would like; or that she was ashamed of the savage ways of her people, for he had heard that the women in Muscovy wear beards and the men are covered with fur from the waist down; that both sexes are smeared with tallow to keep the cold out, tear meat with their fingers and live in huts where an English noble would scruple to keep his cattle; so that he forebore to press her. But on reflection, he concluded that her silence could not be for that reason; she herself was entirely free from hair on the chin; she dressed in velvet and pearls, and her manners were certainly not those of a woman bred in a cattle-shed.

What, then, did she hide from him? The doubt underlying the tremendous force of his feelings was like a quicksand beneath a monument which shifts suddenly and makes the whole pile shake. The agony would seize him suddenly. Then he would blaze out in such wrath that she did not know how to quiet him. Perhaps she did not want to quiet him; perhaps his rages pleased her and she provoked them purposely--such is the curious obliquity of the Muscovitish temperament.

To continue the story--skating farther than their wont that day they reached that part of the river where the ships had anchored and been frozen in midstream. Among them was the ship of the Muscovite Embassy flying its double-headed black eagle from the main mast, which was hung with many-coloured icicles several yards in length. Sasha had left some of her clothing on board, and supposing the ship to be empty they climbed on deck and went in search of it. Remembering certain passages in his own past, Orlando would not have marvelled had some good citizens sought this refuge before them; and so it turned out. They had not ventured far when a fine young man started up from some business of his own behind a coil of rope and saying, apparently, for he spoke Russian, that he was one of the crew and would help the Princess to find what she wanted, lit a lump of candle and disappeared with her into the lower parts of the ship.

Time went by, and Orlando, wrapped in his own dreams, thought only of the pleasures of life; of his jewel; of her rarity; of means for making her irrevocably and indissolubly his own. Obstacles there were and hardships to overcome. She was determined to live in Russia, where there were frozen rivers and wild horses and men, she said, who gashed each other's throats open. It is true that a landscape of pine and snow, habits of lust and slaughter, did not entice him. Nor was he anxious to cease his pleasant country ways of sport and tree-planting; relinquish his office; ruin his career; shoot the reindeer instead of the rabbit; drink vodka instead of canary, and slip a knife up his sleeve--for what purpose, he knew not. Still, all this and more than all this he would do for her sake. As for his marriage to the Lady Margaret, fixed though it was for this day sennight, the thing was so palpably absurd that he scarcely gave it a thought. Her kinsmen would abuse him for deserting a great lady; his friends would deride him for ruining the finest career in the world for a Cossack woman and a waste of snow--it weighed not a straw in the balance compared with Sasha herself. On the first dark night they would fly. They would take ship to Russia. So he pondered; so he plotted as he walked up and down the deck.

He was recalled, turning westward, by the sight of the sun, slung like an orange on the cross of St Paul's. It was blood-red and sinking rapidly. It must be almost evening. Sasha had been gone this hour and more. Seized instantly with those dark forebodings which shadowed even his most confident thoughts of her, he plunged the way he had seen them go into the hold of the ship; and, after stumbling among chests and barrels in the darkness, was made aware by a faint glimmer in a corner that they were seated there. For one second, he had a vision of them; saw Sasha seated on the sailor's knee; saw her bend towards him; saw them embrace before the light was blotted out in a red cloud by his rage. He blazed into such a howl of anguish that the whole ship echoed. Sasha threw herself between them, or the sailor would have been stifled before he could draw his cutlass. Then a deadly sickness came over Orlando, and they had to lay him on the floor and give him brandy to drink before he revived. And then, when he had recovered and was sat upon a heap of sacking on deck, Sasha hung over him, passing before his dizzied eyes softly, sinuously, like the fox that had bit him, now cajoling, now denouncing, so that he came to doubt what he had seen. Had not the candle guttered; had not the shadows moved? The box was heavy, she said; the man was helping her to move it. Orlando believed her one moment--for who can be sure that his rage has not painted what he most dreads to find?--the next was the more violent with anger at her deceit. Then Sasha herself turned white; stamped her foot on deck; said she would go that night, and called upon her Gods to destroy her, if she, a Romanovitch, had lain in the arms of a common seaman. Indeed, looking at them together (which he could hardly bring himself to do) Orlando was outraged by the foulness of his imagination that could have painted so frail a creature in the paw of that hairy sea brute. The man was huge; stood six feet four in his stockings, wore common wire rings in his ears; and looked like a dray horse upon which some wren or robin has perched in its flight. So he yielded; believed her; and asked her pardon. Yet when they were going down the ship's side, lovingly again, Sasha paused with her hand on the ladder, and called back to this tawny wide-cheeked monster a volley of Russian greetings, jests, or endearments, not a word of which Orlando could understand. But there was something in her tone (it might be the fault of the Russian consonants) that reminded Orlando of a scene some nights since, when he had come upon her in secret gnawing a candle-end in a corner, which she had picked from the floor. True, it was pink; it was gilt; and it was from the King's table; but it was tallow, and she gnawed it. Was there not, he thought, handing her on to the ice, something rank in her, something coarse flavoured, something peasant born? And he fancied her at forty grown unwieldy though she was now slim as a reed, and lethargic though she was now blithe as a lark. But again as they skated towards London such suspicions melted in his breast, and he felt as if he had been hooked by a great fish through the nose and rushed through the waters unwillingly, yet with his own consent.

It was an evening of astonishing beauty. As the sun sank, all the domes, spires, turrets, and pinnacles of London rose in inky blackness against the furious red sunset clouds. Here was the fretted cross at Charing; there the dome of St Paul's; there the massy square of the Tower buildings; there like a grove of trees stripped of all leaves save a knob at the end were the heads on the pikes at Temple Bar. Now the Abbey windows were lit up and burnt like a heavenly, many-coloured shield (in Orlando's fancy); now all the west seemed a golden window with troops of angels (in Orlando's fancy again) passing up and down the heavenly stairs perpetually. All the time they seemed to be skating in fathomless depths of air, so blue the ice had become; and so glassy smooth was it that they sped quicker and quicker to the city with the white gulls circling about them, and cutting in the air with their wings the very same sweeps that they cut on the ice with their skates.

Sasha, as if to reassure him, was tenderer than usual and even more delightful. Seldom would she talk about her past life, but now she told him how, in winter in Russia, she would listen to the wolves howling across the steppes, and thrice, to show him, she barked like a wolf. Upon which he told her of the stags in the snow at home, and how they would stray into the great hall for warmth and be fed by an old man with porridge from a bucket. And then she praised him; for his love of beasts; for his gallantry; for his legs. Ravished with her praises and shamed to think how he had maligned her by fancying her on the knees of a common sailor and grown fat and lethargic at forty, he told her that he could find no words to praise her; yet instantly bethought him how she was like the spring and green grass and rushing waters, and seizing her more tightly than ever, he swung her with him half across the river so that the gulls and the cormorants swung too. And halting at length, out of breath, she said, panting slightly, that he was like a million-candled Christmas tree (such as they have in Russia) hung with yellow globes; incandescent; enough to light a whole street by; (so one might translate it) for what with his glowing cheeks, his dark curls, his black and crimson cloak, he looked as if he were burning with his own radiance, from a lamp lit within.

All the colour, save the red of Orlando's cheeks, soon faded. Night came on. As the orange light of sunset vanished it was succeeded by an astonishing white glare from the torches, bonfires, flaming cressets, and other devices by which the river was lit up and the strangest transformation took place. Various churches and noblemen's palaces, whose fronts were of white stone showed in streaks and patches as if floating on the air. Of St Paul's, in particular, nothing was left but a gilt cross. The Abbey appeared like the grey skeleton of a leaf. Everything suffered emaciation and transformation. As they approached the carnival, they heard a deep note like that struck on a tuning-fork which boomed louder and louder until it became an uproar. Every now and then a great shout followed a rocket into the air. Gradually they could discern little figures breaking off from the vast crowd and spinning hither and thither like gnats on the surface of a river. Above and around this brilliant circle like a bowl of darkness pressed the deep black of a winter's night. And then into this darkness there began to rise with pauses, which kept the expectation alert and the mouth open, flowering rockets; crescents; serpents; a crown. At one moment the woods and distant hills showed green as on a summer's day; the next all was winter and blackness again.

By this time Orlando and the Princess were close to the Royal enclosure and found their way barred by a great crowd of the common people, who were pressing as near to the silken rope as they dared. Loth to end their privacy and encounter the sharp eyes that were on the watch for them, the couple lingered there, shouldered by apprentices; tailors; fishwives; horse dealers, cony catchers; starving scholars; maid-servants in their whimples; orange girls; ostlers; sober citizens; bawdy tapsters; and a crowd of little ragamuffins such as always haunt the outskirts of a crowd, screaming and scrambling among people's feet--all the riff-raff of the London streets indeed was there, jesting and jostling, here casting dice, telling fortunes, shoving, tickling, pinching; here uproarious, there glum; some of them with mouths gaping a yard wide; others as little reverent as daws on a house-top; all as variously rigged out as their purse or stations allowed; here in fur and broadcloth; there in tatters with their feet kept from the ice only by a dish-clout bound about them. The main press of people, it appeared, stood opposite a booth or stage something like our Punch and Judy show upon which some kind of theatrical performance was going forward. A black man was waving his arms and vociferating. There was a woman in white laid upon a bed. Rough though the staging was, the actors running up and down a pair of steps and sometimes tripping, and the crowd stamping their feet and whistling, or when they were bored, tossing a piece of orange peel on to the ice which a dog would scramble for, still the astonishing, sinuous melody of the words stirred Orlando like music. Spoken with extreme speed and a daring agility of tongue which reminded him of the sailors singing in the beer gardens at Wapping, the words even without meaning were as wine to him. But now and again a single phrase would come to him over the ice which was as if torn from the depths of his heart. The frenzy of the Moor seemed to him his own frenzy, and when the Moor suffocated the woman in her bed it was Sasha he killed with his own hands.

At last the play was ended. All had grown dark. The tears streamed down his face. Looking up into the sky there was nothing but blackness there too. Ruin and death, he thought, cover all. The life of man ends in the grave. Worms devour us.

Methinks it should be now a huge eclipse Of sun and moon, and that the affrighted globe Should yawn--

Even as he said this a star of some pallor rose in his memory. The night was dark; it was pitch dark; but it was such a night as this that they had waited for; it was on such a night as this that they had planned to fly. He remembered everything. The time had come. With a burst of passion he snatched Sasha to him, and hissed in her ear 'Jour de ma vie!' It was their signal. At midnight they would meet at an inn near Blackfriars. Horses waited there. Everything was in readiness for their flight. So they parted, she to her tent, he to his. It still wanted an hour of the time.

Long before midnight Orlando was in waiting. The night was of so inky a blackness that a man was on you before he could be seen, which was all to the good, but it was also of the most solemn stillness so that a horse's hoof, or a child's cry, could be heard at a distance of half a mile. Many a time did Orlando, pacing the little courtyard, hold his heart at the sound of some nag's steady footfall on the cobbles, or at the rustle of a woman's dress. But the traveller was only some merchant, making home belated; or some woman of the quarter whose errand was nothing so innocent. They passed, and the street was quieter than before. Then those lights which burnt downstairs in the small, huddled quarters where the poor of the city lived moved up to the sleeping-rooms, and then, one by one, were extinguished. The street lanterns in these purlieus were few at most; and the negligence of the night watchman often suffered them to expire long before dawn.

The darkness then became even deeper than before. Orlando looked to the wicks of his lantern, saw to the saddle girths; primed his pistols; examined his holsters; and did all these things a dozen times at least till he could find nothing more needing his attention. Though it still lacked some twenty minutes to midnight, he could not bring himself to go indoors to the inn parlour, where the hostess was still serving sack and the cheaper sort of canary wine to a few seafaring men, who would sit there trolling their ditties, and telling their stories of Drake, Hawkins, and Grenville, till they toppled off the benches and rolled asleep on the sanded floor. The darkness was more compassionate to his swollen and violent heart. He listened to every footfall; speculated on every sound. Each drunken shout and each wail from some poor wretch laid in the straw or in other distress cut his heart to the quick, as if it boded ill omen to his venture. Yet, he had no fear for Sasha. Her courage made nothing of the adventure. She would come alone, in her cloak and trousers, booted like a man. Light as her footfall was, it would hardly be heard, even in this silence.

So he waited in the darkness. Suddenly he was struck in the face by a blow, soft, yet heavy, on the side of his cheek. So strung with expectation was he, that he started and put his hand to his sword. The blow was repeated a dozen times on forehead and cheek. The dry frost had lasted so long that it took him a minute to realize that these were raindrops falling; the blows were the blows of the rain. At first, they fell slowly, deliberately, one by one. But soon the six drops became sixty; then six hundred; then ran themselves together in a steady spout of water. It was as if the hard and consolidated sky poured itself forth in one profuse fountain. In the space of five minutes Orlando was soaked to the skin.

Hastily putting the horses under cover, he sought shelter beneath the lintel of the door whence he could still observe the courtyard. The air was thicker now than ever, and such a steaming and droning rose from the downpour that no foot-fall of man or beast could be heard above it. The roads, pitted as they were with great holes, would be under water and perhaps impassable. But of what effect this would have upon their flight he scarcely thought. All his senses were bent upon gazing along the cobbled pathway--gleaming in the light of the lantern--for Sasha's coming. Sometimes, in the darkness, he seemed to see her wrapped about with rain strokes. But the phantom vanished. Suddenly, with an awful and ominous voice, a voice full of horror and alarm which raised every hair of anguish in Orlando's soul, St Paul's struck the first stroke of midnight. Four times more it struck remorselessly. With the superstition of a lover, Orlando had made out that it was on the sixth stroke that she would come. But the sixth stroke echoed away, and the seventh came and the eighth, and to his apprehensive mind they seemed notes first heralding and then proclaiming death and disaster. When the twelfth struck he knew that his doom was sealed. It was useless for the rational part of him to reason; she might be late; she might be prevented; she might have missed her way. The passionate and feeling heart of Orlando knew the truth. Other clocks struck, jangling one after another. The whole world seemed to ring with the news of her deceit and his derision. The old suspicions subterraneously at work in him rushed forth from concealment openly. He was bitten by a swarm of snakes, each more poisonous than the last. He stood in the doorway in the tremendous rain without moving. As the minutes passed, he sagged a little at the knees. The downpour rushed on. In the thick of it, great guns seemed to boom. Huge noises as of the tearing and rending of oak trees could be heard. There were also wild cries and terrible inhuman groanings. But Orlando stood there immovable till Paul's clock struck two, and then, crying aloud with an awful irony, and all his teeth showing, 'Jour de ma vie!' he dashed the lantern to the ground, mounted his horse and galloped he knew not where.

Some blind instinct, for he was past reasoning, must have driven him to take the river bank in the direction of the sea. For when the dawn broke, which it did with unusual suddenness, the sky turning a pale yellow and the rain almost ceasing, he found himself on the banks of the Thames off Wapping. Now a sight of the most extraordinary nature met his eyes. Where, for three months and more, there had been solid ice of such thickness that it seemed permanent as stone, and a whole gay city had been stood on its pavement, was now a race of turbulent yellow waters. The river had gained its freedom in the night. It was as if a sulphur spring (to which view many philosophers inclined) had risen from the volcanic regions beneath and burst the ice asunder with such vehemence that it swept the huge and massy fragments furiously apart. The mere look of the water was enough to turn one giddy. All was riot and confusion. The river was strewn with icebergs. Some of these were as broad as a bowling green and as high as a house; others no bigger than a man's hat, but most fantastically twisted. Now would come down a whole convoy of ice blocks sinking everything that stood in their way. Now, eddying and swirling like a tortured serpent, the river would seem to be hurtling itself between the fragments and tossing them from bank to bank, so that they could be heard smashing against the piers and pillars. But what was the most awful and inspiring of terror was the sight of the human creatures who had been trapped in the night and now paced their twisting and precarious islands in the utmost agony of spirit. Whether they jumped into the flood or stayed on the ice their doom was certain. Sometimes quite a cluster of these poor creatures would come down together, some on their knees, others suckling their babies. One old man seemed to be reading aloud from a holy book. At other times, and his fate perhaps was the most dreadful, a solitary wretch would stride his narrow tenement alone. As they swept out to sea, some could be heard crying vainly for help, making wild promises to amend their ways, confessing their sins and vowing altars and wealth if God would hear their prayers. Others were so dazed with terror that they sat immovable and silent looking steadfastly before them. One crew of young watermen or post-boys, to judge by their liveries, roared and shouted the lewdest tavern songs, as if in bravado, and were dashed against a tree and sunk with blasphemies on their lips. An old nobleman--for such his furred gown and golden chain proclaimed him--went down not far from where Orlando stood, calling vengeance upon the Irish rebels, who, he cried with his last breath, had plotted this devilry. Many perished clasping some silver pot or other treasure to their breasts; and at least a score of poor wretches were drowned by their own cupidity, hurling themselves from the bank into the flood rather than let a gold goblet escape them, or see before their eyes the disappearance of some furred gown. For furniture, valuables, possessions of all sorts were carried away on the icebergs. Among other strange sights was to be seen a cat suckling its young; a table laid sumptuously for a supper of twenty; a couple in bed; together with an extraordinary number of cooking utensils.

Dazed and astounded, Orlando could do nothing for some time but watch the appalling race of waters as it hurled itself past him. At last, seeming to recollect himself, he clapped spurs to his horse and galloped hard along the river bank in the direction of the sea. Rounding a bend of the river, he came opposite that reach where, not two days ago, the ships of the Ambassadors had seemed immovably frozen. Hastily, he made count of them all; the French; the Spanish; the Austrian; the Turk. All still floated, though the French had broken loose from her moorings, and the Turkish vessel had taken a great rent in her side and was fast filling with water. But the Russian ship was nowhere to be seen. For one moment Orlando thought it must have foundered; but, raising himself in his stirrups and shading his eyes, which had the sight of a hawk's, he could just make out the shape of a ship on the horizon. The black eagles were flying from the mast head. The ship of the Muscovite Embassy was standing out to sea.

Flinging himself from his horse, he made, in his rage, as if he would breast the flood. Standing knee-deep in water he hurled at the faithless woman all the insults that have ever been the lot of her sex. Faithless, mutable, fickle, he called her; devil, adulteress, deceiver; and the swirling waters took his words, and tossed at his feet a broken pot and a little straw.

CHAPTER 2.

The biographer is now faced with a difficulty which it is better perhaps to confess than to gloss over. Up to this point in telling the story of Orlando's life, documents, both private and historical, have made it possible to fulfil the first duty of a biographer, which is to plod, without looking to right or left, in the indelible footprints of truth; unenticed by flowers; regardless of shade; on and on methodically till we fall plump into the grave and write finis on the tombstone above our heads. But now we come to an episode which lies right across our path, so that there is no ignoring it. Yet it is dark, mysterious, and undocumented; so that there is no explaining it. Volumes might be written in interpretation of it; whole religious systems founded upon the signification of it. Our simple duty is to state the facts as far as they are known, and so let the reader make of them what he may.

In the summer of that disastrous winter which saw the frost, the flood, the deaths of many thousands, and the complete downfall of Orlando's hopes--for he was exiled from Court; in deep disgrace with the most powerful nobles of his time; the Irish house of Desmond was justly enraged; the King had already trouble enough with the Irish not to relish this further addition--in that summer Orlando retired to his great house in the country and there lived in complete solitude. One June morning--it was Saturday the 18th--he failed to rise at his usual hour, and when his groom went to call him he was found fast asleep. Nor could he be awakened. He lay as if in a trance, without perceptible breathing; and though dogs were set to bark under his window; cymbals, drums, bones beaten perpetually in his room; a gorse bush put under his pillow; and mustard plasters applied to his feet, still he did not wake, take food, or show any sign of life for seven whole days. On the seventh day he woke at his usual time (a quarter before eight, precisely) and turned the whole posse of caterwauling wives and village soothsayers out of his room, which was natural enough; but what was strange was that he showed no consciousness of any such trance, but dressed himself and sent for his horse as if he had woken from a single night's slumber. Yet some change, it was suspected, must have taken place in the chambers of his brain, for though he was perfectly rational and seemed graver and more sedate in his ways than before, he appeared to have an imperfect recollection of his past life. He would listen when people spoke of the great frost or the skating or the carnival, but he never gave any sign, except by passing his hand across his brow as if to wipe away some cloud, of having witnessed them himself. When the events of the past six months were discussed, he seemed not so much distressed as puzzled, as if he were troubled by confused memories of some time long gone or were trying to recall stories told him by another. It was observed that if Russia was mentioned or Princesses or ships, he would fall into a gloom of an uneasy kind and get up and look out of the window or call one of the dogs to him, or take a knife and carve a piece of cedar wood. But the doctors were hardly wiser then than they are now, and after prescribing rest and exercise, starvation and nourishment, society and solitude, that he should lie in bed all day and ride forty miles between lunch and dinner, together with the usual sedatives and irritants, diversified, as the fancy took them, with possets of newt's slobber on rising, and draughts of peacock's gall on going to bed, they left him to himself, and gave it as their opinion that he had been asleep for a week.

But if sleep it was, of what nature, we can scarcely refrain from asking, are such sleeps as these? Are they remedial measures--trances in which the most galling memories, events that seem likely to cripple life for ever, are brushed with a dark wing which rubs their harshness off and gilds them, even the ugliest and basest, with a lustre, an incandescence? Has the finger of death to be laid on the tumult of life from time to time lest it rend us asunder? Are we so made that we have to take death in small doses daily or we could not go on with the business of living? And then what strange powers are these that penetrate our most secret ways and change our most treasured possessions without our willing it? Had Orlando, worn out by the extremity of his suffering, died for a week, and then come to life again? And if so, of what nature is death and of what nature life? Having waited well over half an hour for an answer to these questions, and none coming, let us get on with the story.

Now Orlando gave himself up to a life of extreme solitude. His disgrace at Court and the violence of his grief were partly the reason of it, but as he made no effort to defend himself and seldom invited anyone to visit him (though he had many friends who would willingly have done so) it appeared as if to be alone in the great house of his fathers suited his temper. Solitude was his choice. How he spent his time, nobody quite knew. The servants, of whom he kept a full retinue, though much of their business was to dust empty rooms and to smooth the coverlets of beds that were never slept in, watched, in the dark of the evening, as they sat over their cakes and ale, a light passing along the galleries, through the banqueting-halls, up the staircase, into the bedrooms, and knew that their master was perambulating the house alone. None dared follow him, for the house was haunted by a great variety of ghosts, and the extent of it made it easy to lose one's way and either fall down some hidden staircase or open a door which, should the wind blow it to, would shut upon one for ever--accidents of no uncommon occurrence, as the frequent discovery of the skeletons of men and animals in attitudes of great agony made evident. Then the light would be lost altogether, and Mrs Grimsditch, the housekeeper, would say to Mr Dupper, the chaplain, how she hoped his Lordship had not met with some bad accident. Mr Dupper would opine that his Lordship was on his knees, no doubt, among the tombs of his ancestors in the Chapel, which was in the Billiard Table Court, half a mile away on the south side. For he had sins on his conscience, Mr Dupper was afraid; upon which Mrs Grimsditch would retort, rather sharply, that so had most of us; and Mrs Stewkley and Mrs Field and old Nurse Carpenter would all raise their voices in his Lordship's praise; and the grooms and the stewards would swear that it was a thousand pities to see so fine a nobleman moping about the house when he might be hunting the fox or chasing the deer; and even the little laundry maids and scullery maids, the Judys and the Faiths, who were handing round the tankards and cakes, would pipe up their testimony to his Lordship's gallantry; for never was there a kinder gentleman, or one more free with those little pieces of silver which serve to buy a knot of ribbon or put a posy in one's hair; until even the Blackamoor whom they called Grace Robinson by way of making a Christian woman of her, understood what they were at, and agreed that his Lordship was a handsome, pleasant, darling gentleman in the only way she could, that is to say by showing all her teeth at once in a broad grin. In short, all his serving men and women held him in high respect, and cursed the foreign Princess (but they called her by a coarser name than that) who had brought him to this pass.

But though it was probably cowardice, or love of hot ale, that led Mr Dupper to imagine his Lordship safe among the tombs so that he need not go in search of him, it may well have been that Mr Dupper was right. Orlando now took a strange delight in thoughts of death and decay, and, after pacing the long galleries and ballrooms with a taper in his hand, looking at picture after picture as if he sought the likeness of somebody whom he could not find, would mount into the family pew and sit for hours watching the banners stir and the moonlight waver with a bat or death's head moth to keep him company. Even this was not enough for him, but he must descend into the crypt where his ancestors lay, coffin piled upon coffin, for ten generations together. The place was so seldom visited that the rats made free with the lead work, and now a thigh bone would catch at his cloak as he passed, or he would crack the skull of some old Sir Malise as it rolled beneath his foot. It was a ghastly sepulchre; dug deep beneath the foundations of the house as if the first Lord of the family, who had come from France with the Conqueror, had wished to testify how all pomp is built upon corruption; how the skeleton lies beneath the flesh: how we that dance and sing above must lie below; how the crimson velvet turns to dust; how the ring (here Orlando, stooping his lantern, would pick up a gold circle lacking a stone, that had rolled into a corner) loses its ruby and the eye which was so lustrous shines no more. 'Nothing remains of all these Princes', Orlando would say, indulging in some pardonable exaggeration of their rank, 'except one digit,' and he would take a skeleton hand in his and bend the joints this way and that. 'Whose hand was it?' he went on to ask. 'The right or the left? The hand of man or woman, of age or youth? Had it urged the war horse, or plied the needle? Had it plucked the rose, or grasped cold steel? Had it--' but here either his invention failed him or, what is more likely, provided him with so many instances of what a hand can do that he shrank, as his wont was, from the cardinal labour of composition, which is excision, and he put it with the other bones, thinking how there was a writer called Thomas Browne, a Doctor of Norwich, whose writing upon such subjects took his fancy amazingly.

So, taking his lantern and seeing that the bones were in order, for though romantic, he was singularly methodical and detested nothing so much as a ball of string on the floor, let alone the skull of an ancestor, he returned to that curious, moody pacing down the galleries, looking for something among the pictures, which was interrupted at length by a veritable spasm of sobbing, at the sight of a Dutch snow scene by an unknown artist. Then it seemed to him that life was not worth living any more. Forgetting the bones of his ancestors and how life is founded on a grave, he stood there shaken with sobs, all for the desire of a woman in Russian trousers, with slanting eyes, a pouting mouth and pearls about her neck. She had gone. She had left him. He was never to see her again. And so he sobbed. And so he found his way back to his own rooms; and Mrs Grimsditch, seeing the light in the window, put the tankard from her lips and said Praise be to God, his Lordship was safe in his room again; for she had been thinking all this while that he was foully murdered.

Orlando now drew his chair up to the table; opened the works of Sir Thomas Browne and proceeded to investigate the delicate articulation of one of the doctor's longest and most marvellously contorted cogitations.

For though these are not matters on which a biographer can profitably enlarge it is plain enough to those who have done a reader's part in making up from bare hints dropped here and there the whole boundary and circumference of a living person; can hear in what we only whisper a living voice; can see, often when we say nothing about it, exactly what he looked like; know without a word to guide them precisely what he thought--and it is for readers such as these that we write--it is plain then to such a reader that Orlando was strangely compounded of many humours--of melancholy, of indolence, of passion, of love of solitude, to say nothing of all those contortions and subtleties of temper which were indicated on the first page, when he slashed at a dead nigger's head; cut it down; hung it chivalrously out of his reach again and then betook himself to the windowseat with a book. The taste for books was an early one. As a child he was sometimes found at midnight by a page still reading. They took his taper away, and he bred glow-worms to serve his purpose. They took the glow-worms away, and he almost burnt the house down with a tinder. To put it in a nutshell, leaving the novelist to smooth out the crumpled silk and all its implications, he was a nobleman afflicted with a love of literature. Many people of his time, still more of his rank, escaped the infection and were thus free to run or ride or make love at their own sweet will. But some were early infected by a germ said to be bred of the pollen of the asphodel and to be blown out of Greece and Italy, which was of so deadly a nature that it would shake the hand as it was raised to strike, and cloud the eye as it sought its prey, and make the tongue stammer as it declared its love. It was the fatal nature of this disease to substitute a phantom for reality, so that Orlando, to whom fortune had given every gift--plate, linen, houses, men-servants, carpets, beds in profusion--had only to open a book for the whole vast accumulation to turn to mist. The nine acres of stone which were his house vanished; one hundred and fifty indoor servants disappeared; his eighty riding horses became invisible; it would take too long to count the carpets, sofas, trappings, china, plate, cruets, chafing dishes and other movables often of beaten gold, which evaporated like so much sea mist under the miasma. So it was, and Orlando would sit by himself, reading, a naked man.

The disease gained rapidly upon him now in his solitude. He would read often six hours into the night; and when they came to him for orders about the slaughtering of cattle or the harvesting of wheat, he would push away his folio and look as if he did not understand what was said to him. This was bad enough and wrung the hearts of Hall, the falconer, of Giles, the groom, of Mrs Grimsditch, the housekeeper, of Mr Dupper, the chaplain. A fine gentleman like that, they said, had no need of books. Let him leave books, they said, to the palsied or the dying. But worse was to come. For once the disease of reading has laid upon the system it weakens it so that it falls an easy prey to that other scourge which dwells in the inkpot and festers in the quill. The wretch takes to writing. And while this is bad enough in a poor man, whose only property is a chair and a table set beneath a leaky roof--for he has not much to lose, after all--the plight of a rich man, who has houses and cattle, maidservants, asses and linen, and yet writes books, is pitiable in the extreme. The flavour of it all goes out of him; he is riddled by hot irons; gnawed by vermin. He would give every penny he has (such is the malignity of the germ) to write one little book and become famous; yet all the gold in Peru will not buy him the treasure of a well-turned line. So he falls into consumption and sickness, blows his brains out, turns his face to the wall. It matters not in what attitude they find him. He has passed through the gates of Death and known the flames of Hell.

Happily, Orlando was of a strong constitution and the disease (for reasons presently to be given) never broke him down as it has broken many of his peers. But he was deeply smitten with it, as the sequel shows. For when he had read for an hour or so in Sir Thomas Browne, and the bark of the stag and the call of the night watchman showed that it was the dead of night and all safe asleep, he crossed the room, took a silver key from his pocket and unlocked the doors of a great inlaid cabinet which stood in the corner. Within were some fifty drawers of cedar wood and upon each was a paper neatly written in Orlando's hand. He paused, as if hesitating which to open. One was inscribed 'The Death of Ajax', another 'The Birth of Pyramus', another 'Iphigenia in Aulis', another 'The Death of Hippolytus', another 'Meleager', another 'The Return of Odysseus',--in fact there was scarcely a single drawer that lacked the name of some mythological personage at a crisis of his career. In each drawer lay a document of considerable size all written over in Orlando's hand. The truth was that Orlando had been afflicted thus for many years. Never had any boy begged apples as Orlando begged paper; nor sweetmeats as he begged ink. Stealing away from talk and games, he had hidden himself behind curtains, in priest's holes, or in the cupboard behind his mother's bedroom which had a great hole in the floor and smelt horribly of starling's dung, with an inkhorn in one hand, a pen in another, and on his knee a roll of paper. Thus had been written, before he was turned twenty-five, some forty-seven plays, histories, romances, poems; some in prose, some in verse; some in French, some in Italian; all romantic, and all long. One he had had printed by John Ball of the Feathers and Coronet opposite St Paul's Cross, Cheapside; but though the sight of it gave him extreme delight, he had never dared show it even to his mother, since to write, much more to publish, was, he knew, for a nobleman an inexpiable disgrace.

Now, however, that it was the dead of night and he was alone, he chose from this repository one thick document called 'Xenophila a Tragedy' or some such title, and one thin one, called simply 'The Oak Tree' (this was the only monosyllabic title among the lot), and then he approached the inkhorn, fingered the quill, and made other such passes as those addicted to this vice begin their rites with. But he paused.

As this pause was of extreme significance in his history, more so, indeed, than many acts which bring men to their knees and make rivers run with blood, it behoves us to ask why he paused; and to reply, after due reflection, that it was for some such reason as this. Nature, who has played so many queer tricks upon us, making us so unequally of clay and diamonds, of rainbow and granite, and stuffed them into a case, often of the most incongruous, for the poet has a butcher's face and the butcher a poet's; nature, who delights in muddle and mystery, so that even now (the first of November 1927) we know not why we go upstairs, or why we come down again, our most daily movements are like the passage of a ship on an unknown sea, and the sailors at the mast-head ask, pointing their glasses to the horizon; Is there land or is there none? to which, if we are prophets, we make answer 'Yes'; if we are truthful we say 'No'; nature, who has so much to answer for besides the perhaps unwieldy length of this sentence, has further complicated her task and added to our confusion by providing not only a perfect rag-bag of odds and ends within us--a piece of a policeman's trousers lying cheek by jowl with Queen Alexandra's wedding veil--but has contrived that the whole assortment shall be lightly stitched together by a single thread. Memory is the seamstress, and a capricious one at that. Memory runs her needle in and out, up and down, hither and thither. We know not what comes next, or what follows after. Thus, the most ordinary movement in the world, such as sitting down at a table and pulling the inkstand towards one, may agitate a thousand odd, disconnected fragments, now bright, now dim, hanging and bobbing and dipping and flaunting, like the underlinen of a family of fourteen on a line in a gale of wind. Instead of being a single, downright, bluff piece of work of which no man need feel ashamed, our commonest deeds are set about with a fluttering and flickering of wings, a rising and falling of lights. Thus it was that Orlando, dipping his pen in the ink, saw the mocking face of the lost Princess and asked himself a million questions instantly which were as arrows dipped in gall. Where was she; and why had she left him?

Was the Ambassador her uncle or her lover? Had they plotted? Was she forced? Was she married? Was she dead?--all of which so drove their venom into him that, as if to vent his agony somewhere, he plunged his quill so deep into the ink-horn that the ink spirted over the table, which act, explain it how one may (and no explanation perhaps is possible--Memory is inexplicable), at once substituted for the face of the Princess a face of a very different sort. But whose was it, he asked himself? And he had to wait, perhaps half a minute, looking at the new picture which lay on top of the old, as one lantern slide is half seen through the next, before he could say to himself, 'This is the face of that rather fat, shabby man who sat in Twitchett's room ever so many years ago when old Queen Bess came here to dine; and I saw him,' Orlando continued, catching at another of those little coloured rags, 'sitting at the table, as I peeped in on my way downstairs, and he had the most amazing eyes,' said Orlando, 'that ever were, but who the devil was he?' Orlando asked, for here Memory added to the forehead and eyes, first, a coarse, grease-stained ruffle, then a brown doublet, and finally a pair of thick boots such as citizens wear in Cheapside. 'Not a Nobleman; not one of us,' said Orlando (which he would not have said aloud, for he was the most courteous of gentlemen; but it shows what an effect noble birth has upon the mind and incidentally how difficult it is for a nobleman to be a writer), 'a poet, I dare say.' By all the laws, Memory, having disturbed him sufficiently, should now have blotted the whole thing out completely, or have fetched up something so idiotic and out of keeping--like a dog chasing a cat or an old woman blowing her nose into a red cotton handkerchief--that, in despair of keeping pace with her vagaries, Orlando should have struck his pen in earnest against his paper. (For we can, if we have the resolution, turn the hussy, Memory, and all her ragtag and bobtail out of the house.) But Orlando paused. Memory still held before him the image of a shabby man with big, bright eyes. Still he looked, still he paused. It is these pauses that are our undoing. It is then that sedition enters the fortress and our troops rise in insurrection. Once before he had paused, and love with its horrid rout, its shawms, its cymbals, and its heads with gory locks torn from the shoulders had burst in. From love he had suffered the tortures of the damned. Now, again, he paused, and into the breach thus made, leapt Ambition, the harridan, and Poetry, the witch, and Desire of Fame, the strumpet; all joined hands and made of his heart their dancing ground. Standing upright in the solitude of his room, he vowed that he would be the first poet of his race and bring immortal lustre upon his name. He said (reciting the names and exploits of his ancestors) that Sir Boris had fought and killed the Paynim; Sir Gawain, the Turk; Sir Miles, the Pole; Sir Andrew, the Frank; Sir Richard, the Austrian; Sir Jordan, the Frenchman; and Sir Herbert, the Spaniard. But of all that killing and campaigning, that drinking and love-making, that spending and hunting and riding and eating, what remained? A skull; a finger. Whereas, he said, turning to the page of Sir Thomas Browne, which lay open upon the table--and again he paused. Like an incantation rising from all parts of the room, from the night wind and the moonlight, rolled the divine melody of those words which, lest they should outstare this page, we will leave where they lie entombed, not dead, embalmed rather, so fresh is their colour, so sound their breathing--and Orlando, comparing that achievement with those of his ancestors, cried out that they and their deeds were dust and ashes, but this man and his words were immortal.

He soon perceived, however, that the battles which Sir Miles and the rest had waged against armed knights to win a kingdom, were not half so arduous as this which he now undertook to win immortality against the English language. Anyone moderately familiar with the rigours of composition will not need to be told the story in detail; how he wrote and it seemed good; read and it seemed vile; corrected and tore up; cut out; put in; was in ecstasy; in despair; had his good nights and bad mornings; snatched at ideas and lost them; saw his book plain before him and it vanished; acted his people's parts as he ate; mouthed them as he walked; now cried; now laughed; vacillated between this style and that; now preferred the heroic and pompous; next the plain and simple; now the vales of Tempe; then the fields of Kent or Cornwall; and could not decide whether he was the divinest genius or the greatest fool in the world.

It was to settle this last question that he decided after many months of such feverish labour, to break the solitude of years and communicate with the outer world. He had a friend in London, one Giles Isham, of Norfolk, who, though of gentle birth, was acquainted with writers and could doubtless put him in touch with some member of that blessed, indeed sacred, fraternity. For, to Orlando in the state he was now in, there was a glory about a man who had written a book and had it printed, which outshone all the glories of blood and state. To his imagination it seemed as if even the bodies of those instinct with such divine thoughts must be transfigured. They must have aureoles for hair, incense for breath, and roses must grow between their lips--which was certainly not true either of himself or Mr Dupper. He could think of no greater happiness than to be allowed to sit behind a curtain and hear them talk. Even the imagination of that bold and various discourse made the memory of what he and his courtier friends used to talk about--a dog, a horse, a woman, a game of cards--seem brutish in the extreme. He bethought him with pride that he had always been called a scholar, and sneered at for his love of solitude and books. He had never been apt at pretty phrases. He would stand stock still, blush, and stride like a grenadier in a ladies' drawing-room. He had twice fallen, in sheer abstraction, from his horse. He had broken Lady Winchilsea's fan once while making a rhyme. Eagerly recalling these and other instances of his unfitness for the life of society, an ineffable hope, that all the turbulence of his youth, his clumsiness, his blushes, his long walks, and his love of the country proved that he himself belonged to the sacred race rather than to the noble--was by birth a writer, rather than an aristocrat--possessed him. For the first time since the night of the great flood he was happy.

He now commissioned Mr Isham of Norfolk to deliver to Mr Nicholas Greene of Clifford's Inn a document which set forth Orlando's admiration for his works (for Nick Greene was a very famous writer at that time) and his desire to make his acquaintance; which he scarcely dared ask; for he had nothing to offer in return;

but if Mr Nicholas Greene would condescend to visit him, a coach and four would be at the corner of Fetter Lane at whatever hour Mr Greene chose to appoint, and bring him safely to Orlando's house. One may fill up the phrases which then followed; and figure Orlando's delight when, in no long time, Mr Greene signified his acceptance of the Noble Lord's invitation; took his place in the coach and was set down in the hall to the south of the main building punctually at seven o'clock on Monday, April the twenty-first.

Many Kings, Queens, and Ambassadors had been received there; Judges had stood there in their ermine. The loveliest ladies of the land had come there; and the sternest warriors. Banners hung there which had been at Flodden and at Agincourt. There were displayed the painted coats of arms with their lions and their leopards and their coronets. There were the long tables where the gold and silver plate was stood; and there the vast fireplaces of wrought Italian marble where nightly a whole oak tree, with its million leaves and its nests of rook and wren, was burnt to ashes. Nicholas Greene, the poet stood there now, plainly dressed in his slouched hat and black doublet, carrying in one hand a small bag.

That Orlando as he hastened to greet him was slightly disappointed was inevitable. The poet was not above middle height; was of a mean figure; was lean and stooped somewhat, and, stumbling over the mastiff on entering, the dog bit him. Moreover, Orlando for all his knowledge of mankind was puzzled where to place him. There was something about him which belonged neither to servant, squire, or noble. The head with its rounded forehead and beaked nose was fine, but the chin receded. The eyes were brilliant, but the lips hung loose and slobbered. It was the expression of the face--as a whole, however, that was disquieting. There was none of that stately composure which makes the faces of the nobility so pleasing to look at; nor had it anything of the dignified servility of a well-trained domestic's face; it was a face seamed, puckered, and drawn together. Poet though he was, it seemed as if he were more used to scold than to flatter; to quarrel than to coo; to scramble than to ride; to struggle than to rest; to hate than to love. This, too, was shown by the quickness of his movements; and by something fiery and suspicious in his glance. Orlando was somewhat taken aback. But they went to dinner.

Here, Orlando, who usually took such things for granted, was, for the first time, unaccountably ashamed of the number of his servants and of the splendour of his table. Stranger still, he bethought him with pride--for the thought was generally distasteful--of that great grandmother Moll who had milked the cows. He was about somehow to allude to this humble woman and her milk-pails, when the poet forestalled him by saying that it was odd, seeing how common the name of Greene was, that the family had come over with the Conqueror and was of the highest nobility in France. Unfortunately, they had come down in the world and done little more than leave their name to the royal borough of Greenwich. Further talk of the same sort, about lost castles, coats of arms, cousins who were baronets in the north, intermarriage with noble families in the west, how some Greens spelt the name with an e at the end, and others without, lasted till the venison was on the table. Then Orlando contrived to say something of Grandmother Moll and her cows, and had eased his heart a little of its burden by the time the wild fowl were before them. But it was not until the Malmsey was passing freely that Orlando dared mention what he could not help thinking a more important matter than the Greens or the cows; that is to say the sacred subject of poetry. At the first mention of the word, the poet's eyes flashed fire; he dropped the fine gentleman airs he had worn; thumped his glass on the table, and launched into one of the longest, most intricate, most passionate, and bitterest stories that Orlando had ever heard, save from the lips of a jilted woman, about a play of his; another poet; and a critic. Of the nature of poetry itself, Orlando only gathered that it was harder to sell than prose, and though the lines were shorter took longer in the writing. So the talk went on with ramifications interminable, until Orlando ventured to hint that he had himself been so rash as to write--but here the poet leapt from his chair. A mouse had squeaked in the wainscot, he said. The truth was, he explained, that his nerves were in a state where a mouse's squeak upset them for a fortnight. Doubtless the house was full of vermin, but Orlando had not heard them. The poet then gave Orlando the full story of his health for the past ten years or so. It had been so bad that one could only marvel that he still lived. He had had the palsy, the gout, the ague, the dropsy, and the three sorts of fever in succession; added to which he had an enlarged heart, a great spleen, and a diseased liver. But, above all, he had, he told Orlando, sensations in his spine which defied description. There was one knob about the third from the top which burnt like fire; another about second from the bottom which was cold as ice. Sometimes he woke with a brain like lead; at others it was as if a thousand wax tapers were alight and people were throwing fireworks inside him. He could feel a rose leaf through his mattress, he said; and knew his way almost about London by the feel of the cobbles. Altogether he was a piece of machinery so finely made and curiously put together (here he raised his hand as if unconsciously, and indeed it was of the finest shape imaginable) that it confounded him to think that he had only sold five hundred copies of his poem, but that of course was largely due to the conspiracy against him. All he could say, he concluded, banging his fist upon the table, was that the art of poetry was dead in England.

How that could be with Shakespeare, Marlowe, Ben Jonson, Browne, Donne, all now writing or just having written, Orlando, reeling off the names of his favourite heroes, could not think.

Greene laughed sardonically. Shakespeare, he admitted, had written some scenes that were well enough; but he had taken them chiefly from Marlowe. Marlowe was a likely boy, but what could you say of a lad who died before he was thirty? As for Browne, he was for writing poetry in prose, and people soon got tired of such conceits as that. Donne was a mountebank who wrapped up his lack of meaning in hard words. The gulls were taken in; but the style would be out of fashion twelve months hence. As for Ben Jonson--Ben Jonson was a friend of his and he never spoke ill of his friends.

No, he concluded, the great age of literature is past; the great age of literature was the Greek; the Elizabethan age was inferior in every respect to the Greek. In such ages men cherished a divine ambition which he might call La Gloire (he pronounced it Glawr, so that Orlando did not at first catch his meaning). Now all young writers were in the pay of the booksellers and poured out any trash that would sell. Shakespeare was the chief offender in this way and Shakespeare was already paying the penalty. Their own age, he said, was marked by precious conceits and wild experiments--neither of which the Greeks would have tolerated for a moment. Much though it hurt him to say it--for he loved literature as he loved his life--he could see no good in the present and had no hope for the future. Here he poured himself out another glass of wine.

Orlando was shocked by these doctrines; yet could not help observing that the critic himself seemed by no means downcast. On the contrary, the more he denounced his own time, the more complacent he became. He could remember, he said, a night at the Cock Tavern in Fleet Street when Kit Marlowe was there and some others. Kit was in high feather, rather drunk, which he easily became, and in a mood to say silly things. He could see him now, brandishing his glass at the company and hiccoughing out, 'Stap my vitals, Bill' (this was to Shakespeare), 'there's a great wave coming and you're on the top of it,' by which he meant, Greene explained, that they were trembling on the verge of a great age in English literature, and that Shakespeare was to be a poet of some importance. Happily for himself, he was killed two nights later in a drunken brawl, and so did not live to see how this prediction turned out. 'Poor foolish fellow,' said Greene, 'to go and say a thing like that. A great age, forsooth--the Elizabethan a great age!'

'So, my dear Lord,' he continued, settling himself comfortably in his chair and rubbing the wine-glass between his fingers, 'we must make the best of it, cherish the past and honour those writers--there are still a few of 'em--who take antiquity for their model and write, not for pay but for Glawr.' (Orlando could have wished him a better accent.) 'Glawr', said Greene, 'is the spur of noble minds. Had I a pension of three hundred pounds a year paid quarterly, I would live for Glawr alone. I would lie in bed every morning reading Cicero. I would imitate his style so that you couldn't tell the difference between us. That's what I call fine writing,' said Greene; 'that's what I call Glawr. But it's necessary to have a pension to do it.'

By this time Orlando had abandoned all hope of discussing his own work with the poet; but this mattered the less as the talk now got upon the lives and characters of Shakespeare, Ben Jonson, and the rest, all of whom Greene had known intimately and about whom he had a thousand anecdotes of the most amusing kind to tell. Orlando had never laughed so much in his life. These, then, were his gods! Half were drunken and all were amorous. Most of them quarrelled with their wives; not one of them was above a lie or an intrigue of the most paltry kind. Their poetry was scribbled down on the backs of washing bills held to the heads of printer's devils at the street door. Thus Hamlet went to press; thus Lear; thus Othello. No wonder, as Greene said, that these plays show the faults they do. The rest of the time was spent in carousings and junketings in taverns and in beer gardens, When things were said that passed belief for wit, and things were done that made the utmost frolic of the courtiers seem pale in comparison. All this Greene told with a spirit that roused Orlando to the highest pitch of delight. He had a power of mimicry that brought the dead to life, and could say the finest things of books provided they were written three hundred years ago.

So time passed, and Orlando felt for his guest a strange mixture of liking and contempt, of admiration and pity, as well as something too indefinite to be called by any one name, but had something of fear in it and something of fascination. He talked incessantly about himself, yet was such good company that one could listen to the story of his ague for ever. Then he was so witty; then he was so irreverent; then he made so free with the names of God and Woman; then he was So full of queer crafts and had such strange lore in his head; could make salad in three hundred different ways; knew all that could be known of the mixing of wines; played half-a-dozen musical instruments, and was the first person, and perhaps the last, to toast cheese in the great Italian fireplace. That he did not know a geranium from a carnation, an oak from a birch tree, a mastiff from a greyhound, a teg from a ewe, wheat from barley, plough land from fallow; was ignorant of the rotation of the crops; thought oranges grew underground and turnips on trees; preferred any townscape to any landscape;--all this and much more amazed Orlando, who had never met anybody of his kind before. Even the maids, who despised him, tittered at his jokes, and the men-servants, who loathed him, hung about to hear his stories. Indeed, the house had never been so lively as now that he was there--all of which gave Orlando a great deal to think about, and caused him to compare this way of life with the old. He recalled the sort of talk he had been used to about the King of Spain's apoplexy or the mating of a bitch; he bethought him how the day passed between the stables and the dressing closet; he remembered how the Lords snored over their wine and hated anybody who woke them up. He bethought him how active and valiant they were in body; how slothful and timid in mind. Worried by these thoughts, and unable to strike a proper balance, he came to the conclusion that he had admitted to his house a plaguey spirit of unrest that would never suffer him to sleep sound again.

At the same moment, Nick Greene came to precisely the opposite conclusion. Lying in bed of a morning on the softest pillows between the smoothest sheets and looking out of his oriel window upon turf which for centuries had known neither dandelion nor dock weed, he thought that unless he could somehow make his escape, he should be smothered alive. Getting up and hearing the pigeons coo, dressing and hearing the fountains fall, he thought that unless he could hear the drays roar upon the cobbles of Fleet Street, he would never write another line. If this goes on much longer, he thought, hearing the footman mend the fire and spread the table with silver dishes next door, I shall fall asleep and (here he gave a prodigious yawn) sleeping die.

So he sought Orlando in his room, and explained that he had not been able to sleep a wink all night because of the silence. (Indeed, the house was surrounded by a park fifteen miles in circumference and a wall ten feet high.) Silence, he said, was of all things the most oppressive to his nerves. He would end his visit, by Orlando's leave, that very morning. Orlando felt some relief at this, yet also a great reluctance to let him go. The house, he thought, would seem very dull without him. On parting (for he had never yet liked to mention the subject), he had the temerity to press his play upon the Death of Hercules upon the poet and ask his opinion of it. The poet took it; muttered something about Glawr and Cicero, which Orlando cut short by promising to pay the pension quarterly; whereupon Greene, with many protestations of affection, jumped into the coach and was gone.

The great hall had never seemed so large, so splendid, or so empty as the chariot rolled away. Orlando knew that he would never have the heart to make toasted cheese in the Italian fireplace again. He would never have the wit to crack jokes about Italian pictures; never have the skill to mix punch as it should be mixed; a thousand good quips and cranks would be lost to him. Yet what a relief to be out of the sound of that querulous voice, what a luxury to be alone once more, so he could not help reflecting, as he unloosed the mastiff which had been tied up these six weeks because it never saw the poet without biting him.

Nick Greene was set down at the corner of Fetter Lane that same afternoon, and found things going on much as he had left them. Mrs Greene, that is to say, was giving birth to a baby in one room; Tom Fletcher was drinking gin in another. Books were tumbled all about the floor; dinner--such as it was--was set on a dressing-table where the children had been making mud pies. But this, Greene felt, was the atmosphere for writing, here he could write, and write he did. The subject was made for him. A noble Lord at home. A visit to a Nobleman in the country--his new poem was to have some such title as that. Seizing the pen with which his little boy was tickling the cat's ears, and dipping it in the egg-cup which served for inkpot, Greene dashed off a very spirited satire there and then. It was so done to a turn that no one could doubt that the young Lord who was roasted was Orlando; his most private sayings and doings, his enthusiasms and folies, down to the very colour of his hair and the foreign way he had of rolling his r's, were there to the life. And if there had been any doubt about it, Greene clinched the matter by introducing, with scarcely any disguise, passages from that aristocratic tragedy, the Death of Hercules, which he found as he expected, wordy and bombastic in the extreme.

The pamphlet, which ran at once into several editions, and paid the expenses of Mrs Greene's tenth lying-in, was soon sent by friends who take care of such matters to Orlando himself. When he had read it, which he did with deadly composure from start to finish, he rang for the footman; delivered the document to him at the end of a pair of tongs; bade him drop it in the filthiest heart of the foulest midden on the estate. Then, when the man was turning to go he stopped him, 'Take the swiftest horse in the stable,' he said, 'ride for dear life to Harwich. There embark upon a ship which you will find bound for Norway. Buy for me from the King's own kennels the finest elk-hounds of the Royal strain, male and female. Bring them back without delay. For', he murmured, scarcely above his breath as he turned to his books, 'I have done with men.'

The footman, who was perfectly trained in his duties, bowed and disappeared. He fulfilled his task so efficiently that he was back that day three weeks, leading in his hand a leash of the finest elk-hounds, one of whom, a female, gave birth that very night under the dinner-table to a litter of eight fine puppies. Orlando had them brought to his bedchamber.

'For', he said, 'I have done with men.'

Nevertheless, he paid the pension quarterly.

Thus, at the age of thirty, or thereabouts, this young Nobleman had not only had every experience that life has to offer, but had seen the worthlessness of them all. Love and ambition, women and poets were all equally vain. Literature was a farce. The night after reading Greene's Visit to a Nobleman in the Country, he burnt in a great conflagration fifty-seven poetical works, only retaining 'The Oak Tree', which was his boyish dream and very short. Two things alone remained to him in which he now put any trust: dogs and nature; an elk-hound and a rose bush. The world, in all its variety, life in all its complexity, had shrunk to that. Dogs and a bush were the whole of it. So feeling quit of a vast mountain of illusion, and very naked in consequence, he called his hounds to him and strode through the Park.

So long had he been secluded, writing and reading, that he had half forgotten the amenities of nature, which in June can be great. When he reached that high mound whence on fine days half of England with a slice of Wales and Scotland thrown in can be seen, he flung himself under his favourite oak tree and felt that if he need never speak to another man or woman so long as he lived; if his dogs did not develop the faculty of speech; if he never met a poet or a Princess again, he might make out what years remained to him in tolerable content.

Here he came then, day after day, week after week, month after month, year after year. He saw the beech trees turn golden and the young ferns unfurl; he saw the moon sickle and then circular; he saw--but probably the reader can imagine the passage which should follow and how every tree and plant in the neighbourhood is described first green, then golden; how moons rise and suns set; how spring follows winter and autumn summer; how night succeeds day and day night; how there is first a storm and then fine weather; how things remain much as they are for two or three hundred years or so, except for a little dust and a few cobwebs which one old woman can sweep up in half an hour; a conclusion which, one cannot help feeling, might have been reached more quickly by the simple statement that 'Time passed' (here the exact amount could be indicated in brackets) and nothing whatever happened.

But Time, unfortunately, though it makes animals and vegetables bloom and fade with amazing punctuality, has no such simple effect upon the mind of man. The mind of man, moreover, works with equal strangeness upon the body of time. An hour, once it lodges in the queer element of the human spirit, may be stretched to fifty or a hundred times its clock length; on the other hand, an hour may be accurately represented on the timepiece of the mind by one second. This extraordinary discrepancy between time on the clock and time in the mind is less known than it should be and deserves fuller investigation. But the biographer, whose interests are, as we have said, highly restricted, must confine himself to one simple statement: when a man has reached the age of thirty, as Orlando now had, time when he is thinking becomes inordinately long; time when he is doing becomes inordinately short. Thus Orlando gave his orders and did the business of his vast estates in a flash; but directly he was alone on the mound under the oak tree, the seconds began to round and fill until it seemed as if they would never fall. They filled themselves, moreover, with the strangest variety of objects. For not only did he find himself confronted by problems which have puzzled the wisest of men, such as What is love? What friendship? What truth? but directly he came to think about them, his whole past, which seemed to him of extreme length and variety, rushed into the falling second, swelled it a dozen times its natural size, coloured it a thousand tints, and filled it with all the odds and ends in the universe.

In such thinking (or by whatever name it should be called) he spent months and years of his life. It would be no exaggeration to say that he would go out after breakfast a man of thirty and come home to dinner a man of fifty-five at least. Some weeks added a century to his age, others no more than three seconds at most. Altogether, the task of estimating the length of human life (of the animals' we presume not to speak) is beyond our capacity, for directly we say that it is ages long, we are reminded that it is briefer than the fall of a rose leaf to the ground. Of the two forces which alternately, and what is more confusing still, at the same moment, dominate our unfortunate numbskulls--brevity and diuturnity--Orlando was sometimes under the influence of the elephant-footed deity, then of the gnat-winged fly. Life seemed to him of prodigious length. Yet even so, it went like a flash. But even when it stretched longest and the moments swelled biggest and he seemed to wander alone in deserts of vast eternity, there was no time for the smoothing out and deciphering of those scored parchments which thirty years among men and women had rolled tight in his heart and brain. Long before he had done thinking about Love (the oak tree had put forth its leaves and shaken them to the ground a dozen times in the process) Ambition would jostle it off the field, to be replaced by Friendship or Literature. And as the first question had not been settled--What is Love?--back it would come at the least provocation or none, and hustle Books or Metaphors of What one lives for into the margin, there to wait till they saw their chance to rush into the field again. What made the process still longer was that it was profusely illustrated, not only with pictures, as that of old Queen Elizabeth, laid on her tapestry couch in rose-coloured brocade with an ivory snuff-box in her hand and a gold-hilted sword by her side, but with scents--she was strongly perfumed--and with sounds; the stags were barking in Richmond Park that winter's day. And so, the thought of love would be all ambered over with snow and winter; with log fires burning; with Russian women, gold swords, and the bark of stags; with old King James' slobbering and fireworks and sacks of treasure in the holds of Elizabethan sailing ships. Every single thing, once he tried to dislodge it from its place in his mind, he found thus cumbered with other matter like the lump of glass which, after a year at the bottom of the sea, is grown about with bones and dragon-flies, and coins and the tresses of drowned women.

'Another metaphor by Jupiter!' he would exclaim as he said this (which will show thc disorderly and circuitous way in which his mind worked and explain why the oak tree flowered and faded so often before he came to any conclusion about Love). 'And what's the point of it?' he would ask himself. 'Why not say simply in so many words--' and then he would try to think for half an hour,--or was it two years and a half?--how to say simply in so many words what love is. 'A figure like that is manifestly untruthful,' he argued, 'for no dragon-fly, unless under very exceptional circumstances, could live at the bottom of the sea. And if literature is not the Bride and Bedfellow of Truth, what is she? Confound it all,' he cried, 'why say Bedfellow when one's already said Bride? Why not simply say what one means and leave it?'

So then he tried saying the grass is green and the sky is blue and so to propitiate the austere spirit of poetry whom still, though at a great distance, he could not help reverencing. 'The sky is blue,' he said, 'the grass is green.' Looking up, he saw that, on the contrary, the sky is like the veils which a thousand Madonnas have let fall from their hair; and the grass fleets and darkens like a flight of girls fleeing the embraces of hairy satyrs from enchanted woods. 'Upon my word,' he said (for he had fallen into the bad habit of speaking aloud), 'I don't see that one's more true than another. Both are utterly false.' And he despaired of being able to solve the problem of what poetry is and what truth is and fell into a deep dejection.

And here we may profit by a pause in his soliloquy to reflect how odd it was to see Orlando stretched there on his elbow on a June day and to reflect that this fine fellow with all his faculties about him and a healthy body, witness cheeks and limbs--a man who never thought twice about heading a charge or fighting a duel--should be so subject to the lethargy of thought, and rendered so susceptible by it, that when it came to a question of poetry, or his own competence in it, he was as shy as a little girl behind her mother's cottage door. In our belief, Greene's ridicule of his tragedy hurt him as much as the Princess' ridicule of his love. But to return:--

Orlando went on thinking. He kept looking at the grass and at the sky and trying to bethink him what a true poet, who has his verses published in London, would say about them. Memory meanwhile (whose habits have already been described) kept steady before his eyes the face of Nicholas Greene, as if that sardonic loose-lipped man, treacherous as he had proved himself, were the Muse in person, and it was to him that Orlando must do homage. So Orlando, that summer morning, offered him a variety of phrases, some plain, others figured, and Nick Greene kept shaking his head and sneering and muttering something about Glawr and Cicero and the death of poetry in our time. At length, starting to his feet (it was now winter and very cold) Orlando swore one of the most remarkable oaths of his lifetime, for it bound him to a servitude than which none is stricter. 'I'll be blasted', he said, 'if I ever write another word, or try to write another word, to please Nick Greene or the Muse. Bad, good, or indifferent, I'll write, from this day forward, to please myself'; and here he made as if he were tearing a whole budget of papers across and tossing them in the face of that sneering loose-lipped man. Upon which, as a cur ducks if you stoop to shy a stone at him, Memory ducked her effigy of Nick Greene out of sight; and substituted for it--nothing whatever.

But Orlando, all the same, went on thinking. He had indeed much to think of. For when he tore the parchment across, he tore, in one rending, the scrolloping, emblazoned scroll which he had made out in his own favour in the solitude of his room appointing himself, as the King appoints Ambassadors, the first poet of his race, the first writer of his age, conferring eternal immortality upon his soul and granting his body a grave among laurels and the intangible banners of a people's reverence perpetually. Eloquent as this all was, he now tore it up and threw it in the dustbin. 'Fame', he said. 'is like' (and since there was no Nick Greene to stop him, he went on to revel in images of which we will choose only one or two of the quietest) 'a braided coat which hampers the limbs; a jacket of silver which curbs the heart; a painted shield which covers a scarecrow,' etc. etc. The pith of his phrases was that while fame impedes and constricts, obscurity wraps about a man like a mist; obscurity is dark, ample, and free; obscurity lets the mind take its way unimpeded. Over the obscure man is poured the merciful suffusion of darkness. None knows where he goes or comes. He may seek the truth and speak it; he alone is free; he alone is truthful; he alone is at peace. And so he sank into a quiet mood, under the oak tree, the hardness of whose roots, exposed above the ground, seemed to him rather comfortable than otherwise.

Sunk for a long time in profound thoughts as to the value of obscurity, and the delight of having no name, but being like a wave which returns to the deep body of the sea; thinking how obscurity rids the mind of the irk of envy and spite; how it sets running in the veins the free waters of generosity and magnanimity; and allows giving and taking without thanks offered or praise given; which must have been the way of all great poets, he supposed (though his knowledge of Greek was not enough to bear him out), for, he thought, Shakespeare must have written like that, and the church builders built like that, anonymously, needing no thanking or naming, but only their work in the daytime and a little ale perhaps at night--'What an admirable life this is,' he thought, stretching his limbs out under the oak tree. 'And why not enjoy it this very moment?' The thought struck him like a bullet. Ambition dropped like a plummet. Rid of the heart-burn of rejected love, and of vanity rebuked, and all the other stings and pricks which the nettle-bed of life had burnt upon him when ambitious of fame, but could no longer inflict upon one careless of glory, he opened his eyes, which had been wide open all the time, but had seen only thoughts, and saw, lying in the hollow beneath him, his house.

There it lay in the early sunshine of spring. It looked a town rather than a house, but a town built, not hither and thither, as this man wished or that, but circumspectly, by a single architect with one idea in his head. Courts and buildings, grey, red, plum colour, lay orderly and symmetrical; the courts were some of them oblong and some square; in this was a fountain; in that a statue; the buildings were some of them low, some pointed; here was a chapel, there a belfry; spaces of the greenest grass lay in between and clumps of cedar trees and beds of bright flowers; all were clasped--yet so well set out was it that it seemed that every part had room to spread itself fittingly--by the roll of a massive wall; while smoke from innumerable chimneys curled perpetually into the air. This vast, yet ordered building, which could house a thousand men and perhaps two thousand horses, was built, Orlando thought, by workmen whose names are unknown. Here have lived, for more centuries than I can count, the obscure generations of my own obscure family. Not one of these Richards, Johns, Annes, Elizabeths has left a token of himself behind him, yet all, working together with their spades and their needles, their love-making and their child-bearing, have left this.

Never had the house looked more noble and humane.

Why, then, had he wished to raise himself above them? For it seemed vain and arrogant in the extreme to try to better that anonymous work of creation; the labours of those vanished hands. Better was it to go unknown and leave behind you an arch, a potting shed, a wall where peaches ripen, than to burn like a meteor and leave no dust. For after all, he said, kindling as he looked at the great house on the greensward below, the unknown lords and ladies who lived there never forgot to set aside something for those who come after; for the roof that will leak; for the tree that will fall. There was always a warm corner for the old shepherd in the kitchen; always food for the hungry; always their goblets were polished, though they lay sick, and their windows were lit though they lay dying. Lords though they were, they were content to go down into obscurity with the molecatcher and the stone-mason. Obscure noblemen, forgotten builders--thus he apostrophized them with a warmth that entirely gainsaid such critics as called him cold, indifferent, slothful (the truth being that a quality often lies just on the other side of the wall from where we seek it)--thus he apostrophized his house and race in terms of the most moving eloquence; but when it came to the peroration--and what is eloquence that lacks a peroration?--he fumbled. He would have liked to have ended with a flourish to the effect that he would follow in their footsteps and add another stone to their building. Since, however, the building already covered nine acres, to add even a single stone seemed superfluous. Could one mention furniture in a peroration? Could one speak of chairs and tables and mats to lie beside people's beds? For whatever the peroration wanted, that was what the house stood in need of. Leaving his speech unfinished for the moment, he strode down hill again resolved henceforward to devote himself to the furnishing of the mansion. The news--that she was to attend him instantly--brought tears to the eyes of good old Mrs Grimsditch, now grown somewhat old. Together they perambulated the house.

The towel horse in the King's bedroom ('and that was King Jamie, my Lord,' she said, hinting that it was many a day since a King had slept under their roof; but the odious Parliament days were over and there was now a Crown in England again) lacked a leg; there were no stands to the ewers in the little closet leading into the waiting room of the Duchess's page; Mr Greene had made a stain on the carpet with his nasty pipe smoking, which she and Judy, for all their scrubbing, had never been able to wash out. Indeed, when Orlando came to reckon up the matter of furnishing with rosewood chairs and cedar-wood cabinets, with silver basins, china bowls, and Persian carpets, every one of the three hundred and sixty-five bedrooms which the house contained, he saw that it would be no light one; and if some thousands of pounds of his estate remained over, these would do little more than hang a few galleries with tapestry, set the dining hall with fine, carved chairs and provide mirrors of solid silver and chairs of the same metal (for which he had an inordinate passion) for the furnishing of the royal bedchambers.

He now set to work in earnest, as we can prove beyond a doubt if we look at his ledgers. Let us glance at an inventory of what he bought at this time, with the expenses totted up in the margin--but these we omit.

'To fifty pairs of Spanish blankets, ditto curtains of crimson and white taffeta; the valence to them of white satin embroidered with crimson and white silk...

'To seventy yellow satin chairs and sixty stools, suitable with their buckram covers to them all...

'To sixty seven walnut tree tables...

'To seventeen dozen boxes containing each dozen five dozen of Venice glasses...

'To one hundred and two mats, each thirty yards long...

'To ninety seven cushions of crimson damask laid with silver parchment lace and footstools of cloth of tissue and chairs suitable...

'To fifty branches for a dozen lights apiece...'

Already--it is an effect lists have upon us--we are beginning to yawn. But if we stop, it is only that the catalogue is tedious, not that it is finished. There are ninety-nine pages more of it and the total sum disbursed ran into many thousands--that is to say millions of our money. And if his day was spent like this, at night again, Lord Orlando might be found reckoning out what it would cost to level a million molehills, if the men were paid tenpence an hour; and again, how many hundredweight of nails at fivepence halfpenny a gill were needed to repair the fence round the park, which was fifteen miles in circumference. And so on and so on.

The tale, we say, is tedious, for one cupboard is much like another, and one molehill not much different from a million. Some pleasant journeys it cost him; and some fine adventures. As, for instance, when he set a whole city of blind women near Bruges to stitch hangings for a silver canopied bed; and the story of his adventure with a Moor in Venice of whom he bought (but only at the sword's point) his lacquered cabinet, might, in other hands, prove worth the telling. Nor did the work lack variety; for here would come, drawn by teams from Sussex, great trees, to be sawn across and laid along the gallery for flooring; and then a chest from Persia, stuffed with wool and sawdust. from which, at last, he would take a single plate, or one topaz ring.

At length, however, there was no room in the galleries for another table; no room on the tables for another cabinet; no room in the cabinet for another rose-bowl; no room in the bowl for another handful of potpourri; there was no room for anything anywhere; in short the house was furnished. In the garden snowdrops, crocuses, hyacinths, magnolias, roses, lilies, asters, the dahlia in all its va-varieties, pear trees and apple trees and cherry trees and mulberry trees, with an enormous quantity of rare and flowering shrubs, of trees evergreen and perennial, grew so thick on each other's roots that there was no plot of earth without its bloom, and no stretch of sward without its shade. In addition, he had imported wild fowl with gay plumage; and two Malay bears, the surliness of whose manners concealed, he was certain, trusty hearts.

All now was ready; and when it was evening and the innumerable silver sconces were lit and the light airs which for ever moved about the galleries stirred the blue and green arras, so that it looked as if the huntsmen were riding and Daphne flying; when the silver shone and lacquer glowed and wood kindled; when the carved chairs held their arms out and dolphins swam upon the walls with mermaids on their backs; when all this and much more than all this was complete and to his liking, Orlando walked through the house with his elk hounds following and felt content. He had matter now, he thought, to fill out his peroration. Perhaps it would be well to begin the speech all over again. Yet, as he paraded the galleries he felt that still something was lacking. Chairs and tables, however richly gilt and carved, sofas, resting on lions' paws with swans' necks curving under them, beds even of the softest swansdown are not by themselves enough. People sitting in them, people lying in them improve them amazingly. Accordingly Orlando now began a series of very splendid entertainments to the nobility and gentry of the neighbourhood. The three hundred and sixty-five bedrooms were full for a month at a time. Guests jostled each other on the fifty-two staircases. Three hundred servants bustled about the pantries. Banquets took place almost nightly. Thus, in a very few years, Orlando had worn the nap off his velvet, and spent the half of his fortune; but he had earned the good opinion of his neighbours. held a score of offices in the county, and was annually presented with perhaps a dozen volumes dedicated to his Lordship in rather fulsome terms by grateful poets. For though he was careful not to consort with writers at that time and kept himself always aloof from ladies of foreign blood, still, he was excessively generous both to women and to poets, and both adored him.

But when the feasting was at its height and his guests were at their revels, he was apt to take himself off to his private room alone. There when the door was shut, and he was certain of privacy, he would have out an old writing book, stitched together with silk stolen from his mother's workbox, and labelled in a round schoolboy hand, 'The Oak Tree, A Poem'. In this he would write till midnight chimed and long after. But as he scratched out as many lines as he wrote in, the sum of them was often, at the end of the year, rather less than at the beginning, and it looked as if in the process of writing the poem would be completely unwritten. For it is for the historian of letters to remark that he had changed his style amazingly. His floridity was chastened; his abundance curbed; the age of prose was congealing those warm fountains. The very landscape outside was less stuck about with garlands and the briars themselves were less thorned and intricate. Perhaps the senses were a little duller and honey and cream less seductive to the palate. Also that the streets were better drained and the houses better lit had its effect upon the style, it cannot be doubted.

One day he was adding a line or two with enormous labour to 'The Oak Tree, A Poem', when a shadow crossed the tail of his eye. It was no shadow, he soon saw, but the figure of a very tall lady in riding hood and mantle crossing the quadrangle on which his room looked out. As this was the most private of the courts, and the lady was a stranger to him, Orlando marvelled how she had got there. Three days later the same apparition appeared again; and on Wednesday noon appeared once more. This time, Orlando was determined to follow her, nor apparently was she afraid to be found, for she slackened her steps as he came up and looked him full in the face. Any other woman thus caught in a Lord's private grounds would have been afraid; any other woman with that face, head-dress, and aspect would have thrown her mantilla across her shoulders to hide it. For this lady resembled nothing so much as a hare; a hare startled, but obdurate; a hare whose timidity is overcome by an immense and foolish audacity; a hare that sits upright and glowers at its pursuer with great, bulging eyes; with ears erect but quivering, with nose pointed, but twitching. This hare, moreover, was six feet high and wore a head-dress into the bargain of some antiquated kind which made her look still taller. Thus confronted, she stared at Orlando with a stare in which timidity and audacity were most strangely combined.

First, she asked him, with a proper, but somewhat clumsy curtsey, to forgive her her intrusion. Then, rising to her full height again, which must have been something over six feet two, she went on to say--but with such a cackle of nervous laughter, so much tee-heeing and haw-hawing that Orlando thought she must have escaped from a lunatic asylum--that she was the Archduchess Harriet Griselda of Finster-Aarhorn and Scand-op-Boom in the Roumanian territory. She desired above all things to make his acquaintance, she said. She had taken lodging over a baker's shop at the Park Gates. She had seen his picture and it was the image of a sister of hers who was--here she guffawed--long since dead. She was visiting the English court. The Queen was her Cousin. The King was a very good fellow but seldom went to bed sober. Here she tee-heed and haw-hawed again. In short, there was nothing for it but to ask her in and give her a glass of wine.

Indoors, her manners regained the hauteur natural to a Roumanian Archduchess; and had she not shown a knowledge of wines rare in a lady, and made some observations upon firearms and the customs of sportsmen in her country, which were sensible enough, the talk would have lacked spontaneity. Jumping to her feet at last, she announced that she would call the following day, swept another prodigious curtsey and departed. The following day, Orlando rode out. The next, he turned his back; on the third he drew his curtain. On the fourth it rained, and as he could not keep a lady in the wet, nor was altogether averse to company, he invited her in and asked her opinion whether a suit of armour, which belonged to an ancestor of his, was the work of Jacobi or of Topp. He inclined to Topp. She held another opinion--it matters very little which. But it is of some importance to the course of our story that, in illustrating her argument, which had to do with the working of the tie pieces, the Archduchess Harriet took the golden shin case and fitted it to Orlando's leg.

That he had a pair of the shapliest legs that any Nobleman has ever stood upright upon has already been said.

Perhaps something in the way she fastened the ankle buckle; or her stooping posture; or Orlando's long seclusion; or the natural sympathy which is between the sexes; or the Burgundy; or the fire--any of these causes may have been to blame; for certainly blame there is on one side or another, when a Nobleman of Orlando's breeding, entertaining a lady in his house, and she his elder by many years, with a face a yard long and staring eyes, dressed somewhat ridiculously too, in a mantle and riding cloak though the season was warm--blame there is when such a Nobleman is so suddenly and violently overcome by passion of some sort that he has to leave the room.

But what sort of passion, it may well be asked, could this be? And the answer is double faced as Love herself. For Love--but leaving Love out of the argument for a moment, the actual event was this:

When the Archduchess Harriet Griselda stooped to fasten the buckle, Orlando heard, suddenly and unaccountably, far off the beating of Love's wings. The distant stir of that soft plumage roused in him a thousand memories of rushing waters, of loveliness in the snow and faithlessness in the flood; and the sound came nearer; and he blushed and trembled; and he was moved as he had thought never to be moved again; and he was ready to raise his hands and let the bird of beauty alight upon his shoulders, when--horror!--a creaking sound like that the crows make tumbling over the trees began to reverberate; the air seemed dark with coarse black wings; voices croaked; bits of straw, twigs, and feathers dropped; and there pitched down upon his shoulders the heaviest and foulest of the birds; which is the vulture. Thus he rushed from the room and sent the footman to see the Archduchess Harriet to her carriage.

For Love, to which we may now return, has two faces; one white, the other black; two bodies; one smooth, the other hairy. It has two hands, two feet, two nails, two, indeed, of every member and each one is the exact opposite of the other. Yet, so strictly are they joined together that you cannot separate them. In this case, Orlando's love began her flight towards him with her white face turned, and her smooth and lovely body outwards. Nearer and nearer she came wafting before her airs of pure delight. All of a sudden (at the sight of the Archduchess presumably) she wheeled about, turned the other way round; showed herself black, hairy, brutish; and it was Lust the vulture, not Love, the Bird of Paradise, that flopped, foully and disgustingly, upon his shoulders. Hence he ran; hence he fetched the footman.

But the harpy is not so easily banished as all that. Not only did the Archduchess continue to lodge at the Baker's, but Orlando was haunted every day and night by phantoms of the foulest kind. Vainly, it seemed, had he furnished his house with silver and hung the walls with arras, when at any moment a dung-bedraggled fowl could settle upon his writing table. There she was, flopping about among the chairs; he saw her waddling ungracefully across the galleries. Now, she perched, top heavy upon a fire screen. When he chased her out, back she came and pecked at the glass till she broke it.

Thus realizing that his home was uninhabitable, and that steps must be taken to end the matter instantly, he did what any other young man would have done in his place, and asked King Charles to send him as Ambassador Extraordinary to Constantinople. The King was walking in Whitehall. Nell Gwyn was on his arm. She was pelting him with hazel nuts. 'Twas a thousand pities, that amorous lady sighed, that such a pair of legs should leave the country.

Howbeit, the Fates were hard; she could do no more than toss one kiss over her shoulder before Orlando sailed.

CHAPTER 3.

It is, indeed, highly unfortunate, and much to be regretted that at this stage of Orlando's career, when he played a most important part in the public life of his country, we have least information to go upon. We know that he discharged his duties to admiration--witness his Bath and his Dukedom. We know that he had a finger in some of the most delicate negotiations between King Charles and the Turks--to that, treaties in the vault of the Record Office bear testimony. But the revolution which broke out during his period of office, and the fire which followed, have so damaged or destroyed all those papers from which any trustworthy record could be drawn, that what we can give is lamentably incomplete. Often the paper was scorched a deep brown in the middle of the most important sentence. Just when we thought to elucidate a secret that has puzzled historians for a hundred years, there was a hole in the manuscript big enough to put your finger through. We have done our best to piece out a meagre summary from the charred fragments that remain; but often it has been necessary to speculate, to surmise, and even to use the imagination.

Orlando's day was passed, it would seem, somewhat in this fashion. About seven, he would rise, wrap himself in a long Turkish cloak, light a cheroot, and lean his elbows on the parapet. Thus he would stand, gazing at the city beneath him, apparently entranced. At this hour the mist would lie so thick that the domes of Santa Sofia and the rest would seem to be afloat; gradually the mist would uncover them; the bubbles would be seen to be firmly fixed; there would be the river; there the Galata Bridge; there the green-turbaned pilgrims without eyes or noses, begging alms; there the pariah dogs picking up offal; there the shawled women; there the innumerable donkeys; there men on horses carrying long poles. Soon, the whole town would be astir with the cracking of whips, the beating of gongs, cryings to prayer, lashing of mules, and rattle of brass-bound wheels, while sour odours, made from bread fermenting and incense, and spice, rose even to the heights of Pera itself and seemed the very breath of the strident multi-coloured and barbaric population.

Nothing, he reflected, gazing at the view which was now sparkling in the sun, could well be less like the counties of Surrey and Kent or the towns of London and Tunbridge Wells. To the right and left rose in bald and stony prominence the inhospitable Asian mountains, to which the arid castle of a robber chief or two might hang; but parsonage there was none, nor manor house, nor cottage, nor oak, elm, violet, ivy, or wild eglantine. There were no hedges for ferns to grow on, and no fields for sheep to graze. The houses were white as egg-shells and as bald. That he, who was English root and fibre, should yet exult to the depths of his heart in this wild panorama, and gaze and gaze at those passes and far heights planning journeys there alone on foot where only the goat and shepherd had gone before; should feel a passion of affection for the bright, unseasonable flowers, love the unkempt pariah dogs beyond even his elk hounds at home, and snuff the acrid, sharp smell of the streets eagerly into his nostrils, surprised him. He wondered if, in the season of the Crusades, one of his ancestors had taken up with a Circassian peasant woman; thought it possible; fancied a certain darkness in his complexion; and, going indoors again, withdrew to his bath.

An hour later, properly scented, curled, and anointed, he would receive visits from secretaries and other high officials carrying, one after another, red boxes which yielded only to his own golden key. Within were papers of the highest importance, of which only fragments, here a flourish, there a seal firmly attached to a piece of burnt silk, now remain. Of their contents then, we cannot speak, but can only testify that Orlando was kept busy, what with his wax and seals, his various coloured ribbons which had to be diversely attached, his engrossing of titles and making of flourishes round capital letters, till luncheon came--a splendid meal of perhaps thirty courses.

After luncheon, lackeys announced that his coach and six was at the door, and he went, preceded by purple Janissaries running on foot and waving great ostrich feather fans above their heads, to call upon the other ambassadors and dignitaries of state. The ceremony was always the same. On reaching the courtyard, the Janissaries struck with their fans upon the main portal, which immediately flew open revealing a large chamber, splendidly furnished. Here were seated two figures, generally of the opposite sexes. Profound bows and curtseys were exchanged. In the first room, it was permissible only to mention the weather. Having said that it was fine or wet, hot or cold, the Ambassador then passed on to the next chamber, where again, two figures rose to greet him. Here it was only permissible to compare Constantinople as a place of residence with London; and the Ambassador naturally said that he preferred Constantinople, and his hosts naturally said, though they had not seen it, that they preferred London. In the next chamber, King Charles's and the Sultan's healths had to be discussed at some length. In the next were discussed the Ambassador's health and that of his host's wife, but more briefly. In the next the Ambassador complimented his host upon his furniture, and the host complimented the Ambassador upon his dress. In the next, sweet meats were offered, the host deploring their badness, the Ambassador extolling their goodness. The ceremony ended at length with the smoking of a hookah and the drinking of a glass of coffee; but though the motions of smoking and drinking were gone through punctiliously there was neither tobacco in the pipe nor coffee in the glass, as, had either smoke or drink been real, the human frame would have sunk beneath the surfeit. For, no sooner had the Ambassador despatched one such visit, than another had to be undertaken. The same ceremonies were gone through in precisely the same order six or seven times over at the houses of the other great officials, so that it was often late at night before the Ambassador reached home. Though Orlando performed these tasks to admiration and never denied that they are, perhaps, the most important part of a diplomatist's duties, he was undoubtedly fatigued by them, and often depressed to such a pitch of gloom that he preferred to take his dinner alone with his dogs. To them, indeed, he might be heard talking in his own tongue. And sometimes, it is said, he would pass out of his own gates late at night so disguised that the sentries did not know him. Then he would mingle with the crowd on the Galata Bridge; or stroll through the bazaars; or throw aside his shoes and join the worshippers in the Mosques. Once, when it was given out that he was ill of a fever, shepherds, bringing their goats to market, reported that they had met an English Lord on the mountain top and heard him praying to his God. This was thought to be Orlando himself, and his prayer was, no doubt, a poem said aloud, for it was known that he still carried about with him, in the bosom of his cloak, a much scored manuscript; and servants, listening at the door, heard the Ambassador chanting something in an odd, sing-song voice when he was alone.

It is with fragments such as these that we must do our best to make up a picture of Orlando's life and character at this time. There exist, even to this day, rumours, legends, anecdotes of a floating and unauthenticated kind about Orlando's life in Constantinople--(we have quoted but a few of them) which go to prove that he possessed, now that he was in the prime of life, the power to stir the fancy and rivet the eye which will keep a memory green long after all that more durable qualities can do to preserve it is forgotten. The power is a mysterious one compounded of beauty, birth, and some rarer gift, which we may call glamour and have done with it. 'A million candles', as Sasha had said, burnt in him without his being at the trouble of lighting a single one. He moved like a stag, without any need to think about his legs. He spoke in his ordinary voice and echo beat a silver gong. Hence rumours gathered round him. He became the adored of many women and some men. It was not necessary that they should speak to him or even that they should see him; they conjured up before them especially when the scenery was romantic, or the sun was setting, the figure of a noble gentleman in silk stockings. Upon the poor and uneducated, he had the same power as upon the rich. Shepherds, gipsies, donkey drivers, still sing songs about the English Lord 'who dropped his emeralds in the well', which undoubtedly refer to Orlando, who once, it seems, tore his jewels from him in a moment of rage or intoxication and flung them in a fountain; whence they were fished by a page boy. But this romantic power, it is well known, is often associated with a nature of extreme reserve. Orlando seems to have made no friends. As far as is known, he formed no attachments. A certain great lady came all the way from England in order to be near him, and pestered him with her attentions, but he continued to discharge his duties so indefatigably that he had not been Ambassador at the Horn for more than two years and a half before King Charles signified his intention of raising him to the highest rank in the peerage. The envious said that this was Nell Gwyn's tribute to the memory of a leg. But, as she had seen him once only, and was then busily engaged in pelting her royal master with nutshells, it is likely that it was his merits that won him his Dukedom, not his calves.

Here we must pause, for we have reached a moment of great significance in his career. For the conferring of the Dukedom was the occasion of a very famous, and indeed, much disputed incident, which we must now describe, picking our way among burnt papers and little bits of tape as best we may. It was at the end of the great fast of Ramadan that the Order of the Bath and the patent of nobility arrived in a frigate commanded by Sir Adrian Scrope; and Orlando made this the occasion for an entertainment more splendid than any that has been known before or since in Constantinople. The night was fine; the crowd immense, and the windows of the Embassy brilliantly illuminated. Again, details are lacking, for the fire had its way with all such records, and has left only tantalizing fragments which leave the most important points obscure. From the diary of John Fenner Brigge, however, an English naval officer, who was among the guests, we gather that people of all nationalities 'were packed like herrings in a barrel' in the courtyard. The crowd pressed so unpleasantly close that Brigge soon climbed into a Judas tree, the better to observe the proceedings. The rumour had got about among the natives (and here is additional proof of Orlando's mysterious power over the imagination) that some kind of miracle was to be performed. 'Thus,' writes Brigge (but his manuscript is full of burns and holes, some sentences being quite illegible), 'when the rockets began to soar into the air, there was considerable uneasiness among us lest the native population should be seized...fraught with unpleasant consequences to all...English ladies in the company, I own that my hand went to my cutlass. Happily,' he continues in his somewhat long-winded style, 'these fears seemed, for the moment, groundless and, observing the demeanour of the natives...I came to the conclusion that this demonstration of our skill in the art of pyrotechny was valuable, if only because it impressed upon them...the superiority of the British...Indeed, the sight was one of indescribable magnificence. I found myself alternately praising the Lord that he had permitted...and wishing that my poor, dear mother...By the Ambassador's orders, the long windows, which are so imposing a feature of Eastern architecture, for though ignorant in many ways...were thrown wide; and within, we could see a tableau vivant or theatrical display in which English ladies and gentlemen...represented a masque the work of one...The words were inaudible, but the sight of so many of our countrymen and women, dressed with the highest elegance and distinction...moved me to emotions of which I am certainly not ashamed, though unable...I was intent upon observing the astonishing conduct of Lady--which was of a nature to fasten the eyes of all upon her, and to bring discredit upon her sex and country, when'--unfortunately a branch of the Judas tree broke, Lieutenant Brigge fell to the ground, and the rest of the entry records only his gratitude to Providence (who plays a very large part in the diary) and the exact nature of his injuries.

Happily, Miss Penelope Hartopp, daughter of the General of that name, saw the scene from inside and carries on the tale in a letter, much defaced too, which ultimately reached a female friend at Tunbridge Wells. Miss Penelope was no less lavish in her enthusiasm than the gallant officer. 'Ravishing,' she exclaims ten times on one page, 'wondrous...utterly beyond description...gold plate...candelabras...negroes in plush breeches... pyramids of ice...fountains of negus...jellies made to represent His Majesty's ships...swans made to represent water lilies...birds in golden cages...gentlemen in slashed crimson velvet...Ladies' headdresses AT LEAST six foot high...musical boxes....Mr Peregrine said I looked QUITE lovely which I only repeat to you, my dearest, because I know...Oh! how I longed for you all!...surpassing anything we have seen at the Pantiles...oceans to drink...some gentlemen overcome...Lady Betty ravishing....Poor Lady Bonham made the unfortunate mistake of sitting down without a chair beneath her...Gentlemen all very gallant...wished a thousand times for you and dearest Betsy...But the sight of all others, the cynosure of all eyes...as all admitted, for none could be so vile as to deny it, was the Ambassador himself. Such a leg! Such a countenance!! Such princely manners!!! To see him come into the room! To see him go out again! And something INTERESTING in the expression, which makes one feel, one scarcely knows why, that he has SUFFERED! They say a lady was the cause of it. The heartless monster!!! How can one of our REPUTED TENDER SEX have had the effrontery!!! He is unmarried, and half the ladies in the place are wild for love of him...A thousand, thousand kisses to Tom, Gerry, Peter, and dearest Mew' [presumably her cat].

From the Gazette of the time, we gather that 'as the clock struck twelve, the Ambassador appeared on the centre Balcony which was hung with priceless rugs. Six Turks of the Imperial Body Guard, each over six foot in height, held torches to his right and left. Rockets rose into the air at his appearance, and a great shout went up from the people, which the Ambassador acknowledged, bowing deeply, and speaking a few words of thanks in the Turkish language, which it was one of his accomplishments to speak with fluency. Next, Sir Adrian Scrope, in the full dress of a British Admiral, advanced; the Ambassador knelt on one knee; the Admiral placed the Collar of the Most Noble Order of the Bath round his neck, then pinned the Star to his breast; after which another gentleman of the diplomatic corps advancing in a stately manner placed on his shoulders the ducal robes, and handed him on a crimson cushion, the ducal coronet.'

At length, with a gesture of extraordinary majesty and grace, first bowing profoundly, then raising himself proudly erect, Orlando took the golden circlet of strawberry leaves and placed it, with a gesture which none that saw it ever forgot, upon his brows. It was at this point that the first disturbance began. Either the people had expected a miracle--some say a shower of gold was prophesied to fall from the skies--which did not happen, or this was the signal chosen for the attack to begin; nobody seems to know; but as the coronet settled on Orlando's brows a great uproar rose. Bells began ringing; the harsh cries of the prophets were heard above the shouts of the people; many Turks fell flat to the ground and touched the earth with their foreheads. A door burst open. The natives pressed into the banqueting rooms. Women shrieked. A certain lady, who was said to be dying for love of Orlando, seized a candelabra and dashed it to the ground. What might not have happened, had it not been for the presence of Sir Adrian Scrope and a squad of British bluejackets, nobody can say. But the Admiral ordered the bugles to be sounded; a hundred bluejackets stood instantly at attention; the disorder was quelled, and quiet, at least for the time being, fell upon the scene.

So far, we are on the firm, if rather narrow, ground of ascertained truth. But nobody has ever known exactly what took place later that night. The testimony of the sentries and others seems, however, to prove that the Embassy was empty of company, and shut up for the night in the usual way by two A.M. The Ambassador was seen to go to his room, still wearing the insignia of his rank, and shut the door. Some say he locked it, which was against his custom. Others maintain that they heard music of a rustic kind, such as shepherds play, later that night in the courtyard under the Ambassador's window. A washer-woman, who was kept awake by toothache, said that she saw a man's figure, wrapped in a cloak or dressing gown, come out upon the balcony. Then, she said, a woman, much muffled, but apparently of the peasant class, was drawn up by means of a rope which the man let down to her on to the balcony. There, the washer-woman said, they embraced passionately 'like lovers', and went into the room together, drawing the curtains so that no more could be seen.

Next morning, the Duke, as we must now call him, was found by his secretaries sunk in profound slumber amid bed clothes that were much tumbled. The room was in some disorder, his coronet having rolled on the floor, and his cloak and garter being flung all of a heap on a chair. The table was littered with papers. No suspicion was felt at first, as the fatigues of the night had been great. But when afternoon came and he still slept, a doctor was summoned. He applied remedies which had been used on the previous occasion, plasters, nettles, emetics, etc., but without success. Orlando slept on. His secretaries then thought it their duty to examine the papers on the table. Many were scribbled over with poetry, in which frequent mention was made of an oak tree. There were also various state papers and others of a private nature concerning the management of his estates in England. But at length they came upon a document of far greater significance. It was nothing less, indeed, than a deed of marriage, drawn up, signed, and witnessed between his Lordship, Orlando, Knight of the Garter, etc., etc., etc., and Rosina Pepita, a dancer, father unknown, but reputed a gipsy, mother also unknown but reputed a seller of old iron in the market-place over against the Galata Bridge. The secretaries looked at each other in dismay. And still Orlando slept. Morning and evening they watched him, but, save that his breathing was regular and his cheeks still flushed their habitual deep rose, he gave no sign of life. Whatever science or ingenuity could do to waken him they did. But still he slept.

On the seventh day of his trance (Thursday, May the 10th) the first shot was fired of that terrible and bloody insurrection of which Lieutenant Brigge had detected the first symptoms. The Turks rose against the Sultan, set fire to the town, and put every foreigner they could find, either to the sword or to the bastinado. A few English managed to escape; but, as might have been expected, the gentlemen of the British Embassy preferred to die in defence of their red boxes, or, in extreme cases, to swallow bunches of keys rather than let them fall into the hands of the Infidel. The rioters broke into Orlando's room, but seeing him stretched to all appearances dead they left him untouched, and only robbed him of his coronet and the robes of the Garter.

And now again obscurity descends, and would indeed that it were deeper! Would, we almost have it in our hearts to exclaim, that it were so deep that we could see nothing whatever through its opacity! Would that we might here take the pen and write Finis to our work! Would that we might spare the reader what is to come and say to him in so many words, Orlando died and was buried. But here, alas, Truth, Candour, and Honesty, the austere Gods who keep watch and ward by the inkpot of the biographer, cry No! Putting their silver trumpets to their lips they demand in one blast, Truth! And again they cry Truth! and sounding yet a third time in concert they peal forth, The Truth and nothing but the Truth!

At which--Heaven be praised! for it affords us a breathing space--the doors gently open, as if a breath of the gentlest and holiest zephyr had wafted them apart, and three figures enter. First, comes our Lady of Purity; whose brows are bound with fillets of the whitest lamb's wool; whose hair is as an avalanche of the driven snow; and in whose hand reposes the white quill of a virgin goose. Following her, but with a statelier step, comes our Lady of Chastity; on whose brow is set like a turret of burning but unwasting fire a diadem of icicles; her eyes are pure stars, and her fingers, if they touch you, freeze you to the bone. Close behind her, sheltering indeed in the shadow of her more stately sisters, comes our Lady of Modesty, frailest and fairest of the three; whose face is only shown as the young moon shows when it is thin and sickle shaped and half hidden among clouds. Each advances towards the centre of the room where Orlando still lies sleeping; and with gestures at once appealing and commanding, OUR LADY OF PURITY speaks first:

'I am the guardian of the sleeping fawn; the snow is dear to me; and the moon rising; and the silver sea. With my robes I cover the speckled hen's eggs and the brindled sea shell; I cover vice and poverty. On all things frail or dark or doubtful, my veil descends. Wherefore, speak not, reveal not. Spare, O spare!'

Here the trumpets peal forth.

'Purity Avaunt! Begone Purity!'

Then OUR LADY OF CHASTITY speaks:

'I am she whose touch freezes and whose glance turns to stone. I have stayed the star in its dancing, and the wave as it falls. The highest Alps are my dwelling place; and when I walk, the lightnings flash in my hair; where my eyes fall, they kill. Rather than let Orlando wake, I will freeze him to the bone. Spare, O spare!'

Here the trumpets peal forth.

'Chastity Avaunt! Begone Chastity!'

Then OUR LADY OF MODESTY speaks, so low that one can hardly hear:

'I am she that men call Modesty. Virgin I am and ever shall be. Not for me the fruitful fields and the fertile vineyard. Increase is odious to me; and when the apples burgeon or the flocks breed, I run, I run; I let my mantle fall. My hair covers my eyes. I do not see. Spare, O spare!'

Again the trumpets peal forth:

'Modesty Avaunt! Begone Modesty!'

With gestures of grief and lamentation the three sisters now join hands and dance slowly, tossing their veils and singing as they go:

'Truth come not out from your horrid den. Hide deeper, fearful Truth. For you flaunt in the brutal gaze of the sun things that were better unknown and undone; you unveil the shameful; the dark you make clear, Hide! Hide! Hide!'

Here they make as if to cover Orlando with their draperies. The trumpets, meanwhile, still blare forth,

'The Truth and nothing but the Truth.'

At this the Sisters try to cast their veils over the mouths of the trumpets so as to muffle them, but in vain, for now all the trumpets blare forth together,

'Horrid Sisters, go!'

The sisters become distracted and wail in unison, still circling and flinging their veils up and down.

'It has not always been so! But men want us no longer; the women detest us. We go; we go. I (PURITY SAYS THIS) to the hen roost. I (CHASTITY SAYS THIS) to the still unravished heights of Surrey. I (MODESTY SAYS THIS) to any cosy nook where there are ivy and curtains in plenty.'

'For there, not here (all speak together joining hands and making gestures of farewell and despair towards the bed where Orlando lies sleeping) dwell still in nest and boudoir, office and lawcourt those who love us; those who honour us, virgins and city men; lawyers and doctors; those who prohibit; those who deny; those who reverence without knowing why; those who praise without understanding; the still very numerous (Heaven be praised) tribe of the respectable; who prefer to see not; desire to know not; love the darkness; those still worship us, and with reason; for we have given them Wealth, Prosperity, Comfort, Ease. To them we go, you we leave. Come, Sisters, come! This is no place for us here.'

They retire in haste, waving their draperies over their heads, as if to shut out something that they dare not look upon and close the door behind them.

We are, therefore, now left entirely alone in the room with the sleeping Orlando and the trumpeters. The trumpeters, ranging themselves side by side in order, blow one terrific blast:--

'THE TRUTH!

at which Orlando woke.

He stretched himself. He rose. He stood upright in complete nakedness before us, and while the trumpets pealed Truth! Truth! Truth! we have no choice left but confess--he was a woman.

***

The sound of the trumpets died away and Orlando stood stark naked. No human being, since the world began, has ever looked more ravishing. His form combined in one the strength of a man and a woman's grace. As he stood there, thc silver trumpets prolonged their note, as if reluctant to leave the lovely sight which their blast had called forth; and Chastity, Purity, and Modesty, inspired, no doubt, by Curiosity, peeped in at the door and threw a garment like a towel at the naked form which, unfortunately, fell short by several inches. Orlando looked himself up and down in a long looking-glass, without showing any signs of discomposure, and went, presumably, to his bath.

We may take advantage of this pause in the narrative to make certain statements. Orlando had become a woman--there is no denying it. But in every other respect, Orlando remained precisely as he had been. The change of sex, though it altered their future, did nothing whatever to alter their identity. Their faces remained, as their portraits prove, practically the same. His memory--but in future we must, for convention's sake, say 'her' for 'his,' and 'she' for 'he'--her memory then, went back through all the events of her past life without encountering any obstacle. Some slight haziness there may have been, as if a few dark drops had fallen into the clear pool of memory; certain things had become a little dimmed; but that was all. The change seemed to have been accomplished painlessly and completely and in such a way that Orlando herself showed no surprise at it. Many people, taking this into account, and holding that such a change of sex is against nature, have been at great pains to prove (1) that Orlando had always been a woman, (2) that Orlando is at this moment a man. Let biologists and psychologists determine. It is enough for us to state the simple fact; Orlando was a man till the age of thirty; when he became a woman and has remained so ever since.

But let other pens treat of sex and sexuality; we quit such odious subjects as soon as we can. Orlando had now washed, and dressed herself in those Turkish coats and trousers which can be worn indifferently by either sex; and was forced to consider her position. That it was precarious and embarrassing in the extreme must be the first thought of every reader who has followed her story with sympathy. Young, noble, beautiful, she had woken to find herself in a position than which we can conceive none more delicate for a young lady of rank. We should not have blamed her had she rung the bell, screamed, or fainted. But Orlando showed no such signs of perturbation. All her actions were deliberate in the extreme,. and might indeed have been thought to show tokens of premeditation. First, she carefully examined the papers on the table; took such as seemed to be written in poetry, and secreted them in her bosom; next she called her Seleuchi hound, which had never left her bed all these days, though half famished with hunger, fed and combed him; then stuck a pair of pistols in her belt; finally wound about her person several strings of emeralds and pearls of the finest orient which had formed part of her Ambassadorial wardrobe. This done, she leant out of the window, gave one low whistle, and descended the shattered and bloodstained staircase, now strewn with the litter of waste-paper baskets, treaties, despatches, seals, sealing wax, etc., and so entered the courtyard. There, in the shadow of a giant fig tree, waited an old gipsy on a donkey. He led another by the bridle. Orlando swung her leg over it; and thus, attended by a lean dog, riding a donkey, in company of a gipsy, the Ambassador of Great Britain at the Court of the Sultan left Constantinople.

They rode for several days and nights and met with a variety of adventures, some at the hands of men, some at the hands of nature, in all of which Orlando acquitted herself with courage. Within a week they reached the high ground outside Broussa, which was then the chief camping ground of the gipsy tribe to which Orlando had allied herself. Often she had looked at those mountains from her balcony at the Embassy; often had longed to be there; and to find oneself where one has longed to be always, to a reflective mind, gives food for thought. For some time, however, she was too well pleased with the change to spoil it by thinking. The pleasure of having no documents to seal or sign, no flourishes to make, no calls to pay, was enough. The gipsies followed the grass; when it was grazed down, on they moved again. She washed in streams if she washed at all; no boxes, red, blue, or green, were presented to her; there was not a key, let alone a golden key, in the whole camp; as for 'visiting', the word was unknown. She milked the goats; she collected brushwood; she stole a hen's egg now and then, but always put a coin or a pearl in place of it; she herded cattle; she stripped vines; she trod the grape; she filled the goat-skin and drank from it; and when she remembered how, at about this time of day, she should have been making the motions of drinking and smoking over an empty coffee-cup and a pipe which lacked tobacco, she laughed aloud, cut herself another hunch of bread, and begged for a puff from old Rustum's pipe, filled though it was with cow dung.

The gipsies, with whom it is obvious that she must have been in secret communication before the revolution, seem to have looked upon her as one of themselves (which is always the highest compliment a people can pay), and her dark hair and dark complexion bore out the belief that she was, by birth, one of them and had been snatched by an English Duke from a nut tree when she was a baby and taken to that barbarous land where people live in houses because they are too feeble and diseased to stand the open air. Thus, though in many ways inferior to them, they were willing to help her to become more like them; taught her their arts of cheese-making and basket-weaving, their science of stealing and bird-snaring, and were even prepared to consider letting her marry among them.

But Orlando had contracted in England some of the customs or diseases (whatever you choose to consider them) which cannot, it seems, be expelled. One evening, when they were all sitting round the camp fire and the sunset was blazing over the Thessalian hills, Orlando exclaimed:

'How good to eat!'

(The gipsies have no word for 'beautiful'. This is the nearest.)

All the young men and women burst out laughing uproariously. The sky good to eat, indeed! The elders, however, who had seen more of foreigners than they had, became suspicious. They noticed that Orlando often sat for whole hours doing nothing whatever, except look here and then there; they would come upon her on some hill-top staring straight in front of her, no matter whether the goats were grazing or straying. They began to suspect that she had other beliefs than their own, and the older men and women thought it probable that she had fallen into the clutches of the vilest and cruellest among all the Gods, which is Nature. Nor were they far wrong. The English disease, a love of Nature, was inborn in her, and here, where Nature was so much larger and more powerful than in England, she fell into its hands as she had never done before. The malady is too well known, and has been, alas, too often described to need describing afresh, save very briefly. There were mountains; there were valleys; there were streams. She climbed the mountains; roamed the valleys; sat on the banks of the streams. She likened the hills to ramparts, to the breasts of doves, and the flanks of kine. She compared the flowers to enamel and the turf to Turkey rugs worn thin. Trees were withered hags, and sheep were grey boulders. Everything, in fact, was something else. She found the tarn on the mountain-top and almost threw herself in to seek the wisdom she thought lay hid there; and when, from the mountain-top, she beheld far off, across the Sea of Marmara, the plains of Greece, and made out (her eyes were admirable) the Acropolis with a white streak or two, which must, she thought, be the Parthenon, her soul expanded with her eyeballs, and she prayed that she might share the majesty of the hills, know the serenity of the plains, etc. etc., as all such believers do. Then, looking down, the red hyacinth, the purple iris wrought her to cry out in ecstasy at the goodness, the beauty of nature; raising her eyes again, she beheld the eagle soaring, and imagined its raptures and made them her own. Returning home, she saluted each star, each peak, and each watch-fire as if they signalled to her alone; and at last, when she flung herself upon her mat in the gipsies' tent, she could not help bursting out again, How good to eat! How good to eat! (For it is a curious fact that though human beings have such imperfect means of communication, that they can only say 'good to eat' when they mean 'beautiful' and the other way about, they will yet endure ridicule and misunderstanding rather than keep any experience to themselves.) All the young gipsies laughed. But Rustum el Sadi, the old man who had brought Orlando out of Constantinople on his donkey, sat silent. He had a nose like a scimitar; his cheeks were furrowed as if from the age-long descent of iron hail; he was brown and keen-eyed, and as he sat tugging at his hookah he observed Orlando narrowly. He had the deepest suspicion that her God was Nature. One day he found her in tears. Interpreting this to mean that her God had punished her, he told her that he was not surprised. He showed her the fingers of his left hand, withered by the frost; he showed her his right foot, crushed where a rock had fallen. This, he said, was what her God did to men. When she said, 'But so beautiful', using the English word, he shook his head; and when she repeated it he was angry. He saw that she did not believe what he believed, and that was enough, wise and ancient as he was, to enrage him.

This difference of opinion disturbed Orlando, who had been perfectly happy until now. She began to think, was Nature beautiful or cruel; and then she asked herself what this beauty was; whether it was in things themselves, or only in herself; so she went on to the nature of reality, which led her to truth, which in its turn led to Love, Friendship, Poetry (as in the days on the high mound at home); which meditations, since she could impart no word of them, made her long, as she had never longed before, for pen and ink.

'Oh! if only I could write!' she cried (for she had the odd conceit of those who write that words written are shared). She had no ink; and but little paper. But she made ink from berries and wine; and finding a few margins and blank spaces in the manuscript of 'The Oak Tree', managed by writing a kind of shorthand, to describe the scenery in a long, blank version poem, and to carry on a dialogue with herself about this Beauty and Truth concisely enough. This kept her extremely happy for hours on end. But the gipsies became suspicious. First, they noticed that she was less adept than before at milking and cheese-making; next, she often hesitated before replying; and once a gipsy boy who had been asleep, woke in a terror feeling her eyes upon him. Sometimes this constraint would be felt by the whole tribe, numbering some dozens of grown men and women. It sprang from the sense they had (and their senses are very sharp and much in advance of their vocabulary) that whatever they were doing crumbled like ashes in their hands. An old woman making a basket, a boy skinning a sheep, would be singing or crooning contentedly at their work, when Orlando would come into the camp, fling herself down by the fire and gaze into the flames. She need not even look at them, and yet they felt, here is someone who doubts; (we make a rough-and-ready translation from the gipsy language) here is someone who does not do the thing for the sake of doing; nor looks for looking's sake; here is someone who believes neither in sheep-skin nor basket; but sees (here they looked apprehensively about the tent) something else. Then a vague but most unpleasant feeling would begin to work in the boy and in the old woman. They broke their withys; they cut their fingers. A great rage filled them. They wished Orlando would leave the tent and never come near them again. Yet she was of a cheerful and willing disposition, they owned; and one of her pearls was enough to buy the finest herd of goats in Broussa.

Slowly, she began to feel that there was some difference between her and the gipsies which made her hesitate sometimes to marry and settle down among them for ever. At first she tried to account for it by saying that she came of an ancient and civilized race, whereas these gipsies were an ignorant people, not much better than savages. One night when they were questioning her about England she could not help with some pride describing the house where she was born, how it had 365 bedrooms and had been in the possession of her family for four or five hundred years. Her ancestors were earls, or even dukes, she added. At this she noticed again that the gipsies were uneasy; but not angry as before when she had praised the beauty of nature. Now they were courteous, but concerned as people of fine breeding are when a stranger has been made to reveal his low birth or poverty. Rustum followed her out of the tent alone and said that she need not mind if her father were a Duke, and possessed all the bedrooms and furniture that she described. They would none of them think the worse of her for that. Then she was seized with a shame that she had never felt before. It was clear that Rustum and the other gipsies thought a descent of four or five hundred years only the meanest possible. Their own families went back at least two or three thousand years. To the gipsy whose ancestors had built the Pyramids centuries before Christ was born, the genealogy of Howards and Plantagenets was no better and no worse than that of the Smiths and the Joneses: both were negligible. Moreover, where the shepherd boy had a lineage of such antiquity, there was nothing specially memorable or desirable in ancient birth; vagabonds and beggars all shared it. And then, though he was too courteous to speak openly, it was clear that the gipsy thought that there was no more vulgar ambition than to possess bedrooms by the hundred (they were on top of a hill as they spoke; it was night; the mountains rose around them) when the whole earth is ours. Looked at from the gipsy point of view, a Duke, Orlando understood, was nothing but a profiteer or robber who snatched land and money from people who rated these things of little worth, and could think of nothing better to do than to build three hundred and sixty-five bedrooms when one was enough, and none was even better than one. She could not deny that her ancestors had accumulated field after field; house after house; honour after honour; yet had none of them been saints or heroes, or great benefactors of the human race. Nor could she counter the argument (Rustum was too much of a gentleman to press it, but she understood) that any man who did now what her ancestors had done three or four hundred years ago would be denounced--and by her own family most loudly--for a vulgar upstart, an adventurer, a nouveau riche.

She sought to answer such arguments by the familiar if oblique method of finding the gipsy life itself rude and barbarous; and so, in a short time, much bad blood was bred between them. Indeed, such differences of opinion are enough to cause bloodshed and revolution. Towns have been sacked for less, and a million martyrs have suffered at the stake rather than yield an inch upon any of the points here debated. No passion is stronger in the breast of man than the desire to make others believe as he believes. Nothing so cuts at the root of his happiness and fills him with rage as the sense that another rates low what he prizes high. Whigs and Tories, Liberal party and Labour party--for what do they battle except their own prestige? It is not love of truth but desire to prevail that sets quarter against quarter and makes parish desire the downfall of parish. Each seeks peace of mind and subserviency rather than the triumph of truth and the exaltation of virtue--but these moralities belong, and should be left to the historian, since they are as dull as ditch water.

'Four hundred and seventy-six bedrooms mean nothing to them,' sighed Orlando.

'She prefers a sunset to a flock of goats,' said the gipsies.

What was to be done, Orlando could not think. To leave the gipsies and become once more an Ambassador seemed to her intolerable. But it was equally impossible to remain for ever where there was neither ink nor writing paper, neither reverence for the Talbots nor respect for a multiplicity of bedrooms. So she was thinking, one fine morning on the slopes of Mount Athos, when minding her goats. And then Nature, in whom she trusted, either played her a trick or worked a miracle--again, opinions differ too much for it to be possible to say which. Orlando was gazing rather disconsolately at the steep hill-side in front of her. It was now midsummer, and if we must compare the landscape to anything, it would have been to a dry bone; to a sheep's skeleton; to a gigantic skull picked white by a thousand vultures. The heat was intense, and the little fig tree under which Orlando lay only served to print patterns of fig-leaves upon her light burnous.

Suddenly a shadow, though there was nothing to cast a shadow, appeared on the bald mountain-side opposite. It deepened quickly and soon a green hollow showed where there had been barren rock before. As she looked, the hollow deepened and widened, and a great park-like space opened in the flank of the hill. Within, she could see an undulating and grassy lawn; she could see oak trees dotted here and there; she could see the thrushes hopping among the branches. She could see the deer stepping delicately from shade to shade, and could even hear the hum of insects and the gentle sighs and shivers of a summer's day in England. After she had gazed entranced for some time, snow began falling; soon the whole landscape was covered and marked with violet shades instead of yellow sunlight. Now she saw heavy carts coming along the roads, laden with tree trunks, which they were taking, she knew, to be sawn for firewood; and then appeared the roofs and belfries and towers and courtyards of her own home. The snow was falling steadily, and she could now hear the slither and flop which it made as it slid down the roof and fell to the ground. The smoke went up from a thousand chimneys. All was so clear and minute that she could see a Daw pecking for worms in the snow. Then, gradually, the violet shadows deepened and closed over the carts and the lawns and the great house itself. All was swallowed up. Now there was nothing left of the grassy hollow, and instead of the green lawns was only the blazing hill-side which a thousand vultures seemed to have picked bare. At this, she burst into a passion of tears, and striding back to the gipsies' camp, told them that she must sail for England the very next day.

It was happy for her that she did so. Already the young men had plotted her death. Honour, they said, demanded it, for she did not think as they did. Yet they would have been sorry to cut her throat; and welcomed the news of her departure. An English merchant ship, as luck would have it, was already under sail in the harbour about to return to England; and Orlando, by breaking off another pearl from her necklace, not only paid her passage but had some banknotes left over in her wallet. These she would have liked to present to the gipsies. But they despised wealth she knew; and she had to content herself with embraces, which on her part were sincere.

CHAPTER 4.

With some of the guineas left from the sale of the tenth pearl on her string, Orlando bought herself a complete outfit of such clothes as women then wore, and it was in the dress of a young Englishwoman of rank that she now sat on the deck of the "Enamoured Lady". It is a strange fact, but a true one, that up to this moment she had scarcely given her sex a thought. Perhaps the Turkish trousers which she had hitherto worn had done something to distract her thoughts; and the gipsy women, except in one or two important particulars, differ very little from the gipsy men. At any rate, it was not until she felt the coil of skirts about her legs and the Captain offered, with the greatest politeness, to have an awning spread for her on deck, that she realized with a start the penalties and the privileges of her position. But that start was not of the kind that might have been expected.

It was not caused, that is to say, simply and solely by the thought of her chastity and how she could preserve it. In normal circumstances a lovely young woman alone would have thought of nothing else; the whole edifice of female government is based on that foundation stone; chastity is their jewel, their centrepiece, which they run mad to protect, and die when ravished of. But if one has been a man for thirty years or so, and an Ambassador into the bargain, if one has held a Queen in one's arms and one or two other ladies, if report be true, of less exalted rank, if one has married a Rosina Pepita, and so on, one does not perhaps give such a very great start about that. Orlando's start was of a very complicated kind, and not to be summed up in a trice. Nobody, indeed, ever accused her of being one of those quick wits who run to the end of things in a minute. It took her the entire length of the voyage to moralize out the meaning of her start, and so, at her own pace, we will follow her.

'Lord,' she thought, when she had recovered from her start, stretching herself out at length under her awning, 'this is a pleasant, lazy way of life, to be sure. But,' she thought, giving her legs a kick, 'these skirts are plaguey things to have about one's heels. Yet the stuff (flowered paduasoy) is the loveliest in the world. Never have I seen my own skin (here she laid her hand on her knee) look to such advantage as now. Could I, however, leap overboard and swim in clothes like these? No! Therefore, I should have to trust to the protection of a blue-jacket. Do I object to that? Now do I?' she wondered, here encountering the first knot in the smooth skein of her argument.

Dinner came before she had untied it, and then it was the Captain himself--Captain Nicholas Benedict Bartolus, a sea-captain of distinguished aspect, who did it for her as he helped her to a slice of corned beef.

'A little of the fat, Ma'm?' he asked. 'Let me cut you just the tiniest little slice the size of your fingernail.' At those words a delicious tremor ran through her frame. Birds sang; the torrents rushed. It recalled the feeling of indescribable pleasure with which she had first seen Sasha, hundreds of years ago. Then she had pursued, now she fled. Which is the greater ecstasy? The man's or the woman's? And are they not perhaps the same? No, she thought, this is the most delicious (thanking the Captain but refusing), to refuse, and see him frown. Well, she would, if he wished it, have the very thinnest, smallest shiver in the world. This was the most delicious of all, to yield and see him smile. 'For nothing,' she thought, regaining her couch on deck, and continuing the argument, 'is more heavenly than to resist and to yield; to yield and to resist. Surely it throws the spirit into such a rapture as nothing else can. So that I'm not sure', she continued, 'that I won't throw myself overboard, for the mere pleasure of being rescued by a blue-jacket after all.'

(It must be remembered that she was like a child entering into possession of a pleasaunce or toy cupboard; her arguments would not commend themselves to mature women, who have had the run of it all their lives.)

'But what used we young fellows in the cockpit of the "Marie Rose" to say about a woman who threw herself overboard for the pleasure of being rescued by a blue-jacket?' she said. 'We had a word for them. Ah! I have it...' (But we must omit that word; it was disrespectful in the extreme and passing strange on a lady's lips.) 'Lord! Lord! she cried again at the conclusion of her thoughts, 'must I then begin to respect the opinion of the other sex, however monstrous I think it? If I wear skirts, if I can't swim, if I have to be rescued by a blue-jacket, by God!' she cried, 'I must!' Upon which a gloom fell over her. Candid by nature, and averse to all kinds of equivocation, to tell lies bored her. It seemed to her a roundabout way of going to work. Yet, she reflected, the flowered paduasoy--the pleasure of being rescued by a blue-jacket--if these were only to be obtained by roundabout ways, roundabout one must go, she supposed. She remembered how, as a young man, she had insisted that women must be obedient, chaste, scented, and exquisitely apparelled. 'Now I shall have to pay in my own person for those desires,' she reflected; 'for women are not (judging by my own short experience of the sex) obedient, chaste, scented, and exquisitely apparelled by nature. They can only attain these graces, without which they may enjoy none of the delights of life, by the most tedious discipline. There's the hairdressing,' she thought, 'that alone will take an hour of my morning, there's looking in the looking-glass, another hour; there's staying and lacing; there's washing and powdering; there's changing from silk to lace and from lace to paduasoy; there's being chaste year in year out...' Here she tossed her foot impatiently, and showed an inch or two of calf. A sailor on the mast, who happened to look down at the moment, started so violently that he missed his footing and only saved himself by the skin of his teeth. 'If the sight of my ankles means death to an honest fellow who, no doubt, has a wife and family to support, I must, in all humanity, keep them covered,' Orlando thought. Yet her legs were among her chiefest beauties. And she fell to thinking what an odd pass we have come to when all a woman's beauty has to be kept covered lest a sailor may fall from a mast-head. 'A pox on them!' she said, realizing for the first time what, in other circumstances, she would have been taught as a child, that is to say, the sacred responsibilities of womanhood.

@'And that's the last oath I shall ever be able to swear,' she thought; 'once I set foot on English soil. And I shall never be able to crack a man over the head, or tell him he lies in his teeth, or draw my sword and run him through the body, or sit among my peers, or wear a coronet, or walk in procession, or sentence a man to death, or lead an army, or prance down Whitehall on a charger, or wear seventy-two different medals on my breast. All I can do, once I set foot on English soil, is to pour out tea and ask my lords how they like it. D'you take sugar? D'you take cream?' And mincing out the words, she was horrified to perceive how low an opinion she was forming of the other sex, the manly, to which it had once been her pride to belong--'To fall from a mast-head', she thought, 'because you see a woman's ankles; to dress up like a Guy Fawkes and parade the streets, so that women may praise you; to deny a woman teaching lest she may laugh at you; to be the slave of the frailest chit in petticoats. and yet to go about as if you were the Lords of creation.--Heavens!' she thought, 'what fools they make of us--what fools we are!' And here it would seem from some ambiguity in her terms that she was censuring both sexes equally, as if she belonged to neither; and indeed, for the time being, she seemed to vacillate; she was man; she was woman; she knew the secrets, shared the weaknesses of each. It was a most bewildering and whirligig state of mind to be in. The comforts of ignorance seemed utterly denied her. She was a feather blown on the gale. Thus it is no great wonder, as she pitted one sex against the other, and found each alternately full of the most deplorable infirmities, and was not sure to which she belonged--it was no great wonder that she was about to cry out that she would return to Turkey and become a gipsy again when the anchor fell with a great splash into the sea; the sails came tumbling on deck, and she perceived (so sunk had she been in thought that she had seen nothing for several days) that the ship was anchored off the coast of Italy. The Captain at once sent to ask the honour of her company ashore with him in the longboat.

When she returned the next morning, she stretched herself on her couch under the awning and arranged her draperies with the greatest decorum about her ankles.

'Ignorant and poor as we are compared with the other sex,' she thought, continuing the sentence which she had left unfinished the other day, 'armoured with every weapon as they are, while they debar us even from a knowledge of the alphabet' (and from these opening words it is plain that something had happened during the night to give her a push towards the female sex, for she was speaking more as a woman speaks than as a man, yet with a sort of content after all), 'still--they fall from the mast-head.' Here she gave a great yawn and fell asleep. When she woke, the ship was sailing before a fair breeze so near the shore that towns on the cliffs' edge seemed only kept from slipping into the water by the interposition of some great rock or the twisted roots of some ancient olive tree. The scent of oranges wafted from a million trees, heavy with the fruit, reached her on deck. A score of blue dolphins, twisting their tails, leapt high now and again into the air. Stretching her arms out (arms, she had learnt already, have no such fatal effects as legs), she thanked Heaven that she was not prancing down Whitehall on a war-horse, nor even sentencing a man to death. 'Better is it', she thought, 'to be clothed with poverty and ignorance, which are the dark garments of the female sex; better to leave the rule and discipline of the world to others; better be quit of martial ambition, the love of power, and all the other manly desires if so one can more fully enjoy the most exalted raptures known to the humane spirit, which are', she said aloud, as her habit was when deeply moved, 'contemplation, solitude, love.'

'Praise God that I'm a woman!' she cried, and was about to run into extreme folly--than which none is more distressing in woman or man either--of being proud of her sex, when she paused over the singular word, which, for all we can do to put it in its place, has crept in at the end of the last sentence: Love. 'Love,' said Orlando. Instantly--such is its impetuosity--love took a human shape--such is its pride. For where other thoughts are content to remain abstract, nothing will satisfy this one but to put on flesh and blood, mantilla and petticoats, hose and jerkin. And as all Orlando's loves had been women, now, through the culpable laggardry of the human frame to adapt itself to convention, though she herself was a woman, it was still a woman she loved; and if the consciousness of being of the same sex had any effect at all, it was to quicken and deepen those feelings which she had had as a man. For now a thousand hints and mysteries became plain to her that were then dark. Now, the obscurity, which divides the sexes and lets linger innumerable impurities in its gloom, was removed, and if there is anything in what the poet says about truth and beauty, this affection gained in beauty what it lost in falsity. At last, she cried, she knew Sasha as she was, and in the ardour of this discovery, and in the pursuit of all those treasures which were now revealed, she was so rapt and enchanted that it was as if a cannon ball had exploded at her ear when a man's voice said, 'Permit me, Madam,' a man's hand raised her to her feet; and the fingers of a man with a three-masted sailing ship tattooed on the middle finger pointed to the horizon.

'The cliffs of England, Ma'am,' said the Captain, and he raised the hand which had pointed at the sky to the salute. Orlando now gave a second start, even more violent than the first.

'Christ Jesus!' she cried.

Happily, the sight of her native land after long absence excused both start and exclamation, or she would have been hard put to it to explain to Captain Bartolus the raging and conflicting emotions which now boiled within her. How tell him that she, who now trembled on his arm, had been a Duke and an Ambassador? How explain to him that she, who had been lapped like a lily in folds of paduasoy, had hacked heads off, and lain with loose women among treasure sacks in the holds of pirate ships on summer nights when the tulips were abloom and the bees buzzing off Wapping Old Stairs? Not even to herself could she explain the giant start she gave, as the resolute right hand of the sea-captain indicated the cliffs of the British Islands.

'To refuse and to yield,' she murmured, 'how delightful; to pursue and conquer, how august; to perceive and to reason, how sublime.' Not one of these words so coupled together seemed to her wrong; nevertheless, as the chalky cliffs loomed nearer, she felt culpable; dishonoured; unchaste, which, for one who had never given the matter a thought, was strange. Closer and closer they drew, till the samphire gatherers, hanging half-way down the cliff, were plain to the naked eye. And watching them, she felt, scampering up and down within her, like some derisive ghost who in another instant will pick up her skirts and flaunt out of sight, Sasha the lost, Sasha the memory, whose reality she had proved just now so surprisingly--Sasha, she felt, mopping and mowing and making all sorts of disrespectful gestures towards the cliffs and the samphire gatherers; and when the sailors began chanting, 'So good-bye and adieu to you, Ladies of Spain', the words echoed in Orlando's sad heart, and she felt that however much landing there meant comfort, meant opulence, meant consequence and state (for she would doubtless pick up some noble Prince and reign, his consort, over half Yorkshire), still, if it meant conventionality, meant slavery, meant deceit, meant denying her love, fettering her limbs, pursing her lips, and restraining her tongue, then she would turn about with the ship and set sail once more for the gipsies.

Among the hurry of these thoughts, however, there now rose, like a dome of smooth, white marble, something which, whether fact or fancy, was so impressive to her fevered imagination that she settled upon it as one has seen a swarm of vibrant dragonflies alight, with apparent satisfaction, upon the glass bell which shelters some tender vegetable. The form of it, by the hazard of fancy, recalled that earliest, most persistent memory--the man with the big forehead in Twitchett's sitting-room, the man who sat writing, or rather looking, but certainly not at her, for he never seemed to see her poised there in all her finery, lovely boy though she must have been, she could not deny it--and whenever she thought of him, the thought spread round it, like the risen moon on turbulent waters, a sheet of silver calm. Now her hand went to her bosom (the other was still in the Captain's keeping), where the pages of her poem were hidden safe. It might have been a talisman that she kept there. The distraction of sex, which hers was, and what it meant, subsided; she thought now only of the glory of poetry, and the great lines of Marlowe, Shakespeare, Ben Jonson, Milton began booming and reverberating, as if a golden clapper beat against a golden bell in the cathedral tower which was her mind. The truth was that the image of the marble dome which her eyes had first discovered so faintly that it suggested a poet's forehead and thus started a flock of irrelevant ideas, was no figment, but a reality; and as the ship advanced down the Thames before a favouring gale, the image with all its associations gave place to the truth, and revealed itself as nothing more and nothing less than the dome of a vast cathedral rising among a fretwork of white spires.

'St Paul's,' said Captain Bartolus, who stood by her side. 'The Tower of London,' he continued. 'Greenwich Hospital, erected in memory of Queen Mary by her husband, his late majesty, William the Third. Westminster Abbey. The Houses of Parliament.' As he spoke, each of these famous buildings rose to view. It was a fine September morning. A myriad of little water-craft plied from bank to bank. Rarely has a gayer, or more interesting, spectacle presented itself to the gaze of a returned traveller. Orlando hung over the prow, absorbed in wonder. Her eyes had been used too long to savages and nature not to be entranced by these urban glories. That, then, was the dome of St Paul's which Mr Wren had built during her absence. Near by, a shock of golden hair burst from a pillar--Captain Bartolus was at her side to inform her that that was the Monument; there had been a plague and a fire during her absence, he said. Do what she could to restrain them, the tears came to her eyes, until, remembering that it is becoming in a woman to weep, she let them flow. Here, she thought, had been the great carnival. Here, where the waves slapped briskly, had stood the Royal Pavilion. Here she had first met Sasha. About here (she looked down into the sparkling waters) one had been used to see the frozen bumboat woman with her apples on her lap. All that splendour and corruption was gone. Gone, too, was the dark night, the monstrous downpour, the violent surges of the flood. Here, where yellow icebergs had raced circling with a crew of terror-stricken wretches on top, a covey of swans floated, orgulous, undulant, superb. London itself had completely changed since she had last seen it. Then, she remembered, it had been a huddle of little black, beetle-browed houses. The heads of rebels had grinned on pikes at Temple Bar. The cobbled pavements had reeked of garbage and ordure. Now, as the ship sailed past Wapping, she caught glimpses of broad and orderly thoroughfares. Stately coaches drawn by teams of well-fed horses stood at the doors of houses whose bow windows, whose plate glass, whose polished knockers, testified to the wealth and modest dignity of the dwellers within. Ladies in flowered silk (she put the Captain's glass to her eye) walked on raised footpaths. Citizens in broidered coats took snuff at street corners under lamp-posts. She caught sight of a variety of painted signs swinging in the breeze and could form a rapid notion from what was painted on them of the tobacco, of the stuff, of the silk, of the gold, of the silver ware, of the gloves, of the perfumes, and of a thousand other articles which were sold within. Nor could she do more as the ship sailed to its anchorage by London Bridge than glance at coffee-house windows where, on balconies, since the weather was fine, a great number of decent citizens sat at ease, with china dishes in front of them, clay pipes by their sides, while one among them read from a news sheet, and was frequently interrupted by the laughter or the comments of the others. Were these taverns, were these wits, were these poets? she asked of Captain Bartolus, who obligingly informed her that even now--if she turned her head a little to the left and looked along the line of his first finger--so--they were passing the Cocoa Tree, where,--yes, there he was--one might see Mr Addison taking his coffee; the other two gentlemen--'there, Ma'am, a little to the right of the lamp-post, one of 'em humped, t'other much the same as you or me'--were Mr

Dryden and Mr Pope.' 'Sad dogs,' said the Captain, by which he meant that they were Papists, 'but men of parts, none the less,' he added, hurrying aft to superintend the arrangements for landing. (The Captain must have been mistaken, as a referencc to any textbook of literatnre will show; but the mistake was a kindly one, and so we let it stand.)

'Addison, Dryden, Pope,' Orlando repeated as if the words were an incantation. For one moment she saw the high mountains above Broussa, the next, she had set her foot upon her native shore.

***

But now Orlando was to learn how little the most tempestuous flutter of excitement avails against the iron countenance of the law; how harder than the stones of London Bridge it is, and than the lips of a cannon more severe. No sooner had she returned to her home in Blackfriars than she was made aware by a succession of Bow Street runners and other grave emissaries from the Law Courts that she was a party to three major suits which had been preferred against her during her absence, as well as innumerable minor litigations, some arising out of, others depending on them. The chief charges against her were (1) that she was dead, and therefore could not hold any property whatsoever; (2) that she was a woman, which amounts to much the same thing; (3) that she was an English Duke who had married one Rosina Pepita, a dancer; and had had by her three sons, which sons now declaring that their father was deceased, claimed that all his property descended to them. Such grave charges as these would, of course, take time and money to dispose of. All her estates were put in Chancery and her titles pronounced in abeyance while the suits were under litigation. Thus it was in a highly ambiguous condition, uncertain whether she was alive or dead, man or woman, Duke or nonentity, that she posted down to her country seat, where, pending the legal judgment, she had the Law's permission to reside in a state of incognito or incognita, as the case might turn out to be.

It was a fine evening in December when she arrived and the snow was falling and the violet shadows were slanting much as she had seen them from the hill-top at Broussa. The great house lay more like a town than a house, brown and blue, rose and purple in the snow, with all its chimneys smoking busily as if inspired with a life of their own. She could not restrain a cry as she saw it there tranquil and massive, couched upon the meadows. As the yellow coach entered the park and came bowling along the drive between the trees, the red deer raised their heads as if expectantly, and it was observed that instead of showing the timidity natural to their kind, they followed the coach and stood about the courtyard when it drew up. Some tossed their antlers, others pawed the ground as the step was let down and Orlando alighted. One, it is said, actually knelt in the snow before her. She had not time to reach her hand towards the knocker before both wings of the great door were flung open, and there, with lights and torches held above their heads, were Mrs Grimsditch, Mr Dupper, and a whole retinue of servants come to greet her. But the orderly procession was interrupted first by the impetuosity of Canute, the elk-hound, who threw himself with such ardour upon his mistress that he almost knocked her to the ground; next, by the agitation of Mrs Grimsditch, who, making as if to curtsey, was overcome with emotion and could do no more than gasp Milord! Milady! Milady! Milord! until Orlando comforted her with a hearty kiss upon both her cheeks. After that, Mr Dupper began to read from a parchment, but the dogs barking, the huntsmen winding their horns, and the stags, who had come into the courtyard in the confusion, baying the moon, not much progress was made, and the company dispersed within after crowding about their Mistress, and testifying in every way to their great joy at her return.

No one showed an instant's suspicion that Orlando was not the Orlando they had known. If any doubt there was in the human mind the action of the deer and the dogs would have been enough to dispel it, for the dumb creatures, as is well known, are far better judges both of identity and character than we are. Moreover, said Mrs Grimsditch, over her dish of china tea, to Mr Dupper that night, if her Lord was a Lady now, she had never seen a lovelier one, nor was there a penny piece to choose between them; one was as well-favoured as the other; they were as like as two peaches on one branch; which, said Mrs Grimsditch, becoming confidential, she had always had her suspicions (here she nodded her head very mysteriously), which it was no surprise to her (here she nodded her head very knowingly), and for her part, a very great comfort; for what with the towels wanting mending and the curtains in the chaplain's parlour being moth-eaten round the fringes, it was time they had a Mistress among them.

'And some little masters and mistresses to come after her,' Mr Dupper added, being privileged by virtue of his holy office to speak his mind on such delicate matters as these.

So, while the old servants gossiped in the servants' hall, Orlando took a silver candle in her hand and roamed once more through the halls, the galleries, the courts, the bedrooms; saw loom down at her again the dark visage of this Lord Keeper, that Lord Chamberlain, among her ancestors; sat now in this chair of state, now reclined on that canopy of delight; observed the arras, how it swayed; watched the huntsmen riding and Daphne flying; bathed her hand, as she had loved to do as a child, in the yellow pool of light which the moonlight made falling through the heraldic Leopard in the window; slid along the polished planks of the gallery, the other side of which was rough timber; touched this silk, that satin; fancied the carved dolphins swam; brushed her hair with King James' silver brush; buried her face in the potpourri, which was made as the Conqueror had taught them many hundred years ago and from the same roses; looked at the garden and imagined the sleeping crocuses, the dormant dahlias; saw the frail nymphs gleaming white in the snow and the great yew hedges, thick as a house, black behind them; saw the orangeries and the giant medlars;--all this she saw, and each sight and sound, rudely as we write it down, filled her heart with such a lust and balm of joy, that at length, tired out, she entered the Chapel and sank into the old red arm-chair in which her ancestors used to hear service. There she lit a cheroot ('twas a habit she had brought back from the East) and opened the Prayer Book.

It was a little book bound in velvet, stitched with gold, which had been held by Mary Queen of Scots on the scaffold, and the eye of faith could detect a brownish stain, said to be made of a drop of the Royal blood. But what pious thoughts it roused in Orlando, what evil passions it soothed asleep, who dare say, seeing that of all communions this with the deity is the most inscrutable? Novelist, poet, historian all falter with their hand on that door; nor does the believer himself enlighten us, for is he more ready to die than other people, or more eager to share his goods? Does he not keep as many maids and carriage horses as the rest? and yet with it all, holds a faith he says which should make goods a vanity and death desirable. In the Queen's prayerbook, along with the blood-stain, was also a lock of hair and a crumb of pastry; Orlando now added to these keepsakes a flake of tobacco, and so, reading and smoking, was moved by the humane jumble of them all--the hair, the pastry, the blood-stain, the tobacco--to such a mood of contemplation as gave her a reverent air suitable in the circumstances, though she had, it is said, no traffic with the usual God. Nothing, however, can be more arrogant, though nothing is commoner than to assume that of Gods there is only one, and of religions none but the speaker's. Orlando, it seemed, had a faith of her own. With all the religious ardour in the world, she now reflected upon her sins and the imperfections that had crept into her spiritual state. The letter S, she reflected, is the serpent in the poet's Eden. Do what she would there were still too many of these sinful reptiles in the first stanzas of 'The Oak Tree'. But 'S' was nothing, in her opinion, compared with the termination 'ing'. The present participle is the Devil himself, she thought, now that we are in the place for believing in Devils. To evade such temptations is the first duty of the poet, she concluded, for as the ear is the antechamber to the soul, poetry can adulterate and destroy more surely than lust or gunpowder. The poet's, then, is the highest office of all, she continued. His words reach where others fall short. A silly song of Shakespeare's has done more for the poor and the wicked than all the preachers and philanthropists in the world. No time, no devotion, can be too great, therefore, which makes the vehicle of our message less distorting. We must shape our words till they are the thinnest integument for our thoughts. Thoughts are divine, etc. Thus it is obvious that she was back in the confines of her own religion which time had only strengthened in her absence, and was rapidly acquiring the intolerance of belief.

'I am growing up,' she thought, taking her taper at last. 'I am losing some illusions,' she said, shutting Queen Mary's book, 'perhaps to acquire others,' and she descended among the tombs where the bones of her ancestors lay.

But even the bones of her ancestors, Sir Miles, Sir Gervase, and the rest, had lost something of their sanctity since Rustum el Sadi had waved his hand that night in the Asian mountains. Somehow the fact that only three or four hundred years ago these skeletons had been men with their way to make in the world like any modern upstart, and that they had made it by acquiring houses and offices, garters and ribbands, as any other upstart does, while poets, perhaps, and men of great mind and breeding had preferred the quietude of the country, for which choice they paid the penalty by extreme poverty, and now hawked broadsheets in the Strand, or herded sheep in the fields, filled her with remorse. She thought of the Egyptian pyramids and what bones lie beneath them as she stood in the crypt; and the vast, empty hills which lie above the Sea of Marmara seemed, for the moment, a finer dwelling-place than this many-roomed mansion in which no bed lacked its quilt and no silver dish its silver cover.

'I am growing up,' she thought, taking her taper. 'I am losing my illusions, perhaps to acquire new ones,' and she paced down the long gallery to her bedroom. It was a disagreeable process, and a troublesome. But it was interesting, amazingly, she thought, stretching her legs out to her log fire (for no sailor was present), and she reviewed, as if it were an avenue of great edifices, the progress of her own self along her own past.

How she had loved sound when she was a boy, and thought the volley of tumultuous syllables from the lips the finest of all poetry. Then--it was the effect of Sasha and her disillusionment perhaps--into this high frenzy was let fall some black drop, which turned her rhapsody into sluggishness. Slowly there had opened within her something intricate and many-chambered, which one must take a torch to explore, in prose not verse; and she remembered how passionately she had studied that doctor at Norwich, Browne, whose book was at her hand there. She had formed here in solitude after her affair with Greene, or tried to form, for Heaven knows these growths are agelong in coming, a spirit capable of resistance. 'I will write,' she had said, 'what I enjoy writing'; and so had scratched out twenty-six volumes. Yet still, for all her travels and adventures and profound thinkings and turnings this way and that, she was only in process of fabrication. What the future might bring, Heaven only knew. Change was incessant, and change perhaps would never cease. High battlements of thought, habits that had seemed durable as stone, went down like shadows at the touch of another mind and left a naked sky and fresh stars twinkling in it. Here she went to the window, and in spite of the cold could not help unlatching it. She leant out into the damp night air. She heard a fox bark in the woods, and the clutter of a pheasant trailing through the branches. She heard the snow slither and flop from the roof to the ground. 'By my life,' she exclaimed, 'this is a thousand times better than Turkey. Rustum,' she cried, as if she were arguing with the gipsy (and in this new power of bearing an argument in mind and continuing it with someone who was not there to contradict she showed again the development of her soul), 'you were wrong. This is better than Turkey. Hair, pastry, tobacco--of what odds and ends are we compounded,' she said (thinking of Queen Mary's prayer-book). 'What a phantasmagoria the mind is and meeting-place of dissemblables! At one moment we deplore our birth and state and aspire to an ascetic exaltation; the next we are overcome by the smell of some old garden path and weep to hear the thrushes sing.' And so bewildered as usual by the multitude of things which call for explanation and imprint their message without leaving any hint as to their meaning, she threw her cheroot out of the window and went to bed.

Next morning, in pursuance of these thoughts, she had out her pen and paper. and started afresh upon 'The Oak Tree', for to have ink and paper in plenty when one has made do with berries and margins is a delight not to be conceived. Thus she was now striking out a phrase in the depths of despair, now in the heights of ecstasy writing one in, when a shadow darkened the page. She hastily hid her manuscript.

As her window gave on to the most central of the courts, as she had given orders that she would see no one, as she knew no one and was herself legally unknown, she was first surprised at the shadow, then indignant at it, then (when she looked up and saw what caused it) overcome with merriment. For it was a familiar shadow, a grotesque shadow, the shadow of no less a personage than the Archduchess Harriet Griselda of Finster-Aarhorn and Scand-op-Boom in the Roumanian territory. She was loping across the court in her old black riding-habit and mantle as before. Not a hair of her head was changed. This then was the woman who had chased her from England! This was the eyrie of that obscene vulture--this the fatal fowl herself! At the thought that she had fled all the way to Turkey to avoid her seductions (now become excessively flat), Orlando laughed aloud. There was something inexpressibly comic in the sight. She resembled, as Orlando had thought before, nothing so much as a monstrous hare. She had the staring eyes, the lank cheeks, the high headdress of that animal. She stopped now, much as a hare sits erect in the corn when thinking itself unobserved, and stared at Orlando, who stared back at her from the window. After they had stared like this for a certain time, there was nothing for it but to ask her in, and soon the two ladies were exchanging compliments while the Archduchess struck the snow from her mantle.

'A plague on women,' said Orlando to herself, going to the cupboard to fetch a glass of wine, 'they never leave one a moment's peace. A more ferreting, inquisiting, busybodying set of people don't exist. It was to escape this Maypole that I left England, and now'--here she turned to present the Archduchess with the salver, and behold--in her place stood a tall gentleman in black. A heap of clothes lay in the fender. She was alone with a man.

Recalled thus suddenly to a consciousness of her sex, which she had completely forgotten, and of his, which was now remote enough to be equally upsetting, Orlando felt seized with faintness.

'La!' she cried, putting her hand to her side, 'how you frighten me!'

'Gentle creature,' cried the Archduchess, falling on one knee and at the same time pressing a cordial to Orlando's lips, 'forgive me for the deceit I have practised on you!'

Orlando sipped the wine and the Archduke knelt and kissed her hand.

In short, they acted the parts of man and woman for ten minutes with great vigour and then fell into natural discourse. The Archduchess (but she must in future be known as the Archduke) told his story--that he was a man and always had been one; that he had seen a portrait of Orlando and fallen hopelessly in love with him; that to compass his ends, he had dressed as a woman and lodged at the Baker's shop; that he was desolated when he fled to Turkey; that he had heard of her change and hastened to offer his services (here he teed and heed intolerably).

For to him, said the Archduke Harry, she was and would ever be the Pink, the Pearl, the Perfection of her sex. The three p's would have been more persuasive if they had not been interspersed with tee-hees and haw-haws of the strangest kind. 'If this is love,' said Orlando to herself, looking at the Archduke on the other side of the fender, and now from the woman's point of view, 'there is something highly ridiculous about it.'

Falling on his knees, the Archduke Harry made the most passionate declaration of his suit. He told her that he had something like twenty million ducats in a strong box at his castle. He had more acres than any nobleman in England. The shooting was excellent: he could promise her a mixed bag of ptarmigan and grouse such as no English moor, or Scotch either, could rival. True, the pheasants had suffered from the gape in his absence, and the does had slipped their young, but that could be put right, and would be with her help when they lived in Roumania together.

As he spoke, enormous tears formed in his rather prominent eyes and ran down the sandy tracts of his long and lanky cheeks.

That men cry as frequently and as unreasonably as women, Orlando knew from her own experience as a man; but she was beginning to be aware that women should be shocked when men display emotion in their presence, and so, shocked she was.

The Archduke apologized. He commanded himself sufficiently to say that he would leave her now, but would return on the following day for his answer.

That was a Tuesday. He came on Wednesday; he came on Thursday; he came on Friday; and he came on Saturday. It is true that each visit began, continued, or concluded with a declaration of love, but in between there was much room for silence. They sat on either side of the fireplace and sometimes the Archduke knocked over the fire-irons and Orlando picked them up again. Then the Archduke would bethink him how he had shot an elk in Sweden, and Orlando would ask, was it a very big elk, and the Archduke would say that it was not as big as the reindeer which he shot in Norway; and Orlando would ask, had he ever shot a tiger, and the Archduke would say he had shot an albatross, and Orlando would say (half hiding her yawn) was an albatross as big as an elephant, and the Archduke would say--something very sensible, no doubt, but Orlando heard it not, for she was looking at her writing-table, out of the window, at the door. Upon which the Archduke would say, 'I adore you', at the very same moment that Orlando said 'Look, it's beginning to rain', at which they were both much embarrassed, and blushed scarlet, and could neither of them think what to say next. Indeed, Orlando was at her wit's end what to talk about and had she not bethought her of a game called Fly Loo, at which great sums of money can be lost with very little expense of spirit, she would have had to marry him, she supposed; for how else to get rid of him she knew not. By this device, however, and it was a simple one, needing only three lumps of sugar and a sufficiency of flies, the embarrassment of conversation was overcome and the necessity of marriage avoided. For now, the Archduke would bet her five hundred pounds to a tester that a fly would settle on this lump and not on that. Thus, they would have occupation for a whole morning watching the flies (who were naturally sluggish at this season and often spent an hour or so circling round the ceiling) until at length some fine bluebottle made his choice and the match was won. Many hundreds of pounds changed hands between them at this game, which the Archduke, who was a born gambler, swore was every bit as good as horse racing, and vowed he could play at for ever. But Orlando soon began to weary.

What's the good of being a fine young woman in the prime of life', she asked, 'if I have to pass all my mornings watching blue-bottles with an Archduke?'

She began to detest the sight of sugar; flies made her dizzy. Some way out of the difficulty there must be, she supposed, but she was still awkward in the arts of her sex, and as she could no longer knock a man over the head or run him through the body with a rapier, she could think of no better method than this. She caught a blue-bottle, gently pressed the life out of it (it was half dead already; or her kindness for the dumb creatures would not have permitted it) and secured it by a drop of gum arabic to a lump of sugar. While the Archduke was gazing at the ceiling, she deftly substituted this lump for the one she had laid her money on, and crying 'Loo Loo!' declared that she had won her bet. Her reckoning was that the Archduke, with all his knowledge of sport and horseracing, would detect the fraud and, as to cheat at Loo is the most heinous of crimes, and men have been banished from the society of mankind to that of apes in the tropics for ever because of it, she calculated that he would be manly enough to refuse to have anything further to do with her. But she misjudged the simplicity of the amiable nobleman. He was no nice judge of flies. A dead fly looked to him much the same as a living one. She played the trick twenty times on him and he paid her over 17,250 pounds (which is about 40,885 pounds 6 shillings and 8 pence of our own money) before Orlando cheated so grossly that even he could be deceived no longer. When he realized the truth at last, a painful scene ensued. The Archduke rose to his full height. He coloured scarlet. Tears rolled down his cheeks one by one. That she had won a fortune from him was nothing--she was welcome to it; that she had deceived him was something--it hurt him to think her capable of it; but that she had cheated at Loo was everything. To love a woman who cheated at play was, he said, impossible. Here he broke down completely. Happily, he said, recovering slightly, there were no witnesses. She was, after all, only a woman, he said. In short, he was preparing in the chivalry of his heart to forgive her and had bent to ask her pardon for the violence of his language, when she cut the matter short, as he stooped his proud head, by dropping a small toad between his skin and his shirt.

In justice to her, it must be said that she would infinitely have preferred a rapier. Toads are clammy things to conceal about one's person a whole morning. But if rapiers are forbidden; one must have recourse to toads. Moreover toads and laughter between them sometimes do what cold steel cannot. She laughed. The Archduke blushed. She laughed. The Archduke cursed. She laughed. The Archduke slammed the door.

'Heaven be praised!' cried Orlando still laughing. She heard the sound of chariot wheels driven at a furious pace down the courtyard. She heard them rattle along the road. Fainter and fainter the sound became. Now it faded away altogether.

'I am alone,' said Orlando, aloud since there was no one to hear.

That silence is more profound after noise still wants the confirmation of science. But that loneliness is more apparent directly after one has been made love to, many women would take their oath. As the sound of the Archduke's chariot wheels died away, Orlando felt drawing further from her and further from her an Archduke (she did not mind that), a fortune (she did not mind that), a title (she did not mind that), the safety and circumstance of married life (she did not mind that), but life she heard going from her, and a lover. 'Life and a lover,' she murmured; and going to her writing-table she dipped her pen in the ink and wrote:

'Life and a lover'--a line which did not scan and made no sense with what went before--something about the proper way of dipping sheep to avoid the scab. Reading it over she blushed and repeated,

'Life and a lover.' Then laying her pen aside she went into her bedroom, stood in front of her mirror, and arranged her pearls about her neck. Then since pearls do not show to advantage against a morning gown of sprigged cotton, she changed to a dove grey taffeta; thence to one of peach bloom; thence to a wine-coloured brocade. Perhaps a dash of powder was needed, and if her hair were disposed--so--about her brow, it might become her. Then she slipped her feet into pointed slippers, and drew an emerald ring upon her finger. 'Now,' she said when all was ready and lit the silver sconces on either side of the mirror. What woman would not have kindled to see what Orlando saw then burning in the snow--for all about the looking-glass were snowy lawns, and she was like a fire, a burning bush, and the candle flames about her head were silver leaves; or again, the glass was green water, and she a mermaid, slung with pearls, a siren in a cave, singing so that oarsmen leant from their boats and fell down, down to embrace her; so dark, so bright, so hard, so soft, was she, so astonishingly seductive that it was a thousand pities that there was no one there to put it in plain English, and say outright, 'Damn it, Madam, you are loveliness incarnate,' which was the truth. Even Orlando (who had no conceit of her person) knew it, for she smiled the involuntary smile which women smile when their own beauty, which seems not their own, forms like a drop falling or a fountain rising and confronts them all of a sudden in the glass--this smile she smiled and then she listened for a moment and heard only the leaves blowing and the sparrows twittering, and then she sighed, 'Life, a lover,' and then she turned on her heel with extraordinary rapidity; whipped her pearls from her neck, stripped the satins from her back, stood erect in the neat black silk knickerbockers of an ordinary nobleman, and rang the bell. When the servant came, she told him to order a coach and six to be in readiness instantly. She was summoned by urgent affairs to London. Within an hour of the Archduke's departure, off she drove.

And as she drove, we may seize the opportunity, since the landscape was of a simple English kind which needs no description, to draw the reader's attention more particularly than we could at the moment to one or two remarks which have slipped in here and there in the course of the narrative. For example, it may have been observed that Orlando hid her manuscripts when interrupted. Next, that she looked long and intently in the glass; and now, as she drove to London, one might notice her starting and suppressing a cry when the horses galloped faster than she liked. Her modesty as to her writing, her vanity as to her person, her fears for her safety all seems to hint that what was said a short time ago about there being no change in Orlando the man and Orlando the woman, was ceasing to be altogether true. She was becoming a little more modest, as women are, of her brains, and a little more vain, as women are, of her person. Certain susceptibilities were asserting themselves, and others were diminishing. The change of clothes had, some philosophers will say, much to do with it. Vain trifles as they seem, clothes have, they say, more important offices than merely to keep us warm. They change our view of the world and the world's view of us. For example, when Captain Bartolus saw Orlando's skirt, he had an awning stretched for her immediately, pressed her to take another slice of beef, and invited her to go ashore with him in the long-boat. These compliments would certainly not have been paid her had her skirts, instead of flowing, been cut tight to her legs in the fashion of breeches. And when we are paid compliments, it behoves us to make some return. Orlando curtseyed; she complied; she flattered the good man's humours as she would not have done had his neat breeches been a woman's skirts, and his braided coat a woman's satin bodice. Thus, there is much to support the view that it is clothes that wear us and not we them; we may make them take the mould of arm or breast, but they mould our hearts, our brains, our tongues to their liking. So, having now worn skirts for a considerable time, a certain change was visible in Orlando, which is to be found if the reader will look at @ above, even in her face. If we compare the picture of Orlando as a man with that of Orlando as a woman we shall see that though both are undoubtedly one and the same person, there are certain changes. The man has his hand free to seize his sword, the woman must use hers to keep the satins from slipping from her shoulders. The man looks the world full in the face, as if it were made for his uses and fashioned to his liking. The woman takes a sidelong glance at it, full of subtlety, even of suspicion. Had they both worn the same clothes, it is possible that their outlook might have been the same.

That is the view of some philosophers and wise ones, but on the whole, we incline to another. The difference between the sexes is, happily, one of great profundity. Clothes are but a symbol of something hid deep beneath. It was a change in Orlando herself that dictated her choice of a woman's dress and of a woman's sex. And perhaps in this she was only expressing rather more openly than usual--openness indeed was the soul of her nature--something that happens to most people without being thus plainly expressed. For here again, we come to a dilemma. Different though the sexes are, they intermix. In every human being a vacillation from one sex to the other takes place, and often it is only the clothes that keep the male or female likeness, while underneath the sex is the very opposite of what it is above. Of the complications and confusions which thus result everyone has had experience; but here we leave the general question and note only the odd effect it had in the particular case of Orlando herself.

For it was this mixture in her of man and woman, one being uppermost and then the other, that often gave her conduct an unexpected turn. The curious of her own sex would argue, for example, if Orlando was a woman, how did she never take more than ten minutes to dress? And were not her clothes chosen rather at random, and sometimes worn rather shabby? And then they would say, still, she has none of the formality of a man, or a man's love of power. She is excessively tender-hearted. She could not endure to see a donkey beaten or a kitten drowned. Yet again, they noted, she detested household matters, was up at dawn and out among the fields in summer before the sun had risen. No farmer knew more about the crops than she did. She could drink with the best and liked games of hazard. She rode well and drove six horses at a gallop over London Bridge. Yet again, though bold and active as a man, it was remarked that the sight of another in danger brought on the most womanly palpitations. She would burst into tears on slight provocation. She was unversed in geography, found mathematics intolerable, and held some caprices which are more common among women than men, as for instance that to travel south is to travel downhill. Whether, then, Orlando was most man or woman, it is difficult to say and cannot now be decided. For her coach was now rattling on the cobbles. She had reached her home in the city. The steps were being let down; the iron gates were being opened. She was entering her father's house at Blackfriars, which though fashion was fast deserting that end of the town, was still a pleasant, roomy mansion, with gardens running down to the river, and a pleasant grove of nut trees to walk in.

Here she took up her lodging and began instantly to look about her for what she had come in search of--that is to say, life and a lover. About the first there might be some doubt; the second she found without the least difficulty two days after her arrival. It was a Tuesday that she came to town. On Thursday she went for a walk in the Mall, as was then the habit of persons of quality. She had not made more than a turn or two of the avenue before she was observed by a little knot of vulgar people who go there to spy upon their betters. As she came past them, a common woman carrying a child at her breast stepped forward, peered familiarly into Orlando's face, and cried out, 'Lawk upon us, if it ain't the Lady Orlando!' Her companions came crowding round, and Orlando found herself in a moment the centre of a mob of staring citizens and tradesmen's wives, all eager to gaze upon the heroine of the celebrated lawsuit. Such was the interest that the case excited in the minds of the common people. She might, indeed, have found herself gravely discommoded by the pressure of the crowd--she had forgotten that ladies are not supposed to walk in public places alone--had not a tall gentleman at once stepped forward and offered her the protection of his arm. It was the Archduke. She was overcome with distress and yet with some amusement at the sight. Not only had this magnanimous nobleman forgiven her, but in order to show that he took her levity with the toad in good part, he had procured a jewel made in the shape of that reptile which he pressed upon her with a repetition of his suit as he handed her to her coach.

What with the crowd, what with the Duke, what with the jewel, she drove home in the vilest temper imaginable. Was it impossible then to go for a walk without being half-suffocated, presented with a toad set in emeralds, and asked in marriage by an Archduke? She took a kinder view of the case next day when she found on her breakfast table half a dozen billets from some of the greatest ladies in the land--Lady Suffolk, Lady Salisbury, Lady Chesterfield, Lady Tavistock, and others who reminded her in the politest manner of old alliances between their families and her own, and desired the honour of her acquaintance. Next day, which was a Saturday, many of these great ladies waited on her in person. On Tuesday, about noon, their footmen brought cards of invitation to various routs, dinners, and assemblies in the near future; so that Orlando was launched without delay, and with some splash and foam at that, upon the waters of London society.

To give a truthful account of London society at that or indeed at any other time, is beyond the powers of the biographer or the historian. Only those who have little need of the truth, and no respect for it--the poets and the novelists--can be trusted to do it, for this is one of the cases where the truth does not exist. Nothing exists. The whole thing is a miasma--a mirage. To make our meaning plain--Orlando could come home from one of these routs at three or four in the morning with cheeks like a Christmas tree and eyes like stars. She would untie a lace, pace the room a score of times, untie another lace, stop, and pace the room again. Often the sun would be blazing over Southwark chimneys before she could persuade herself to get into bed, and there she would lie, pitching and tossing, laughing and sighing for an hour or longer before she slept at last. And what was all this stir about? Society. And what had society said or done to throw a reasonable lady into such an excitement? In plain language, nothing. Rack her memory as she would, next day Orlando could never remember a single word to magnify into the name something. Lord O. had been gallant. Lord A. polite. The Marquis of C. charming. Mr M. amusing. But when she tried to recollect in what their gallantry, politeness, charm, or wit had consisted, she was bound to suppose her memory at fault, for she could not name a thing. It was the same always. Nothing remained over the next day, yet the excitement of the moment was intense. Thus we are forced to conclude that society is one of those brews such as skilled housekeepers serve hot about Christmas time, whose flavour depends upon the proper mixing and stirring of a dozen different ingredients. Take one out, and it is in itself insipid. Take away Lord O., Lord A., Lord C., or Mr M. and separately each is nothing. Stir them all together and they combine to give off the most intoxicating of flavours, the most seductive of scents. Yet this intoxication, this seductiveness, entirely evade our analysis. At one and the same time, therefore, society is everything and society is nothing. Society is the most powerful concoction in the world and society has no existence whatsoever. Such monsters the poets and the novelists alone can deal with; with such something-nothings their works are stuffed out to prodigious size; and to them with the best will in the world we are content to leave it.

Following the example of our predecessors, therefore, we will only say that society in the reign of Queen Anne was of unparalleled brilliance. To have the entry there was the aim of every well-bred person. The graces were supreme. Fathers instructed their sons, mothers their daughters. No education was complete for either sex which did not include the science of deportment, the art of bowing and curtseying, the management of the sword and the fan, the care of the teeth, the conduct of the leg, the flexibility of the knee, the proper methods of entering and leaving the room, with a thousand etceteras, such as will immediately suggest themselves to anybody who has himself been in society. Since Orlando had won the praise of Queen Elizabeth for the way she handed a bowl of rose water as a boy, it must be supposed that she was sufficiently expert to pass muster. Yet it is true that there was an absentmindedness about her which sometimes made her clumsy; she was apt to think of poetry when she should have been thinking of taffeta; her walk was a little too much of a stride for a woman, perhaps, and her gestures, being abrupt, might endanger a cup of tea on occasion.

Whether this slight disability was enough to counterbalance the splendour of her bearing, or whether she inherited a drop too much of that black humour which ran in the veins of all her race, certain it is that she had not been in the world more than a score of times before she might have been heard to ask herself, had there been anybody but her spaniel Pippin to hear her, 'What the devil is the matter with me?' The occasion was Tuesday, the 16th of June 1712; she had just returned from a great ball at Arlington House; the dawn was in the sky, and she was pulling off her stockings. 'I don't care if I never meet another soul as long as I live,' cried Orlando, bursting into tears. Lovers she had in plenty, but life, which is, after all, of some importance in its way, escaped her. 'Is this', she asked--but there was none to answer, 'is this', she finished her sentence all the same, 'what people call life?' The spaniel raised her forepaw in token of sympathy. The spaniel licked Orlando with her tongue. Orlando stroked the spaniel with her hand. Orlando kissed the spaniel with her lips. In short, there was the truest sympathy between them that can be between a dog and its mistress, and yet it cannot be denied that the dumbness of animals is a great impediment to the refinements of intercourse. They wag their tails; they bow the front part of the body and elevate the hind; they roll, they jump, they paw, they whine, they bark, they slobber, they have all sorts of ceremonies and artifices of their own, but the whole thing is of no avail, since speak they cannot. Such was her quarrel, she thought, setting the dog gently on to the floor, with the great people at Arlington House. They, too, wag their tails, bow, roll, jump, paw, and slobber, but talk they cannot. 'All these months that I've been out in the world', said Orlando, pitching one stocking across the room, 'I've heard nothing but what Pippin might have said. I'm cold. I'm happy. I'm hungry. I've caught a mouse. I've buried a bone. Please kiss my nose.' And it was not enough.

How, in so short a time, she had passed from intoxication to disgust we will only seek to explain by supposing that this mysterious composition which we call society, is nothing absolutely good or bad in itself, but has a spirit in it, volatile but potent, which either makes you drunk when you think it, as Orlando thought it, delightful, or gives you a headache when you think it, as Orlando thought it, repulsive. That the faculty of speech has much to do with it either way, we take leave to doubt. Often a dumb hour is the most ravishing of all; brilliant wit can be tedious beyond description. But to the poets we leave it, and so on with our story.

Orlando threw the second stocking after the first and went to bed dismally enough, determined that she would forswear society for ever. But again as it turned out, she was too hasty in coming to her conclusions. For the very next morning she woke to find, among the usual cards of invitation upon her table, one from a certain great Lady, the Countess of R. Having determined overnight that she would never go into society again, we can only explain Orlando's behaviour--she sent a messenger hot-foot to R-- House to say that she would attend her Ladyship with all the pleasure in the world--by the fact that she was still suffering from the effect of three honeyed words dropped into her ear on the deck of the "Enamoured Lady" by Captain Nicholas Benedict Bartolus as they sailed down the Thames. Addison, Dryden, Pope, he had said, pointing to the Cocoa Tree, and Addison, Dryden, Pope had chimed in her head like an incantation ever since. Who can credit such folly? but so it was. All her experience with Nick Greene had taught her nothing. Such names still exercised over her the most powerful fascination. Something, perhaps, we must believe in, and as Orlando, we have said, had no belief in the usual divinities she bestowed her credulity upon great men--yet with a distinction. Admirals, soldiers, statesmen, moved her not at all. But the very thought of a great writer stirred her to such a pitch of belief that she almost believed him to be invisible. Her instinct was a sound one. One can only believe entirely, perhaps, in what one cannot see. The little glimpse she had of these great men from the deck of the ship was of the nature of a vision. That the cup was china, or the gazette paper, she doubted. When Lord O. said one day that he had dined with Dryden the night before, she flatly disbelieved him. Now, the Lady R.'s reception room had the reputation of being the antechamber to the presence room of genius; it was the place where men and women met to swing censers and chant hymns to the bust of genius in a niche in the wall. Sometimes the God himself vouchsafed his presence for a moment. Intellect alone admitted the suppliant, and nothing (so the report ran) was said inside that was not witty.

It was thus with great trepidation that Orlando entered the room. She found a company already assembled in a semicircle round the fire. Lady R., an oldish lady, of dark complexion, with a black lace mantilla on her head, was seated in a great arm-chair in the centre. Thus being somewhat deaf, she could control the conversation on both sides of her. On both sides of her sat men and women of the highest distinction. Every man, it was said, had been a Prime Minister and every woman, it was whispered, had been the mistress of a king. Certain it is that all were brilliant, and all were famous. Orlando took her seat with a deep reverence in silence...After three hours, she curtseyed profoundly and left.

But what, the reader may ask with some exasperation, happened in between. In three hours, such a company must have said the wittiest, the profoundest, the most interesting things in the world. So it would seem indeed. But the fact appears to be that they said nothing. It is a curious characteristic which they share with all the most brilliant societies that the world has seen. Old Madame du Deffand and her friends talked for fifty years without stopping. And of it all, what remains? Perhaps three witty sayings. So that we are at liberty to suppose either that nothing was said, or that nothing witty was said, or that the fraction of three witty sayings lasted eighteen thousand two hundred and fifty nights, which does not leave a liberal allowance of wit for any one of them.

The truth would seem to be--if we dare use such a word in such a connection--that all these groups of people lie under an enchantment. The hostess is our modern Sibyl. She is a witch who lays her guests under a spell. In this house they think themselves happy; in that witty; in a third profound. It is all an illusion (which is nothing against it, for illusions are the most valuable and necessary of all things, and she who can create one is among the world's greatest benefactors), but as it is notorious that illusions are shattered by conflict with reality, so no real happiness, no real wit, no real profundity are tolerated where the illusion prevails. This serves to explain why Madame du Deffand said no more than three witty things in the course of fifty years. Had she said more, her circle would have been destroyed. The witticism, as it left her lips, bowled over the current conversation as a cannon ball lays low the violets and the daisies. When she made her famous 'mot de Saint Denis' the very grass was singed. Disillusionment and desolation followed. Not a word was uttered. 'Spare us another such, for Heaven's sake, Madame!' her friends cried with one accord. And she obeyed. For almost seventeen years she said nothing memorable and all went well. The beautiful counterpane of illusion lay unbroken on her circle as it lay unbroken on the circle of Lady R. The guests thought that they were happy, thought that they were witty, thought that they were profound, and, as they thought this, other people thought it still more strongly; and so it got about that nothing was more delightful than one of Lady R.'s assemblies; everyone envied those who were admitted; those who were admitted envied themselves because other people envied them; and so there seemed no end to it--except that which we have now to relate.

For about the third time Orlando went there a certain incident occurred. She was still under the illusion that she was listening to the most brilliant epigrams in the world, though, as a matter of fact, old General C. was only saying, at some length, how the gout had left his left leg and gone to his right, while Mr L. interrupted when any proper name was mentioned, 'R.? Oh! I know Billy R. as well as I know myself. S.? My dearest friend. T.? Stayed with him a fortnight in Yorkshire'--which, such is the force of illusion, sounded like the wittiest repartee, the most searching comment upon human life, and kept the company in a roar; when the door opened and a little gentleman entered whose name Orlando did not catch.

Soon a curiously disagreeable sensation came over her. To judge from their faces, the rest began to feel it as well. One gentleman said there was a draught. The Marchioness of C. feared a cat must be under the sofa. It was as if their eyes were being slowly opened after a pleasant dream and nothing met them but a cheap wash-stand and a dirty counterpane. It was as if the fumes of some delicious wine were slowly leaving them. Still the General talked and still Mr L. remembered. But it became more and more apparent how red the General's neck was, how bald Mr L.'s head was. As for what they said--nothing more tedious and trivial could be imagined. Everybody fidgeted and those who had fans yawned behind them. At last Lady R. rapped with hers upon the arm of her great chair. Both gentlemen stopped talking.

Then the little gentleman said, He said next, He said finally (These sayings are too well known to require repetition, and besides, they are all to be found in his published works.),

Here, it cannot be denied, was true wit, true wisdom, true profundity. The company was thrown into complete dismay. One such saying was bad enough; but three, one after another, on the same evening! No society could survive it.

'Mr Pope,' said old Lady R. in a voice trembling with sarcastic fury, 'you are pleased to be witty.' Mr Pope flushed red. Nobody spoke a word. They sat in dead silence some twenty minutes. Then, one by one, they rose and slunk from the room. That they would ever come back after such an experience was doubtful. Link-boys could be heard calling their coaches all down South Audley Street. Doors were slammed and carriages drove off. Orlando found herself near Mr Pope on the staircase. His lean and misshapen frame was shaken by a variety of emotions. Darts of malice, rage, triumph, wit, and terror (he was shaking like a leaf) shot from his eyes. He looked like some squat reptile set with a burning topaz in its forehead. At the same time, the strangest tempest of emotion seized now upon the luckless Orlando. A disillusionment so complete as that inflicted not an hour ago leaves the mind rocking from side to side. Everything appears ten times more bare and stark than before. It is a moment fraught with the highest danger for the human spirit. Women turn nuns and men priests in such moments. In such moments, rich men sign away their wealth; and happy men cut their throats with carving knives. Orlando would have done all willingly, but there was a rasher thing still for her to do, and this she did. She invited Mr Pope to come home with her.

For if it is rash to walk into a lion's den unarmed, rash to navigate the Atlantic in a rowing boat, rash to stand on one foot on the top of St Paul's, it is still more rash to go home alone with a poet. A poet is Atlantic and lion in one. While one drowns us the other gnaws us. If we survive the teeth, we succumb to the waves. A man who can destroy illusions is both beast and flood. Illusions are to the soul what atmosphere is to the earth. Roll up that tender air and the plant dies, the colour fades. The earth we walk on is a parched cinder. It is marl we tread and fiery cobbles scorch our feet. By the truth we are undone. Life is a dream. 'Tis waking that kills us. He who robs us of our dreams robs us of our life--(and so on for six pages if you will, but the style is tedious and may well be dropped).

On this showing, however, Orlando should have been a heap of cinders by the time the chariot drew up at her house in Blackfriars. That she was still flesh and blood, though certainly exhausted, is entirely due to a fact to which we drew attention earlier in the narrative. The less we see the more we believe. Now the streets that lie between Mayfair and Blackfriars were at that time very imperfectly lit. True, the lighting was a great improvement upon that of the Elizabethan age. Then the benighted traveller had to trust to the stars or the red flame of some night watchman to save him from the gravel pits at Park Lane or the oak woods where swine rootled in the Tottenham Court Road. But even so it wanted much of our modern efficiency. Lamp-posts lit with oil-lamps occurred every two hundred yards or so, but between lay a considerable stretch of pitch darkness. Thus for ten minutes Orlando and Mr Pope would be in blackness; and then for about half a minute again in the light. A very strange state of mind was thus bred in Orlando. As the light faded, she began to feel steal over her the most delicious balm. 'This is indeed a very great honour for a young woman to be driving with Mr Pope,' she began to think, looking at the outline of his nose. 'I am the most blessed of my sex. Half an inch from me--indeed, I feel the knot of his knee ribbons pressing against my thigh--is the greatest wit in Her Majesty's dominions. Future ages will think of us with curiosity and envy me with fury.' Here came the lamp-post again. 'What a foolish wretch I am!' she thought. 'There is no such thing as fame and glory. Ages to come will never cast a thought on me or on Mr Pope either. What's an "age", indeed? What are "we"?' and their progress through Berkeley Square seemed the groping of two blind ants, momentarily thrown together without interest or concern in common, across a blackened desert. She shivered. But here again was darkness. Her illusion revived. 'How noble his brow is,' she thought (mistaking a hump on a cushion for Mr Pope's forehead in the darkness). 'What a weight of genius lives in it! What wit, wisdom, and truth--what a wealth of all those jewels, indeed, for which people are ready to barter their lives! Yours is the only light that burns for ever. But for you the human pilgrimage would be performed in utter darkness'; (here the coach gave a great lurch as it fell into a rut in Park Lane) 'without genius we should be upset and undone. Most august, most lucid of beams,'--thus she was apostrophizing the hump on the cushion when they drove beneath one of the street lamps in Berkeley Square and she realized her mistake. Mr Pope had a forehead no bigger than another man's. 'Wretched man,' she thought, 'how you have deceived me! I took that hump for your forehead. When one sees you plain, how ignoble, how despicable you are! Deformed and weakly, there is nothing to venerate in you, much to pity, most to despise.'

Again they were in darkness and her anger became modified directly she could see nothing but the poet's knees.

'But it is I that am a wretch,' she reflected, once they were in complete obscurity again, 'for base as you may be, am I not still baser? It is you who nourish and protect me, you who scare the wild beast, frighten the savage, make me clothes of the silkworm's wool, and carpets of the sheep's. If I want to worship, have you not provided me with an image of yourself and set it in the sky? Are not evidences of your care everywhere? How humble, how grateful, how docile, should I not be, therefore? Let it be all my joy to serve, honour, and obey you.'

Here they reached the big lamp-post at the corner of what is now Piccadilly Circus. The light blazed in her eyes, and she saw, besides some degraded creatures of her own sex, two wretched pigmies on a stark desert land. Both were naked, solitary, and defenceless. The one was powerless to help the other. Each had enough to do to look after itself. Looking Mr Pope full in the face, 'It is equally vain', she thought; 'for you to think you can protect me, or for me to think I can worship you. The light of truth beats upon us without shadow, and the light of truth is damnably unbecoming to us both.'

All this time, of course, they went on talking agreeably, as people of birth and education use, about the Queen's temper and the Prime Minister's gout, while the coach went from light to darkness down the Haymarket, along the Strand, up Fleet Street, and reached, at length, her house in Blackfriars. For some time the dark spaces between the lamps had been becoming brighter and the lamps themselves less bright--that is to say, the sun was rising, and it was in the equable but confused light of a summer's morning in which everything is seen but nothing is seen distinctly that they alighted, Mr Pope handing Orlando from her carriage and Orlando curtseying Mr Pope to precede her into her mansion with the most scrupulous attention to the rites of the Graces.

From the foregoing passage, however, it must not be supposed that genius (but the disease is now stamped out in the British Isles, the late Lord Tennyson, it is said, being the last person to suffer from it) is constantly alight, for then we should see everything plain and perhaps should be scorched to death in the process. Rather it resembles the lighthouse in its working, which sends one ray and then no more for a time; save that genius is much more capricious in its manifestations and may flash six or seven beams in quick succession (as Mr Pope did that night) and then lapse into darkness for a year or for ever. To steer by its beams is therefore impossible, and when the dark spell is on them men of genius are, it is said, much like other people.

It was happy for Orlando, though at first disappointing, that this should be so, for she now began to live much in the company of men of genius. Nor were they so different from the rest of us as one might have supposed. Addison, Pope, Swift, proved, she found, to be fond of tea. They liked arbours. They collected little bits of coloured glass. They adored grottos. Rank was not distasteful to them. Praise was delightful. They wore plum-coloured suits one day and grey another. Mr Swift had a fine malacca cane. Mr Addison scented his handkerchiefs. Mr Pope suffered with his head. A piece of gossip did not come amiss. Nor were they without their jealousies. (We are jotting down a few reflections that came to Orlando higgledy-piggledy.) At first, she was annoyed with herself for noticing such trifles, and kept a book in which to write down their memorable sayings, but the page remained empty. All the same, her spirits revived, and she took to tearing up her cards of invitation to great parties; kept her evenings free; began to look forward to Mr Pope's visit, to Mr Addison's, to Mr Swift's--and so on and so on. If the reader will here refer to the "Rape of the Lock", to the "Spectator", to "Gulliver's Travels", he will understand precisely what these mysterious words may mean. Indeed, biographers and critics might save themselves all their labours if readers would only take this advice. For when we read:

Whether the Nymph shall break Diana's Law, Or some frail China Jar receive a Flaw, Or stain her Honour, or her new Brocade, Forget her Pray'rs or miss a Masquerade, Or lose her Heart, or Necklace, at a Ball.

--we know as if we heard him how Mr Pope's tongue flickered like a lizard's, how his eyes flashed, how his hand trembled, how he loved, how he lied, how he suffered. In short, every secret of a writer's soul, every experience of his life; every quality of his mind is written large in his works; yet we require critics to explain the one and biographers to expound the other. That time hangs heavy on people's hands is the only explanation of the monstrous growth.

So, now that we have read a page or two of the "Rape of the Lock", we know exactly why Orlando was so much amused and so much frightened and so very bright-cheeked and bright-eyed that afternoon.

Mrs Nelly then knocked at the door to say that Mr Addison waited on her Ladyship. At this, Mr Pope got up with a wry smile, made his congee, and limped off. In came Mr Addison. Let us, as he takes his seat, read the following passage from the "Spectator":

'I consider woman as a beautiful, romantic animal, that may be adorned with furs and feathers, pearls and diamonds, ores and silks. The lynx shall cast its skin at her feet to make her a tippet, the peacock, parrot and swan shall pay contributions to her muff; the sea shall be searched for shells, and the rocks for gems, and every part of nature furnish out its share towards the embellishment of a creature that is the most consummate work of it. All this, I shall indulge them in, but as for the petticoat I have been speaking of, I neither can, nor will allow it.'

We hold that gentleman, cocked hat and all, in the hollow, of our hands. Look once more into the crystal. Is he not clear to the very wrinkle in his stocking? Does not every ripple and curve of his wit lie exposed before us, and his benignity and his timidity and his urbanity and the fact that he would marry a Countess and die very respectably in the end? All is clear. And when Mr Addison has said his say, there is a terrific rap at the door, and Mr Swift, who had these arbitrary ways with him, walks in unannounced. One moment, where is "Gulliver's Travels"? Here it is! Let us read a passage from the voyage to the Houyhnhnms:

'I enjoyed perfect Health of Body and Tranquillity of Mind; I did not find the Treachery or Inconstancy of a Friend, nor the Injuries of a secret or open Enemy. I had no occasion of bribing, flattering or pimping, to procure the Favour of any great Man or of his Minion. I wanted no Fence against Fraud or Oppression; Here was neither Physician to destroy my Body, nor Lawyer to ruin my Fortune; No Informer to watch my Words, and Actions, or forge Accusations against me for Hire: Here were no Gibers, Censurers, Backbiters, Pickpockets, Highwaymen,

Housebreakers, Attorneys, Bawds, Buffoons, Gamesters, Politicians, Wits, splenetick tedious Talkers...'

But stop, stop your iron pelt of words, lest you flay us all alive, and yourself too! Nothing can be plainer than that violent man. He is so coarse and yet so clean; so brutal, yet so kind; scorns the whole world, yet talks baby language to a girl, and will die, can we doubt it? in a madhouse.

So Orlando poured out tea for them all; and sometimes, when the weather was fine, she carried them down to the country with her, and feasted them royally in the Round Parlour, which she had hung with their pictures all in a circle, so that Mr Pope could not say that Mr Addison came before him, or the other way about. They were very witty, too (but their wit is all in their books) and taught her the most important part of style, which is the natural run of the voice in speaking--a quality which none that has not heard it can imitate, not Greene even, with all his skill; for it is born of the air, and breaks like a wave on the furniture, and rolls and fades away, and is never to be recaptured, least of all by those who prick up their ears, half a century later, and try. They taught her this, merely by the cadence of their voices in speech; so that her style changed somewhat, and she wrote some very pleasant, witty verses and characters in prose. And so she lavished her wine on them and put bank-notes, which they took very kindly, beneath their plates at dinner, and accepted their dedications, and thought herself highly honoured by the exchange.

Thus time ran on, and Orlando could often be heard saying to herself with an emphasis which might, perhaps, make the hearer a little suspicious, 'Upon my soul, what a life this is!' (For she was still in search of that commodity.) But circumstances soon forced her to consider the matter more narrowly.

One day she was pouring out tea for Mr Pope while, as anyone can tell from the verses quoted above, he sat very bright-eyed, observant, and all crumpled up in a chair by her side.

'Lord,' she thought, as she raised the sugar tongs, 'how women in ages to come will envy me! And yet--' she paused; for Mr Pope needed her attention. And yet--let us finish her thought for her--when anybody says 'How future ages will envy me', it is safe to say that they are extremely uneasy at the present moment. Was this life quite so exciting, quite so flattering, quite so glorious as it sounds when the memoir writer has done his work upon it? For one thing, Orlando had a positive hatred of tea; for another, the intellect, divine as it is, and all-worshipful, has a habit of lodging in the most seedy of carcases, and often, alas, acts the cannibal among the other faculties so that often, where the Mind is biggest, the Heart, the Senses, Magnanimity, Charity, Tolerance, Kindliness, and the rest of them scarcely have room to breathe. Then the high opinion poets have of themselves; then the low one they have of others; then the enmities, injuries, envies, and repartees in which they are constantly engaged; then the volubility with which they impart them; then the rapacity with which they demand sympathy for them; all this, one may whisper, lest the wits may overhear us, makes pouring out tea a more precarious and, indeed, arduous occupation than is generally allowed. Added to which (we whisper again lest the women may overhear us), there is a little secret which men share among them; Lord Chesterfield whispered it to his son with strict injunctions to secrecy, 'Women are but children of a larger growth...A man of sense only trifles with them, plays with them, humours and flatters them', which, since children always hear what they are not meant to, and sometimes, even, grow up, may have somehow leaked out, so that the whole ceremony of pouring out tea is a curious one. A woman knows very well that, though a wit sends her his poems, praises her judgment, solicits her criticism, and drinks her tea, this by no means signifies that he respects her opinions, admires her understanding, or will refuse, though the rapier is denied him, to run her through the body with his pen. All this, we say, whisper it as low as we can, may have leaked out by now; so that even with the cream jug suspended and the sugar tongs distended the ladies may fidget a little, look out of the window a little, yawn a little, and so let the sugar fall with a great plop--as Orlando did now--into Mr Pope's tea. Never was any mortal so ready to suspect an insult or so quick to avenge one as Mr Pope. He turned to Orlando and presented her instantly with the rough draught of a certain famous line in the 'Characters of Women'. Much polish was afterwards bestowed on it, but even in the original it was striking enough. Orlando received it with a curtsey. Mr Pope left her with a bow. Orlando, to cool her cheeks, for really she felt as if the little man had struck her, strolled in the nut grove at the bottom of the garden. Soon the cool breezes did their work. To her amazement she found that she was hugely relieved to find herself alone. She watched the merry boatloads rowing up the river. No doubt the sight put her in mind of one or two incidents in her past life. She sat herself down in profound meditation beneath a fine willow tree. There she sat till the stars were in the sky. Then she rose, turned, and went into the house, where she sought her bedroom and locked the door. Now she opened a cupboard in which hung still many of the clothes she had worn as a young man of fashion, and from among them she chose a black velvet suit richly trimmed with Venetian lace. It was a little out of fashion, indeed, but it fitted her to perfection and dressed in it she looked the very figure of a noble Lord. She took a turn or two before the mirror to make sure that her petticoats had not lost her the freedom of her legs, and then let herself secretly out of doors.

It was a fine night early in April. A myriad stars mingling with the light of a sickle moon, which again was enforced by the street lamps, made a light infinitely becoming to the human countenance and to the architecture of Mr Wren. Everything appeared in its tenderest form, yet, just as it seemed on the point of dissolution, some drop of silver sharpened it to animation. Thus it was that talk should be, thought Orlando (indulging in foolish reverie); that society should be, that friendship should be, that love should be. For, Heaven knows why, just as we have lost faith in human intercourse some random collocation of barns and trees or a haystack and a waggon presents us with so perfect a symbol of what is unattainable that we begin the search again.

She entered Leicester Square as she made these observations. The buildings had an airy yet formal symmetry not theirs by day. The canopy of the sky seemed most dexterously washed in to fill up the outline of roof and chimney. A young woman who sat dejectedly with one arm drooping by her side, the other reposing in her lap, on a seat beneath a plane tree in the middle of the square seemed the very figure of grace, simplicity, and desolation. Orlando swept her hat off to her in the manner of a gallant paying his addresses to a lady of fashion in a public place. The young woman raised her head. It was of the most exquisite shapeliness. The young woman raised her eyes. Orlando saw them to be of a lustre such as is sometimes seen on teapots but rarely in a human face. Through this silver glaze the young woman looked up at him (for a man he was to her) appealing, hoping, trembling, fearing. She rose; she accepted his arm. For--need we stress the point?--she was of the tribe which nightly burnishes their wares, and sets them in order on the common counter to wait the highest bidder. She led Orlando to the room in Gerrard Street which was her lodging. To feel her hanging lightly yet like a suppliant on her arm, roused in Orlando all the feelings which become a man. She looked, she felt, she talked like one. Yet, having been so lately a woman herself, she suspected that the girl's timidity and her hesitating answers and the very fumbling with the key in the latch and the fold of her cloak and the droop of her wrist were all put on to gratify her masculinity. Upstairs they went, and the pains which the poor creature had been at to decorate her room and hide the fact that she had no other deceived Orlando not a moment. The deception roused her scorn; the truth roused her pity. One thing showing through the other bred the oddest assortment of feeling, so that she did not know whether to laugh or to cry. Meanwhile Nell, as the girl called herself, unbuttoned her gloves; carefully concealed the left-hand thumb, which wanted mending; then drew behind a screen, where, perhaps, she rouged her cheeks, arranged her clothes, fixed a new kerchief round her neck--all the time prattling as women do, to amuse her lover, though Orlando could have sworn, from the tone of her voice, that her thoughts were elsewhere. When all was ready, out she came, prepared--but here Orlando could stand it no longer. In the strangest torment of anger, merriment, and pity she flung off all disguise and admitted herself a woman.

At this, Nell burst into such a roar of laughter as might have been heard across the way.

'Well, my dear,' she said, when she had somewhat recovered, 'I'm by no means sorry to hear it. For the plain Dunstable of the matter is' (and it was remarkable how soon, on discovering that they were of the same sex, her manner changed and she dropped her plaintive, appealing ways), 'the plain Dunstable of the matter is, that I'm not in the mood for the society of the other sex to-night. Indeed, I'm in the devil of a fix.' Whereupon, drawing up the fire and stirring a bowl of punch, she told Orlando the whole story of her life. Since it is Orlando's life that engages us at present, we need not relate the adventures of the other lady, but it is certain that Orlando had never known the hours speed faster or more merrily, though Mistress Nell had not a particle of wit about her, and when the name of Mr Pope came up in talk asked innocently if he were connected with the perruque maker of that name in Jermyn Street. Yet, to Orlando, such is the charm of ease and the seduction of beauty, this poor girl's talk, larded though it was with the commonest expressions of the street corners, tasted like wine after the fine phrases she had been used to, and she was forced to the conclusion that there was something in the sneer of Mr Pope, in the condescension of Mr Addison, and in the secret of Lord Chesterfield which took away her relish for the society of wits, deeply though she must continue to respect their works.

These poor creatures, she ascertained, for Nell brought Prue, and Prue Kitty, and Kitty Rose, had a society of their own of which they now elected her a member. Each would tell the story of the adventures which had landed her in her present way of life. Several were the natural daughters of earls and one was a good deal nearer than she should have been to the King's person. None was too wretched or too poor but to have some ring or handkerchief in her pocket which stood her in lieu of pedigree. So they would draw round the punch-bowl which Orlando made it her business to furnish generously, and many were the fine tales they told and many the amusing observations they made, for it cannot be denied that when women get together--but hist--they are always careful to see that the doors are shut and that not a word of it gets into print. All they desire is--but hist again--is that not a man's step on the stair? All they desire, we were about to say when the gentleman took the very words out of our mouths. Women have no desires, says this gentleman, coming into Nell's parlour; only affectations. Without desires (she has served him and he is gone) their conversation cannot be of the slightest interest to anyone. 'It is well known', says Mr S. W., 'that when they lack the stimulus of the other sex, women can find nothing to say to each other. When they are alone, they do not talk, they scratch.' And since they cannot talk together and scratching cannot continue without interruption and it is well known (Mr T. R. has proved it) 'that women are incapable of any feeling of affection for their own sex and hold each other in the greatest aversion', what can we suppose that women do when they seek out each other's society?

As that is not a question that can engage the attention of a sensible man, let us, who enjoy the immunity of all biographers and historians from any sex whatever, pass it over, and merely state that Orlando professed great enjoyment in the society of her own sex, and leave it to the gentlemen to prove, as they are very fond of doing, that this is impossible.

But to give an exact and particular account of Orlando's life at this time becomes more and more out of the question. As we peer and grope in the ill-lit, ill-paved, ill-ventilated courtyards that lay about Gerrard Street and Drury Lane at that time, we seem now to catch sight of her and then again to lose it. The task is made still more difficult by the fact that she found it convenient at this time to change frequently from one set of clothes to another. Thus she often occurs in contemporary memoirs as 'Lord' So-and-so, who was in fact her cousin; her bounty is ascribed to him, and it is he who is said to have written the poems that were really hers. She had, it seems, no difficulty in sustaining the different parts, for her sex changed far more frequently than those who have worn only one set of clothing can conceive; nor can there be any doubt that she reaped a twofold harvest by this device; the pleasures of life were increased and its experiences multiplied. For the probity of breeches she exchanged the seductiveness of petticoats and enjoyed the love of both sexes equally.

So then one may sketch her spending her morning in a China robe of ambiguous gender among her books; then receiving a client or two (for she had many scores of suppliants) in the same garment; then she would take a turn in the garden and clip the nut trees--for which knee-breeches were convenient; then she would change into a flowered taffeta which best suited a drive to Richmond and a proposal of marriage from some great nobleman; and so back again to town, where she would don a snuff-coloured gown like a lawyer's and visit the courts to hear how her cases were doing,--for her fortune was wasting hourly and the suits seemed no nearer consummation than they had been a hundred years ago; and so, finally, when night came, she would more often than not become a nobleman complete from head to toe and walk the streets in search of adventure.

Returning from some of these junketings--of which there were many stories told at the time, as, that she fought a duel, served on one of the King's ships as a captain, was seen to dance naked on a balcony, and fled with a certain lady to the Low Countries where the lady's husband followed them--but of the truth or otherwise of these stories, we express no opinion--returning from whatever her occupation may have been, she made a point sometimes of passing beneath the windows of a coffee house, where she could see the wits without being seen, and thus could fancy from their gestures what wise, witty, or spiteful things they were saying without hearing a word of them; which was perhaps an advantage; and once she stood half an hour watching three shadows on the blind drinking tea together in a house in Bolt Court.

Never was any play so absorbing. She wanted to cry out, Bravo! Bravo! For, to be sure, what a fine drama it was--what a page torn from the thickest volume of human life! There was the little shadow with the pouting lips, fidgeting this way and that on his chair, uneasy, petulant, officious; there was the bent female shadow, crooking a finger in the cup to feel how deep the tea was, for she was blind; and there was the Roman-looking rolling shadow in the big armchair--he who twisted his fingers so oddly and jerked his head from side to side and swallowed down the tea in such vast gulps. Dr Johnson, Mr Boswell, and Mrs Williams,--those were the shadows' names. So absorbed was she in the sight, that she forgot to think how other ages would have envied her, though it seems probable that on this occasion they would. She was content to gaze and gaze. At length Mr Boswell rose. He saluted the old woman with tart asperity. But with what humility did he not abase himself before the great Roman shadow, who now rose to its full height and rocking somewhat as he stood there rolled out the most magnificent phrases that ever left human lips; so Orlando thought them, though she never heard a word that any of the three shadows said as they sat there drinking tea.

At length she came home one night after one of these saunterings and mounted to her bedroom. She took off her laced coat and stood there in shirt and breeches looking out of the window. There was something stirring in the air which forbade her to go to bed. A white haze lay over the town, for it was a frosty night in midwinter and a magnificent vista lay all round her. She could see St Paul's, the Tower, Westminster Abbey, with all the spires and domes of the city churches, the smooth bulk of its banks, the opulent and ample curves of its halls and meeting-places. On the north rose the smooth, shorn heights of Hampstead, and in the west the streets and squares of Mayfair shone out in one clear radiance. Upon this serene and orderly prospect the stars looked down, glittering, positive, hard, from a cloudless sky. In the extreme clearness of the atmosphere the line of every roof, the cowl of every chimney, was perceptible; even the cobbles in the streets showed distinct one from another, and Orlando could not help comparing this orderly scene with the irregular and huddled purlieus which had been the city of London in the reign of Queen Elizabeth. Then, she remembered, the city, if such one could call it, lay crowded, a mere huddle and conglomeration of houses, under her windows at Blackfriars. The stars reflected themselves in deep pits of stagnant water which lay in the middle of the streets. A black shadow at the corner where the wine shop used to stand was, as likely as not, the corpse of a murdered man. She could remember the cries of many a one wounded in such night brawlings, when she was a little boy, held to the diamond-paned window in her nurse's arms. Troops of ruffians, men and women, unspeakably interlaced, lurched down the streets, trolling out wild songs with jewels flashing in their ears, and knives gleaming in their fists. On such a night as this the impermeable tangle of the forests on Highgate and Hampstead would be outlined, writhing in contorted intricacy against the sky. Here and there, on one of the hills which rose above London, was a stark gallows tree, with a corpse nailed to rot or parch on its cross; for danger and insecurity, lust and violence, poetry and filth swarmed over the tortuous Elizabethan highways and buzzed and stank--Orlando could remember even now the smell of them on a hot night--in the little rooms and narrow pathways of the city. Now--she leant out of her window--all was light, order, and serenity. There was the faint rattle of a coach on the cobbles. She heard the faraway cry of the night watchman--'Just twelve o'clock on a frosty morning'. No sooner had the words left his lips than the first stroke of midnight sounded. Orlando then for the first time noticed a small cloud gathered behind the dome of St Paul's. As the strokes sounded, the cloud increased, and she saw it darken and spread with extraordinary speed. At the same time a light breeze rose and by the time the sixth stroke of midnight had struck the whole of the eastern sky was covered with an irregular moving darkness, though the sky to the west and north stayed clear as ever. Then the cloud spread north. Height upon height above the city was engulfed by it. Only Mayfair, with all its lights shining. burnt more brilliantly than ever by contrast. With the eighth stroke, some hurrying tatters of cloud sprawled over Piccadilly. They seemed to mass themselves and to advance with extraordinary rapidity towards the west end. As the ninth, tenth, and eleventh strokes struck, a huge blackness sprawled over the whole of London. With the twelfth stroke of midnight, the darkness was complete. A turbulent welter of cloud covered the city. All was darkness; all was doubt; all was confusion. The Eighteenth century was over; the Nineteenth century had begun.

CHAPTER 5.

The great cloud which hung, not only over London, but over the whole of the British Isles on the first day of the nineteenth century stayed, or rather, did not stay, for it was buffeted about constantly by blustering gales, long enough to have extraordinary consequences upon those who lived beneath its shadow. A change seemed to have come over the climate of England. Rain fell frequently, but only in fitful gusts, which were no sooner over than they began again. The sun shone, of course, but it was so girt about with clouds and the air was so saturated with water, that its beams were discoloured and purples, oranges, and reds of a dull sort took the place of the more positive landscapes of the eighteenth century. Under this bruised and sullen canopy the green of the cabbages was less intense, and the white of the snow was muddied. But what was worse, damp now began to make its way into every house--damp, which is the most insidious of all enemies, for while the sun can be shut out by blinds, and the frost roasted by a hot fire, damp steals in while we sleep; damp is silent, imperceptible, ubiquitous. Damp swells the wood, furs the kettle, rusts the iron, rots the stone. So gradual is the process, that it is not until we pick up some chest of drawers, or coal scuttle, and the whole thing drops to pieces in our hands, that we suspect even that the disease is at work.

Thus, stealthily and imperceptibly, none marking the exact day or hour of the change, the constitution of England was altered and nobody knew it. Everywhere the effects were felt. The hardy country gentleman, who had sat down gladly to a meal of ale and beef in a room designed, perhaps by the brothers Adam, with classic dignity, now felt chilly. Rugs appeared; beards were grown; trousers were fastened tight under the instep. The chill which he felt in his legs the country gentleman soon transferred to his house; furniture was muffled; walls and tables were covered; nothing was left bare. Then a change of diet became essential. The muffin was invented and the crumpet. Coffee supplanted the after-dinner port, and, as coffee led to a drawing-room in which to drink it, and a drawing-room to glass cases, and glass cases to artificial flowers, and artificial flowers to mantelpieces, and mantelpieces to pianofortes, and pianofortes to drawing-room ballads, and drawing-room ballads (skipping a stage or two) to innumerable little dogs, mats, and china ornaments, the home--which had become extremely important--was completely altered.

Outside the house--it was another effect of the damp--ivy grew in unparalleled profusion. Houses that had been of bare stone were smothered in greenery. No garden, however formal its original design, lacked a shrubbery, a wilderness, a maze. What light penetrated to the bedrooms where children were born was naturally of an obfusc green, and what light penetrated to the drawing-rooms where grown men and women lived came through curtains of brown and purple plush. But the change did not stop at outward things. The damp struck within. Men felt the chill in their hearts; the damp in their minds. In a desperate effort to snuggle their feelings into some sort of warmth one subterfuge was tried after another. Love, birth, and death were all swaddled in a variety of fine phrases. The sexes drew further and further apart. No open conversation was tolerated. Evasions and concealments were sedulously practised on both sides. And just as the ivy and the evergreen rioted in the damp earth outside, so did the same fertility show itself within. The life of the average woman was a succession of childbirths. She married at nineteen and had fifteen or eighteen children by the time she was thirty; for twins abounded. Thus the British Empire came into existence; and thus--for there is no stopping damp; it gets into the inkpot as it gets into the woodwork--sentences swelled, adjectives multiplied, lyrics became epics, and little trifles that had been essays a column long were now encyclopaedias in ten or twenty volumes. But Eusebius Chubb shall be our witness to the effect this all had upon the mind of a sensitive man who could do nothing to stop it. There is a passage towards the end of his memoirs where he describes how, after writing thirty-five folio pages one morning 'all about nothing' he screwed the lid of his inkpot and went for a turn in his garden. Soon he found himself involved in the shrubbery. Innumerable leaves creaked and glistened above his head. He seemed to himself 'to crush the mould of a million more under his feet'. Thick smoke exuded from a damp bonfire at the end of the garden. He reflected that no fire on earth could ever hope to consume that vast vegetable encumbrance. Wherever he looked, vegetation was rampant. Cucumbers 'came scrolloping across the grass to his feet'. Giant cauliflowers towered deck above deck till they rivalled, to his disordered imagination, the elm trees themselves. Hens laid incessantly eggs of no special tint. Then, remembering with a sigh his own fecundity and his poor wife Jane, now in the throes of her fifteenth confinement indoors, how, he asked himself, could he blame the fowls? He looked upwards into the sky. Did not heaven itself, or that great frontispiece of heaven, which is the sky, indicate the assent, indeed, the instigation of the heavenly hierarchy? For there, winter or summer, year in year out, the clouds turned and tumbled, like whales, he pondered, or elephants rather; but no, there was no escaping the simile which was pressed upon him from a thousand airy acres; the whole sky itself as it spread wide above the British Isles was nothing but a vast feather bed; and the undistinguished fecundity of the garden, the bedroom and the henroost was copied there. He went indoors, wrote the passage quoted above, laid his head in a gas oven, and when they found him later he was past revival.

While this went on in every part of England, it was all very well for Orlando to mew herself in her house at Blackfriars and pretend that the climate was the same; that one could still say what one liked and wear knee-breeches or skirts as the fancy took one. Even she, at length, was forced to acknowledge that times were changed. One afternoon in the early part of the century she was driving through St James's Park in her old panelled coach when one of those sunbeams, which occasionally, though not often, managed to come to earth, struggled through, marbling the clouds with strange prismatic colours as it passed. Such a sight was sufficiently strange after the clear and uniform skies of the eighteenth century to cause her to pull the window down and look at it. The puce and flamingo clouds made her think with a pleasurable anguish, which proves that she was insensibly afflicted with the damp already, of dolphins dying in Ionian seas. But what was her surprise when, as it struck the earth, the sunbeam seemed to call forth, or to light up, a pyramid, hecatomb, or trophy (for it had something of a banquet-table air)--a conglomeration at any rate of the most heterogeneous and ill-assorted objects, piled higgledy-piggledy in a vast mound where the statue of Queen Victoria now stands! Draped about a vast cross of fretted and floriated gold were widow's weeds and bridal veils; hooked on to other excrescences were crystal palaces, bassinettes, military helmets, memorial wreaths, trousers, whiskers, wedding cakes, cannon, Christmas trees, telescopes, extinct monsters, globes, maps, elephants, and mathematical instruments--the whole supported like a gigantic coat of arms on the right side by a female figure clothed in flowing white; on the left by a portly gentleman wearing a frock-coat and sponge-bag trousers. The incongruity of the objects, the association of the fully clothed and the partly draped, the garishness of the different colours and their plaid-like juxtapositions afflicted Orlando with the most profound dismay. She had never, in all her life, seen anything at once so indecent, so hideous, and so monumental. It might, and indeed it must be, the effect of the sun on the water-logged air; it would vanish with the first breeze that blew; but for all that, it looked, as she drove past, as if it were destined to endure for ever. Nothing, she felt, sinking back into the corner of her coach, no wind, rain, sun, or thunder, could ever demolish that garish erection. Only the noses would mottle and the trumpets would rust; but there they would remain, pointing east, west, south, and north, eternally. She looked back as her coach swept up Constitution Hill. Yes, there it was, still beaming placidly in a light which--she pulled her watch out of her fob--was, of course, the light of twelve o'clock mid-day. None other could be so prosaic, so matter-of-fact, so impervious to any hint of dawn or sunset, so seemingly calculated to last for ever. She was determined not to look again. Already she felt the tides of her blood run sluggishly. But what was more peculiar a blush, vivid and singular, overspread her cheeks as she passed Buckingham Palace and her eyes seemed forced by a superior power down upon her knees. Suddenly she saw with a start that she was wearing black breeches. She never ceased blushing till she had reached her country house, which, considering the time it takes four horses to trot thirty miles, will be taken, we hope, as a signal proof of her chastity.

Once there, she followed what had now become the most imperious need of her nature and wrapped herself as well as she could in a damask quilt which she snatched from her bed. She explained to the Widow Bartholomew (who had succeeded good old Grimsditch as housekeeper) that she felt chilly.

'So do we all, m'lady,' said the Widow, heaving a profound sigh. 'The walls is sweating,' she said, with a curious, lugubrious complacency, and sure enough, she had only to lay her hand on the oak panels for the finger-prints to be marked there. The ivy had grown so profusely that many windows were now sealed up. The kitchen was so dark that they could scarcely tell a kettle from a cullender. A poor black cat had been mistaken for coals and shovelled on the fire. Most of the maids were already wearing three or four red-flannel petticoats, though the month was August.

'But is it true, m'lady,' the good woman asked, hugging herself, while the golden crucifix heaved on her bosom, 'that the Queen, bless her, is wearing a what d'you call it, a--,' the good woman hesitated and blushed.

'A crinoline,' Orlando helped her out with it (for the word had reached Blackfriars). Mrs Bartholomew nodded. The tears were already running down her cheeks, but as she wept she smiled. For it was pleasant to weep. Were they not all of them weak women? wearing crinolines the better to conceal the fact; the great fact; the only fact; but, nevertheless, the deplorable fact; which every modest woman did her best to deny until denial was impossible; the fact that she was about to bear a child? to bear fifteen or twenty children indeed, so that most of a modest woman's life was spent, after all, in denying what, on one day at least of every year, was made obvious.

'The muffins is keepin' 'ot,' said Mrs Bartholomew, mopping up her tears, 'in the liberry.'

And wrapped in a damask bed quilt, to a dish of muffins Orlando now sat down.

'The muffins is keepin' 'ot in the liberry'--Orlando minced out the horrid cockney phrase in Mrs Bartholomew's refined cockney accents as she drank--but no, she detested the mild fluid--her tea. It was in this very room, she remembered, that Queen Elizabeth had stood astride the fireplace with a flagon of beer in her hand, which she suddenly dashed on the table when Lord Burghley tactlessly used the imperative instead of the subjunctive. 'Little man, little man,'--Orlando could hear her say--'is "must" a word to be addressed to princes?' And down came the flagon on the table: there was the mark of it still.

But when Orlando leapt to her feet, as the mere thought of that great Queen commanded, the bed quilt tripped her up, and she fell back in her arm-chair with a curse. Tomorrow she would have to buy twenty yards or more of black bombazine, she supposed, to make a skirt. And then (here she blushed), she would have to buy a crinoline, and then (here she blushed) a bassinette, and then another crinoline, and so on...The blushes came and went with the most exquisite iteration of modesty and shame imaginable. One might see the spirit of the age blowing, now hot, now cold, upon her cheeks. And if the spirit of the age blew a little unequally, the crinoline being blushed for before the husband, her ambiguous position must excuse her (even her sex was still in dispute) and the irregular life she had lived before.

At length the colour on her cheeks resumed its stability and it seemed as if the spirit of the age--if such indeed it were--lay dormant for a time. Then Orlando felt in the bosom of her shirt as if for some locket or relic of lost affection, and drew out no such thing, but a roll of paper, sea-stained, blood-stained, travel-stained--the manuscript of her poem, 'The Oak Tree'. She had carried this about with her for so many years now, and in such hazardous circumstances, that many of the pages were stained, some were torn, while the straits she had been in for writing paper when with the gipsies, had forced her to overscore the margins and cross the lines till the manuscript looked like a piece of darning most conscientiously carried out. She turned back to the first page and read the date, 1586, written in her own boyish hand. She had been working at it for close three hundred years now. It was time to make an end. Meanwhile she began turning and dipping and reading and skipping and thinking as she read, how very little she had changed all these years. She had been a gloomy boy, in love with death, as boys are; and then she had been amorous and florid; and then she had been sprightly and satirical; and sometimes she had tried prose and sometimes she had tried drama. Yet through all these changes she had remained, she reflected, fundamentally the same. She had the same brooding meditative temper, the same love of animals and nature, the same passion for the country and the seasons.

'After all,' she thought, getting up and going to the window, 'nothing has changed. The house, the garden are precisely as they were. Not a chair has been moved, not a trinket sold. There are the same walks, the same lawns, the same trees, and the same pool, which, I dare say, has the same carp in it. True, Queen Victoria is on the throne and not Queen Elizabeth, but what difference...'

No sooner had the thought taken shape, than, as if to rebuke it, the door was flung wide and in marched Basket, the butler, followed by Bartholomew, the housekeeper, to clear away tea. Orlando, who had just dipped her pen in the ink, and was about to indite some reflection upon the eternity of all things, was much annoyed to be impeded by a blot, which spread and meandered round her pen. It was some infirmity of the quill, she supposed; it was split or dirty. She dipped it again. The blot increased. She tried to go on with what she was saying; no words came. Next she began to decorate the blot with wings and whiskers, till it became a round-headed monster, something between a bat and a wombat. But as for writing poetry with Basket and Bartholomew in the room, it was impossible. No sooner had she said 'Impossible' than, to her astonishment and alarm, the pen began to curve and caracole with the smoothest possible fluency. Her page was written in the neatest sloping Italian hand with the most insipid verse she had ever read in her life:

I am myself but a vile link Amid life's weary chain, But I have spoken hallow'd words, Oh, do not say in vain!

Will the young maiden, when her tears, Alone in moonlight shine, Tears for the absent and the loved, Murmur--

she wrote without a stop as Bartholomew and Basket grunted and groaned about the room, mending the fire, picking up the muffins.

Again she dipped her pen and off it went:--

She was so changed, the soft carnation cloud Once mantling o'er her cheek like that which eve Hangs o'er the sky, glowing with roseate hue, Had faded into paleness, broken by Bright burning blushes, torches of the tomb,

but here, by an abrupt movement she spilt the ink ever the page and blotted it from human sight she hoped for ever. She was all of a quiver, all of a stew. Nothing more repulsive could be imagined than to feel the ink flowing thus in cascades of involuntary inspiration. What had happened to her? Was it the damp, was it Bartholomew, was it Basket, what was it? she demanded. But the room was empty. No one answered her, unless the dripping of the rain in the ivy could be taken for an answer.

Meanwhile, she became conscious, as she stood at the window, of an extraordinary tingling and vibration all over her, as if she were made of a thousand wires upon which some breeze or errant fingers were playing scales. Now her toes tingled; now her marrow. She had the queerest sensations about the thigh bones. Her hairs seemed to erect themselves. Her arms sang and twanged as the telegraph wires would be singing and twanging in twenty years or so. But all this agitation seemed at length to concentrate in her hands; and then in one hand, and then in one finger of that hand, and then finally to contract itself so that it made a ring of quivering sensibility about the second finger of the left hand. And when she raised it to see what caused this agitation, she saw nothing--nothing but the vast solitary emerald which Queen Elizabeth had given her. And was that not enough? she asked. It was of the finest water. It was worth ten thousand pounds at least. The vibration seemed, in the oddest way (but remember we are dealing with some of the darkest manifestations of the human soul) to say No, that is not enough; and, further, to assume a note of interrogation, as though it were asking, what did it mean, this hiatus, this strange oversight? till poor Orlando felt positively ashamed of the second finger of her left hand without in the least knowing why. At this moment, Bartholomew came in to ask which dress she should lay out for dinner, and Orlando, whose senses were much quickened, instantly glanced at Bartholomew's left hand, and instantly perceived what she had never noticed before--a thick ring of rather jaundiced yellow circling the third finger where her own was bare.

'Let me look at your ring, Bartholomew,' she said, stretching her hand to take it.

At this, Bartholomew made as if she had been struck in the breast by a rogue. She started back a pace or two, clenched her hand and flung it away from her with a gesture that was noble in the extreme. 'No,' she said, with resolute dignity, her Ladyship might look if she pleased, but as for taking off her wedding ring, not the Archbishop nor the Pope nor Queen Victoria on her throne could force her to do that. Her Thomas had put it on her finger twenty-five years, six months, three weeks ago; she had slept in it; worked in it; washed in it; prayed in it; and proposed to be buried in it. In fact, Orlando understood her to say, but her voice was much broken with emotion; that it was by the gleam on her wedding ring that she would be assigned her station among the angels and its lustre would be tarnished for ever if she let it out of her keeping for a second.

'Heaven help us,' said Orlando, standing at the window and watching the pigeons at their pranks, 'what a world we live in! What a world to be sure!' Its complexities amazed her. It now seemed to her that the whole world was ringed with gold. She went in to dinner. Wedding rings abounded. She went to church. Wedding rings were everywhere. She drove out. Gold, or pinchbeck, thin, thick, plain, smooth, they glowed dully on every hand. Rings filled the jewellers' shops, not the flashing pastes and diamonds of Orlando's recollection, but simple bands without a stone in them. At the same time, she began to notice a new habit among the town people. In the old days, one would meet a boy trifling with a girl under a hawthorn hedge frequently enough. Orlando had flicked many a couple with the tip of her whip and laughed and passed on. Now, all that was changed. Couples trudged and plodded in the middle of the road indissolubly linked together. The woman's right hand was invariably passed through the man's left and her fingers were firmly gripped by his. Often it was not till the horses' noses were on them that they budged, and then, though they moved it was all in one piece, heavily, to the side of the road. Orlando could only suppose that some new discovery had been made about the race; that they were somehow stuck together, couple after couple, but who had made it and when, she could not guess. It did not seem to be Nature. She looked at the doves and the rabbits and the elk-hounds and she could not see that Nature had changed her ways or mended them, since the time of Elizabeth at least. There was no indissoluble alliance among the brutes that she could see. Could it be Queen Victoria then, or Lord Melbourne? Was it from them that the great discovery of marriage proceeded? Yet the Queen, she pondered, was said to be fond of dogs, and Lord Melbourne, she had heard, was said to be fond of women. It was strange--it was distasteful; indeed, there was something in this indissolubility of bodies which was repugnant to her sense of decency and sanitation. Her ruminations, however, were accompanied by such a tingling and twanging of the afflicted finger that she could scarcely keep her ideas in order. They were languishing and ogling like a housemaid's fancies. They made her blush. There was nothing for it but to buy one of those ugly bands and wear it like the rest. This she did, slipping it, overcome with shame, upon her finger in the shadow of a curtain; but without avail. The tingling persisted more violently, more indignantly than ever. She did not sleep a wink that night. Next morning when she took up the pen to write, either she could think of nothing, and the pen made one large lachrymose blot after another, or it ambled off, more alarmingly still, into mellifluous fluencies about early death and corruption, which were worse than no thinking at all. For it would seem--her case proved it--that we write, not with the fingers, but with the whole person. The nerve which controls the pen winds itself about every fibre of our being, threads the heart, pierces the liver. Though the seat of her trouble seemed to be the left hand, she could feel herself poisoned through and through, and was forced at length to consider the most desperate of remedies, which was to yield completely and submissively to the spirit of the age, and take a husband.

That this was much against her natural temperament has been sufficiently made plain. When the sound of the Archduke's chariot wheels died away, the cry that rose to her lips was 'Life! A Lover!' not 'Life! A Husband!' and it was in pursuit of this aim that she had gone to town and run about the world as has been shown in the previous chapter. Such is the indomitable nature of the spirit of the age, however, that it batters down anyone who tries to make stand against it far more effectually than those who bend its own way. Orlando had inclined herself naturally to the Elizabethan spirit, to the Restoration spirit, to the spirit of the eighteenth century, and had in consequence scarcely been aware of the change from one age to the other. But the spirit of the nineteenth century was antipathetic to her in the extreme, and thus it took her and broke her, and she was aware of her defeat at its hands as she had never been before. For it is probable that the human spirit has its place in time assigned to it; some are born of this age, some of that; and now that Orlando was grown a woman, a year or two past thirty indeed, the lines of her character were fixed, and to bend them the wrong way was intolerable.

So she stood mournfully at the drawing-room window (Bartholomew had so christened the library) dragged down by the weight of the crinoline which she had submissively adopted. It was heavier and more drab than any dress she had yet worn. None had ever so impeded her movements. No longer could she stride through the garden with her dogs, or run lightly to the high mound and fling herself beneath the oak tree. Her skirts collected damp leaves and straw. The plumed hat tossed on the breeze. The thin shoes were quickly soaked and mud-caked. Her muscles had lost their pliancy. She became nervous lest there should be robbers behind the wainscot and afraid, for the first time in her life, of ghosts in the corridors. All these things inclined her, step by step, to submit to the new discovery, whether Queen Victoria's or another's, that each man and each woman has another allotted to it for life, whom it supports, by whom it is supported, till death them do part. It would be a comfort, she felt, to lean; to sit down; yes, to lie down; never, never, never to get up again. Thus did the spirit work upon her, for all her past pride, and as she came sloping down the scale of emotion to this lowly and unaccustomed lodging-place, those twangings and tinglings which had been so captious and so interrogative modulated into the sweetest melodies, till it seemed as if angels were plucking harp-strings with white fingers and her whole being was pervaded by a seraphic harmony.

But whom could she lean upon? She asked that question of the wild autumn winds. For it was now October, and wet as usual. Not the Archduke; he had married a very great lady and had hunted hares in Roumania these many years now; nor Mr M.; he was become a Catholic; nor the Marquis of C.; he made sacks in

Botany Bay; nor the Lord O.; he had long been food for fishes. One way or another, all her old cronies were gone now, and the Nells and the Kits of Drury Lane, much though she favoured them, scarcely did to lean upon.

'Whom', she asked, casting her eyes upon the revolving clouds, clasping her hands as she knelt on the window-sill, and looking the very image of appealing womanhood as she did so, 'can I lean upon?' Her words formed themselves, her hands clasped themselves, involuntarily, just as her pen had written of its own accord. It was not Orlando who spoke, but the spirit of the age. But whichever it was, nobody answered it. The rooks were tumbling pell-mell among the violet clouds of autumn. The rain had stopped at last and there was an iridescence in the sky which tempted her to put on her plumed hat and her little stringed shoes and stroll out before dinner.

'Everyone is mated except myself,' she mused, as she trailed disconsolately across the courtyard. There were the rooks; Canute and Pippin even--transitory as their alliances were, still each this evening seemed to have a partner. 'Whereas, I, who am mistress of it all,' Orlando thought, glancing as she passed at the innumerable emblazoned windows of the hall, 'am single, am mateless, am alone.'

Such thoughts had never entered her head before. Now they bore her down unescapably. Instead of thrusting the gate open, she tapped with a gloved hand for the porter to unfasten it for her. One must lean on someone, she thought, if it is only on a porter; and half wished to stay behind and help him to grill his chop on a bucket of fiery coals, but was too timid to ask it. So she strayed out into the park alone, faltering at first and apprehensive lest there might be poachers or gamekeepers or even errand-boys to marvel that a great lady should walk alone.

At every step she glanced nervously lest some male form should be hiding behind a furze bush or some savage cow be lowering its horns to toss her. But there were only the rooks flaunting in the sky. A steel-blue plume from one of them fell among the heather. She loved wild birds' feathers. She had used to collect them as a boy. She picked it up and stuck it in her hat. The air blew upon her spirit somewhat and revived it. As the rooks went whirling and wheeling above her head and feather after feather fell gleaming through the purplish air, she followed them, her long cloak floating behind her, over the moor, up the hill. She had not walked so far for years. Six feathers had she picked from the grass and drawn between her fingers and pressed to her lips to feel their smooth, glinting plumage, when she saw, gleaming on the hill-side, a silver pool, mysterious as the lake into which Sir Bedivere flung the sword of Arthur. A single feather quivered in the air and fell into the middle of it. Then, some strange ecstasy came over her. Some wild notion she had of following the birds to the rim of the world and flinging herself on the spongy turf and there drinking forgetfulness, while the rooks' hoarse laughter sounded over her. She quickened her pace; she ran; she tripped; the tough heather roots flung her to the ground. Her ankle was broken. She could not rise. But there she lay content. The scent of the bog myrtle and the meadow-sweet was in her nostrils. The rooks' hoarse laughter was in her ears. 'I have found my mate,' she murmured. 'It is the moor. I am nature's bride,' she whispered, giving herself in rapture to the cold embraces of the grass as she lay folded in her cloak in the hollow by the pool. 'Here will I lie. (A feather fell upon her brow.) I have found a greener laurel than the bay. My forehead will be cool always. These are wild birds' feathers--the owl's, the nightjar's. I shall dream wild dreams. My hands shall wear no wedding ring,' she continued, slipping it from her finger. 'The roots shall twine about them. Ah!' she sighed, pressing her head luxuriously on its spongy pillow, 'I have sought happiness through many ages and not found it; fame and missed it; love and not known it; life--and behold, death is better. I have known many men and many women,' she continued; 'none have I understood. It is better that I should lie at peace here with only the sky above me--as the gipsy told me years ago. That was in Turkey.' And she looked straight up into the marvellous golden foam into which the clouds had churned themselves, and saw next moment a track in it, and camels passing in single file through the rocky desert among clouds of red dust; and then, when the camels had passed, there were only mountains, very high and full of clefts and with pinnacles of rock, and she fancied she heard goat bells ringing in their passes, and in their folds were fields of irises and gentian. So the sky changed and her eyes slowly lowered themselves down and down till they came to the rain-darkened earth and saw the great hump of the South Downs, flowing in one wave along the coast; and where the land parted, there was the sea, the sea with ships passing; and she fancied she heard a gun far out at sea, and thought at first, 'That's the Armada,' and then thought 'No, it's Nelson', and then remembered how those wars were over and the ships were busy merchant ships; and the sails on the winding river were those of pleasure boats. She saw, too, cattle sprinkled on the dark fields, sheep and cows, and she saw the lights coming here and there in farm-house windows, and lanterns moving among the cattle as the shepherd went his rounds and the cowman; and then the lights went out and the stars rose and tangled themselves about the sky. Indeed, she was falling asleep with the wet feathers on her face and her ear pressed to the ground when she heard, deep within, some hammer on an anvil, or was it a heart beating? Tick-tock, tick-tock, so it hammered, so it beat, the anvil, or the heart in the middle of the earth; until, as she listened, she thought it changed to the trot of a horse's hoofs; one, two, three, four, she counted; then she heard a stumble; then, as it came nearer and nearer, she could hear the crack of a twig and the suck of the wet bog in its hoofs. The horse was almost on her. She sat upright. Towering dark against the yellow-slashed sky of dawn, with the plovers rising and falling about him, she saw a man on horseback. He started. The horse stopped.

'Madam,' the man cried, leaping to the ground, 'you're hurt!'

'I'm dead, sir!' she replied.

A few minutes later, they became engaged.

The morning after, as they sat at breakfast, he told her his name. It was Marmaduke Bonthrop Shelmerdine, Esquire.

'I knew it!' she said, for there was something romantic and chivalrous, passionate, melancholy, yet determined about him which went with the wild, dark-plumed name--a name which had, in her mind, the steel-blue gleam of rooks' wings, the hoarse laughter of their caws, the snake-like twisting descent of their feathers in a silver pool, and a thousand other things which will be described presently.

'Mine is Orlando,' she said. He had guessed it. For if you see a ship in full sail coming with the sun on it proudly sweeping across the Mediterranean from the South Seas, one says at once, 'Orlando', he explained.

In fact, though their acquaintance had been so short, they had guessed, as always happens between lovers, everything of any importance about each other in two seconds at the utmost, and it now remained only to fill in such unimportant details as what they were called; where they lived; and whether they were beggars or people of substance. He had a castle in the Hebrides, but it was ruined, he told her. Gannets feasted in the banqueting hall. He had been a soldier and a sailor, and had explored the East. He was on his way now to join his brig at Falmouth, but the wind had fallen and it was only when the gale blew from the South-west that he could put out to sea. Orlando looked hastily from the breakfast-room window at the gilt leopard on the weather vane. Mercifully its tail pointed due east and was steady as a rock. 'Oh! Shel, don't leave me!' she cried. 'I'm passionately in love with you,' she said. No sooner had the words left her mouth than an awful suspicion rushed into both their minds simultaneously.

'You're a woman, Shel!' she cried.

'You're a man, Orlando!' he cried.

Never was there such a scene of protestation and demonstration as then took place since the world began. When it was over and they were seated again she asked him, what was this talk of a South-west gale? Where was he bound for?

'For the Horn,' he said briefly, and blushed. (For a man had to blush as a woman had, only at rather different things.) It was only by dint of great pressure on her side and the use of much intuition that she gathered that his life was spent in the most desperate and splendid of adventures--which is to voyage round Cape Horn in the teeth of a gale. Masts had been snapped off; sails torn to ribbons (she had to drag the admission from him). Sometimes the ship had sunk, and he had been left the only survivor on a raft with a biscuit.

'It's about all a fellow can do nowadays,' he said sheepishly, and helped himself to great spoonfuls of strawberry jam. The vision which she had thereupon of this boy (for he was little more) sucking peppermints, for which he had a passion, while the masts snapped and the stars reeled and he roared brief orders to cut this adrift, to heave that overboard, brought the tears to her eyes, tears, she noted, of a finer flavour than any she had cried before: 'I am a woman,' she thought, 'a real woman, at last.' She thanked Bonthrop from the bottom of her heart for having given her this rare and unexpected delight. Had she not been lame in the left foot, she would have sat upon his knee.

'Shel, my darling,' she began again, 'tell me...' and so they talked two hours or more, perhaps about Cape Horn, perhaps not, and really it would profit little to write down what they said, for they knew each other so well that they could say anything, which is tantamount to saying nothing, or saying such stupid, prosy things as how to cook an omelette, or where to buy the best boots in London, things which have no lustre taken from their setting, yet are positively of amazing beauty within it. For it has come about, by the wise economy of nature, that our modern spirit can almost dispense with language; the commonest expressions do, since no expressions do; hence the most ordinary conversation is often the most poetic, and the most poetic is precisely that which cannot be written down. For which reasons we leave a great blank here, which must be taken to indicate that the space is filled to repletion.

After some days more of this kind of talk,

'Orlando, my dearest,' Shel was beginning, when there was a scuffling outside, and Basket the butler entered with the information that there was a couple of Peelers downstairs with a warrant from the Queen.

'Show 'em up,' said Shelmerdine briefly, as if on his own quarter-deck, taking up, by instinct, a stand with his hands behind him in front of the fireplace. Two officers in bottlegreen uniforms with truncheons at their hips then entered the room and stood at attention. Formalities being over, they gave into Orlando's own hands, as their commission was, a legal document of some very impressive sort; judging by the blobs of sealing wax, the ribbons, the oaths, and the signatures, which were all of the highest importance.

Orlando ran her eyes through it and then, using the first finger of her right hand as pointer, read out the following facts as being most germane to the matter.

'The lawsuits are settled,' she read out...'some in my favour, as for example...others not. Turkish marriage annulled (I was ambassador in Constantinople, Shel,' she explained) 'Children pronounced illegitimate, (they said I had three sons by Pepita, a Spanish dancer). So they don't inherit, which is all to the good...Sex? Ah! what about sex? My sex', she read out with some solemnity, 'is pronounced indisputably, and beyond the shadow of a doubt (what I was telling you a moment ago, Shel?), female. The estates which are now desequestrated in perpetuity descend and are tailed and entailed upon the heirs male of my body, or in default of marriage'--but here she grew impatient with this legal verbiage, and said, 'but there won't be any default of marriage, nor of heirs either, so the rest can be taken as read.' Whereupon she appended her own signature beneath Lord Palmerston's and entered from that moment into the undisturbed possession of her titles, her house, and her estate--which was now so much shrunk, for the cost of the lawsuits had been prodigious, that, though she was infinitely noble again, she was also excessively poor.

When the result of the lawsuit was made known (and rumour flew much quicker than the telegraph which has supplanted it), the whole town was filled with rejoicings.

[Horses were put into carriages for the sole purpose of being taken out. Empty barouches and landaus were trundled up and down the High Street incessantly. Addresses were read from the Bull. Replies were made from the Stag. The town was illuminated. Gold caskets were securely sealed in glass cases. Coins were well and duly laid under stones. Hospitals were founded. Rat and Sparrow clubs were inaugurated. Turkish women by the dozen were burnt in effigy in the market-place, together with scores of peasant boys with the label 'I am a base Pretender', lolling from their mouths. The Queen's cream-coloured ponies were soon seen trotting up the avenue with a command to Orlando to dine and sleep at the Castle, that very same night. Her table, as on a previous occasion, was snowed under with invitations from the Countess if R., Lady Q., Lady Palmerston, the Marchioness of P., Mrs W.E. Gladstone and others, beseeching the pleasure of her company, reminding her of ancient alliances between their family and her own, etc.]--all of which is properly enclosed in square brackets, as above, for the good reason that a parenthesis it was without any importance in Orlando's life. She skipped it, to get on with the text. For when the bonfires were blazing in the marketplace, she was in the dark woods with Shelmerdine alone. So fine was the weather that the trees stretched their branches motionless above them, and if a leaf fell, it fell, spotted red and gold, so slowly that one could watch it for half an hour fluttering and falling till it came to rest at last, on Orlando's foot.

'Tell me, Mar,' she would say (and here it must be explained, that when she called him by the first syllable of his first name, she was in a dreamy, amorous, acquiescent mood, domestic, languid a little, as if spiced logs were burning, and it was evening, yet not time to dress, and a thought wet perhaps outside, enough to make the leaves glisten, but a nightingale might be singing even so among the azaleas, two or three dogs barking at distant farms, a cock crowing--all of which the reader should imagine in her voice)--'Tell me, Mar,' she would say, 'about Cape Horn.' Then Shelmerdine would make a little model on the ground of the Cape with twigs and dead leaves and an empty snail shell or two.

'Here's the north,' he would say. 'There's the south. The wind's coming from hereabouts. Now the brig is sailing due west; we've just lowered the top-boom mizzen: and so you see--here, where this bit of grass is, she enters the current which you'll find marked--where's my map and compasses, Bo'sun? Ah! thanks, that'll do, where the snail shell is. The current catches her on the starboard side, so we must rig the jib-boom or we shall be carried to the larboard, which is where that beech leaf is,--for you must understand my dear--' and so he would go on, and she would listen to every word; interpreting them rightly, so as to see, that is to say, without his having to tell her, the phosphorescence on the waves; the icicles clanking in the shrouds; how he went to the top of the mast in a gale; there reflected on the destiny of man; came down again; had a whisky and soda; went on shore; was trapped by a black woman; repented; reasoned it out; read Pascal; determined to write philosophy; bought a monkey; debated the true end of life; decided in favour of Cape Horn, and so on. All this and a thousand other things she understood him to say, and so when she replied, Yes, negresses are seductive, aren't they? he having told her that the supply of biscuits now gave out, he was surprised and delighted to find how well she had taken his meaning.

'Are you positive you aren't a man?' he would ask anxiously, and she would echo,

'Can it be possible you're not a woman?' and then they must put it to the proof without more ado. For each was so surprised at the quickness of the other's sympathy, and it was to each such a revelation that a woman could be as tolerant and free-spoken as a man, and a man as strange and subtle as a woman, that they had to put the matter to the proof at once.

And so they would go on talking or rather, understanding, which has become the main art of speech in an age when words are growing daily so scanty in comparison with ideas that 'the biscuits ran out' has to stand for kissing a negress in the dark when one has just read Bishop Berkeley's philosophy for the tenth time. (And from this it follows that only the most profound masters of style can tell the truth, and when one meets a simple one-syllable writer, one may conclude, without any doubt at all, that the poor man is lying.)

So they would talk; and then, when her feet were fairly covered with spotted autumn leaves, Orlando would rise and stroll away into the heart of the woods in solitude, leaving Bonthrop sitting there among the snail shells, making models of Cape Horn. 'Bonthrop,' she would say, 'I'm off,' and when she called him by his second name, 'Bonthrop', it should signify to the reader that she was in a solitary mood, felt them both as specks on a desert, was desirous only of meeting death by herself, for people die daily, die at dinner tables, or like this, out of doors in the autumn woods; and with the bonfires blazing and Lady Palmerston or Lady Derby asking her out every night to dinner, the desire for death would overcome her, and so saying 'Bonthrop', she said in effect, 'I'm dead', and pushed her way as a spirit might through the spectre-pale beech trees, and so oared herself deep into solitude as if the little flicker of noise and movement were over and she were free now to take her way--all of which the reader should hear in her voice when she said 'Bonthrop,' and should also add, the better to illumine the word, that for him too the same word signified, mystically, separation and isolation and the disembodied pacing the deck of his brig in unfathomable seas.

After some hours of death, suddenly a jay shrieked 'Shelmerdine', and stooping, she picked up one of those autumn crocuses which to some people signify that very word, and put it with the jay's feather that came tumbling blue through the beech woods, in her breast. Then she called 'Shelmerdine' and the word went shooting this way and that way through the woods and struck him where he sat, making models out of snail shells in the grass. He saw her, and heard her coming to him with the crocus and the jay's feather in her breast, and cried 'Orlando', which meant (and it must be remembered that when bright colours like blue and yellow mix themselves in our eyes, some of it rubs off on our thoughts) first the bowing and swaying of bracken as if something were breaking through; which proved to be a ship in full sail, heaving and tossing a little dreamily, rather as if she had a whole year of summer days to make her voyage in; and so the ship bears down, heaving this way, heaving that way, nobly, indolently, and rides over the crest of this wave and sinks into the hollow of that one, and so, suddenly stands over you (who are in a little cockle shell of a boat, looking up at her) with all her sails quivering, and then, behold, they drop all of a heap on deck--as Orlando dropped now into the grass beside him.

Eight or nine days had been spent thus, but on the tenth, which was the 26th of October, Orlando was lying in the bracken, while Shelmerdine recited Shelley (whose entire works he had by heart), when a leaf which had started to fall slowly enough from a treetop whipped briskly across Orlando's foot. A second leaf followed and then a third. Orlando shivered and turned pale. It was the wind. Shelmerdine--but it would be more proper now to call him Bonthrop--leapt to his feet.

'The wind!' he cried.

Together they ran through the woods, the wind plastering them with leaves as they ran, to the great court and through it and the little courts, frightened servants leaving their brooms and their saucepans to follow after till they reached the Chapel, and there a scattering of lights was lit as fast as could be, one knocking over this bench, another snuffing out that taper. Bells were rung. People were summoned. At length there was Mr Dupper catching at the ends of his white tie and asking where was the prayer book. And they thrust Queen Mary's prayer book in his hands and he searched, hastily fluttering the pages, and said, 'Marmaduke Bonthrop Shelmerdine, and Lady Orlando, kneel down'; and they knelt down, and now they were bright and now they were dark as the light and shadow came flying helter-skelter through the painted windows; and among the banging of innumerable doors and a sound like brass pots beating, the organ sounded, its growl coming loud and faint alternately, and Mr Dupper, who was grown a very old man, tried now to raise his voice above the uproar and could not be heard and then all was quiet for a moment, and one word--it might be 'the jaws of death'--rang out clear, while all the estate servants kept pressing in with rakes and whips still in their hands to listen, and some sang loud and others prayed, and now a bird was dashed against the pane, and now there was a clap of thunder, so that no one heard the word Obey spoken or saw, except as a golden flash, the ring pass from hand to hand. All was movement and confusion. And up they rose with the organ booming and the lightning playing and the rain pouring, and the Lady Orlando, with her ring on her finger, went out into the court in her thin dress and held the swinging stirrup, for the horse was bitted and bridled and the foam was still on his flank, for her husband to mount, which he did with one bound, and the horse leapt forward and Orlando, standing there, cried out Marmaduke Bonthrop Shelmerdine! and he answered her Orlando! and the words went dashing and circling like wild hawks together among the belfries and higher and higher, further and further, faster and faster they circled, till they crashed and fell in a shower of fragments to the ground; and she went in.

CHAPTER 6.

Orlando went indoors. It was completely still. It was very silent. There was the ink pot: there was the pen; there was the manuscript of her poem, broken off in the middle of a tribute to eternity. She had been about to say, when Basket and Bartholomew interrupted with the tea things, nothing changes. And then, in the space of three seconds and a half, everything had changed--she had broken her ankle, fallen in love, married Shelmerdine.

There was the wedding ring on her finger to prove it. It was true that she had put it there herself before she met Shelmerdine, but that had proved worse than useless. She now turned the ring round and round, with superstitious reverence, taking care lest it should slip past the joint of her finger.

'The wedding ring has to be put on the third finger of the left hand', she said, like a child cautiously repeating its lesson, 'for it to be of any use at all.'

She spoke thus, aloud and rather more pompously than was her wont, as if she wished someone whose good opinion she desired to overhear her. Indeed, she had in mind, now that she was at last able to collect her thoughts, the effect that her behaviour would have had upon the spirit of the age. She was extremely anxious to be informed whether the steps she had taken in the matter of getting engaged to Shelmerdine and marrying him met with its approval. She was certainly feeling more herself. Her finger had not tingled once, or nothing to count, since that night on the moor. Yet, she could not deny that she had her doubts. She was married, true; but if one's husband was always sailing round Cape Horn, was it marriage? If one liked him, was it marriage? If one liked other people, was it marriage? And finally, if one still wished, more than anything in the whole world, to write poetry, was it marriage? She had her doubts.

But she would put it to the test. She looked at the ring. She looked at the ink pot. Did she dare? No, she did not. But she must. No, she could not. What should she do then? Faint, if possible. But she had never felt better in her life.

'Hang it all!' she cried, with a touch of her old spirit. 'Here goes!'

And she plunged her pen neck deep in the ink. To her enormous surprise, there was no explosion. She drew the nib out. It was wet, but not dripping. She wrote. The words were a little long in coming, but come they did. Ah! but did they make sense? she wondered, a panic coming over her lest the pen might have been at some of its involuntary pranks again. She read,

And then I came to a field where the springing grass Was dulled by the hanging cups of fritillaries, Sullen and foreign-looking, the snaky flower, Scarfed in dull purple, like Egyptian girls:--

As she wrote she felt some power (remember we are dealing with the most obscure manifestations of the human spirit) reading over her shoulder, and when she had written 'Egyptian girls', the power told her to stop. Grass, the power seemed to say, going back with a ruler such as governesses use to the beginning, is all right; the hanging cups of fritillaries--admirable; the snaky flower--a thought, strong from a lady's pen, perhaps, but Wordsworth no doubt, sanctions it; but--girls? Are girls necessary? You have a husband at the Cape, you say? Ah, well, that'll do.

And so the spirit passed on.

Orlando now performed in spirit (for all this took place in spirit) a deep obeisance to the spirit of her age, such as--to compare great things with small--a traveller, conscious that he has a bundle of cigars in the corner of his suit case, makes to the customs officer who has obligingly made a scribble of white chalk on the lid. For she was extremely doubtful whether, if the spirit had examined the contents of her mind carefully, it would not have found something highly contraband for which she would have had to pay the full fine. She had only escaped by the skin of her teeth. She had just managed, by some dexterous deference to the spirit of the age, by putting on a ring and finding a man on a moor, by loving nature and being no satirist, cynic, or psychologist--any one of which goods would have been discovered at once--to pass its examination successfully. And she heaved a deep sigh of relief, as, indeed, well she might, for the transaction between a writer and the spirit of the age is one of infinite delicacy, and upon a nice arrangement between the two the whole fortune of his works depends. Orlando had so ordered it that she was in an extremely happy position; she need neither fight her age, nor submit to it; she was of it, yet remained herself. Now, therefore, she could write, and write she did. She wrote. She wrote. She wrote.

It was now November. After November, comes December. Then January, February, March, and April. After April comes May. June, July, August follow. Next is September. Then October, and so, behold, here we are back at November again, with a whole year accomplished.

This method of writing biography, though it has its merits, is a little bare, perhaps, and the reader, if we go on with it, may complain that he could recite the calendar for himself and so save his pocket whatever sum the Hogarth Press may think proper to charge for this book. But what can the biographer do when his subject has put him in the predicament into which Orlando has now put us? Life, it has been agreed by everyone whose opinion is worth consulting, is the only fit subject for novelist or biographer; life, the same authorities have decided, has nothing whatever to do with sitting still in a chair and thinking. Thought and life are as the poles asunder. Therefore--since sitting in a chair and thinking is precisely what Orlando is doing now--there is nothing for it but to recite the calendar, tell one's beads, blow one's nose, stir the fire, look out of the window, until she has done. Orlando sat so still that you could have heard a pin drop. Would, indeed, that a pin had dropped! That would have been life of a kind. Or if a butterfly had fluttered through the window and settled on her chair, one could write about that. Or suppose she had got up and killed a wasp. Then, at once, we could out with our pens and write. For there would be blood shed, if only the blood of a wasp. Where there is blood there is life. And if killing a wasp is the merest trifle compared with killing a man, still it is a fitter subject for novelist or biographer than this mere wool-gathering; this thinking; this sitting in a chair day in, day out, with a cigarette and a sheet of paper and a pen and an ink pot. If only subjects, we might complain (for our patience is wearing thin), had more consideration for their biographers! What is more irritating than to see one's subject, on whom one has lavished so much time and trouble, slipping out of one's grasp altogether and indulging--witness her sighs and gasps, her flushing, her palings, her eyes now bright as lamps, now haggard as dawns--what is more humiliating than to see all this dumb show of emotion and excitement gone through before our eyes when we know that what causes it--thought and imagination--are of no importance whatsoever?

But Orlando was a woman--Lord Palmerston had just proved it. And when we are writing the life of a woman, we may, it is agreed, waive our demand for action, and substitute love instead. Love, the poet has said, is woman's whole existence. And if we look for a moment at Orlando writing at her table, we must admit that never was there a woman more fitted for that calling. Surely, since she is a woman, and a beautiful woman, and a woman in the prime of life, she will soon give over this pretence of writing and thinking and begin at least to think of a gamekeeper (and as long as she thinks of a man, nobody objects to a woman thinking). And then she will write him a little note (and as long as she writes little notes nobody objects to a woman writing either) and make an assignation for Sunday dusk and Sunday dusk will come; and the gamekeeper will whistle under the window--all of which is, of course, the very stuff of life and the only possible subject for fiction. Surely Orlando must have done one of these things? Alas,--a thousand times, alas, Orlando did none of them. Must it then be admitted that Orlando was one of those monsters of iniquity who do not love? She was kind to dogs, faithful to friends, generosity itself to a dozen starving poets, had a passion for poetry. But love--as the male novelists define it--and who, after all, speak with greater authority?--has nothing whatever to do with kindness, fidelity, generosity, or poetry. Love is slipping off one's petticoat and--But we all know what love is. Did Orlando do that? Truth compels us to say no, she did not. If then, the subject of one's biography will neither love nor kill, but will only think and imagine, we may conclude that he or she is no better than a corpse and so leave her.

The only resource now left us is to look out of the window. There were sparrows; there were starlings; there were a number of doves, and one or two rooks, all occupied after their fashion. One finds a worm, another a snail. One flutters to a branch, another takes a little run on the turf. Then a servant crosses the courtyard, wearing a green baize apron. Presumably he is engaged on some intrigue with one of the maids in the pantry, but as no visible proof is offered us, in the courtyard, we can but hope for the best and leave it. Clouds pass, thin or thick, with some disturbance of the colour of the grass beneath. The sun-dial registers the hour in its usual cryptic way. One's mind begins tossing up a question or two, idly, vainly, about this same life. Life, it sings, or croons rather, like a kettle on a hob. Life, life, what art thou? Light or darkness, the baize apron of the under-footman or the shadow of the starling on the grass?

Let us go, then, exploring, this summer morning, when all are adoring the plum blossom and the bee. And humming and hawing, let us ask of the starling (who is a more sociable bird than the lark) what he may think on the brink of the dustbin, whence he picks among the sticks combings of scullion's hair. What's life, we ask, leaning on the farmyard gate; Life, Life, Life! cries the bird, as if he had heard, and knew precisely, what we meant by this bothering prying habit of ours of asking questions indoors and out and peeping and picking at daisies as the way is of writers when they don't know what to say next. Then they come here, says the bird, and ask me what life is; Life, Life, Life!

We trudge on then by the moor path, to the high brow of the wine-blue purple-dark hill, and fling ourselves down there, and dream there and see there a grass-hopper, carting back to his home in the hollow, a straw. And he says (if sawings like his can be given a name so sacred and tender) Life's labour, or so we interpret the whirr of his dust-choked gullet. And the ant agrees and the bees, but if we lie here long enough to ask the moths, when they come at evening, stealing among the paler heather bells, they will breathe in our ears such wild nonsense as one hears from telegraph wires in snow storms; tee hee, haw haw. Laughter, Laughter! the moths say.

Having asked then of man and of bird and the insects, for fish, men tell us, who have lived in green caves, solitary for years to hear them speak, never, never say, and so perhaps know what life is--having asked them all and grown no wiser, but only older and colder (for did we not pray once in a way to wrap up in a book something so hard, so rare, one could swear it was life's meaning?) back we must go and say straight out to the reader who waits a-tiptoe to hear what life is--alas, we don't know.

At this moment, but only just in time to save the book from extinction, Orlando pushed away her chair, stretched her arms, dropped her pen, came to the window, and exclaimed, 'Done!'

She was almost felled to the ground by the extraordinary sight which now met her eyes. There was the garden and some birds. The world was going on as usual. All the time she was writing the world had continued.

'And if I were dead, it would be just the same!' she exclaimed.

Such was the intensity of her feelings that she could even imagine that she had suffered dissolution, and perhaps some faintness actually attacked her. For a moment she stood looking at the fair, indifferent spectacle with staring eyes. At length she was revived in a singular way. The manuscript which reposed above her heart began shuffling and beating as if it were a living thing, and, what was still odder, and showed how fine a sympathy was between them, Orlando, by inclining her head, could make out what it was that it was saying. It wanted to be read. It must be read. It would die in her bosom if it were not read. For the first time in her life she turned with violence against nature. Elk-hounds and rose bushes were about her in profusion. But elk-hounds and rose bushes can none of them read. It is a lamentable oversight on the part of Providence which had never struck her before. Human beings alone are thus gifted. Human beings had become necessary. She rang the bell. She ordered the carriage to take her to London at once.

'There's just time to catch the eleven forty five, M'Lady,' said Basket. Orlando had not yet realized the invention of the steam engine, but such was her absorption in the sufferings of a being, who, though not herself, yet entirely depended on her, that she saw a railway train for the first time, took her seat in a railway carriage, and had the rug arranged about her knees without giving a thought to 'that stupendous invention, which had (the historians say) completely changed the face of Europe in the past twenty years' (as, indeed, happens much more frequently than historians suppose). She noticed only that it was extremely smutty; rattled horribly; and the windows stuck. Lost in thought, she was whirled up to London in something less than an hour and stood on the platform at Charing Cross, not knowing where to go.

The old house at Blackfriars, where she had spent so many pleasant days in the eighteenth century, was now sold, part to the Salvation Army, part to an umbrella factory. She had bought another in Mayfair which was sanitary, convenient, and in the heart of the fashionable world, but was it in Mayfair that her poem would be relieved of its desire? Pray God, she thought, remembering the brightness of their ladyships' eyes and the symmetry of their lordship's legs, they haven't taken to reading there. For that would be a thousand pities. Then there was Lady R.'s. The same sort of talk would be going on there still, she had no doubt. The gout might have shifted from the General's left leg to his right, perhaps. Mr L. might have stayed ten days with R. instead of T. Then Mr Pope would come in. Oh! but Mr Pope was dead. Who were the wits now, she wondered--but that was not a question one could put to a porter, and so she moved on. Her ears were now distracted by the jingling of innumerable bells on the heads of innumerable horses. Fleets of the strangest little boxes on wheels were drawn up by the pavement. She walked out into the Strand. There the uproar was even worse. Vehicles of all sizes, drawn by blood horses and by dray horses, conveying one solitary dowager or crowded to the top by whiskered men in silk hats, were inextricably mixed. Carriages, carts, and omnibuses seemed to her eyes, so long used to the look of a plain sheet of foolscap, alarmingly at loggerheads; and to her ears, attuned to a pen scratching, the uproar of the street sounded violently and hideously cacophonous. Every inch of the pavement was crowded. Streams of people, threading in and out between their own bodies and the lurching and lumbering traffic with incredible agility, poured incessantly east and west. Along the edge of the pavement stood men, holding out trays of toys, and bawled. At corners, women sat beside great baskets of spring flowers and bawled. Boys running in and out of the horses' noses, holding printed sheets to their bodies, bawled too, Disaster! Disaster! At first Orlando supposed that she had arrived at some moment of national crisis; but whether it was happy or tragic, she could not tell. She looked anxiously at people's faces. But that confused her still more. Here would come by a man sunk in despair, muttering to himself as if he knew some terrible sorrow. Past him would nudge a fat, jolly-faced fellow, shouldering his way along as if it were a festival for all the world. Indeed, she came to the conclusion that there was neither rhyme nor reason in any of it. Each man and each woman was bent on his own affairs. And where was she to go?

She walked on without thinking, up one street and down another, by vast windows piled with handbags, and mirrors, and dressing gowns, and flowers, and fishing rods, and luncheon baskets; while stuff of every hue and pattern, thickness or thinness, was looped and festooned and ballooned across and across. Sometimes she passed down avenues of sedate mansions, soberly numbered 'one', 'two', 'three', and so on right up to two or three hundred, each the copy of the other, with two pillars and six steps and a pair of curtains neatly drawn and family luncheons laid on tables, and a parrot looking out of one window and a man servant out of another, until her mind was dizzied with the monotony. Then she came to great open squares with black shiny, tightly buttoned statues of fat men in the middle, and war horses prancing, and columns rising and fountains falling and pigeons fluttering. So she walked and walked along pavements between houses until she felt very hungry, and something fluttering above her heart rebuked her with having forgotten all about it. It was her manuscript. 'The Oak Tree'.

She was confounded at her own neglect. She stopped dead where she stood. No coach was in sight. The street, which was wide and handsome, was singularly empty. Only one elderly gentleman was approaching. There was something vaguely familiar to her in his walk. As he came nearer, she felt certain that she had met him at some time or other. But where? Could it be that this gentleman, so neat, so portly, so prosperous, with a cane in his hand and a flower in his buttonhole, with a pink, plump face, and combed white moustaches, could it be, Yes, by jove, it was!--her old, her very old friend, Nick Greene!

At the same time he looked at her; remembered her; recognized her. 'The Lady Orlando!' he cried, sweeping his silk hat almost in the dust.

'Sir Nicholas!' she exclaimed. For she was made aware intuitively by something in his bearing that the scurrilous penny-a-liner, who had lampooned her and many another in the time of Queen Elizabeth, was now risen in the world and become certainly a Knight and doubtless a dozen other fine things into the bargain.

With another bow, he acknowledged that her conclusion was correct; he was a Knight; he was a Litt.D.; he was a Professor. He was the author of a score of volumes. He was, in short, the most influential critic of the Victorian age.

A violent tumult of emotion besieged her at meeting the man who had caused her, years ago, so much pain. Could this be the plaguy, restless fellow who had burnt holes in her carpets, and toasted cheese in the Italian fireplace and told such merry stories of Marlowe and the rest that they had seen the sun rise nine nights out of ten? He was now sprucely dressed in a grey morning suit, had a pink flower in his button-hole, and grey suede gloves to match. But even as she marvelled, he made another bow, and asked her whether she would honour him by lunching with him? The bow was a thought overdone perhaps, but the imitation of fine breeding was creditable. She followed him, wondering, into a superb restaurant, all red plush, white table-cloths, and silver cruets, as unlike as could be the old tavern or coffee house with its sanded floor, its wooden benches, its bowls of punch and chocolate, and its broadsheets and spittoons. He laid his gloves neatly on the table beside him. Still she could hardly believe that he was the same man. His nails were clean; where they used to be an inch long. His chin was shaved; where a black beard used to sprout. He wore gold sleeve-links; where his ragged linen used to dip in the broth. It was not, indeed, until he had ordered the wine, which he did with a care that reminded her of his taste in Malmsey long ago, that she was convinced he was the same man. 'Ah!' he said, heaving a little sigh, which was yet comfortable enough, 'ah! my dear lady, the great days of literature are over. Marlowe, Shakespeare, Ben Jonson--those were the giants. Dryden, Pope, Addison--those were the heroes. All, all are dead now. And whom have they left us? Tennyson, Browning, Carlyle!'--he threw an immense amount of scorn into his voice. 'The truth of it is,' he said, pouring himself a glass of wine, 'that all our young writers are in the pay of the booksellers. They turn out any trash that serves to pay their tailor's bills. It is an age', he said, helping himself to hors-d'oeuvres, 'marked by precious conceits and wild experiments--none of which the Elizabethans would have tolerated for an instant.'

'No, my dear lady,' he continued, passing with approval the turbot au gratin, which the waiter exhibited for his sanction, 'the great days are over. We live in degenerate times. We must cherish the past; honour those writers--there are still a few left of 'em--who take antiquity for their model and write, not for pay but--' Here Orlando almost shouted 'Glawr!' Indeed she could have sworn that she had heard him say the very same things three hundred years ago. The names were different, of course, but the spirit was the same. Nick Greene had not changed, for all his knighthood. And yet, some change there was. For while he ran on about taking Addison as one's model (it had been Cicero once, she thought) and lying in bed of a morning (which she was proud to think her pension paid quarterly enabled him to do) rolling the best works of the best authors round and round on one's tongue for an hour, at least, before setting pen to paper, so that the vulgarity of the present time and the deplorable condition of our native tongue (he had lived long in America, she believed) might be purified--while he ran on in much the same way that Greene had run on three hundred years ago, she had time to ask herself, how was it then that he had changed? He had grown plump; but he was a man verging on seventy. He had grown sleek: literature had been a prosperous pursuit evidently; but somehow the old restless, uneasy vivacity had gone. His stories, brilliant as they were, were no longer quite so free and easy. He mentioned, it is true, 'my dear friend Pope' or 'my illustrious friend Addison' every other second, but he had an air of respectability about him which was depressing, and he preferred, it seemed, to enlighten her about the doings and sayings of her own blood relations rather than tell her, as he used to do, scandal about the poets.

Orlando was unaccountably disappointed. She had thought of literature all these years (her seclusion, her rank, her sex must be her excuse) as something wild as the wind, hot as fire, swift as lightning; something errant, incalculable, abrupt, and behold, literature was an elderly gentleman in a grey suit talking about duchesses. The violence of her disillusionment was such that some hook or button fastening the upper part of her dress burst open, and out upon the table fell 'The Oak Tree', a poem.

'A manuscript!' said Sir Nicholas, putting on his gold pince-nez. 'How interesting, how excessively interesting! Permit me to look at it.' And once more, after an interval of some three hundred years, Nicholas Greene took Orlando's poem and, laying it down among the coffee cups and the liqueur glasses, began to read it. But now his verdict was very different from what it had been then. It reminded him, he said as he turned over the pages, of Addison's "Cato". It compared favourably with Thomson's "Seasons". There was no trace in it, he was thankful to say, of the modern spirit. It was composed with a regard to truth, to nature, to the dictates of the human heart, which was rare indeed, in these days of unscrupulous eccentricity. It must, of course, be published instantly.

Really Orlando did not know what he meant. She had always carried her manuscripts about with her in the bosom of her dress. The idea tickled Sir Nicholas considerably.

'But what about royalties?' he asked.

Orlando's mind flew to Buckingham Palace and some dusky potentates who happened to be staying there.

Sir Nicholas was highly diverted. He explained that he was alluding to the fact that Messrs -- (here he mentioned a well-known firm of publishers) would be delighted, if he wrote them a line, to put the book on their list. He could probably arrange for a royalty of ten per cent on all copies up to two thousand; after that it would be fifteen. As for the reviewers, he would himself write a line to Mr --, who was the most influential; then a compliment--say a little puff of her own poems--addressed to the wife of the editor of the -- never did any harm. He would call --. So he ran on. Orlando understood nothing of all this, and from old experience did not altogether trust his good nature, but there was nothing for it but to submit to what was evidently his wish and the fervent desire of the poem itself. So Sir Nicholas made the blood-stained packet into a neat parcel; flattened it into his breast pocket, lest it should disturb the set of his coat; and with many compliments on both sides, they parted.

Orlando walked up the street. Now that the poem was gone,--and she felt a bare place in her breast where she had been used to carry it--she had nothing to do but reflect upon whatever she liked--the extraordinary chances it might be of the human lot. Here she was in St James's Street; a married woman; with a ring on her finger; where there had been a coffee house once there was now a restaurant; it was about half past three in the afternoon; the sun was shining; there were three pigeons; a mongrel terrier dog; two hansom cabs and a barouche landau. What then, was Life? The thought popped into her head violently, irrelevantly (unless old Greene were somehow the cause of it). And it may be taken as a comment, adverse or favourable, as the reader chooses to consider it upon her relations with her husband (who was at the Horn), that whenever anything popped violently into her head, she went straight to the nearest telegraph office and wired to him. There was one, as it happened, close at hand. 'My God Shel', she wired; 'life literature Greene toady--' here she dropped into a cypher language which they had invented between them so that a whole spiritual state of the utmost complexity might be conveyed in a word or two without the telegraph clerk being any wiser, and added the words 'Rattigan Glumphoboo', which summed it up precisely. For not only had the events of the morning made a deep impression on her, but it cannot have escaped the reader's attention that Orlando was growing up--which is not necessarily growing better--and 'Rattigan Glumphoboo' described a very complicated spiritual state--which if the reader puts all his intelligence at our service he may discover for himself.

There could be no answer to her telegram for some hours; indeed, it was probable, she thought, glancing at the sky, where the upper clouds raced swiftly past, that there was a gale at Cape Horn, so that her husband would be at the masthead, as likely as not, or cutting away some tattered spar, or even alone in a boat with a biscuit. And so, leaving the post office, she turned to beguile herself into the next shop, which was a shop so common in our day that it needs no description, yet, to her eyes, strange in the extreme; a shop where they sold books. All her life long Orlando had known manuscripts; she had held in her hands the rough brown sheets on which Spenser had written in his little crabbed hand; she had seen Shakespeare's script and Milton's. She owned, indeed, a fair number of quartos and folios, often with a sonnet in her praise in them and sometimes a lock of hair. But these innumerable little volumes, bright, identical, ephemeral, for they seemed bound in cardboard and printed on tissue paper, surprised her infinitely. The whole works of Shakespeare cost half a crown, and could be put in your pocket. One could hardly read them, indeed, the print was so small, but it was a marvel, none the less. 'Works'--the works of every writer she had known or heard of and many more stretched from end to end of the long shelves. On tables and chairs, more 'works' were piled and tumbled, and these she saw, turning a page or two, were often works about other works by Sir Nicholas and a score of others whom, in her ignorance, she supposed, since they were bound and printed, to be very great writers too. So she gave an astounding order to the bookseller to send her everything of any importance in the shop and left.

She turned into Hyde Park, which she had known of old (beneath that cleft tree, she remembered, the Duke of Hamilton fell run through the body by Lord Mohun), and her lips, which are often to blame in the matter, began framing the words of her telegram into a senseless singsong; life literature Greene toady Rattigan Glumphoboo; so that several park keepers looked at her with suspicion and were only brought to a favourable opinion of her sanity by noticing the pearl necklace which she wore. She had carried off a sheaf of papers and critical journals from the book shop, and at length, flinging herself on her elbow beneath a tree, she spread these pages round her and did her best to fathom the noble art of prose composition as these masters practised it. For still the old credulity was alive in her; even the blurred type of a weekly newspaper had some sanctity in her eyes. So she read, lying on her elbow, an article by Sir Nicholas on the collected works of a man she had once known--John Donne. But she had pitched herself, without knowing it, not far from the Serpentine. The barking of a thousand dogs sounded in her ears. Carriage wheels rushed ceaselessly in a circle. Leaves sighed overhead. Now and again a braided skirt and a pair of tight scarlet trousers crossed the grass within a few steps of her. Once a gigantic rubber ball bounced on the newspaper. Violets, oranges, reds, and blues broke through the interstices of the leaves and sparkled in the emerald on her finger. She read a sentence and looked up at the sky; she looked up at the sky and looked down at the newspaper. Life? Literature? One to be made into the other? But how monstrously difficult! For--here came by a pair of tight scarlet trousers--how would Addison have put that? Here came two dogs dancing on their hind legs. How would Lamb have described that? For reading Sir Nicholas and his friends (as she did in the intervals of looking about her), she somehow got the impression--here she rose and walked--they made one feel--it was an extremely uncomfortable feeling--one must never, never say what one thought. (She stood on the banks of the Serpentine. It was a bronze colour; spider-thin boats were skimming from side to side.) They made one feel, she continued, that one must always, always write like somebody else. (The tears formed themselves in her eyes.) For really, she thought, pushing a little boat off with her toe, I don't think I could (here the whole of Sir Nicholas' article came before her as articles do, ten minutes after they are read, with the look of his room, his head, his cat, his writing-table, and the time of the day thrown in), I don't think I could, she continued, considering the article from this point of view, sit in a study, no, it's not a study, it's a mouldy kind of drawing-room, all day long, and talk to pretty young men, and tell them little anecdotes, which they mustn't repeat, about what Tupper said about Smiles; and then, she continued, weeping bitterly, they're all so manly; and then, I do detest Duchesses; and I don't like cake; and though I'm spiteful enough, I could never learn to be as spiteful as all that, so how can I be a critic and write the best English prose of my time? Damn it all! she exclaimed, launching a penny steamer so vigorously that the poor little boat almost sank in the bronze-coloured waves.

Now, the truth is that when one has been in a state of mind (as nurses call it)--and the tears still stood in Orlando's eyes--the thing one is looking at becomes, not itself, but another thing, which is bigger and much more important and yet remains the same thing. If one looks at the Serpentine in this state of mind, the waves soon become just as big as the waves on the Atlantic; the toy boats become indistinguishable from ocean liners. So Orlando mistook the toy boat for her husband's brig; and the wave she had made with her toe for a mountain of water off

Cape Horn; and as she watched the toy boat climb the ripple, she thought she saw Bonthrop's ship climb up and up a glassy wall; up and up it went, and a white crest with a thousand deaths in it arched over it; and through the thousand deaths it went and disappeared--'It's sunk!' she cried out in an agony--and then, behold, there it was again sailing along safe and sound among the ducks on the other side of the Atlantic.

'Ecstasy!' she cried. 'Ecstasy! Where's the post office?' she wondered. 'For I must wire at once to Shel and tell him...' And repeating 'A toy boat on the Serpentine', and 'Ecstasy', alternately, for the thoughts were interchangeable and meant exactly the same thing, she hurried towards Park Lane.

'A toy boat, a toy boat, a toy boat,' she repeated, thus enforcing upon herself the fact that it is not articles by Nick Greene on John Donne nor eight-hour bills nor covenants nor factory acts that matter; it's something useless, sudden, violent; something that costs a life; red, blue, purple; a spirit; a splash; like those hyacinths (she was passing a fine bed of them); free from taint, dependence, soilure of humanity or care for one's kind; something rash, ridiculous, like my hyacinth, husband I mean, Bonthrop: that's what it is--a toy boat on the Serpentine, ecstasy--it's ecstasy that matters. Thus she spoke aloud, waiting for the carriages to pass at Stanhope Gate, for the consequence of not living with one's husband, except when the wind is sunk, is that one talks nonsense aloud in Park Lane. It would no doubt have been different had she lived all the year round with him as Queen Victoria recommended. As it was the thought of him would come upon her in a flash. She found it absolutely necessary to speak to him instantly. She did not care in the least what nonsense it might make, or what dislocation it might inflict on the narrative. Nick Greene's article had plunged her in the depths of despair; the toy boat had raised her to the heights of joy. So she repeated: 'Ecstasy, ecstasy', as she stood waiting to cross.

But the traffic was heavy that spring afternoon, and kept her standing there, repeating, ecstasy, ecstasy, or a toy boat on the Serpentine, while the wealth and power of England sat, as if sculptured, in hat and cloak, in four-in-hand, victoria and barouche landau. It was as if a golden river had coagulated and massed itself in golden blocks across Park Lane. The ladies held card-cases between their fingers; the gentlemen balanced gold-mounted canes between their knees. She stood there gazing, admiring, awe-struck. One thought only disturbed her, a thought familiar to all who behold great elephants, or whales of an incredible magnitude, and that is: how do these leviathans to whom obviously stress, change, and activity are repugnant, propagate their kind? Perhaps, Orlando thought, looking at the stately, still faces, their time of propagation is over; this is the fruit; this is the consummation. What she now beheld was the triumph of an age. Portly and splendid there they sat. But now, the policeman let fall his hand; the stream became liquid; the massive conglomeration of splendid objects moved, dispersed, and disappeared into Piccadilly.

So she crossed Park Lane and went to her house in Curzon Street, where, when the meadow-sweet blew there, she could remember curlew calling and one very old man with a gun.

She could remember, she thought, stepping across the threshold of her house, how Lord Chesterfield had said--but her memory was checked. Her discreet eighteenth-century hall, where she could see Lord Chesterfield putting his hat down here and his coat down there with an elegance of deportment which it was a pleasure to watch, was now completely littered with parcels. While she had been sitting in Hyde Park the bookseller had delivered her order, and the house was crammed--there were parcels slipping down the staircase--with the whole of Victorian literature done up in grey paper and neatly tied with string. She carried as many of these packets as she could to her room, ordered footmen to bring the others, and, rapidly cutting innumerable strings, was soon surrounded by innumerable volumes.

Accustomed to the little literatures of the sixteenth, seventeenth, and eighteenth centuries, Orlando was appalled by the consequences of her order. For, of course, to the Victorians themselves Victorian literature meant not merely four great names separate and distinct but four great names sunk and embedded in a mass of Alexander Smiths, Dixons, Blacks, Milmans, Buckles, Taines, Paynes, Tuppers, Jamesons--all vocal, clamorous, prominent, and requiring as much attention as anybody else. Orlando's reverence for print had a tough job set before it but drawing her chair to the window to get the benefit of what light might filter between the high houses of Mayfair, she tried to come to a conclusion.

And now it was clear that there are only two ways of coming to a conclusion upon Victorian literature--one is to write it out in sixty volumes octavo, the other is to squeeze it into six lines of the length of this one. Of the two courses, economy, since time runs short, leads us to choose the second; and so we proceed. Orlando then came to the conclusion (opening half-a-dozen books) that it was very odd that there was not a single dedication to a nobleman among them; next (turning over a vast pile of memoirs) that several of these writers had family trees half as high as her own; next, that it would be impolitic in the extreme to wrap a ten-pound note round the sugar tongs when Miss Christina Rossetti came to tea; next (here were half-a-dozen invitations to celebrate centenaries by dining) that literature since it ate all these dinners must be growing very corpulent; next (she was invited to a score of lectures on the Influence of this upon that; the Classical revival; the Romantic survival, and other titles of the same engaging kind) that literature since it listened to all these lectures must be growing very dry; next (here she attended a reception given by a peeress) that literature since it wore all those fur tippets must be growing very respectable; next (here she visited Carlyle's sound-proof room at Chelsea) that genius since it needed all this coddling must be growing very delicate; and so at last she reached her final conclusion, which was of the highest importance but which, as we have already much overpassed our limit of six lines, we must omit.

Orlando, having come to this conclusion, stood looking out of the window for a considerable space of time. For, when anybody comes to a conclusion it is as if they had tossed the ball over the net and must wait for the unseen antagonist to return it to them. What would be sent her next from the colourless sky above Chesterfield House, she wondered? And with her hands clasped, she stood for a considerable space of time wondering. Suddenly she started--and here we could only wish that, as on a former occasion, Purity, Chastity, and Modesty would push the door ajar and provide, at least, a breathing space in which we could think how to wrap up what now has to be told delicately, as a biographer should. But no! Having thrown their white garment at the naked Orlando and seen it fall short by several inches, these ladies had given up all intercourse with her these many years; and were now otherwise engaged. Is nothing then, going to happen this pale March morning to mitigate, to veil, to cover, to conceal, to shroud this undeniable event whatever it may be? For after giving that sudden, violent start, Orlando--but Heaven be praised, at this very moment there struck up outside one of these frail, reedy, fluty, jerky, old-fashioned barrel-organs which are still sometimes played by Italian organ-grinders in back streets. Let us accept the intervention, humble though it is, as if it were the music of the spheres, and allow it, with all its gasps and groans, to fill this page with sound until the moment comes when it is impossible to deny its coming; which the footman has seen coming and the maid-servant; and the reader will have to see too; for Orlando herself is clearly unable to ignore it any longer--let the barrel-organ sound and transport us on thought, which is no more than a little boat, when music sounds, tossing on the waves; on thought, which is, of all carriers, the most clumsy, the most erratic, over the roof tops and the back gardens where washing is hanging to--what is this place? Do you recognize the Green and in the middle the steeple, and the gate with a lion couchant on either side? Oh yes, it is Kew! Well, Kew will do. So here we are at Kew, and I will show you to-day (the second of March) under the plum tree, a grape hyacinth, and a crocus, and a bud, too, on the almond tree; so that to walk there is to be thinking of bulbs, hairy and red, thrust into the earth in October; flowering now; and to be dreaming of more than can rightly be said, and to be taking from its case a cigarette or cigar even, and to be flinging a cloak under (as the rhyme requires) an oak, and there to sit, waiting the kingfisher, which, it is said, was seen once to cross in the evening from bank to bank.

Wait! Wait! The kingfisher comes; the kingfisher comes not.

Behold, meanwhile, the factory chimneys and their smoke; behold the city clerks flashing by in their outrigger. Behold the old lady taking her dog for a walk and the servant girl wearing her new hat for the first time not at the right angle. Behold them all. Though Heaven has mercifully decreed that the secrets of all hearts are hidden so that we are lured on for ever to suspect something, perhaps, that does not exist; still through our cigarette smoke, we see blaze up and salute the splendid fulfilment of natural desires for a hat, for a boat, for a rat in a ditch; as once one saw blazing--such silly hops and skips the mind takes when it slops like this all over the saucer and the barrel-organ plays--saw blazing a fire in a field against minarets near Constantinople.

Hail! natural desire! Hail! happiness! divine happiness! and pleasure of all sorts, flowers and wine, though one fades and the other intoxicates; and half-crown tickets out of London on Sundays, and singing in a dark chapel hymns about death, and anything, anything that interrupts and confounds the tapping of typewriters and filing of letters and forging of links and chains, binding the Empire together. Hail even the crude, red bows on shop girls' lips (as if Cupid, very clumsily, dipped his thumb in red ink and scrawled a token in passing). Hail, happiness! kingfisher flashing from bank to bank, and all fulfilment of natural desire, whether it is what the male novelist says it is; or prayer; or denial; hail! in whatever form it comes, and may there be more forms, and stranger. For dark flows the stream--would it were true, as the rhyme hints 'like a dream'--but duller and worser than that is our usual lot; without dreams, but alive, smug, fluent, habitual, under trees whose shade of an olive green drowns the blue of the wing of the vanishing bird when he darts of a sudden from bank to bank.

Hail, happiness, then, and after happiness, hail not those dreams which bloat the sharp image as spotted mirrors do the face in a country-inn parlour; dreams which splinter the whole and tear us asunder and wound us and split us apart in the night when we would sleep; but sleep, sleep, so deep that all shapes are ground to dust of infinite softness, water of dimness inscrutable, and there, folded, shrouded, like a mummy, like a moth, prone let us lie on the sand at the bottom of sleep.

But wait! but wait! we are not going, this time, visiting the blind land. Blue, like a match struck right in the ball of the innermost eye, he flies, burns, bursts the seal of sleep; the kingfisher; so that now floods back refluent like a tide, the red, thick stream of life again; bubbling, dripping; and we rise, and our eyes (for how handy a rhyme is to pass us safe over the awkward transition from death to life) fall on--(here the barrel-organ stops playing abruptly).

'It's a very fine boy, M'Lady,' said Mrs Banting, the midwife, putting her first-born child into Orlando's arms. In other words Orlando was safely delivered of a son on Thursday, March the 20th, at three o'clock in the morning.

Once more Orlando stood at the window, but let the reader take courage; nothing of the same sort is going to happen to-day, which is not, by any means, the same day. No--for if we look out of the window, as Orlando was doing at the moment, we shall see that Park Lane itself has considerably changed. Indeed one might stand there ten minutes or more, as Orlando stood now, without seeing a single barouche landau. 'Look at that!' she exclaimed, some days later when an absurd truncated carriage without any horses began to glide about of its own accord. A carriage without any horses indeed! She was called away just as she said that, but came back again after a time and had another look out of the window. It was odd sort of weather nowadays. The sky itself, she could not help thinking, had changed. It was no longer so thick, so watery, so prismatic now that King Edward--see, there he was, stepping out of his neat brougham to go and visit a certain lady opposite--had succeeded Queen Victoria. The clouds had shrunk to a thin gauze; the sky seemed made of metal, which in hot weather tarnished verdigris, copper colour or orange as metal does in a fog. It was a little alarming--this shrinkage. Everything seemed to have shrunk. Driving past Buckingham Palace last night, there was not a trace of that vast erection which she had thought everlasting; top hats, widows' weeds, trumpets, telescopes, wreaths, all had vanished and left not a stain, not a puddle even, on the pavement. But it was now--after another interval she had come back again to her favourite station in the window--now, in the evening, that the change was most remarkable. Look at the lights in the houses! At a touch, a whole room was lit; hundreds of rooms were lit; and one was precisely the same as the other. One could see everything in the little square-shaped boxes; there was no privacy; none of those lingering shadows and odd corners that there used to be; none of those women in aprons carrying wobbly lamps which they put down carefully on this table and on that. At a touch, the whole room was bright. And the sky was bright all night long; and the pavements were bright; everything was bright. She came back again at mid-day. How narrow women have grown lately! They looked like stalks of corn, straight, shining, identical. And men's faces were as bare as the palm of one's hand. The dryness of the atmosphere brought out the colour in everything and seemed to stiffen the muscles of the cheeks. It was harder to cry now. Water was hot in two seconds. Ivy had perished or been scraped off houses. Vegetables were less fertile; families were much smaller. Curtains and covers had been frizzled up and the walls were bare so that new brilliantly coloured pictures of real things like streets, umbrellas, apples, were hung in frames, or painted upon the wood. There was something definite and distinct about the age, which reminded her of the eighteenth century, except that there was a distraction, a desperation--as she was thinking this, the immensely long tunnel in which she seemed to have been travelling for hundreds of years widened; the light poured in; her thoughts became mysteriously tightened and strung up as if a piano tuner had put his key in her back and stretched the nerves very taut; at the same time her hearing quickened; she could hear every whisper and crackle in the room so that the clock ticking on the mantelpiece beat like a hammer. And so for some seconds the light went on becoming brighter and brighter, and she saw everything more and more clearly and the clock ticked louder and louder until there was a terrific explosion right in her ear. Orlando leapt as if she had been violently struck on the head. Ten times she was struck. In fact it was ten o'clock in the morning. It was the eleventh of October. It was 1928. It was the present moment.

No one need wonder that Orlando started, pressed her hand to her heart, and turned pale. For what more terrifying revelation can there be than that it is the present moment? That we survive the shock at all is only possible because the past shelters us on one side and the future on another. But we have no time now for reflections; Orlando was terribly late already. She ran downstairs, she jumped into her motorcar, she pressed the self-starter and was off. Vast blue blocks of building rose into the air; the red cowls of chimneys were spotted irregularly across the sky; the road shone like silver-headed nails; omnibuses bore down upon her with sculptured white-faced drivers; she noticed sponges, bird-cages, boxes of green American cloth. But she did not allow these sights to sink into her mind even the fraction of an inch as she crossed the narrow plank of the present, lest she should fall into the raging torrent beneath. 'Why don't you look where you're going to?...Put your hand out, can't you?'--that was all she said sharply, as if the words were jerked out of her. For the streets were immensely crowded; people crossed without looking where they were going. People buzzed and hummed round the plate-glass windows within which one could see a glow of red, a blaze of yellow, as if they were bees, Orlando thought--but her thought that they were bees was violently snipped off and she saw, regaining perspective with one flick of her eye, that they were bodies. 'Why don't you look where you're going?' she snapped out.

At last, however, she drew up at Marshall & Snelgrove's and went into the shop. Shade and scent enveloped her. The present fell from her like drops of scalding water. Light swayed up and down like thin stuffs puffed out by a summer breeze. She took a list from her bag and began reading in a curious stiff voice at first, as if she were holding the words--boy's boots, bath salts, sardines--under a tap of many-coloured water. She watched them change as the light fell on them. Bath and boots became blunt, obtuse; sardines serrated itself like a saw. So she stood in the ground-floor department of Messrs Marshall & Snelgrove; looked this way and that; snuffed this smell and that and thus wasted some seconds. Then she got into the lift, for the good reason that the door stood open; and was shot smoothly upwards. The very fabric of life now, she thought as she rose, is magic. In the eighteenth century we knew how everything was done; but here I rise through the air; I listen to voices in America; I see men flying--but how its done I can't even begin to wonder. So my belief in magic returns. Now the lift gave a little jerk as it stopped at the first floor; and she had a vision of innumerable coloured stuffs flaunting in a breeze from which came distinct, strange smells; and each time the lift stopped and flung its doors open, there was another slice of the world displayed with all the smells of that world clinging to it. She was reminded of the river off Wapping in the time of Elizabeth, where the treasure ships and the merchant ships used to anchor. How richly and curiously they had smelt! How well she remembered the feel of rough rubies running through her fingers when she dabbled them in a treasure sack! And then lying with Sukey--or whatever her name was--and having Cumberland's lantern flashed on them! The Cumberlands had a house in Portland Place now and she had lunched with them the other day and ventured a little joke with the old man about almshouses in the Sheen Road. He had winked. But here as the lift could go no higher, she must get out--Heaven knows into what 'department' as they called it. She stood still to consult her shopping list, but was blessed if she could see, as the list bade her, bath salts, or boy's boots anywhere about. And indeed, she was about to descend again, without buying anything, but was saved from that outrage by saying aloud automatically the last item on her list; which happened to be 'sheets for a double bed'.

'Sheets for a double bed,' she said to a man at a counter and, by a dispensation of Providence, it was sheets that the man at that particular counter happened to sell. For Grimsditch, no, Grimsditch was dead; Bartholomew, no, Bartholomew was dead; Louise then--Louise had come to her in a great taking the other day, for she had found a hole in the bottom of the sheet in the royal bed. Many kings and queens had slept there--Elizabeth; James; Charles; George; Victoria; Edward; no wonder the sheet had a hole in it. But Louise was positive she knew who had done it. It was the Prince Consort.

'Sale bosch!' she said (for there had been another war; this time against the Germans).

'Sheets for a double bed,' Orlando repeated dreamily, for a double bed with a silver counterpane in a room fitted in a taste which she now thought perhaps a little vulgar--all in silver; but she had furnished it when she had a passion for that metal. While the man went to get sheets for a double bed, she took out a little looking-glass and a powder puff. Women were not nearly as roundabout in their ways, she thought, powdering herself with the greatest unconcern, as they had been when she herself first turned woman and lay on the deck of the "Enamoured Lady". She gave her nose the right tint deliberately. She never touched her cheeks. Honestly, though she was now thirty-six, she scarcely looked a day older. She looked just as pouting, as sulky, as handsome, as rosy (like a million-candled Christmas tree, Sasha had said) as she had done that day on the ice, when the Thames was frozen and they had gone skating--

'The best Irish linen, Ma'am,' said the shopman, spreading the sheets on the counter,--and they had met an old woman picking up sticks. Here, as she was fingering the linen abstractedly, one of the swing-doors between the departments opened and let through, perhaps from the fancy-goods department, a whiff of scent, waxen, tinted as if from pink candles, and the scent curved like a shell round a figure--was it a boy's or was it a girl's--young, slender, seductive--a girl, by God! furred, pearled, in Russian trousers; but faithless, faithless!

'Faithless!' cried Orlando (the man had gone) and all the shop seemed to pitch and toss with yellow water and far off she saw the masts of the Russian ship standing out to sea, and then, miraculously (perhaps the door opened again) the conch which the scent had made became a platform, a dais, off which stepped a fat, furred woman, marvellously well preserved, seductive, diademed, a Grand Duke's mistress; she who, leaning over the banks of the Volga, eating sandwiches, had watched men drown; and began walking down the shop towards her.

'Oh Sasha!' Orlando cried. Really, she was shocked that she should have come to this; she had grown so fat; so lethargic; and she bowed her head over the linen so that this apparition of a grey woman in fur, and a girl in Russian trousers, with all these smells of wax candles, white flowers, and old ships that it brought with it might pass behind her back unseen.

'Any napkins, towels, dusters today, Ma'am?' the shopman persisted. And it is enormously to the credit of the shopping list, which Orlando now consulted, that she was able to reply with every appearance of composure, that there was only one thing in the world she wanted and that was bath salts; which was in another department.

But descending in the lift again--so insidious is the repetition of any scene--she was again sunk far beneath the present moment; and thought when the lift bumped on the ground, that she heard a pot broken against a river bank. As for finding the right department, whatever it might be, she stood engrossed among the handbags, deaf to the suggestions of all the polite, black, combed, sprightly shop assistants, who descending as they did equally and some of them, perhaps, as proudly, even from such depths of the past as she did, chose to let down the impervious screen of the present so that today they appeared shop assistants in Marshall & Snelgrove's merely. Orlando stood there hesitating. Through the great glass doors she could see the traffic in Oxford Street. Omnibus seemed to pile itself upon omnibus and then to jerk itself apart. So the ice blocks had pitched and tossed that day on the Thames. An old nobleman--in furred slippers had sat astride one of them. There he went--she could see him now--calling down maledictions upon the Irish rebels. He had sunk there, where her car stood.

'Time has passed over me,' she thought, trying to collect herself; 'this is the oncome of middle age. How strange it is! Nothing is any longer one thing. I take up a handbag and I think of an old bumboat woman frozen in the ice. Someone lights a pink candle and I see a girl in Russian trousers. When I step out of doors--as I do now,' here she stepped on to the pavement of Oxford Street, 'what is it that I taste? Little herbs. I hear goat bells. I see mountains. Turkey? India? Persia?' Her eyes filled with tears.

That Orlando had gone a little too far from the present moment will, perhaps, strike the reader who sees her now preparing to get into her motor-car with her eyes full of tears and visions of Persian mountains. And indeed, it cannot be denied that the most successful practitioners of the art of life, often unknown people by the way, somehow contrive to synchronize the sixty or seventy different times which beat simultaneously in every normal human system so that when eleven strikes, all the rest chime in unison, and the present is neither a violent disruption nor completely forgotten in the past. Of them we can justly say that they live precisely the sixty-eight or seventy-two years allotted them on the tombstone. Of the rest some we know to be dead though they walk among us; some are not yet born though they go through the forms of life; others are hundreds of years old though they call themselves thirty-six. The true length of a person's life, whatever the "Dictionary of National Biography" may say, is always a matter of dispute. For it is a difficult business--this time-keeping; nothing more quickly disorders it than contact with any of the arts; and it may have been her love of poetry that was to blame for making Orlando lose her shopping list and start home without the sardines, the bath salts, or the boots. Now as she stood with her hand on the door of her motor-car, the present again struck her on the head. Eleven times she was violently assaulted.

'Confound it all!' she cried, for it is a great shock to the nervous system, hearing a clock strike--so much so that for some time now there is nothing to be said of her save that she frowned slightly, changed her gears admirably, and cried out, as before, 'Look where you're going!' 'Don't you know your own mind?' 'Why didn't you say so then?' while the motor-car shot, swung, squeezed, and slid, for she was an expert driver, down Regent Street, down Haymarket, down Northumberland Avenue, over Westminster Bridge, to the left, straight on, to the right, straight on again...

The Old Kent Road was very crowded on Thursday, the eleventh of October 1928. People spilt off the pavement. There were women with shopping bags. Children ran out. There were sales at drapers' shops. Streets widened and narrowed. Long vistas steadily shrunk together. Here was a market. Here a funeral. Here a procession with banners upon which was written 'Ra--Un', but what else? Meat was very red. Butchers stood at the door. Women almost had their heels sliced off. Amor Vin-- that was over a porch. A woman looked out of a bedroom window, profoundly contemplative, and very still. Applejohn and Applebed, Undert--. Nothing could be seen whole or read from start to finish. What was seen begun--like two friends starting to meet each other across the street--was never seen ended. After twenty minutes the body and mind were like scraps of torn paper tumbling from a sack and, indeed, the process of motoring fast out of London so much resembles the chopping up small of identity which precedes unconsciousness and perhaps death itself that it is an open question in what sense Orlando can be said to have existed at the present moment. Indeed we should have given her over for a person entirely disassembled were it not that here, at last, one green screen was held out on the right, against which the little bits of paper fell more slowly; and then another was held out on the left so that one could see the separate scraps now turning over by themselves in the air; and then green screens were held continuously on either side, so that her mind regained the illusion of holding things within itself and she saw a cottage, a farmyard and four cows, all precisely life-size.

When this happened, Orlando heaved a sigh of relief, lit a cigarette, and puffed for a minute or two in silence. Then she called hesitatingly, as if the person she wanted might not be there, 'Orlando? For if there are (at a venture) seventy-six different times all ticking in the mind at once, how many different people are there not--Heaven help us--all having lodgment at one time or another in the human spirit? Some say two thousand and fifty-two. So that it is the most usual thing in the world for a person to call, directly they are alone, Orlando? (if that is one's name) meaning by that, Come, come! I'm sick to death of this particular self. I want another. Hence, the astonishing changes we see in our friends. But it is not altogether plain sailing, either, for though one may say, as Orlando said (being out in the country and needing another self presumably) Orlando? still the Orlando she needs may not come; these selves of which we are built up, one on top of another, as plates are piled on a waiter's hand, have attachments elsewhere, sympathies, little constitutions and rights of their own, call them what you will (and for many of these things there is no name) so that one will only come if it is raining, another in a room with green curtains, another when Mrs Jones is not there, another if you can promise it a glass of wine--and so on; for everybody can multiply from his own experience the different terms which his different selves have made with him--and some are too wildly ridiculous to be mentioned in print at all.

So Orlando, at the turn by the barn, called 'Orlando?' with a note of interrogation in her voice and waited. Orlando did not come.

'All right then,' Orlando said, with the good humour people practise on these occasions; and tried another. For she had a great variety of selves to call upon, far more than we have been able to find room for, since a biography is considered complete if it merely accounts for six or seven selves, whereas a person may well have as many thousand. Choosing then, only those selves we have found room for, Orlando may now have called on the boy who cut the nigger's head down; the boy who strung it up again; the boy who sat on the hill; the boy who saw the poet; the boy who handed the Queen the bowl of rose water; or she may have called upon the young man who fell in love with Sasha; or upon the Courtier; or upon the Ambassador; or upon the Soldier; or upon the Traveller; or she may have wanted the woman to come to her; the Gipsy; the Fine Lady; the Hermit; the girl in love with life; the Patroness of Letters; the woman who called Mar (meaning hot baths and evening fires) or Shelmerdine (meaning crocuses in autumn woods) or Bonthrop (meaning the death we die daily) or all three together--which meant more things than we have space to write out--all were different and she may have called upon any one of them.

Perhaps; but what appeared certain (for we are now in the region of 'perhaps' and 'appears') was that the one she needed most kept aloof, for she was, to hear her talk, changing her selves as quickly as she drove--there was a new one at every corner--as happens when, for some unaccountable reason, the conscious self, which is the uppermost, and has the power to desire, wishes to be nothing but one self. This is what some people call the true self, and it is, they say, compact of all the selves we have it in us to be; commanded and locked up by the Captain self, the Key self, which amalgamates and controls them all. Orlando was certainly seeking this self as the reader can judge from overhearing her talk as she drove (and if it is rambling talk, disconnected, trivial, dull, and sometimes unintelligible, it is the reader's fault for listening to a lady talking to herself; we only copy her words as she spoke them, adding in brackets which self in our opinion is speaking, but in this we may well be wrong).

'What then? Who then?' she said. 'Thirty-six; in a motor-car; a woman. Yes, but a million other things as well. A snob am I? The garter in the hall? The leopards? My ancestors? Proud of them? Yes! Greedy, luxurious, vicious? Am I? (here a new self came in). Don't care a damn if I am. Truthful? I think so. Generous? Oh, but that don't count (here a new self came in). Lying in bed of a morning listening to the pigeons on fine linen; silver dishes; wine; maids; footmen. Spoilt? Perhaps. Too many things for nothing. Hence my books (here she mentioned fifty classical titles; which represented, so we think, the early romantic works that she tore up). Facile, glib, romantic. But (here another self came in) a duffer, a fumbler. More clumsy I couldn't be. And--and--(here she hesitated for a word and if we suggest 'Love' we may be wrong, but certainly she laughed and blushed and then cried out--) A toad set in emeralds! Harry the Archduke! Blue-bottles on the ceiling! (here another self came in). But Nell, Kit, Sasha? (she was sunk in gloom: tears actually shaped themselves and she had long given over crying). Trees, she said. (Here another self came in.) I love trees (she was passing a clump) growing there a thousand years. And barns (she passed a tumbledown barn at the edge of the road). And sheep dogs (here one came trotting across the road. She carefully avoided it). And the night. But people (here another self came in). People? (She repeated it as a question.) I don't know. Chattering, spiteful, always telling lies. (Here she turned into the High Street of her native town, which was crowded, for it was market day, with farmers, and shepherds, and old women with hens in baskets.) I like peasants. I understand crops. But (here another self came skipping over the top of her mind like the beam from a lighthouse). Fame! (She laughed.) Fame! Seven editions. A prize. Photographs in the evening papers (here she alluded to the 'Oak Tree' and 'The Burdett Coutts' Memorial Prize which she had won; and we must snatch space to remark how discomposing it is for her biographer that this culmination to which the whole book moved, this peroration with which the book was to end, should be dashed from us on a laugh casually like this; but the truth is that when we write of a woman, everything is out of place--culminations and perorations; the accent never falls where it does with a man). Fame! she repeated. A poet--a charlatan; both every morning as regularly as the post comes in. To dine, to meet; to meet, to dine; fame--fame! (She had here to slow down to pass through the crowd of market people. But no one noticed her. A porpoise in a fishmonger's shop attracted far more attention than a lady who had won a prize and might, had she chosen, have worn three coronets one on top of another on her brow.) Driving very slowly she now hummed as if it were part of an old song, 'With my guineas I'll buy flowering trees, flowering trees, flowering trees and walk among my flowering trees and tell my sons what fame is'. So she hummed, and now all her words began to sag here and there like a barbaric necklace of heavy beads. 'And walk among my flowering trees,' she sang, accenting the words strongly, 'and see the moon rise slow, the waggons go...' Here she stopped short and looked ahead of her intently at the bonnet of the car in profound meditation.

'He sat at Twitchett's table,' she mused, 'with a dirty ruff on...Was it old Mr Baker come to measure the timber? Or was it Sh-p--re? (for when we speak names we deeply reverence to ourselves we never speak them whole.) She gazed for ten minutes ahead of her, letting the car come almost to a standstill.

'Haunted!' she cried, suddenly pressing the accelerator. 'Haunted! ever since I was a child. There flies the wild goose. It flies past the window out to sea. Up I jumped (she gripped the steering-wheel tighter) and stretched after it. But the goose flies too fast. I've seen it, here--there--there--England, Persia, Italy. Always it flies fast out to sea and always I fling after it words like nets (here she flung her hand out) which shrivel as I've seen nets shrivel drawn on deck with only seaweed in them; and sometimes there's an inch of silver--six words--in the bottom of the net. But never the great fish who lives in the coral groves.' Here she bent her head, pondering deeply.

And it was at this moment, when she had ceased to call 'Orlando' and was deep in thoughts of something else, that the Orlando whom she had called came of its own accord; as was proved by the change that now came over her (she had passed through the lodge gates and was entering the park).

The whole of her darkened and settled, as when some foil whose addition makes the round and solidity of a surface is added to it, and the shallow becomes deep and the near distant; and all is contained as water is contained by the sides of a well. So she was now darkened, stilled, and become, with the addition of this Orlando, what is called, rightly or wrongly, a single self, a real self. And she fell silent. For it is probable that when people talk aloud, the selves (of which there may be more than two thousand) are conscious of disseverment, and are trying to communicate, but when communication is established they fall silent.

Masterfully, swiftly, she drove up the curving drive between the elms and oaks through the falling turf of the park whose fall was so gentle that had it been water it would have spread the beach with a smooth green tide. Planted here and in solemn groups were beech trees and oak trees. The deer stepped among them, one white as snow, another with its head on one side, for some wire netting had caught in its horns. All this, the trees, deer, and turf, she observed with the greatest satisfaction as if her mind had become a fluid that flowed round things and enclosed them completely. Next minute she drew up in the courtyard where, for so many hundred years she had come, on horseback or in coach and six, with men riding before or coming after; where plumes had tossed, torches flashed, and the same flowering trees that let their leaves drop now had shaken their blossoms. Now she was alone. The autumn leaves were falling. The porter opened the great gates. 'Morning, James,' she said, 'there're some things in the car. Will you bring 'em in?' words of no beauty, interest, or significance themselves, it will be conceded, but now so plumped out with meaning that they fell like ripe nuts from a tree, and proved that when the shrivelled skin of the ordinary is stuffed out with meaning it satisfies the senses amazingly. This was true indeed of every movement and action now, usual though they were; so that to see Orlando change her skirt for a pair of whipcord breeches and leather jacket, which she did in less than three minutes, was to be ravished with the beauty of movement as if Madame Lopokova were using her highest art. Then she strode into the dining-room where her old friends Dryden, Pope, Swift, Addison regarded her demurely at first as who should say Here's the prize winner! but when they reflected that two hundred guineas was in question, they nodded their heads approvingly. Two hundred guineas, they seemed to say; two hundred guineas are not to be sniffed at. She cut herself a slice of bread and ham, clapped the two together and began to eat, striding up and down the room, thus shedding her company habits in a second, without thinking. After five or six such turns, she tossed off a glass of red Spanish wine, and, filling another which she carried in her hand, strode down the long corridor and through a dozen drawing-rooms and so began a perambulation of the house, attended by such elk-hounds and spaniels as chose to follow her.

This, too, was all in the day's routine. As soon would she come home and leave her own grandmother without a kiss as come back and leave the house unvisited. She fancied that the rooms brightened as she came in; stirred, opened their eyes as if they had been dozing in her absence. She fancied, too, that, hundreds and thousands of times as she had seen them, they never looked the same twice, as if so long a life as theirs had stored in them a myriad moods which changed with winter and summer, bright weather and dark, and her own fortunes and the people's characters who visited them. Polite, they always were to strangers, but a little weary: with her, they were entirely open and at their ease. Why not indeed? They had known each other for close on four centuries now. They had nothing to conceal. She knew their sorrows and joys. She knew what age each part of them was and its little secrets--a hidden drawer, a concealed cupboard, or some deficiency perhaps, such as a part made up, or added later. They, too, knew her in all her moods and changes. She had hidden nothing from them; had come to them as boy and woman, crying and dancing, brooding and gay. In this window-seat, she had written her first verses; in that chapel, she had been married. And she would be buried here, she reflected, kneeling on the window-sill in the long gallery and sipping her Spanish wine. Though she could hardly fancy it, the body of the heraldic leopard would be making yellow pools on the floor the day they lowered her to lie among her ancestors. She, who believed in no immortality, could not help feeling that her soul would come and go forever with the reds on the panels and the greens on the sofa. For the room--she had strolled into the Ambassador's bedroom--shone like a shell that has lain at the bottom of the sea for centuries and has been crusted over and painted a million tints by the water; it was rose and yellow, green and sand-coloured. It was frail as a shell, as iridescent and as empty. No Ambassador would ever sleep there again. Ah, but she knew where the heart of the house still beat. Gently opening a door, she stood on the threshold so that (as she fancied) the room could not see her and watched the tapestry rising and falling on the eternal faint breeze which never failed to move it. Still the hunter rode; still Daphne flew. The heart still beat, she thought, however faintly, however far withdrawn; the frail indomitable heart of the immense building.

Now, calling her troop of dogs to her she passed down the gallery whose floor was laid with whole oak trees sawn across. Rows of chairs with all their velvets faded stood ranged against the wall holding their arms out for Elizabeth, for James, for Shakespeare it might be, for Cecil, who never came. The sight made her gloomy. She unhooked the rope that fenced them off. She sat on the Queen's chair; she opened a manuscript book lying on Lady Betty's table; she stirred her fingers in the aged rose leaves; she brushed her short hair with King James' silver brushes: she bounced up and down upon his bed (but no King would ever sleep there again, for all Louise's new sheets) and pressed her cheek against the worn silver counterpane that lay upon it. But everywhere were little lavender bags to keep the moth out and printed notices, 'Please do not touch', which, though she had put them there herself, seemed to rebuke her. The house was no longer hers entirely, she sighed. It belonged to time now; to history; was past the touch and control of the living. Never would beer be spilt here any more, she thought (she was in the bedroom that had been old Nick Greene's), or holes burnt in the carpet. Never two hundred servants come running and brawling down the corridors with warming pans and great branches for the great fireplaces. Never would ale be brewed and candles made and saddles fashioned and stone shaped in the workshops outside the house. Hammers and mallets were silent now. Chairs and beds were empty; tankards of silver and gold were locked in glass cases. The great wings of silence beat up and down the empty house.

So she sat at the end of the gallery with her dogs couched round her, in Queen Elizabeth's hard armchair. The gallery stretched far away to a point where the light almost failed. It was as a tunnel bored deep into the past. As her eyes peered down it, she could see people laughing and talking; the great men she had known; Dryden, Swift, and Pope; and statesmen in colloquy; and lovers dallying in the window-seats; and people eating and drinking at the long tables; and the wood smoke curling round their heads and making them sneeze and cough. Still further down, she saw sets of splendid dancers formed for the quadrille. A fluty, frail, but nevertheless stately music began to play. An organ boomed. A coffin was borne into the chapel. A marriage procession came out of it. Armed men with helmets left for the wars. They brought banners back from Flodden and Poitiers and stuck them on the wall. The long gallery filled itself thus, and still peering further, she thought she could make out at the very end, beyond the Elizabethans and the Tudors, some one older, further, darker, a cowled figure, monastic, severe, a monk, who went with his hands clasped, and a book in them, murmuring--

Like thunder, the stable clock struck four. Never did any earthquake so demolish a whole town. The gallery and all its occupants fell to powder. Her own face, that had been dark and sombre as she gazed, was lit as by an explosion of gunpowder. In this same light everything near her showed with extreme distinctness. She saw two flies circling round and noticed the blue sheen on their bodies; she saw a knot in the wood where her foot was, and her dog's ear twitching. At the same time, she heard a bough creaking in the garden, a sheep coughing in the park, a swift screaming past the window. Her own body quivered and tingled as if suddenly stood naked in a hard frost. Yet, she kept, as she had not done when the clock struck ten in London, complete composure (for she was now one and entire, and presented, it may be, a larger surface to the shock of time). She rose, but without precipitation, called her dogs, and went firmly but with great alertness of movement down the staircase and out into the garden. Here the shadows of the plants were miraculously distinct. She noticed the separate grains of earth in the flower beds as if she had a microscope stuck to her eye. She saw the intricacy of the twigs of every tree. Each blade of grass was distinct and the marking of veins and petals. She saw Stubbs, the gardener, coming along the path, and every button on his gaiters was visible; she saw Betty and Prince, the cart horses, and never had she marked so clearly the white star on Betty's forehead, and the three long hairs that fell down below the rest on Prince's tail. Out in the quadrangle the old grey walls of the house looked like a scraped new photograph; she heard the loud speaker condensing on the terrace a dance tune that people were listening to in the red velvet opera house at Vienna. Braced and strung up by the present moment she was also strangely afraid, as if whenever the gulf of time gaped and let a second through some unknown danger might come with it. The tension was too relentless and too rigorous to be endured long without discomfort. She walked more briskly than she liked, as if her legs were moved for her, through the garden and out into the park. Here she forced herself, by a great effort, to stop by the carpenter's shop, and to stand stock-still watching Joe Stubbs fashion a cart wheel. She was standing with her eye fixed on his hand when the quarter struck. It hurtled through her like a meteor, so hot that no fingers can hold it. She saw with disgusting vividness that the thumb on Joe's right hand was without a finger nail and there was a raised saucer of pink flesh where the nail should have been. The sight was so repulsive that she felt faint for a moment, but in that moment's darkness, when her eyelids flickered, she was relieved of the pressure of the present. There was something strange in the shadow that the flicker of her eyes cast, something which (as anyone can test for himself by looking now at the sky) is always absent from the present--whence its terror, its nondescript character--something one trembles to pin through the body with a name and call beauty, for it has no body, is as a shadow without substance or quality of its own, yet has the power to change whatever it adds itself to. This shadow now, while she flickered her eye in her faintness in the carpenter's shop, stole out, and attaching itself to the innumerable sights she had been receiving, composed them into something tolerable, comprehensible. Her mind began to toss like the sea. Yes, she thought, heaving a deep sigh of relief, as she turned from the carpenter's shop to climb the hill, I can begin to live again. I am by the Serpentine, she thought, the little boat is climbing through the white arch of a thousand deaths. I am about to understand...

Those were her words, spoken quite distinctly, but we cannot conceal the fact that she was now a very indifferent witness to the truth of what was before her and might easily have mistaken a sheep for a cow, or an old man called Smith for one who was called Jones and was no relation of his whatever. For the shadow of faintness which the thumb without a nail had cast had deepened now, at the back of her brain (which is the part furthest from sight), into a pool where things dwell in darkness so deep that what they are we scarcely know. She now looked down into this pool or sea in which everything is reflected--and, indeed, some say that all our most violent passions, and art and religion, are the reflections which we see in the dark hollow at the back of the head when the visible world is obscured for the time. She looked there now, long, deeply, profoundly, and immediately the ferny path up the hill along which she was walking became not entirely a path, but partly the Serpentine; the hawthorn bushes were partly ladies and gentlemen sitting with card-cases and gold-mounted canes; the sheep were partly tall Mayfair houses; everything was partly something else, as if her mind had become a forest with glades branching here and there; things came nearer, and further, and mingled and separated and made the strangest alliances and combinations in an incessant chequer of light and shade. Except when Canute, the elk-hound, chased a rabbit and so reminded her that it must be about half past four--it was indeed twenty-three minutes to six--she forgot the time.

The ferny path led, with many turns and windings, higher and higher to the oak tree, which stood on the top. The tree had grown bigger, sturdier, and more knotted since she had known it, somewhere about the year 1588, but it was still in the prime of life. The little sharply frilled leaves were still fluttering thickly on its branches. Flinging herself on the ground, she felt the bones of the tree running out like ribs from a spine this way and that beneath her. She liked to think that she was riding the back of the world. She liked to attach herself to something hard. As she flung herself down a little square book bound in red cloth fell from the breast of her leather jacket--her poem 'The Oak Tree'. 'I should have brought a trowel,' she reflected. The earth was so shallow over the roots that it seemed doubtful if she could do as she meant and bury the book here. Besides, the dogs would dig it up. No luck ever attends these symbolical celebrations, she thought. Perhaps it would be as well then to do without them. She had a little speech on the tip of her tongue which she meant to speak over the book as she buried it. (It was a copy of the first edition, signed by author and artist.) 'I bury this as a tribute,' she was going to have said, 'a return to the land of what the land has given me,' but Lord! once one began mouthing words aloud, how silly they sounded! She was reminded of old Greene getting upon a platform the other day comparing her with Milton (save for his blindness) and handing her a cheque for two hundred guineas. She had thought then, of the oak tree here on its hill, and what has that got to do with this, she had wondered? What has praise and fame to do with poetry? What has seven editions (the book had already gone into no less) got to do with the value of it? Was not writing poetry a secret transaction, a voice answering a voice? So that all this chatter and praise and blame and meeting people who admired one and meeting people who did not admire one was as ill suited as could be to the thing itself--a voice answering a voice. What could have been more secret, she thought, more slow, and like the intercourse of lovers, than the stammering answer she had made all these years to the old crooning song of the woods, and the farms and the brown horses standing at the gate, neck to neck, and the smithy and the kitchen and the fields, so laboriously bearing wheat, turnips, grass, and the garden blowing irises and fritillaries?

So she let her book lie unburied and dishevelled on the ground, and watched the vast view, varied like an ocean floor this evening with the sun lightening it and the shadows darkening it. There was a village with a church tower among elm trees; a grey domed manor house in a park; a spark of light burning on some glass-house; a farmyard with yellow corn stacks. The fields were marked with black tree clumps, and beyond the fields stretched long woodlands, and there was the gleam of a river, and then hills again. In the far distance Snowdon's crags broke white among the clouds; she saw the far Scottish hills and the wild tides that swirl about the Hebrides. She listened for the sound of gun-firing out at sea.

No--only the wind blew. There was no war to-day. Drake had gone; Nelson had gone. 'And there', she thought, letting her eyes, which had been looking at these far distances, drop once more to the land beneath her, 'was my land once: that Castle between the downs was mine; and all that moor running almost to the sea was mine.' Here the landscape (it must have been some trick of the fading light) shook itself, heaped itself, let all this encumbrance of houses, castles, and woods slide off its tent-shaped sides. The bare mountains of Turkey were before her. It was blazing noon. She looked straight at the baked hill-side. Goats cropped the sandy tufts at her feet. An eagle soared above. The raucous voice of old Rustum, the gipsy, croaked in her ears, 'What is your antiquity and your race, and your possessions compared with this? What do you need with four hundred bedrooms and silver lids on all your dishes, and housemaids dusting?'

At this moment some church clock chimed in the valley. The tent-like landscape collapsed and fell. The present showered down upon her head once more, but now that the light was fading, gentlier than before, calling into view nothing detailed, nothing small, but only misty fields, cottages with lamps in them, the slumbering bulk of a wood, and a fan-shaped light pushing the darkness before it along some lane. Whether it had struck nine, ten, or eleven, she could not say. Night had come--night that she loved of all times, night in which the reflections in the dark pool of the mind shine more clearly than by day. It was not necessary to faint now in order to look deep into the darkness where things shape themselves and to see in the pool of the mind now Shakespeare, now a girl in Russian trousers, now a toy boat on the Serpentine, and then the Atlantic itself, where it storms in great waves past Cape Horn. She looked into the darkness. There was her husband's brig, rising to the top of the wave! Up, it went, and up and up. The white arch of a thousand deaths rose before it. Oh rash, oh ridiculous man, always sailing, so uselessly, round Cape Horn in the teeth of a gale! But the brig was through the arch and out on the other side; it was safe at last!

'Ecstasy!' she cried, 'ecstasy!' And then the wind sank, the waters grew calm; and she saw the waves rippling peacefully in the moonlight.

'Marmaduke Bonthrop Shelmerdine!' she cried, standing by the oak tree.

The beautiful, glittering name fell out of the sky like a steel-blue feather. She watched it fall, turning and twisting like a slow-falling arrow that cleaves the deep air beautifully. He was coming, as he always came, in moments of dead calm; when the wave rippled and the spotted leaves fell slowly over her foot in the autumn woods; when the leopard was still; the moon was on the waters, and nothing moved in between sky and sea. Then he came.

All was still now. It was near midnight. The moon rose slowly over the weald. Its light raised a phantom castle upon earth. There stood the great house with all its windows robed in silver. Of wall or substance there was none. All was phantom. All was still. All was lit as for the coming of a dead Queen. Gazing below her, Orlando saw dark plumes tossing in the courtyard, and torches flickering and shadows kneeling. A Queen once more stepped from her chariot.

'The house is at your service, Ma'am,' she cried, curtseying deeply. 'Nothing has been changed. The dead Lord, my father, shall lead you in.'

As she spoke, the first stroke of midnight sounded. The cold breeze of the present brushed her face with its little breath of fear. She looked anxiously into the sky. It was dark with clouds now. The wind roared in her ears. But in the roar of the wind she heard the roar of an aeroplane coming nearer and nearer.

'Here! Shel, here!' she cried, baring her breast to the moon (which now showed bright) so that her pearls glowed--like the eggs of some vast moon-spider. The aeroplane rushed out of the clouds and stood over her head. It hovered above her. Her pearls burnt like a phosphorescent flare in the darkness.

And as Shelmerdine, now grown a fine sea captain, hale, fresh-coloured, and alert, leapt to the ground, there sprang up over his head a single wild bird.

'It is the goose!' Orlando cried. 'The wild goose...'

And the twelfth stroke of midnight sounded; the twelfth stroke of midnight, Thursday, the eleventh of October, Nineteen hundred and Twenty Eight.

THE END

A Room of One's Own

This essay is based upon two papers read to the Arts Society at Newnharn and the Odtaa at Girton in October 1928. The papers were too long to be read in full, and have since been altered and expanded.

ONE

But, you may say, we asked you to speak about women and fiction--what, has that got to do with a room of one's own? I will try to explain. When you asked me to speak about women and fiction I sat down on the banks of a river and began to wonder what the words meant. They might mean simply a few remarks about Fanny Burney; a few more about Jane Austen; a tribute to the Brontës and a sketch of Haworth Parsonage under snow; some witticisms if possible about Miss Mitford; a respectful allusion to George Eliot; a reference to Mrs Gaskell and one would have done. But at second sight the words seemed not so simple. The title women and fiction might mean, and you may have meant it to mean, women and what they are like, or it might mean women and the fiction that they write; or it might mean women and the fiction that is written about them, or it might mean that somehow all three are inextricably mixed together and you want me to consider them in that light. But when I began to consider the subject in this last way, which seemed the most interesting, I soon saw that it had one fatal drawback. I should never be able to come to a conclusion. I should never be able to fulfil what is, I understand, the first duty of a lecturer to hand you after an hour's discourse a nugget of pure truth to wrap up between the pages of your notebooks and keep on the mantelpiece for ever. All I could do was to offer you an opinion upon one minor point--a woman must have money and a room of her own if she is to write fiction; and that, as you will see, leaves the great problem of the true nature of woman and the true nature of fiction unsolved. I have shirked the duty of coming to a conclusion upon these two questions--women and fiction remain, so far as I am concerned, unsolved problems. But in order to make some amends I am going to do what I can to show you how I arrived at this opinion about the room and the money. I am going to develop in your presence as fully and freely as I can the train of thought which led me to think this. Perhaps if I lay bare the ideas, the prejudices, that lie behind this statement you will find that they have some bearing upon women and some upon fiction. At any rate, when a subject is highly controversial--and any question about sex is that--one cannot hope to tell the truth. One can only show how one came to hold whatever opinion one does hold. One can only give one's audience the chance of drawing their own conclusions as they observe the limitations, the prejudices, the idiosyncrasies of the speaker. Fiction here is likely to contain more truth than fact. Therefore I propose, making use of all the liberties and licences of a novelist, to tell you the story of the two days that preceded my coming here--how, bowed down by the weight of the subject which you have laid upon my shoulders, I pondered it, and made it work in and out of my daily life. I need not say that what I am about to describe has no existence; Oxbridge is an invention; so is Fernham; 'I' is only a convenient term for somebody who has no real being. Lies will flow from my lips, but there may perhaps be some truth mixed up with them; it is for you to seek out this truth and to decide whether any part of it is worth keeping. If not, you will of course throw the whole of it into the waste-paper basket and forget all about it.

Here then was I (call me Mary Beton, Mary Seton, Mary Carmichael or by any name you please--it is not a matter of any importance) sitting on the banks of a river a week or two ago in fine October weather, lost in thought. That collar I have spoken of, women and fiction, the need of coming to some conclusion on a subject that raises all sorts of prejudices and passions, bowed my head to the ground. To the right and left bushes of some sort, golden and crimson, glowed with the colour, even it seemed burnt with the heat, of fire. On the further bank the willows wept in perpetual lamentation, their hair about their shoulders. The river reflected whatever it chose of sky and bridge and burning tree, and when the undergraduate had oared his boat through the reflections they closed again, completely, as if he had never been. There one might have sat the clock round lost in thought. Thought--to call it by a prouder name than it deserved--had let its line down into the stream. It swayed, minute after minute, hither and thither among the reflections and the weeds, letting the water lift it and sink it until--you know the little tug--the sudden conglomeration of an idea at the end of one's line: and then the cautious hauling of it in, and the careful laying of it out? Alas, laid on the grass how small, how insignificant this thought of mine looked; the sort of fish that a good fisherman puts back into the water so that it may grow fatter and be one day worth cooking and eating. I will not trouble you with that thought now, though if you look carefully you may find it for yourselves in the course of what I am going to say.

But however small it was, it had, nevertheless, the mysterious property of its kind--put back into the mind, it became at once very exciting, and important; and as it darted and sank, and flashed hither and thither, set up such a wash and tumult of ideas that it was impossible to sit still. It was thus that I found myself walking with extreme rapidity across a grass plot. Instantly a man's figure rose to intercept me. Nor did I at first understand that the gesticulations of a curious-looking object, in a cut-away coat and evening shirt, were aimed at me. His face expressed horror and indignation. Instinct rather than reason came to my help, he was a Beadle; I was a woman. This was the turf; there was the path. Only the Fellows and Scholars are allowed here; the gravel is the place for me. Such thoughts were the work of a moment. As I regained the path the arms of the Beadle sank, his face assumed its usual repose, and though turf is better walking than gravel, no very great harm was done. The only charge I could bring against the Fellows and Scholars of whatever the college might happen to be was that in protection of their turf, which has been rolled for 300 years in succession they had sent my little fish into hiding.

What idea it had been that had sent me so audaciously trespassing I could not now remember. The spirit of peace descended like a cloud from heaven, for if the spirit of peace dwells anywhere, it is in the courts and quadrangles of Oxbridge on a fine October morning. Strolling through those colleges past those ancient halls the roughness of the present seemed smoothed away; the body seemed contained in a miraculous glass cabinet through which no sound could penetrate, and the mind, freed from any contact with facts (unless one trespassed on the turf again), was at liberty to settle down upon whatever meditation was in harmony with the moment. As chance would have it, some stray memory of some old essay about revisiting Oxbridge in the long vacation brought Charles Lamb to mind--Saint Charles, said Thackeray, putting a letter of Lamb's to his forehead. Indeed, among all the dead (I give you my thoughts as they came to me), Lamb is one of the most congenial; one to whom one would have liked to say, Tell me then how you wrote your essays? For his essays are superior even to Max Beerbohm's, I thought, with all their perfection, because of that wild flash of imagination, that lightning crack of genius in the middle of them which leaves them flawed and imperfect, but starred with poetry. Lamb then came to Oxbridge perhaps a hundred years ago. Certainly he wrote an essay--the name escapes me--about the manuscript of one of Milton's poems which he saw here. It was LYCIDAS perhaps, and Lamb wrote how it shocked him to think it possible that any word in LYCIDAS could have been different from what it is. To think of Milton changing the words in that poem seemed to him a sort of sacrilege. This led me to remember what I could of LYCIDAS and to amuse myself with guessing which word it could have been that Milton had altered, and why. It then occurred to me that the very manuscript itself which Lamb had looked at was only a few hundred yards away, so that one could follow Lamb's footsteps across the quadrangle to that famous library where the treasure is kept. Moreover, I recollected, as I put this plan into execution, it is in this famous library that the manuscript of Thackeray's ESMOND is also preserved. The critics often say that ESMOND is Thackeray's most perfect novel. But the affectation of the style, with its imitation of the eighteenth century, hampers one, so far as I can remember; unless indeed the eighteenth-century style was natural to Thackeray--a fact that one might prove by looking at the manuscript and seeing whether the alterations were for the benefit of the style or of the sense. But then one would have to decide what is style and what is meaning, a question which--but here I was actually at the door which leads into the library itself. I must have opened it, for instantly there issued, like a guardian angel barring the way with a flutter of black gown instead of white wings, a deprecating, silvery, kindly gentleman, who regretted in a low voice as he waved me back that ladies are only admitted to the library if accompanied by a Fellow of the College or furnished with a letter of introduction.

That a famous library has been cursed by a woman is a matter of complete indifference to a famous library. Venerable and calm, with all its treasures safe locked within its breast, it sleeps complacently and will, so far as I am concerned, so sleep for ever. Never will I wake those echoes, never will I ask for that hospitality again, I vowed as I descended the steps in anger. Still an hour remained before luncheon, and what was one to do? Stroll on the meadows? sit by the river? Certainly it was a lovely autumn morning; the leaves were fluttering red to the ground; there was no great hardship in doing either. But the sound of music reached my ear. Some service or celebration was going forward. The organ complained magnificently as I passed the chapel door. Even the sorrow of Christianity sounded in that serene air more like the recollection of sorrow than sorrow itself; even the groanings of the ancient organ seemed lapped in peace. I had no wish to enter had I the right, and this time the verger might have stopped me, demanding perhaps my baptismal certificate, or a letter of introduction from the Dean. But the outside of these magnificent buildings is often as beautiful as the inside. Moreover, it was amusing enough to watch the congregation assembling, coming in and going out again, busying themselves at the door of the chapel like bees at the mouth of a hive. Many were in cap and gown; some had tufts of fur on their shoulders; others were wheeled in bath-chairs; others, though not past middle age, seemed creased and crushed into shapes so singular that one was reminded of those giant crabs and crayfish who heave with difficulty across the sand of an aquarium. As I leant against the wall the University indeed seemed a sanctuary in which are preserved rare types which would soon be obsolete if left to fight for existence on the pavement of the Strand. Old stories of old deans and old dons came back to mind, but before I had summoned up courage to whistle--it used to be said that at the sound of a whistle old Professor ---- instantly broke into a gallop--the venerable congregation had gone inside. The outside of the chapel remained. As you know, its high domes and pinnacles can be seen, like a sailing-ship always voyaging never arriving, lit up at night and visible for miles, far away across the hills. Once, presumably, this quadrangle with its smooth lawns, its massive buildings and the chapel itself was marsh too, where the grasses waved and the swine rootled. Teams of horses and oxen, I thought, must have hauled the stone in wagons from far countries, and then with infinite labour the grey blocks in whose shade I was now standing were poised in order one on top of another. and then the painters brought their glass for the windows, and the masons were busy for centuries up on that roof with putty and cement, spade and trowel. Every Saturday somebody must have poured gold and silver out of a leathern purse into their ancient fists, for they had their beer and skittles presumably of an evening. An unending stream of gold and silver, I thought, must have flowed into this court perpetually to keep the stones coming and the masons working; to level, to ditch, to dig and to drain. But it was then the age of faith, and money was poured liberally to set these stones on a deep foundation, and when the stones were raised, still more money was poured in from the coffers of kings and queens and great nobles to ensure that hymns should be sung here and scholars taught. Lands were granted; tithes were paid. And when the age of faith was over and the age of reason had come, still the same flow of gold and silver went on; fellowships were founded; lectureships endowed; only the gold and silver flowed now, not from the coffers of the king. but from the chests of merchants and manufacturers, from the purses of men who had made, say, a fortune from industry, and returned, in their wills, a bounteous share of it to endow more chairs, more lectureships, more fellowships in the university where they had learnt their craft. Hence the libraries and laboratories; the observatories; the splendid equipment of costly and delicate instruments which now stands on glass shelves, where centuries ago the grasses waved and the swine rootled. Certainly, as I strolled round the court, the foundation of gold and silver seemed deep enough; the pavement laid solidly over the wild grasses. Men with trays on their heads went busily from staircase to staircase. Gaudy blossoms flowered in window-boxes. The strains of the gramophone blared out from the rooms within. It was impossible not to reflect--the reflection whatever it may have been was cut short. The clock struck. it was time to find one's way to luncheon.

It is a curious fact that novelists have a way of making us believe that luncheon parties are invariably memorable for something very witty that was said, or for something very wise that was done. But they seldom spare a word for what was eaten. It is part of the novelist's convention not to mention soup and salmon and ducklings, as if soup and salmon and ducklings were of no importance whatsoever, as if nobody ever smoked a cigar or drank a glass of wine. Here, however, I shall take the liberty to defy that convention and to tell you that the lunch on this occasion began with soles, sunk in a deep dish, over which the college cook had spread a counterpane of the whitest cream, save that it was branded here and there with brown spots like the spots on the flanks of a doe. After that came the partridges, but if this suggests a couple of bald, brown birds on a plate you are mistaken. The partridges, many and various, came with all their retinue of sauces and salads, the sharp and the sweet, each in its order; their potatoes, thin as coins but not so hard; their sprouts, foliated as rosebuds but more succulent. And no sooner had the roast and its retinue been done with than the silent servingman, the Beadle himself perhaps in a milder manifestation, set before us, wreathed in napkins, a confection which rose all sugar from the waves. To call it pudding and so relate it to rice and tapioca would be an insult. Meanwhile the wineglasses had flushed yellow and flushed crimson; had been emptied; had been filled. And thus by degrees was lit, half-way down the spine, which is the seat of the soul, not that hard little electric light which we call brilliance, as it pops in and out upon our lips, but the more profound, subtle and subterranean glow which is the rich yellow flame of rational intercourse. No need to hurry. No need to sparkle. No need to be anybody but oneself. We are all going to heaven and Vandyck is of the company--in other words, how good life seemed, how sweet its rewards, how trivial this grudge or that grievance, how admirable friendship and the society of one's kind, as, lighting a good cigarette, one sunk among the cushions in the window-seat.

If by good luck there had been an ash-tray handy, if one had not knocked the ash out of the window in default, if things had been a little different from what they were, one would not have seen, presumably, a cat without a tail. The sight of that abrupt and truncated animal padding softly across the quadrangle changed by some fluke of the subconscious intelligence the emotional light for me. It was as if someone had let fall a shade. Perhaps the excellent hock was relinquishing its hold. Certainly, as I watched the Manx cat pause in the middle of the lawn as if it too questioned the universe, something seemed lacking, something seemed different. But what was lacking, what was different, I asked myself, listening to the talk? And to answer that question I had to think myself out of the room, back into the past, before the war indeed, and to set before my eyes the model of another luncheon party held in rooms not very far distant from these; but different. Everything was different. Meanwhile the talk went on among the guests, who were many and young, some of this sex, some of that; it went on swimmingly, it went on agreeably, freely, amusingly. And as it went on I set it against the background of that other talk, and as I matched the two together I had no doubt that one was the descendant, the legitimate heir of the other. Nothing was changed; nothing was different save only here I listened with all my ears not entirely to what was being said, but to the murmur or current behind it. Yes, that was it--the change was there. Before the war at a luncheon party like this people would have said precisely the same things but they would have sounded different, because in those days they were accompanied by a sort of humming noise, not articulate, but musical, exciting, which changed the value of the words themselves. Could one set that humming noise to words? Perhaps with the help of the poets one could.. A book lay beside me and, opening it, I turned casually enough to Tennyson. And here I found Tennyson was singing:

There has fallen a splendid tear From the passion-flower at the gate. She is coming, my dove, my dear; She is coming, my life, my fate; The red rose cries, 'She is near, she is near'; And the white rose weeps, 'She is late'; The larkspur listens, 'I hear, I hear'; And the lily whispers, 'I wait.'

Was that what men hummed at luncheon parties before the war? And the women?

My heart is like a singing bird Whose nest is in a water'd shoot; My heart is like an apple tree Whose boughs are bent with thick-set fruit, My heart is like a rainbow shell That paddles in a halcyon sea; My heart is gladder than all these Because my love is come to me.

Was that what women hummed at luncheon parties before the war?

There was something so ludicrous in thinking of people humming such things even under their breath at luncheon parties before the war that I burst out laughing. and had to explain my laughter by pointing at the Manx cat, who did look a little absurd, poor beast, without a tail, in the middle of the lawn. Was he really born so, or had he lost his tail in an accident? The tailless cat, though some are said to exist in the Isle of Man, is rarer than one thinks. It is a queer animal, quaint rather than beautiful. It is strange what a difference a tail makes--you know the sort of things one says as a lunch party breaks up and people are finding their coats and hats.

This one, thanks to the hospitality of the host, had lasted far into the afternoon. The beautiful October day was fading and the leaves were falling from the trees in the avenue as I walked through it. Gate after gate seemed to close with gentle finality behind me. Innumerable beadles were fitting innumerable keys into well-oiled locks; the treasure-house was being made secure for another night. After the avenue one comes out upon a road--I forget its name--which leads you, if you take the right turning, along to Fernham. But there was plenty of time. Dinner was not till half-past seven. One could almost do without dinner after such a luncheon. It is strange how a scrap of poetry works in the mind and makes the legs move in time to it along the road. Those words----

There has fallen a splendid tear From the passion-flower at the gate. She is coming, my dove, my dear----

sang in my blood as I stepped quickly along towards Headingley. And then, switching off into the other measure, I sang, where the waters are churned up by the weir:

My heart is like a singing bird Whose nest is in a water'd shoot; My heart is like an apple tree . . .

What poets, I cried aloud, as one does in the dusk, what poets they were!

In a sort of jealousy, I suppose, for our own age, silly and absurd though these comparisons are, I went on to wonder if honestly one could name two living poets now as great as Tennyson and Christina Rossetti were then. Obviously it is impossible, I thought, looking into those foaming waters, to compare them. The very reason why that poetry excites one to such abandonment, such rapture, is that it celebrates some feeling that one used to have (at luncheon parties before the war perhaps), so that one responds easily, familiarly, without troubling to check the feeling, or to compare it with any that one has now. But the living poets express a feeling that is actually being made and torn out of us at the moment. One does not recognize it in the first place; often for some reason one fears it; one watches it with keenness and compares it jealously and suspiciously with the old feeling that one knew. Hence the difficulty of modern poetry; and it is because of this difficulty that one cannot remember more than two consecutive lines of any good modern poet. For this reason--that my memory failed me--the argument flagged for want of material. But why, I continued, moving on towards Headingley, have we stopped humming under our breath at luncheon parties? Why has Alfred ceased to sing

She is coming, my dove, my dear.

Why has Christina ceased to respond

My heart is gladder than all these Because my love is come to me?

Shall we lay the blame on the war? When the guns fired in August 1914, did the faces of men and women show so plain in each other's eyes that romance was killed? Certainly it was a shock (to women in particular with their illusions about education, and so on) to see the faces of our rulers in the light of the shell-fire. So ugly they looked--German, English, French--so stupid. But lay the blame where one will, on whom one will, the illusion which inspired Tennyson and Christina

Rossetti to sing so passionately about the coming of their loves is far rarer now than then. One has only to read, to look, to listen, to remember. But why say 'blame'? Why, if it was an illusion, not praise the catastrophe, whatever it was, that destroyed illusion and put truth in its place? For truth . . . those dots mark the spot where, in search of truth, I missed the turning up to Fernham. Yes indeed, which was truth and which was illusion? I asked myself. What was the truth about these houses, for example, dim and festive now with their red windows in the dusk, but raw and red and squalid, with their sweets and their bootlaces, at nine o'clock in the morning? And the willows and the river and the gardens that run down to the river, vague now with the mist stealing over them, but gold and red in the sunlight--which was the truth, which was the illusion about them? I spare you the twists and turns of my cogitations, for no conclusion was found on the road to Headingley, and I ask You to suppose that I soon found out my mistake about the turning and retraced my steps to Fernham.

As I have said already that it was an October day, I dare not forfeit your respect and imperil the fair name of fiction by changing the season and describing lilacs hanging over garden walls, crocuses, tulips and other flowers of spring. Fiction must stick to facts, and the truer the facts the better the fiction--so we are told. Therefore it was still autumn and the leaves were still yellow and falling, if anything, a little faster than before, because it was now evening (seven twenty-three to be precise) and a breeze (from the south-west to be exact) had risen. But for all that there was something odd at work:

My heart is like a singing bird Whose nest is in a water'd shoot; My heart is like an apple tree Whose boughs are bent with thick-set fruit--

perhaps the words of Christina Rossetti were partly responsible for the folly of the fancy--it was nothing of course but a fancy--that the lilac was shaking its flowers over the garden walls, and the brimstone butterflies were scudding hither and thither, and the dust of the pollen was in the air. A wind blew, from what quarter I know not, but it lifted the half-grown leaves so that there was a flash of silver grey in the air. It was the time between the lights when colours undergo their intensification and purples and golds burn in window-panes like the beat of an excitable heart; when for some reason the beauty of the world revealed and yet soon to perish (here I pushed into the garden, for, unwisely, the door was left open and no beadles seemed about), the beauty of the world which is so soon to perish, has two edges, one of laughter, one of anguish, cutting the heart asunder. The gardens of Fernham lay before me in the spring twilight, wild and open, and in the long grass, sprinkled and carelessly flung, were daffodils and bluebells, not orderly perhaps at the best of times, and now wind-blown and waving as they tugged at their roots. The windows of the building, curved like ships' windows among generous waves of red brick, changed from lemon to silver under the flight of the quick spring clouds. Somebody was in a hammock, somebody, but in this light they were phantoms only, half guessed, half seen, raced across the grass--would no one stop her?--and then on the terrace, as if popping out to breathe the air, to glance at the garden, came a bent figure, formidable yet humble, with her great forehead and her shabby dress--could it be the famous scholar, could it be J---- H---- herself? All was dim, yet intense too, as if the scarf which the dusk had flung over the garden were torn asunder by star or sword--the gash of some terrible reality leaping, as its way is, out of the heart of the spring. For youth----

Here was my soup. Dinner was being served in the great dining-hall. Far from being spring it was in fact an evening in October. Everybody was assembled in the big dining-room. Dinner was ready. Here was the soup. It was a plain gravy soup. There was nothing to stir the fancy in that. One could have seen through the transparent liquid any pattern that there might have been on the plate itself. But there was no pattern. The plate was plain. Next came beef with its attendant greens and potatoes--a homely trinity, suggesting the rumps of cattle in a muddy market, and sprouts curled and yellowed at the edge, and bargaining and cheapening and women with string bags on Monday morning. There was no reason to complain of human nature's daily food, seeing that the supply was sufficient and coal-miners doubtless were sitting down to less. Prunes and custard followed. And if anyone complains that prunes, even when mitigated by custard, are an uncharitable vegetable (fruit they are not), stringy as a miser's heart and exuding a fluid such as might run in misers' veins who have denied themselves wine and warmth for eighty years and yet not given to the poor, he should reflect that there are people whose charity embraces even the prune. Biscuits and cheese came next, and here the water-jug was liberally passed round, for it is the nature of biscuits to be dry, and these were biscuits to the core. That was all. The meal was over. Everybody scraped their chairs back; the swing-doors swung violently to and fro; soon the hall was emptied of every sign of food and made ready no doubt for breakfast next morning. Down corridors and up staircases the youth of England went banging and singing. And was it for a guest, a stranger (for I had no more right here in Fernham than in Trinity or Somerville or Girton or Newnham or Christchurch), to say, 'The dinner was not good,' or to say (we were now, Mary Seton and I, in her sitting-room), 'Could we not have dined up here alone?' for if I had said anything of the kind I should have been prying and searching into the secret economies of a house which to the stranger wears so fine a front of gaiety and courage. No, one could say nothing of the sort. Indeed, conversation for a moment flagged. The human frame being what it is, heart, body and brain all mixed together, and not contained in separate compartments as they will be no doubt in another million years, a good dinner is of great importance to good talk. One cannot think well, love well, sleep well, if one has not dined well. The lamp in the spine does not light on beef and prunes. We are all PROBABLY going to heaven, and Vandyck is, we HOPE, to meet us round the next corner--that is the dubious and qualifying state of mind that beef and prunes at the end of the day's work breed between them. Happily my friend, who taught science, had a cupboard where there was a squat bottle and little glasses--(but there should have been sole and partridge to begin with)--so that we were able to draw up to the fire and repair some of the damages of the day's living. In a minute or so we were slipping freely in and out among all those objects of curiosity and interest which form in the mind in the absence of a particular person, and are naturally to be discussed on coming together again--how somebody has married, another has not; one thinks this, another that; one has improved out of all knowledge, the other most amazingly gone to the bad--with all those speculations upon human nature and the character of the amazing world we live in which spring naturally from such beginnings. While these things were being said, however, I became shamefacedly aware of a current setting in of its own accord and carrying everything forward to an end of its own. One might be talking of Spain or Portugal, of book or racehorse, but the real interest of whatever was said was none of those things, but a scene of masons on a high roof some five centuries ago. Kings and nobles brought treasure in huge sacks and poured it under the earth. This scene was for ever coming alive in my mind and placing itself by another of lean cows and a muddy market and withered greens and the stringy hearts of old men--these two pictures, disjointed and disconnected and nonsensical as they were, were for ever coming together and combating each other and had me entirely at their mercy. The best course, unless the whole talk was to be distorted, was to expose what was in my mind to the air, when with good luck it would fade and crumble like the head of the dead king when they opened the coffin at Windsor. Briefly, then, I told Miss Seton about the masons who had been all those years on the roof of the chapel, and about the kings and queens and nobles bearing sacks of gold and silver on their shoulders, which they shovelled into the earth; and then how the great financial magnates of our own time came and laid cheques and bonds, I suppose, where the others had laid ingots and rough lumps of gold. All that lies beneath the colleges down there, I said; but this college, where we are now sitting, what lies beneath its gallant red brick and the wild unkempt grasses of the garden? What force is behind that plain china off which we dined, and (here it popped out of my mouth before I could stop it) the beef, the custard and the prunes?

Well, said Mary Seton, about the year 1860--Oh, but you know the story, she said, bored, I suppose, by the recital. And she told me--rooms were hired. Committees met. Envelopes were addressed. Circulars were drawn up. Meetings were held; letters were read out; so-and-so has promised so much; on the contrary, Mr ---- won't give a penny. The SATURDAY REVIEW has been very rude. How can we raise a fund to pay for offices? Shall we hold a bazaar? Can't we find a pretty girl to sit in the front row? Let us look up what John Stuart Mill said on the subject. Can anyone persuade the editor of the ---- to print a letter? Can we get Lady ---- to sign it? Lady ---- is out of town. That was the way it was done, presumably, sixty years ago, and it was a prodigious effort, and a great deal of time was spent on it. And it was only after a long struggle and with the utmost difficulty that they got thirty thousand pounds together[1]. So obviously we cannot have wine and par-

[1] We are told that we ought to ask for £30,000 at least. . . . It is not a large sum, considering that there is to be but one college of this sort for Great Britain, Ireland and the Colonies, and considering how easy it is to raise immense sums for boys' schools. But

tridges and servants carrying tin dishes on their heads, she said. We cannot have sofas and separate rooms. 'The amenities,' she said, quoting from some book or other, 'will have to wait.'[1]

At the thought of all those women working year after year and finding it hard to get two thousand pounds together, and as much as they could do to get thirty thousand pounds, we burst out in scorn at the reprehensible poverty of our sex. What had our mothers been doing then that they had no wealth to leave us? Powdering their noses? Looking in at shop windows? Flaunting in the sun at Monte Carlo? There were some photographs on the mantelpiece. Mary's mother--if that was her picture--may have been a wastrel in her spare time (she had thirteen children by a minister of the church), but if so her gay and dissipated life had left too few traces of its pleasures on her face. She was a homely body; an old lady in a plaid shawl which was fastened by a large cameo; and she sat in a basket-chair, encouraging a spaniel to look at the camera, with the amused, yet strained expression of one who is sure that the dog will move directly the bulb is pressed. Now if she had gone into business; had become a manufacturer of artificial silk or a magnate on the Stock Exchange; if she had left two or three hundred thousand pounds to Fernham, we could have been sitting at our ease to-night and the subject of our talk might have been archaeology, botany, anthropology, physics, the nature of the atom, mathematics, astronomy, relativity, geography. If only Mrs Seton and her mother and her mother before her had learnt the great art of making money and had left their money, like their fathers and their grandfathers before them, to found fellowships and lectureships and prizes and scholarships appropriated to the use of their own sex, we might have dined very tolerably up here alone off a bird and a bottle of wine; we might have looked forward without undue confidence to a pleasant and honourable lifetime spent in the shelter of one of the liberally endowed professions. We might have been exploring or writing; mooning about the venerable places of the earth; sitting contemplative on the steps of the Parthenon, or going at ten to an office and coming home comfortably at half-past four to write a little poetry. Only, if Mrs Seton and her like had gone into business at the age of fifteen, there would have been--that was the snag in the argument--no Mary. What, I asked, did Mary think of that? There between the curtains was the October night, calm and lovely, with a star or two caught in the yellowing trees. Was she ready to resign her share of it and her memories (for they had been a happy family, though a large one) of games and quarrels up in Scotland, which she is never tired of praising for the fineness of its air and the quality of its cakes, in order that Fernham might have been endowed with fifty thousand pounds or so by a stroke of the pen? For, to endow a college would necessitate the suppression of families altogether. Making a fortune and bearing thirteen children--no human

---

considering how few people really wish women to be educated, it is a good deal.'--LADY STEPHEN, EMILY DAVIES AND GIRTON COLLEGE.

[1] Every penny which could be scraped together was set aside for building, and the amenities had to be postponed.--R. STRACHEY, THE CAUSE.

being could stand it. Consider the facts, we said. First there are nine months before the baby is born. Then the baby is born. Then there are three or four months spent in feeding the baby. After the baby is fed there are certainly five years spent in playing with the baby. You cannot, it seems, let children run about the streets. People who have seen them running wild in Russia say that the sight is not a pleasant one. People say, too, that human nature takes its shape in the years between one and five. If Mrs Seton, I said, had been making money, what sort of memories would you have had of games and quarrels? What would you have known of Scotland, and its fine air and cakes and all the rest of it? But it is useless to ask these questions, because you would never have come into existence at all. Moreover, it is equally useless to ask what might have happened if Mrs Seton and her mother and her mother before her had amassed great wealth and laid it under the foundations of college and library, because, in the first place, to earn money was impossible for them, and in the second, had it been possible, the law denied them the right to possess what money they earned. It is only for the last forty-eight years that Mrs Seton has had a penny of her own. For all the centuries before that it would have been her husband's property--a thought which, perhaps, may have had its share in keeping Mrs Seton and her mothers off the Stock Exchange. Every penny I earn, they may have said, will be taken from me and disposed of according to my husband's wisdom--perhaps to found a scholarship or to endow a fellowship in Balliol or Kings, so that to earn money, even if I could earn money, is not a matter that interests me very greatly. I had better leave it to my husband.

At any rate, whether or not the blame rested on the old lady who was looking at the spaniel, there could be no doubt that for some reason or other our mothers had mismanaged their affairs very gravely. Not a penny could be spared for 'amenities'; for partridges and wine, beadles and turf, books and cigars, libraries and leisure. To raise bare walls out of bare earth was the utmost they could do.

So we talked standing at the window and looking, as so many thousands look every night, down on the domes and towers of the famous city beneath us. It was very beautiful, very mysterious in the autumn moonlight. The old stone looked very white and venerable. One thought of all the books that were assembled down there; of the pictures of old prelates and worthies hanging in the panelled rooms; of the painted windows that would be throwing strange globes and crescents on the pavement; of the tablets and memorials and inscriptions; of the fountains and the grass; of the quiet rooms looking across the quiet quadrangles. And (pardon me the thought) I thought, too, of the admirable smoke and drink and the deep armchairs and the pleasant carpets: of the urbanity, the geniality, the dignity which are the offspring of luxury and privacy and space. Certainly our mothers had not provided us with any thing comparable to all this--our mothers who found it difficult to scrape together thirty thousand pounds, our mothers who bore thirteen children to ministers of religion at St Andrews.

So I went back to my inn, and as I walked through the dark streets I pondered this and that, as one does at the end of the day's work. I pondered why it was that

Mrs Seton had no money to leave us; and what effect poverty has on the mind; and what effect wealth has on the mind; and I thought of the queer old gentlemen I had seen that morning with tufts of fur upon their shoulders; and I remembered how if one whistled one of them ran; and I thought of the organ booming in the chapel and of the shut doors of the library; and I thought how unpleasant it is to be locked out; and I thought how it is worse perhaps to be locked in; and, thinking of the safety and prosperity of the one sex and of the poverty and insecurity of the other and of the effect of tradition and of the lack of tradition upon the mind of a writer, I thought at last that it was time to roll up the crumpled skin of the day, with its arguments and its impressions and its anger and its laughter, and cast it into the hedge. A thousand stars were flashing across the blue wastes of the sky. One seemed alone with an inscrutable society. All human beings were laid asleep--prone, horizontal, dumb. Nobody seemed stirring in the streets of Oxbridge. Even the door of the hotel sprang open at the touch of an invisible hand--not a boots was sitting up to light me to bed, it was so late.

TWO

The scene, if I may ask you to follow me, was now changed. The leaves were still falling, but in London now, not Oxbridge; and I must ask you to imagine a room, like many thousands, with a window looking across people's hats and vans and motor-cars to other windows, and on the table inside the room a blank sheet of paper on which was written in large letters WOMEN AND FICTION, but no more. The inevitable sequel to lunching and dining at Oxbridge seemed, unfortunately, to be a visit to the British Museum. One must strain off what was personal and accidental in all these impressions and so reach the pure fluid, the essential oil of truth. For that visit to Oxbridge and the luncheon and the dinner had started a swarm of questions. Why did men drink wine and women water? Why was one sex so prosperous and the other so poor? What effect has poverty on fiction? What conditions are necessary for the creation of works of art?--a thousand questions at once suggested themselves. But one needed answers, not questions; and an answer was only to be had by consulting the learned and the unprejudiced, who have removed themselves above the strife of tongue and the confusion of body and issued the result of their reasoning and research in books which are to be found in the British Museum. If truth is not to be found on the shelves of the British Museum, where, I asked myself, picking up a notebook and a pencil, is truth?

Thus provided, thus confident and enquiring, I set out in the pursuit of truth. The day, though not actually wet, was dismal, and the streets in the neighbourhood of the Museum were full of open coal-holes, down which sacks were showering; four-wheeled cabs were drawing up and depositing on the pavement corded boxes containing, presumably, the entire wardrobe of some Swiss or Italian family seeking fortune or refuge or some other desirable commodity which is to be found in the boarding-houses of Bloomsbury in the winter. The usual hoarse-voiced men paraded the streets with plants on barrows. Some shouted; others sang. London was like a workshop. London was like a machine. We were all being shot backwards and forwards on this plain foundation to make some pattern. The British Museum was another department of the factory. The swing-doors swung open; and there one stood under the vast dome, as if one were a thought in the huge bald forehead which is so splendidly encircled by a band of famous names. One went to the counter; one took a slip of paper; one opened a volume of the catalogue, and the five dots here indicate five separate minutes of stupefaction, wonder and bewilderment. Have you any notion of how many books are written about women in the course of one year? Have you any notion how many are written by men? Are you aware that you are, perhaps, the most discussed animal in the universe? Here had I come with a notebook and a pencil proposing to spend a morning reading, supposing that at the end of the morning I should have transferred the truth to my notebook. But I should need to be a herd of elephants, I thought, and a wilderness of spiders, desperately referring to the animals that are reputed longest lived and most multitudinously eyed, to cope with all this. I should need claws of steel and beak of brass even to penetrate the husk. How shall I ever find the grains of truth embedded in all this mass of paper? I asked myself, and in despair began running my eye up and down the long list of titles. Even the names of the books gave me food for thought. Sex and its nature might well attract doctors and biologists; but what was surprising and difficult of explanation was the fact that sex--woman, that is to say--also attracts agreeable essayists, light-fingered novelists, young men who have taken the M.A. degree; men who have taken no degree; men who have no apparent qualification save that they are not women. Some of these books were, on the face of it, frivolous and facetious; but many, on the other hand, were serious and prophetic, moral and hortatory. Merely to read the titles suggested innumerable schoolmasters, innumerable clergymen mounting their platforms and pulpits and holding forth with loquacity which far exceeded the hour usually alloted to such discourse on this one subject. It was a most strange phenomenon; and apparently--here I consulted the letter M--one confined to the male sex. Women do not write books about men--a fact that I could not help welcoming with relief, for if I had first to read all that men have written about women, then all that women have written about men, the aloe that flowers once in a hundred years would flower twice before I could set pen to paper. So, making a perfectly arbitrary choice of a dozen volumes or so, I sent my slips of paper to lie in the wire tray, and waited in my stall, among the other seekers for the essential oil of truth.

What could be the reason, then, of this curious disparity, I wondered, drawing cart-wheels on the slips of paper provided by the British taxpayer for other purposes. Why are women, judging from this catalogue, so much more interesting to men than men are to women? A very curious fact it seemed, and my mind wandered to picture the lives of men who spend their time in writing books about women; whether they were old or young, married or unmarried, red-nosed or hump-backed--anyhow, it was flattering, vaguely, to feel oneself the object of such attention provided that it was not entirely bestowed by the crippled and the infirm--so I pondered until all such frivolous thoughts were ended by an avalanche of books sliding down on to the desk in front of me. Now the trouble began. The student who has been trained in research at Oxbridge has no doubt some method of shepherding his question past all distractions till it runs into his answer as a sheep runs into its pen. The student by my side, for instance, who was copying assiduously from a scientific manual, was, I felt sure, extracting pure nuggets of the essential ore every ten minutes or so. His little grunts of satisfaction indicated so much. But if, unfortunately, one has had no training in a university, the question far from being shepherded to its pen flies like a frightened flock hither and thither, helter-skelter, pursued by a whole pack of hounds. Professors, schoolmasters, sociologists, clergymen, novelists, essayists, journalists, men who had no qualification save that they were not women, chased my simple and single question--Why are some women poor?--until it became fifty questions; until the fifty questions leapt frantically into midstream and were carried away. Every page in my notebook was scribbled over with notes. To show the state of mind I was in, I will read you a few of them, explaining that the page was headed quite simply, WOMEN AND POVERTY, in block letters; but what followed was something like this:

Condition in Middle Ages of, Habits in the Fiji Islands of, Worshipped as goddesses by, Weaker in moral sense than, Idealism of, Greater conscientiousness of, South Sea Islanders, age of puberty among, Attractiveness of, Offered as sacrifice to, Small size of brain of, Profounder sub-consciousness of, Less hair on the body of, Mental, moral and physical inferiority of, Love of children of, Greater length of life of, Weaker muscles of, Strength of affections of, Vanity of, Higher education of, Shakespeare's opinion of, Lord Birkenhead's opinion of, Dean Inge's opinion of, La Bruyere's opinion of, Dr Johnson's opinion of, Mr Oscar Browning's opinion of, . . .

Here I drew breath and added, indeed, in the margin, Why does Samuel Butler say, 'Wise men never say what they think of women'? Wise men never say anything else apparently. But, I continued, leaning back in my chair and looking at the vast dome in which I was a single but by now somewhat harassed thought, what is so unfortunate is that wise men never think the same thing about women. Here is Pope:

Most women have no character at all.

And here is La Bruyère:

Les femmes sont extrêmes, elles sont meilleures ou pires que les hommes---

a direct contradiction by keen observers who were contemporary. Are they capable of education or incapable? Napoleon thought them incapable. Dr Johnson thought the opposite[1]. Have they souls or have they not souls? Some savages say they have none. Others, on the contrary, maintain that women are half divine and worship them on that account[2]. Some sages hold that they are shallower in the brain; others that they are deeper in the consciousness. Goethe honoured them; Mussolini despises them. Wherever one looked men thought about women and

---

[1] '"Men know that women are an overmatch for them, and therefore they choose the weakest or the most ignorant. If they did not think so, they never could be afraid of women knowing as much as themselves." . . . In justice to the sex, I think it but candid to acknowledge that, in a subsequent conversation, he told me that he was serious in what he said.'--BOSWELL, THE JOURNAL OF A TOUR TO THE HEBRIDES.

[2] The ancient Germans believed that there was something holy in women, and accordingly consulted them as oracles.'--FRAZER, GOLDEN BOUGH.

thought differently. It was impossible to make head or tail of it all, I decided, glancing with envy at the reader next door who was making the neatest abstracts, headed often with an A or a B or a C, while my own notebook rioted with the wildest scribble of contradictory jottings. It was distressing, it was bewildering, it was humiliating. Truth had run through my fingers. Every drop had escaped.

I could not possibly go home, I reflected, and add as a serious contribution to the study of women and fiction that women have less hair on their bodies than men, or that the age of puberty among the South Sea Islanders is nine--or is it ninety?--even the handwriting had become in its distraction indecipherable. It was disgraceful to have nothing more weighty or respectable to show after a whole morning's work. And if I could not grasp the truth about W. (as for brevity's sake I had come to call her) in the past, why bother about W. in the future? It seemed pure waste of time to consult all those gentlemen who specialize in woman and her effect on whatever it may be--politics, children, wages, morality--numerous and learned as they are. One might as well leave their books unopened.

But while I pondered I had unconsciously, in my listlessness, in my desperation, been drawing a picture where I should, like my neighbour, have been writing a conclusion. I had been drawing a face, a figure. It was the face and the figure of Professor von X engaged in writing his monumental work entitled THE MENTAL, MORAL, AND PHYSICAL INFERIORITY OF THE FEMALE SEX. He was not in my picture a man attractive to women. He was heavily built; he had a great jowl; to balance that he had very small eyes; he was very red in the face. His expression suggested that he was labouring under some emotion that made him jab his pen on the paper as if he were killing some noxious insect as he wrote, but even when he had killed it that did not satisfy him; he must go on killing it; and even so, some cause for anger and irritation remained. Could it be his wife, I asked, looking at my picture? Was she in love with a cavalry officer? Was the cavalry officer slim and elegant and dressed in astrakhan? Had he been laughed at, to adopt the Freudian theory, in his cradle by a pretty girl? For even in his cradle the professor, I thought, could not have been an attractive child. Whatever the reason, the professor was made to look very angry and very ugly in my sketch, as he wrote his great book upon the mental, moral and physical inferiority of women. Drawing pictures was an idle way of finishing an unprofitable morning's work. Yet it is in our idleness, in our dreams, that the submerged truth sometimes comes to the top. A very elementary exercise in psychology, not to be dignified by the name of psychoanalysis, showed me, on looking at my notebook, that the sketch of the angry professor had been made in anger. Anger had snatched my pencil while I dreamt. But what was anger doing there? Interest, confusion, amusement, boredom--all these emotions I could trace and name as they succeeded each other throughout the morning. Had anger, the black snake, been lurking among them? Yes, said the sketch, anger had. It referred me unmistakably to the one book, to the one phrase, which had roused the demon; it was the professor's statement about the mental, moral and physical inferiority of women. My heart had leapt. My cheeks had burnt. I had flushed with anger. There was nothing specially remarkable, however foolish, in that. One does not like to be told that one is naturally the inferior of a little man--I looked at the student next me--who breathes hard, wears a ready-made tie, and has not shaved this fortnight. One has certain foolish vanities. It is only human nature, I reflected, and began drawing cartwheels and circles over the angry professor's face till he looked like a burning bush or a flaming comet--anyhow, an apparition without human semblance or significance. The professor was nothing now but a faggot burning on the top of Hampstead Heath. Soon my own anger was explained and done with; but curiosity remained. How explain the anger of the professors? Why were they angry? For when it came to analysing the impression left by these books there was always an element of heat. This heat took many forms; it showed itself in satire, in sentiment, in curiosity, in reprobation. But there was another element which was often present and could not immediately be identified. Anger, I called it. But it was anger that had gone underground and mixed itself with all kinds of other emotions. To judge from its odd effects, it was anger disguised and complex, not anger simple and open.

Whatever the reason, all these books, I thought, surveying the pile on the desk, are worthless for my purposes. They were worthless scientifically, that is to say, though humanly they were full of instruction, interest, boredom, and very queer facts about the habits of the Fiji Islanders. They had been written in the red light of emotion and not in the white light of truth. Therefore they must be returned to the central desk and restored each to his own cell in the enormous honeycomb. All that I had retrieved from that morning's work had been the one fact of anger. The professors--I lumped them together thus--were angry. But why, I asked myself, having returned the books, why, I repeated, standing under the colonnade among the pigeons and the prehistoric canoes, why are they angry? And, asking myself this question, I strolled off to find a place for luncheon. What is the real nature of what I call for the moment their anger? I asked. Here was a puzzle that would last all the time that it takes to be served with food in a small restaurant somewhere near the British Museum. Some previous luncher had left the lunch edition of the evening paper on a chair, and, waiting to be served, I began idly reading the headlines. A ribbon of very large letters ran across the page. Somebody had made a big score in South Africa. Lesser ribbons announced that Sir Austen Chamberlain was at Geneva. A meat axe with human hair on it had been found in a cellar. Mr justice ---- commented in the Divorce Courts upon the Shamelessness of Women. Sprinkled about the paper were other pieces of news. A film actress had been lowered from a peak in California and hung suspended in mid-air. The weather was going to be foggy. The most transient visitor to this planet, I thought, who picked up this paper could not fail to be aware, even from this scattered testimony, that England is under the rule of a patriarchy. Nobody in their senses could fail to detect the dominance of the professor. His was the power and the money and the influence. He was the proprietor of the paper and its editor and sub-editor. He was the Foreign Secretary and the judge. He was the cricketer; he owned the racehorses and the yachts. He was the director of the company that pays two hundred per cent to its shareholders. He left millions to charities and colleges that were ruled by himself. He suspended the film actress in mid-air. He will decide if the hair on the meat axe is human; he it is who will acquit or convict the murderer, and hang him, or let him go free. With the exception of the fog he seemed to control everything. Yet he was angry. I knew that he was angry by this token. When I read what he wrote about women--I thought, not of what he was saying, but of himself. When an arguer argues dispassionately he thinks only of the argument; and the reader cannot help thinking of the argument too. If he had written dispassionately about women, had used indisputable proofs to establish his argument and had shown no trace of wishing that the result should be one thing rather than another, one would not have been angry either. One would have accepted the fact, as one accepts the fact that a pea is green or a canary yellow. So be it, I should have said. But I had been angry because he was angry. Yet it seemed absurd, I thought, turning over the evening paper, that a man with all this power should be angry. Or is anger, I wondered, somehow, the familiar, the attendant sprite on power? Rich people, for example, are often angry because they suspect that the poor want to seize their wealth. The professors, or patriarchs, as it might be more accurate to call them, might be angry for that reason partly, but partly for one that lies a little less obviously on the surface. Possibly they were not 'angry' at all; often, indeed, they were admiring, devoted, exemplary in the relations of private life. Possibly when the professor insisted a little too emphatically upon the inferiority of women, he was concerned not with their inferiority, but with his own superiority. That was what he was protecting rather hot-headedly and with too much emphasis, because it was a jewel to him of the rarest price. Life for both sexes--and I looked at them, shouldering their way along the pavement--is arduous, difficult, a perpetual struggle. It calls for gigantic courage and strength. More than anything, perhaps, creatures of illusion as we are, it calls for confidence in oneself. Without self-confidence we are as babes in the cradle. And how can we generate this imponderable quality, which is yet so invaluable, most quickly? By thinking that other people are inferior to one self. By feeling that one has some innate superiority--it may be wealth, or rank, a straight nose, or the portrait of a grandfather by Romney--for there is no end to the pathetic devices of the human imagination--over other people. Hence the enormous importance to a patriarch who has to conquer, who has to rule, of feeling that great numbers of people, half the human race indeed, are by nature inferior to himself. It must indeed be one of the chief sources of his power. But let me turn the light of this observation on to real life, I thought. Does it help to explain some of those psychological puzzles that one notes in the margin of daily life? Does it explain my astonishment of the other day when Z, most humane, most modest of men, taking up some book by Rebecca West and reading a passage in it, exclaimed, 'The arrant feminist! She says that men are snobs!' The exclamation, to me so surprising--for why was Miss West an arrant feminist for making a possibly true if uncomplimentary statement about the other sex?--was not merely the cry of wounded vanity; it was a protest against some infringement of his power to believe in himself. Women have served all these centuries as looking-glasses possessing the magic and delicious power of reflecting the figure of man at twice its natural size. Without that power probably the earth would still be swamp and jungle. The glories of all our wars would he unknown. We should still be scratching the outlines of deer on the remains of mutton bones and bartering flints for sheep skins or whatever simple ornament took our unsophisticated taste. Supermen and Fingers of Destiny would never have existed. The Czar and the Kaiser would never have worn crowns or lost them. Whatever may be their use in civilized societies, mirrors are essential to all violent and heroic action. That is why Napoleon and Mussolini both insist so emphatically upon the inferiority of women, for if they were not inferior, they would cease to enlarge. That serves to explain in part the necessity that women so often are to men. And it serves to explain how restless they are under her criticism; how impossible it is for her to say to them this book is bad, this picture is feeble, or whatever it may be, without giving far more pain and rousing far more anger than a man would do who gave the same criticism. For if she begins to tell the truth, the figure in the looking-glass shrinks; his fitness for life is diminished. How is he to go on giving judgement, civilizing natives, making laws, writing books, dressing up and speechifying at banquets, unless he can see himself at breakfast and at dinner at least twice the size he really is? So I reflected, crumbling my bread and stirring my coffee and now and again looking at the people in the street. The looking-glass vision is of supreme importance because it charges the vitality; it stimulates the nervous system. Take it away and man may die, like the drug fiend deprived of his cocaine. Under the spell of that illusion, I thought, looking out of the window, half the people on the pavement are striding to work. They put on their hats and coats in the morning under its agreeable rays. They start the day confident, braced, believing themselves desired at Miss Smith's tea party; they say to themselves as they go into the room, I am the superior of half the people here, and it is thus that they speak with that self-confidence, that self-assurance, which have had such profound consequences in public life and lead to such curious notes in the margin of the private mind.

But these contributions to the dangerous and fascinating subject of the psychology of the other sex--it is one, I hope, that you will investigate when you have five hundred a year of your own--were interrupted by the necessity of paying the bill. It came to five shillings and ninepence. I gave the waiter a ten-shilling note and he went to bring me change. There was another ten-shilling note in my purse; I noticed it, because it is a fact that still takes my breath away the power of my purse to breed ten-shilling notes automatically. I open it and there they are. Society gives me chicken and coffee, bed and lodging, in return for a certain number of pieces of paper which were left me by an aunt, for no other reason than that I share her name.

My aunt, Mary Beton, I must tell you, died by a fall from her horse when she was riding out to take the air in Bombay. The news of my legacy reached me one night about the same time that the act was passed that gave votes to women. A solicitor's letter fell into the post-box and when I opened it I found that she had left me five hundred pounds a year for ever. Of the two--the vote and the money--the money, I own, seemed infinitely the more important. Before that I had made my living by cadging odd jobs from newspapers, by reporting a donkey show here or a wedding there; I had earned a few pounds by addressing envelopes, reading to old ladies, making artificial flowers, teaching the alphabet to small children in a kindergarten. Such were the chief occupations that were open to women before 1918. I need not, I am afraid, describe in any detail the hardness of the work, for you know perhaps women who have done it; nor the difficulty of living on the money when it was earned, for you may have tried. But what still remains with me as a worse infliction than either was the poison of fear and bitterness which those days bred in me. To begin with, always to be doing work that one did not wish to do, and to do it like a slave, flattering and fawning, not always necessarily perhaps, but it seemed necessary and the stakes were too great to run risks; and then the thought of that one gift which it was death to hide--a small one but dear to the possessor--perishing and with it my self, my soul,--all this became like a rust eating away the bloom of the spring, destroying the tree at its heart. However, as I say, my aunt died; and whenever I change a ten-shilling note a little of that rust and corrosion is rubbed off, fear and bitterness go. Indeed, I thought, slipping the silver into my purse, it is remarkable, remembering the bitterness of those days, what a change of temper a fixed income will bring about. No force in the world can take from me my five hundred pounds. Food, house and clothing are mine forever. Therefore not merely do effort and labour cease, but also hatred and bitterness. I need not hate any man; he cannot hurt me. I need not flatter any man; he has nothing to give me. So imperceptibly I found myself adopting a new attitude towards the other half of the human race. It was absurd to blame any class or any sex, as a whole. Great bodies of people are never responsible for what they do. They are driven by instincts which are not within their control. They too, the patriarchs, the professors, had endless difficulties, terrible drawbacks to contend with. Their education had been in some ways as faulty as my own. It had bred in them defects as great. True, they had money and power, but only at the cost of harbouring in their breasts an eagle, a vulture, forever tearing the liver out and plucking at the lungs--the instinct for possession, the rage for acquisition which drives them to desire other people's fields and goods perpetually; to make frontiers and flags; battleships and poison gas; to offer up their own lives and their children's lives. Walk through the Admiralty Arch (I had reached that monument), or any other avenue given up to trophies and cannon, and reflect upon the kind of glory celebrated there. Or watch in the spring sunshine the stockbroker and the great barrister going indoors to make money and more money and more money when it is a fact that five hundred pounds a year will keep one alive in the sunshine. These arc unpleasant instincts to harbour, I reflected. They are bred of the conditions of life; of the lack of civilization, I thought, looking at the statue of the Duke of Cambridge, and in particular at the feathers in his cocked hat, with a fixity that they have scarcely ever received before. And, as I realized these drawbacks, by degrees fear and bitterness modified themselves into pity and toleration; and then in a year or two, pity and toleration went, and the greatest release of all came, which is freedom to think of things in themselves. That building, for example, do I like it or not? Is that picture beautiful or not? Is that in my opinion a good book or a bad? Indeed my aunt's legacy unveiled the sky to me, and substituted for the large and imposing figure of a gentleman, which Milton recommended for my perpetual adoration, a view of the open sky.

So thinking, so speculating I found my way back to my house by the river. Lamps were being lit and an indescribable change had come over London since the morning hour. It was as if the great machine after labouring all day had made with our help a few yards of something very exciting and beautiful--a fiery fabric flashing with red eyes, a tawny monster roaring with hot breath. Even the wind seemed flung like a flag as it lashed the houses and rattled the hoardings.

In my little street, however, domesticity prevailed. The house painter was descending his ladder; the nursemaid was wheeling the perambulator carefully in and out back to nursery tea; the coal-heaver was folding his empty sacks on top of each other; the woman who keeps the green grocer's shop was adding up the day's takings with her hands in red mittens. But so engrossed was I with the problem you have laid upon my shoulders that I could not see even these usual sights without referring them to one centre. I thought how much harder it is now than it must have been even a century ago to say which of these employments is the higher, the more necessary. Is it better to be a coal-heaver or a nursemaid; is the charwoman who has brought up eight children of less value to the world than, the barrister who has made a hundred thousand pounds? it is useless to ask such questions; for nobody can answer them. Not only do the comparative values of charwomen and lawyers rise and fall from decade to decade, but we have no rods with which to measure them even as they are at the moment. I had been foolish to ask my professor to furnish me with 'indisputable proofs' of this or that in his argument about women. Even if one could state the value of any one gift at the moment, those values will change; in a century's time very possibly they will have changed completely. Moreover, in a hundred years, I thought, reaching my own doorstep, women will have ceased to be the protected sex. Logically they will take part in all the activities and exertions that were once denied them. The nursemaid will heave coal. The shopwoman will drive an engine. All assumptions founded on the facts observed when women were the protected sex will have disappeared--as, for example (here a squad of soldiers marched down the street), that women and clergymen and gardeners live longer than other people. Remove that protection, expose them to the same exertions and activities, make them soldiers and sailors and engine-drivers and dock labourers, and will not women die off so much younger, so much quicker, than men that one will say, 'I saw a woman today', as one used to say, 'I saw an aeroplane'. Anything may happen when womanhood has ceased to be a protected occupation, I thought, opening the door. But what bearing has all this upon the subject of my paper, Women and Fiction? I asked, going indoors.

THREE

It was disappointing not to have brought back in the evening some important statement, some authentic fact. Women are poorer than men because--this or that. Perhaps now it would be better to give up seeking for the truth, and receiving on one's head an avalanche of opinion hot as lava, discoloured as dish-water. It would be better to draw the curtains; to shut out distractions; to light the lamp; to narrow the enquiry and to ask the historian, who records not opinions but facts, to describe under what conditions women lived, not throughout the ages, but in England, say, in the time of Elizabeth.

For it is a perennial puzzle why no woman wrote a word of that extraordinary literature when every other man, it seemed, was capable of song or sonnet. What were the conditions in which women lived? I asked myself; for fiction, imaginative work that is, is not dropped like a pebble upon the ground, as science may be; fiction is like a spider's web, attached ever so lightly perhaps, but still attached to life at all four corners. Often the attachment is scarcely perceptible; Shakespeare's plays, for instance, seem to hang there complete by themselves. But when the web is pulled askew, hooked up at the edge, torn in the middle, one remembers that these webs are not spun in mid-air by incorporeal creatures, but are the work of suffering human beings, and are attached to grossly material things, like health and money and the houses we live in.

I went, therefore, to the shelf where the histories stand and took down one of the latest, Professor Trevelyan's HISTORY OF ENGLAND. Once more I looked up Women, found 'position of' and turned to the pages indicated. 'Wife-beating', I read, 'was a recognized right of man, and was practised without shame by high as well as low. . . . Similarly,' the historian goes on, 'the daughter who refused to marry the gentleman of her parents' choice was liable to be locked up, beaten and flung about the room, without any shock being inflicted on public opinion. Marriage was not an affair of personal affection, but of family avarice, particularly in the "chivalrous" upper classes. . . . Betrothal often took place while one or both of the parties was in the cradle, and marriage when they were scarcely out of the nurses' charge.' That was about 1470, soon after Chaucer's time. The next reference to the position of women is some two hundred years later, in the time of the Stuarts. 'It was still the exception for women of the upper and middle class to choose their own husbands, and when the husband had been assigned, he was lord and master, so far at least as law and custom could make him. Yet even so,' Professor Trevelyan concludes, 'neither Shakespeare's women nor those of authentic seventeenth-century memoirs, like the Verneys and the Hutchinsons, seem wanting in personality and character.' Certainly, if we consider it, Cleopatra must have had a way with her; Lady Macbeth, one would suppose, had a will of her own; Rosalind, one might conclude, was an attractive girl. Professor Trevelyan is speaking no more than the truth when he remarks that Shakespeare's women do not seem wanting in personality and character. Not being a historian, one might go even further and say that women have burnt like beacons in all the works of all the poets from the beginning of time--Clytemnestra, Antigone, Cleopatra, Lady Macbeth, Phedre, Cressida, Rosalind, Desdemona, the Duchess of Malfi, among the dramatists; then among the prose writers: Millamant, Clarissa, Becky Sharp, Anna Karenina, Emma Bovary, Madame de Guermantes--the names flock to mind, nor do they recall women 'lacking in personality and character.' Indeed, if woman had no existence save in the fiction written by men, one would imagine her a person of the utmost importance; very various; heroic and mean; splendid and sordid; infinitely beautiful and hideous in the extreme; as great as a man, some think even greater[1]. But this is woman in fiction. In fact, as Professor Trevelyan points out, she was locked up, beaten and flung about the room.

A very queer, composite being thus emerges. Imaginatively she is of the highest importance; practically she is completely insignificant. She pervades poetry from cover to cover; she is all but absent from history. She dominates the lives of kings and conquerors in fiction; in fact she was the slave of any boy whose parents forced a ring upon her finger. Some of the most inspired words, some of the most profound thoughts in literature fall from her lips; in real life she could hardly read, could scarcely spell, and was the property of her husband.

It was certainly an odd monster that one made up by reading the historians first and the poets afterwards--a worm winged like an eagle; the spirit of life and beauty in a kitchen chopping up suet. But these monsters, however amusing to the imagination, have no existence in fact. What one must do to bring her to life was

---

[1] 'It remains a strange and almost inexplicable fact that in Athena's city, where women were kept in almost Oriental suppression as odalisques or drudges, the stage should yet have produced figures like Clytemnestra and Cassandra Atossa and Antigone, Phedre and Medea, and all the other heroines who dominate play after play of the "misogynist" Euripides. But the paradox of this world where in real life a respectable woman could hardly show her face alone in the street, and yet on the stage woman equals or surpasses man, has never been satisfactorily explained. In modern tragedy the same predominance exists. At all events, a very cursory survey of Shakespeare's work (similarly with Webster, though not with Marlowe or Jonson) suffices to reveal how this dominance, this initiative of women, persists from Rosalind to Lady Macbeth. So too in Racine; six of his tragedies bear their heroines' names; and what male characters of his shall we set against Hermione and Andromaque, Berenice and Roxane, Phedre and Athalie? So again with Ibsen; what men shall we match with Solveig and Nora, Heda and Hilda Wangel and Rebecca West?'--F. L. LUCAS, TRAGEDY, pp. 114-15.

to think poetically and prosaically at one and the same moment, thus keeping in touch with fact--that she is Mrs Martin, aged thirty-six, dressed in blue, wearing a black hat and brown shoes; but not losing sight of fiction either--that she is a vessel in which all sorts of spirits and forces are coursing and flashing perpetually. The moment, however, that one tries this method with the Elizabethan woman, one branch of illumination fails; one is held up by the scarcity of facts. One knows nothing detailed, nothing perfectly true and substantial about her. History scarcely mentions her. And I turned to Professor Trevelyan again to see what history meant to him. I found by looking at his chapter headings that it meant----

'The Manor Court and the Methods of Open-field Agriculture . . . The Cistercians and Sheep-farming . . . The Crusades . . . The University . . . The House of Commons . . . The Hundred Years' War . . . The Wars of the Roses . . . The Renaissance Scholars . . . The Dissolution of the Monasteries . . . Agrarian and Religious Strife . . . The Origin of English Sea-power. . . The Armada. . .' and so on. Occasionally an individual woman is mentioned, an Elizabeth, or a Mary; a queen or a great lady. But by no possible means could middle-class women with nothing but brains and character at their command have taken part in any one of the great movements which, brought together, constitute the historian's view of the past. Nor shall we find her in collection of anecdotes. Aubrey hardly mentions her. She never writes her own life and scarcely keeps a diary; there are only a handful of her letters in existence. She left no plays or poems by which we can judge her. What one wants, I thought--and why does not some brilliant student at Newnham or Girton supply it?--is a mass of information; at what age did she marry; how many children had she as a rule; what was her house like, had she a room to herself; did she do the cooking; would she be likely to have a servant? All these facts lie somewhere, presumably, in parish registers and account books; the life of the average Elizabethan woman must be scattered about somewhere, could one collect it and make a book of it. It would be ambitious beyond my daring, I thought, looking about the shelves for books that were not there, to suggest to the students of those famous colleges that they should rewrite history, though I own that it often seems a little queer as it is, unreal, lop-sided; but why should they not add a supplement to history, calling it, of course, by some inconspicuous name so that women might figure there without impropriety? For one often catches a glimpse of them in the lives of the great, whisking away into the back ground, concealing, I sometimes think, a wink, a laugh, perhaps a tear. And, after all, we have lives enough of Jane Austen; it scarcely seems necessary to consider again the influence of the tragedies of Joanna Baillie upon the poetry of Edgar Allan Poe; as for myself, I should not mind if the homes and haunts of Mary Russell Mitford were closed to the public for a century at least. But what I find deplorable, I continued, looking about the bookshelves again, is that nothing is known about women before the eighteenth century. I have no model in my mind to turn about this way and that. Here am I asking why women did not write poetry in the Elizabethan age, and I am not sure how they were educated; whether they were taught to write; whether they had sitting-rooms to themselves; how many women had children before they were twenty-one; what, in short, they did from eight in the morning till eight at night. They had no money evidently; according to Professor Trevelyan they were married whether they liked it or not before they were out of the nursery, at fifteen or sixteen very likely. It would have been extremely odd, even upon this showing, had one of them suddenly written the plays of Shakespeare, I concluded, and I thought of that old gentleman, who is dead now, but was a bishop, I think, who declared that it was impossible for any woman, past, present, or to come, to have the genius of Shakespeare. He wrote to the papers about it. He also told a lady who applied to him for information that cats do not as a matter of fact go to heaven, though they have, he added, souls of a sort. How much thinking those old gentlemen used to save one! How the borders of ignorance shrank back at their approach! Cats do not go to heaven. Women cannot write the plays of Shakespeare.

Be that as it may, I could not help thinking, as I looked at the works of Shakespeare on the shelf, that the bishop was right at least in this; it would have been impossible, completely and entirely, for any woman to have written the plays of Shakespeare in the age of Shakespeare. Let me imagine, since facts are so hard to come by, what would have happened had Shakespeare had a wonderfully gifted sister, called Judith, let us say. Shakespeare himself went, very probably,--his mother was an heiress--to the grammar school, where he may have learnt Latin--Ovid, Virgil and Horace--and the elements of grammar and logic. He was, it is well known, a wild boy who poached rabbits, perhaps shot a deer, and had, rather sooner than he should have done, to marry a woman in the neighbourhood, who bore him a child rather quicker than was right. That escapade sent him to seek his fortune in London. He had, it seemed, a taste for the theatre; he began by holding horses at the stage door. Very soon he got work in the theatre, became a successful actor, and lived at the hub of the universe, meeting everybody, knowing everybody, practising his art on the boards, exercising his wits in the streets, and even getting access to the palace of the queen. Meanwhile his extraordinarily gifted sister, let us suppose, remained at home. She was as adventurous, as imaginative, as agog to see the world as he was. But she was not sent to school. She had no chance of learning grammar and logic, let alone of reading Horace and Virgil. She picked up a book now and then, one of her brother's perhaps, and read a few pages. But then her parents came in and told her to mend the stockings or mind the stew and not moon about with books and papers. They would have spoken sharply but kindly, for they were substantial people who knew the conditions of life for a woman and loved their daughter--indeed, more likely than not she was the apple of her father's eye. Perhaps she scribbled some pages up in an apple loft on the sly but was careful to hide them or set fire to them. Soon, however, before she was out of her teens, she was to be betrothed to the son of a neighbouring wool-stapler. She cried out that marriage was hateful to her, and for that she was severely beaten by her father. Then he ceased to scold her. He begged her instead not to hurt him, not to shame him in this matter of her marriage. He would give her a chain of beads or a fine petticoat, he said; and there were tears in his eyes. How could she disobey him? How could she break his heart? The force of her own gift alone drove her to it. She made up a small parcel of her belongings, let herself down by a rope one summer's night and took the road to London. She was not seventeen. The birds that sang in the hedge were not more musical than she was. She had the quickest fancy, a gift like her brother's, for the tune of words. Like him, she had a taste for the theatre. She stood at the stage door; she wanted to act, she said. Men laughed in her face. The manager--a fat, looselipped man--guffawed. He bellowed something about poodles dancing and women acting--no woman, he said, could possibly be an actress. He hinted--you can imagine what. She could get no training in her craft. Could she even seek her dinner in a tavern or roam the streets at midnight? Yet her genius was for fiction and lusted to feed abundantly upon the lives of men and women and the study of their ways. At last--for she was very young, oddly like Shakespeare the poet in her face, with the same grey eyes and rounded brows--at last Nick Greene the actor-manager took pity on her; she found herself with child by that gentleman and so--who shall measure the heat and violence of the poet's heart when caught and tangled in a woman's body?--killed herself one winter's night and lies buried at some cross-roads where the omnibuses now stop outside the Elephant and Castle.

That, more or less, is how the story would run, I think, if a woman in Shakespeare's day had had Shakespeare's genius. But for my part, I agree with the deceased bishop, if such he was--it is unthinkable that any woman in Shakespeare's day should have had Shakespeare's genius. For genius like Shakespeare's is not born among labouring, uneducated, servile people. It was not born in England among the Saxons and the Britons. It is not born to-day among the working classes. How, then, could it have been born among women whose work began, according to Professor Trevelyan, almost before they were out of the nursery, who were forced to it by their parents and held to it by all the power of law and custom? Yet genius of a sort must have existed among women as it must have existed among the working classes. Now and again an Emily Brontë or a Robert Burns blazes out and proves its presence. But certainly it never got itself on to paper. When, however, one reads of a witch being ducked, of a woman possessed by devils, of a wise woman selling herbs, or even of a very remarkable man who had a mother, then I think we are on the track of a lost novelist, a suppressed poet, of some mute and inglorious Jane Austen, some Emily Brontë who dashed her brains out on the moor or mopped and mowed about the highways crazed with the torture that her gift had put her to. Indeed, I would venture to guess that Anon, who wrote so many poems without singing them, was often a woman. It was a woman Edward Fitzgerald, I think, suggested who made the ballads and the folk-songs, crooning them to her children, beguiling her spinning with them, or the length of the winter's night.

This may be true or it may be false--who can say?--but what is true in it, so it seemed to me, reviewing the story of Shakespeare's sister as I had made it, is that any woman born with a great gift in the sixteenth century would certainly have gone crazed, shot herself, or ended her days in some lonely cottage outside the village, half witch, half wizard, feared and mocked at. For it needs little skill in psychology to be sure that a highly gifted girl who had tried to use her gift for poetry would have been so thwarted and hindered by other people, so tortured and pulled asunder by her own contrary instincts, that she must have lost her health and sanity to a certainty. No girl could have walked to London and stood at a stage door and forced her way into the presence of actor-managers without doing herself a violence and suffering an anguish which may have been irrational--for chastity may be a fetish invented by certain societies for unknown reasons--but were none the less inevitable. Chastity had then, it has even now, a religious importance in a woman's life, and has so wrapped itself round with nerves and instincts that to cut it free and bring it to the light of day demands courage of the rarest. To have lived a free life in London in the sixteenth century would have meant for a woman who was poet and playwright a nervous stress and dilemma which might well have killed her. Had she survived, whatever she had written would have been twisted and deformed, issuing from a strained and morbid imagination. And undoubtedly, I thought, looking at the shelf where there are no plays by women, her work would have gone unsigned. That refuge she would have sought certainly. It was the relic of the sense of chastity that dictated anonymity to women even so late as the nineteenth century. Currer Bell, George Eliot, George Sand, all the victims of inner strife as their writings prove, sought ineffectively to veil themselves by using the name of a man. Thus they did homage to the convention, which if not implanted by the other sex was liberally encouraged by them (the chief glory of a woman is not to be talked of, said Pericles, himself a much-talked-of man) that publicity in women is detestable. Anonymity runs in their blood. The desire to be veiled still possesses them. They are not even now as concerned about the health of their fame as men are, and, speaking generally, will pass a tombstone or a signpost without feeling an irresistible desire to cut their names on it, as Alf, Bert or Chas. must do in obedience to their instinct, which murmurs if it sees a fine woman go by, or even a dog, Ce chien est a moi. And, of course, it may not be a dog, I thought, remembering Parliament Square, the Sieges Allee and other avenues; it may be a piece of land or a man with curly black hair. It is one of the great advantages of being a woman that one can pass even a very fine negress without wishing to make an Englishwoman of her.

That woman, then, who was born with a gift of poetry in the sixteenth century, was an unhappy woman, a woman at strife against herself. All the conditions of her life, all her own instincts, were hostile to the state of mind which is needed to set free whatever is in the brain. But what is the state of mind that is most propitious to the act of creation? I asked. Can one come by any notion of the state that furthers and makes possible that strange activity? Here I opened the volume containing the Tragedies of Shakespeare. What was Shakespeare's state of mind, for instance, when he wrote LEAR and ANTONY AND CLEOPATRA? It was certainly the state of mind most favourable to poetry that there has ever existed. But Shakespeare himself said nothing about it. We only know casually and by chance that he 'never blotted a line'. Nothing indeed was ever said by the artist himself about his state of mind until the eighteenth century perhaps. Rousseau perhaps began it. At any rate, by the nineteenth century self-consciousness had developed so far that it was the habit for men of letters to describe their minds in confessions and autobiographies. Their lives also were written, and their letters were printed after their deaths. Thus, though we do not know what Shakespeare went through when he wrote LEAR, we do know what Carlyle went through when he wrote the FRENCH REVOLUTION; what Flaubert went through when he wrote MADAME BOVARY; what Keats was going through when he tried to write poetry against the coming death and the indifference of the world.

And one gathers from this enormous modern literature of confession and self-analysis that to write a work of genius is almost always a feat of prodigious difficulty. Everything is against the likelihood that it will come from the writer's mind whole and entire. Generally material circumstances are against it. Dogs will bark; people will interrupt; money must be made; health will break down. Further, accentuating all these difficulties and making them harder to bear is the world's notorious indifference. It does not ask people to write poems and novels and histories; it does not need them. It does not care whether Flaubert finds the right word or whether Carlyle scrupulously verifies this or that fact. Naturally, it will not pay for what it does not want. And so the writer, Keats, Flaubert, Carlyle, suffers, especially in the creative years of youth, every form of distraction and discouragement. A curse, a cry of agony, rises from those books of analysis and confession. 'Mighty poets in their misery dead'--that is the burden of their song. If anything comes through in spite of all this, it is a miracle, and probably no book is born entire and uncrippled as it was conceived.

But for women, I thought, looking at the empty shelves, these difficulties were infinitely more formidable. In the first place, to have a room of her own, let alone a quiet room or a sound-proof room, was out of the question, unless her parents were exceptionally rich or very noble, even up to the beginning of the nineteenth century. Since her pin money, which depended on the goodwill of her father, was only enough to keep her clothed, she was debarred from such alleviations as came even to Keats or Tennyson or Carlyle, all poor men, from a walking tour, a little journey to France, from the separate lodging which, even if it were miserable enough, sheltered them from the claims and tyrannies of their families. Such material difficulties were formidable; but much worse were the immaterial. The indifference of the world which Keats and Flaubert and other men of genius have found so hard to bear was in her case not indifference but hostility. The world did not say to her as it said to them, Write if you choose; it makes no difference to me. The world said with a guffaw, Write? What's the good of your writing? Here the psychologists of Newnham and Girton might come to our help, I thought, looking again at the blank spaces on the shelves. For surely it is time that the effect of discouragement upon the mind of the artist should be measured, as I have seen a dairy company measure the effect of ordinary milk and Grade A milk upon the body of the rat. They set two rats in cages side by side, and of the two one was furtive, timid and small, and the other was glossy, bold and big. Now what food do we feed women as artists upon? I asked, remembering, I suppose, that dinner of prunes and custard. To answer that question I had only to open the evening paper and to read that Lord Birkenhead is of opinion--but really I am not going to trouble to copy out Lord Birkenhead's opinion upon the writing of women. What Dean Inge says I will leave in peace. The Harley Street specialist may be allowed to rouse the echoes of Harley Street with his vociferations without raising a hair on my head. I will quote, however, Mr Oscar Browning, because Mr Oscar Browning was a great figure in Cambridge at one time, and used to examine the students at Girton and Newnham. Mr Oscar Browning was wont to declare 'that the impression left on his mind, after looking over any set of examination papers, was that, irrespective of the marks he might give, the best woman was intellectually the inferior of the worst man'. After saying that Mr Browning went back to his rooms--and it is this sequel that endears him and makes him a human figure of some bulk and majesty--he went back to his rooms and found a stable-boy lying on the sofa--'a mere skeleton, his cheeks were cavernous and sallow, his teeth were black, and he did not appear to have the full use of his limbs. . . . "That's Arthur" [said Mr Browning]. "He's a dear boy really and most high-minded."' The two pictures always seem to me to complete each other. And happily in this age of biography the two pictures often do complete each other, so that we are able to interpret the opinions of great men not only by what they say, but by what they do.

But though this is possible now, such opinions coming from the lips of important people must have been formidable enough even fifty years ago. Let us suppose that a father from the highest motives did not wish his daughter to leave home and become writer, painter or scholar. 'See what Mr Oscar Browning says,' he would say; and there so was not only Mr Oscar Browning; there was the SATURDAY REVIEW; there was Mr Greg--the 'essentials of a woman's being', said Mr Greg emphatically, 'are that THEY ARE SUPPORTED BY, AND THEY MINISTER TO, MEN'--there was an enormous body of masculine opinion to the effect that nothing could be expected of women intellectually. Even if her father did not read out loud these opinions, any girl could read them for herself; and the reading, even in the nineteenth century, must have lowered her vitality, and told profoundly upon her work. There would always have been that assertion--you cannot do this, you are incapable of doing that--to protest against, to overcome. Probably for a novelist this germ is no longer of much effect; for there have been women novelists of merit. But for painters it must still have some sting in it; and for musicians, I imagine, is even now active and poisonous in the extreme. The woman composer stands where the actress stood in the time of Shakespeare. Nick Greene, I thought, remembering the story I had made about Shakespeare's sister, said that a woman acting put him in mind of a dog dancing. Johnson repeated the phrase two hundred years later of women preaching. And here, I said, opening a book about music, we have the very words used again in this year of grace, 1928, of women who try to write music. 'Of Mlle. Germaine Tailleferre one can only repeat Dr Johnson's dictum concerning, a woman preacher, transposed into terms of music. "Sir, a woman's composing is like a dog's walking on his hind legs. It is not done well, but you are surprised to find it done at all."'[1] So accurately does history repeat itself.

Thus, I concluded, shutting Mr Oscar Browning's life and pushing away the rest, it is fairly evident that even in the nineteenth century a woman was not encouraged to be an artist. On the contrary, she was snubbed, slapped, lectured and exhorted. Her mind must have been strained and her vitality lowered by the need of opposing this, of disproving that. For here again we come within range of that very interesting and obscure masculine complex which has had so much influence upon the woman's movement; that deep-seated desire, not so much that SHE shall be inferior as that HE shall be superior, which plants him wherever one looks, not only in front of the arts, but barring the way to politics too, even when the risk to himself seems infinitesimal and the suppliant humble and devoted. Even Lady Bessborough, I remembered, with all her passion for politics, must humbly bow herself and write to Lord Granville Leveson-Gower: '. . . notwithstanding all my violence in politicks and talking so much on that subject, I perfectly agree with you that no woman has any business to meddle with that or any other serious business, farther than giving her opinion (if she is ask'd).' And so she goes on to spend her enthusiasm where it meets with no obstacle whatsoever, upon that immensely important subject, Lord Granville's maiden speech in the House of Commons. The spectacle is certainly a strange one, I thought. The history of men's opposition to women's emancipation is more interesting perhaps than the story of that emancipation itself. An amusing book might be made of it if some young student at Girton or Newnham would collect examples and deduce a theory,--but she would need thick gloves on her hands, and bars to protect her of solid gold.

But what is amusing now, I recollected, shutting Lady Bessborough, had to be taken in desperate earnest once. Opinions that one now pastes in a book labelled cock-a-doodledum and keeps for reading to select audiences on summer nights once drew tears, I can assure you. Among your grandmothers and great-grandmothers there were many that wept their eyes out. Florence Nightingale shrieked aloud in her agony[2]. Moreover, it is all very well for you, who have got yourselves to college and enjoy sitting-rooms--or is it only bed-sitting-rooms?--of your own to say that genius should disregard such opinions; that genius should be above caring what is said of it. Unfortunately, it is precisely the men or women of genius who mind most what is said of them. Remember Keats. Remember the words he had cut on his tombstone. Think of Tennyson; think but I need hardly multiply instances of the undeniable, if very fortunate, fact that it is the nature of the artist to mind excessively what is said about him. Literature is strewn with the wreckage of men who have minded beyond reason the opinions of others.

---

[1] A SURVEY OF CONTEMPORARY MUSIC, Cecil Gray, P. 246.

[2] See CASSANDRA, by Florence Nightingale, printed in THE CAUSE, by R. Strachey.

And this susceptibility of theirs is doubly unfortunate, I thought, returning again to my original enquiry into what state of mind is most propitious for creative work, because the mind of an artist, in order to achieve the prodigious effort of freeing whole and entire the work that is in him, must be incandescent, like Shakespeare's mind, I conjectured, looking at the book which lay open at ANTONY AND CLEOPATRA. There must be no obstacle in it, no foreign matter unconsumed.

For though we say that we know nothing about Shakespeare's state of mind, even as we say that, we are saying something about Shakespeare's state of mind. The reason perhaps why we know so little of Shakespeare--compared with Donne or Ben Jonson or Milton--is that his grudges and spites and antipathies are hidden from us. We are not held up by some 'revelation' which reminds us of the writer. All desire to protest, to preach, to proclaim an injury, to pay off a score, to make the world the witness of some hardship or grievance was fired out of him and consumed. Therefore his poetry flows from him free and unimpeded. If ever a human being got his work expressed completely, it was Shakespeare. If ever a mind was incandescent, unimpeded, I thought, turning again to the bookcase, it was Shakespeare's mind.

FOUR

That one would find any woman in that state of mind in the sixteenth century was obviously impossible. One has only to think of the Elizabethan tombstones with all those children kneeling with clasped hands; and their early deaths; and to see their houses with their dark, cramped rooms, to realize that no woman could have written poetry then. What one would expect to find would be that rather later perhaps some great lady would take advantage of her comparative freedom and comfort to publish something with her name to it and risk being thought a monster. Men, of course, are not snobs, I continued, carefully eschewing 'the arrant feminism' of Miss Rebecca West; but they appreciate with sympathy for the most part the efforts of a countess to write verse. One would expect to find a lady of title meeting with far greater encouragement than an unknown Miss Austen or a Miss Brontë at that time would have met with. But one would also expect to find that her mind was disturbed by alien emotions like fear and hatred and that her poems showed traces of that disturbance. Here is Lady Winchilsea, for example, I thought, taking down her poems. She was born in the year 1661; she was noble both by birth and by marriage; she was childless; she wrote poetry, and one has only to open her poetry to find her bursting out in indignation against the position of women:

How we are fallen! fallen by mistaken rules, And Education's more than Nature's fools; Debarred from all improvements of the mind, And to be dull, expected and designed;

And if someone would soar above the rest, With warmer fancy, and ambition pressed, So strong the opposing faction still appears, The hopes to thrive can ne'er outweigh the fears.

Clearly her mind has by no means 'consumed all impediments and become incandescent'. On the contrary, it is harassed and distracted with hates and grievances. The human race is split up for her into two parties. Men are the 'opposing faction'; men are hated and feared, because they have the power to bar her way to what she wants to do--which is to write.

Alas! a woman that attempts the pen, Such a presumptuous creature is esteemed, The fault can by no virtue be redeemed. They tell us we mistake our sex and way; Good breeding, fashion, dancing, dressing, play, Are the accomplishments we should desire; To write, or read, or think, or to enquire, Would cloud our beauty, and exhaust our time, And interrupt the conquests of our prime. Whilst the dull manage of a servile house Is held by some our utmost art and use.

Indeed she has to encourage herself to write by supposing that what she writes will never be published; to soothe herself with the sad chant:

To some few friends, and to thy sorrows sing, For groves of laurel thou wert never meant; Be dark enough thy shades, and be thou there content.

Yet it is clear that could she have freed her mind from hate and fear and not heaped it with bitterness and resentment, the fire was hot within her. Now and again words issue of pure poetry:

Nor will in fading silks compose, Faintly the inimitable rose.

--they are rightly praised by Mr Murry, and Pope, it is thought, remembered and appropriated those others:

Now the jonquille o'ercomes the feeble brain; We faint beneath the aromatic pain.

It was a thousand pities that the woman who could write like that, whose mind was tuned to nature and reflection, should have been forced to anger and bitterness. But how could she have helped herself? I asked, imagining the sneers and the laughter, the adulation of the toadies, the scepticism of the professional poet. She must have shut herself up in a room in the country to write, and been torn asunder by bitterness and scruples perhaps, though her husband was of the kindest, and their married life perfection. She 'must have', I say, because when one comes to seek out the facts about Lady Winchilsea, one finds, as usual, that almost nothing is known about her. She suffered terribly from melancholy, which we can explain at least to some extent when we find her telling us how in the grip of it she would imagine:

My lines decried, and my employment thought An useless folly or presumptuous fault:

The employment, which was thus censured, was, as far as one can see, the harmless one of rambling about the fields and dreaming:

My hand delights to trace unusual things, And deviates from the known and common way, Nor will in fading silks compose, Faintly the inimitable rose.

Naturally, if that was her habit and that was her delight, she could only expect to be laughed at; and, accordingly, Pope or Gay is said to have satirized her 'as a blue-stocking with an itch for scribbling'. Also it is thought that she offended Gay by laughing at him. She said that his TRIVIA showed that 'he was more proper to walk before a chair than to ride in one'. But this is all 'dubious gossip' and, says Mr Murry, 'uninteresting'. But there I do not agree with him, for I should have liked to have had more even of dubious gossip so that I might have found out or made up some image of this melancholy lady, who loved wandering in the fields and thinking about unusual things and scorned, so rashly, so unwisely, 'the dull manage of a servile house'. But she became diffuse, Mr Murry says. Her gift is all grown about with weeds and bound with briars. It had no chance of showing itself for the fine distinguished gift it was. And so, putting, her back on the shelf, I turned to the other great lady, the Duchess whom Lamb loved, hare-brained, fantastical Margaret of Newcastle, her elder, but her contemporary. They were very different, but alike in this that both were noble and both childless, and both were married to the best of husbands. In both burnt the same passion for poetry and both are disfigured and deformed by the same causes. Open the Duchess and one finds the same outburst of rage. 'Women live like Bats or Owls, labour like Beasts, and die like Worms. . . .' Margaret too might have been a poet; in our day all that activity would have turned a wheel of some sort. As it was, what could bind, tame or civilize for human use that wild, generous, untutored intelligence? It poured itself out, higgledy-piggledy, in torrents of rhyme and prose, poetry and philosophy which stand congealed in quartos and folios that nobody ever reads. She should have had a microscope put in her hand. She should have been taught to look at the stars and reason scientifically. Her wits were turned with solitude and freedom. No one checked her. No one taught her. The professors fawned on her. At Court they jeered at her. Sir Egerton Brydges complained of her coarseness--'as flowing from a female of high rank brought up in the Courts'. She shut herself up at Welbeck alone.

What a vision of loneliness and riot the thought of Margaret Cavendish brings to mind! as if some giant cucumber had spread itself over all the roses and carnations in the garden and choked them to death. What a waste that the woman who wrote 'the best bred women are those whose minds are civilest' should have frittered her time away scribbling nonsense and plunging ever deeper into obscurity and folly till the people crowded round her coach when she issued out. Evidently the crazy Duchess became a bogey to frighten clever girls with. Here, I remembered, putting away the Duchess and opening Dorothy Osborne's letters, is Dorothy writing to Temple about the Duchess's new book. 'Sure the poore woman is a little distracted, shee could never bee soe rediculous else as to venture at writeing book's and in verse too, if I should not sleep this fortnight I should not come to that.'

And so, since no woman of sense and modesty could write books, Dorothy, who was sensitive and melancholy, the very opposite of the Duchess in temper, wrote nothing. Letters did not count. A woman might write letters while she was sitting by her father's sick-bed. She could write them by the fire whilst the men talked without disturbing them. The strange thing is, I thought, turning over the pages of Dorothy's letters, what a gift that untaught and solitary girl had for the framing of a sentence, for the fashioning of a scene. Listen to her running on:

'After dinner wee sitt and talk till Mr B. com's in question and then I am gon. the heat of the day is spent in reading or working and about sixe or seven a Clock, I walke out into a Common that lyes hard by the house where a great many young wenches keep Sheep and Cow's and sitt in the shades singing of Ballads; I goe to them and compare their voyces and Beauty's to some Ancient Shepherdesses that I have read of and finde a vaste difference there, but trust mee I think these are as innocent as those could bee. I talke to them, and finde they want nothing to make them the happiest People in the world, but the knoledge that they are soe. most commonly when we are in the middest of our discourse one looks aboute her and spyes her Cow's goeing into the Corne and then away they all run, as if they had wing's at theire heels. I that am not soe nimble stay behinde, and when I see them driveing home theire Cattle I think tis time for mee to retyre too. when I have supped I goe into the Garden and soe to the syde of a small River that runs by it where I sitt downe and wish you with mee. . . .'

One could have sworn that she had the makings of a writer in her. But 'if I should not sleep this fortnight I should not come to that'--one can measure the opposition that was in the air to a woman writing when one finds that even a woman with a great turn for writing has brought herself to believe that to write a book was to be ridiculous, even to show oneself distracted. And so we come, I continued, replacing the single short volume of Dorothy Osborne's letters upon the shelf, to Mrs Behn.

And with Mrs Behn we turn a very important corner on the road. We leave behind, shut up in their parks among their folios, those solitary great ladies who wrote without audience or criticism, for their own delight alone. We come to town and rub shoulders with ordinary people in the streets. Mrs Behn was a middle-class woman with all the plebeian virtues of humour, vitality and courage; a woman forced by the death of her husband and some unfortunate adventures of her own to make her living by her wits. She had to work on equal terms with men. She made, by working very hard, enough to live on. The importance of that fact outweighs anything that she actually wrote, even the splendid 'A Thousand Martyrs I have made', or 'Love in Fantastic Triumph sat', for here begins the freedom of the mind, or rather the possibility that in the course of time the mind will be free to write what it likes. For now that Aphra Behn had done it, girls could go to their parents and say, You need not give me an allowance; I can make money by my pen. Of course the answer for many years to come was, Yes, by living the life of Aphra Behn! Death would be better! and the door was slammed faster than ever. That profoundly interesting subject, the value that men set upon women's chastity and its effect upon their education, here suggests itself for discussion, and might provide an interesting book if any student at Girton or Newnham cared to go into the matter. Lady Dudley, sitting in diamonds among the midges of a Scottish moor, might serve for frontispiece. Lord Dudley, THE TIMES said when Lady Dudley died the other day, 'a man of cultivated taste and many accomplishments, was benevolent and bountiful, but whimsically despotic. He insisted upon his wife's wearing full dress, even at the remotest shooting-lodge in the Highlands; he loaded her with gorgeous jewels', and so on, 'he gave her everything--always excepting any measure of responsibility'. Then Lord Dudley had a stroke and she nursed him and ruled his estates with supreme competence for ever after. That whimsical despotism was in the nineteenth century too.

But to return. Aphra Behn proved that money could be made by writing at the sacrifice, perhaps, of certain agreeable qualities; and so by degrees writing became not merely a sign of folly and a distracted mind, but was of practical importance. A husband might die, or some disaster overtake the family. Hundreds of women began as the eighteenth century drew on to add to their pin money, or to come to the rescue of their families by making translations or writing the innumerable bad novels which have ceased to be recorded even in text-books, but are to be picked up in the fourpenny boxes in the Charing Cross Road. The extreme activity of mind which showed itself in the later eighteenth century among women--the talking, and the meeting, the writing of essays on Shakespeare, the translating of the classics--was founded on the solid fact that women could make money by writing. Money dignifies what is frivolous if unpaid for. It might still be well to sneer at 'blue stockings with an itch for scribbling', but it could not be denied that they could put money in their purses. Thus, towards the end of the eighteenth century a change came about which, if I were rewriting history, I should describe more fully and think of greater importance than the Crusades or the Wars of the Roses.

The middle-class woman began to write. For if PRIDE AND PREJUDICE matters, and MIDDLEMARCH and VILLETTE and WUTHERING HEIGHTS matter, then it matters far more than I can prove in an hour's discourse that women generally, and not merely the lonely aristocrat shut up in her country house among her folios and her flatterers, took to writing. Without those forerunners, Jane Austen and the Brontës and George Eliot could no more have written than Shakespeare could have written without Marlowe, or Marlowe without Chaucer, or Chaucer without those forgotten poets who paved the ways and tamed the natural savagery of the tongue. For masterpieces are not single and solitary births; they are the outcome of many years of thinking in common, of thinking by the body of the people, so that the experience of the mass is behind the single voice. Jane Austen should have laid a wreath upon the grave of Fanny Burney, and George Eliot done homage to the robust shade of Eliza Carter--the valiant old woman who tied a bell to her bedstead in order that she might wake early and learn Greek. All women together ought to let flowers fall upon the tomb of Aphra Behn, which is, most scandalously but rather appropriately, in Westminster Abbey, for it was she who earned them the right to speak their minds. It is she--shady and amorous as she was--who makes it not quite fantastic for me to say to you to-night: Earn five hundred a year by your wits.

Here, then, one had reached the early nineteenth century. And here, for the first time, I found several shelves given up entirely to the works of women. But why, I could not help asking, as I ran my eyes over them, were they, with very few exceptions, all novels? The original impulse was to poetry. The 'supreme head of song' was a poetess. Both in France and in England the women poets precede the women novelists. Moreover, I thought, looking at the four famous names, what had George Eliot in common with Emily Brontë? Did not Charlotte Brontë fail entirely to understand Jane Austen? Save for the possibly relevant fact that not one of them had a child, four more incongruous characters could not have met together in a room--so much so that it is tempting to invent a meeting and a dialogue between them. Yet by some strange force they were all compelled when they wrote, to write novels. Had it something to do with being born of the middle class, I asked; and with the fact, which Miss Emily Davies a little later was so strikingly to demonstrate, that the middle-class family in the early nineteenth century was possessed only of a single sitting-room between them? If a woman wrote, she would have to write in the common sitting-room. And, as Miss Nightingale was so vehemently to complain,--"women never have an half hour . . . that they can call their own"--she was always interrupted. Still it would be easier to write prose and fiction there than to write poetry or a play. Less concentration is required. Jane Austen wrote like that to the end of her days. 'How she was able to effect all this', her nephew writes in his Memoir, 'is surprising, for she had no separate study to repair to, and most of the work must have been done in the general sitting-room, subject to all kinds of casual interruptions. She was careful that her occupation should not be suspected by servants or visitors or any persons beyond her own family party[1]. Jane Austen hid her manuscripts or covered them with a piece of blotting-paper. Then, again, all the literary training that a woman had in the early nineteenth century was training in the observation of character, in the analysis of emotion. Her sensibility had been educated for centuries by the influences of the common sitting-room. People's feelings were impressed on her; personal relations were always before her eyes. Therefore, when the middle-class woman took to writing, she naturally wrote novels, even though, as seems evident enough, two of the four famous women here named were not by nature novelists. Emily Brontë should have written poetic plays; the overflow of George Eliot's capacious mind should have spread itself when the creative impulse was spent upon history or biography. They wrote novels, however; one may even go further, I said, taking PRIDE AND PREJUDICE from the shelf, and say that they wrote good novels. Without boasting or giving pain to the opposite sex, one may say that PRIDE AND PREJUDICE is a good book. At any rate, one would not have been ashamed to have been caught in the act of writing PRIDE AND PREJUDICE. Yet Jane Austen was glad that a hinge creaked, so that she might hide her manuscript before anyone came in. To Jane Austen there was something discreditable in writing PRIDE AND PREJUDICE. And, I wondered, would PRIDE AND PREJUDICE have been a better novel if Jane Austen had not thought it necessary to hide her manuscript from visitors? I read a page or two to see; but I could not find any signs that her circumstances had harmed her work in the slightest. That, perhaps, was the chief miracle about it. Here was a woman about the year 1800 writing without hate, without bitterness, without fear, without protest, without preaching. That was how Shakespeare wrote, I thought, looking at ANTONY AND CLEOPATRA; and when people compare Shakespeare and Jane Austen, they may mean that the minds of both had consumed all impediments; and for that reason we do not know Jane Austen and we do not know Shakespeare, and for that reason Jane Austen pervades every word that she wrote, and so does Shakespeare. If Jane Austen suffered in any way from her circumstances it was in the narrowness of life that was imposed upon her. It was impossible for a woman to go about alone. She never travelled; she never drove

---

[1] MEMOIR OF JANE AUSTEN, by her nephew, James Edward Austen-Leigh.

through London in an omnibus or had luncheon in a shop by herself. But perhaps it was the nature of Jane Austen not to want what she had not. Her gift and her circumstances matched each other completely. But I doubt whether that was true of Charlotte Brontë, I said, opening JANE EYRE and laying it beside PRIDE AND PREJUDICE.

I opened it at chapter twelve and my eye was caught by the phrase 'Anybody may blame me who likes'. What were they blaming Charlotte Brontë for? I wondered. And I read how Jane Eyre used to go up on to the roof when Mrs Fairfax was making jellies and looked over the fields at the distant view. And then she longed--and it was for this that they blamed her--that 'then I longed for a power of vision which might overpass that limit; which might reach the busy world, towns, regions full of life I had heard of but never seen: that then I desired more of practical experience than I possessed; more of intercourse with my kind, of acquaintance with variety of character than was here within my reach. I valued what was good in Mrs Fairfax, and what was good in Adele; but I believed in the existence of other and more vivid kinds of goodness, and what I believed in I wished to behold.

'Who blames me? Many, no doubt, and I shall he called discontented. I could not help it: the restlessness was in my nature; it agitated me to pain sometimes. . . .

'It is vain to say human beings ought to be satisfied with tranquillity: they must have action; and they will make it if they cannot find it. Millions are condemned to a stiller doom than mine, and millions are in silent revolt against their lot. Nobody knows how many rebellions ferment in the masses of life which people earth. Women are supposed to be very calm generally: but women feel just as men feel; they need exercise for their faculties and a field for their efforts as much as their brothers do; they suffer from too rigid a restraint, too absolute a stagnation, precisely as men would suffer; and it is narrow-minded in their more privileged fellow-creatures to say that they ought to confine themselves to making puddings and knitting stockings, to playing on the piano and embroidering bags. It is thoughtless to condemn them, or laugh at them, if they seek to do more or learn more than custom has pronounced necessary for their sex.

'When thus alone I not unfrequently heard Grace Poole's laugh. . . .'

That is an awkward break, I thought. It is upsetting to come upon Grace Poole all of a sudden. The continuity is disturbed. One might say, I continued, laying the book down beside PRIDE AND PREJUDICE, that the woman who wrote those pages had more genius in her than Jane Austen; but if one reads them over and marks that jerk in them, that indignation, one sees that she will never get her genius expressed whole and entire. Her books will be deformed and twisted. She will write in a rage where she should write calmly. She will write foolishly where she should write wisely. She will write of herself where she should write of her characters. She is at war with her lot. How could she help but die young, cramped and thwarted?

One could not but play for a moment with the thought of what might have happened if Charlotte Brontë had possessed say three hundred a year--but the foolish woman sold the copyright of her novels outright for fifteen hundred pounds; had somehow possessed more knowledge of the busy world, and towns and regions full of life; more practical experience, and intercourse with her kind and acquaintance with a variety of character. In those words she puts her finger exactly not only upon her own defects as a novelist but upon those of her sex at that time. She knew, no one better, how enormously her genius would have profited if it had not spent itself in solitary visions over distant fields; if experience and intercourse and travel had been granted her. But they were not granted; they were withheld; and we must accept the fact that all those good novels, VILLETTE, EMMA, WUTHERING HEIGHTS, MIDDLEMARCH, were written by women without more experience of life than could enter the house of a respectable clergyman; written too in the common sitting-room of that respectable house and by women so poor that they could not afford to buy more than a few quires of paper at a time upon which to write WUTHERING HEIGHTS or JANE EYRE. One of them, it is true, George Eliot, escaped after much tribulation, but only to a secluded villa in St John's Wood. And there she settled down in the shadow of the world's disapproval. 'I wish it to be understood', she wrote, 'that I should never invite anyone to come and see me who did not ask for the invitation'; for was she not living in sin with a married man and might not the sight of her damage the chastity of Mrs Smith or whoever it might be that chanced to call? One must submit to the social convention, and be 'cut off from what is called the world'. At the same time, on the other side of Europe, there was a young man living freely with this gypsy or with that great lady; going to the wars; picking up unhindered and uncensored all that varied experience of human life which served him so splendidly later when he came to write his books. Had Tolstoi lived at the Priory in seclusion with a married lady 'cut off from what is called the world', however edifying the moral lesson, he could scarcely, I thought, have written WAR AND PEACE.

But one could perhaps go a little deeper into the question of novel-writing and the effect of sex upon the novelist. If one shuts one's eyes and thinks of the novel as a whole, it would seem to be a creation owning a certain looking-glass likeness to life, though of course with simplifications and distortions innumerable. At any rate, it is a structure leaving a shape on the mind's eye, built now in squares, now pagoda shaped, now throwing out wings and arcades, now solidly compact and domed like the Cathedral of Saint Sofia at Constantinople. This shape, I thought, thinking back over certain famous novels, starts in one the kind of emotion that is appropriate to it. But that emotion at once blends itself with others, for the 'shape' is not made by the relation of stone to stone, but by the relation of human being to human being. Thus a novel starts in us all sorts of antagonistic and opposed emotions. Life conflicts with something that is not life. Hence the difficulty of coming to any agreement about novels, and the immense sway that our private prejudices have upon us. On the one hand we feel You--John the hero--must live, or I shall be in the depths of despair. On the other, we feel, Alas, John, you must die, because the shape of the book requires it. Life conflicts with something that is not life. Then since life it is in part, we judge it as life. James is the sort of man I most detest, one says. Or, This is a farrago of absurdity. I could never feel anything of the sort myself. The whole structure, it is obvious, thinking back on any famous novel, is one of infinite complexity, because it is thus made up of so many different judgements, of so many different kinds of emotion. The wonder is that any book so composed holds together for more than a year or two, or can possibly mean to the English reader what it means for the Russian or the Chinese. But they do hold together occasionally very remarkably. And what holds them together in these rare instances of survival (I was thinking of WAR AND PEACE) is something that one calls integrity, though it has nothing to do with paying one's bills or behaving honourably in an emergency. What one means by integrity, in the case of the novelist, is the conviction that he gives one that this is the truth. Yes, one feels, I should never have thought that this could be so; I have never known people behaving like that. But you have convinced me that so it is, so it happens. One holds every phrase, every scene to the light as one reads--for Nature seems, very oddly, to have provided us with an inner light by which to judge of the novelist's integrity or disintegrity. Or perhaps it is rather that Nature, in her most irrational mood, has traced in invisible ink on the walls of the mind a premonition which these great artists confirm; a sketch which only needs to be held to the fire of genius to become visible. When one so exposes it and sees it come to life one exclaims in rapture, But this is what I have always felt and known and desired! And one boils over with excitement, and, shutting the book even with a kind of reverence as if it were something very precious, a stand-by to return to as long as one lives, one puts it back on the shelf, I said, taking WAR AND PEACE and putting it back in its place. If, on the other hand, these poor sentences that one takes and tests rouse first a quick and eager response with their bright colouring and their dashing gestures but there they stop: something seems to check them in their development: or if they bring to light only a faint scribble in that corner and a blot over there, and nothing appears whole and entire, then one heaves a sigh of disappointment and says. Another failure. This novel has come to grief somewhere.

And for the most part, of course, novels do come to grief somewhere. The imagination falters under the enormous strain. The insight is confused; it can no longer distinguish between the true and the false, it has no longer the strength to go on with the vast labour that calls at every moment for the use of so many different faculties. But how would all this be affected by the sex of the novelist, I wondered, looking at JANE EYRE and the others. Would the fact of her sex in any way interfere with the integrity of a woman novelist--that integrity which I take to be the backbone of the writer? Now, in the passages I have quoted from JANE EYRE, it is clear that anger was tampering with the integrity of Charlotte Brontë the novelist. She left her story, to which her entire devotion was due, to attend to some personal grievance. She remembered that she had been starved of her proper due of experience--she had been made to stagnate in a parsonage mending stockings when she wanted to wander free over the world. Her imagination swerved from indignation and we feel it swerve. But there were many more influences than anger tugging at her imagination and deflecting it from its path. Ignorance, for instance. The portrait of Rochester is drawn in the dark. We feel the influence of fear in it; just as we constantly feel an acidity which is the result of oppression, a buried suffering smouldering beneath her passion, a rancour which contracts those books, splendid as they are, with a spasm of pain.

And since a novel has this correspondence to real life, its values are to some extent those of real life. But it is obvious that the values of women differ very often from the values which have been made by the other sex; naturally, this is so. Yet it is the masculine values that prevail. Speaking crudely, football and sport are 'important'; the worship of fashion, the buying of clothes 'trivial'. And these values are inevitably transferred from life to fiction. This is an important book, the critic assumes, because it deals with war. This is an insignificant book because it deals with the feelings of women in a drawing-room. A scene in a battle-field is more important than a scene in a shop--everywhere and much more subtly the difference of value persists. The whole structure, therefore, of the early nineteenth-century novel was raised, if one was a woman, by a mind which was slightly pulled from the straight, and made to alter its clear vision in deference to external authority. One has only to skim those old forgotten novels and listen to the tone of voice in which they are written to divine that the writer was meeting criticism; she was saying this by way of aggression, or that by way of conciliation. She was admitting that she was 'only a woman', or protesting that she was 'as good as a man'. She met that criticism as her temperament dictated, with docility and diffidence, or with anger and emphasis. It does not matter which it was; she was thinking of something other than the thing itself. Down comes her book upon our heads. There was a flaw in the centre of it. And I thought of all the women's novels that lie scattered, like small pock-marked apples in an orchard, about the second-hand book shops of London. It was the flaw in the centre that had rotted them. She had altered her values in deference to the opinion of others.

But how impossible it must have been for them not to budge either to the right or to the left. What genius, what integrity it must have required in face of all that criticism, in the midst of that purely patriarchal society, to hold fast to the thing as they saw it without shrinking. Only Jane Austen did it and Emily Brontë. It is another feather, perhaps the finest, in their caps. They wrote as women write, not as men write. Of all the thousand women who wrote novels then, they alone entirely ignored the perpetual admonitions of the eternal pedagogue--write this, think that. They alone were deaf to that persistent voice, now grumbling, now patronizing, now domineering, now grieved, now shocked, now angry, now avuncular, that voice which cannot let women alone, but must be at them, like some too-conscientious governess, adjuring them, like Sir Egerton Brydges, to be refined;

dragging even into the criticism of poetry criticism of sex;[1] admonishing them, if they would be good and win, as I suppose, some shiny prize, to keep within certain limits which the gentleman in question thinks suitable--'. . . female novelists should only aspire to excellence by courageously acknowledging the limitations of their sex'.[2] That puts the matter in a nutshell, and when I tell you, rather to your surprise, that this sentence was written not in August 1828 but in August 1928, you will agree, I think, that however delightful it is to us now, it represents a vast body of opinion--I am not going to stir those old pools; I take only what chance has floated to my feet--that was far more vigorous and far more vocal a century ago. It would have needed a very stalwart young woman in 1828 to disregard all those snubs and chidings and promises of prizes. One must have been something of a firebrand to say to oneself, Oh, but they can't buy literature too. Literature is open to everybody. I refuse to allow you, Beadle though you are, to turn me off the grass. Lock up your libraries if you like; but there is no gate, no lock, no bolt, that you can set upon the freedom of my mind.

But whatever effect discouragement and criticism had upon their writing--and I believe that they had a very great effect--that was unimportant compared with the other difficulty which faced them (I was still considering those early nineteenth-century novelists) when they came to set their thoughts on paper--that is that they had no tradition behind them, or one so short and partial that it was of little help. For we think back through our mothers if we are women. It is useless to go to the great men writers for help, however much one may go to them for pleasure. Lamb, Browne, Thackeray, Newman, Sterne, Dickens, De Quincey--whoever it may be--never helped a woman yet, though she may have learnt a few tricks of them and adapted them to her use. The weight, the pace, the stride of a man's mind are too unlike her own for her to lift anything substantial from him successfully. The ape is too distant to be sedulous. Perhaps the first thing she would find, setting pen to paper, was that there was no common sentence ready for her use. All the great novelists like Thackeray and Dickens and Balzac have written a natural prose, swift but not slovenly, expressive but not precious, taking their own tint without ceasing to be common property. They have based it on the sentence that was current at the time. The sentence that was current at the beginning of the nineteenth century ran something like this perhaps: 'The grandeur of their works was an argument with them, not to stop short, but to proceed. They could have no higher excitement or satisfaction than in the exercise of their art

---

[1] [She] has a metaphysical purpose, and that is a dangerous obsession, especially with a woman, for women rarely possess men's healthy love of rhetoric. It is a strange lack in the sex which is in other things more primitive and more materialistic.'--NEW CRITERION, June 1928.

[2] 'If, like the reporter, you believe that female novelists should only aspire to excellence by courageously acknowledging the limitations of their sex (Jane Austen [has] demonstrated how gracefully this gesture can be accomplished . . .).'--LIFE AND LETTERS, August 1928.

and endless generations of truth and beauty. Success prompts to exertion; and habit facilitates success.' That is a man's sentence; behind it one can see Johnson, Gibbon and the rest. It was a sentence that was unsuited for a woman's use. Charlotte Brontë, with all her splendid gift for prose, stumbled and fell with that clumsy weapon in her hands. George Eliot committed atrocities with it that beggar description. Jane Austen looked at it and laughed at it and devised a perfectly natural, shapely sentence proper for her own use and never departed from it. Thus, with less genius for writing than Charlotte Brontë, she got infinitely more said. Indeed, since freedom and fullness of expression are of the essence of the art, such a lack of tradition, such a scarcity and inadequacy of tools, must have told enormously upon the writing of women. Moreover, a book is not made of sentences laid end to end, but of sentences built, if an image helps, into arcades or domes. And this shape too has been made by men out of their own needs for their own uses. There is no reason to think that the form of the epic or of the poetic play suit a woman any more than the sentence suits her. But all the older forms of literature were hardened and set by the time she became a writer. The novel alone was young enough to be soft in her hands another reason, perhaps, why she wrote novels. Yet who shall say that even now 'the novel' (I give it inverted commas to mark my sense of the words' inadequacy), who shall say that even this most pliable of all forms is rightly shaped for her use? No doubt we shall find her knocking that into shape for herself when she has the free use of her limbs; and providing some new vehicle, not necessarily in verse, for the poetry in her. For it is the poetry that is still denied outlet. And I went on to ponder how a woman nowadays would write a poetic tragedy in five acts. Would she use verse?--would she not use prose rather?

But these are difficult questions which lie in the twilight of the future. I must leave them, if only because they stimulate me to wander from my subject into trackless forests where I shall be lost and, very likely, devoured by wild beasts. I do not want, and I am sure that you do not want me, to broach that very dismal subject, the future of fiction. so that I will only pause here one moment to draw your attention to the great part which must be played in that future so far as women are concerned by physical conditions. The book has somehow to be adapted to the body, and at a venture one would say that women's books should be shorter, more concentrated, than those of men, and framed so that they do not need long hours of steady and uninterrupted work. For interruptions there will always be. Again, the nerves that feed the brain would seem to differ in men and women, and if you are going to make them work their best and hardest, you must find out what treatment suits them--whether these hours of lectures, for instance, which the monks devised, presumably, hundreds of years ago, suit them--what alternations of work and rest they need, interpreting rest not as doing nothing but as doing something but something that is different; and what should that difference be? All this should be discussed and discovered; all this is part of the question of women and fiction. And yet, I continued, approaching the bookcase again, where shall I find that elaborate study of the psychology of women by a woman? If through their incapacity to play football women are not going to be allowed to practise medicine--

Happily my thoughts were now given another turn.

FIVE

I had come at last, in the course of this rambling, to the shelves which hold books by the living; by women and by men; for there are almost as many books written by women now as by men. Or if that is not yet quite true, if the male is still the voluble sex, it is certainly true that women no longer write novels solely. There are Jane Harrison's books on Greek archaeology; Vernon Lee's books on aesthetics; Gertrude Bell's books on Persia. There are books on all sorts of subjects which a generation ago no woman could have touched. There are poems and plays and criticism; there are histories and biographies, books of travel and books of scholarship and research; there are even a few philosophies and books about science and economics. And though novels predominate, novels themselves may very well have changed from association with books of a different feather. The natural simplicity, the epic age of women's writing, may have gone. Reading and criticism may have given her a wider range, a greater subtlety. The impulse towards autobiography may be spent. She may be beginning to use writing as an art, not as a method of selfexpression. Among these new novels one might find an answer to several such questions.

I took down one of them at random. It stood at the very end of the shelf, was called LIFE'S ADVENTURE, or some such title, by Mary Carmichael, and was published in this very month of October. It seems to be her first book, I said to myself, but one must read it as if it were the last volume in a fairly long series, continuing all those other books that I have been glancing at--Lady Winchilsea's poems and Aphra Behn's plays and the novels of the four great novelists. For books continue each other, in spite of our habit of judging them separately. And I must also consider her--this unknown woman--as the descendant of all those other women whose circumstances I have been glancing at and see what she inherits of their characteristics and restrictions. So, with a sigh, because novels so often provide an anodyne and not an antidote, glide one into torpid slumbers instead of rousing one with a burning brand, I settled down with a notebook and a pencil to make what I could of Mary Carmichael's first novel, LIFE'S ADVENTURE.

To begin with, I ran my eye up and down the page. I am going to get the hang of her sentences first, I said, before I load my memory with blue eyes and brown and the relationship that there may be between Chloe and Roger. There will be time for that when I have decided whether she has a pen in her hand or a pickaxe.

So I tried a sentence or two on my tongue. Soon it was obvious that something was not quite in order. The smooth gliding of sentence after sentence was interrupted. Something tore, something scratched; a single word here and there flashed its torch in my eyes. She was 'unhanding' herself as they say in the old plays. She is like a person striking a match that will not light, I thought. But why, I asked her as if she were present, are Jane Austen's sentences not of the right shape for you? Must they all be scrapped because Emma and Mr Woodhouse are dead? Alas, I sighed, that it should be so. For while Jane Austen breaks from melody to melody as Mozart from song to song, to read this writing was like being out at sea in an open boat. Up one went, down one sank. This terseness, this short-windedness, might mean that she was afraid of something; afraid of being called 'sentimental' perhaps; or she remembers that women's writing has been called flowery and so provides a superfluity of thorns; but until I have read a scene with some care, I cannot be sure whether she is being herself or someone else. At any rate, she does not lower one's vitality, I thought, reading more carefully. But she is heaping up too many facts. She will not be able to use half of them in a book of this size. (It was about half the length of JANE EYRE.) However, by some means or other she succeeded in getting us all--Roger, Chloe, Olivia, Tony and Mr Bigham--in a canoe up the river. Wait a moment, I said, leaning back in my chair, I must consider the whole thing more carefully before I go any further.

I am almost sure, I said to myself, that Mary Carmichael is playing a trick on us. For I feel as one feels on a switchback railway when the car, instead of sinking, as one has been led to expect, swerves up again. Mary is tampering with the expected sequence. First she broke the sentence; now she has broken the sequence. Very well, she has every right to do both these things if she does them not for the sake of breaking, but for the sake of creating. Which of the two it is I cannot be sure until she has faced herself with a situation. I will give her every liberty, I said, to choose what that situation shall be; she shall make it of tin cans and old kettles if she likes; but she must convince me that she believes it to be a situation; and then when she has made it she must face it. She must jump. And, determined to do my duty by her as reader if she would do her duty by me as writer, I turned the page and read . . . I am sorry to break off so abruptly. Are there no men present? Do you promise me that behind that red curtain over there the figure of Sir Charles Biron is not concealed? We are all women you assure me? Then I may tell you that the very next words I read were these--'Chloe liked Olivia . . .' Do not start. Do not blush. Let us admit in the privacy of our own society that these things sometimes happen. Sometimes women do like women.

'Chloe liked Olivia,' I read. And then it struck me how immense a change was there. Chloe liked Olivia perhaps for the first time in literature. Cleopatra did not like Octavia. And how completely ANTONY AND CLEOPATRA would have been altered had she done so! As it is, I thought, letting my mind, I am afraid, wander a little from LIFE'S ADVENTURE, the whole thing is simplified, conventionalized, if one dared say it, absurdly. Cleopatra's only feeling about Octavia is one of jealousy. Is she taller than I am? How does she do her hair? The play, perhaps, required no more. But how interesting it would have been if the relationship between the two women had been more complicated. All these relationships between women, I thought, rapidly recalling the splendid gallery of fictitious women, are too simple. So much has been left out, unattempted. And I tried to remember any case in the course of my reading where two women are represented as friends. There is an attempt at it in DIANA OF THE CROSSWAYS. They are confidantes, of course, in Racine and the Greek tragedies. They are now and then mothers and daughters. But almost without exception they are shown in their relation to men. It was strange to think that all the great women of fiction were, until Jane Austen's day, not only seen by the other sex, but seen only in relation to the other sex. And how small a part of a woman's life is that; and how little can a man know even of that when he observes it through the black or rosy spectacles which sex puts upon his nose. Hence, perhaps, the peculiar nature of woman in fiction; the astonishing extremes of her beauty and horror; her alternations between heavenly goodness and hellish depravity--for so a lover would see her as his love rose or sank, was prosperous or unhappy. This is not so true of the nineteenth-century novelists, of course. Woman becomes much more various and complicated there. Indeed it was the desire to write about women perhaps that led men by degrees to abandon the poetic drama which, with its violence, could make so little use of them, and to devise the novel as a more fitting receptacle. Even so it remains obvious, even in the writing of Proust, that a man is terribly hampered and partial in his knowledge of women, as a woman in her knowledge of men.

Also, I continued, looking down at the page again, it is becoming evident that women, like men, have other interests besides the perennial interests of domesticity. 'Chloe liked Olivia. They shared a laboratory together. . ..' I read on and discovered that these two young women were engaged in mincing liver, which is, it seems, a cure for pernicious anaemia; although one of them was married and had--I think I am right in stating--two small children. Now all that, of course, has had to be left out, and thus the splendid portrait of the fictitious woman is much too simple and much too monotonous. Suppose, for instance, that men were only represented in literature as the lovers of women, and were never the friends of men, soldiers, thinkers, dreamers; how few parts in the plays of Shakespeare could be allotted to them; how literature would suffer! We might perhaps have most of Othello; and a good deal of Antony; but no Caesar, no Brutus, no Hamlet, no Lear, no Jaques--literature would be incredibly impoverished, as indeed literature is impoverished beyond our counting by the doors that have been shut upon women. Married against their will, kept in one room, and to one occupation, how could a dramatist give a full or interesting or truthful account of them? Love was the only possible interpreter. The poet was forced to be passionate or bitter, unless indeed he chose to 'hate women', which meant more often than not that he was unattractive to them.

Now if Chloe likes Olivia and they share a laboratory, which of itself will make their friendship more varied and lasting because it will be less personal; if Mary Carmichael knows how to write, and I was beginning to enjoy some quality in her style; if she has a room to herself, of which I am not quite sure; if she has five hundred a year of her own--but that remains to be proved--then I think that something of great importance has happened.

For if Chloe likes Olivia and Mary Carmichael knows how to express it she will light a torch in that vast chamber where nobody has yet been. It is all half lights and profound shadows like those serpentine caves where one goes with a candle peering up and down, not knowing where one is stepping. And I began to read the book again, and read how Chloe watched Olivia put a jar on a shelf and say how it was time to go home to her children. That is a sight that has never been seen since the world began, I exclaimed. And I watched too, very curiously. For I wanted to see how Mary Carmichael set to work to catch those unrecorded gestures, those unsaid or half-said words, which form themselves, no more palpably than the shadows of moths on the ceiling, when women are alone, unlit by the capricious and coloured light of the other sex. She will need to hold her breath, I said, reading on, if she is to do it; for women are so suspicious of any interest that has not some obvious motive behind it, so terribly accustomed to concealment and suppression, that they are off at the flicker of an eye turned observingly in their direction. The only way for you to do it, I thought, addressing Mary Carmichael as if she were there, would be to talk of something else, looking steadily out of the window, and thus note, not with a pencil in a notebook, but in the shortest of shorthand, in words that are hardly syllabled yet, what happens when Olivia--this organism that has been under the shadow of the rock these million years--feels the light fall on it, and sees coming her way a piece of strange food--knowledge, adventure, art. And she reaches out for it, I thought, again raising my eyes from the page, and has to devise some entirely new combination of her resources, so highly developed for other purposes, so as to absorb the new into the old without disturbing the infinitely intricate and elaborate balance of the whole.

But, alas, I had done what I had determined not to do; I had slipped unthinkingly into praise of my own sex. 'Highly developed'--'infinitely intricate'--such are undeniably terms of praise, and to praise one's own sex is always suspect, often silly; moreover, in this case, how could one justify it? One could not go to the map and say Columbus discovered America and Columbus was a woman; or take an apple and remark, Newton discovered the laws of gravitation and Newton was a woman; or look into the sky and say aeroplanes are flying overhead and aeroplanes were invented by women. There is no mark on the wall to measure the precise height of women. There are no yard measures, neatly divided into the fractions of an inch, that one can lay against the qualities of a good mother or the devotion of a daughter, or the fidelity of a sister, or the capacity of a housekeeper. Few women even now have been graded at the universities; the great trials of the professions, army and navy, trade, politics and diplomacy have hardly tested them. They remain even at this moment almost unclassified. But if I want to know all that a human being can tell me about Sir Hawley Butts, for instance, I have only to open Burke or Debrett and I shall find that he took such and such a degree; owns a hall; has an heir; was Secretary to a Board; represented Great Britain in Canada; and has received a certain number of degrees, offices, medals and other distinctions by which his merits are stamped upon him indelibly. Only Providence can know more about Sir Hawley Butts than that.

When, therefore, I say 'highly developed', 'infinitely intricate' of women, I am unable to verify my words either in Whitaker, Debrett or the University Calendar. In this predicament what can I do? And I looked at the bookcase again. There were the biographies: Johnson and Goethe and Carlyle and Sterne and Cowper and Shelley and Voltaire and Browning and many others. And I began thinking of all those great men who have for one reason or another admired, sought out, lived with, confided in, made love to, written of, trusted in, and shown what can only be described as some need of and dependence upon certain persons of the opposite sex. That all these relationships were absolutely Platonic I would not affirm, and Sir William Joynson Hicks would probably deny. But we should wrong these illustrious men very greatly if we insisted that they got nothing from these alliances but comfort, flattery and the pleasures of the body. What they got, it is obvious, was something that their own sex was unable to supply; and it would not be rash, perhaps, to define it further, without quoting the doubtless rhapsodical words of the poets, as some stimulus; some renewal of creative power which is in the gift only of the opposite sex to bestow. He would open the door of drawing-room or nursery, I thought, and find her among her children perhaps, or with a piece of embroidery on her knee--at any rate, the centre of some different order and system of life, and the contrast between this world and his own, which might be the law courts or the House of Commons, would at once refresh and invigorate; and there would follow, even in the simplest talk, such a natural difference of opinion that the dried ideas in him would be fertilized anew; and the sight of her creating in a different medium from his own would so quicken his creative power that insensibly his sterile mind would begin to plot again, and he would find the phrase or the scene which was lacking when he put on his hat to visit her. Every Johnson has his Thrale, and holds fast to her for some such reasons as these, and when the Thrale marries her Italian music master Johnson goes half mad with rage and disgust, not merely that he will miss his pleasant evenings at Streatham, but that the light of his life will be 'as if gone out'.

And without being Dr Johnson or Goethe or Carlyle or Voltaire, one may feel, though very differently from these great men, the nature of this intricacy and the power of this highly developed creative faculty among women. One goes into the room--but the resources of the English language would he much put to the stretch, and whole flights of words would need to wing their way illegitimately into existence before a woman could say what happens when she goes into a room. The rooms differ so completely; they are calm or thunderous; open on to the sea, or, on the contrary, give on to a prison yard; are hung with washing; or alive with opals and silks; are hard as horsehair or soft as feathers--one has only to go into any room in any street for the whole of that extremely complex force of femininity to fly in one's face. How should it be otherwise? For women have sat indoors all these millions of years, so that by this time the very walls are permeated by their creative force, which has, indeed, so overcharged the capacity of bricks and mortar that it must needs harness itself to pens and brushes and business and politics. But this creative power differs greatly from the creative power of men. And one must conclude that it would be a thousand pities if it were hindered or wasted, for it was won by centuries of the most drastic discipline, and there is nothing to take its place. It would be a thousand pities if women wrote like men, or lived like men, or looked like men, for if two sexes are quite inadequate, considering the vastness and variety of the world, how should we manage with one only? Ought not education to bring out and fortify the differences rather than the similarities? For we have too much likeness as it is, and if an explorer should come back and bring word of other sexes looking through the branches of other trees at other skies, nothing would he of greater service to humanity; and we should have the immense pleasure into the bargain of watching Professor X rush for his measuring-rods to prove himself 'superior'.

Mary Carmichael, I thought, still hovering at a little distance above the page, will have her work cut out for her merely as an observer. I am afraid indeed that she will be tempted to become, what I think the less interesting branch of the species--the naturalist-novelist, and not the contemplative. There are so many new facts for her to observe. She will not need to limit herself any longer to the respectable houses of the upper middle classes. She will go without kindness or condescension, but in the spirit of fellowship, into those small, scented rooms where sit the courtesan, the harlot and the lady with the pug dog. There they still sit in the rough and ready-made clothes that the male writer has had perforce to clap upon their shoulders. But Mary Carmichael will have out her scissors and fit them close to every hollow and angle. It will be a curious sight, when it comes, to see these women as they are, but we must wait a little, for Mary Carmichael will still be encumbered with that self-consciousness in the presence of 'sin' which is the legacy of our sexual barbarity. She will still wear the shoddy old fetters of class on her feet.

However, the majority of women are neither harlots nor courtesans; nor do they sit clasping pug dogs to dusty velvet all through the summer afternoon. But what do they do then? and there came to my mind's eye one of those long streets somewhere south of the river whose infinite rows are innumerably populated. With the eye of the imagination I saw a very ancient lady crossing the street on the arm of a middle-aged woman, her daughter, perhaps, both so respectably booted and furred that their dressing in the afternoon must be a ritual, and the clothes themselves put away in cupboards with camphor, year after year, throughout the summer months. They cross the road when the lamps are being lit (for the dusk is their favourite hour), as they must have done year after year. The elder is close on eighty; but if one asked her what her life has meant to her, she would say that she remembered the streets lit for the battle of Balaclava, or had heard the guns fire in Hyde Park for the birth of King Edward the Seventh. And if one asked her, longing to pin down the moment with date and season, but what were you doing on the fifth of April 1868, or the second of November 1875, she would look vague and say that she could remember nothing. For all the dinners are cooked; the plates and cups washed; the children sent to school and gone out into the world. Nothing remains of it all. All has vanished. No biography or history has a word to say about it. And the novels, without meaning to, inevitably lie.

All these infinitely obscure lives remain to be recorded, I said, addressing Mary Carmichael as if she were present; and went on in thought through the streets of London feeling in imagination the pressure of dumbness, the accumulation of unrecorded life, whether from the women at the street corners with their arms akimbo, and the rings embedded in their fat swollen fingers, talking with a gesticulation like the swing of Shakespeare's words; or from the violet-sellers and match-sellers and old crones stationed under doorways; or from drifting girls whose faces, like waves in sun and cloud, signal the coming of men and women and the flickering lights of shop windows. All that you will have to explore, I said to Mary Carmichael, holding your torch firm in your hand. Above all, you must illumine your own soul with its profundities and its shallows, and its vanities and its generosities, and say what your beauty means to you or your plainness, and what is your relation to the everchanging and turning world of gloves and shoes and stuffs swaying up and down among the faint scents that come through chemists' bottles down arcades of dress material over a floor of pseudo-marble. For in imagination I had gone into a shop; it was laid with black and white paving; it was hung, astonishingly beautifully, with coloured ribbons. Mary Carmichael might well have a look at that in passing, I thought, for it is a sight that would lend itself to the pen as fittingly as any snowy peak or rocky gorge in the Andes. And there is the girl behind the counter too--I would as soon have her true history as the hundred and fiftieth life of Napoleon or seventieth study of Keats and his use of Miltonic inversion which old Professor Z and his like are now inditing. And then I went on very warily, on the very tips of my toes (so cowardly am I, so afraid of the lash that was once almost laid on my own shoulders), to murmur that she should also learn to laugh, without bitterness, at the vanities--say rather at the peculiarities, for it is a less offensive word--of the other sex. For there is a spot the size of a shilling at the back of the head which one can never see for oneself. It is one of the good offices that sex can discharge for sex--to describe that spot the size of a shilling at the back of the head. Think how much women have profited by the comments of Juvenal; by the criticism of Strindberg. Think with what humanity and brilliancy men, from the earliest ages, have pointed out to women that dark place at the back of the head! And if Mary were very brave and very honest, she would go behind the other sex and tell us what she found there. A true picture of man as a whole can never be painted until a woman has described that spot the size of a shilling. Mr Woodhouse and Mr Casuabon are spots of that size and nature. Not of course that anyone in their senses would counsel her to hold up to scorn and ridicule of set purpose--literature shows the futility of what is written in that spirit. Be truthful, one would say, and the result is bound to be amazingly interesting. Comedy is bound to be enriched. New facts are bound to be discovered.

However, it was high time to lower my eyes to the page again. It would be better, instead of speculating what Mary Carmichael might write and should write, to see what in fact Mary Carmichael did write. So I began to read again. I remembered that I had certain grievances against her. She had broken up Jane Austen's sentence, and thus given me no chance of pluming myself upon my impeccable taste, my fastidious ear. For it was useless to say, 'Yes, yes, this is very nice; but Jane Austen wrote much better than you do', when I had to admit that there was no point of likeness between them. Then she had gone further and broken the sequence--the expected order. Perhaps she had done this unconsciously, merely giving things their natural order, as a woman would, if she wrote like a woman. But the effect was somehow baffling; one could not see a wave heaping itself, a crisis coming round the next corner. Therefore I could not plume myself either upon the depths of my feelings and my profound knowledge of the human heart. For whenever I was about to feel the usual things in the usual places, about love, about death, the annoying creature twitched me away, as if the important point were just a little further on. And thus she made it impossible for me to roll out my sonorous phrases about 'elemental feelings', the 'common stuff of humanity', 'the depths of the human heart', and ail those other phrases which support us in our belief that, however clever we may be on top, we are very serious, very profound and very humane underneath. She made me feel, on the contrary, that instead of being serious and profound and humane, one might be--and the thought was far less seductive--merely lazy minded and conventional into the bargain.

But I read on, and noted certain other facts. She was no 'genius' that was evident. She had nothing like the love of Nature, the fiery imagination, the wild poetry, the brilliant wit, the brooding wisdom of her great predecessors, Lady Winchilsea, Charlotte Brontë, Emily Brontë, Jane Austen and George Eliot; she could not write with the melody and the dignity of Dorothy Osborne--indeed she was no more than a clever girl whose books will no doubt be pulped by the publishers in ten years' time. But, nevertheless, she had certain advantages which women of far greater gift lacked even half a century ago. Men were no longer to her 'the opposing faction'; she need not waste her time railing against them; she need not climb on to the roof and ruin her peace of mind longing for travel, experience and a knowledge of the world and character that were denied her. Fear and hatred were almost gone, or traces of them showed only in a slight exaggeration of the joy of freedom, a tendency to the caustic and satirical, rather than to the romantic, in her treatment of the other sex. Then there could be no doubt that as a novelist she enjoyed some natural advantages of a high order. She had a sensibility that was very wide, eager and free. It responded to an almost imperceptible touch on it. It feasted like a plant newly stood in the air on every sight and sound that came its way. It ranged, too, very subtly and curiously, among almost unknown or unrecorded things; it lighted on small things and showed that perhaps they were not small after all. It brought buried things to light and made one wonder what need there had been to bury them. Awkward though she was and without the unconscious bearing of long descent which makes the least turn of the pen of a

Thackeray or a Lamb delightful to the ear, she had--I began to think--mastered the first great lesson; she wrote as a woman, but as a woman who has forgotten that she is a woman, so that her pages were full of that curious sexual quality which comes only when sex is unconscious of itself.

All this was to the good. But no abundance of sensation or fineness of perception would avail unless she could build up out of the fleeting and the personal the lasting edifice which remains unthrown. I had said that I would wait until she faced herself with 'a situation'. And I meant by that until she proved by summoning, beckoning and getting together that she was not a skimmer of surfaces merely, but had looked beneath into the depths. Now is the time, she would say to herself at a certain moment, when without doing anything violent I can show the meaning of all this. And she would begin--how unmistakable that quickening is!--beckoning and summoning, and there would rise up in memory, half forgotten, perhaps quite trivial things in other chapters dropped by the way. And she would make their presence felt while someone sewed or smoked a pipe as naturally as possible, and one would feel, as she went on writing, as if one had gone to the top of the world and seen it laid out, very majestically, beneath.

At any rate, she was making the attempt. And as I watched her lengthening out for the test, I saw, but hoped that she did not see, the bishops and the deans, the doctors and the professors, the patriarchs and the pedagogues all at her shouting warning and advice. You can't do this and you shan't do that! Fellows and scholars only allowed on the grass! Ladies not admitted without a letter of introduction! Aspiring and graceful female novelists this way! So they kept at her like the crowd at a fence on the racecourse, and it was her trial to take her fence without looking to right or to left. If you stop to curse you are lost, I said to her; equally, if you stop to laugh. Hesitate or fumble and you are done for. Think only of the jump, I implored her, as if I had put the whole of my money on her back; and she went over it like a bird. But there was a fence beyond that and a fence beyond that. Whether she had the staying power I was doubtful, for the clapping and the crying were fraying to the nerves. But she did her best. Considering that Mary Carmichael was no genius, but an unknown girl writing her first novel in a bed-sitting-room, without enough of those desirable things, time, money and idleness, she did not do so badly, I thought.

Give her another hundred years, I concluded, reading the last chapter--people's noses and bare shoulders showed naked against a starry sky, for someone had twitched the curtain in the drawing-room--give her a room of her own and five hundred a year, let her speak her mind and leave out half that she now puts in, and she will write a better book one of these days. She will be a poet, I said, putting LIFE'S ADVENTURE, by Mary Carmichael, at the end of the shelf, in another hundred years' time.

SIX

Next day the light of the October morning was falling in dusty shafts through the uncurtained windows, and the hum of traffic rose from the street. London then was winding itself up again; the factory was astir; the machines were beginning. It was tempting, after all this reading, to look out of the window and see what London was doing on the morning of the 26th of October 1928. And what was London doing? Nobody, it seemed, was reading ANTONY AND CLEOPATRA. London was wholly indifferent, it appeared, to Shakespeare's plays. Nobody cared a straw--and I do not blame them--for the future of fiction, the death of poetry or the development by the average woman of a prose style completely expressive of her mind. If opinions upon any of these matters had been chalked on the pavement, nobody would have stooped to read them. The nonchalance of the hurrying feet would have rubbed them out in half an hour. Here came an errand-boy; here a woman with a dog on a lead. The fascination of the London street is that no two people are ever alike; each seems bound on some private affair of his own. There were the business-like, with their little bags; there were the drifters rattling sticks upon area railings; there were affable characters to whom the streets serve for clubroom, hailing men in carts and giving information without being asked for it. Also there were funerals to which men, thus suddenly reminded of the passing of their own bodies, lifted their hats. And then a very distinguished gentleman came slowly down a doorstep and paused to avoid collision with a bustling lady who had, by some means or other, acquired a splendid fur coat and a bunch of Parma violets. They all seemed separate, self-absorbed, on business of their own.

At this moment, as so often happens in London, there was a complete lull and suspension of traffic. Nothing came down the street; nobody passed. A single leaf detached itself from the plane tree at the end of the street, and in that pause and suspension fell. Somehow it was like a signal falling, a signal pointing to a force in things which one had overlooked. It seemed to point to a river, which flowed past, invisibly, round the corner, down the street, and took people and eddied them along, as the stream at Oxbridge had taken the undergraduate in his boat and the dead leaves. Now it was bringing from one side of the street to the other diagonally a girl in patent leather boots, and then a young man in a maroon overcoat; it was also bringing a taxi-cab; and it brought all three together at a point directly beneath my window; where the taxi stopped; and the girl and the young man stopped; and they got into the taxi; and then the cab glided off as if it were swept on by the current elsewhere.

The sight was ordinary enough; what was strange was the rhythmical order with which my imagination had invested it; and the fact that the ordinary sight of two people getting into a cab had the power to communicate something of their own seeming satisfaction. The sight of two people coming down the street and meeting at the corner seems to ease the mind of some strain, I thought, watching the taxi turn and make off. Perhaps to think, as I had been thinking these two days, of one sex as distinct from the other is an effort. It interferes with the unity of the mind. Now that effort had ceased and that unity had been restored by seeing two people come together and get into a taxicab. The mind is certainly a very mysterious organ, I reflected, drawing my head in from the window, about which nothing whatever is known, though we depend upon it so completely. Why do I feel that there are severances and oppositions in the mind, as there are strains from obvious causes on the body? What does one mean by 'the unity of the mind'? I pondered, for clearly the mind has so great a power of concentrating at any point at any moment that it seems to have no single state of being. It can separate itself from the people in the street, for example, and think of itself as apart from them, at an upper window looking down on them. Or it can think with other people spontaneously, as, for instance, in a crowd waiting to hear some piece of news read out. it can think back through its fathers or through its mothers, as I have said that a woman writing thinks back through her mothers. Again if one is a woman one is often surprised by a sudden splitting off of consciousness, say in walking down Whitehall, when from being the natural inheritor of that civilization, she becomes, on the contrary, outside of it, alien and critical. Clearly the mind is always altering its focus, and bringing the world into different perspectives. But some of these states of mind seem, even if adopted spontaneously, to be less comfortable than others. In order to keep oneself continuing in them one is unconsciously holding something back, and gradually the repression becomes an effort. But there may be some state of mind in which one could continue without effort because nothing is required to be held back. And this perhaps, I thought, coming in from the window, is one of them. For certainly when I saw the couple get into the taxicab the mind felt as if, after being divided, it had come together again in a natural fusion. The obvious reason would be that it is natural for the sexes to co-operate. One has a profound, if irrational, instinct in favour of the theory that the union of man and woman makes for the greatest satisfaction, the most complete happiness. But the sight of the two people getting into the taxi and the satisfaction it gave me made me also ask whether there are two sexes in the mind corresponding to the two sexes in the body, and whether they also require to be united in order to get complete satisfaction and happiness? And I went on amateurishly to sketch a plan of the soul so that in each of us two powers preside, one male, one female; and in the man's brain the man predominates over the woman, and in the woman's brain the woman predominates over the man. The normal and comfortable state of being is that when the two live in harmony together, spiritually co-operating. If one is a man, still the woman part of his brain must have effect; and a woman also must have intercourse with the man in her. Coleridge perhaps meant this when he said that a great mind is androgynous. It is when this fusion takes place that the mind is fully fertilized and uses all its faculties. Perhaps a mind that is purely masculine cannot create, any more than a mind that is purely feminine, I thought. But it would he well to test what one meant by man-womanly, and conversely by woman-manly, by pausing and looking at a book or two.

Coleridge certainly did not mean, when he said that a great mind is androgynous, that it is a mind that has any special sympathy with women; a mind that takes up their cause or devotes itself to their interpretation. Perhaps the androgynous mind is less apt to make these distinctions than the single-sexed mind. He meant, perhaps, that the androgynous mind is resonant and porous; that it transmits emotion without impediment; that it is naturally creative, incandescent and undivided. In fact one goes back to Shakespeare's mind as the type of the androgynous, of the man-womanly mind, though it would be impossible to say what Shakespeare thought of women. And if it be true that it is one of the tokens of the fully developed mind that it does not think specially or separately of sex, how much harder it is to attain that condition now than ever before. Here I came to the books by living writers, and there paused and wondered if this fact were not at the root of something that had long puzzled me. No age can ever have been as stridently sex-conscious as our own; those innumerable books by men about women in the British Museum are a proof of it. The Suffrage campaign was no doubt to blame. It must have roused in men an extraordinary desire for self-assertion; it must have made them lay an emphasis upon their own sex and its characteristics which they would not have troubled to think about had they not been challenged. And when one is challenged, even by a few women in black bonnets, one retaliates, if one has never been challenged before, rather excessively. That perhaps accounts for some of the characteristics that I remember to have found here, I thought, taking down a new novel by Mr A, who is in the prime of life and very well thought of, apparently, by the reviewers. I opened it. Indeed, it was delightful to read a man's writing again. It was so direct, so straightforward after the writing of women. It indicated such freedom of mind, such liberty of person, such confidence in himself. One had a sense of physical well-being in the presence of this well-nourished, well-educated, free mind, which had never been thwarted or opposed, but had had full liberty from birth to stretch itself in whatever way it liked. All this was admirable. But after reading a chapter or two a shadow seemed to lie across the page. it was a straight dark bar, a shadow shaped something like the letter 'I'. One began dodging this way and that to catch a glimpse of the landscape behind it. Whether that was indeed a tree or a woman walking I was not quite sure. Back one was always hailed to the letter 'I'. One began to be tired of 'I'. Not but what this 'I' was a most respectable 'I'; honest and logical; as hard as a nut, and polished for centuries by good teaching and good feeding. I respect and admire that 'I' from the bottom of my heart. But--here I turned a page or two, looking for something or other--the worst of it is that in the shadow of the letter 'I' all is shapeless as mist. Is that a tree? No, it is a woman. But . . . she has not a bone in her body, I thought, watching Phoebe, for that was her name, coming across the beach. Then Alan got up and the shadow of Alan at once obliterated Phoebe. For Alan had views and Phoebe was quenched in the flood of his views. And then Alan, I thought, has passions; and here I turned page after page very fast, feeling that the crisis was approaching, and so it was. It took place on the beach under the sun. It was done very openly. It was done very vigorously. Nothing could have been more indecent. But . . . I had said 'but' too often. One cannot go on saying 'but'. One must finish the sentence somehow, I rebuked myself. Shall I finish it, 'But--I am bored!' But why was I bored? Partly because of the dominance of the letter 'I' and the aridity, which, like the giant beech tree, it casts within its shade. Nothing will grow there. And partly for some more obscure reason. There seemed to be some obstacle, some impediment in Mr A's mind which blocked the fountain of creative energy and shored it within narrow limits. And remembering the lunch party at Oxbridge, and the cigarette ash and the Manx cat and Tennyson and Christina Rossetti all in a bunch, it seemed possible that the impediment lay there. As he no longer hums under his breath, 'There has fallen a splendid tear from the passion-flower at the gate', when Phoebe crosses the beach, and she no longer replies, 'My heart is like a singing bird whose nest is in a water'd shoot', when Alan approaches what can he do? Being honest as the day and logical as the sun, there is only one thing he can do. And that he does, to do him justice, over and over (I said turning the pages) and over again. And that, I added, aware of the awful nature of the confession, seems somehow dull. Shakespeare's indecency uproots a thousand other things in one's mind, and is far from being dull. But Shakespeare does it for pleasure; Mr A, as the nurses say, does it on purpose. He does it in protest. He is protesting against the equality of the other sex by asserting his own superiority. He is therefore impeded and inhibited and self-conscious as Shakespeare might have been if he too had known Miss Clough and Miss Davies. Doubtless Elizabethan literature would have been very different from what it is if the women's movement had begun in the sixteenth century and not in the nineteenth.

What, then, it amounts to, if this theory of the two sides of the mind holds good, is that virility has now become self-conscious--men, that is to say, are now writing only with the male side of their brains. It is a mistake for a woman to read them, for she will inevitably look for something that she will not find. It is the power of suggestion that one most misses, I thought, taking Mr B the critic in my hand and reading, very carefully and very dutifully, his remarks upon the art of poetry. Very able they were, acute and full of learning; but the trouble was that his feelings no longer communicated; his mind seemed separated into different chambers; not a sound carried from one to the other. Thus, when one takes a sentence of Mr B into the mind it falls plump to the ground--dead; but when one takes a sentence of Coleridge into the mind, it explodes and gives birth to all kinds of other ideas, and that is the only sort of writing of which one can say that it has the secret of perpetual life.

But whatever the reason may be, it is a fact that one must deplore. For it means--here I had come to rows of books by Mr Galsworthy and Mr Kipling--that some of the finest works of our greatest living writers fall upon deaf ears. Do what she will a woman cannot find in them that fountain of perpetual life which the critics assure her is there. It is not only that they celebrate male virtues, enforce male values and describe the world of men; it is that the emotion with which these books are permeated is to a woman incomprehensible. It is coming, it is gathering, it is about to burst on one's head, one begins saying long before the end. That picture will fall on old Jolyon's head; he will die of the shock; the old clerk will speak over him two or three obituary words; and all the swans on the Thames will simultaneously burst out singing. But one will rush away before that happens and hide in the gooseberry bushes, for the emotion which is so deep, so subtle, so symbolical to a man moves a woman to wonder. So with Mr Kipling's officers who turn their Backs; and his Sowers who sow the Seed; and his Men who are alone with their Work; and the Flag--one blushes at all these capital letters as if one had been caught eavesdropping at some purely masculine orgy. The fact is that neither Mr Galsworthy nor Mr Kipling has a spark of the woman in him. Thus all their qualities seem to a woman, if one may generalize, crude and immature. They lack suggestive power. And when a book lacks suggestive power, however hard it hits the surface of the mind it cannot penetrate within.

And in that restless mood in which one takes books out and puts them back again without looking at them I began to envisage an age to come of pure, of self-assertive virility, such as the letters of professors (take Sir Walter Raleigh's letters, for instance) seem to forebode, and the rulers of Italy have already brought into being. For one can hardly fail to be impressed in Rome by the sense of unmitigated masculinity; and whatever the value of unmitigated masculinity upon the state, one may question the effect of it upon the art of poetry. At any rate, according to the newspapers, there is a certain anxiety about fiction in Italy. There has been a meeting of academicians whose object it is 'to develop the Italian novel'. 'Men famous by birth, or in finance, industry or the Fascist corporations' came together the other day and discussed the matter, and a telegram was sent to the Duce expressing the hope 'that the Fascist era would soon give birth to a poet worthy of it'. We may all join in that pious hope, but it is doubtful whether poetry can come of an incubator. Poetry ought to have a mother as well as a father. The Fascist poem, one may fear, will be a horrid little abortion such as one sees in a glass jar in the museum of some county town. Such monsters never live long, it is said; one has never seen a prodigy of that sort cropping grass in a field. Two heads on one body do not make for length of life.

However, the blame for all this, if one is anxious to lay blame, rests no more upon one sex than upon the other. All seducers and reformers are responsible: Lady Bessborough when she lied to Lord Granville; Miss Davies when she told the truth to Mr Greg. All who have brought about a state of sex-consciousness are to blame, and it is they who drive me, when I want to stretch my faculties on a book, to seek it in that happy age, before Miss Davies and Miss Clough were born, when the writer used both sides of his mind equally. One must turn back to Shakespeare then, for Shakespeare was androgynous; and so were Keats and Sterne and Cowper and Lamb and Coleridge. Shelley perhaps was sexless. Milton and Ben Jonson had a dash too much of the male in them. So had Wordsworth and Tolstoi. In our time Proust was wholly androgynous, if not perhaps a little too much of a woman. But that failing is too rare for one to complain of it, since without some mixture of the kind the intellect seems to predominate and the other faculties of the mind harden and become barren. However, I consoled myself with the reflection that this is perhaps a passing phase; much of what I have said in obedience to my promise to give you the course of my thoughts will seem out of date; much of what flames in my eyes will seem dubious to you who have not yet come of age.

Even so, the very first sentence that I would write here, I said, crossing over to the writing-table and taking up the page headed Women and Fiction, is that it is fatal for anyone who writes to think of their sex. It is fatal to be a man or woman pure and simple; one must be woman-manly or man-womanly. It is fatal for a woman to lay the least stress on any grievance; to plead even with justice any cause; in any way to speak consciously as a woman. And fatal is no figure of speech; for anything written with that conscious bias is doomed to death. It ceases to be fertilized. Brilliant and effective, powerful and masterly, as it may appear for a day or two, it must wither at nightfall; it cannot grow in the minds of others. Some collaboration has to take place in the mind between the woman and the man before the art of creation can be accomplished. Some marriage of opposites has to be consummated. The whole of the mind must lie wide open if we are to get the sense that the writer is communicating his experience with perfect fullness. There must be freedom and there must be peace. Not a wheel must grate, not a light glimmer. The curtains must be close drawn. The writer, I thought, once his experience is over, must lie back and let his mind celebrate its nuptials in darkness. He must not look or question what is being done. Rather, he must pluck the petals from a rose or watch the swans float calmly down the river. And I saw again the current which took the boat and the under-graduate and the dead leaves; and the taxi took the man and the woman, I thought, seeing them come together across the street, and the current swept them away, I thought, hearing far off the roar of London's traffic, into that tremendous stream.

Here, then, Mary Beton ceases to speak. She has told you how she reached the conclusion--the prosaic conclusion--that it is necessary to have five hundred a year and a room with a lock on the door if you are to write fiction or poetry. She has tried to lay bare the thoughts and impressions that led her to think this. She has asked you to follow her flying into the arms of a Beadle, lunching here, dining there, drawing pictures in the British Museum, taking books from the shelf, looking out of the window. While she has been doing all these things, you no doubt have been observing her failings and foibles and deciding what effect they have had on her opinions. You have been contradicting her and making whatever additions and deductions seem good to you. That is all as it should be, for in a question like this truth is only to be had by laying together many varieties of error. And I will end now in my own person by anticipating two criticisms, so obvious that you can hardly fail to make them.

No opinion has been expressed, you may say, upon the comparative merits of the sexes even as writers. That was done purposely, because, even if the time had come for such a valuation--and it is far more important at the moment to know how much money women had and how many rooms than to theorize about their capacities--even if the time had come I do not believe that gifts, whether of mind or character, can be weighed like sugar and butter, not even in Cambridge, where they are so adept at putting people into classes and fixing caps on their heads and letters after their names. I do not believe that even the Table of Precedency which you will find in Whitaker's ALMANAC represents a final order of values, or that there is any sound reason to suppose that a Commander of the Bath will ultimately walk in to dinner behind a Master in Lunacy. All this pitting of sex against sex, of quality against quality; all this claiming of superiority and imputing of inferiority, belong to the private-school stage of human existence where there are 'sides', and it is necessary for one side to beat another side, and of the utmost importance to walk up to a platform and receive from the hands of the Headmaster himself a highly ornamental pot. As people mature they cease to believe in sides or in Headmasters or in highly ornamental pots. At any rate, where books are concerned, it is notoriously difficult to fix labels of merit in such a way that they do not come off. Are not reviews of current literature a perpetual illustration of the difficulty of judgement? 'This great book', 'this worthless book', the same book is called by both names. Praise and blame alike mean nothing. No, delightful as the pastime of measuring may be, it is the most futile of all occupations, and to submit to the decrees of the measurers the most servile of attitudes. So long as you write what you wish to write, that is all that matters; and whether it matters for ages or only for hours, nobody can say. But to sacrifice a hair of the head of your vision, a shade of its colour, in deference to some Headmaster with a silver pot in his hand or to some professor with a measuring-rod up his sleeve, is the most abject treachery, and the sacrifice of wealth and chastity which used to be said to be the greatest of human disasters, a mere flea-bite in comparison.

Next I think that you may object that in all this I have made too much of the importance of material things. Even allowing a generous margin for symbolism, that five hundred a year stands for the power to contemplate, that a lock on the door means the power to think for oneself, still you may say that the mind should rise above such things; and that great poets have often been poor men. Let me then quote to you the words of your own Professor of Literature, who knows better than I do what goes to the making of a poet. Sir Arthur Quiller-Couch writes[1]:

---

[1] THE ART OF WRITING, by Sir Arthur Quiller-Couch.

'What are the great poetical names of the last hundred years or so? Coleridge, Wordsworth, Byron, Shelley, Landor, Keats, Tennyson, Browning, Arnold, Morris, Rossetti, Swinburne--we may stop there. Of these, all but Keats, Browning, Rossetti were University men, and of these three, Keats, who died young, cut off in his prime, was the only one not fairly well to do. It may seem a brutal thing to say, and it is a sad thing to say: but, as a matter of hard fact, the theory that poetical genius bloweth where it listeth, and equally in poor and rich, holds little truth. As a matter of hard fact, nine out of those twelve were University men: which means that somehow or other they procured the means to get the best education England can give. As a matter of hard fact, of the remaining three you know that Browning was well to do, and I challenge you that, if he had not been well to do, he would no more have attained to write SAUL or THE RING AND THE BOOK than Ruskin would have attained to writing MODERN PAINTERS if his father had not dealt prosperously in business. Rossetti had a small private income; and, moreover, he painted. There remains but Keats; whom Atropos slew young, as she slew John Clare in a mad-house, and James Thomson by the laudanum he took to drug disappointment. These are dreadful facts, but let us face them. It is--however dishonouring to us as a nation--certain that, by some fault in our commonwealth, the poor poet has not in these days, nor has had for two hundred years, a dog's chance. Believe me--and I have spent a great part of ten years in watching some three hundred and twenty elementary schools, we may prate of democracy, but actually, a poor child in England has little more hope than had the son of an Athenian slave to be emancipated into that intellectual freedom of which great writings are born.'

Nobody could put the point more plainly. 'The poor poet has not in these days, nor has had for two hundred years, a dog's chance . . . a poor child in England has little more hope than had the son of an Athenian slave to be emancipated into that intellectual freedom of which great writings are born.' That is it. Intellectual freedom depends upon material things. Poetry depends upon intellectual freedom. And women have always been poor, not for two hundred years merely, but from the beginning of time. Women have had less intellectual freedom than the sons of Athenian slaves. Women, then, have not had a dog's chance of writing poetry. That is why I have laid so much stress on money and a room of one's own. However, thanks to the toils of those obscure women in the past, of whom I wish we knew more, thanks, curiously enough to two wars, the Crimean which let Florence Nightingale out of her drawing-room, and the European War which opened the doors to the average woman some sixty years later, these evils are in the way to be bettered. Otherwise you would not be here tonight, and your chance of earning five hundred pounds a year, precarious as I am afraid that it still is, would be minute in the extreme.

Still, you may object, why do you attach so much importance to this writing of books by women when, according to you, it requires so much effort, leads perhaps to the murder of one's aunts, will make one almost certainly late for luncheon, and may bring one into very grave disputes with certain very good fellows? My motives, let me admit, are partly selfish. Like most uneducated Englishwomen, I like reading--I like reading books in the bulk. Lately my diet has become a trifle monotonous; history is too much about wars; biography too much about great men; poetry has shown, I think, a tendency to sterility, and fiction but I have sufficiently exposed my disabilities as a critic of modern fiction and will say no more about it. Therefore I would ask you to write all kinds of books, hesitating at no subject however trivial or however vast. By hook or by crook, I hope that you will possess yourselves of money enough to travel and to idle, to contemplate the future or the past of the world, to dream over books and loiter at street corners and let the line of thought dip deep into the stream. For I am by no means confining you to fiction. If you would please me--and there are thousands like me--you would write books of travel and adventure, and research and scholarship, and history and biography, and criticism and philosophy and science. By so doing you will certainly profit the art of fiction. For books have a way of influencing each other. Fiction will be much the better for standing cheek by jowl with poetry and philosophy. Moreover, if you consider any great figure of the past, like Sappho, like the Lady Murasaki, like Emily Brontë, you will find that she is an inheritor as well as an originator, and has come into existence because women have come to have the habit of writing naturally; so that even as a prelude to poetry such activity on your part would be invaluable.

But when I look back through these notes and criticize my own train of thought as I made them, I find that my motives were not altogether selfish. There runs through these comments and discursions the conviction--or is it the instinct?--that good books are desirable and that good writers, even if they show every variety of human depravity, are still good human beings. Thus when I ask you to write more books I am urging you to do what will be for your good and for the good of the world at large. How to justify this instinct or belief I do not know, for philosophic words, if one has not been educated at a university, are apt to play one false. What is meant by 'reality'? It would seem to be something very erratic, very undependable--now to be found in a dusty road, now in a scrap of newspaper in the street, now a daffodil in the sun. It lights up a group in a room and stamps some casual saying. It overwhelms one walking home beneath the stars and makes the silent world more real than the world of speech--and then there it is again in an omnibus in the uproar of Piccadilly. Sometimes, too, it seems to dwell in shapes too far away for us to discern what their nature is. But whatever it touches, it fixes and makes permanent. That is what remains over when the skin of the day has been cast into the hedge; that is what is left of past time and of our loves and hates. Now the writer, as I think, has the chance to live more than other people in the presence of this reality. It is his business to find it and collect it and communicate it to the rest of us. So at least I infer from reading LEAR or EMMA or LA RECHERCHE DU TEMPS PERDU. For the reading of these books seems to perform a curious couching operation on the senses; one sees more intensely afterwards; the world seems bared of its covering and given an intenser life. Those are the enviable people who live at enmity with unreality; and those are the pitiable who are knocked on the head by the thing done without knowing or caring. So that when I ask you to earn money and have a room of your own, I am asking you to live in the presence of reality, an invigorating life, it would appear, whether one can impart it or not.

Here I would stop, but the pressure of convention decrees that every speech must end with a peroration. And a peroration addressed to women should have something, you will agree, particularly exalting and ennobling about it. I should implore you to remember your responsibilities, to be higher, more spiritual; I should remind, you how much depends upon you, and what an influence you can exert upon the future. But those exhortations can safely, I think, be left to the other sex, who will put them, and indeed have put them, with far greater eloquence than I can compass. When I rummage in my own mind I find no noble sentiments about being companions and equals and influencing the world to higher ends. I find myself saying briefly and prosaically that it is much more important to be oneself than anything else. Do not dream of influencing other people, I would say, if I knew how to make it sound exalted. Think of things in themselves.

And again I am reminded by dipping into newspapers and novels and biographies that when a woman speaks to women she should have something very unpleasant up her sleeve. Women are hard on women. Women dislike women. Women--but are you not sick to death of the word? I can assure you that I am. Let us agree, then, that a paper read by a woman to women should end with something particularly disagreeable.

But how does it go? What can I think of? The truth is, I often like women. I like their unconventionality. I like their completeness. I like their anonymity. I like--but I must not run on in this way. That cupboard there,--you say it holds clean table-napkins only; but what if Sir Archibald Bodkin were concealed among them? Let me then adopt a sterner tone. Have I, in the preceding words, conveyed to you sufficiently the warnings and reprobation of mankind? I have told you the very low opinion in which you were held by Mr Oscar Browning. I have indicated what Napoleon once thought of you and what Mussolini thinks now. Then, in case any of you aspire to fiction, I have copied out for your benefit the advice of the critic about courageously acknowledging the limitations of your sex. I have referred to Professor X and given prominence to his statement that women are intellectually, morally and physically inferior to men. I have handed on all that has come my way without going in search of it, and here is a final warning--from Mr John Langdon Davies[1]. Mr John Langdon Davies warns women 'that when children cease to be altogether desirable, women cease to be altogether necessary'. I hope you will make a note of it.

How can I further encourage you to go about the business of life? Young women, I would say, and please attend, for the peroration is beginning, you are, in my opinion, disgracefully ignorant. You have never made a discovery of any sort of importance. You have never shaken an empire or led an army into battle. The

---

[1] A SHORT HISTORY OF WOMEN, by John Langdon Davies.

plays of Shakespeare are not by you, and you have never introduced a barbarous race to the blessings of civilization. What is your excuse? It is all very well for you to say, pointing to the streets and squares and forests of the globe swarming with black and white and coffee-coloured inhabitants, all busily engaged in traffic and enterprise and love-making, we have had other work on our hands. Without our doing, those seas would be unsailed and those fertile lands a desert. We have borne and bred and washed and taught, perhaps to the age of six or seven years, the one thousand six hundred and twenty-three million human beings who are, according to statistics, at present in existence, and that, allowing that some had help, takes time.

There is truth in what you say--I will not deny it. But at the same time may I remind you that there have been at least two colleges for women in existence in England since the year 1866; that after the year 1880 a married woman was allowed by law to possess her own property; and that in 1919--which is a whole nine years ago she was given a vote? May I also remind you that most of the professions have been open to you for close on ten years now? When you reflect upon these immense privileges and the length of time during which they have been enjoyed, and the fact that there must be at this moment some two thousand women capable of earning over five hundred a year in one way or another, you will agree that the excuse of lack of opportunity, training, encouragement, leisure and money no longer holds good. Moreover, the economists are telling us that Mrs Seton has had too many children. You must, of course, go on bearing children, but, so they say, in twos and threes, not in tens and twelves.

Thus, with some time on your hands and with some book learning in your brains--you have had enough of the other kind, and are sent to college partly, I suspect, to be uneducated--surely you should embark upon another stage of your very long, very laborious and highly obscure career. A thousand pens are ready to suggest what you should do and what effect you will have. My own suggestion is a little fantastic, I admit; I prefer, therefore, to put it in the form of fiction.

I told you in the course of this paper that Shakespeare had a sister; but do not look for her in Sir Sidney Lee's life of the poet. She died young--alas, she never wrote a word. She lies buried where the omnibuses now stop, opposite the Elephant and Castle. Now my belief is that this poet who never wrote a word and was buried at the cross-roads still lives. She lives in you and in me, and in many other women who are not here to-night, for they are washing up the dishes and putting the children to bed. But she lives; for great poets do not die; they are continuing presences; they need only the opportunity to walk among us in the flesh. This opportunity, as I think, it is now coming within your power to give her. For my belief is that if we live another century or so--I am talking of the common life which is the real life and not of the little separate lives which we live as individuals--and have five hundred a year each of us and rooms of our own; if we have the habit of freedom and the courage to write exactly what we think; if we escape a little from the common sitting-room and see human beings not always in their relation to each other but in relation to reality; and the sky, too, and the trees or whatever it may be in themselves; if we look past Milton's bogey, for no human being should shut out the view; if we face the fact, for it is a fact, that there is no arm to cling to, but that we go alone and that our relation is to the world of reality and not only to the world of men and women, then the opportunity will come and the dead poet who was Shakespeare's sister will put on the body which she has so often laid down. Drawing her life from the lives of the unknown who were her forerunners, as her brother did before her, she will be born. As for her coming without that preparation, without that effort on our part, without that determination that when she is born again she shall find it possible to live and write her poetry, that we cannot expect, for that would be impossible. But I maintain that she would come if we worked for her, and that so to work, even in poverty and obscurity, is worth while.

THE END

Charles Williams Omnibus - War in Heaven, Many Dimensions, The Place of the Lion, Shadows of Ecstasy, The Greater Trumps, Descent into Hell, All Hallows' Eve, & Et in Sempiternum Pereant
Charles Williams
Oxford City Press, 2012
1068 pages
ISBN: 978-1-78139-146-4

Available from www.amazon.com, www.amazon.co.uk

This book is an omnibus edition containing the seven novels that Charles Williams wrote as well as a short story that he wrote for the London Mercury: War in Heaven (1930) - The Holy Grail is discovered in a small country parish and becomes both a sacramental object to protect or a cup of power to exploit. Many Dimensions (1931) - The Stone of Suleiman is illegally acquired from its Islamic guardian in Baghdad and taken to England, it is discovered the stone allows its possessor to transcend the barriers of space and time. The Place of the Lion (1931) - Platonic archetypes begin to appear in an English market town, wreaking havoc and unveiling the spiritual strengths and flaws of the townspeople. Shadows of Ecstasy (1931) - A man discovers that by focusing his energies inward he can extend his life almost indefinitely. He undertakes an experiment using to die and resurrect his own body in order to attain immortality. The Greater Trumps (1932) - The original Tarot is used to unlock immense power, allowing those who possess it to see across space and time, create matter, and create powerful natural storms. Descent into Hell (1937) - An academic fetishizes a woman to the extent that his perversion takes the form of a female demon. The cycle of sin brings about the necessity for redemptive acts. All Hallows' Eve (1945) - Explores the meaning of suffering and empathy by removing the barrier between the living and the dead through both black magic and divine love. Et in Sempiternum Pereant (1935) - In this short story a retired Lord Chief Justice is on a walk in the countryside when he enters a burning house and encounters a troubled spirit on its way to Hell. This is the only tale of this kind that Williams wrote - sketchy in detail but terrifying through implication. Williams was admired by his contemporaries including T. S. Eliot and W. H. Auden, his especially by C. S. Lewis, whose novel That Hideous Strength is considered to be entirely inspired by Williams's work. When he moved to Oxford he participated regularly in Lewis's literary society known as the Inklings. This enabled Williams to read and improve his final published novel, All Hallows' Eve, as well as to hear J. R. R. Tolkien read some of his early drafts of The Lord of the Rings aloud to the group.

On the Eve
Ivan Turgenev
Benediction Classics, 2011
176 pages
ISBN: 978-1-84902-310-8

Available from www.amazon.com, www.amazon.co.uk

On the Eve is the third novel written by the famous Russian writer Ivan Turgenev, best known for his novel Fathers and Sons. It is a story, set in 1853, of love during the Crimean War and at a time of social upheaval. The heroine, Elena, is a charming, serious and courageous young woman. She is concerned about justice, but this finds no outlet in her middle class world, until she is introduced Insarov, a man below her social status, but whose idealism matches her own. He becomes Elena's husband and changes her life.

Here and Beyond
Edith Wharton
Benediction Classics, 2011
150 pages
ISBN: 978-1-84902-421-1

Available from www.amazon.com, www.amazon.co.uk

Edith Wharton (1862 - 1937), was a Pulitzer Prize-winning American novelist and short story writer. She grew up in upper-class pre-WWI society and many of her stories critique this culture, using subtle irony. Here and Beyond was written in 1926 and includes ghost stories, social dramas and character studies set in Brittany, New England, and Morocco.

Also from Benediction Books ...
Wandering Between Two Worlds: Essays on Faith and Art
Anita Mathias
Benediction Books, 2007
152 pages
ISBN: 0955373700

Available from www.amazon.com, www.amazon.co.uk

In these wide-ranging lyrical essays, Anita Mathias writes, in lush, lovely prose, of her naughty Catholic childhood in Jamshedpur, India; her large, eccentric family in Mangalore, a sea-coast town converted by the Portuguese in the sixteenth century; her rebellion and atheism as a teenager in her Himalayan boarding school, run by German missionary nuns, St. Mary's Convent, Nainital; and her abrupt religious conversion after which she entered Mother Teresa's convent in Calcutta as a novice. Later rich, elegant essays explore the dualities of her life as a writer, mother, and Christian in the United States-- Domesticity and Art, Writing and Prayer, and the experience of being "an alien and stranger" as an immigrant in America, sensing the need for roots.

About the Author

Anita Mathias is the author of *Wandering Between Two Worlds: Essays on Faith and Art*. She has a B.A. and M.A. in English from Somerville College, Oxford University, and an M.A. in Creative Writing from the Ohio State University, USA. Anita won a National Endowment of the Arts fellowship in Creative Non-fiction in 1997. She lives in Oxford, England with her husband, Roy, and her daughters, Zoe and Irene.

Anita's website:
    http://www.anitamathias.com, and
Anita's blog Dreaming Beneath the Spires:
    http://dreamingbeneaththespires.blogspot.com

The Church That Had Too Much
Anita Mathias
Benediction Books, 2010
52 pages
ISBN: 9781849026567

Available from www.amazon.com, www.amazon.co.uk

The Church That Had Too Much was very well-intentioned. She wanted to love God, she wanted to love people, but she was both hampered by her muchness and the abundance of her possessions, and beset by ambition, power struggles and snobbery. Read about the surprising way The Church That Had Too Much began to resolve her problems in this deceptively simple and enchanting fable.

About the Author

Anita Mathias is the author of *Wandering Between Two Worlds: Essays on Faith and Art*. She has a B.A. and M.A. in English from Somerville College, Oxford University, and an M.A. in Creative Writing from the Ohio State University, USA. Anita won a National Endowment of the Arts fellowship in Creative Non-fiction in 1997. She lives in Oxford, England with her husband, Roy, and her daughters, Zoe and Irene.

Anita's website:
http://www.anitamathias.com, and
Anita's blog Dreaming Beneath the Spires:
http://dreamingbeneaththespires.blogspot.com

www.ingramcontent.com/pod-product-compliance
Lightning Source LLC
Chambersburg PA
CBHW081128300726
48982CB00005B/884
* 9 7 8 1 7 8 1 3 9 2 0 7 2 *